A MAN
RIDES
THROUGH

By Stephen R. Donaldson
Published by Ballantine Books:

THE CHRONICLES OF THOMAS COVENANT
Book One: Lord Foul's Bane
Book Two: The Illearth War
Book Three: The Power That Preserves

THE SECOND CHRONICLES OF
THOMAS COVENANT
Book One: The Wounded Land
Book Two: The One Tree
Book Three: White Gold Wielder

DAUGHTER OF REGALS AND OTHER TALES

MORDANT'S NEED
Volume One: The Mirror of Her Dreams
Volume Two: A Man Rides Through

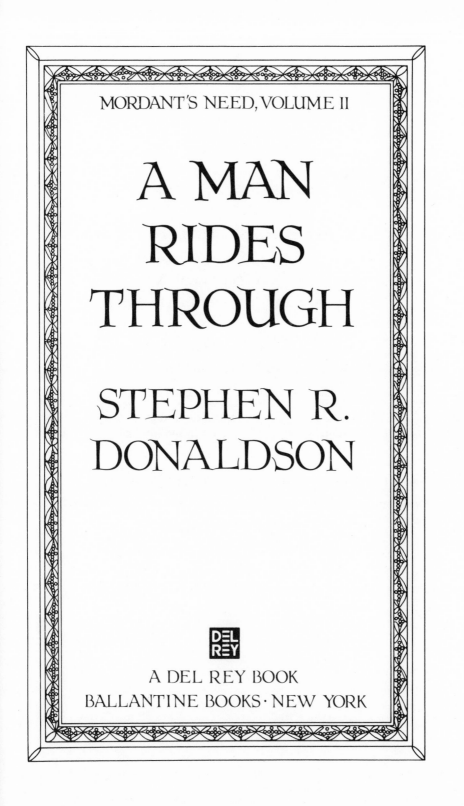

MORDANT'S NEED, VOLUME II

A MAN RIDES THROUGH

STEPHEN R. DONALDSON

A DEL REY BOOK

BALLANTINE BOOKS · NEW YORK

A Del Rey Book
Published by Ballantine Books

Copyright © 1987 by Stephen R. Donaldson

Library of Congress Cataloging-in-Publication Data

Donaldson, Stephen R.
  A man rides through.

  (Mordant's need; book 2)
  "A Del Rey book."
  Includes index.
  I. Title. II. Series: Donaldson, Stephen R. Mordant's
need; bk. 2.
PS3554.0469M36 1987   813'.54   87-47741
ISBN 0-345-33299-7

Manufactured in the United States of America
Design by Holly Johnson

First Edition: November 1987

10 9 8 7 6 5 4 3 2 1

CONTENTS

To Perryn Laura Donaldson:
for sunshine and flowers
        whenever you need them
and love
        whenever you want it

A MAN
RIDES
THROUGH

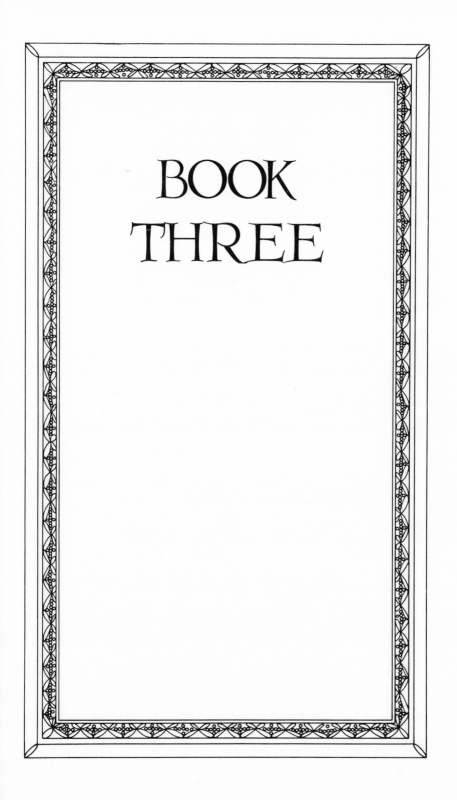

BOOK
THREE

TWENTY-SEVEN: THE PRINCE'S SIEGE

arly the next morning, the siege of Orison began.

The huge, rectangular pile of the castle stood on slightly lower ground, surrounded by bare dirt and straggling grass—and surrounded, too, by the Alend army, with its supporting horde of servants and camp followers. From Prince Kragen's perspective, Orison looked too massive—and the ring of attackers around it too thin—for the siege to succeed. He understood sieges, however. He knew his force was strong enough to take the castle.

Nevertheless the Prince didn't risk any men. He felt the pressure of time, of course: he could almost taste High King Festten's army marching out of Cadwal against him, a sensation as disturbing as a stench borne along on the edges of the raw wind. And that army was large—the Prince knew this because he had captured a number of the Perdon's wounded men on their way to Orison and had taken the information from them. Composed half of mercenaries, half of his own troops, the High King's troops numbered at least twenty thousand. And of the Alend Monarch's men there were barely ten thousand.

So Kragen had to hurry. He needed to take Orison and fortify it before those twenty thousand Cadwals crossed the Broadwine into the Demesne. Otherwise when the High King came he would have no choice but to retreat ignominiously. Unless he was willing to lose his entire force in an effort to help Joyse keep the Congery out of Cadwal's hands. The lady Elega's plan to paralyze Orison from within had failed, and now time was not on the Alend Contender's side.

Still he didn't risk any men. He was going to need them soon enough.

Instead, he ordered his catapults into position to heave rocks at the scant curtain-wall which protected the hole in the side of the castle.

He had seen that wound from a similar vantage point the day after the Congery's mad champion had blasted his way to freedom, the day when as the Alend Monarch's ambassador he had formally departed Orison: a smoking breach with a look of death about it torn in one face of the blunt stone. The damage had been impressive then, seen against a background of cold and snow, like a fatal hurt that steamed because the corpse was still warm. The sight of it had simultaneously lifted and chilled Prince Kragen's heart, promising as it did that Orison could be taken—that a power which had once ruled Mordant and controlled the ancient conflict between Alend and Cadwal was doomed.

In some ways, however, King Joyse's seat looked more vulnerable now. The inadequacies of the curtain-wall were so simple that a child could measure them. Considering his circumstances, Castellan Lebbick had done well—quite well, in fact. But circumstantial excuses wouldn't help the wall stand against siege engines. The Prince's captain of catapults was privately taking bets as to whether the curtain-wall could survive more than one good hit.

No, the obvious question facing Prince Kragen was not whether he could break into Orison, but rather how hard the castle would defend itself. The lady Elega had failed to poison Lebbick's guards— but she *had* poisoned the reservoir, putting the badly overcrowded castle into a state of severe rationing. And as for King Joyse— He wasn't just the leader of his people: he was their hero, the man who had given them identity as well as ideals. Now he had lost his mind. Leaderless and desperate, how fiercely would the Mordants fight?

They might find it in themselves to fight very fiercely, if Joyse kept his word. He had certainly lost his mind, there was no doubt about that. Yet he had met Alend's demand for surrender with the one threat which might give heart to his followers: *King Joyse intends to unleash the full force of the Congery against you and rout you from the Earth!*

Elega didn't believe that, but the Prince lacked her confidence. If Joyse did indeed *unleash the Congery,* then what happened to Alend's army might be worse than a rout. It might be complete ruin.

So Prince Kragen held his troops back from the walls of Orison. Wearing his spiked helmet over his curly black hair, with his moustache waxed to a bold gloss that matched his eyes, and his longsword and breastplate exposed by the negligent way he wore his white fur robe, he was the image of assurance and vitality as he readied his forces, warned back the army's camp followers, discussed weights and trajectories with his captain of catapults. Nevertheless every thought in his head was hedged with doubts. He didn't intend to risk any men until he had to. He was afraid that he might soon need them all.

The terrain suited catapults. For one thing, it was clear. Except for the trees edging the roads, the ground was uncluttered: virtually all the natural brush had been cut away, and even the grass struggling to come out for the spring was having a hard time because of the chill and the lack of rain. And the roads weren't in Kragen's way: they met some distance outside Orison's gates to the northeast of the castle, and the wound in the wall faced more toward the northwest. For another, Orison's immediate setting was either level with or slightly lower than the positions of Alend's army. As Prince Kragen's military teachers and advisors had drummed into him for years, it was exceptionally difficult to aim catapults uphill. Here, however, the shot which actually presented itself to his siege engines was an easy one.

The lady Elega came to his side while the most powerful of the catapults was being loaded. His mind was preoccupied; but she had the capacity to get his attention at any time, and he greeted her with a smile that was warmer than his distracted words.

"My lady, we are about to begin."

Clutching her robe about her, she looked hard at her home. "What will happen, my lord Prince?" she murmured as if she didn't expect an answer. "Will the curtain-wall hold? The Castellan is a cunning old veteran. Surely he had done his best for Orison."

Prince Kragen studied her face while she studied the castle. Because he loved her, even admired her—and because he was reluctant to acknowledge that he didn't entirely trust a woman who had tried so hard to betray her own father—it was difficult for him to admit that she wasn't at her best under these conditions. Cold and wind took the spark out of her vivid eyes, turning them sore and puffy; stark sunlight made her look wan, bloodless, like a woman with no heart. She was only lovely when she was within doors, seen by the light of candles and intrigue. Yet her present lack of beauty only caused the Prince to love her more. He knew that she did indeed have a heart. The fingers that held her robe closed were pale and urgent. Every word she said, and every line of her stance, told him that she was mourning.

"Oh, the wall will fall," he replied in the same distracted tone. "We will have it down before sunset—perhaps before noon. It was raised in winter. Let Lebbick be as cunning and experienced as you wish." Kragen didn't much like the dour Castellan. "He has had nothing to use for mortar. If he took all the sand of the Congery—and then butchered every Imager for blood—he would still be unable to seal those stones against us."

The lady winced slightly. "And when it comes down?" she asked, pursuing an unspoken worry. "What then?"

"When this blow is struck," he said, suddenly harsh, "there will be no turning back. Alend will be at war with Mordant. And we cannot wait for thirst and fear to do our work for us. The Perdon is all that stands between us and High King Festten. We will make the breach as large as we can. Then we will fight our way in." A moment later, however, he took pity on her and added, "Orison will be given every conceivable opportunity to surrender. I want no slaughter. Every man, woman, and child there will be needed against Cadwal."

Elega looked at him, mute gratitude on her chafed and swollen face. She thought for a while, then nodded. "Castellan Lebbick will never surrender. My father has never surrendered in his life."

"Then they must begin here," snapped the Prince.

He believed that. He believed that the curtain-wall couldn't hold—that apart from Imagery, Orison didn't have the resources to withstand his assault. Yet doubts he could hardly name tightened their grip on his stomach as he ordered the captain to throw the first stone.

In unison, two brawny men swung mallets against the hooks on either side of the catapult; the great arm leaped forward and slammed against its stops; a boulder as heavy as a man arced out of the cup. The throw raised a shout of anticipation from the army, but Prince

Kragen watched it go grimly. The flat smack of the mallets, the groan
of stress in the timbers, the thud of the stops and the protest of the
wheels: he seemed to feel them in his chest, as if they were blows
struck against him—as if he could tell simply by the sound that the
stone was going to miss.

It did.

Not entirely, of course: Orison was too big a target for that.
But the boulder hit high and to the left, away from the curtain-wall.

The impact left a scar on the face of the castle. That was trivial,
however: the projectile itself shattered. The plain purple swath of
the King's personal banner continued to snap and flutter, untouched,
unconcerned.

Under his breath, Kragen cursed the wind, although he knew
it had nothing to do with the miss. In fact, a miss was normal: a hit
would have been uncommon. The captain of catapults needed a few
throws to adjust his engine, get the range. Yet Prince Kragen felt
an irrational pang, as if the miss were an omen.

Perhaps it was. Before the captain's men could start hauling on
the tackle which pulled back the arm of the catapult, the entire
besieging force heard the cry of a trumpet.

It wasn't one of the familiar fanfares, announcing messengers
or defiance. It was a high, shrill wail on one note, as if the trumpeter
himself didn't know what he was doing, but had simply been instructed to attract attention.

Kragen glanced at the lady Elega, implicitly asking for an explanation. She shrugged and nodded toward Orison.

From his present position, the Prince couldn't see the castle
gates. They must have been opened, however, because a man on a
horse came around the corner of the wall, riding in the direction of
the catapult.

He was a small man—too small for his mount, Prince Kragen
gauged automatically. And not accustomed to horses, judging by the
precarious way he kept his seat. If he carried any weapons or armor,
they were hidden under his thick mantle.

But over his shoulders, outside his mantle, he wore the yellow
chasuble of a Master. The wind made the ends of the chasuble flap
so that they couldn't be missed.

The Prince cocked a black eyebrow, but didn't let anything else
show. Conscious that everything he said would be heard and reported

throughout the army, he murmured calmly, "Interesting. An Imager.
A Master of the Congery. Do you know him, my lady?"

She waited until there was no possibility of mistake. Then she
responded softly, "Quillon, my lord Prince." She was frowning hard.
"Why him? He has never been important, either to the Congery or
to my father."

Prince Kragen smiled toward the approaching Master. So that
only Elega could hear him, he commented, "I suspect we will learn
the answer shortly."

Master Quillon came forward, red-faced and laughable on his
oversized mount. His eyes watered as if he were weeping, though
there was no sorrow in his expression. His nose twitched like a rabbit's; his lips exposed his protruding teeth. But as the Master brought
his horse to a halt in front of Prince Kragen and the lady Elega—as
Quillon dismounted almost as if he were falling, blown out of his
seat by the wind—the Alend Contender had no difficulty suppressing
his mirth. Regardless of what Quillon looked like, he was an Imager.
If he had a mirror with him, he might be able to do considerable
damage before he was taken prisoner or killed.

"My lord Prince," he said without preamble—without a glance
at King Joyse's daughter or a bow for the Alend Monarch's son—
"I have come to warn you."

The men around the Prince stiffened; the captain of catapults
put his hand on his sword. But Prince Kragen's demeanor gave no
hint of offense.

"To warn us, Master Quillon?" His tone was smooth, despite
the piercing glitter of his gaze. "That is an unexpected courtesy. I
distinctly heard Castellan Lebbick threaten to 'unleash the Congery'
against us. Have I misunderstood your King's intent? Have I not
already been warned? Or"—he held Quillon's eyes sharply—"is your
warning different in some way? Does your presence here imply that
the Congery is no longer under Joyse's rule?"

"No, my lord Prince." The Imager had such an appearance of
being frightened that the assertion in his voice sounded unnatural,
unexpectedly ominous. "You rush to conclusions. That is a dangerous weakness in a leader of men. If you wish to survive this war,
you must show greater care."

"Must I?" replied the Prince, still smoothly. "I beg your pardon.
You have misled me. Your own incaution in coming to speak to me
inspired my incautious speculations. If you mean merely to repeat

the Castellan's threats, you could have spared yourself an uncomfortable ride."

"I mean nothing of the kind. I came to warn you that we will destroy this catapult. If you remain near it, you may be injured— perhaps killed. King Joyse does not wish you killed. This war is not of his doing, and he has no interest in your death."

A cold, unfamiliar tingle ran across Kragen's scalp and down the back of his neck. *We will destroy*— Like everyone else he had ever known, he was afraid of Imagers, afraid of the strange power to produce atrocities out of nothing more than glass and talent. One consequence of this was that he had distorted the shape of his siege to avoid the crossroads because he knew from Elega that the Perdon had once been attacked by Imagery there. And Quillon's manner made his words seem mad—unpredictable and therefore perilous. *King Joyse does not wish you killed.*

At the same time, Margonal's son was the Alend Contender: he occupied a position, and carried a responsibility, which no one had forced on him. In other lands, other princes might become kings whether they deserved the place or not; but the Alend Monarch's Seat in Scarab could only be earned, never inherited. And Kragen wanted that Seat, both because he trusted his father and because he trusted himself. More than anyone else who desired to rule Alend, he believed in what his father was doing. And he felt sure that none of his competitors was better qualified than himself.

So there was no fear in the way he looked at Quillon, or in the way he stood, or in the way he spoke. There was only watchfulness— and a superficial amusement which wasn't intended to fool anybody.

"What, no interest at all?" he asked easily. "Even though I have taken his daughter from him and brought the full strength of the Alend Monarch to the gates of Orison? Forgive me if I seem skeptical, Master Quillon. Your King's concern for my life appears to be—I mean no offense—a little eccentric." As if he were bowing, he nodded his head; but his men understood him and closed around Quillon, blocking the Imager's retreat. "And you risk much to make me aware of his regard for me."

Master Quillon's gaze flicked from side to side, trying to watch everything at once. "Not so much," he commented as if he hadn't noticed his own anxiety. "Only my life. I prefer to live, but nothing of importance will be lost if I am killed. This catapult will still be destroyed. Every catapult which you presume to aim against us will be destroyed. As I say, King Joyse has no interest in your death. If you insist on dying, however, he will not prohibit you.

"The risk to my life is your assurance that I speak the truth."

"Fascinating," drawled the Prince. "From this distance, you will destroy my siege engines? What new horror has the Congery devised, that you are now able to project destruction so far from your glass?"

The Master didn't answer that question. "Withdraw or not, as you choose," he said. "Kill me or not." The twitching of his nose was unmistakably rabbitlike. "But do not make the error of believing that you will be permitted to enter or occupy Orison. Rather than surrender his Seat and his strength, King Joyse will allow you to be crushed between the hammer of Cadwal and the anvil of the Congery."

The lady Elega couldn't restrain herself. "Quillon, this is madness." Her protest sounded at once angry and forlorn. "You are a minor Imager, a lesser member of the Congery. You admit that your life has no importance. Yet you dare threaten the Alend Monarch and his son. How have you gained such stature, that you claim to speak with my father's voice?"

For the first time, Master Quillon looked at her. Suddenly, his face knotted, and an incongruous note of ferocity sharpened his tone. "My lady, I have been given my stature by the King's command. I am the mediator of the Congery." Without moving, he confronted her as if he had abruptly become taller. "Unlike his daughter, I have not betrayed him."

Loyal to their Prince, the Alend soldiers tensed; a number of them put their hands on their swords.

But Elega met the Master's reply squarely. She had a King's daughter's pride, as well as a King's daughter's commitment to what she was doing. "That is unjust," she snapped. "He has betrayed all Mordant. You cannot be blind to the truth. You cannot—"

Deliberately, Master Quillon turned away as if she had ceased to exist for him.

Unheeded, her protest trailed into silence. In the chill spring wind she looked like she might weep.

With difficulty, Prince Kragen checked his anger. The Master's attitude infuriated him because he understood it too well. Nevertheless he resisted the impulse to have Quillon struck down. Instead, he murmured through his teeth, "You risk more than you realize, Master Quillon. Perhaps you do not consider death to be of great importance, but I assure you that you will attach more significance to pain."

At that, Elega's head jerked, and her gaze widened, as if she were shocked. The Prince and the Imager faced each other, however, ignoring her reaction.

Master Quillon's eyes flicked; his nose twitched. He might have been on the verge of panic. But his tone contradicted that impression. It cut fearlessly.

"Is that your answer to what you do not understand, my lord Prince? Torture? Or do you inflict pain for the simple pleasure of it? Be warned again, son of the Alend Monarch, you are being tested here, as surely as you were tested in Orison, at the hop-board table—and elsewhere. I do not advise you to prove unworthy."

Without Prince Kragen's permission, Quillon left. He mounted his horse awkwardly, gathered up the reins. He was surrounded by Alends; yet when he pulled his mount's head toward Orison the soldiers seemed to open a path for him involuntarily, without instructions from their captain or their Prince, as if they were ruled by the Imager's peculiar dignity.

Looking slightly ridiculous—or perhaps valiant—on his big horse, he rode back the way he had come. In a short time, he rounded the corner of Orison and disappeared from sight.

Kragen chewed his lips under his moustache as he turned to the lady. *You are being tested here*— He would have asked, What was the meaning of *that?* but the darkness in her eyes stopped him.

"Elega?" he inquired softly.

Her jaw tightened as she met his gaze. " 'Pain,' my lord Prince?"

Her indignation made him want to shout at her. We are at *war* here, my lady. Do you believe that we can fight a *war* without hurting anyone? He restrained himself, however, because he was also a little ashamed of having threatened Master Quillon.

It was certainly true that in the old days of the constant struggle between Alend and Cadwal, no supporter or adherent of the Alend Monarch would have hesitated to twist a few screams out of any Mordant or Cadwal. And the barons of the Lieges still tended to be a bloodthirsty lot. But since his defeat at King Joyse's hands, Margonal hadn't failed to notice that his opponent was able to rule Mordant with considerable ease by winning loyalty rather than extorting it. Never a stupid man, the Alend Monarch had experimented with techniques of kingship other than those which hinged upon fear, violence, and pain, and had been pleased with the results. Even the barons were becoming easier to command.

That was one of the things Margonal had done which Prince Kragen believed in. He wanted to make more such experiments himself.

So despite the fact that he was angry and alarmed and full of doubt, he lowered his guard enough to offer Elega a piece of difficult honesty.

"I said more than I meant. The Imager affronted you, my lady. I do not like it when you are affronted."

His explanation seemed to give her what she needed. Slowly, her expression cleared; moisture softened her gaze until it looked like a promise. "I should not be so easily offended," she replied. "Surely it is obvious that anyone who still trusts my father will be unable to trust me." Then, as if she were trying to match his candor, she added, "Yet I thank you for your anger, my lord Prince. It is a comfort that you consider me worth defending."

For a moment, Prince Kragen studied her, measuring his hunger for her against the exigencies of the situation. Then he bowed and turned away.

The wind seemed to be getting colder. Spring had come early—therefore it was possible that winter would return. That, the Prince thought bitterly, would be just what he and his army needed: to be encamped and paralyzed by winter outside Orison like curs outside a village, cold and hungry, and helpless to do anything except hope for table scraps. Yes, that would be perfect.

But he kept his bile to himself. To his captain of catapults, he said briskly, as if he were sure of what he was doing, "We will heed the Imager's warning, I think. Withdraw all who are unnecessary, and prepare the rest to retreat. Then resume the attack."

The captain saluted, began to issue orders. Men obeyed with nervous alacrity, artificially quick to demonstrate that they weren't concerned. Taking Elega with him, Prince Kragen walked in the direction of his father's tents until he had put nearly a hundred yards between himself and the catapult. There he turned to watch.

He didn't have to wait long for Master Quillon's threat to be carried out. The mediator of the Congery must have given the signal almost as soon as he entered the courtyard of the castle. Moments after the Prince began to study Orison's heavy gray profile for some hint of what was coming, he saw a brown shape as imprecise as a puff of smoke lift off the ramparts of the northwest wall.

It looked like it would dissipate like smoke; yet it held together. It looked like it was no bigger than a large dog, no more than twice the size of a buzzard; yet the way it rose seething and shifting into the sky made it seem as dangerous as a thunderbolt. A bit of brown smoke— Like nearly ten thousand other men and virtually all his army's adherents, Prince Kragen craned his neck and squinted his eyes to trace the shape's movement against the dull background of the clouds.

So high that it was almost certainly beyond arrow range, even for the iron-trussed crossbows some of the Alends carried, the brown shape sailed out toward the catapult and over it and away again, back in the direction of the castle. The Prince thought he heard a faint, thin cry, like the wail of a seabird.

And from out of the smoke as it passed overhead came plummeting a rock as big as the one which the catapult had pitched at Orison.

Powerful with the force of its fall, the rock struck the catapult and shattered the wood as easily as if the engine had been built of kindling. Splinters and bolts burst loose on all sides; chunks of timber arced away from the impact and hit the ground like rubble. Two of the men fleeing from the catapult went down, one with a ragged stave driven through his leg, the other with his skull crushed by a bit of the engine's iron. The rest were luckier.

The vague brown shape had already dropped out of sight beyond the parapets of the castle.

A shout went up from the army—anger and fear demanding an outlet, calling for blood. But Prince Kragen stood still, his face impassive, as if he had never been surprised in his life. Only the white lines of his mouth hidden under his moustache betrayed what he felt.

"My lady," he said to Elega in a tone of grim nonchalance, "you have lived for years in the proximity of Imagers. Surely Orison has always been full of rumors concerning the Congery. Have you ever heard of or seen such a thing before?"

She shook her head dumbly and studied the wreckage of the catapult as if she couldn't believe her eyes.

"It is possible," he muttered for her ears alone, "that during King Joyse's peace we have forgotten too much of the abomination of Imagery. Clearly the Masters have not been inactive under his rule.

"My lady"—he closed his eyes just for a moment and allowed himself to be appalled—"the Congery *must not* fall into the hands of High King Festten."

Then the Prince took command of himself again and left her. First he ordered the captain of catapults to bring forward another siege engine and try again, taking whatever precautions were necessary to protect the men. After that, he went to talk to his father.

The Alend Monarch's tents were sumptuous by his standards. Margonal liked to travel in comfort. Also he knew that upon occasion a grand public display was good for morale. Nevertheless High King Festten would have considered the Monarch's quarters a hovel. Alend lacked the seaports and hence the trade of Cadwal. Compared to Festten, Margonal was no wealthier than one of his Lieges. If Mordant hadn't lain between Cadwal and Alend—and if the Cares of Mordant hadn't been so contentious, so difficult to rule—a quality which made them an effective buffer—the High King and the forces which his wealth could procure would long since have swallowed up his ancient enemy.

Prince Kragen was conscious of this, not because he was jealous of the High King's riches, but because he felt acutely vulnerable to Cadwal, as he pushed the canvas door-flap aside and was admitted to his father's presence. He could feel Alend's peril in the cold wind that curled about his neck like a garotte.

The Alend Monarch sat in the fore-tent where he held councils and consultations. The Prince could see him well enough: braziers intended for warmth gave off a flickering illumination that danced among the tentpoles and around the meeting chairs. But there was no other light. The seams of the tent were sealed with flaps, and Margonal didn't permit lamps or torches or even candles in his presence. Privately, Prince Kragen considered this arbitrary prohibition a vestige of the tyranny to which his father had formerly been accustomed. Nevertheless he accepted it without question. As anyone who looked on the Alend Monarch's face in good light could see, Margonal was stone blind.

It was unimaginable that any vision could penetrate the white film which covered his eyes like curtains.

Obviously, his battles with King Joyse hadn't been his only

losses in life. And it had been when he had begun to lose his sight
that he had first started to search for surer ways to rule, safer means
of preserving the kingship for himself and his successor. As he had
repeated until everyone near him was sick of it, "Loss teaches many
things." Again privately, however—and without any disrespect—
Prince Kragen dropped *loss* and substituted *fear*. A man who couldn't
see his enemies couldn't strike at them. For that reason, he had to
find new ways to protect himself. Kragen understood his father's fear
and honored it. A lesser man than Margonal would have retreated
into terror and violence.

Old and no longer strong, the Alend Monarch sprawled in the
most comfortable of the meeting chairs and turned his head toward
the sound of his son's entrance. Because he was punctilious, he didn't
speak until the Alend Contender had been announced, and had
greeted him in the formal manner prescribed by custom. Then he
sighed as if he were especially tired. "Well, my son. My guards have
already been here, whispering lurid reports which they were unable
to explain. Perhaps you will tell me something comprehensible."

"My lord," Prince Kragen replied, "I fear I can only increase
the range of your incomprehension." Succinctly, he described Master
Quillon's visit and the destruction of the catapult. When he was done,
he told his father what he was thinking.

"The Imager's actions were strange, unquestionably. But to my
mind the great mystery is that King Joyse behaves as if he had not
made himself weak—as if we were nothing more than an annoyance
to a sovereign in an invulnerable position. And he is able to command
men such as Castellan Lebbick and Master Quillon to preserve that
illusion.

"Yet we know it *is* an illusion. Cadwal marches against him. He
has a hole in his wall, few men to defend it, and no water for them
to drink. Despite his control over the Congery, the Imagers who
serve his enemies are more powerful. They are able to strike him at
will anywhere in Mordant or Orison, passing through flat glass as if
they were immune to madness. In addition, there are Masters on the
Congery who would abandon his cause if they could. Men such as
Eremis may be loyal to Mordant, but they are no longer committed
to their King.

"His lords will not help him. The Armigite is a coward. The
Termigan values nothing but his own affairs. And the Perdon resists
Cadwal, not for King Joyse, but for his own survival. Of the Cares,

only Domne, Tor, and Fayle are truly loyal. Yet the Domne does
not fight. The Tor is old, sodden with wine—and *here,* where he is
unable to muster his people. And the Fayle cannot come to Orison's
aid because we stand in his way.

"And *still* King Joyse treats us as if we lack the means to harm
him."

The more he thought about it, the more unsure the Prince
became. For a moment, he chewed on his moustache while his doubts
chewed on him. Then he concluded, "In truth, my lord, I cannot
decide in my own mind whether his audacity constitutes raving or
deep policy."

Again, the Alend Monarch sighed. With apparent irrelevance,
he murmured, "I suffered an uncomfortable night. The loss of sight
has sharpened my powers of recollection. Instead of sleeping, I saw
every trick and subterfuge he has ever practiced against me. I felt
every blow of our battles. Such memories would curdle the blood
of a young sovereign with his eyes clear in his head. For me, they
are fatal."

Facing his son as if he could see, Margonal asked in a husky
voice, "Can you think of anything—anything at all—that a king such
as Joyse might gain by feigning weakness—by allowing Imagers to
bring atrocities down on the heads of his people—by permitting us
to invest him when his defenses are so poor?"

"No." Prince Kragen shook his head for his own benefit. "It is
madness. It must be madness."

"And the lady Elega? She is his daughter. Her knowledge of
him is greater than yours—greater even than mine. Can she think
of anything that he might gain?"

Again, the Prince said, "No." He trusted her, didn't he? He
believed what she believed about her father, didn't he?

Abruptly, the Alend Monarch raised his voice. "Then he is a
madman, a *madman.* He must be rooted out of his stronghold and
made to pay for this. Do you hear me? It is unsufferable!"

As if he didn't know what they were doing, his fists began to
beat on the arms of his chair.

"I understand his desire to take Mordant from us and rule it as
his own. He was able to do it—therefore he did it. Who would not?
And I understand his desire to gather all the resources of Imagery
for himself. Again he was able to do it—therefore he did it. Who
would not? And perhaps I understand also his restraint when he had

created the Congery, his refusal to use his power for conquest. That is not what Festten would have done. It is not what *I* would have done. But perhaps in that he was saner than we.

"But *this*—*!* To create all he has created, and then abandon it to destruction!" Now the Alend Monarch was shouting. "To forge such a weapon as the Congery, and then make himself vulnerable to attack, neglect responsibility, turn his back on those who serve and trust him, so that his enemies have no choice but to attempt to wrest his weapon from him for their own survival!" Margonal half rose from his seat, as if he intended to go to demand sense from King Joyse in person. "I say it is *unsufferable!* It must not *continue!*"

As quickly as it had come up, however, his passion subsided. Sinking back, he wiped his hands across his face.

"My son," he whispered hoarsely, "when I received your message asking us to march, a chill went into my heart. I cannot warm it away. I *know* that man. He has beaten me too often. I fear that he has lured us here to destroy us—that his weakness is a pose to bring us and Cadwal within reach, so we can be crushed at his ease, instead of met in honest battle. You say this cannot be true. The lady Elega says it cannot be true. My own reason says it cannot be true—if only because in fifty years he has never shown any desire to crush us. And yet I fear it.

"He has witched me. We have come here to our doom."

Prince Kragen stared at what his father was saying and tried not to shudder. Fear teaches many things, he thought. Have all the rest of us been blind? Why have we never believed that Joyse is malign? Softly, he answered, "My lord, say the word, and we will retreat. You are the Alend Monarch. And I trust your wisdom. We will—"

"No!" Margonal's refusal sounded more like pain than anger or protest. "No," he repeated almost at once, in a steadier tone. "He has witched me, I say. I am certain of only one thing—I cannot make decisions where he is concerned.

"No, my son, this siege is yours. You are the Alend Contender. I have given our doom into your hands." A moment later, he added in warning, "If you choose retreat, be very certain that you can answer for your decision to the others who seek my Seat."

Mutely, the Prince nodded. He had caught Margonal's chill much earlier: long before this conversation, the cold of the wind had crept into his vitals. But the Alend Monarch had named his doubt for him—and the name seemed to make the doubt more palpable, more potent. *We have come here to our doom.* When his father asked, "What will you do?" he chewed his lip and replied, "I do not know."

"Choose soon." Now Margonal spoke to him harshly, as he himself had spoken harshly to the lady Elega. "Festten will not be patient with your uncertainty."

In response, Kragen stiffened his spine. "Perhaps not, my lord. Nevertheless our doom will be Cadwal's as well. Until the issue is proven, I will do my best to teach the High King better uses for his impatience."

Slowly, the Alend Monarch relaxed until he was sprawling in his chair once again. Unexpectedly, he smiled. "Festten, I have heard, has many sons. I have only one. I am inclined to think, however, that I have already bested him in the matter."

Because he didn't know what else to do, Prince Kragen bowed deeply. Then he withdrew from his father's presence and went to watch a vague brown shape rise above the walls of Orison and wreck another of his best catapults.

Fortunately, his men escaped without injury this time.

His face showed nothing but confidence as he went to consult with all his captains.

TWENTY-EIGHT: A DAY OF TROUBLE

astellan Lebbick stood with the three Imagers on the ramparts of the northwest wall and watched as the brown shape which Adept Havelock had translated reduced the second Alend catapult to firewood and splinters. At this elevation, behind the defensive parapet built into Orison's outward face, he had a good view despite the distance.

Judging by the old scowl cut into the lines of his face, the knot of his jaw muscles, the bleak glare in his eyes, he wasn't impressed.

He ought to have been impressed. He had had no idea that this mirror existed—or that a creature with no more definition than dense smoke could be translated *and controlled*, could be made to carry rocks as heavy as a man anywhere the Adept commanded. And that wasn't all. In plain fact, he had had no idea that Havelock was still sane enough to cooperate in Orison's defense—that plans could be designed on the assumption that the Adept would carry out his part in them. In some way, the Castellan's warrior spirit probably was impressed. Unquestionably he ought to have been.

He wasn't conscious of it, however. He certainly didn't show it. The truth was that only a harsh act of will enabled him to keep his mind on what he was doing, pay any attention to the situation at all.

"Well done," Master Quillon breathed as the airborne shape returned to Havelock's glass, gusting easily across the wind. "You surpass yourself, indeed you do." And he actually patted the Adept's shoulder like an old friend—which would have surprised Lebbick under other circumstances, since Havelock's lunacy had made friendship with him impossible for everyone except King Joyse. Who was himself, the Castellan thought sourly, no longer particularly sane.

"Fornication," Adept Havelock replied negligently, as if he normally performed such feats of Imagery standing on his head. "Piss on the slut." In spite of his tone, however, he was concentrating so hard that his misaimed eyes bulged slightly.

"Of course," murmured Master Eremis. "My thought exactly." He was the only other man near the mirror, although a number of guards and several Apts were clustered a short distance away, watching raptly. "Yet it occurs to me that you have been a bit too coy with your talents, Adept Havelock."

Nominally, Eremis was here only because the Castellan wasn't done with him. Too many questions remained to be answered. Nevertheless his interest in what happened was intense: his wedge-shaped head followed everything, studied every movement; his eyes gleamed as if he were having a wonderful time. "If the Congery had known of your resources, we might have made different decisions entirely."

Master Quillon glanced rapidly at the taller Imager. "Is that so? Such as?"

In response, Master Eremis smiled distinctly at the Castellan. "We might have decided to defend Mordant ourselves, rather than waiting politely for our beloved King to fall off the precarious perch of his reason."

Lebbick really should have replied to that jibe. Eremis intended to provoke him—and provocation was his bread and meat. It fed the fires of dedication and outrage which kept him going, sustained him so that he could continue to serve his King past the point where his own common sense rebelled and his instinct for fidelity turned against him. In addition, he had work to do where Master Eremis was concerned—issues to resolve, explanations to obtain. But this time the Master's sarcasm didn't touch him. His heart was elsewhere, and without it he wasn't able to think clearly.

His heart was in the dungeon, where he had left that woman.

Curse her, anyway, *curse* her. She was the source of all the trouble, all the harm. He was even starting to think that she was the reason for King Joyse's weakness, even though the King had been

walking that path for years before her first appearance. But now
Lebbick would get the truth out of her. He would tear her limbs off
if necessary to get the truth out of her. He would take the soft flesh
of her body in his hands—

He would do anything he wanted to her. He had permission.

*Now you've done it, woman. You've done something so heinous that
nobody is going to protect you.* That was true. The Tor had tried—and
failed. *You've helped a murderer escape.*

Now you are mine.

Even though he had been warned.

Mine.

If only he could control the way he trembled whenever he
thought of her.

He answered Master Eremis for no reason at all except to mask
what was happening to him, disguise the tremors in his muscles.

But he wasn't thinking about what he said. He couldn't. He was
too busy remembering the way her arms felt when he ground his
fingers into them.

"No," he heard her whisper. Her protest was like the horror
in her soft brown eyes, like the quivering of her delicately cleft chin.
She was afraid of him, deeply afraid. His anger touched a sore place
in her—he could see that vividly, even though she had stood up to
him in the past, had lied to him, forced him to swallow his passion
against her time and again. She feared him as if she deserved to be
terrified, as if she already knew that anything he might do to her was
justified. "No," she whispered, but it wasn't his accusations she denied; it was *him,* the Castellan himself, his violence and authority.

"Yes," he replied through his teeth, smiling at her fiercely as
if she made him happy for the last time in his life.

Holding her as hard as he wished, without regard for her pain—
or for the way the Masters and guards looked at him despite the
chaos of Nyle's murder and Geraden's disappearance—he escorted
her to the dungeon himself.

Along the way, she babbled.

"No, you don't understand, it's a trick, Geraden didn't kill Nyle,
please listen to me, *listen* to me, Eremis did this somehow, it's a
trick."

He liked that. He liked her fear. He wanted her prostrate in
front of him. At the same time, however, her reaction disturbed him.
For some reason, it reminded him of his wife.

For no good reason, obviously, since his wife hadn't been a babbler. In fact, she hadn't been afraid of anything, not since King Joyse had rescued them from the Alend garrison commander who was having her raped so imaginatively. Not since he, Lebbick, had ripped that dogshit Alend apart with his teeth.

But before that she had been afraid. Yes, he remembered her fear as well. She babbled. Yes. He heard her—watched her—was forced to watch her—and couldn't do anything about it, anything at all. He heard and saw her do every desperate and terrible thing she could think of to try to make those men stop.

Castellan Lebbick wasn't going to stop. Never. Let her babble to her heart's content, cry out, scream if she wanted to. She was *his*.

Yet it disturbed him.

When he thrust her into her cell so that she nearly sprawled on the cot against the far wall, he had no intention of stopping. But he didn't start right away. Instead, he closed the iron door behind him without bothering to lock it, folded his arms across his chest to keep them from shaking, and faced her past the light of the single lamp. Its wick needed trimming; the flame guttered wildly, making shadows dance fright over her pale features.

Still smiling through his teeth, he demanded, "How?"

"I don't know." Babbling. "Somehow. To get rid of Geraden. Geraden is the only one who doesn't trust him." Terrified. "Eremis and Gilbur are working together. And Vagel. He lied to the Congery." Trying to distract him. "Eremis brought Nyle to the meeting of the Congery. He said Nyle would prove Geraden is a traitor, but that was a lie. They set this up together. They planned it." Trying to create the illusion that she made sense. "It's a fake. They staged it. They must have."

Deaf to the illogic of her own defense, she insisted, "Nyle is still alive."

Watching her, the Castellan wanted to crow for joy. "No, woman." His jaws throbbed with the effort of not sinking his teeth into her. "Tell me *how*. How did he escape? How did you help him escape?"

Finally she caught hold of herself, closed her mouth on her panic. Shadows flickered in and out of her eyes; she looked as desirable as an immolation.

"*He's* no Imager," Lebbick went on. "And there isn't any way he could have left those rooms except by Imagery. So *you* did it. You translated him somewhere.

"Where is he, woman? I want him."

She stared at him. Her dismay seemed to become a kind of calm; she was less frantic simply because she was so afraid. "You've gone crazy," she whispered. "You've snapped. It's been too much for you."

"I won't hurt him." The Castellan's face felt like it was being split apart by the stress of restraint. "It isn't really his fault. I know that. You seduced him into it. Until you arrived, he was just another son of the Domne—too clumsy for his own good, but a decent boy. Everybody liked him, even though he couldn't do anything right. You changed that. You involved him in treachery. When I get my hands on him, I won't even punish him. I just want him to tell me the truth."

Suddenly, like dry brush on a smoldering blaze, Lebbick yelled at her, "*Where* IS *he?*"

She flinched, cowered. Just for a second, he believed that she was going to answer. But then something inside her stiffened. She raised her head and faced him squarely.

"Go to hell."

At that, he laughed. He couldn't help himself: he laughed as if his heart were breaking. "You little whore," he chortled, "don't try to defy *me*. You aren't strong enough."

At once, he began to speak more precisely, more formally, tapping words into her fear like coffin nails. "I'm going to start by taking off your clothes. I might do it gently, just for fun. Women are especially vulnerable when they don't have any clothes on.

"Then I'll begin to hurt you." He took a step toward her, but didn't release his arms from his chest. "Just a little at first. One breast or the other. Or perhaps a few barbs across your belly. A rough piece of wood between your legs. Just to get your attention." He wished she could see what he saw: his wife being stretched out in the dirt by those Alends, her limbs spread-eagled and staked so that she couldn't move, the delicate things the garrison commander had done to her with small knives. "Then I'll begin to hurt you in earnest.

"You'll beg me to stop. You'll tell me everything I desire, and you'll beg me to stop. But it will be too late. Your chance will be lost. Once I begin to hurt you, I will never stop. I will never stop."

She was so vividly appalled—the fright on her face was so

stark—that the sight of it cost him his grip on himself. His arms
burst out of his control; his hands caught her shoulders. Snatching
her to him, he covered her mouth with his and kissed her as hard
as a blow, aching to consume her with his passion before it tore him
to pieces. Then he hugged her, hugged her so urgently that the muscles in his shoulders stood out like iron.

"Tell me the truth." His voice shook, feverish with distress.
"Don't make me hurt you."

She had her arms between them, her hands against his chest.
But she didn't struggle: she surrendered to his embrace as if the
resistance had been squeezed out of her. If he had released her without warning, she would have fallen.

Nevertheless when she spoke all she said was, "Please don't do
this. Please." The way he held her muffled her words in his shoulder,
but he could still hear them. "I'll beg now, if that's what you want.
Please don't do this to me."

For a moment, the gloom in the cell grew unexpectedly darker.
It rose up around the Castellan, swept over his head; it made a roaring
noise like a black torrent in his ears. Then it cleared, and the back
of his hand hurt. The woman was slumped on the floor; the wall
barely braced her up in a sitting position. Blood oozed like midnight
from the corner of her mouth. Her eyes seemed glazed, as if she
were scarcely conscious.

"The lady Terisa is too polite," someone else said. "I will not
speak so courteously. The next blow will be your last. If you strike
her again, I will not rest until you are sent to the gallows."

Staggering, Castellan Lebbick turned and saw the Tor at the
entrance of the cell.

"My lord Tor—" The Castellan croaked as if he were choking.
"This isn't your concern. Crimes committed in Orison are *my*
responsibility."

The old lord was as fat as a holiday goose and as pasty-faced as
poorly kneaded dough. Yet his small eyes glinted in the lamplight
as if he were capable of murder. Under his fat, there was strength
which enabled him to support his immense weight. "Then," he shot
back, "you will be especially responsible for crimes you commit yourself. What if she is innocent?"

"'Innocent'?"

Lebbick was ashamed to hear himself cry out the word like a

man who was about to start weeping. With a savage effort, he regained control of himself.

"'Innocent'?" he repeated more steadily. "You weren't there,
my lord. You didn't see Geraden kill his brother. I caught her helping
him escape—helping a *murderer* escape, my lord Tor. You have
strange ideas of innocence."

"And your ideas of guilt have cost you your *reason,* Castellan."
The Tor's outrage sounded as acute as Lebbick's own. "You accuse
her of helping a murderer *escape,* not of shedding blood herself. When
I heard that you had brought her here, I could hardly believe my
ears. You have no right and no *reason* to punish her until King Joyse
has judged her guilt for himself and given you his consent."

"Do you think he'll refuse me?" countered Castellan Lebbick,
fighting to shore up his self-command. "*Now,* when Orison is besieged, and all his enemies are conspiring against him? My lord, you
misjudge him. *This*"—he made a slapping gesture in that woman's
direction—"is one problem he'll leave to me."

Without hesitation, the Tor snapped, "Shall we ask him?"

The Castellan had no choice; he couldn't refuse. In spite of the
way his bones ached and his guts shook, so that he seemed to be
dying on his feet, he turned his back on that woman and went with
the Tor to talk to King Joyse.

When Lebbick demanded an audience, the King answered in his
nightshirt.

Instead of admitting the Castellan and the Tor to his presence,
he opened the door of his formal rooms and stood there between
the guards, blinking his watery old eyes at the lamplight as if he had
become timid—as if he feared he might not be safe in his own castle
in the middle of the night. He hadn't been asleep: he had come to
the door too promptly for that. And he neglected or forgot to close
it behind him. The Castellan saw that King Joyse already had
company.

Two men sat in front of his hearth, looking over their shoulders
toward the door.

Adept Havelock. Of course. And Master Quillon, the recently
designated mediator of the Congery.

Master Quillon, who had *accidentally* contrived to help Geraden
escape by tripping Lebbick. Master Quillon, who had *mistakenly*

given that woman time to help Geraden by sending the guards away from the rooms where the mirrors were kept.

The Castellan ground curses between his teeth.

King Joyse gaped at Castellan Lebbick and then the Tor with a foolish expression on his face. His beard was tangled in all directions; his white hair jutted wildly around the rim of his tattered and lumpy nightcap—a cap, Lebbick happened to know, which Queen Madin had given him nearly twenty years ago. His hands were swollen with arthritis, and his back stooped for the same reason. The result was that he looked small and a little silly, too much reduced in physical and mental stature to be a credible ruler for his people.

And yet the Castellan loved him. Looking at him now, Lebbick found that what he missed most wasn't Joyse's former leadership— or his former trust. It was the Queen: blunt, beautiful, pragmatic Madin. She had done everything in her power to keep King Joyse from becoming so much less than he was. She wouldn't have let anybody see him in this condition.

That recognition surprised Castellan Lebbick out of the fierce speech he was primed to make. Instead of spitting his bitter demands in Joyse's face, he muttered almost gently, "Forgive the intrusion, my lord King. Couldn't you sleep?"

"No," King Joyse assented in a vague tone. "I meant what I told you to tell Kragen. I want to use the Congery. But I didn't know how. It was keeping me awake. So I sent for Quillon." As if he believed this to be the reason Castellan Lebbick had come to him, he asked distractedly, "If you were them, what would you do tomorrow?"

Involuntarily, Lebbick exchanged a glance of incomprehension with the Tor. "'Them,' my lord King? The Masters?"

"The Alends," King Joyse explained without impatience. "Prince Kragen. What's he going to do tomorrow?"

That question didn't require thought. "Catapults. He'll try to break down the curtain-wall."

King Joyse nodded. "That's what I thought." He seemed too sleepy to concentrate well. "Quillon and Havelock are going to do something about it." As an afterthought, he added, "They'll need advice. And you need to know what they're doing. Meet Quillon at dawn.

"Good night." He turned back toward his rooms.

"My lord King." It was the Tor who spoke.

The King raised his eyebrows tiredly. "Was there something else?"

"Yes," the Tor said sharply before Castellan Lebbick could break in. "Yes, my lord King. Lebbick has put the lady Terisa of Morgan in the dungeon. He struck her. He means to question her with pain. And he may"—the Tor looked at Lebbick and fought to contain his anger—"may have other intentions as well.

"He must be stopped."

The Castellan started to protest, then caught himself. To his astonishment, King Joyse was glaring at the Tor as if the old lord had begun to stink in some way.

"What difference does it make to you, my lord Tor?" retorted the King. "Nyle was *killed*. Maybe you didn't realize that. The son of the *Domne,* my lord Tor—the son of a *friend.*" He spoke as if he had forgotten why the old lord had come to Orison in the first place. "Lebbick is just doing his job."

In response, the Tor's expression turned to nausea; his mouth opened and closed stupidly. He was so appalled that a moment passed before he was able to breathe; then he said as if he were suppressing an attack of apoplexy, "Do I understand you, my lord King?" His lips stretched tight, baring his wine-stained teeth. "Does Castellan Lebbick have your permission to torture and rape the lady Terisa of Morgan?"

A muscle in King Joyse's cheek twitched. Suddenly, his eyes were no longer watery: they flashed blue fire. "That's enough!" Echoes of the man he used to be rang off the walls as he articulated distinctly, "You fat, old, useless sot, you've interfered with me enough. I'm sick of your self-righteousness. I'm sick of being judged. Castellan Lebbick has my permission to *do his job.*"

Behind his constant scowl, inside his clenched heart, Lebbick felt like cheering.

The Tor's face swelled purple; his eyes bulged. His fists came up trembling, as if he were in the throes of a seizure—as if he had finally been provoked to strike his King. When he lowered them again, the act cost him a supreme effort. As the blood left his face, his skin became waxen.

"I do not believe you. You are my King. My friend." His voice rattled in his throat; his gaze was no longer focused on anything. "I, too, have lost a son. I will not believe you.

"Be warned, Castellan. You will suffer for it if you believe him."

His flesh seemed to slump on his bones as he moved away and went slowly down the stairs, carrying himself as if his years had caught up with him without warning and made him frail.

Softly, so that he wouldn't betray his jubilation, Castellan Lebbick murmured, "My lord King."

At once, King Joyse turned on him. The King's blue eyes continued to burn, but now they were unexpectedly rimmed with red. "That woman must be pushed," he rasped under his breath. "She must be made to declare herself—or to discover herself." Then he thrust a crooked finger into Lebbick's face and snarled, "Be ready to answer for everything you do."

Without allowing Lebbick time to reply, he reentered his rooms and slammed the door.

Since the guards were studiously not looking at him, Castellan Lebbick glowered at them to conceal his satisfaction. He hadn't forgotten the rest of his job: Master Quillon, Master Eremis, Nyle; the organization and defense of Orison. But those things carried no emotional weight with him now; he would deal with them simply to get them out of his way. King Joyse had given him permission. His King trusted him to discover that woman's secrets.

His King's trust was the only answer he needed. The answer for everything.

Deliberately postponing the pleasure he desired most, he didn't return to the dungeon. Instead, he went looking for Master Eremis— and Nyle's body. *Nyle is still alive.* He had time before dawn to give himself the luxury of confirming that that woman had lied.

He found the Imager in the corridor leading away from the section of Orison where all the Masters had their quarters. Eremis was striding purposefully in Lebbick's direction, and he greeted the Castellan by saying without preamble, "Nyle is still alive."

Castellan Lebbick halted, braced his fists on his hips, faced the Imager fiercely. Now that Eremis had his attention, he remembered why he hated the tall, lean Master so much. He hated the lively and sardonic superiority in Eremis' gaze, the combination of intelligence and ridicule in Eremis' manner. Most of all, however, he hated Eremis' success with women. Women whose faces wore an implicit sneer for the Castellan spread their legs for Eremis whenever the Master simply lifted an eyebrow at them. It probably wasn't surprising that the sluttish maid Saddith was eager for the prestige she

could get from a Master. But it knotted the Castellan's guts to recollect the mute yearning he had occasionally seen in his prisoner's
expression at the mere mention of Master Eremis.

Lebbick himself would have been tempted to kill any woman
who acquiesced to him without being his wife.

Unfortunately, he didn't have time to hate Eremis at the moment. Too much was happening; the Master's words seemed to open
an abyss under his feet. "Alive?" he snapped. "What're you talking
about?"

"I hoped this was possible," replied Master Eremis as if the
Castellan had asked his question politely. "That is why I rushed him
to my rooms. I have never seen Geraden do anything well, so I hoped
that he might find it impossible to murder his brother successfully.
Apparently, his knife missed Nyle's heart."

At once, relief reeled through Lebbick's head. That woman *was*
lying. She still belonged to him. For a moment, he was so giddy that
he couldn't pull his thoughts together enough to speak.

"Underwell is with him," continued Eremis. Underwell was one
of the best physicians in Orison. In fact, he was the physician Castellan Lebbick himself would have chosen to take care of Nyle. "If
he can be saved, Underwell will do it.

"In addition, I took the liberty of making a few demands on
your guards." The Master's eyes glittered with mirth or malice, as if
he could read Lebbick's confusion plainly. "If Geraden wants his
brother dead badly enough, he may try again. It seems clear that he
is in league with Gilbur as well as Gart—and almost certainly with
the arch-Imager also. You may recall that they are apparently able
to come and go in Orison as they wish. So I insisted on being obeyed
by four of your men. Two of them are with Underwell and Nyle.
The other two guard my door.

"Do you approve of my arrangements"—Master Eremis smiled
amiably—"good Castellan?"

With some difficulty, the Castellan imposed a bit of order on
his inner riot. He *did* approve of Eremis' arrangements. They were
right. No, more than that: they were so right that they made that
woman's accusations against Master Eremis look ludicrous. Just for
a second, he found himself wondering whether Eremis had jilted
her, whether her behavior could be explained by jealousy. But speculations like that only led him back into turmoil. What he needed
at the moment was to forget about her for a while.

"They'll do for now," he replied, speaking roughly because he resented the necessity of giving Eremis even that much satisfaction. "In the meantime, I want you to come with me. I want some answers, but I haven't got time to stand here talking."

Master Eremis frowned, although his eyes continued smiling. With a hint of acid, he said, "My time is valuable also, Castellan. Our brave King threatened the Alend army with the strength of the Congery, did he not? And yet we have made no plans to back up his threat. It seems likely that our new mediator will call a second meeting of the Congery before this night ends." The Imager's tone gave nothing away. "If he does, I must attend."

Lebbick consulted his mental hourglass and retorted, "I don't think so. There isn't time." His anger matched Eremis'. "I've been commanded to meet Quillon at dawn. You can talk to him then.

"Come on."

He almost hoped that Eremis would refuse. The Castellan would have enjoyed having the insolent Imager tied up and dragged along behind him. On the other hand, he had too much else on his mind and wouldn't be able to give an experience like that the attention it deserved. So he waited until Master Eremis acceded; then he strode away.

His questions were the same ones which had come up during that ill-fated meeting of the Congery earlier in the evening. How did Eremis account for the fact that he was the only man in Orison who had been consistently able to know where that woman was when the High King's Monomach attacked her? And why was Gart trying to kill her anyway, if he and Geraden were plotting together and Geraden loved her? And what had the lords of the Cares and Prince Kragen said to each other when they had treacherously met at Eremis' instigation? And what was that story about an attack of Imagery on Geraden—translated insects trying to kill him? With or without Eremis' knowledge?

Of course, Master Eremis had replied to all those questions during the meeting. But Castellan Lebbick hadn't liked the answers. Taken together, they all contained one fatal flaw: they all presupposed that Geraden was a smooth and expert traitor; that he not only possessed but concealed unprecedented talents; that he had allied himself with Gart and Cadwal long before that woman's translation into Orison; that all his clumsiness, his appearance of being a confused puppy, was a sham.

Lebbick found the whole idea incredible.

He believed that Geraden had tried to kill Nyle: he had seen it with his own eyes. But Geraden secretly plotting Mordant's downfall? Artagel's brother in league with Gart? The son of the Domne seducing that woman to crimes she wouldn't otherwise have committed? Those things Castellan Lebbick didn't believe. No, the crimes and the plotting and the seduction were hers, not Geraden's.

And Eremis was a fool for blaming him. Or else the Master hadn't started to tell the truth yet.

So while he went about readying Orison to meet the dawn, Castellan Lebbick made Master Eremis go through all his explanations again, with more care, in greater detail. After a day without water, the castle was already experiencing considerable distress. Strict rationing created hundreds of hardships; dozens of people cheated—or tried to cheat—and had to be dealt with. On the other hand, the difficulties were much less now than they would be soon. Severity was Orison's only hope. Therefore Lebbick dispensed severity everywhere he went. And Eremis watched him. Answered his questions. Betrayed nothing.

Perhaps that was why Castellan Lebbick couldn't think of a good retort when Eremis goaded him about his loyalty to the King, on the ramparts of Orison after Adept Havelock had demonstrated the effectiveness of his defense against catapults. The Master had betrayed nothing. *We might have decided to defend Mordant ourselves, rather than waiting politely for our beloved King to fall off the precarious perch of his reason.* Some reply was essential: Lebbick knew that. But he couldn't seem to pull his yearning spirit this far away from the dungeon. Without paying much attention to what he said, he muttered, "Prove it. Get me water."

Then he didn't want to look at Eremis anymore. The tall Master's smile had become abruptly intolerable: it was too bemused, too secretly triumphant. Instead, he did his best to concentrate on what Havelock and Quillon were doing.

At first glance, the Adept seemed to be in a state of unnatural self-possession, even though the obscenities he muttered as he worked were so extravagant that they would have earned him a round of applause from any squad of the Castellan's guard. Lebbick wasn't used to seeing him do what was asked of him. The mad walleyed old goat who capered and jeered in the hall of audiences—or who incinerated important prisoners before they could be questioned—was the Havelock Lebbick knew: the man working with Master Quillon was a relative stranger. A throwback to the potent and cunning Imager who had helped King Joyse found and secure Mordant. Only the Adept's appearance seemed unchanged. He wore nothing but an ancient, unclean surcoat; what was left of his hair stuck out from his skull in wild tufts. Between the craziness of his imperfectly focused eyes and the trembling, sybaritic flesh of his lips, his nose jutted fiercely.

But a closer look showed the cost of Adept Havelock's self-possession.

He was sweating, despite the chill of the breeze. His whole body shook as if he were in the grip of a fever—as if he stood where he was and worked his Imagery by an act of will so harsh that his entire frame rebelled against it. With an unexpected pang, Lebbick noticed that there was blood running down Havelock's chin. The Adept had chewed on his lower lip until he had torn it to shreds.

For all practical purposes, he was Orison's only defense against catapults. Master Quillon had made it clear that the Congery possessed no other mirrors which could meet this particular need. Everything the Castellan had ever served or cared about depended on Havelock—and Havelock obviously wasn't going to last much longer.

"Dogswater!" Roughly, Castellan Lebbick took hold of Quillon's arm, demanded the Master's attention. "How much longer can he keep going?"

Before Quillon could answer, the Adept swung away from his glass, cackling like a demented crone.

"Long enough! Hee-hee! Long *enough!*" Havelock brandished a mouth full of bloody teeth toward Lebbick, but neither of his eyes succeeded at aiming itself at the Castellan. His voice scaled higher, tittering on the verge of hysteria. "They're throwing *rocks* at him, rocks rocks rocks rocks rocks! And *we're* the only friends he has left! *We're the only friends he has left!*"

Moving too quickly to be stopped, he wiped blood from his chin onto his hands and slapped them across Lebbick's cheeks, smearing red into the grizzled stubble of the Castellan's whiskers. "And *you've* lost your *mind!*"

Suddenly wild, Castellan Lebbick knocked Havelock's arms

away. He snatched at his sword, barely stopped himself from sweeping it out and gutting the Adept where he stood. Trembling as badly as Havelock, he jammed his blade back into its scabbard, then clamped his arms across his chest. "Whelp of a slut," he muttered through his teeth. "You should have been locked up years ago."

For a moment, Adept Havelock grinned blood at the Castellan. Then he turned to Master Quillon. Jerking a thumb at Lebbick, he whispered as if no one but Quillon could hear him, "Did you ever know his wife?" Havelock stressed the word *know* suggestively. "I did." Without warning, he started to cackle again. "She was a better man than he'll ever be."

Still laughing, he returned to his mirror.

Master Eremis also was laughing; his eyes sparkled with mirth. "Master Quillon," he chuckled to the pained consternation in Quillon's face, "we are well and truly fortunate that only one of the King's last friends has lost his mind."

The Alend forces wheeled a third catapult into position. Adept Havelock, the King's Dastard, caused it to be destroyed also. After that, no more catapults were advanced against the castle for a while. Prince Kragen had apparently decided to reconsider his options.

But Castellan Lebbick didn't stay to watch. The mention of his wife made him so angry that he could barely endure it—and in any case his guards were perfectly capable of reporting whatever happened to him. While the blood dried on his cheeks, he stormed back into Orison and headed toward the dungeon, taking Master Eremis with him.

After a moment, of course, he realized that the last thing he wanted was to have the leering Imager with him when he confronted that woman again. Luckily, he was able to deflect his course before Eremis could guess where he was going. Instead of exposing his obsession, he led Eremis toward the Masters' quarters to check on Nyle.

"A good thought," Master Eremis commented when it became clear where Lebbick was headed. "I wish for news of Nyle's condition myself."

"Sure you do," rasped the Castellan. "He's the one who was going to prove your innocence. He was going to prove his own brother is the real traitor. Isn't that what you said?"

"Indeed." Obviously, Eremis wasn't afraid of Lebbick at all. "You find it impossible to believe that I am concerned about him

for his own sake. I understand perfectly. Considering your attitude
toward me, I am gratified that you believe I wish him well for my
own reasons." The Master's sarcasm seemed to contain an undercurrent of hilarity; he sounded like he was trying to conceal his enjoyment of a good joke. "As I said, he is my proof that I am innocent
of Geraden's accusations."

Lebbick kept on walking. When he replied, he hardly cared
whether Eremis heard him or not. Primarily for his own benefit, he
muttered under his breath, "Laugh now, you goat-rutting bastard.
Someday I'm going to learn the truth about you. When I do, I'll have
an excuse to feed you your balls."

He was so clenched inside himself, so obsessed with his own
thoughts, that he didn't expect a retort. After Master Eremis spoke,
the Castellan wasn't sure that he had heard his companion correctly.

"Try it."

Behind his bland smile, Eremis looked as eager as an axe.

Grinding his teeth, Castellan Lebbick strode down the corridor
toward the Imager's quarters.

They were reached by a short hall like a cul-de-sac, with servants' doors on either side and the main entrance at the end. Master
Eremis' ostentatious rosewood door made Lebbick sneer: it was
carved in a bas-relief of the Imager himself, representing clearly his
sense of his own superiority. But the door itself wasn't important;
it changed nothing. No, what mattered—Castellan Lebbick clung to
what mattered with both fists—was that the door was properly
closed, and that two reliable guards were on duty in the hall, controlling access to Master Eremis' chambers.

The guards saluted, and Lebbick demanded a report.

"Underwell and two of our men have been in there all night,
Castellan," the senior guard said. "Nyle must still be alive, or Underwell would have come out. But we haven't heard anything."

Master Eremis said, "Good," but the Castellan ignored him.
Brushing past the guards, Lebbick jerked the door open.

Then for a long moment he just stood there and stared dumbly
into the room, trying as if all his common sense and reason had
evaporated to figure out why the guards hadn't heard anything. That
much carnage should have made some noise.

Behind him, his men stifled curses. Master Eremis murmured,
"Excrement of a pig!" and began whistling thinly between his teeth.

There were three men in Eremis' sitting room, the two guards and Nyle. All three of them had been slaughtered.

Well, not *slaughtered,* exactly. Lebbick's brain struggled to function. The dead men hadn't actually been cut to pieces. The damage didn't look like it had been done with any kind of blade. No, instead of being victims of slaughter, human butchery, the men resembled carcases on which predators had gorged. Huge predators, with jaws that took hunks the size of helmets out of the chest and guts and limbs of his guards, *his guards.* The bodies lay in a slop of blood and entrails and splintered bones.

As for Nyle—

In some ways, he was in better condition; in some ways, worse. He hadn't been as thoroughly chewed on as the guards. But both his arms were gone, one at the elbow, the other at the shoulder. And his head had been bitten open to the brain: his whole face was gone. He was recognizable only by his general size and shape, and by his position on Eremis' sumptuous divan.

The Castellan started grinning. He wanted to laugh. He couldn't help himself: despair was the only joke he understood. Almost cheerfully, he said, "You aren't going to be seducing any women here for a while, Imager. You won't be able to get all this blood out. You'll have to replace everything."

Eremis didn't seem to hear. He was asking softly, "Underwell? Underwell?"

Of course, there should have been *four* men here: Lebbick knew that. His two guards. Nyle. And Underwell. With a feral smile, he sent a guard to search the other rooms. He still had that much self-possession. But he was sure the physician was gone. Why would Underwell want to stay and get caught after committing treachery like this?

For some reason, the fact that what had happened should have been impossible didn't bother Lebbick.

"Castellan," the senior guard said in a constricted voice, as if the air were being squeezed from his chest, "nobody went in or out. I swear it."

"Imagery." Castellan Lebbick relished the word: it hurt so much that he seemed to enjoy it. "They must have been hit too hard, too fast. Maybe it was that firecat. Or those round things with teeth the Perdon talked about." The desire to at least chuckle was almost unsupportable. "They didn't even have a chance to shout. Imagery."

"I fear so." Master Eremis' manner was unusually subdued, but his eyes shone like bits of glass. "Our enemies have been able to do such things ever since the lady Terisa of Morgan was brought here."

"And in your quarters, Imager." Lebbick kept on grinning. "In your care. Protected by arrangements you made."

At that, Eremis' eyes widened; he blinked at the Castellan. "Are you serious? Do you blame me for this?"

"It was done by imagery. You're an Imager. They're your rooms."

"He was alive when I left him," Master Eremis protested. "Ask your guards." For the first time, Lebbick saw him look worried. "And I have spent all the rest of my time with you."

The Master's point was reasonable, but Castellan Lebbick ignored it. "You're an Imager," he repeated. As he spoke, his voice took on a slight singsong tone, as if deep inside himself he were trying to rock his hurt like a sick child. "You think you're a good one. Do you expect me to believe 'our enemies' have a flat glass that shows your rooms and you don't know about it? They made it and then never used it, never gave you any kind of hint, never did anything that might possibly have made a good Imager like you aware of what they had? Are *you* serious?"

To his astonishment, Lebbick discovered that he was almost in tears. His men had never had a chance to defend themselves, and there was nothing he could do to help them now, no way he could ever bring them back. Grinning as hard as he could, he twisted his voice down into a snarl. "I don't like it when my men are slaughtered."

"An admirable sentiment." Master Eremis' face was tight; the concern in his eyes had become anger. "It does you credit. But it has no relevance. *Our* enemies appear to have flat glass which admits them everywhere. If I knew how that trick is done, I would do it myself. But that also has no relevance. Nyle was alive when I left him. A blind man could see that I was with you when he was killed. I am not to blame for this."

"Prove it," retorted the Castellan as if he were recovering his good humor. "I know you didn't do this yourself. The traitors you're in league with did it. But *you* set it up. All *you* did"—with difficulty, he resisted a tremendous impulse to hit Eremis a few times—"*all* you did was bring Nyle here so that Gart and Gilbur and the rest of your *friends* could get at him."

He wanted to roar, *All you did was have my men slaughtered!* But the words caught in his throat, choking him.

"Castellan Lebbick, listen to me. Listen to me." Master Eremis spoke as if he had been trying to get Lebbick's attention for some time—as if Lebbick were in the grip of delirium. "That makes no sense.

"If you believe I am responsible for Nyle's death, then you must believe he would not have defended me from Geraden's accusations. Therefore you must believe I had no reason to take him to the meeting of the Congery. What, so that he could speak against me? I say that makes no sense.

"And if you believe I am responsible for his death, you must also believe I have the means to leave Orison whenever I wish—by the same glass which enabled Gilbur to escape. Then why do I remain? Why did I go to face Geraden before the Congery, when I could have fled his charges so easily? Why have I submitted myself to this siege? Castellan, that makes *no sense.*

"I am not a traitor. I serve Mordant and Orison. I am not to blame for Nyle's death."

Unable to think coherently, Lebbick rasped again, "Prove it." He wanted to howl. Eremis' argument was too persuasive: he didn't know what was wrong with it. "Talk doesn't mean anything. You can say whatever you want." And yet there had to be something wrong with it. There *had* to be, because he needed that so badly. He needed to do something with his despair. "Just prove it."

Unfortunately, Master Eremis had recovered his confidence. The Imager's expression was again full of secrets—hidden facts or intentions which made Eremis want to laugh, restored his look of untarnished superiority.

Smiling amiably, hatefully, he remarked, "You said that once before. Out on the battlements. Do you remember?"

The gentle suggestion that Lebbick might not remember—that he might not have that much grasp on what he was doing—infuriated him enough to restore some of his self-command. "I remember," he shot back, relieved to hear himself sound trenchant and familiar. "You didn't do anything about it then, either."

"No," the Master agreed. "But a possibility occurred to me. I was about to discuss it when the Adept treated us to another of his fits. That distracted me, and I forgot my thought until now."

"You mentioned water."

Involuntarily, Castellan Lebbick froze. Water! Complex pressures seized his heart: he could hardly breathe.

"I can provide it."

Orison was desperate for water. The lack of water hurt a lot of people. And it was Lebbick's job to supervise that hurt. Because of his duties, he was responsible, culpable, as if he caused the hurt himself.

But he would have preferred to be gutted by whores than to accept any vital help from Master Eremis.

"I have a glass," Eremis explained, "which shows a scene in which the rain is incessant. The Image is always in a state of torrential downpour. I can take that mirror to the reservoir and translate rain to replenish our supply of water." He shrugged slightly. "The process may take some time. The volume of rain that I can bring out at any given instant will be limited. But surely I can ease the need for rationing. Perhaps in a few days I can refill the reservoir."

Deliberately, he smiled as if he knew precisely how much distress he was causing Lebbick. "Will that prove my loyalty, good Castellan? Will that demonstrate the sincerity of my desire to serve Orison and Mordant?"

Castellan Lebbick made a rattling noise far back in his throat. Eremis' offer was so bitter to him that he was in danger of strangling on it. He couldn't refuse it, he knew that. It was just what King Joyse had always wanted from the Congery, from Imagery: the ability to heal wounds, solve problems, rectify losses without doing any injustice—real or theoretical—to the Images themselves. And it was just what Orison needed.

With enough water to keep them going, the castle's defenders might prove strong enough to repulse Alend, even if that bastard Kragen's catapults succeeded at tearing down the curtain-wall.

The offer had to be accepted. There was no way around it. The Castellan had to swallow it somehow, had to sacrifice that much more of himself for the sake of his duty. But he could not, *could* not choke down such a mortification directly. Instead of replying to Master Eremis, he turned on the senior guard so savagely that the veteran flinched.

"Pay attention," he snapped unnecessarily. "You were supposed to protect these people, and you did a great job of it. This is your chance to redeem yourself.

"Take this Imager to the King. Make him tell the King what

happened here. Make sure he tells the King everything he just told me. Beat it out of him if you have to. Then take him to get that mirror of his. Take him up to the reservoir. Make him do what he promised.

"Use as many men as you need. He's your problem until that reservoir is full.

"Do it now."

"Yes, Castellan." Shock, fear, and anger made the guard zealous. Glad for something specific and physical to do, he clamped a fist around Master Eremis' arm. "Are you coming, or do I have to drag you?"

In response, the expression on Master Eremis' face became positively blissful.

He had more strength than Lebbick suspected—and better leverage. A twist freed his arm: a nudge knocked the guard off balance: a strategically placed knee doubled the man over. With sarcastic elegance, Eremis adjusted his jet cloak, straightened his chasuble. Then, in an excessively polite tone, he commented, "Good Castellan, I fear that your men are not trained well enough for this siege."

Before Lebbick could find words for his fury, the Master turned to the guard. "Shall we go? I believe the Castellan wishes me to speak to King Joyse."

Flourishing his arms, he left the hallway.

Paralyzed by pain and consternation, the guard stayed where he was. After a moment, however, the murder in Castellan Lebbick's glare sent him hobbling after Master Eremis with his comrade.

Lebbick remained alone. He didn't look at Nyle's mutilated corpse again, or at the bodies of his men. Slowly and steadily, unconscious of what he was doing, he beat his forehead against the wall until he had regained enough self-possession to call for more guards without howling. Then he had the dead carried out and gave orders for the sealing of the rooms, in case Geraden or his allies wanted to use this way into Orison again.

Geraden wasn't just a murderer. He was a butcher, crazy with hate for his own brother, and nothing made sense anymore.

For the rest of the day, Castellan Lebbick concentrated on keeping himself busy, so that he wouldn't go down to the dungeon. Eremis' innocence seemed to weaken him in ways he couldn't explain, cut the ground out from under his rage. He was afraid that if he saw that woman now he would end up begging her to forgive him.

———

Keeping himself busy was easy: he had plenty of duties. While he heard reports about the state of the siege, however, while he settled disputes among Orison's overcrowded population, or discussed tactical alternatives in case Adept Havelock became ineffective against the Alend catapults, he didn't say anything about water to anyone. He didn't want to raise any hopes until Master Eremis proved himself. Nevertheless he sent men to adjust all the valves of the water system and incurred the outrage of hundreds of thirsty people by using the little water which the castle's spring had accumulated to flush any possible residue of the lady Elega's poison out of the pipes.

And when one of his men finally brought him word that Master Eremis was at work in the reservoir, he went to watch.

The Imager was doing what he had said he could do. In the high, cathedral-like vault of the reservoir, he stood on the stone lip of the empty pool and held his mirror leaning out over the edge. The glass was nearly as tall as he was, and set in an ornate frame; therefore it was heavy: even a man with his unexpected strength wouldn't be able to support its weight in that position for any length of time. He had solved the problem, however, by bringing two Apts to help him. One braced the bottom of the mirror to keep it steady; the other held the top of the mirror by means of a rope looped over one of the timbers which propped up the network of pipes and screens above the pool. The assistance of the Apts enabled Master Eremis to concentrate exclusively on his translation.

As he stroked the frame and murmured whatever invocations triggered the relationship between his talent and the glass, rain came gushing from the uneven surface of the mirror.

He was right: the process was going to take time. However torrential the rain was, the amount which could be translated through the mirror was small compared to the size of the pool and Orison's need. Nevertheless Castellan Lebbick could see that the glass gave significantly more water than the spring. If Master Eremis was able to keep going—and if the water was good.

Lebbick tested one worry by requiring the Imager to drink two cups of the rainwater himself—which Master Eremis did with no discernible hesitation. But a close look at him only increased the Castellan's other concern.

Master Eremis was sweating in the cool air of the reservoir. His breathing was deep and hard, and his features had the tight pallor of clenched knuckles. His expression was uncharacteristically simple: for once, what he was doing required him to concentrate so acutely, exert himself so fully, that he had no energy to spare for secrets.

He had been at work for only a short time, and already the strain had begun to tell on him. To keep his translation going, he would need more than unexpected strength. He would need the stamina of an iron bar.

Castellan Lebbick didn't bother to curse. He could feel something inside him failing: the Imager was beating him. This was just perfect. Eremis was going to save Orison—but that wasn't enough for him, oh, no, not enough at all. He was going to save Orison *heroically,* exhausting himself with a translation which would leave no doubt in anyone's mind about where his loyalties lay.

A curious weakness dragged at Lebbick's muscles. He had trouble keeping his back straight. His cheeks felt unnaturally stiff; when he rubbed them, dried blood came off on his fingers. Maybe Havelock was right about him. Maybe he had lost his mind. Two of his men and Nyle had been *slaughtered,* and it was his fault, not because he had trusted Eremis, whom he hated, but because he had refused to believe that bright, clumsy, likable Geraden was sick with evil. Geraden had translated atrocities to butcher his own brother. Or he had made someone else do it for him.

The Castellan wanted his wife. He wanted to hide his face against her shoulder and feel her arms around him. But she was dead, and he was never going to be comforted again.

Master Eremis wasn't cold now, but he would be chilled as soon as he stopped for rest. Mortifying himself further, Castellan Lebbick ordered a cot and food, warmer clothes, a fire on the edge of the pool, brandy. Then, when he had done everything he could think of for Orison's savior, he went back to his duties.

During the afternoon, the Alends brought up a catapult against Orison's gates—the only other part of the castle which might prove vulnerable without a prolonged assault. Master Quillon roused Havelock from a loud snooze, and the two Imagers took the Adept's mirror around to Orison's long northeast face to protect the gates. Castellan Lebbick, however, remained out of sight above the curtain-wall. When several hundred Alends rushed forward suddenly, carrying scaling ladders, the Castellan was ready for them. His archers forced them to retreat.

That success relieved some of his weakness. But it wasn't enough. Nothing was enough anymore. To keep himself from foundering, he fell back on the one distinct, comprehensible instruction he had received from his King.

To do his job.

That woman must be pushed.

After dark, when the loss of light alleviated the threat of catapults, allowing the guards to concentrate on defending Orison from simpler forms of attack, Castellan Lebbick went back to the dungeon to do what King Joyse had told him.

TWENTY-NINE:
TERISA HAS
VISITORS

fter the Castellan hit her and left, Terisa Morgan remained against the wall for a long time, held up in a sitting position more by the blank stone than by any desire to keep herself from crumpling.

It's a trick. She told him that, didn't she? *Eremis did this somehow.* Yes, she told him. *To get rid of Geraden.* She told him all that. She even tried to beg—tried to call on the part of herself which had babbled and pleaded with her parents, her father, No, I didn't do it, it isn't my fault, I'll never do it again, *please don't do this.* Don't lock me in the closet. That's where I fade. It's dark, and it sucks me away, and I stop existing. *Nyle is still alive.*

But the Castellan didn't listen to her. He took hold of her shoulders and kissed her like a blow. Then he did hit her; she staggered against the wall and fell. It was the second time he had hit her. The first time, she had been full of audacity. She had told him that his wife would have been ashamed of him. She could almost have foreseen that he would hit her. But this time she was begging. *Please don't do this to me.* And he hit her anyway. Like her father, he didn't stop.

The third time was going to be the end of her. She felt sure of that. He had promised to hurt her, and he was going to keep his promise. *Just a little at first. One breast or the other. Or perhaps a few*

barbs across your belly. A rough piece of wood between your legs. He was
going to hit and hurt her until she broke.

She didn't understand why he kissed her. She didn't want to
understand. *Go to hell.* All she wanted was to fade. The cell was cold,
and the lamp was afflicted with a ghoulish flicker like a promise that
it might go out at any moment, plunging her into blackness. When
she was a child, the prospect of fading had always terrified her. It
still did. But soon being locked in the closet had reminded her of
the safety of the dark, had taught her again that she could fade to
escape from being alone and unloved, scarcely able to breathe. If
she didn't exist, she couldn't be hurt.

If she didn't exist, she couldn't be hurt.

Go to hell.

But now, when she needed it most, it was taken away from her.
She couldn't fade: she had lost the trick of letting go. The Castellan
was going to hurt her in a way she had never experienced before.
That wasn't like the relatively passive violence of being locked in a
closet. It wasn't like being left alone to save herself or go mad. It
was a new kind of pain—

And Geraden—

Oh, Geraden!

She needed to fade, *had* to escape, in order to protect him, just
in case he was still alive, just in case he had somehow succeeded at
working another impossible translation. Fading was her only defense
against the pressure to betray him. If she were gone, she wouldn't
be able to tell the Castellan where he was.

And yet he was the other reason she couldn't let go. She was
too afraid for him. She couldn't forget the way she had last seen him,
the poignant mixture of anguish and iron in his face, the fatal authority in his voice and movements. The sweet and openhearted
young man she loved wasn't gone. No. That would have been bad
enough, but what had happened to him was worse. He had been
melted and beaten to iron without losing any of his vulnerabilities,
so that the strength or desperation which led him to cast himself into
a mirror wasn't a measure of how hard he had become, but rather
of how much pain he was in.

She had cried, *I'm not an Imager! I can't help you!* And he had
turned away from her because he didn't have any other choice. She
wasn't the answer to his need. He had flung himself into the glass
and was gone, unreachable, so far beyond hope or help that he didn't

even appear in the Image of the mirror. Even an Adept couldn't have
brought him back.

That was how she knew where he was.

If he were still alive at all. And if the translation hadn't cost
him his sanity.

She should have gone with him.

Yes. She should have gone with him. That was another reason
she couldn't fade: she couldn't forget that she had already failed him.
And failed herself at the same time. She loved him, didn't she? Wasn't
that what she had learned in their last day together?—that he was
more important to her even than Master Eremis' strange power to
draw a response from her body? that she believed in him and trusted
him no matter what the evidence against him was? that she cared
about him too much to take any side but his in the machinations and
betrayals which embroiled Mordant? Then what was she doing *here?*
Why had she stood still and simply watched him risk his life and his
mind, without making the slightest effort to go with him?

She should have gone.

She was blocked from escaping inside herself by her fear of the
Castellan. By her fear for Geraden. And by shame.

After a while, the wall began to pain her back. Imperfectly fitted
pieces of granite pressed against her spine, her shoulder blades. Cold
seemed to soak into her from the floor, despite the warm riding
clothes Mindlin had made for her, despite her boots. Perhaps it
would be wiser if she got up and went to the cot. But she didn't
have the heart to move, or the strength.

Now you are mine.

Geraden, forgive me.

"My lady."

She couldn't see who spoke. Nevertheless his voice didn't
frighten her, so after a while she was able to raise her head.

The Tor stood at the door of her cell. His voice shook as he
murmured again, "My lady." His fat fists gripped the bars of the door
as if he were the one who had been locked up—as if he were im-
prisoned and she were free. Dully, she noticed the lamplit tears
spreading across his cheeks.

"My lady, help me."

His appeal reached her. He was her friend, one of the few
people in Orison who seemed to wish her well. He had saved her
from the Castellan. More than once. Biting back a groan, she shifted

onto her hands and knees. Then she got her feet under her and
tottered upright.

Swaying and afraid that she might faint, she moved closer to
the door. For the moment, that was the best she could do.

"My lady, you must help me." The old lord's voice shook, not
because he was urgent, but because he was fighting grief. "King Joyse
has given Lebbick permission to do anything he wants to you."

She didn't understand. Like the Castellan's kiss, this was incomprehensible. Somehow, she found herself sitting on the floor
again, hunched forward so that her graceless and untended hair hid
her face. *Permission to do anything.* King Joyse had smiled at her, and
his smile was wonderful, a sunrise that could have lit the dark of her
life. She could have loved that smile, as she loved Geraden. But it
was all a lie. *Anything he wants to you.* It was all a lie, and there was
no hope left.

"Please," the Tor breathed in supplication. "My lady. Terisa."
He was barely able to contain his distress. "In the name of everything
you respect—everything you would find good and worthy about him,
if he had not fallen so far below himself. Tell us where Geraden has
gone."

Involuntarily, her head jerked up. Her eyes were full of shadows. You, too? Nausea closed around her stomach. You've turned
against him, too? She couldn't reply: there weren't any words. If she
tried to say anything, she would start to cry herself. Or throw up.
Not you, *too.*

"You will not hurt him, my lady." The Tor was pleading. He
was an old man and carried every pound of his weight as if it were
burdensome. "I care nothing for his guilt. If he lives, he is far from
here, safe from Lebbick's outrage. We are besieged. Lebbick cannot
pursue him. And no one else can use his glass. It will cost him nothing
if you speak.

"But King Joyse—" The lord's throat closed convulsively.
When he was able to speak again, his voice rattled in his chest like
a hint of mortality. "King Joyse has trusted the Castellan too long.
And he is no longer himself. He does not understand the permission
he has given. He does not know that Lebbick is mad.

"My lady, he is my friend. I have served him with my life, and
with the lives of all my Care, for decades. Now he is not what he
was. I acknowledge that. At one time, he was the hero of all Mordant.
Now it is the best he can do to defend Orison intelligently.

"But he has only become smaller, my lady, not less good. He means well. I swear to you on my heart that he means well.

"If you defy Lebbick, the Castellan will do his worst. And when King Joyse understands what his permission has done to you, he will lose the little of himself that remains.

"Help me, my lady. Save him. Tell us where Geraden has gone, so that Lebbick will have no excuse to hurt you."

Terisa couldn't focus her eyes. All she seemed to see was the light reflecting on his cheeks. He was asking her to rescue herself. After all, he was right: if she revealed where Geraden was, the Castellan would have no more excuse to harm her. And in the process King Joyse would be saved from doing something cruel. And the Tor himself—the only one of the three she cared about—might be able to stop crying.

With more strength than she knew she had, she got to her feet. "King Joyse is your friend." To herself, she sounded dry and unmoved, vaguely heartless. "Geraden is mine." Then, trying to ease the old man's distress, she murmured, "I'm sorry."

"'Sorry'?" His voice broke momentarily. "Why are you sorry? You will suffer—and perhaps you will die—out of loyalty to a man who has killed his own brother, and it will do him no good. Perhaps he will never know that you have done it. You will endure the worst Lebbick can do to you and accomplish nothing." His hands struggled with the bars. "You have no cause to be sorry. In all Orison, you alone will pay a higher price for your loyalty than King Joyse will.

"No, my lady. The sorrow is mine." The rattle in the Tor's chest made every word he said painful to hear. "It is *mine*. You will meet your agony heroically, and you will either speak or hold still, as you are able. But I am left to watch my friend bring to ruin everything he loves.

"I did not come to you with this at once. Do not think that. Since King Joyse gave his orders, I have been in torment, wracking my heart for the means to persuade him, move him—to understand him. I have begged at his door. I have bullied servants and guards. Do not think that I bring my pain to you lightly.

"But I have nowhere else to turn.

"My lady, your loyalty is too expensive.

"Whatever I have done, I have done in my King's name. He is all that remains to me. I beg of you—do not let him destroy himself."

"No." Terisa couldn't bear the sight any longer, so she turned her back on the Tor's dismay. "Geraden is innocent. Eremis set this all up." She spoke as if she were reciting a litany, fitting pieces of faith together in an effort to build conviction. "He faked Nyle's death to make Geraden look bad, because he knew Nyle was never going to support his accusations against Geraden. If the King lets me be hurt"—a moment of dizziness swirled through her, and she nearly fell—"he's going to have to live with the consequences. Geraden is innocent."

"No, my lady," the Tor repeated; but now she heard something new in his voice—a different kind of distress, almost a note of horror. "In this you are wrong. I care nothing for Geraden's guilt. I have said that. Only the King matters to me. But you have placed your trust in someone evil."

She stood still, her pulse loud in her ears and doubt gathering in her gut.

"Nyle is unquestionably dead." The lord sounded as sick as she felt. "I have seen his body myself."

Unquestionably dead. That made her move. Groping, she found her way to the cot. It smelled of stale straw and old damp, but she sat down on it gratefully. Then she closed her eyes. She had to have a little rest. In a minute or two, when her heart had stopped quaking, she would answer the Tor. Surely she would be able to think of an answer? Surely Geraden *was* innocent?

But a moment later the thought that Nyle really had been murdered cut through her, and everything inside her seemed to spill away. Unconscious of what she was doing, she stretched out on the cot and covered her face with her hands.

Eventually, the Tor gave up and left, but she didn't hear him go.

At noon, the guards brought her a meal—hard bread and some watery stew. She panicked at their approach because she thought they might be the Castellan; her relief when she saw who they were left her too weak to get off the cot.

In fact, she felt too weak to eat at all, to take care of herself in any way. As soon as Castellan Lebbick spoke to her, she would tell him anything he wanted. But that wouldn't stop him. She could see his face in her mind, and she knew the truth. He didn't want to stop. Now that he had King Joyse's permission, nothing would stop him.

Where were the people who had shown her courtesy or kindness, the people who might be supposed to have some interest in her? Elega had gone with Prince Kragen. Myste had left Orison on a crazy quest to help the Congery's lost and rampaging champion. Adept Havelock was mad. Master Quillon had become mediator of the Congery because that was what King Joyse wanted—and King Joyse had given the Castellan permission to do whatever he wished to her. Saddith? She was only a maid, in spite of her ambitions. Maybe she *had* inadvertently betrayed Terisa to Eremis. That didn't mean there was anything she could do to correct the situation. Ribuld, the coarse veteran who had fought for Terisa more than once? He was only a guard—not even a captain.

She couldn't lift the whole weight of Mordant's need by herself. She was hardly able to lift her head off the lumpy pallet which served as her mattress. The Tor had seen Nyle's body. Geraden's brother was *unquestionably dead.*

Why should she bother to eat? What was the point?

Maybe if she got hungry enough, she would regain the ability to let go of her own existence.

She tried to sleep—tried to relax so that the tension and reality would flow out of her muscles—but another set of boots stumbled toward her down the corridor. Just one: someone was coming in her direction alone. A slow, limping stride, hesitant or frail. Deliberately, she closed her eyes again. She didn't want to know who it was. She didn't want to be distracted.

For the first time, he called her by her name.

"Terisa."

It wasn't a good omen.

Startled, she raised her head and saw Geraden's brother at the door of her cell.

"Artagel?"

He wore a nightshirt and breeches—clothes which seemed to increase his family resemblance to Geraden and Nyle because they weren't right for a swordsman. His dress and his way of standing as if someone had just stuck a knife in his side made it clear that he was still supposed to be in bed. He had been too weak yesterday— was it really only yesterday?—to support Geraden in front of the Congery. Obviously, he was too weak to walk around in the dungeon alone today.

Yet he was here.

It was definitely not a good omen that he had called her *Terisa.*

Forgetting her own lack of strength, she swung her legs off the cot and went toward him. "Oh, Artagel, I'm so glad to see you, I'm in so much trouble, I need you, I need a friend, Artagel, they think Geraden killed Nyle, they—"

His pallor stopped her. The sweat of strain on his forehead and the tremor of pain in his mouth stopped her. His eyes were glazed, as if he were about to lose consciousness. Gart, the High King's Monomach, had wounded him severely, and he drove himself into relapses by struggling out of bed when he should have been resting. The fact that Gart had beaten him; Nyle's treasonous alliance with Prince Kragen and the lady Elega; the accusations against Geraden: things like that tormented the Domne's most famous son, goading him to fight his weakness—and his recovery.

"Artagel," she groaned, "you shouldn't be here. You should be in bed. You're making yourself sick again."

"No." The word came out like a gurgle. With one arm, he clamped his other hand against his side. "No." Because he was too sick to remain standing without help, he leaned on the door, pressing his forehead against the bars. The dullness in his eyes made him look like he was going blind. "This is your doing."

She halted: pain went through her like a burn. "Artagel?" There were, after all, more kinds of pain in the world than she would ever have guessed. Except for Geraden, Artagel was the best friend she had. She would have trusted him without question. "You don't mean that." He thought *she* was responsible? "You can't."

"I didn't mean to say it." He was having trouble with his respiration. His breath seemed to struggle past an obstruction in his chest. "That isn't why I'm here. Lebbick is going to take care of you. I just want to know where Geraden is.

"I'm going to hunt him down and cut his heart out."

Suddenly, she was filled with a desire to wail or weep. It would have done her good to cry out. But this was too important. Somehow, she kept her cry down. Panting because the cell was too small and if she didn't get more air soon she was going to fail, she protested, "No. Eremis did this. It's a trick. I tell you, it's a *trick.* The Tor says he's seen the body and Nyle is really dead, but I don't believe it. Geraden didn't have anything to do with this."

"Ah!" Artagel gasped as if he were hurt and furious. "Don't lie to me. Don't lie to me anymore." Now his eyes were clear and hot, bright with passion or fever. "I've seen the body myself."

And while she reeled inside herself he continued, "After Geraden stabbed him, he was still alive. That much is true. Eremis rushed
him to his own rooms and got a physician for him. That was his only
chance to stay alive. Eremis got him that chance. Then Eremis put
guards on him—inside the room and outside the door. In case Geraden tried again.

"It didn't work." Artagel's forehead seemed to bulge between
the bars; he might have been trying to break his skull. "Lebbick found
them. The guards were killed. Some kind of beast fed off them.
Geraden must have translated something into the room—something
they couldn't fight.

"Nyle was killed. It chewed his face off."

Just for a second, that image struck her so horribly that she
quailed. Oh, Nyle! Oh, my God. Visceral revulsion churned inside
her, and her hands leaped to cover her mouth. Geraden, no!

She should have gone with him. To prevent all this.

But then she saw iron and anguish, and Geraden came back to
her. She knew him. And she loved him. *Terisa, I did not kill my
brother.* Without warning, she was angry. Years of outrage which she
had stored away in the secret places of her heart abruptly sprang out,
touching her with fire.

"Say that again," she breathed, panted. "Go on. Say it."

Artagel was beyond the reach of surprise. Baring his teeth in a
snarl, he repeated, "Nyle was killed. The beast chewed his face off."

"And you believe *Geraden* did that?" She lashed her protest at
him. "Are you out of your mind? Has everybody in this whole place
gone crazy?"

He blinked dumbly; for one brief moment, he seemed to regard
her in a different light. Almost at once, however, his own horror
returned. His legs were failing. Slowly, he began to slip down the
bars.

"I saw his body. I held it. I've still got his blood on my clothes."

That was true. Her lamp was bright enough to reveal the dried
stains on his nightshirt.

"I don't care." She was too angry to imagine what the experience
had been like for him—to hold his own brother's outraged corpse
in his arms and have no way to bring the body back to life. "Geraden
is your brother. You've known him all his life. You know him better
than that."

Artagel continued slipping. His side hurt too much: apparently, he couldn't use his hands. She reached through the bars and grabbed his nightshirt to support him somehow; but he was too heavy for her. Finally he bent his legs and caught his weight on his knees. "I tell you I've seen his body."

He pulled her down with him until she was on her knees as well. Raging into his face, she gasped, "I don't care. *Geraden* didn't do it."

"And I tell you I've seen his body." In spite of weakness and fever, Artagel met her with the unflinching passion which had twice led him to hurl himself against the High King's Monomach. "You deny it, but it isn't going to go away. An Imager did it. Translation is the only way a beast could get into that room and out again. But it wasn't Eremis. He was with Lebbick the whole time.

"Right now, he's up in the reservoir translating a new water supply. He's the only reason we've got any hope at all. I took Geraden's side against him"—Artagel's voice seemed to be thick with blood—"and I was wrong. He's *saving* us.

"Geraden killed Nyle. I'm going to track him down whether you tell me where he is or not. The only difference it's going to make is time."

"And then you're going to cut his heart out." Terisa couldn't bear any more. He made her want to shriek. With an effort of will, she let go of his shirt, drew back from him. "Get out of here," she muttered. "I don't want to hear this." The image of what had happened to Nyle sucked at her concentration. She thrust it away with both hands. "Just get out of here."

Then the sight of him—fierce and in pain on his knees against her bars—touched her, and she relented a little. "You really ought to be in bed. You aren't going to be hunting anybody for a while. If the Castellan doesn't tear it out of me—and if he lets me live— I promise I'll tell you everything I can when you're well enough to do something about it."

He didn't raise his head for a long time. When he finally looked up, the light had gone out of his gaze.

Tortuously, like an old man whose joints had begun to betray him, he pulled himself up the bars, regained his feet. "I always trusted him," he murmured as if he were alone, deaf and blind to her presence. "More than Nyle or any of the others. He was so clumsy and decent. And smarter than I am. I can't figure it out.

"You came along, and I thought that was good because it gave him something to fight for. It gave him a reason to stop letting those Masters humiliate him. So then he kills Nyle, kills"—Artagel shuddered, his eyes focused on nothing—"and you're the only explanation I can think of, you must be evil in some terrible way I don't understand, but you want me to go on trusting him. I can't figure it out.

"I saw his body." Like an old man, he turned from the door and began shuffling down the corridor. "I picked it up and held it." Brushing at the dried stains on his nightshirt, he passed beyond Terisa's range of vision. His boots scuffed along the floor until she couldn't hear them anymore.

She stood rigidly and watched the empty passage for a while, as erect as a witness testifying to what she believed. Like the Tor, he said that Nyle was dead. And he could hardly be wrong. He ought to be able to identify his own brother's body. And yet she didn't recant. Unexpectedly, she found that she was supported by a lifetime's anger. A childhood of punishment and neglect had taught her many things—and she was only now starting to realize what some of those things were.

Her hands shook. She steadied them as well as she could and began to eat the bread and stew she had been brought, pacing back and forth across the cell as she ate. She needed strength, needed to pull all her resources together. King Joyse had told her to think, to *reason*. Now more than at any other time in her life, she needed the stamina and determination to think clearly.

To the extent that it was possible for anyone to do so, she intended to defy the Castellan.

When he came at last—several hours and another meal later—she was almost glad to see him. Waiting was no doubt much easier to bear than rape or torture, but it was harder than defiance. Solitude eroded courage. Half a dozen times during those hours, she quailed, and her resolution ran out of her. Once she panicked so badly that afterward she found herself on the floor in the corner with her knees hugged against her chest and no idea how she got there.

But she was brought back from failure of nerve by the fact that she knew how to survive waiting alone in a cold, ill-lit cell. She had recovered her ability to blank out the dark and the fear. Paradoxically, the decision to meet her danger head on restored her capacity for escape. And when she surrendered to fading, she rediscovered the safety hidden in it and felt better.

For this she didn't need a mirror. Mirrors helped her fight the erosion of her existence; they weren't necessary if she wanted to let go. And it was letting go, not desperate clinging, which had kept her sane when her parents had locked her in the closet.

Nevertheless the time and the waiting, the cold and the inadequate food exacted their toll. There were limits to how far she could stretch her determination. She was almost glad to see him when the stamp of boots announced his coming and Castellan Lebbick appeared past the stone edge of her cell.

Now he would hurt her as much as he could. And she would find out what she was good for.

But the sight of him shocked her: it wasn't what she had expected. She was braced for rage and violence, for the intensity like hate in his glare and his knotted jaws, for the potential murder tightly coiled in all his muscles. She wasn't ready for the distracted man, noticeably shorter than she was, who entered her cell with no swagger in his shoulders and no authority on his face.

The Castellan looked like someone who had suffered an essential defeat.

Dully, he let himself into the cell. Again, he didn't bother to lock the door behind him. He was enough of a bar to her escape. And if she got past him and out of her cell, where could she go? She could run the corridors like a trapped rat, but she couldn't get out of the dungeon without passing through the guardroom. Castellan Lebbick didn't need to lock the door.

For a moment, he didn't meet her gaze; he glanced around the cell, glanced up and down her body without quite looking at her face. Then he murmured as if he were speaking primarily to himself, "You're better. The last time I saw you, you were about to fall apart. Now you look like you want to fight." Without sarcasm, he commented, "I had no idea being thrown in the dungeon was going to be good for you."

Terisa shrugged, studying him hard. "I've had time to think."

At last, he raised his eyes to hers. The smolder she was accustomed to seeing in them had been extinguished—or tamped down, at any rate. He seemed almost calm, almost stable—almost lost. "Does that mean," he asked quietly, "you're going to tell me where he is?"

She shook her head.

In the same tone, the Castellan continued, "Are you going to tell me what you've been plotting? Are you going to tell me why he did it?"

Once more, she shook her head. For some reason, her throat had gone dry. Lebbick's uncharacteristic demeanor began to frighten her.

"That doesn't surprise me." He seemed to have no sarcasm left. Turning away, he started to walk back and forth in front of the bars. His manner was almost casual; he might have been out for a stroll. "King Joyse told me to push you. He wants you to declare yourself. Does that surprise you?" The question was rhetorical. "It should. It isn't like him. He was always able to get what he wanted without beating up women.

"I've been looking forward to it all day.

"But now—" He spread his hands in a way that almost gave the impression he was asking her for help. "Everything is inside out. Clumsy, decent, *loyal* Geraden has turned rotten. Crazy Adept Havelock spent most of the day protecting us from catapults. Master Eremis is busy refilling the reservoir." Apparently, he didn't know that she had been visited by both the Tor and Artagel, that she was already aware of the things he told her. "And King Joyse wants me to hurt you. He wants me to find out who you are—what you are."

A suggestion of yearning came into Lebbick's voice, a hint of wistfulness. "Sometimes—a long time ago—he used to let me get even with his enemies. Sometimes. Men like that garrison commander— But he's never given me permission to hurt someone like you."

Then the Castellan faced her—and still he seemed almost casual, almost lost. "He must be afraid of you. He must be more afraid of you than he's ever been of Margonal or Festten or Gart or even Vagel.

"Why is that? What are you?"

Meeting his extinguished, unreadable gaze, Terisa swallowed roughly. She didn't understand what had happened to him, what had taken the fire out of him or stifled his hate; but this was the best chance she would ever get to distract him, deflect his intentions against her.

"I don't know," she said as steadily as she could. "You're asking the wrong questions."

"The wrong questions?"

"I can't tell you why King Joyse is afraid of me. *If* he's afraid of me. And I won't tell you where Geraden is. Because he didn't do it. I'm not going to give him away.

"But I'll tell you anything else."

"Anything else?" Castellan Lebbick sounded no more than mildly interested in the idea. "Like what?"

His manner gave her a moment of panic. She was afraid that he had become unreachable—that whatever was happening to him had taken him beyond the point where anybody could talk to him, argue with him, guess what he would do next. Breathing deeply to shore up her courage, she replied, "Like how did I survive when Gart tried to kill me the first night I was here. Like what was I using that secret passage in my rooms for. Like what really happened the night Eremis had his meeting with the lords and Prince Kragen. Like what happened the first time Geraden was attacked." Her own passion mounted against the Castellan's blankness. "Like how I can be sure Eremis is lying."

At that, something like a spark showed in Lebbick's eyes. His posture didn't shift, but his whole body seemed to become unnaturally still. "Tell me."

"It all fits together," she answered. King Joyse had told her to *reason,* and *reason* was the only weapon she had. "I can even tell you why they're afraid of Geraden—Vagel and Eremis and Gilbur—why they're trying so hard to get him out of their way."

Lebbick didn't blink. "Tell me," he repeated.

So she told him. As clearly as she could, she told him how Adept Havelock had saved her from the High King's Monomach. She described how Havelock and Master Quillon had used the passage hidden behind her wardrobe. She related every detail she could remember about Eremis' clandestine meeting with the lords of the Cares, including Artagel's role in saving her. And then she told the Castellan what conclusions she drew.

"The first time Gart tried to kill me, he obviously didn't know about that secret passage. The last time, he did. How did he find out? You knew it was there. Myste and Elega knew." Lebbick didn't react to this revelation. "Quillon and Havelock, of course. Geraden knew. And Saddith, my maid. But Myste and Elega and Havelock and Quillon all knew about it long before I came here. They could have told Gart that first night. Forget them. What about Geraden?

He didn't know when I first moved into those rooms. You think he's in with Gart. Well, I told him about it the next morning. After I talked to you. Why did he wait all that time before letting Gart know the best way to kill me?

"On the other hand"—she was determined to hold back nothing that might help her—"Saddith and Eremis are lovers. She could have told him about the passage—and she could have taken a long time to do it.

"She could have told him where I was that first night."

"I know all that," the Castellan murmured without inflection. "Tell me something I don't know. Tell me why Eremis rescued you. Gart came through the passage, and Eremis could have gotten rid of you both at the same time. How do you explain that?"

Because she was only guessing, Terisa did her best to sound plausible. "There were witnesses. If Gart just killed me, Geraden would see that Eremis let it happen. And if Gart tried to get both of us, the guards outside might catch him at it. All they had to do was open the door. Either way, everyone would know Eremis is a traitor.

"What he thought he was going to do"—she forced herself to say this also—"was make love to me. And then while I was asleep or distracted Gart would sneak in and kill me. And no one would ever know Eremis had been there.

"He wasn't expecting Geraden to interrupt."

Still the Castellan didn't show what he was thinking. All he said was, "Go on."

Grimly, Terisa continued.

"Eremis controlled every detail of that meeting with the lords. He arranged the location, the time, who was going to be there. He arranged where I would be afterward. Geraden couldn't have known any of his plans. The only thing Eremis didn't arrange was Artagel. He didn't arrange for me to be saved.

"When Gart attacked, he obviously came and went through a mirror. I don't know how he did that without losing his mind—but Artagel and I figured out where the point of translation was, the place in the Image. He and Geraden and I went to look at the place again, and the same mirror translated those insects. Artagel told you about that. They almost killed all three of us.

"Eremis says it was a feint, a trick to make Geraden look innocent, but that's nonsense. If Havelock hadn't rescued him, he would have died. And no one could have predicted that the Adept would show up there to help us. And Eremis knows all about it, even though he wasn't there and no one told him. He says I did, but I didn't. He must have been on the other side of the glass, watching."

Lebbick had begun to scowl. His eyes gave out glints of dark fire. For better or worse, Terisa was bringing the banked heat in him to flame. If that was a mistake, she was sealing her own doom. Nevertheless she kept going.

"They want Geraden dead or ruined because he really is an Imager—a kind of Imager no one has ever seen before."

Obliquely, it occurred to her that she should have grasped this before. But she hadn't forced herself to think until now. And because of that Geraden was paying a fearful price. At the moment, however, she had no time for regret. She was too busy defending herself from the Castellan.

"That's why he isn't able to recognize what he is for himself. He can do translations that don't have anything to do with the Image in his mirror. He got me out of a glass that showed the champion the Congery wanted. And Eremis knew that was going to happen. Or Gilbur did, anyway. He taught Geraden how to make that mirror. He must have seen Geraden wasn't making it right. When the mirror was made wrong and it still showed the Image with the champion, Gilbur must have realized what Geraden can do.

"If he ever figures out what his power is or how to use it, he'll be the strongest Master there ever was. And he's loyal to King Joyse. Even though it's breaking his heart. Gilbur and Vagel and Eremis have to get rid of him before he learns how to fight them.

"That's why they attacked him with insects, tried to kill him. And that's why they set him up to look like he killed Nyle. They're afraid of him. And he's trying to expose them. They need to get rid of him in a way that makes them look innocent.

"Nyle isn't really dead. He can't be. Eremis couldn't have used him like that without his cooperation—and he wouldn't have cooperated if he thought he was going to be killed."

Distinctly, the Castellan said, "Pigshit." The muscles bunched along his jaw; his eyes glared balefully. "My men are dead, and I saw his body. His entire face was eaten through to the brain." She had succeeded at restoring his outrage. "Eremis is at the reservoir right now *saving us*. He's the hero of Orison. No one will believe a word you say." His raised his fists in front of her face, hammered them at the unresisting air. "That whoreson physician betrayed us, and *two of my men are dead!*"

Now it was her turn to stare at him, stunned with surprise. "Physician?" Artagel hadn't mentioned a physician.

"*Underwell,* you bitch! The best physician in Orison. Eremis did everything perfectly. He got Nyle to his rooms fast. He got Underwell. He set guards. While you were out helping Geraden escape and that pisspot Quillon was getting in my way, Eremis was actually trying to *save Nyle.*"

She should have been afraid of his new rage, but she wasn't. "Physician?" Instead, she was astonished by the sudden clarity of her thoughts. "What happened to him? Didn't he see what attacked your men and Nyle?"

"*Escaped!*" snarled Lebbick. "What do you think? Did you expect him to wait around and let us catch him?" Rage swelled the cords of his neck. "He was translated away the same way Geraden's bloody creature was translated in."

"But why?"

"How should *I* know? I've never looked inside his head. Maybe he just hated Nyle. Maybe Festten offered to make him rich. Maybe Gart took his relatives hostage. I don't know and I don't care. As far as I'm concerned, he just *did* it."

"No," Terisa said as if now she had nothing to fear. "That isn't what I meant. Why did he do it that way? Why have the guards killed? Why—?" Why do that horrible thing to Nyle? "They might have been interrupted. They might have been caught. What about the noise? Wouldn't being attacked by some kind of beast make noise— warn the guards outside? Why take the chance?"

Fuming, the Castellan started to spit an explanation at her. But she didn't want to hear him say anything more against Geraden. She ignored him.

"He's a physician," she said. "'The best physician in Orison.' He didn't need any help getting rid of Nyle. And he didn't need to make himself look like a traitor. Don't you understand?" Lebbick's slowness to grasp the implications surprised her almost as much as her own certainty. "All he had to do was *fail.* Let Nyle die. Put something toxic in the wound and cover it with bandages. No one would ever know. No one would even suspect.

"Why take the stupid, *stupid* risk of all that bloodshed?"

Castellan Lebbick stared at her as if she were growing noxious in front of him. "So maybe he didn't do it."

"Then where is he?" shot back Terisa.

"He wouldn't let them kill Nyle without trying to stop them—without trying to get help." Lebbick was making a visible effort to understand her. "Maybe they killed him, too, and took the body with them."

"Why?" she repeated. "Why bother? To create the illusion they had a confederate they didn't need? To make you think Underwell is guilty when he really isn't? What does that accomplish? What would be the point?"

"*Right!*" The Castellan clenched his fury in both fists. "*What would be the point?*"

And still she wasn't afraid. *His entire face was eaten*—Calmly, she asked, "What did Underwell look like?"

Lebbick made a strangling noise. " 'Look like'?"

"Compared to Nyle," she explained. "Were they about the same height? The same weight? About the same coloring?"

"NO!" the Castellan yelled as if she had gone too far, as if this time she had finally pushed him past the point where he could hold back his hands. And then, an instant later, what she was getting at hit him, and he stopped.

In a thin voice, he said, "Yes. About the same."

Quietly, as if she didn't mean anything personal, she pursued her argument. "If you put Underwell in Nyle's clothes, would you still be able to recognize him? If you gave him wounds to match the ones Nyle was supposed to have—and if you disfigured him—and if you covered the rest of him with blood—would you still be able to recognize him?"

Castellan Lebbick stared at her with apoplexy on his face.

"I think Nyle is alive," she finished, not because she thought the Castellan still didn't understand her, but simply because she had to say something to control the silence, keep him from exploding. "I think the poor man who got butchered was Underwell."

With an effort, Lebbick pulled a breath between his teeth. "All that," he chewed out distinctly, "you think all that, and you haven't set foot outside this cell. Sheep-rut! How do you do it? What do you use for reasons? What do you use for proof?"

Now that she had arrived at her conclusion, she lost her invulnerability. He was beginning to scare her again. "I've already explained it." She was determined not to let her voice shake. "Eremis wants to shift the blame onto Geraden. Partly to get him out of the way, so he can't understand his talent and start using it. And partly because Eremis isn't ready to betray you yet. Maybe his plans aren't finished. If he sprang his trap now, Prince Kragen would get Orison. Alend would get the Congery. Isn't that right? But Eremis is in with Gart—with High King Festten and Cadwal. He wants to keep us all safe until Cadwal gets here—until Alend is out of the way.

"If Geraden is working with Gart—if he really does serve Cadwal—he wouldn't have done any of this. He wouldn't have risked accusing Eremis, he wouldn't have done anything to undermine Orison. Until Cadwal got here. He wouldn't have ruined his own position by killing his brother."

She would have gone on, trying to build a wall of words between herself and the Castellan, but he cut her off. "That's enough!" he snapped fiercely. "It's just talk. It isn't a reason. It isn't *proof.* You've been in this cell all day. What makes you think you know what's going on? You say he's doing everything because he's guilty—but he would do exactly the same things if he was innocent. I want *proof.* If you expect me to go arrest the 'hero of Orison,' you'll have to give me *proof.*"

Just for a second, Terisa nearly failed. Proof. Her mind went dark; a lid closed over her courage. What kind of proof *was* there, in a world like this? If Underwell had been stretched out naked in front of her, she wouldn't have been able to tell the difference between him and Nyle. She didn't know men. Only the crudest physical characteristics would have enabled her to distinguish between him and, say, Eremis. Or Barsonage.

Then, abruptly, the answer came to her. In sudden, giddy relief, she said, "Ask Artagel."

"Artagel?" demanded the Castellan suspiciously. "*Geraden's* brother?"

"And Nyle's," she countered. "Make him look at the body. Take the clothes off and make him look. He ought to be able to recognize his own brother's body."

Lebbick glared at that idea as if he found it offensive. Under one eye, a muscle twitched, giving his gaze a manic cast. She had gone too far, said something wrong, accidentally convinced him her arguments were false. He was going to do what he had come for in the first place. He was going to hurt her.

He didn't. He said, "All right. I'll try that.

"It's too bad Underwell doesn't have any family here. It would be better to look at this from both sides. But I'll try Artagel."

Terisa felt faint. She wanted to sit down. The Castellan's scowl was still fixed on her, however. He made no move to leave. After a moment, he said, "While I'm gone, remember something. Even if that *is* Underwell's corpse, it doesn't prove Nyle is alive. It doesn't prove anything about Geraden or Eremis. All it proves is that some shit-lover is still plotting something. If you want me to arrest the whore-bait 'hero of Orison,' don't show me Underwell is dead. Show me Nyle is alive."

Then he left. The cell door banged; the key scraped in the lock; hard bootheels echoed away on the stone of the passage.

Terisa sat down on the cot, leaned her back against the wall, and let herself evaporate for a while.

THIRTY:
ODD CHOICES

he bars of the cell were of old, rough iron, crudely forged and cast. Little marks of rust pitted the metal like smallpox; it looked ancient and corrupt. Nevertheless the bars were still intact, despite their age. Against the gnawing of rust, which the rude workmanship and the damp atmosphere aggravated, the iron was defended by generations of human oil and fear. Since the dungeons were first constructed, dozens or hundreds of men and women and perhaps children had stood in this cell, holding the bars because they didn't have anything else to do with their need. And now the ooze of sweat and dirt left behind by their knotted, aching, condemned hands protected the metal from its accumulated years. Sections of iron could be brought to a dull shine, if Terisa rubbed them with the sleeve of her new shirt.

So. He was right. It didn't prove Nyle was alive. She couldn't argue with that.

So the Castellan would be coming back.

She wondered whether the places where people suffered were always made stronger by the residue of pain. And—not for the first time—she wondered how many different kinds of pain it was possible to feel.

When he came back, whatever he did would be out of her control. She had used up all her weapons. She wasn't Saddith: she couldn't use her body to protect her spirit, even though he apparently desired her. Even if she had been willing to make the attempt—a purely theoretical question—she lacked the knowledge, the experience. And somewhere between the poles of love and violence Castellan Lebbick had lost his way. He might no longer be able to distinguish between them.

She should have gone with Geraden.

She should have come to her own conclusions about him earlier, much earlier.

She should have stuck a knife in Master Eremis when she had the chance. If, in fact, she had ever had the chance.

The Castellan would be coming back.

What hope was there for her now? Only one: that Artagel might look at the body and be sure it wasn't Nyle's. If that happened—if she were proved right on that point—the Castellan might doubt his own rage enough to treat her more carefully. He might. She had to hope for *something,* now that she couldn't hope to be left alone.

She had to hope that Geraden's talent was strong enough to save him. Somehow, he had bent his mirror away from its Image in order to appear in her apartment and translate her to Orison. That was one thing. But to bend the same mirror so that it functioned as if it were flat—that was something else. A more hazardous attempt altogether. And yet she had reason to think it was within his abilities. With that same glass, he had put her partway into a scene which bore no resemblance to the Image, a scene which he called "the Closed Fist" in the Care of Domne, and she hadn't gone mad. If he could do that for her, surely he could do it for himself?

Surely?

Oh, Geraden.

The truth was that she wasn't sure of anything anymore. She wasn't accustomed to the confidence she had projected in front of Castellan Lebbick: it was easier to forget than to sustain. Unfortunately, there wasn't anything inevitable about the explanation of events she had urged on him. Like her capacity for love, it was purely theoretical. She knew how Master Eremis would laugh, if anyone told him what she had said. At bottom, her defense of herself rested entirely and exclusively on the conviction that Geraden was innocent. If she was wrong about that—

The implications were intolerable, so she tried to close her mind to them. Because she didn't know whether the Castellan would come back soon or late—and either way it could mean anything, good or bad—she made an effort to distract herself by counting the granite blocks which formed the walls of the cell.

Both of the end walls had been built in the same way. At a glance, the construction looked careless: ill-fitting blocks had simply been piled on top of each other. So it might be possible to work some of them loose, especially up near the ceiling. But time and use had worn off the rough edges, leaving a surface that couldn't be hurt. In contrast, the back of the cell was flat, seamless stone—cut, not built. No doubt the work had been done by the Mordant-born slaves of Alend or Cadwal, during the long years of conflict between those powers.

And now she was a prisoner of the same conflict. In a sense, dungeons never gave up their victims. The faces and the bodies changed—died and were dragged away—but the old stone clung to its purpose, and the anguish of the men and women locked within it never changed. King Joyse hadn't gone far enough when he had altered Orison to make it a place of peace. Much of the extensive dungeons had been given over to the Congery for a laborium: that was good—but not good enough. The whole place should have been put to some other use. Then perhaps the Castellan wouldn't have spent so many years thinking about the things he could do to people who offended him.

She didn't know what to say to him.

She had never known what to say to her father, either. So far, however, she had had better luck with the Castellan. But that was finished. She had done everything she could think of. Now she was at the mercy of events and attitudes she couldn't control, men who were losing their minds, men who hated, men who—

"Deep in thought, I see, my lady," said Master Eremis. "It makes you especially lovely."

She turned, her heart thudding in her throat, and saw him at the door of her cell. With one hand, he twirled the ends of his chasuble negligently. His relaxed stance suggested that he had been watching her for several minutes.

"You are quite remarkable," he continued. "Ordinarily, cogitation in a woman produces only ugliness. Were you thinking of me?"

She opened her mouth to say his name, but she couldn't swallow her heart; it was beating too hard. Staring at him as if she had been stricken dumb, she took an involuntary step backward.

"That would explain this increased beauty—if you were thinking of me. My lady"—he smiled as if she were naked in front of him—"I have certainly been thinking of you."

"How—?" She fought to regain her voice. "How did you get in here?"

At that, he laughed. "On my legs, my lady. I walked."

"No." She shook her head. Slowly, her immediate panic receded. "You're supposed to be up at the reservoir. Saving Orison. Castellan Lebbick wouldn't let you just walk in here."

"Unfortunately, no," the Master agreed. His tone became marginally more sober. "I was forced to resort to a little chicanery. Some cayenne in my wine to produce a sweat, so that he would be impressed by the strain of my exertions. A gentle potion in the brandy I offered to the men he set to guard me, so that they would sleep. A passage which has been secretly built from my workrooms in the laborium into an unused part of the dungeons—tremendous forethought on my part, do you not agree? considering that it was never possible for me to be certain Lebbick would arrest you."

Terisa ignored the cayenne and the potion; they meant nothing to her. But a secret passage out of the dungeon— A way of escape— She had to take hold of herself with both hands to keep her sudden, irrational hope under command.

Struggling to muffle the tremor in her voice, she said, "You went to a lot of trouble. What do you want? Do you expect me to tell you where Geraden is?"

Again, Master Eremis laughed. "Oh, no, my lady." She was beginning to loathe his laugh. "You told me that a long time ago."

When he said that, a sting of panic went through her—a fear different than all her other frights and alarms. She forgot about the secret passage; it was secondary. She wanted to shout, No, I didn't, I never did that! But as soon as he said it she knew it was true.

She had refused the Tor and Artagel and Castellan Lebbick—but Eremis already knew.

"Then why?" she demanded as though she were genuinely capable of belligerence. "Have you come to kill me? Do you want to keep me from talking to the Castellan? You're too late. I've already told him everything."

"'Everything'?" The Imager's dark gaze glinted as if he were no longer as amused as he sounded. "Which 'everything' is that, my lady? Did you tell him that I have held your sweet breasts in my hands? Did you tell him that I have tasted your nipples with my tongue?"

The recollection twisted her stomach. More angrily, she retorted, "I told him you faked Nyle's death. You and Nyle set it up as an attack on Geraden. So no one would believe the things he said about you.

"I told him Nyle is still alive. You ambushed Underwell and those guards so everyone would think Geraden came back and killed him, but he's still alive. You've got him hidden somewhere. You talked him into being on your side somehow—maybe he hates Geraden for stopping him when he tried to help Elega and Prince Kragen—and now you've got him safe somewhere.

"That's what I told the Castellan."

In the uncertain lamplight, Master Eremis' smile seemed to grow harder, sharper. "Then I am glad it was never my intention to harm you. If I were to hurt you now, everyone would assume that there is some justice in your accusations.

"But I do not hold a grievance against you. I will demonstrate," he said smoothly, "the injustice of those accusations."

"How?" she shot back, trying to shore up her courage—trying not to think about the fact that she had betrayed Geraden to the Imager. "What new lies have you got in mind?"

His smile flashed like a blade. "No lies at all, my lady. I will not lie to you again. Behold!" Flourishing one hand, he produced a long iron key from the sleeve of his cloak. "I have come to let you out."

She stared at him; shock made her want to lie down and close her eyes. He had a key to the cell. He wanted to let her out, help her escape—he wanted to get her away from the Castellan. She was too confused, she couldn't think. Start over again. He had a key to the cell. He wanted— It didn't make any sense.

"Why?" she murmured, asking herself the question, not expecting him to answer.

"Because," he said distinctly, "your body is mine. I have claimed it, and I mean to have it. I do not allow my desires to be frustrated or refused. Other women have such skin and loins as yours, such breasts—but they do not prefer a gangling, stupid, inept Apt after I have offered myself to them. When I conceive a desire, my lady, I satisfy it."

"No," she said again, "no," not because she meant to argue with him, but because he had given her a way to think. "You wouldn't risk it. You wouldn't take the chance you might get caught here. You want to use me for something."

Then it came to her.

"Does Geraden really scare you that badly?"

Master Eremis' smile turned crooked and faded from his face; his eyes burned at her. "Have you lost your senses, my lady? *Scare* me? *Geraden?* Forgive my bluntness—but if you believe that Geraden Fumblefoot frightens me in any way, you are out of your wits. Lebbick and his dungeon have cost you your mind."

"I don't think so." In a manner that strangely resembled the Castellan's, she clenched her fists and tapped them on the sides of her legs as if to emphasize the rhythm of her thoughts, the inevitability. "I don't think so.

"You know what he can do. You pretend you don't, but you know what he can do better than anybody—better than he does. Gilbur watched him make that mirror. You knew something unexpected was going to happen when the Congery decided to let him go ahead and try to translate the champion. That's why you argued against him. You weren't trying to protect him. You wanted to keep him from discovering who he is.

"The reason you tried to get him accepted into the Congery was just to distract him, confuse him—make it harder for him to understand.

"When Gilbur translated the champion"—she swung her fists harder, harder—"you left Geraden and me in front of the mirror, *directly* in front of the mirror. You probably pushed him. You wanted the champion to kill him." To kill both of us. The Master had been trying to take her life as well for a long time. But that was the only flaw in her convictions, the only thing which didn't make any sense: why anybody would want to have her killed. "There isn't any doubt about it. You're definitely afraid of him."

This time, the bark of Master Eremis' laugh held no humor, no mirth at all. "You misjudge me, my lady. You misjudge me badly."

She didn't stop; it was too late to draw back. "That's why you're here," she said, beating out the words against her thighs. "Why you want to let me out. You want me to be your prisoner. You know he cares about me," *cares* about me, oh, Geraden! "and you want to use me against him. You think if you threaten to hurt me he'll do whatever you want."

"You misjudge me, I say. It is not fear. Fear *that* puppy? I would rather lose my manhood."

She heard him, but she didn't slow down. "The only thing"—which was already a lie, but she had no intention of telling him the truth—"the only thing I don't understand is why you didn't just send Gart to kill the lords of the Cares and Prince Kragen. Why else did you get them all together? You didn't want any alliance—you knew that meeting would fail. You were just trying to undermine all of Cadwal's enemies at the same time.

"Why didn't you finish the job? With the lords and Prince Kragen dead, Alend and Mordant and even Orison would be in chaos. What were you afraid of?"

Abruptly, Master Eremis swung his own fists and hit the bars so hard that the door clanged against its latch. "*It was not fear.* Are you *deaf?* Do you have the arrogance to ignore me? It was not *fear!*

"It was *policy.*"

Terisa stared at him past the bars, past the stark conflict of lamplight and shadows on his face, and murmured softly, in recognition, "Oh."

"I did not send Gart against the lords and Kragen," he said harshly, "because it was impossible to be sure that he would succeed. The Termigan and the Perdon and Kragen are all fierce fighters. Kragen had bodyguards. And any man who killed the Tor might drown in all his blood. Also it was much too soon to risk revealing my intentions. The gamble I chose to take was safer.

"When Gilbur performed his translation, the champion came to us facing the direction we wanted him to go—in toward the most crowded parts of Orison, the rooms and towers where his havoc would be most likely to bring the lords and Kragen to ruin. That was why I wanted him, the only reason I permitted his translation to take place.

"Of course," the Master said in digression, "once he had been translated, it was necessary to preserve him from Lebbick. I could not allow some bizarre happenstance to bring him into alliance with Orison and Mordant. Let him rampage now and do harm as he wishes, without friends or understanding. That also serves me. But my chief intent was more immediate.

"I wanted him to gut Orison, destroying all my principal enemies at once. If he had gone that way—if you had not turned him, my lady—my gamble would have brought a rich return.

"*Policy,* my lady. If it succeeds, I succeed with it. If it fails, I remain to pursue my ends by other means.

"And what I have done where Geraden is concerned is also *policy,* not *fear.* He is my enemy—and he appears to possess a strange talent. Therefore I will destroy him. But I will destroy him in a way that serves my ends rather than risks them. I do not"—vehemence bared his teeth—"*fear* that ignorant and impossible son of a coward."

So he admitted it. She was right about him—she had reasoned her way to the truth. That discovery simultaneously relieved and terrified her. She was right about him, *right* about him. Geraden was innocent, and she had reached the truth alone, without anyone to help or rescue her. It was an intense relief just to recollect that he had never been able to finish anything he started with her: that he hadn't gotten her killed—or into his bed; hadn't gotten her confused enough to turn her back on Geraden.

On the other hand, there were no witnesses; no one else had heard him. She was alone with her knowledge—alone with him.

And he had a key to her cell.

Without meaning to do it, she had stripped herself of her only protection—the appearance of incomprehension that let him think she wasn't a threat to him, led him to believe he could do anything he wanted with her.

In quick panic, she tried to fake a defense. "Prove it," she replied, groaning inwardly at the way her voice shook. "Leave me here. Go back to the reservoir and save Orison from Alend. If you aren't afraid of him, you don't need me."

Her own alarm was too obvious: it seemed to restore his humor, his equanimity. He began to smile again, voraciously.

"Tush, my lady," he said in deprecation, "you do not truly wish that. I have touched you in places you will never forget. No man will ever treasure the ardor of your loins or the supplication of your breasts as I do—most assuredly not that lout Geraden, whose clumsiness will make his every caress a misery to you. If you consult your heart, you will accompany me willingly.

"If you should prove useful to me, how does that harm you? You will still be my lady. And you will be rewarded. I am going to *win* this contest. King Joyse considers it a mere game, an exercise in hop-board, and that is one of many reasons why Mordant will be defeated. Alend will be defeated, and Cadwal will be consumed. When I am done, there will be no power left in all this world which

is not *mine*. Then the woman who stands with me will have riches
and indulgence beyond her wildest imaginings.

"You would look well in that place, my lady. If you accompany
me willingly, it will be yours."

Terisa studied him hard. She didn't listen to what he was saying;
his offer meant nothing to her. But the fact that he made it meant
something. It *meant* something. When he stopped, she muttered,
"Take Saddith. She wants the job," speaking aloud for her own benefit, so that the sound of the words would help her think. "I'm still
trying to figure out why you bother pretending to seduce me. You've
got a key. You're bigger than I am. Why don't you just come in here,
rape me, club me over the head, and let Gilbur or Vagel translate
me to some other dungeon where you can use me without having
to be nice about it?"

"Because"—he had recovered from the unpleasant surprise she
had given him; now he was very sure of himself—"that is not what
you truly wish, my lady. Your deepest desire is not to defy me, but
to open yourself so that I may teach you the joy of your body—and
mine."

She shook her head, hardly hearing him. Any explanation he
gave was automatically false. Still for her own benefit, she went on,
"You're not just afraid of Geraden. You're afraid of *me*." She felt a
growing sense of wonder and dismay. "You're trying to trick me for
the same reason you've been trying to have me killed. You're *afraid*
of me."

This time when Master Eremis laughed his amusement was un-
forced and unmistakable. "Oh, my lady," he chortled, "you are a
wonderment. You flatter yourself beyond recognition. If you were
not so earnest, I would believe you drunk with pride.

"Nevertheless I will respect what you say. Perhaps you desire
a little force. Perhaps that will add spice to your eventual surrender.
Since you suggest it—"

With a final chuckle, he pushed the key into the lock and
turned it.

Without a second's hesitation, Terisa reared back and yelled at
the top of her lungs, "Guards!"

Master Eremis froze. His gaze flicked away down the passage,
then sprang back to her in instant fury.

She put her whole heart into it:

"Guards!"

A door clanged in the distance. A rumor of boots ran along the corridor.

The Imager snarled a curse. "Very well, my lady," he hissed savagely. "That was your last chance, and you have lost it." In a swirl of darkness, he turned to leave. "Now you will face the consequences of your foolishness. When Lebbick is done with you"—he spoke sharply enough to raise echoes after him, so that she could hear him as he left—"expect worse from me."

Then he was gone.

His departure was so abrupt—and the approach of the guards sounded so ominous—that just for an instant she thought she had made a mistake.

That concern evaporated almost immediately, however: it was burned away by the swift, hot awareness that she preferred being left to the Castellan's mercy. He was unpredictable and violent, capable of almost any atrocity when his loyalties were outraged. Yet he was *faithful*—far more trustworthy than the people in whom he had placed his faith. In fact, that discrepancy was what drove him wild. She would rather fight a man like him, who was at least true to his King, than be seduced by a man like Master Eremis, who was false to everybody.

The guards arrived at her cell, demanded an explanation threateningly because Castellan Lebbick might take them to task for anything they did in regard to her. For a moment, she was right on the edge of telling them what had happened. Master Eremis was here. He's got a secret entrance to the dungeons. He's a traitor. But her instinct for subterfuge made her swallow the words. No. She might need them. The Castellan would be back: she might need everything she could possibly tell him.

Facing the guards as if she had become bold, she replied, "I want to see him."

The two men gaped at her. One of them asked stupidly, "Who? The Castellan?"

She nodded.

The other leered, "Waste of effort. Last time a woman wanted to *see* him, he had her stripped and flogged and thrown out of Orison." He grinned at the memory. "Had nice tits, too. Would have done better to come to me."

Terisa closed her eyes to control an upswelling of disgust. "Tell him," she demanded. "Just tell him."

The guards looked at each other. The first one said, "He isn't going to like it." But the other shrugged.

Walking loudly, they went away.

She sat down on her cot and tried to believe that she knew what she was doing.

She didn't have much time to prepare herself. Scant moments after the guards left, she heard Castellan Lebbick's rage echoing along the corridor.

"I don't give a trough of horseshit who she wants to see! You irresponsible sons-of-sheep are going to be cleaning latrines before morning! You're going to clean latrines until everything you eat tastes like piss and your wives and even your children stink as bad as you do! Who gave you the fornicating permission to let her have *visitors?*"

Then the door between the guardroom and the dungeons rang viciously against its frame; and boots came, as hard as hate, along the damp stone corridor.

Shocked, she found herself murmuring helplessly, Oh, no, oh, no, oh, no, on the verge of panic.

The Castellan stamped to the front of her cell like a man with murder on his mind. The glare in his eyes was fierce enough to wither what little courage she had left; his jaws were knotted with violence. Like a blow, he rammed the key into the lock, turned it, and slammed the door open. The door hit the bars so hard that they belled like a carillon.

"You heartless *slut!*" He came into the cell, came straight at her. "I've been tearing my guts out over you all day, and you've been having *visitors!*"

Involuntarily, she flinched back onto the cot, cowered against the wall. "The Tor!" she cried out, trying to keep him from hitting her. "Artagel! They came here. I didn't ask to see them."

"You didn't *have* to!" His fists caught her shirt, wrenched her off the cot so fiercely that the seam at one shoulder parted and the fabric ripped like a wail. "Artagel is still too sick to get out of bed, and King Joyse personally told the Tor to let me do my job with you. So instead they both came to see *you.*

"What are you plotting? Did they tell you what to say to me? They must have. I half believed that dogpiss story about Eremis and Gart. You couldn't make that up yourself—you don't know enough.

No, you're all doing this together. Those riders with the red fur came
from the Care of Tor. Artagel is Geraden's brother." Convulsive with
anger, he twisted her shirt so that it tore down one seam to the hem.
"What are you plotting?"

"Nothing." She ought to be able to resist him, but her strength
had deserted her. "Nothing." His fury was thrust so closely into her
face that she could hardly focus her eyes on it, hardly see him at all;
he was a darkness roaring in front of her, clawing at her—too much
hate to be endured. She couldn't do anything more than whimper
in protest. "Nothing."

"You're *lying!*" His intensity seemed to strangle him. "You're
lying to me!" His voice was like a howl stuck in his throat, too congested for utterance. "You've got friends, allies. Even when you're
locked in the dungeon, I can't stop you from plotting. You're going
to *destroy* us! You're going to destroy *me!*"

She felt him gathering force as if he rose up to consume her;
he blotted out her vision. A spasm of his grip nearly dislocated her
shoulders. Then he caught his arms around her and began to kiss
her as if he had been starving for her so long that the pressure of
his need had snapped his self-command.

She sank into his embrace, into the dark. She let herself fall
limp, so that she scarcely felt the violence of his kisses, scarcely felt
the iron of his breastplate against her chest. The darkness sucked
her away, out of herself, out of existence—out of danger. It took
her to a place where he couldn't touch her and she was safe—

No. Fading wasn't the answer. She had to do better than this.
It accomplished nothing. Oh, it kept her safe, kept her spirit hidden
among the secrets of her heart—but her body would still be harmed.
And no one would be left to help Geraden. No one would be left
to stop Master Eremis. No one would be left to champion Orison
against the real enemy, against Master Eremis and his dire alliance
with Master Gilbur and the arch-Imager Vagel, with Gart and Cadwal. It came down to her in the end. Myste had said, *Problems should
be solved by those who see them.* There wasn't anybody else.

She was terrified—but the fact that she was capable of escape
gave her courage. She remained limp, lifeless, until the Castellan
eased his embrace and shifted his hands to the waistband of her pants,
bending her backward over the cot. Then she opened her eyes and
looked at him.

She could see him clearly now, the distress bulging along the line of his jaw, the pale intensity on either side of his nose, the darkness like mania in his eyes. He scared her down to the bottom of her soul, where her fear of her father still lived and burned, distorting her. Nevertheless she caught at his wrists and held them as hard as she could, trying to stop him.

As if his kisses had made her lucid and crazy, immune to fright, she said, "You didn't ask them why they came to see me. You didn't bother. You didn't ask Artagel to look at Nyle's body. You didn't even *try* to find out the truth. You just want to hurt me more than anything else in the world, and they finally gave you an excuse."

Roaring almost silently behind the constriction in his chest, he let go of her and drew back his arm. He was going to hit her hard enough to crush her skull against the wall.

"They came to see me," she said—lucid and completely out of touch with the reality of her plight—"because they want me to tell you where Geraden is."

While his arm rose and his teeth flashed, he stopped. Surprise or doubt or self-disgust seemed to seize hold of him, cramp all his muscles. Hoarsely, he panted, "You're lying. You're still lying."

"No." She shook her head calmly. It was madness to be so calm. "Is it true that you didn't ask Artagel to look at Nyle's body?"

The Castellan was going to hit her. Or else he was going to break down right there in front of her. Precariously balanced between the extremes, he choked, "I asked. He's had another relapse. Too sick to understand the question."

Steady and unafraid, she shrugged away her disappointment as if it were trivial. "Never mind," she murmured. She might have been trying to console Castellan Lebbick. "I had another visitor. One you don't know about.

"Master Eremis was here.

"Now I can prove he's a traitor."

Lamplight flickered in the Castellan's gaze. He straightened his back and stood over her as though his body had become stone; he held himself back from bloodshed with an effort of will so savage that it made him gasp for air.

"How?"

Unnatural quiet and clenched wildness, Terisa and the Castellan spoke to each other.

"He put cayenne in his wine to make himself sweat, so you would think he was exhausted."

"You'll never prove that."

"He gave your guards a potion to make them sleep, so he could get away."

"If they're awake when I check on them, you'll never prove *that,* either."

"He has a secret way into the dungeon. It comes from his workroom in the laborium. You ought to be able to find it without too much trouble."

When she said that, Castellan Lebbick flinched backward. He didn't loosen his grip on himself, but his eyes betrayed a vast accumulation of pain.

"If he came here," he asked, still breathing hard, "why didn't you go with him? Why didn't you escape?"

For some reason, that question cracked her mad calm. She seemed to feel herself shattering, like an eggshell. Without transition, she went from lucidity to the edge of hysteria.

"Because—" Her voice broke, and her heart hammered as if it couldn't bear the strain any longer. "Because he wanted to use me against Geraden. The same way he used Nyle."

A muscle began to twitch in the Castellan's right cheek. The twitch spread until the whole side of his face felt the spasm. He was losing control.

"So if you're telling the truth"—for the first time since she had met him, he sounded like a man who might weep—"Geraden has always been true to King Joyse. *True,* when almost nobody else is. And you're true to Geraden. And I've been hurting my King by distrusting you—by trying to protect him from you."

Dumbly, Terisa nodded.

Without warning, the Castellan whirled away. "I've got to see this 'secret way' for myself." Slamming the cell door so hard that flakes of rust scattered to the stone, he started down the corridor.

Almost at once, he broke into a run. His voice echoed across the sound of his boots as he shouted as if he were calling farewell to her—or to himself—"I am loyal to my King!"

Stricken numb and hardly able to care what happened to her at the moment, Terisa pulled the torn seam of her shirt closed as well as she could. Grief threatened to overwhelm her: her own; the Castellan's; the hurt and sorrow of anyone who had to bear the consequences of King Joyse's decline. No, *decline* wasn't the right word. He still knew what he was doing. He had brought Mordant and

Orison to this dilemma deliberately. Dully, she thought about that to keep herself from considering how close she and Castellan Lebbick had come to destroying each other.

When she finally looked up from her futile attempt to make her shirt decent—or at least warm—she saw Master Quillon inexplicably standing outside the bars of her cell.

"That was bravely done, my lady," he said in a distant tone. "Unfortunately, it was a mistake."

She looked at him, gaped at him; her mouth hung open, and there was nothing she could do about it.

"Master Eremis lied to you. He has no passage from his workroom into the dungeon. He came to you by translation.

"When the Castellan learns that no passage exists, he will not believe another word you say. His rage will be so great that I fear he will be unable to hold himself back from killing you."

It was too much. Fear and loneliness filled Terisa's chest, and she started crying.

THIRTY-ONE:
HOP-BOARD

After a while, she felt a hand on her shoulder.

She was crying hard; but the touch was unexpected, and it startled her. She looked up to find Master Quillon beside her. His nose was twitching, and his eyes were gentle; clearly, he intended to comfort her.

"My lady," he murmured, "it has been painful for you, I know. And it must seem unjustified. You asked for none of this. And though we did not choose you, we have not hesitated to use you. I will give you all the help I can."

Help, she thought through her tears. All the help I can. It was too late. The Castellan was too strong. He had too much power. She couldn't prove anything against Master Eremis. Nobody was going to be able to help her.

But Master Quillon was standing beside her. With his hand on her shoulder. Inside her cell. When she blinked her eyes clear, she saw that the door was open.

The Imager glanced where she was looking and commented like a shrug, "Fortunately, the Castellan was in such dudgeon that he forgot to lock it. I doubt that any of the guards would be willing to open it for us when he is at this level of outrage."

By degrees, the open door and Master Quillon's unexplained presence fixed her attention. The pressure of sobs receded in her chest; her breathing grew steadier. Without meeting the Master's gaze, she muttered, "Did Havelock send you this time?"

"Indirectly," Quillon replied. "I am here for his benefit—and for the King's. To save all Mordant. But primarily"—his grip on her shoulder tightened a bit—"I have come to let you out of this prison."

Let me out—? Her eyes jerked to his: she stared at him, unable to control the way her face suddenly burned with yearning and hope. Her mouth shaped words she couldn't find her voice to say out loud: You're going to set me *free?*

Abruptly, Master Quillon took his hand from her shoulder and sat down next to her on the cot. Now his gaze studied the floor instead of meeting hers. "My lady," he said to the stones, "it pains me to see you so surprised. And it pains me even more to know that we deserve your surprise. I do not like some of the things we have done to you. And I lack King Joyse's talent for risks. We deserve any recrimination you might make against us."

Then his tone became more sardonic. "The truth is that we deserve to be betrayed—by you as well as by Geraden, if by no one else. But a blind man could see now that you are faithful to him, and so you will not betray us. In that we are exceptionally fortunate. Perhaps our good fortune is as great as our need."

Because she was too confused to follow what he was saying, she asked, "Is this going to be another lecture?"

He winced; perhaps he thought she was being sarcastic. But he didn't back down. "Not if you do not wish it, my lady. If you wish me to keep my mouth shut, I will simply take you away from here and let you do whatever you choose without argument—or explanation. But I tell you plainly"—then he did look at her, letting her see the pain on his face—"that you will wound me if you do not permit me to explain. And I think you will increase the difficulty of your own decisions."

She could hardly believe what she heard. To be helped, to be offered explanations, to be offered *freedom*—! Far from resenting him, as he apparently expected, she was hard pressed to restrain herself from weeping again in gratitude.

But she had to have more self-command than *this.* Otherwise it would all be wasted on her. She would go wrong. So she didn't jump to accept his offer. Instead, she did her best to *think* again, to make her brain resume functioning. Tentatively, groping for what she wanted to understand first, she asked, "How do you know Master Eremis doesn't have a secret way in here? How do you know what he said to me?"

"I *heard* him," Master Quillon retorted with sudden sharpness. He didn't seem to like what he had heard. "I have been secreted down here since noon, when Prince Kragen stopped bringing up catapults against us. I heard your conversations with both the Castellan and Eremis—and with the Castellan again." He made an effort to speak more softly. "That is how I became certain of your loyalty to Geraden."

As if he thought she wasn't asking the right questions—not being hard enough on him—he said almost at once, "You will ask why I did not intervene when the Castellan threatened you. My lady, please believe that I would have done so. You found your own answer to his violence, however. Because he must not know my part in all this, if that can be avoided, I left you to deal with him alone."

"No," she said reflexively, abstract with concentration. He was right: that was something she wanted to ask him, a subject she wanted to pursue. But not yet. "Tell me about that later." First things first. She had to pull her mind into some kind of order. "He said he built a secret way from his workroom into the dungeon. How can you be sure that isn't true?"

The Master rubbed his nose to make it stop twitching. "It would be impossible to do such work secretly, with so many Apts everywhere in the laborium. Regardless of that, however, I know Eremis did not use a passage to come here. I saw him arrive and depart. He was translated."

"You mean—" He can pass through flat glass, too, and not lose his mind? Can *everybody* do it? "You mean he has a mirror with this dungeon in its Image?"

How is it possible to fight people who can pass through flat glass without going mad?

"I fear so, my lady. I suspect it is the same mirror which translated those hunting insects against Geraden. The passages of Orison are confusing, I know, but actually we are not far from the translation point they used—and Gart used when he attacked you and the Prince. There is considerable stone between this cell and that corridor, but of course stone would be no obstacle to an Image, if the focus of its glass could be shifted that far.

"Incidentally, you may wonder why your enemies do not send

more of those insects against you while you are here and helpless."
Actually, she hadn't wondered anything of the kind, but Master Quillon went on anyway, "It is the Adept's opinion that they must be given the scent of their victim before they will hunt. For anyone associated with the Congery, it would be easy to obtain something belonging to Geraden—a small possession, a piece of clothing. But opportunities to loot your rooms or wardrobes have been kept as near to nonexistent as possible. Without your scent, the insects cannot be sent against you."

Involuntarily, Terisa shuddered. She didn't want to think about those hideous—

Master Quillon saved her. He continued talking.

"Considering that Eremis wants you—perhaps as a hostage, perhaps as a lover—wants you enough to risk coming here, it is an interesting question why he has not used his mirror to translate you away. You would be entirely in his power then. But I suspect that the focus of his mirror has already been shifted as far as it will go.

"He must find it quite exasperating that the perfect solution to his dilemma is denied him by the small fact that you are *here* rather than eight cells farther down the corridor. As I say, we have been more fortunate than we deserve."

The Master had done it again, gone off at a tangent, distracted her. Sudden frustration welled up in her. "Then why don't you *stop* him?" She turned toward Quillon, demanding an answer with her whole body. "Get the Castellan to arrest him. Lock him up somewhere safe. He's going to betray *everybody*. You've got to *stop* him."

"My lady"—Master Quillon's voice was soft, and his eyes studied her as if he wondered how much of the truth she would be able to bear—"it is too soon."

Too *soon?* Too *soon?* She gaped at him, unable to speak.

"We do not know where his strength is located. We do not know how this trick of translation is done. We do not know how far his alliances extend, or how many powers he is prepared to bring out of his mirrors against us. We do not know what his plans are—how he means to destroy us. Until his trap is sprung, we have no effective way to strike back at him."

Still she gaped at him. Her head was spinning. With an effort, she asked thinly, " 'We'?"

The Master smiled slightly, sourly. "Yes, my lady. King Joyse, for the most part. And Adept Havelock, when he is able. I follow their instructions." He paused while she went pale with shock; then he admitted, "Not a very impressive cabal, I fear. There is no one else."

A moment later—perhaps because she couldn't stop staring at him—he seemed to take pity on her. "We cannot afford allies," he explained. "It is the essence of the King's policy to appear weak. Confused in his priorities. Unable to achieve decisions. Careless of his kingdom. And it would be impossible to create that appearance if his intentions were not kept secret. If Queen Madin knew the truth, would she turn her back on her husband in his time of gravest peril? If the Tor knew the truth, how well would he play the part of the forlorn and hectoring friend? If Castellan Lebbick knew the truth— No, it would be disastrous. He has no subterfuge in him. And no one would believe that King Joyse had lost his will or his wits, while Lebbick remained confident."

We, she murmured to herself, *King Joyse*, as if the words made no sense, *We cannot afford allies. It was all deliberate.*

"The fact is," said Quillon, "that everyone who loves the King would behave differently if they understood him. And so it would all come to nothing. I am trusted only because throughout Orison I am so easily taken for granted—and because King Joyse must have *one* friend and Imager who is more reliable than the Adept."

"But *why?*" The words burst from Terisa. "*Why?* Mordant is falling! Orison is under siege! Everybody who loves him or is loyal to him has been hurt!" *All deliberate. Of course. She knew that. But the reason—!* "He's destroying his whole world, the world *he* created. Why would he do such a terrible thing?"

Abruptly, the Imager jerked to his feet. He was suddenly angry: he bristled with indignation. Quietly, but with such intensity that he shocked her to silence, he replied, "So that he would attack here."

What—?

"We did not know who he was, my lady. Remember that. We did not know who he was until last night, when he erred by trying to make us believe that Geraden had killed Nyle. Before that, we had few suspicions—and less proof. *We did not know who he was.*" Red spots flamed on the Master's cheeks. "We knew only that he was powerful—that he had the ability, unprecedented in the history of Imagery, to inflict his translations wherever he chose. We had no way to find him, no way to combat him. No way to protect Mordant from him.

"But worse than the danger to Mordant was the threat to Alend and Cadwal, that had no Imagers to defend them. *That* King Joyse had accomplished with his ideal of the Congery and peace, that Cadwal and Alend were more helpless than Mordant against the enemy. *That* he was responsible for. His past victories have left Alend and Cadwal at the mercy of his new foes.

"Therefore"—Master Quillon gritted his teeth to keep from shouting—"King Joyse set himself to save the world.

"His weakness is an ambush. He lures the enemy to strike *here* rather than elsewhere—to inflict their peril and harm *here* rather than on the people he has made vulnerable—to attack Mordant and Orison rather than first swallowing Cadwal and Alend and thereby growing too strong to be defeated. We did not know who he was."

Roughly, Quillon shrugged, trying to restrain his anger. "That is the reason for everything King Joyse has done. That—and the Congery's augury—and Geraden's strange translation, which brought you here. When you came among us, your importance was obvious at once. Clearly, it was vital to make you aware of the world you had entered, so that you could choose your own role in Mordant's need. Even a good person may do ill out of ignorance, but only a destructive one would do ill out of knowledge. The augury made it clear that we had to trust you or die.

"But Geraden was also at risk—and his importance was also plain in the augury. His only protection lay in King Joyse's weakness. If Geraden were granted the ability to elicit intelligent, decisive action from his King, the enemy would surely kill him. In addition, the belief that you were ignorant was a form of protection for you. So it was vital also to spurn Geraden's loyalty—and then to make you aware of Mordant's history in secret.

"My lady, I argued against that decision. From the beginning, I found it difficult to trust you—a woman of such passivity. What hope did you represent to us? But King Joyse insisted. That is why Adept Havelock and I approached you and spoke to you, giving you in secret the knowledge which both the Congery and the King had denied to you publicly."

Oh, of course, now I understand. Terisa felt herself smiling into the quagmire of her own stupidity. Had she really spent her entire life like this—helpless, passive, unable to think?

"The translation of the Congery's champion," rasped Quillon, "presented a similar problem in a different guise. Again, the champion's importance in the augury is plain. Therefore King Joyse must oppose that translation, in order to appear determined on his own defeat. And yet he must be too weak to oppose the translation successfully. And I was at risk there, in addition to Geraden and yourself. My loyalties had to be concealed. So King Joyse had no choice but to refuse to hear the Fayle's warnings—and to ensure that Castellan Lebbick did not learn what transpired until the translation could no longer be stopped.

"My lady"—now Master Quillon faced her squarely, and Terisa saw that some of his anger was directed at her—"it will be easy for you to be outraged at what we have done. You have already said that everybody who loves King Joyse or is loyal to him has been hurt—and you are right. His policy is dangerous. Therefore the only way he can save those who love him is to drive them away—to make them distance themselves from the seat of peril he has chosen for himself. He succeeded with Queen Madin. But his failure with such men as the Tor and Geraden haunts him. If harm comes to them, he will carry the fault on his own head, even though they have chosen to do what they do.

"Nevertheless you should understand what he does before you protest against it. He hazards himself so that thousands of men and women from the mountains of Alend to the coast of Cadwal will be spared. He tears his own heart so that the people he loves may be spared. He places the kingdom that he built with his own hands in danger so that his traditional enemies can be spared.

"If you cannot trust him or serve him, my lady, you must at least respect him. He created his own dilemma, and he accepts its consequences. He does what he is *able* to do, so that the harm his enemies do will be suffered by a few instead of by many."

Because the Imager was angry at her—and because she was angry herself and didn't know how to conceal it—she turned away. The light seemed to be failing; maybe the lamp was running out of oil. Darkness gathered in all the corners: fatal implications spilled past the bars from the corridor into the cell. *You must at least respect him.* A man whose idea of wise policy was to twist a knife in his friends' hearts and leave his enemies unscathed. Of course she had to respect that. Sure.

She could hear Castellan Lebbick crying like a farewell, *I am loyal to my King!*

With more bitterness than she had realized she contained, more indignation than she had ever been aware of possessing, she asked softly, "What about the Castellan?"

"What about him?" returned Master Quillon. Perhaps he was too irate to guess what she meant.

"Maybe the Tor and Geraden have made their own choices. They're more stable than he is. What choice did you ever give *him?* If he tried to quit serving, King Joyse would have to stop him. This whole *policy*"—she sneered the word—"depends on the Castellan. If he doesn't stay faithful—if he doesn't do his utter best to keep Orison strong while King Joyse is busy being weak—then the whole thing collapses. When King Joyse finally decides to fight, he won't have anything to fight *with*. Unless the Castellan stays faithful."

Master Quillon nodded. "That is true. What is your point?"

"He doesn't have any choice, and it's *killing him*." Sudden pity surged up through her bitterness. The man Lebbick had once been would probably have treated her with nothing more terrible than detached sarcasm or kindness. But the entire weight of King Joyse's *policy* had come down on his shoulders, and now he could hardly refrain from raping or murdering her. "Don't you *see* that? What you're doing is expensive, and you're making him pay for all of it." Without warning, she began to weep again. Her distress and the Castellan's were too intimately interconnected. "You and your precious King are destroying him."

She expected Master Quillon to yell at her. She was ready for that: she didn't care how angry he got, what he said. Somehow she had gone past the point where mere outrage could threaten her. She had anger of her own, and it was no longer hidden away. If her father had appeared before her there and lost his temper, she would have known how to respond.

The Imager didn't yell at her, however. He didn't raise his voice. Slowly, he moved to the door of the cell. Perhaps he intended to leave, give up on her: she didn't know—and didn't care. But he didn't do that, either. He waited until she looked up at him, lifted her head defiantly and glared at him through her tears. Then he said quietly, "We didn't know this was going to happen. We thought he was stronger."

Just for a second, she almost stopped crying in order to laugh. Imagine it. An aging King and a madman and a minor Imager got together to save the world—and the best plan they could come up with required them to drive the only man in Orison who knew how to fight for them out of his mind. It was funny, really. The only thing she didn't understand was, what made them think it would work? How could they possibly believe—?

The sound of a door rang down the passage: iron hit stone with such savagery that the echo seemed to carry a hint of snapped hinges.

"Lying slut!" howled the Castellan. "I'll have you *gutted* for this!"

His boots started toward her from the guardroom.

Terisa froze in shock. Castellan Lebbick was coming to get her. He was coming to get her, and there was nothing she could do. Master Quillon said something, but she didn't hear what it was. In her mind, she saw the corridor from the guardroom: one turn; another; then the long line of the cells. The Castellan was coming hard, but he wasn't running; he might run as he drew closer, but he wasn't running yet; he was at the first turn—on his way to the next. He would reach her cell in half a minute. Her life had that many seconds left. No more.

"Are you deaf?" Quillon grabbed her wrist and hauled her off the cot. "I said, *Come on.*"

She didn't have a chance to think, to choose. He wrenched her through the open door out into the passage. But he was pulling on her too hard, away from the guardroom: she staggered against the far wall and fell; her weight twisted her wrist from his grasp.

As she scrambled to her feet again, she saw Castellan Lebbick come into view past the second turn.

He saw her as well. For an instant, their eyes met across the distance, as if they had become astonishing to each other.

Then he let out a roar of fury—and she skittered in the opposite direction, her boots slipping on the rotten straw.

She could hear him coming after her. That was impossible; her feet and breathing and Master Quillon's shouts made too much noise. Nevertheless her sense of his overwhelming rage, his ache for destruction, made his pursuit loud in her mind. She could feel his hate reaching out—

And ahead of her the Imager was losing ground. He slowed his flight; took the time to turn and beckon frantically.

A second later, he whipped open the door to another cell, dashed inside.

She followed without thinking. She had no time to think. Deflecting her momentum against the bars, she flung herself into the cell faster than Master Quillon was moving and nearly ran him down when he stopped.

Quickly, he opened a door in the side wall.

It was well hidden: the spring that released it was so cunningly concealed that she would never have found it for herself; and until he hit the spring she couldn't see the door itself. Then it swung wide, moving smoothly, as if it were counterbalanced on its hinges and controlled by weights. It must have been built in when this cell was first constructed.

That was how Master Quillon had gained access to the dungeon. How he had been able to listen to her conversations with Eremis and Lebbick. Another secret passage. But she didn't have time to be surprised. As soon as the door opened, Quillon caught at her arm again and thrust her forward, into the unlit passage.

He followed on her heels. Trying to make room for him without advancing into the dark, she found a wall and put her back to it. He was only a silhouette against the dim reflection from the dungeon lamps. At once, he tripped the mechanism that moved the weights to close and seal the door—   ·

—and Castellan Lebbick burst into the cell.

He was too late: he wasn't going to be able to prevent the door from shutting. And once it was shut he would have to find the spring to open it again.

Nevertheless he was fast, and his sword was already in his hands. Driving wildly to spit Terisa through the closing of the door, he plunged forward, hurled himself headlong toward her.

The door's weight swept his thrust aside. His swordtip missed her by several inches.

Then his sword was caught in the crack of the door. The iron held, jamming the stone so that it couldn't seal.

His body thudded against the door; he recoiled, staggering.

A moment later, his voice came, muffled, into the dark. "Guards! *Guards!*"

"Come on!" hissed Master Quillon. He took Terisa by the wrist once more and tugged her away from the thin slit of illumination. "Curse him! As soon as his men arrive, he will be able to open that door. We must escape *now*."

Struggling for balance, she hurried after her rescuer into a blind passage.

Stone seemed to whirl about her head like a swarm of bats,

probing for some way to strike at her. There was no light—no light of any kind. Except for his grip, Master Quillon had ceased to exist. Her shoulders kept hitting the walls as if she were reeling. She couldn't keep up this pace; she had no idea where the passage went, or how it got there. "Slow down!" she panted. "I can't see."

"You do not need to see," Quillon snapped. "You need to hurry."

Still trying to make him slacken speed, she protested, "How long?"

Without warning, he halted. At the same time, he let go of her. She collided with him, stumbled against the wall again, flung up her arms to protect her head.

"Not long," he muttered acerbically. "This passage was put in when the dungeons were rebuilt to provide room for the laborium. In other words, it is relatively recent. So it does not connect to the more extensive passage systems."

Unseen beside her, he tripped another release, and the wall she had just hit opened, letting cold air wash over her. Her torn shirt couldn't keep the chill out.

The space into which the door gave admittance was dim, almost black; but after a moment her eyes adjusted, and she saw ahead of her a truncated bit of hall leading to a wider corridor. Lanterns out of sight along the corridor in one direction or the other supplied just enough reflected glow to soften the gloom.

When she caught her breath to listen, the sound which came to her was the delicate spatter of dripping water.

Cold and wet. And a side passage too short to be worth lighting with a lantern of its own. A passage that seemed to go nowhere, as long as this door was closed and hidden.

Despite the distractions of fear, exertion, and surprise, her nerves turned to ice as if she had been here before.

"Now, my lady," whispered Master Quillon, "we must be both quick and quiet. These are the disused passages beneath the foundations of Orison, where twice you were attacked. They are back in use now, housing our increased population, but that is not our chief worry. Those people will be asleep—or too confused to hinder us. No, the difficulty is that these halls are now guarded to keep the peace—regularly patrolled. Somehow, we must avoid the Castellan's men."

No, she thought dumbly. That isn't right. Her brain felt like rock, impermeable to understanding. She had never seen the hall from this side, but it looked the same; the hairs on her forearms lifted as if the hall were the same. When Master Quillon started forward, she managed to reach out and stop him.

"No," she whispered, almost croaking. "This is the place. I'm sure of it."

He stood motionless and studied her narrowly. "What place?" The air grew colder on her skin while he stared at her.

"The translation point." The cold made her shiver. Long tremors seemed to start in her bones and build outward until her voice shook. "Where those insects came through to get Geraden. And Gart—"

Closing her arms across her chest, she hugged herself to silence.

"What, here?" the Imager asked in surprise. "Exactly here?"

She nodded as well as she could.

"We did not know that," he muttered; he appeared to be thinking rapidly. "We knew the general area, of course." His quick eyes studied the passage. "But the Adept did not observe the actual translations. And we could hardly afford to betray our interest by asking you or Artagel to show us specifically where the attacks took place."

Terisa ignored what he was saying; it didn't matter. What mattered was the mirror which brought people who wanted to kill her into Orison. "We can't go there," she breathed through her shivers. "I can't go there. They'll see us."

They'll come after us.

"A good point, my lady." Master Quillon's nose twitched as though he were trying to sniff out a way of escape. "If they saw us in the Image—and if they were ready for us—"

A grunting noise, a sound of strain or protest, carried along the passage from the entrance to the dungeons behind them.

The Master and Terisa froze.

"Put your backs into it, shit-lickers." Castellan Lebbick's voice was obscured by stone and distance, but unmistakable. "Get that door open before we lose them completely."

Terisa wanted to groan, but she couldn't stop shivering.

"Glass and splinters!" Quillon swore under his breath. "This is a tidy predicament."

An instant later, however, he grabbed her by the shoulders and shook her to get her attention. "My lady, listen.

"The focus of that glass was shifted. I saw Eremis translated into the dungeon. I saw him depart. He must have used the same mirror which brought your attackers here. Why else was I permitted to eavesdrop on him—to hear him reveal his intentions? Had his allies seen me enter the passage this way, they would have had no difficulty in disposing of me. Therefore they did not see me. Therefore the translation point of that mirror has been shifted."

"They could shift it back," she objected.

"They could be watching us right now," he retorted. "But if that is true, why are we still unharmed?"

The groan of stressed ropes and counterbalances came quietly out of the dark. A man gasped, and Castellan Lebbick barked, "That does it!"

"We must take the risk!" Master Quillon hissed.

Again, Terisa nodded. But she remained still, caught between fears. Gart was there somewhere, the High King's Monomach. And from that translation point had come four lumbering assailants who had themselves been eaten alive from the inside by the most terrible—

"You must go first!" Urgency made Quillon's rabbity face slightly ludicrous. "First is safest. Any man will need a moment to react when he sees us.

"*Go.*"

He shoved her, and she went.

Two stumbling steps toward the main corridor; three; four. For some reason, the strength had gone out of her legs. She felt like a woman in a nightmare, frantic to run, but powerless to do anything except ache with fright while her enemies rushed toward her.

Master Quillon caught up with her and shoved her again to keep her going.

For the second time, she felt *a touch of cold as thin as a feather and as sharp as steel slide straight through the center of her abdomen.*

Running now, but hardly aware of it, hardly conscious of what she was doing at all, she reached the main passage and the light and turned, whirled around in time to see Master Quillon following her and a black shape with a face full of hate and glee rising behind him, clutching a long dagger to strike him down.

No, Quillon! *Quillon!*

The shape rose and swept after him while she tried to cry out a warning and couldn't do it fast enough: black arms rose and then plunged down viciously, driving the dagger into the joining of his shoulders with such fury that blood burst from his mouth and the blade came through his chest and he was crushed to the floor as if he had been hit with a sledgehammer.

"*Got* you, you insipid rodent!" Master Gilbur barked in guttural triumph. "That is the *last* time you will interfere with anything we wish to do!"

When he wrenched his blade out of Quillon's back, blood ran from his hands like water.

Oh, Quillon!

Terisa remembered Master Gilbur's hands. They looked strong enough to bend iron bars; strong enough to grind bones. Their backs were covered with black hair—hair that contrasted starkly with his white beard. The hunch in his spine only seemed to increase his physical power; the flesh of his face was knotted with murder.

Gloating, he looked up from Quillon's corpse. "My lady," he coughed like a curse, "this is fortuitous. I had not expected the pleasure of killing you. That was intended to be Gart's task, after Eremis had finished with you. But my vigilance has been rewarded. Neither Festten's dog nor cocksure Eremis were with me when I found you in the Image."

She watched him as if he were a snake, waited for him to strike.

"It is a delight to rid the world of Quillon at last"—Gilbur licked spittle from his thick lips as he stepped over the body at his feet— "but to twist my knife in your soft flesh will be plain ecstasy."

Reaching out with his blade and his bloody hands, he started toward her.

She turned and fled.

She ran with all her heart this time, pushed all her strength through her legs. In spite of his crooked back, Master Gilbur was fast. His first blow nearly caught her. The gap she opened between them as she sped was less than a stride; then two; then three and a bit more. Instinctively, she had run to the left; she was taking the same direction she and Geraden had taken when they had fled from the insects.

Black arms rose and then plunged down—

Now she would have been glad—delirious with relief—to encounter a guard. An old codger hunting for the public lavatories. A servant. Anyone to witness what was happening, distract Gilbur. But the corridor was deserted. Master Gilbur spat curses as he pursued her. She was young, and running for her life; slowly, she widened the gap. But the air had already become fire in her lungs, and he didn't seem to be tiring.

Plunged down—

In one way, she had no idea where she was going. She didn't know these passages, had never been down here without a guide. The only thought in her mind was to find help. Before she faltered. She could feel her strength ebbing now. In another way, however, her instinctive sense of direction was sure, and she followed it unhesitatingly. To escape the fierce Imager, she tapped resources in herself that she didn't know she possessed.

She took the route to Adept Havelock's quarters.

There: the side passage. A thick wooden door, apparently the entrance to a storeroom. Yes, the entrance to a storeroom. A storeroom which hadn't been appropriated to help house Orison's increased population. She heaved the door open, pulled it shut behind her. It had a bolt. Didn't it have a bolt? It had to have a bolt—*had* to have—but she couldn't find it, couldn't see, there was no light in the storeroom, no illumination except thin yellow slivers from the cracks around the door.

Master Gilbur's bulk blocked even that light—

—and her fingers found the bolt, slapped it home just as he crashed against the door, trying to crush her with the weight of the wood and his own momentum.

The bolt twisted against its staples. But it held.

It wasn't going to hold for long. Gilbur hit the door again, raging at it and her. She couldn't see the bolt—but she could hear the metallic screaming noise as iron rusted into wood was forced out. The staples were going to give. It was only a matter of time.

Ignoring her frantic need for air and rest, she groped across the storeroom toward the door hidden at the back—the entrance to Adept Havelock's secret rooms.

Because she was moving by instinct rather than conscious thought, she didn't remember the possibility that the hidden door might be bolted until she found it open. Master Quillon had probably left it that way. He had probably intended to bring her here himself. Weak with relief and need, she opened the door and hurried into the lighted passage which led to Havelock's domain.

The first room she came to was cluttered with mirrors.

Nothing had changed since her last visit here. The disarray was composed of full-length mirrors so uneven in shape and color that they showed Images she couldn't begin to interpret; bits of flat glass that would have fit in her pocket; mirrors the right size for a dressing table, but piled on top of each other and scattered as if to keep anyone from seeing what they showed. All of them had been gleaned by King Joyse during his wars and never restored to the Congery; all of them were set in rich or loving frames which belied the neglect of their present circumstances. And all of them were useless. The Imagers who had made them were dead.

They didn't have anything to do with her. She rushed past them.

The passage took two or three turns, but she didn't lose her way. In a moment, she reached another door. She thought she could hear Master Gilbur still pounding to get into the storeroom—or perhaps the sound was simply caused by panic beating in her ears— so she pulled the door open and stumbled into the large, square chamber which Adept Havelock used as a study, and which gave him access to Orison's networks of secret passages.

The air was musty, disused—something had gone wrong with the ventilation. There were too many people in the castle. Smoke from lamps with wicks that needed trimming curled lazily around the pillar which held up the center of the ceiling.

The Adept was there, lurking in his madness like a spider.

Master Quillon had asked Terisa to believe that Havelock had helped King Joyse plan the destruction of Mordant. Quillon had expected her to believe it—expected her to believe that the old Adept's insanity didn't prevent him from wisdom or cunning. And perhaps her dead rescuer was right. Perhaps only a madman like Havelock could have conceived a strategy which relied for its sole chance of success on Castellan Lebbick's stability.

Nevertheless Terisa had nowhere else to turn now. Surely Quillon would have brought her here, if he had lived. The Adept had to help her. He had helped her in the past. He had tried to answer her questions. And Master Gilbur might catch up with her at any moment. He might kill the Adept as well, if he got the opportunity. And the Castellan was still after her.

"Havelock!" she gasped, wracking her lungs to force out words, "Gilbur killed Master Quillon. He's after me. I need help. You've got to help me."

Got to. As soon as she stopped running, she knew that she wouldn't be able to stay on her feet much longer.

The Adept stood beside his hop-board table, hunching over it as if he had a game in progress, studying the board intently even though there were no men on it. He didn't look up until she spoke; then, however, he raised his head and smiled amiably. Smoke eddied around him. One eye considered her casually; the other began a scrutiny of the wall behind her.

"My lady Terisa of Morgan," he said in a tone of loopy mildness. "What a pleasant surprise. Fornicate you between the eyes. I trust you are well?"

"*Havelock,*" she insisted. "Listen to me. I need help. Gilbur killed Master Quillon. He's right behind me."

The Adept's smile showed his teeth. "I'm glad to hear it," he replied as if she had just indulged in a pleasantry. "You certainly *look* well. Rest and peace do wonders for the female complexion.

"Now, tell me what you would like to know. I'm completely at your service today."

Horror welled up in her; she could hardly control it. The strain of defending Orison had finished him. He was gone, entirely out of touch with sanity. The air was too thick to give her lungs any relief. Quillon had been killed, and she was going to be killed, and the Adept himself was probably going to be killed. She didn't know how to get through to him. Nearly weeping, she cried, "Don't you understand? Can't you hear me? *Gilbur just killed Master Quillon.* He's coming *here.*"

Abruptly, he switched eyes, regarded her with the orb which had been staring at the wall. His nose cut the air like the beak of a hawk. On the other hand, his fleshy smile didn't waver.

"My lady Terisa of Morgan," he said again, "it would be my very great pleasure to rip the rest of your clothes off and throw you in a pigsty. Today I can answer questions. Ask me anything you want.

"But," he commented as if this particular detail were trivial, "I can't help you. Not today."

She stopped and stared at him, almost retching for air and aid. I can't help you. Not today.

Oh, Quillon!

"Almost everybody," he went on in the same tone of relaxed good cheer, "wants to know why I burned up that creature of Imagery who tried to get Geraden. Timing, that's the answer. Good timing. It doesn't matter what you look like. It doesn't even matter what you smell like. Anybody will lick your ass if you've got good timing. We weren't ready. If Lebbick found out who our enemies are from that creature, it would all collapse. We wouldn't be weak enough to defend ourselves."

"*Havelock!*" Terisa wanted to hit him, curse at him, tear her hair. "Master Quillon was your *friend!* Gilbur just killed him! Don't you even *care?*"

Without transition, Adept Havelock passed from amiable lunacy to wild fury. "Cunt!" With a roar, he brandished his right hand, pinching the fingers together as if he held a checker. "This is you!" Wheeling to the table, he banged his hand down on the board several times, jumping imaginary pieces; then he mimed flinging his checker savagely into the corner of the room. "Gone! Do you understand me? *Gone!*

"Don't you think I *want* to be sane? Don't you think I *want* to help? He was the only one who knew how to help *me*. But I used it all up! This morning—against those catapults! *I used it all up!*"

Dumb with shock, Terisa gaped at him. He was too far gone. She didn't know how to reach him.

An instant later, however, his rage disappeared as suddenly as it had come. Both his eyes seemed to grow glassy with sorrow, and he turned his back on her slowly. "Today I can't help you," he murmured to the blank checkerboard. "Go deal with Gilbur yourself."

He lowered himself into a chair near the table. His shoulders began to shake, and a high, small whine came from his clenched throat. After a moment, Terisa realized that he was sobbing.

Lost and numb, she left him alone there and went to deal with Gilbur herself.

She was so sick with dread and dismay and grief that she didn't even wince when she heard the Adept bolting his door after her, locking her away from any possibility of escape.

Like a sleepwalker—like a woman trying to locate herself, discover who she was, in a glass made from the pure sand of dreams— she returned to the room where Havelock kept his mirrors.

Master Gilbur was already there.

He didn't notice her. He was too full of wonder at what he had found: mirrors he had never known existed, dozens of them; a priceless treasure for any Imager with the talent to use them, any Adept. She could have tried to hide. The look on his face made her think that it might even be possible to sneak past him. He was so caught up in what he was seeing—

With a forlorn shrug, she took one of the small mirrors stacked on a trestle table near her and tossed it to the floor so that it shattered in all directions.

A cloud of dust billowed from the impact, softening the sound. The whole room was thick in dust; the mirrors apparently hadn't been cleaned in decades.

Nevertheless the sound of breakage got his attention. He jerked around to face her, raised his massive fists. His eyes burned; fury seemed to fume from his beard. "You dare!" he coughed. "You dare to destroy such wealth, such power! For that, I will not simply kill you. I will hack you apart."

"No, you won't." To her astonishment, her voice was steady. Perhaps she was too numb to be afraid any longer. As if she did this kind of thing all the time, she put the trestle table between them so that it blocked his approach. "If you take one step toward me, I'll break another mirror. Every time you do anything to threaten me, I'll break another mirror. Maybe I'll break everything here before you get your hands on me."

Numbness was a good start. It led to fading. She could stand here and confront Master Gilbur with all his hate like a woman full of courage—and at the same time she could go away, evaporate from in front of him. Give up her existence and follow mist and smoke to safety. By the time he got his hands on her—she knew he was going to get his hands on her somehow—she would be gone.

And in the meantime she might delay him long enough—

"You would not!" protested Gilbur, momentarily surprised out of his rage.

Terisa picked up another mirror and measured the distance to the Master's head. "Try me."

Numbness. Fading.

Time.

"No, my lady." His features gathered into their familiar scowl. He was breathing heavily, as if his back pained him. "*You* try *me*. All this glass is beyond price—in the abstract. In practice, it is useless. A mirror can only be used by the man who made it. There are new talents in the world, and mine is one of them. I can make mirrors with a speed and accuracy which would astound the Congery, if those pompous fools only knew of it. But only an Adept has the talent to work translations with a glass he did not make.

"If you believe I will not kill you, you are stupid as well as foolish."

He took a step toward her.

She threw the glass at him and snatched up another.

The delicate tinkling noise of broken glass shrouded by dust filled the room.

He halted.

"Maybe nobody except Havelock actually has that talent," she said, nobody except Havelock, for all the good that did her, "but you think you might be able to learn it. It might be a skill, not a talent. You've never had a chance to find out the truth because other Imagers won't let you experiment with their mirrors. With these, you could do all the experimenting you want. You could learn anything there is to learn."

Fading. Time. With her peripheral vision, she picked out the mirror she wanted—a flat glass in a rosewood frame, nearly as tall as she was. Through a layer of dust, its Image showed a bare sand dune, nothing else. Somewhere in Cadwal, she guessed. One of the less hospitable portions of High King Festten's land. In the Image, the wind was blowing hard enough to raise sand from the dune like steam.

Carefully, she edged toward it.

"But I'm not going to let you have them," she continued without pausing. "Not if you try to get me."

Master Gilbur faced her as if he ached to leap for her throat. One hand clutched his dagger; the other curled in anticipation. He restrained himself, however. "A clever point," he snarled. "You are cleverer than I thought. But it is futile. You cannot leave this room without coming within my reach. Or without moving out of reach of the mirrors. In either case, I will cut you down instantly. What do you hope to gain?"

Time. It was amazing how little fear she felt. Her substance was leaching away before his eyes, and he was blind to it. Now she could ease herself into the dark whenever she wished, and then there would be nothing he could do to hurt her. Nothing that would make any difference. All she wanted was time.

She took another small step toward the glass she had chosen.

Then she went still because she thought she heard boots.

"I'm not greedy." Now her voice tried to shake, but she didn't let it. Instead, she began to speak louder, doing what she could to hold the Master's attention. "I don't want much. I just want to frustrate you.

"You and Eremis are so arrogant— You manipulate, you kill. You don't have the slightest interest in what happens to the people you hurt. You're *sick* with arrogance. It's worth breaking a few mirrors just to upset you."

Suddenly, she saw movement in the passage behind him.

Trying to gain all the time she could—trying to strike some kind of blow in Master Quillon's name, and Geraden's, and her own—she flung the mirror she held at Gilbur's head.

He dodged her throw effortlessly.

And even that went wrong for her. Her life had become such a disaster that she couldn't even throw something at a man who hated her without saving him. Dodging, he pivoted and leaped toward the table to close on her. As a result, the first guard charging into the room missed his swing.

Before the man could recover, Master Gilbur hammered him to the floor with a fist like a bludgeon.

The second guard had the opposite problem: he had to check the sweep of his sword in order to avoid his companion. That took only an instant—but an instant was all the time Gilbur needed to plant his dagger in the guard's throat.

Castellan Lebbick entered the room behind his men alone.

He held his longsword poised; the tip of the blade moved warily. He glanced at Terisa, then returned his gaze to the Master. He was coiled to fight, ready and dangerous. She thought that she had never seen him look so calm. This was what he needed: a chance to do battle for Orison and King Joyse.

"So here it is," he commented distinctly. "The truth at last. Geraden's seducer and a renegade Imager, together. And poor Quillon dead in the corridor. Did he try to stop you? I thought it was him helping her escape, but I must have been wrong. The light isn't very good.

"You're lucky you're alive. If she hadn't thrown that glass, my men would have cut you down."

Master Gilbur's face twisted with laughter.

Terisa was past caring what the Castellan thought of her. She took another small step toward the mirror she wanted. Despite the intervening layer of dust, the sand in the Image seemed real to her, more solid than she was herself.

"Drop that pigsticker," Lebbick growled at Master Gilbur. "It isn't going to help you. Lie down. Put your face on the floor. I'm going to tie you up. I'd rather kill you, but King Joyse will want you alive. Maybe he'll let me question you.

"Do it *now*. Before I change my mind."

As if the provocation had become too great to be endured, Gilbur let out a harsh guffaw. "My lady," he said, scowling thunderously, "tell Lebbick why we are not going to let him take us prisoner."

She started to retort. The suggestion that she really was an ally of his nearly broke her careful hold on fading. Her anger had come out of hiding, and she wanted to scathe the Master's skin from his bones.

Unfortunately, his ploy had already accomplished its purpose: it had tricked Castellan Lebbick into glancing at her again.

During that brief glance, Master Gilbur pitched a handful of dust into the Castellan's face.

Cursing, the Castellan recoiled; he swung his blade defensively. His balance and reflexes were so good that he almost saved himself. Without sight, however, he couldn't counter Gilbur's quickness; he couldn't prevent Gilbur from picking up one of the guard's swords and clubbing him senseless.

Terisa paused in front of the mirror she had chosen. Her only rational hope was gone. Now nothing stood between her and whatever the Master might do. She should have been terrified. Yet she wasn't. Her capacity for surrender protected her. The hope she had placed in the Castellan hadn't been hope for herself, but only hope against Gilbur. She hadn't lost anything crucial. Inside herself, she was on the verge of extinction, and Master Gilbur had no way to stop her. When he looked up from Lebbick's body, she asked, "Why don't you kill him?"

"I have a better idea," he snarled, feral with glee. "I will take you with me. When he comes back to consciousness, he will report that we are allies. Joyse and his fools will have no conception of their real danger until we destroy them."

He was right, of course. The Castellan would be believed. Master Quillon was dead—her sole witness to Master Eremis' admission of guilt. And Quillon certainly hadn't had time to tell anyone what he had learned. Gilbur would come after her in a moment. She might be able to slow him down by breaking a few more mirrors, but that would only postpone the inevitable. He had won. If he called this winning.

Deliberately, she began to let go.

Nevertheless on the outside she continued to challenge him. "Someone will stop you," she said as if she were accustomed to defiance. Defiance was what led to being locked in the closet. "If Geraden doesn't do it, I will. You're going to be stopped."

"Geraden?" spat Gilbur. *"You?"* He really was remarkably quick. In the space between one heartbeat and the next, he ducked under the trestle table and came upright again, bringing his knife toward her. Every knot and fold of his expression promised butchery. "How are *you* going to stop me?"

How?

Like this.

She didn't need to say it aloud. He was still bearing down on her with his bloody hands when he seemed to run into a wall. Surprise wiped the violence from his face: his eyes sprang wide as he saw what was happening to the mirror behind her.

"Vagel's balls," he muttered. "How did you do *that?*"

She didn't look. The last time she had done this, she had done it entirely by accident, without knowing what she was doing; she didn't try to coerce it now. In any case, at the moment she didn't care whether she lived or died. She only cared about escape.

Still astonished, but recovering his wits, Master Gilbur reached for her.

Gently, Terisa closed her eyes and drifted backward into the dark.

THIRTY-TWO:
THE BENEFIT
OF SONS

he lay still for a long time. The fact was that she went
to sleep. Two nights ago, the lady Elega had poisoned
the reservoir of Orison. Last night, Geraden had faced
Master Eremis in front of the Congery, and she, Terisa,
had become the Castellan's prisoner. And tonight— She was exhausted. Master Gilbur reached for her, but he must have missed.
Even though her eyes were closed, she knew the light was gone. And
as the light vanished, she felt herself enter the zone of transition,
where time and distance contradicted each other. It was working:
she was being translated. Somewhere.

That was enough. The sensation that she had taken a vast, eternal plunge in no time at all sucked the last bit of her out of herself,
completed her self-erasure; and she slept.

The cold wasn't what awakened her. The dungeon had been as
cold as this. No, it was the faint, damp smell of grass, and the breeze
curling kindly through the tear in her shirt, and the high calling of
birds, and the impression of space. When she opened her eyes, she
saw that she was covered from horizon to horizon by the wide sky.
It was still purple with dawn, but already the birds had begun to flit
through it everywhere, looking as swift and keen as their own songs
against the heavens.

Then she heard the rich chuckle of running water.

She raised her head and looked down the hillside toward a fast stream. The melted snow of spring filled its banks and made it hurry, eager to go on its downland journey. In that direction, the water ran toward a valley still shrouded by the receding night; upstream, it came from a high, dark silhouette piled against the purple sky, a sense of mountains.

The air was as cold as the dungeon, but not as dank, as oppressive; the life hadn't been squeezed out of it by Orison's great weight and overloaded ventilation. She took a deep breath, put her hands into the new grass to push herself onto her feet, and stood up.

Almost at once, the mountains in the distance took light. The sun was rising. For no reason except that it was morning and the air was clear and she was alive, her heart started to sing like the birds, and she knew what she was going to see before the sun reached the massed shadow from which the stream emerged.

The Closed Fist.

There.

Starting from the west, sunshine caught the heavy stone pillar which guarded the stream's egress from the hills on that side. Then it touched the eastside pillar, and the defile between them came clear, the narrow, secret cut from which the Broadwine River ran toward the heart of the Care of Domne.

The Closed Fist. Geraden had played here as a boy. The jumble of rocks inside the defile must have been wonderful for children, a source of endless climbing games and cunning hideaways.

And she had brought herself here. Against all the odds. Despite her utter ignorance of Imagery—and despite Master Eremis' best efforts to confuse her. She had translated herself to safety using a flat glass. And she hadn't lost her mind.

Abruptly, her eyes filled with tears, and she wanted to cry out in relief and joy.

"Terisa."

She heard feet running over the grass. Through her tears, she glimpsed a shape, a man blurred by weeping. She turned to face him—to face the sun—and as its clean, new light shone through her, she found herself in Geraden's arms.

"Terisa."

Oh, Geraden. Oh, love.

"Thank the stars! I thought I was never going to see you again."

You're here. You made it. You made it.

Then he pulled back. "Let me look at you."

She blinked her sight clear and saw him gazing at her hungrily through his own tears.

"I've been watching for you, waiting, almost ever since I got here. It was the only hope I had. I just went in to Houseldon to tell my family what's going on. They didn't want me to come back alone, but I couldn't bear it any other way. I couldn't bear having somebody watch me wait. I left you there—with Eremis and Lebbick—and I thought I was never going to see you again."

She wanted to say, Did you think they could keep me away? The delight of him shone like the sun in front of her. He was the same Geraden he had always been—openhearted, vulnerable, dear. His tears made him look hardly older than a boy. His chestnut hair curled in all directions, full of possibilities above his strong forehead; his bright gaze and his good face were like birdsong in the spring air. I fought Eremis and the Castellan and Master Gilbur for you. Did you think they could keep me away?

But then he took in her rent shirt, her battered appearance, the strain impacted around her eyes; and his face changed.

The bones underlying his features seemed to become iron; his eyes seemed to catch and reflect light like tempered and polished iron. As completely as if he had been translated, the boy was gone, and in his place stood a man she hardly knew, a man who resembled Nyle more than Artagel—Nyle when he had set himself to do something which would both humiliate him and hurt the people he cared about. The metal of Geraden's character had been tempered by bitterness, polished by dismay. When he spoke again, his voice was thick with muffled strength—and veiled threats.

"Why didn't Eremis kill you? It looks like he tried."

Terisa put out her arms to him; she wanted to hug him again, embrace him, bring back the Geraden she had first learned to love. The Geraden who had willingly taken on so many different kinds of pain for her. But he only gripped her hands and held them still, requiring her to stand before him with all her sufferings exposed.

So she had to try to match him, to meet him where he was. She shook her head—not contradicting him, but denying her desire for comfort—and said, "Oh, he tried. Or Master Gilbur tried for him. But the Castellan did this."

Distinctly, like the sound of a breaking twig, he said, "Lebbick."

The skin of his face was tight over his iron bones. His threats weren't directed at her. "Tell me."

Involuntarily, she faltered. She wanted to be equal to him—to be worthy of him—but she couldn't do it. Tears filled her eyes again. "There's so much—"

"Terisa."

At least he could still be reached. He put his arms around her again and let her cling to him as hard as she was able. Then he murmured, "You're cold. And you look like you could use some food." He hadn't become softer: he was simply holding himself back. Turning her with his arm on her waist, he started her moving up the hillside in the direction of the pillars. "My camp is over there."

She nodded, unable to speak—unable to separate the joy and the grief of seeing him.

"When I first came through the mirror," he explained distantly, "when I discovered I was still alive, I planned to hide up here. It's the best place I could think of. And I didn't want to put Houseldon in danger, if Eremis tried to get me again. And I'd already lost you. I thought I would go crazy if anybody else got hurt trying to protect me.

"But we finally figured out what Nyle is doing. There's no way I can keep my family out of danger. So there's no point in hiding. I just came back here because somebody had to do it—in case you managed to get through somehow and then couldn't find Houseldon—and it might as well be me because I was going to spend all my time waiting for you anyway."

The sun had risen farther. The valley below the Closed Fist would remain in shadow for some time; but now there was enough light to reveal two horses tethered near the rocks ahead. One of them looked up at Terisa and Geraden. The other went on cropping grass unconcernedly. With an effort, she cleared her throat. "It sounds like you've figured out a lot of things."

He snorted sardonically. "After that last day we spent together, I knew Eremis was a traitor. When I finally realized I do have a talent for Imagery—an unprecedented talent—it wasn't too hard to start drawing conclusions. Then all I had to do was hope you really have a talent, too—and you would find it—and you would be able to get at a mirror.

"On the whole, it seemed more plausible that Eremis would

just fall down dead and save us that way, but I didn't have anything else left."

There were a couple of packs on the ground near the horses, and a small jumble of blankets—Geraden's bed. As he and Terisa entered the shadow of the rocks, he dropped his arm and hurried ahead to pick up one of the blankets. At once, he draped it over her shoulders. "I don't have a fire," he muttered. "I didn't want to be exposed, in case the wrong people came after me."

She shrugged: the blanket was enough. Grateful for its warmth, she asked, "What did you figure out about Nyle?" She dreaded every-thing she would have to say to him about Nyle.

Without meeting her gaze, he squatted to his packs and began pulling out foodskins, a jug, some fruit. His tone was harsh as he replied, "Falling in love with Elega and letting her talk him into betraying Mordant for Prince Kragen—that was bad enough, but it sort of makes sense. Quiss—that's Tholden's wife—she says Nyle has been unhappy enough to do something like that for years. Not everybody agrees with her"—he grimaced—"but I do. The Domne does.

"But faking his own murder to ruin me and help Master Eremis, right after he heard us prove Eremis was the only man in Orison who could have been working with the High King's Monomach—*That* doesn't make sense. It doesn't sound like him. He came back and saved my life, remember? Right after he rode away to betray Mordant. Helping a known traitor isn't something he would do of his own free will.

"He must have been pushed."

Geraden put cheese, dried apples, and a hunk of mutton on a plate of flat bread. Terisa accepted it and sank to the grass to start eating. Nevertheless her attention was fixed on him.

"Pushed how?" he went on. "What kind of threat or bribe would make him do something like that? What does he value that Eremis could give him—or take away?" Again, Geraden grimaced. He got out food for himself, but didn't eat it. "His family. What else? Eremis must have a mirror that gives him access to the Care of Domne—to Houseldon. He can send those insects here—or creatures with red fur and too many arms—or even Gart. He must have threatened Nyle with something like that."

A pang seized Terisa's heart, and she nearly dropped her food; she stared at him through the shadow. "Then they're still in danger.

Your home—your whole family— He might attack any time. Especially now—now that I got away from him.

"He knows where you are." She had told Eremis that, she had told him that herself.

Geraden jerked up his head.

"He can guess I'm here," she rushed on. "He saw that mirror change—the day you tried to find a way for me to go home. Master Gilbur saw what I was doing. How can they protect themselves? What are they doing to protect themselves?"

He met her alarm squarely. Gloom veiled his eyes, but his voice was iron. "Everything they can."

His tone halted her panic. She was still afraid, however, and there were so many things she had to say which might hurt him. Trying to swallow her shame, she said, "He really does know where you are. I'm sorry—that's my fault. I never told you—" His gaze made it hard for her to speak, but she forced herself. "That day you tried to get me back to my apartment. When you translated me into your mirror. You never asked where I went. I didn't go to the champion—but I didn't go to my apartment, either. I came here." She felt like she was confessing to an essential infidelity. "I never told you, but I told him."

Keeping himself clenched and neutral, he asked, "Why?"

Despite his restraint, he put his finger on the sore place. She could have made excuses. He hypnotized me. He was the first man I knew who ever wanted me. But Geraden deserved better than that. And she was responsible for what had happened. No one else.

"I was wrong," she said. "I thought I wanted him."

Geraden was silent until she looked up at him again. She still wasn't able to read his expression, but he didn't seem angry. His voice only sounded sad as he murmured, "I wish you'd told me the mirror didn't take you to the champion. I would have had an easier time doing what I did. I would have felt less like I was throwing myself away."

She felt the pain he didn't express more acutely than the regret he did. In an effort to make amends somehow, she offered, "But Nyle is still alive. I'm sure of that. Eremis admitted it."

As coherently as she could, she described what had happened to the physician and guards who had been left with Nyle's supposed corpse. The thought of their devoured bodies twisted in her belly; she forced herself to concentrate on her reasoning.

Geraden listened without showing any reaction. He was too tight to react. When she was finished, he said absently, "Poor Nyle. Right now he probably wishes he actually were dead. Being used like that must be horrible for him. As long as Eremis has him, he can be hurt again. He can be used against us again.

"It's my fault, of course. If I hadn't stopped him from going to the Perdon—if I hadn't tried to make his decisions for him, he never would have been vulnerable to this. He wouldn't have been in the dungeon, where Eremis could get at him." Geraden sighed as if blame were a part of what made him strong. "I don't know how much of it he can stand."

Must be horrible. That was true. She knew the feeling. She had come this far herself so that she wouldn't be used against the people she cared for.

Softly, she asked, "What're you going to do, when you try to fight him, and he tells you to surrender or he'll kill Nyle?"

Unexpectedly, Geraden snorted again. If he hadn't been so angry, he might have laughed. "I'm not going to fight him."

You're what? She stared at him through the shadow as if he had struck her. Not going to fight him? The world was full of different kinds of pain, ways of being hurt—more than she had ever suspected. The wrenching sensation she felt now was new to her. I'm not going to fight him. Just for a second, her own anger began to blaze, and she wanted to rage at him.

He hadn't looked away, however. He was facing her like a hard wall; anything she hurled might simply hit him and fall to the ground. He had been that badly hurt himself: she seemed to see the sources of his pain as if the gloom were full of them. He had been hurt by the desperation which had made him translate himself away from Orison with no clear hope of ever being able to return—or to control where he was going. And by all the implications of what he had discovered about Master Eremis. By the fact that no one in Orison trusted or valued him enough to believe him—not one of the Masters, not Castellan Lebbick, not even King Joyse.

By the threat to his home.

And everything else he had ever tried to do with his life had failed. He was even responsible for Nyle's plight. How could she be angry at him now? What gave her the right?

She had to swallow the thick sensation of grief in her throat before she was able to ask, "What *are* you going to do?"

Her quietness seemed to ease him in some way. His posture became marginally less rigid; his features relaxed a bit. With a faint echo of his former humor, he said, "First I'm going to get you to tell me what happened to you. Then I'm going to take you back to Houseldon for a decent shirt."

Involuntarily, she winced. "You know that isn't what I meant."

"All right." The iron came back into his voice. "I'm going to make a mirror. Any mirror, it doesn't matter—as long as it's big enough—as long as it isn't flat. I'm an Imager now. I know how to do it. I always went wrong before because I was trying to do the wrong thing, trying to use my talent wrong. Now I know better.

"I'm going to make a mirror. And I'm going to kill any son of a whore who comes here and tries to hurt my family."

Terisa held her breath to keep herself still.

He shrugged stiffly. "Is that what you wanted to hear?"

Oh, Geraden.

She didn't know what to do for him—but she had to do *some-thing*. She couldn't bear to see him like this. He needed a better way to deal with what had been done to him.

That realization gave her the strength to start talking herself.

"You asked what happened to me. I think I better tell you."

It was easier than she had expected: she was able to leave so much out. On a practical level, she discreetly excised the information that both the Tor and Artagel had asked her to betray him. He didn't need any more of that kind of hurt. And emotionally she could talk as if the Castellan's fury and her own terror hadn't touched her. In any case, she had no language for such things—or for the way they had changed her. Instead, she concentrated on Master Eremis.

"He has them fooled, Geraden," she said after she had described her time in the dungeon, her visits from the Castellan and Eremis and Master Quillon, her escape with Quillon—after she had told him about Gilbur and Havelock, and about Quillon's murder. "What he did with Nyle is just an example. That physician, Underwell, is dead, and everybody thinks you're a butcher, and the only person in Orison who looks innocent is Master Eremis. He's making himself a hero by refilling the reservoir—but that's only an excuse, he's just doing that so he can sneak around while everyone thinks he's busy. He's in league with Gart and Cadwal, and he's just waiting until his plans are ready."

Policy, my lady. If it succeeds, I succeed with it. If it fails, I remain to pursue my ends by other means. In spite of her determination to be detached, the memory made her shudder.

"He's going to spring some kind of terrible trap, and no one knows he's the one behind it all. Master Quillon is my only witness, and he's dead. Since the Castellan saw me with Master Gilbur, he thinks *I* killed Quillon."

Her own anger gathered as she spoke; she was full of accumulated outrage. She didn't want to put pressure on Geraden, she wanted to persuade him. But she simply couldn't think about Eremis without trembling.

"Geraden, he's going to destroy *them all,* and they don't even know it's him. What King Joyse is trying to do is crazy anyway, but it's hopeless if nobody knows who his enemy is. Everything he ever fought for, everything he ever made, Mordant and the Congery, all his ideals," everything that made you love him, "Eremis is going to destroy them all."

Out of the mountains' dusk, Geraden made a cutting gesture, silencing her. His face might have been stone. "'Eremis is going to destroy them all.' Of course. And you want me to stop him. You think there's something I can do to stop him."

She tightened her grip on herself, forced herself to speak softly. "Somebody has to warn them. Otherwise they don't stand a chance."

What about the augury? What about Mordant's need?

Abruptly, he surged to his feet. For a moment, he stalked away as if he never intended to come back; then he swung around harshly and returned to confront her over the new grass and the neglected food.

"You want me to warn them," he rasped. *"Do you think I haven't already considered that?* Talk is easy. Do you know how *far* Orison is from here? Do you know how long it would take me to get there? The siege has already started. Cadwal is already marching. Everything he wants to destroy will be in ruins before I get halfway there. I'll arrive like a good boy, panting and desperate, wanting something to save, and he'll just laugh at me.

"He'll just *laugh* at me.

"Terisa"—he was controlling himself with a visible effort, holding down a desire to yell at her—"I am very, very tired of being laughed at."

All her insides ached as she watched him; he made her so sad that her anger faded, at least temporarily. She didn't know what to say. What could she have said? She understood: of course she understood. He was beaten, and he was trying to accept it. But what she did or didn't understand changed nothing. It didn't help him—or Mordant. Yet she had to give him something. If she didn't, she was going to start crying again.

Quietly, stifling her unhappiness, she asked, "What do you want me to do?"

He had considered that as well. "You're an arch-Imager," he said promptly. "Like Vagel. You've just proved that. You can pass through a mirror without changing worlds. And without losing your mind. But you're more than that, too. You can change the Images themselves. You can do the same thing with flat glass that I do with a normal mirror. Together, we're two of the most powerful people in Mordant. All we need is practice. And mirrors. I want you to stay here and help me defend the only thing left that's worth fighting for."

In the same tone, she asked, "Do you have any glass at all?"

"No, not yet. We've got a bit of equipment and tinct my father confiscated from some sort of hedgerow Imager back in the early days of Mordant's peace, but we've never used it.

"I was worried while you were back in Orison, where Eremis could attack you—or put pressure on you by attacking me. But after what you've just told me, I don't think we need to hurry. We aren't much of a threat to him right now. He's got us out of Orison, and he still looks innocent. We can't hurt him where we are. And he's got a lot of other things on his mind. He's got to spring this trap of his—whatever it is. I think he'll leave us alone until he's done with Orison. He won't worry about cleaning up minor problems like us until afterward."

Terisa sighed softly. "We're 'two of the most powerful people in Mordant,' but we're only a 'minor problem.'"

"All we need is practice," he repeated as if that would reassure her. "By the time he gets around to us, we'll be ready for him. If he tries to touch Domne, we're going to tear his hand off at the wrist."

After a pause, he concluded like a man affirming an article of faith, "There isn't anything else."

Maybe that was true—she didn't know. She had gone as far as she could at the moment. He assumed she would do what he wanted: that was enough. It would give her time to think. Time to *rest*. She needed rest badly. With everything still unresolved, she looked up

at him and said, "Speaking of Domne, I think you ought to take me
to Houseldon. I want to meet your family."

She couldn't be sure in the dim light, but she thought she saw
him almost smile.

For some reason, however, her acquiescence—and the idea of returning home—didn't improve his mood. If he did smile, he did so
in a way which denied laughter. His bitterness may have lifted a bit,
but the dour humor which replaced it was equally iron and ungiving.

With a crisp accuracy entirely unlike the eager, accident-prone
manner she remembered, he repacked his supplies, then watered the
horses and saddled them. "Take the bay," he said, indicating one of
the mounts. "Quiss had her trained to carry pregnant women. Quiss
has been pregnant a lot. I think Tholden wants to have seven sons,
too." His tone seemed gentler when he talked about such things,
but that impression may have been created by what he was saying
rather than by the way he said it. "But so far he only has five children,
and two of them are daughters."

The air was warmer now; nevertheless Terisa kept the blanket
over her shoulders as she climbed onto the bay. This was only her
second experience with a horse, and the saddle seemed dangerously
high. The blanket was awkward to hold closed—but not as awkward
as her torn shirt. The last thing she wanted at a time like this was
to ride into Houseldon with her chest exposed.

When she was seated, he adjusted her stirrups. Then he swung
up onto his own mount, an appaloosa with a look of harmless lunacy
in its eyes, and led her away.

The hillside sloped downward from the Closed Fist for some
distance, then became rumpled, like a rucked-up skirt. Even in the
shadow of the mountains, the light was strong enough now so that
she could see wildflowers scattered across the grass; but she didn't
realize how bright they were—how much brighter they were than
she remembered them—until she and Geraden reached the direct
sunshine. Then color seemed to burst from the grass wherever she
looked: blue and lavender; mauve; yellow shot with orange; the rich,
rich red of poppies. There were trees on the hillsides, too, but most
of them grew down in the folds of the terrain, along the river. Mountains with snow still on them ranged north and east as well as south
of her, so that she and Geraden seemed to be riding out from between their arms. As far as she could see toward the northeast, how-

ever, toward the Care of Domne, the hills were primarily covered
with open grass and wildflowers.

Geraden was right: the bay was easy to ride; her gait instilled
confidence. He and Terisa were soon down among the low hills, and
she began to feel secure enough to attempt a trot. The whole sensation—the horse, the morning sunshine, his presence beside her—
was so much more pleasant than the time she had gone riding with
him and Argus that she couldn't hold in a smile.

"Yes," she heard him murmur as if he were answering a question. "The Care of Domne is beautiful. It's always beautiful, no matter what happens to it—or to Mordant. No matter who lives or dies,
no matter what changes. Some things—" He looked around in an
effort to see everything at once. "Some things remain."

He thought for a moment, then said, "Maybe that's why the
Domne was never willing to fight. And why King Joyse loved him
anyway."

"I don't understand."

Geraden shrugged. "In a way, my father *is* the Care of Domne.
The things he values most don't need to be fought for because they
can't be hurt."

Terisa concentrated on her seat while the horses worked their
way up a steeper hillside. After that, the ground seemed to have
been smoothed out by the hand of the sun. It wasn't level, but the
slopes were long and comfortable, and the grass appeared to flow
all the way to the horizon.

She probably should have been thinking about her strange talent
for Imagery. After any number of denials, she had discovered that
her talent was real. Surely that changed her situation, her responsibilities? But she didn't feel that anything had changed. She had
already chosen her loyalties in the struggle for Mordant, committed
herself. And without glass there was nothing she could do to explore
or define her abilities—whatever they actually were.

At the moment, she wasn't interested in herself. She was interested in Geraden.

"Tell me about your family," she suggested. "You've talked
about them before, but it feels like a long time ago. I'd like to know
who I'm going to meet."

"Well, you won't meet Wester," Geraden answered absently,
as if his family had nothing to do with what he was thinking. "He's
away rallying the farmsteads. That's probably just as well. He's the

handsome one. Women fall in love with him all the time. But he'll
break your heart. The only thing he cares about is wool. If wool
were glass, he'd be the greatest Imager in the world. We aren't sure
he knows women even exist.

"Tholden is the oldest, of course. He's the heir—he'll be the
Domne when our father dies—and he takes that very seriously. He
wants to *be* the Care the same way our father is. And he's good at
it. But he'd be better if he trusted himself enough to relax.

"He and the Domne can be pretty funny sometimes. He's a
compulsive fertilizer—he wants everything to grow like crazy. So he
goes around shoveling manure onto anything that has a root system.
And my father follows him with a pruning saw, muttering about waste
and cutting back everything Tholden just encouraged to grow."

In the distance, Terisa saw a flock of sheep, moving gently like
foam rolling on the green sea of the grass. Two small dogs and a
shepherd kept the flock together without much difficulty: the day
was untroubled, and the animals were placid. Geraden and the shepherd waved at each other, but neither of them risked disturbing the
flock with a shout.

"The sheep are still out," Geraden commented. "We could drive
them into Houseldon, but what good would that do? They're probably safer as far away as they can get."

He rode for a while in silence before returning to her question.
"Anyway, you'll meet Tholden's wife, Quiss. And their children.
She'll make you comfortable in Houseldon, or die trying.

"Minick is the second son. He's married, too, but you probably
won't see his wife. She hardly ever leaves the house. That's too bad—
I like her. But she's so shy she gets in a flutter when you just smile
at her. Once she ruined her best gown by curtseying to the Domne
in a mud puddle.

"I like Minick, too, but he's a little dim. He's the only man I
know who thinks shearing sheep is fun. He and his wife are perfect
for each other.

"That leaves Stead, the family scapegrace. He's in bed right now
with a broken collarbone and several cracked ribs. He just couldn't
keep his hands off the wife of a traveling tinker, and the tinker
expressed his disapproval with the handle of a pitchfork.

"The strange thing is that Stead means well. He works hard.
He's generous. Every day is a new joy. He simply adores women—
and he can't imagine why any man doesn't make love to every woman

there is. They're too precious to belong to anyone. *He* isn't jealous of the husbands he cuckolds. Why should *they* be jealous of him?

"Other than that, only about three hundred people live in Houseldon. It's the seat of the Domne. What serves as government in this Care is there. Anywhere else, Houseldon would be just another village, but in Domne it's the marketplace as well as the counting-house and the court of justice.

"Also the military camp. The Domne maintains six trained bowmen, mainly in case a bear or two or a pack of wolves comes out of the mountains and starts raiding sheep. But it's also their job to do things like rescue Stead from that tinker, or sit on people who get belligerent when they've had too much ale. On the rare occasions when the Domne decides he has to fine somebody for something, they collect it.

"That's what we have to defend ourselves with," Geraden concluded as if this were the question Terisa had asked. "Six bowmen, plus farmers with hoes and shepherds with crooks—as many as Wester can talk into it.

"That's why Houseldon needs us."

The way he drifted from his subject disturbed her. She had always liked hearing him talk about his relatives. Sometimes, the contrast to her own family had saddened her; today it was a pleasure. She was looking forward to meeting his father and brothers. She wasn't ready to start thinking again about the trouble which had driven her here.

And what he suggested didn't sound right, coming from him. To give up everything to which he had ever aspired in order to do nothing more than fight for his home: that didn't sound like him. Like Artagel and Nyle in their different ways, he had never been able to stay at home. He had too much itch for the rest of the world, too much sense of possibility: he couldn't contain himself in Domne. She didn't question his love for Houseldon and the Care, for his father and brothers. But she felt strongly that he was the wrong man for the job he had chosen. He had chosen it as much out of bitterness as out of love: it didn't fit him.

She saw another flock of sheep. Then the ground became more level; fields appeared, watered by ditches from the river and streaked with the delicate green shoots of new corn; the horses reached a road. She and Geraden were the only people on it, but that came as no surprise to her. Everyone except the shepherds was probably busy preparing for the defense of Houseldon.

Then she saw Houseldon itself ahead.

She had forgotten that Geraden had called it a stockade.

The whole village was walled by timbers taller than she was; from horseback, she was barely able to see the thatched roofs of the houses past the top of the stockade. The timbers had been set into the ground and then lashed together with vines of some kind. To her, the idea of a stockade didn't sound especially impressive; she had grown up with concrete and steel. But when she actually saw that timber wall, she thought it looked remarkably sturdy. Mere men on horses wouldn't be able to break it down. Red-furred creatures armed with scimitars and hate wouldn't be able to break it down. They would need a catapult or a battering ram.

Or fire.

Thinking about fire, she clutched the blanket around her shoulders and shivered.

The gate, a massive shutter of timbers trussed with strips of iron, stood open. The men guarding it hailed Geraden in a way that suggested they knew where he had gone, and why. Houseldon wasn't a place for people who liked secrets.

As he and Terisa rode through the gate, Geraden asked the guards, "Where's the Domne?"

One of them shrugged. "At home? With that leg, he doesn't get around as easily as he used to."

Geraden nodded and led Terisa down the main street of the village.

She wanted to ask what was wrong with the Domne's leg, but she was too busy looking around. The dirt street was little more than a lane; yet it served as a thoroughfare for wagons and cattle as well as people. If the street had been busy, she and Geraden would have had trouble getting through. This morning, however, they caused most of the traffic themselves: it was composed almost entirely of people who came out to see Geraden—and her.

In contrast to the lane, the square-fronted buildings on either side were substantial: solidly erected as well as large. They had stone foundations, deep porches, windows covered with oiled sheepskins. Working with rough planks and mud plaster, the inhabitants of Houseldon had constructed homes and shops meant to endure; and the characteristic thatch of the roofs was apparently used because it was practical—cool in summer, warm in winter, easy to replace—rather than because it was cheap. In that way, the houses were like the people, who were dressed primarily in tough fabrics and simple styles, intended to last.

The spectators looked at Geraden and studied Terisa with unabashed curiosity. One rowdy spirit—she didn't see who it was—shouted unexpectedly, "Looks like you made a good choice, Geraden!" but Geraden didn't react.

He certainly didn't need to defend himself. Several voices muttered imprecations at the rowdy spirit on his behalf, and one old man said clearly, "Hold your tongue, puppy. If you had his problems, you would drown yourself in the Broadwine."

Just for a second, the gloom in the background of Geraden's expression lifted, and his eyes sparkled a little.

Terisa was abashed by the realization that she was blushing.

For several minutes, he steered her horse past a number of intersecting lanes and paths—past public watering troughs, a granary or two, a shop that sold foodstuffs and utensils, at least six merchantries which dealt in wool and sheepskins, and one tavern rendered unmistakable by a huge sign over the door that announced succinctly: TAVERN. Then, without warning, he stopped in front of a house and swung off his mount.

This building was somewhat larger than its neighbors. Apart from its size, however, its only distinguishing feature was the plain, brown-and-russet pennon that fluttered from a pole jutting out of its thatch. Geraden tossed his reins over the porch rail, then turned to offer Terisa a lift down, muttering, "This is it."

There was a woman on the porch. A line of rope ran from one end of the porch to the other, and over it hung a large rug, rag-woven from scraps of wool. The woman held a short flail in one hand, and the air around her was dim with dust: apparently, she had been beating the rug. Terisa was immediately struck by her corn silk hair and sky blue eyes, by the flush of exertion on her cheeks and the strength in her hands. She had the bosom of an Earth Mother and the shoulders of a stonemason, and she propped her fists on her hips to greet Geraden as if she weren't entirely ready to let him enter her house.

A child only a little bigger than a toddler peered from behind her skirts, then ducked into hiding.

"You took long enough," she said in a voice that directly contradicted the severity of her manner. "Da's been fretting."

"Quiss," he replied like a man who had forgotten how to laugh and didn't want to get angry, "this is Terisa. The lady Terisa of Morgan. She's an arch-Imager." He seemed to fear that Quiss wouldn't take his companion seriously enough. "After Vagel, she's the most powerful Imager in the country."

Quiss raised her blue eyes to Terisa's face. She didn't smile, but her gaze felt as friendly as sunshine. All at once, Terisa forgot to be self-conscious.

"She's also cold and tired, and probably hungry," Quiss pronounced, "and she isn't used to horses. What are you waiting for? Bring her in."

Terisa smiled helplessly.

Geraden reached up for her hand. His eyes gave away nothing: he was too iron to be dented by Quiss' manner. Terisa included him with her smile, then lost it because she suddenly began to ache for the Geraden who would have chuckled happily at Tholden's wife. When he didn't respond, either to her smile or to her sadness, she took a deep breath for courage and let him help her off the bay.

Her legs began to shake as soon as her feet hit the ground—a consequence of her unfamiliarity with horseback riding—but after she took a step or two the trembling eased. Geraden might have wanted to withdraw his hand, but she didn't give him the chance; she clung to him as she went up the steps onto the porch.

Still without smiling, Quiss unexpectedly took hold of Terisa's shoulders and gave her a quick hug, a kiss on the cheek. "Welcome, Terisa of Morgan," she said. "I don't know anything about Imagery— but I know Geraden. You are very welcome here."

Terisa had no reply. An awkward moment passed while she groped for a way to explain how glad she was to be here. Then the child hiding behind Quiss' skirts broke the silence.

"Ma, the lady don't smell good."

Quiss started to turn. "'Doesn't,' Ruesha. Not 'don't.' And that's no way to talk to a lady."

Geraden was faster, however. "Imp!" he barked. "Come here. I'm going to paddle your behind until you can't walk for a week."

Squealing with an obvious lack of fright, the child sprinted into the house. Geraden followed, thundering his boots on the floorboards as he pretended to run.

This time, Quiss did smile, half in apology, half in pleasure. "Ruesha says what she thinks," she said, "like too many of her uncles." Then she wrinkled her nose humorously. "But it's true, you know. You don't smell good. They must have treated you pretty badly after Geraden got away."

Terisa was smiling herself; a small trill of music ran around her heart. There was hope for Geraden yet. Perhaps just for a second, he had been surprised out of his defeat. She sounded incongruously happy as she replied, "They put me in the dungeon."

Quiss' eyes resumed their sky blue sobriety. "A dungeon they haven't cleaned for decades, apparently." The bare idea affronted her. "Come. I'll introduce you to the Domne. Then we can go get you a bath. And some clean clothes. That will give his father a chance to try to make sense out of Geraden."

With one strong arm wrapped companionably around Terisa's shoulders, Quiss steered her into the house.

The room they entered was so dark that she could hardly see. The only light came from the coals in the hearth, the barely translucent window covers, and the reflection of daylight through the doorway. As her eyes adjusted, however, shapes began to emerge from the dimness: a bulky cast-iron stove beside the fireplace, several doors into other rooms, a rectangular wooden table long enough to seat ten or twelve people.

At the head of the table sat a man with one leg propped on a stool.

"Did you see Geraden, Da?" Quiss asked.

"He went through here," a warm voice rumbled. "He was too busy trying to beat the spit out of your youngest to talk to his mere father. But he's back in one piece—and he's got a woman with him. I gather something good has happened."

"I think so," said Quiss briskly. "Da, this is Terisa—the lady Terisa of Morgan. As soon as you tell her how welcome she is, I'm going to take her and get her a bath and clothes and food. In the meantime—"She paused significantly before saying. "Now that she's here, maybe he'll unbend enough to tell you what's going on.

"My lady Terisa of Morgan, this is the Domne."

Through the gloom, Terisa saw that the Domne was a tall man, as lean and curved as an axe handle. He had Geraden's face, and Artagel's, and Nyle's, but more so in some way, as if they were attractive yet inaccurate copies of him. The hair on his head was thick, but he had no beard. The silver streaks at his temples were the only obvious signs of his age. Perhaps because the light was weak, he didn't appear to be more than half as old as King Joyse.

The leg propped on the stool was plump with bandages. He had a pair of canes nearby, but he made no attempt to rise when Quiss introduced him. Instead, he said, "My lady," in a voice as warm as a hug, "you're welcome in Houseldon—and in my house. If we could do it, we would put on a feast for you, a celebration. But I'm afraid we're a little too busy. Geraden seems to think we might be attacked. That doesn't happen every day, and we have to brace ourselves.

"But don't worry about that right now. I've wanted him to bring a woman home with him for a long time. That's the benefit of sons. When they marry—or only fall in love—or merely feel like flirting a bit—they bring their women home with them. Quiss is a good example. If she were my daughter, and Tholden was someone else's son, she would have left to go with him, and we would have been lost without her."

At that, Quiss snorted affectionately. "Sons, is it? Is that why you treat Ruesha like she's worth the weight of her three brothers in fine brandy?"

The Domne didn't deign to acknowledge this jibe. Noticing the direction of Terisa's gaze, he explained, "A hunting accident. I'm afraid I finally have to admit that I'm not a young man. Occasionally, packs of wild pigs wander into Domne from the Care of Termigan. I'd be willing to let them wander, but unfortunately they can trample an entire cornfield overnight, so we're forced to hunt them. This time, one of my sons had the bad sense to suggest that I was getting too old to hunt wild pig. The truth must be told, Quiss, it was Tholden. Naturally, I insisted on leading the hunt myself.

"When the boar charged, my thrice-cursed horse panicked and threw me. Then at last I had to admit that indeed I have put on a few years since my youth. I simply wasn't spry enough to prevent the pig from sticking his tusk in my leg.

"It heals slowly, alas," he sighed. "Another sign of age."

Almost at once, Terisa found that she liked the Domne. The relaxed way he talked put her at ease, made her feel more welcome than any elaborate speech or feast; made her feel at home. "My lord," she said impulsively because she didn't have any other words for her gratitude, "I'm very glad to be here."

"'My lord'?" the Domne returned humorously. "I hope not. The last time a woman insisted on calling me 'my lord,' I had to marry her to make her stop."

Smiling, Terisa asked, "What should I call you?"

"'Da,'" he answered without hesitation. "It's probably presumptuous of me, but I like it. My sons refuse, of course. Another benefit of sons—they keep me humble. In the name of my dignity. If I have any—which I doubt, sitting here half crippled because I wasn't able to get out of the way of a pig. But the rest of my family won't call me anything else."

"Da," she murmured experimentally. It had a nice sound. She had never called her own father anything except *Father*.

"Thank you," said the Domne as if she had done him a favor.

"Come, Terisa." Quiss put an arm on Terisa's shoulders again. "If I let you stay, he'll keep you talking until lunchtime. That's a 'benefit of sons' he doesn't mention. When they were small, he always had someone to listen to him. They taught him bad habits. Any daughter with sense in her head would have known better."

The Domne nodded gravely. "We can talk later, Terisa, when you've had a chance to rest and refresh yourself.

"If you find Geraden," he added to Quiss, "tell him I want to see him. I refuse to be ignored all morning merely because Ruesha wants to play."

"Yes, Da," Quiss replied in a tone of gently mocking subservience. With her arm, she took Terisa out of the room.

Almost immediately, they encountered a serving girl in the hall. Quiss instructed her to bring hot water for a bath, then to fetch Geraden for the Domne. The girl bobbed an acknowledgment, and Quiss and Terisa walked on.

The house was big—bigger than Terisa had realized. Behind its wide front, it seemed to sprawl for a considerable distance. Beyond the room where the Domne sat, the windows were open, letting light and spring air into the hall, and she found that she could see the grain in the polished hardwood of the floor, the fitted planks of the walls. Here she realized for herself how strong the odor of the dungeon was on her—realized it because everything around her smelled of soap, beeswax, and old resin. Years of wear and polish had brought out a glow from the floorboards down the center of the hall, and that warmer hue seemed to mark the way ahead like a path, a way of making sure that no one got lost.

Quiss took her past a door that stood slightly ajar. As they crossed the opening, a plaintive voice called out, "Quiss! In the name of decency!" The tone of the appeal was both lugubrious and funny. "I'm dying."

"And about time, too," muttered Quiss without stopping—or letting Terisa pause.

"Who was that?" Terisa asked in surprise.

Then she was surprised even further to see Quiss' entire face turn red.

"Stead. One of the sons Da seems to value so highly. He hasn't had a woman since a tinker broke his collarbone, and he wants me to bed him. As soon as he learns you're here, he'll get the same idea about you.

"Take my advice," Quiss continued primly. "Have nothing to do with him. He's the only one of the Domne's sons who has no sense at all. Personally, I won't even let the serving girls go in his room. A groom and one of the shearers are taking care of him."

Terisa made an effort to keep from laughing. "What does he think he can do—with a broken collarbone?"

Quiss stopped in the hall and gave Terisa the full force of her bright blue eyes. Softly, she said, "You must not have much experience with men. It isn't what he thinks he can do. It's what he thinks you can do."

Her expression, however, suggested that she wasn't listening to herself—that her own thoughts had gone in a different direction. She had become grave, almost somber; perplexity knotted her brows. "Before yesterday," she murmured, "none of us knew you existed. Then Geraden arrived out of nowhere, breathing fire about a possible attack and at the same time acting like all the heart and hope had been beaten out of him. He said he left a woman behind who was probably being tortured because she was his friend. Now that I see you, it seems astonishing how little he actually told us about you.

"He never mentioned that you could have any man you wanted."

Terisa bit back an impulse to ask, Is that really what you think? She wanted to believe that she was pretty; and Quiss' opinion seemed to have tremendous value. But Tholden's wife obviously wanted to get reassurance, not give it. She wanted to believe that Geraden wouldn't be hurt anymore. Deliberately, Terisa put her questions aside.

"They put me in the dungeon," she said, "because I wouldn't tell them where he was. He rescued me when my old life was going nowhere. He's risked himself for me any number of times. He even tried to fight the High King's Monomach for me once." Quiss was impressed; but Terisa didn't stop. "He's the only reason I'm alive— the only reason I'm here. Even if I didn't like him so much, I wouldn't be interested in anybody else."

Certainly not Stead, who sounded suspiciously like Master Eremis.

That was what Quiss wanted to hear. She didn't smile—apparently, she rarely smiled when she was happy—but warmth shone from her. "Then I'll stop worrying about him and leave him to you. If anybody can get him out of the pig wallow he's in, you can."

Briskly, she moved Terisa again in the direction of a bath.

Three turns, two doorways, and another long hall brought them to a bedroom with a low, flat cot that contrasted strangely with the rest of the furnishings: the heavy armchairs and the sturdy washstand. "This is Artagel's room," Quiss explained. "It's relatively private, but I can get you a softer bed if his cot is too hard. I don't know how he sleeps on it. Sometimes I think he may actually be as tough as he thinks he is."

"I'll try it and let you know," said Terisa. The bed in her former apartment had had the firmest mattress she could find.

"The advantage," Quiss went on, "is that you get your own bathroom." She pointed at the other door to the room. "Why don't you get started? There's water—and the hot water should be here in a minute. I'll go find you some clothes."

Terisa agreed gratefully. As soon as Tholden's wife left, she closed the bedroom door, pulled off her boots, and went into the bathroom.

It had no running water—apparently the Care of Domne didn't know as much about plumbing as Orison did—but clay pipes had been set in the floor to carry bathwater and waste away. Which explained, now that she thought about it, why she hadn't seen water, not to mention sewage, standing in the ditches alongside Houseldon's streets: underground drains. And that perception, in turn, made her laugh softly at herself. Her time in Orison, and Elega's attempt on the reservoir, had taught her some strange lessons. The woman she used to be would never have noticed plumbing or drains unless they didn't work.

As Quiss had said, however, there was water, plenty of it in a vat beside the wooden bathtub.

Instead of filling the tub right away, however, Terisa went back into the bedroom, sat down on Artagel's hard cot, closed her eyes, and tried to absorb the fact that she was here and safe; that she had finally made her way to a place where she could feel the sun's warmth in the wood of the wall beside the bed, and where the people around her were moved by simple things like family and friendship and wool, rather than by treachery, ambition, and revenge.

She sat there, soaking up the peace of the house, until two serving girls arrived with four buckets of hot water between them. Then she gave herself what felt like the most luxurious bath she had ever had in her life.

Some time later, she dried her scrubbed body and her now-lustrous hair, drained the tub, and tried on the clothes Quiss had left for her.

The undergarments were of fine linen; the shirt and skirt, of unlined sheepskin, supple and delicate against her skin, yet remarkably tough. The long skirt was wide around the hem, and had been slit to the knees both in front and in back, so that it could be worn on horseback; the shirt was decorated only by its buttons, which appeared to be polished pieces of obsidian. Both the shirt and the skirt went well with her winter boots.

Now all she needed was earrings to match the buttons. And a mirror, so that she could do something with her hair.

Of course, she didn't really want a mirror—not for something as simple as vanity. What she actually desired was a chance to see what she looked like, so that she might begin to believe in herself— to believe that Geraden would notice her enough, and care enough about what he saw, to let her reach him.

Get him out of the pig wallow—

She didn't trust any of the conclusions he had reached. And she couldn't bear to see him like that.

When Quiss came to take her back to the Domne, she went both hesitantly and eagerly, unsure of herself, and yet sure that what she wished to do was worth doing.

"Da likes an early lunch," Quiss explained, "and he doesn't like to admit that he's too impatient to wait while you eat, so he asks you to eat with him. Also Tholden is here, and I'm sure he wants to question you. If you don't mind."

Terisa couldn't think of a quick way to describe how important the Domne and his concerns were to her, so she replied simply, "I don't mind."

In the front room, the light had been improved by the raising of the window covers and the altered angle of the sun. Two men sat at the table, and as Terisa entered the room she had no difficulty seeing that one of them was the Domne—or that his companion was huge.

"Ah, Terisa," said the Domne in his warm, comfortable voice, "I'm glad you could join us. I want someone to share my lunch. And Tholden thinks he can't wait to talk to you." Gesturing toward the huge man, he went on, "Terisa, this is Tholden, my eldest. Another of the benefits of sons is that one of them is bound to be the right man to inherit their father's place. Tholden is the right man for mine.

"That's fortunate, since he's also"—the Domne laughed softly—"the only one of my sons who wants the responsibility."

Tholden stood beside his father like a bear; his stiff hair nearly brushed the beams of the ceiling; his beard was so long and wild that it made his chest seem even thicker—and his chest was already thick enough to create the illusion that his shoulders were round and stooped. When he sketched a bow toward her, Terisa saw that his hands were ridged with calluses: they looked more like gardening implements than normal hands.

She also noticed that he had straw and a few twigs caught in his beard. Involuntarily, she smiled. Then, trying to recover her manners, she said, "I'm glad to meet you. Geraden talks about you a lot."

Tholden grinned—a smile which lifted his beard, but didn't soften his expression. "I'm sure he does." His voice was unexpectedly high and gentle; he sounded like a man who wasn't able to shout. "Quiss and I had the doubtful pleasure of raising him after our mother passed away. He probably remembers every beating he deserved in agonizing detail."

Quiss went to the stove and began pulling a meal together. Politely, Terisa replied, "No, nothing like that. He has a higher opinion of you than you think." Then she asked, "Where is he, by the way?"

"He was here," said the Domne. "We talked for a while—"

"Then I sent him to help Minick." Tholden let his smile drop. "Minick is trying to explain to an assortment of farmers, shepherds, merchants, and servants how we want them to defend the walls. He's the most meticulous man in Houseldon, and he's certainly thorough, but he can be a bit slow, and his explanations have a tendency to confuse people. Geraden will get more done in less time, even if he has lost his sense of humor."

Terisa glanced at the Domne, then looked up at Tholden again. "In other words, you want to talk to me alone."

The Domne began chuckling to himself.

From the stove, Quiss said, "I warned you subtlety would be wasted on her." Her tone made it clear that she wasn't laughing at Terisa.

"Silence, upstart woman." Without so much as glancing in his wife's direction, Tholden swung his arm and managed to slap her across the bottom. "Don't be pert. Women should be seen and not heard. As much as possible."

Rather than retorting, Quiss looked at Terisa and rolled her eyes in mock-despair.

Terisa herself wasn't amused, however. Holding herself still, she asked in a neutral tone, "What's the matter? Don't you trust him?"

Tholden opened his mouth as if he had been stung; the Domne waved him silent. "Terisa," the older man said quietly, and this time she could hear his years in his voice, "I would sell my soul at the word of any of my sons. Even Nyle, who seems to have forgotten who he is. But this Geraden who came storming into Houseldon only yesterday, warning of imminent destruction—who is he? He isn't the Geraden who left us for Orison with more hope in his heart than most simple flesh and blood can hold. It's not just that he has become hard. I know him better than that, Terisa. He has become closed. He talks about defending his home as if the mere idea was terrible.

"A change like that"—the Domne spread his hands—"it could mean anything."

"And you want me to explain it," said Terisa stiffly.

The lord and Tholden nodded together. Quiss watched mutely from the stove. "I will sell my soul for him now, if I must," murmured the Domne, "without another word from you—or from him. But I would prefer to understand what I'm trusting."

Without warning, Terisa found that she wanted to say, It isn't your fault. It isn't anything you did. He's just been so badly beaten— He's failed you, he's failed Artagel and Nyle, he's failed Orison and

King Joyse—and now, when it's too late to do any good, he finds
out he really is an Imager. He could have made a difference. He
went through all those years of humiliation, and now it's too late.

But the words refused to be spoken. They weren't hers to say:
they were his. She could feel it in the room that she couldn't try to
explain him without erecting a wall between him and his family—a
wall with pity on one side and loneliness on the other. The more
they knew about his pain, the more difficulty they would have confronting it, challenging it. She herself was almost paralyzed by knowing too much. If he didn't speak for himself, he would never be whole
again.

So she said, "I'm sorry. That's between you and him. He'll have
to tell you himself."

Then she said, "But *I* trust him."

Tholden was scowling. Quiss concentrated on her pots and pans
as if she were leery of what she might say if she spoke. But the
Domne smiled at Terisa with sunlight in his eyes.

Distinctly, Tholden asked, "Do you consider yourself a friend
of his?"

Almost without interrupting her preparations, Quiss swung an
elbow into her husband's ribs. Then, ignoring his muffled grunt, his
sharp glare, she lifted two platters heaped with food and carried them
to the table. "Sit down, Terisa," she said, "eat," placing one platter
in front of the Domne, the other before the chair nearest Terisa. "If
I've given you too much, don't worry about it. I'm used to cooking
for this great ox and the farmers he consorts with."

A bland expression on her face, Quiss pulled out the chair and
held it for Terisa.

On the platter, Terisa saw fried yams, panbread, greens, some
kind of meat covered with gravy, and what looked like apple fritters.
If she ate all that, she wouldn't be able to move for two days.

"I'm sorry," said Tholden. With a hand like a shovel, he gestured
toward the chair. "Please sit down. Eat."

When Terisa still didn't move, he added, "I don't mean to question your integrity. I'm just scared. I don't like the way Geraden has
changed. I don't like the news from Orison. I don't like what he says
it means. Houseldon has never been very good at defending itself."

"Good enough," put in the Domne gently.

"So far," countered Tholden. "But I don't want to watch people

I've known and worked with all my life get killed because something horrendous has happened to Geraden."

The Domne pointed at the chair Quiss held. "Terisa, *sit down*. I haven't heard him apologize that much in twenty years. In another minute, you're going to hurt his feelings."

Terisa sat down and let Quiss adjust the chair.

Now it was her turn. "I'm sorry," she said again. "I'm scared, too. And I'm groping. Quiss says Geraden didn't tell you much about me. He didn't tell you I'm new at all this. I've never been in a place like this. I've never met people like you." I've never been *important* before. "And I'm not used to having enemies.

"I want to help. I'll do anything I can. I just don't want to talk about things that Geraden ought to tell you himself."

Tholden studied her hard for a moment. Then he grinned—a new smile that brightened his whole face. Abruptly, he swept a chair out of his way and sat down opposite her. "When you're done eating, push that plate over here. I could use a snack."

From the stove, Quiss gave Terisa a look of grave, sky blue gladness. Then, wiping her hands on her apron, she turned to the Domne. "Da, I've heard a rumor that some of the women are panicking. They don't know where to hide their daughters—or themselves. With your permission, I'll go try to talk some sense into them."

The Domne nodded. "Of course."

"Tell them to come here if we're attacked," said Tholden. "This house will be our last bastion, if everything else goes down. We'll put the women and children down in the beer cellar, and the rest of us will protect them as long as we can."

With one hand, Quiss placed a brief touch of affection on her husband's shoulder. Nodding to Terisa, she left the room and the house.

Calmly, as if everything were normal, the Domne picked up his knife and fork, and began to eat.

Terisa was moderately hungry, but she couldn't force herself to tackle all that food. These people were seriously considering the necessity of hiding their women and children in a beer cellar while Houseldon was destroyed. Facing Tholden, she said, "Ask me something. Let me help."

Tholden met her gaze squarely. "When Geraden got here yesterday, he thought we were going to be attacked almost immediately.

Now he says we've got time to plan our defense. As long as you're here, he thinks Master Eremis doesn't have any reason to attack us right away. What do you think?"

Without hesitation, she said, "I think he's wrong."

The Domne cocked an eyebrow. His mouth full of yams, he asked, "Why?"

"I don't think he realizes how dangerous he is. Or how dangerous Eremis thinks he is. Eremis has been working hard for a long time now to keep him from understanding his own talent. And he's tried to have him killed. I don't think Eremis will believe he's safe until Geraden is dead."

"That's speculation," murmured Tholden.

"This isn't." Terisa spoke with the confidence of a woman who had been able to outthink Castellan Lebbick. "Eremis can't possibly know how Geraden's feeling. And he can't possibly know there aren't any mirrors here. Now that Geraden knows what his talent is, Eremis has to be afraid of being attacked himself.

"And that's not all. Geraden thinks Eremis will postpone attacking Houseldon until after he's done with Orison. But the last thing he was doing in Orison was refilling the reservoir. That doesn't sound like a man with a trap ready to spring. It sounds like a man who wants to help Orison fight off Prince Kragen until Cadwal is in position.

"If I'm right, Eremis has time to strike at you right now.

"And he knows I'm here." This had to be said, although it was difficult for her. The Domne and his son needed to know the extent of their danger. "Master Gilbur saw the mirror change. He knows I've discovered my talent, too. He knows I can go anywhere in Mordant—or Cadwal or Alend, for that matter—if I just know what it looks like. If I just know how to visualize it. I could show up in his rooms some night when he's asleep and nail him to the bed.

"He's not just afraid of Geraden. He's afraid of me."

He needs to be afraid of me. I'm going to make him afraid of me. Somehow.

The Domne continued to eat without any obvious concern; but Tholden watched Terisa with growing chagrin on his face. When she was done, he muttered as if no one were listening to him, "Sheepdung. I'm not used to this myself. I'm not Artagel—I never wanted to be a soldier. What am I supposed to do?"

The Domne put down his knife and fork. "What *are* you doing?"

Tholden made a dismissive gesture. "You know what. Wester is sending farmers and their families here as fast as he can talk them into it. Every empty hogshead and barrel we've got is being filled with water and positioned around the stockade, in case of fire. Every pitchfork and scythe and axe in Houseldon is being sharpened." Slowly, a frantic look came into his eyes, and his hands knotted on the table in front of him; but he kept his voice steady. "Banquettes are being knocked together inside the wall, so that anyone with a bow will have a place to stand. Minick—and Geraden, I hope—are laying out lines of retreat. They're trying to explain to the men with bows how to retreat—how to use the houses for cover, how to set ambushes.

"What good is that going to do against Imagery?"

Listening to him, Terisa understood how he felt.

The Domne was undismayed, however. "Who knows?" he said calmly. "I don't. I can't see the future.

"But I can see you're the right man for the job. You've already thought of things that wouldn't have occurred to me. You'll think of more. If Artagel were here, he wouldn't be able to defend Houseldon any better."

Tholden wasn't convinced. With a sour snort, he asked, "Is this what you call selling your soul at the word of one of your sons?"

At that, the Domne sat up straighter in his chair; his eyes flashed. "Tholden, I know you think you're a grown man, but you still aren't too old to be punished for disrespect. Maybe I'm only your father, and half crippled as well, but I'm still man enough to prune your apricots within an inch of their lives. Consider *that* before you risk being pert with me."

Involuntarily, Tholden smiled. His beard rustled on his chest. Nevertheless his eyes remained full of trouble, and his smile didn't last long. Too worried to sit where he was, he pushed himself up from the table. "Excuse me, Terisa," he murmured. "I'm afraid you'll have to eat lunch without my help. I've lost my appetite."

With the hunched gait of a man who was accustomed to ducking under doorways and low ceilings, he left the house.

The Domne watched him go and sighed. "You don't know it, Terisa," he commented after Tholden was gone, "but those are the saddest words anyone has said in my house for a long time. 'I've lost my appetite.' I hope you aren't planning to tell me the same thing."

Terisa meant to say Yes. The pile of food on the platter daunted her. The size and consequences of the danger she and Geraden had brought to Houseldon daunted her. Yet the way the Domne looked at her seemed so warm and companionable, so willing to accept whatever she represented, that when she opened her mouth the word which came out was, "No."

He smiled approvingly as she lifted her fork to sample Quiss' panbread and gravy.

For several minutes while she ate a little of everything on the platter, he sat in silence, gazing out into the sunshine through the nearest window. She had the impression that he was waiting for her to finish; but he didn't seem impatient. In fact, he appeared quite content to look out on the street and nod amiably at anyone who caught his eye. If war was coming to Houseldon, it didn't show on the face of the Domne. Geraden had said of him, *The things he values most don't need to be fought for because they can't be hurt.* Yet Terisa wasn't sure that was accurate. Despite his look of contentment, she thought he cared deeply about a number of things which could be hurt very easily.

When she put down her utensils to indicate that she was done, he glanced over at her, then returned his gaze to the window. In a relaxed way, as if he were continuing an earlier conversation, he asked, "What was your impression of Nyle?"

Her stomach knotted around the food she had just eaten. Cautiously, she countered, "What did Geraden tell you?"

The Domne's manner disarmed anxiety. "That you think Nyle is still alive. That this Master Eremis still wants to use him against us. That's not what I want to know. What did you think of him? How is he?"

Because the answer was painful, she said shortly, "He's miserable."

"Ah," sighed the Domne as if he had both expected and feared her reply.

This time, she let herself say, "I don't blame him. Everything he believed that got him into trouble—everything about King Joyse and Orison and Elega and Prince Kragen—it was all plausible. King Joyse has been working for years, setting himself up to be betrayed. Nyle was just unlucky enough to fall into the trap—the same trap Elega fell into herself. He believed what his King wanted him to believe."

Ignoring the Domne's reputation as one of the King's dearest friends, she went on, "He's really just a victim. Eremis probably would never have been able to get his hands on Nyle if Nyle hadn't been stuck in the dungeon with nowhere to turn for hope."

If anything she said offended the Domne, however, he didn't show it. "Families," he murmured mildly. "They are endlessly interesting. Elega and her father. Geraden and Nyle. Sometimes I think the fate of the world depends on how people feel about their families.

"What sort of family do you come from, Terisa? Did you have sisters? Not *six* sisters, by any chance?"

The idea was so absurd that she almost laughed aloud. "No, Da. I was an only child."

He looked at her again, more sharply this time. "Do you mean to say that after you your parents were able to restrain their enthusiasm for children? Were you that bad? Or were you so good that any other child would be a disappointment?"

"No," she answered as candidly as she could. "I was an accident. My father sure didn't have time for children. And he didn't want my mother to have time either."

"'Didn't have time'?" Abruptly, the Domne pushed his sore leg off the stool. Grimacing, he shifted the position of the stool so that he could face her more directly, then heaved his leg back onto it. Propped straight with his elbows on the table, he asked, "What vital and consuming work did your father do, that he 'didn't have time for children'?"

Unsure of where the discussion was headed—and uncomfortable because she was always uncomfortable when she talked about her parents—Terisa replied briefly, "He made money."

Odd how both she and the Domne were speaking of her father in the past tense. But she thought about him in the past, as part of something which wasn't true anymore.

"For what purpose?" inquired the Domne.

She shrugged. "To make more money. I don't think he had any other reason for doing it. He did it because that was what he was good at." She thought about conversations she had overheard from the dining room while she sat out of sight on the stairs, listening when her parents thought she had gone to bed. "Money was the best way to get things that weren't his. Social standing. Political influence." Then she remembered some of the valets her father had hired. Muscle.

"He made money because he believed if you can do that you can buy everything else."

"Very strange," pronounced the Domne. "He would have flourished in Cadwal.

"And what did your mother do while your father made money?"

With an understated vehemence which unsettled her, Terisa said, "I think she practiced."

"'Practiced'?"

"Being ornamental. So my father could show her off whenever he was in the mood."

"'Women should be seen and not heard'?" The Domne couldn't restrain a burst of laughter. "That explains where you got your beauty. Terisa, I don't know how to tell you this—but I think you've already met High King Festten. Even though you wouldn't recognize him if you saw him."

Terisa tried to smile, but she didn't succeed.

The Domne studied her; sunlight from the windows reflected in his eyes. "However, that raises a fascinating question. How did you get here from there? How did the daughter of parents like that become the kind of woman my youngest son—perhaps my best son—would kill for?"

She wanted to answer him. At the same time, she wanted to stop talking about her parents. Roughly, she told him something that she hadn't revealed to anyone else in Mordant, not even to Geraden.

"When I did something my father didn't like, he used to lock me in a closet until I got scared enough to stop crying."

For a long moment, the Domne stared at her without expression, as if the energy of life had been wiped off his face. Then, slowly, carefully, he turned away. He took his leg from the stool in order to put it back in its former position, toward the window. He settled himself again with his leg up and his spine stretched against the back of the chair; he might have been getting comfortable for a nap.

After that, one at a time, he picked up his canes and flung them out the window. The first sailed clear; the second clattered against the frame and fell just outside.

So fiercely that she winced, he whispered, "What are you doing to me, Joyse? Everybody who is worth anything in your entire kingdom is being hurt, and I'm sitting here crippled. What are you *doing?*"

There was nothing she could say. Geraden had surely told his father what she knew about the King's intentions. There was nothing else.

Briefly, the Domne put his hands over his face, and his shoulders clenched. Almost at once, however, he rubbed his cheeks briskly, as if he were scrubbing passion off his features; with a long, slow exhalation, he let his anger go.

"It's remarkable, don't you think," he murmured, "that we're such good friends, King Joyse and I?

"Of course, that isn't the reason our friendship is famous. It's famous because I refused to fight in any of his wars. I refused to let him make me into one of his soldiers. People consider that strange. Don't I think Mordant is worth fighting for? Of course I do. Don't I think his ideal of a Congery that turns Imagery into something benign is worth fighting for? Of course I do. Then why don't I fight? What's the matter with me?

"But I think our friendship is more remarkable than anything I have or haven't refused to do in my life."

"What do you mean?" Terisa asked, wanting him to go on.

"Well—" The Domne spread his hands. "We have next to nothing in common. For one thing, he has little sense of humor. He's not incapable of seeing the funny side. He just thinks on such an heroic scale. Everything is serious—everything is a matter of life and death. You don't have much time for jokes when you're busy saving the world.

"Terisa, it would never occur to *me* to save the world. I don't object to the world being saved. In fact, I want it to be saved. I just can't imagine that it has anything to do with me.

"There's a cottonwood tree down by the river. It lost a branch in a heavy snowfall this winter, and now sap is starting to leak from the wound. If someone doesn't go down there soon, trim the stump, and cover it with pitch, that tree is going to die. Blights or parasites will get in through the wound.

"*That* has something to do with me.

"One of our shepherds has a ewe that keeps dropping stillborn lambs. *That* has something to do with me. There's a woman in a farmstead a few miles away who suffers from a strange fever, and the only thing that helps her is a brew made from the bark of a tree that doesn't grow in Domne. It grows in the Care of Armigite. *That* has something to do with me.

"If you asked me to save the world, I wouldn't know how.

"King Joyse knows how. Or he thinks he does, anyway."

Terisa thought that perhaps King Joyse and his old friend had more in common than the Domne appeared to realize. *Problems should be solved by those who see them.* But she preferred the Domne's way of doing it. Controlling her tendency to get angry whenever she thought about the King, she inquired, "Then why *are* you friends?"

"I'm not sure I can explain it," he said musingly. "We need each other.

"When I first met him—when he chased away the minor Cadwal prince who had been using the Care of Domne as his private vassalage for the better part of a decade and set us free—I hadn't thought to refuse anything. I had as much fire in my blood as any young man who had just been released from a servitude he hated, and I seem to recall that I was perfectly willing to start learning how to use a sword.

"But when I actually met him—

"Terisa, that smile of his went right through my heart. As if it came down to me from the sky, I knew that I loved him. And I knew that the Care of Domne was never going to be what I wanted it to be if he didn't protect it. And I knew that he needed something from me—something he wasn't going to be able to get from anybody else."

"Like what?"

"*Balance,*" replied the Domne distinctly. "He needed *balance.* He wanted to save the world. Do you have any idea how dangerous that is? Men who want to save the world—and who make a few mistakes—become tyrants. The things they really want and love slip out of their fingers, and they end up clinging to the power because it's all they have left. The possibility was written all over him. He was the brightest and keenest man I had ever met—the kind of man who just naturally makes you want to lie down in the dirt for him—and I simply couldn't bear the idea that he might go too far and turn all the good in him rotten.

"It all came to me in a burst, like a sunrise. And it terrified me, because if I refused him he might just ride away and leave the Care of Domne to fend for itself. But it was necessary. We needed each other.

"He rode into Houseldon, as bright as a new day, but I stood my ground as if I had the right to it. 'Well, my lord Domne,' he said with that smile, wringing my heart because until he came I'd never believed that I would be lord of my own land, 'you're free. At least for a while. How many men can you give me?'

"'None, my lord King,' I said.

"'What, none?' He stopped smiling. I seem to remember he put his hand on his sword.

"I was terrified, but I said, 'This is the foaling season. I need every man I have.'

"He was angry, furious. But he was also perplexed. 'Let me understand you,' he said. 'Domne has been butchered back and forth between Alend and Cadwal for generations. You've been a vassal yourself your entire life until today. And all you care about is your *sheep?*'

"I swear to you, Terisa, his anger nearly blinded me. And I was getting a crick in my neck from staring up at him. 'I didn't say that, my lord King,' I replied. 'You asked how many men I can send away to be killed in your wars. The answer is, none. I need help with my foals.'

"He really has very little sense of humor. But he has a wonderful sense of joy. Or had. Instead of splitting my head open, he started to laugh.

"That night, we had one of the best feasts I've ever attended. I thought he was going to laugh for days. He kept saying, 'Sheep. *Sheep,*' and falling out of his chair.

"We've been friends ever since."

Terisa was surprised to find that she felt like crying. She knew what King Joyse's smile was like. From the first, she had wanted to like him, please him; she had wanted to serve him. The Domne reminded her of that—and of the fact that it was impossible. King Joyse himself had made it impossible.

In a soft voice, she asked, "And now? Are you still friends now?" After what he did to Nyle and Geraden and his own daughters? After what he's doing to the Congery and Mordant?

Slowly, the Domne turned his head, shifted his gaze from the window to look at her. His eyes seemed partially blind—adjusted to the brightness outside and unable to make her out clearly.

"He isn't responsible for Nyle's choices. He isn't even responsible for Castellan Lebbick's sanity. Both of them could have trusted him. At the same time, he went to a lot of trouble to keep you and Geraden as safe as he could.

"He's still my friend, Terisa. We need each other. Do you really want me to turn my back on him?"

After a while, she found that she was able to say, "No." In spite of her anger, she had no intention of turning her own back on the King.

THIRTY-THREE:
PEACE IN
HOUSELDON

She was determined to do something for Geraden.

Unfortunately, she didn't know what.

In an odd way, her conversation with the Domne had crystallized her resolve. At the same time, the things he had revealed about his family and King Joyse hadn't shed any useful light. So she wanted to help Geraden. Good: so what? When she got right down to it, what could she actually say to him? Don't be so hurt, it isn't worth it? Nonsense. Snap out of it, you're just feeling sorry for yourself? Ridiculous. I'm sure you can beat Master Eremis if you put your mind to it? Perfect.

Thinking about him wrung her heart, but she didn't know what to do.

Soon the Domne became even less helpful. Gazing out the window with his arms folded over his lean chest, he slipped abruptly into a nap. He was older than he looked, after all. Terisa studied his posture for a moment to make sure that he wasn't about to fall out of his chair. Then she got to her feet; she wanted to go outside and see more of Houseldon.

Before she reached the door, it opened, and a man came in off the porch.

He was brown: that was her first impression. Years of outdoor labor had left his skin the same deep color as his leather jerkin and breeches. His hair was the color of the new mud on his old boots.

And his eyes were nearly the same hue as his skin and clothes; they seemed to get lost in his general brownness. In fact, most of the details of his face and expression were blurred. Behind the brown, he looked like a cross between a turnip and a fence post.

But then he smiled—shyly, almost deferentially—and his smile pulled his features into definition. Immediately, it became obvious that he was one of Geraden's brothers.

He glanced at the Domne, saw that his father was asleep. Gesturing for silence, he put a hand on Terisa's arm and drew her outside. As soon as they reached the porch, however, he let go of her as if he felt his touch was presumptuous and had only risked it to avoid disturbing the Domne. He even backed a step or two away from her.

"Hello, Terisa," he said earnestly, without quite meeting her eyes. "I'm Minick. Geraden sent me to get you."

"Hello, Minick," she replied. "I'm glad to meet you."

As if she had surprised him, he asked, "You are?"

She nodded. "I'm glad to meet Geraden's family. I'm glad to be in Houseldon—in the Care of Domne." This was so true that she didn't know how to explain it. "I've wanted to meet all of you for a long time."

Minick seemed to recognize the inadequacy behind her words. "Well, I'm glad to meet you, too. I wasn't sure before. I don't like it when Geraden's unhappy. But now I am."

He baffled her a bit. "What makes you sure?"

He indicated the house with a lift of one shoulder. "You were in the room with the Domne," he explained, "and now he's taking a nap. He trusts you. So you must be all right. You aren't the reason Geraden's unhappy."

Minick's confidence was so unjustified that Terisa felt compelled to say, "It's probably more complicated than that. Sometimes I think I *am* the reason he's unhappy—sort of. I have a lot to do with a lot of things that hurt him."

"No." Minick shook his head mildly. "It isn't complicated. You're like him. He always thinks things are complicated. But they aren't. Important things are simple. He needs somebody to love him. That's simple. The Domne trusts you. That's simple. So now I can be glad to meet you, when I wasn't sure before."

Unexpectedly, she found herself relaxing. "I guess you're right."

A world of difficulties apparently evaporated when Minick touched them. "I hadn't thought of it that way.

"Let's go see Geraden."

"Oh, no." Minick became suddenly serious. "That isn't what he wants. He's too busy." For a second, the brown man almost shuddered. "When he gets like this, he yells at people a lot. He thinks they're fast. He's fast, and he thinks they are, too. But they aren't fast. They're just farmers and shepherds. They're like me. They like having things explained to them."

The thought of Geraden ranting with impatience was so incongruous that Terisa nearly laughed aloud. At the same time, it gave her a pang. Poor man, he must be almost out of his mind. Deliberately, she controlled herself. "I don't understand. I thought you said he sent you to get me."

Minick nodded. "He did. I thought he was just making an excuse to send me away. But since you're glad to be here I guess I was wrong.

"He sent me to show you around. The Domne can't walk very far, and Tholden is too busy, and Quiss prefers to stay at home with Ruesha. Geraden said, 'She likes tours. She might like a tour of Houseldon.' So I came to get you."

Terisa accepted the suggestion, despite the vexed spirit in which Geraden had probably made it. She understood how he felt. And she wanted to see more of Houseldon. She suspected—in an entirely uncritical way—that there wasn't a great deal to see. On the other hand, if Master Eremis launched an attack soon, she might need to know everything she could learn about the Domne's seat.

Giving Minick a smile which would have astonished Reverend Thatcher—or her father—she went with him to explore Houseldon.

In fact, there was more to see in Houseldon than she had expected.

At any rate, Minick thought there was a great deal to see. And he liked to see it all thoroughly, with an attention to detail which was both loving and analytical. For instance, Houseldon contained no less than three livery stables, to accommodate the numbers of people who came here from all over the Care, as well as from other regions of Mordant. Each of these was exactly what it claimed to be: a place where horses were left and cared for while their masters transacted business, visited relatives, appealed for justice, pursued crafts or apprenticeships. Yet to Minick each was worth looking at closely; each had virtues and drawbacks which required evaluation; each prospered or declined according to factors which he took pains to understand.

And he was a motherlode of information. He knew exactly where all the drainage pipes had been laid, and when, and how many square yards of leachfield they required. He knew who had first conceived the idea of trussing the eaves-thatch of the roofs with *that* particular kind of binding, and why it was superior to the way eaves-thatch used to be trussed. He knew where Houseldon's supplies of tallow came from, and how long they would last in an emergency. And he knew every child he saw by name, parentage, and predilection for mischief.

In a short time, Terisa realized that she had only two choices. She could cut off the tour now, before he drove her to distraction. Or she could relax and let him do whatever he wanted. With him there wasn't any middle ground.

Well, that fit, she mused. In their separate ways, Geraden, Artagel, and Nyle were all intolerant of middle ground. Wester was said to be a fanatic about wool. Stead couldn't keep his hands off women. Geraden had called Tholden *a compulsive fertilizer.* The Domne himself had given up on middle ground when he first met King Joyse. Why should Minick be any different?

Just for a minute, she considered stopping him—telling him that she had had enough, going her own way. But then she noticed that in his company she did very little except smile; he filled her alternately with amusement and affection. He was perfectly capable of distinguishing precisely between good workmanship and bad, sensible husbandry and careless, forethought and its absence; but he liked everybody around him; he loved the details he expounded for her. The more he talked, the more gentle and companionable he seemed. And the more she listened, the more she could feel her tensions and fears going to sleep.

Instead of stopping, she relaxed and let him give her the whole tour.

As a result, the day seemed to evaporate the way complexities did when he analyzed them. He began showing her around a little before noon—and then the shadows were slanting toward late afternoon, and her legs hurt gently with so much walking and standing, and her boots had rubbed a sore place onto one of her toes, and her heart was full of rest for the first time since she could remember.

Minick wasn't just amusing, likable, and meticulous: he was a healer. Somewhere in Houseldon, she knew, preparations were being made for battle—but they didn't come near him; he seemed to carry peace with him wherever he went. Now, she thought, all she needed was one really good night's sleep, and then she would be ready to start thinking again.

So when he brought her back to the Domne's house and started to say good-bye, she didn't want him to leave. "Where are you going?" she asked to forestall him.

This time his grin was shy in a new way, self-conscious about things which hadn't come up before. "I like to go home before supper," he murmured, "and play with the children for a while. It gives their mother a chance to cook. And it uses up some of their energy so they go to bed more easily."

The thought of this earnest brown man playing with his children delighted her—and reminded her that during the whole afternoon he hadn't said anything personal about himself or his life. Maybe he would have considered it presumptuous to talk about himself. Impulsively, because he had done her so much good and hadn't asked her for anything, she leaned forward and thanked him with a quick kiss.

His eyes widened; he stared at her for a moment. Then he ducked his head as if he were blushing.

"I think I'm not going to tell my wife you did that," he said softly. "She might not be pleased." It was obvious that he was enormously pleased. "I like her to be pleased. She's the only other woman who's ever been so patient with me.

"Good-bye, Terisa."

After he left, she went up the steps, across the porch, and into the bustle of Quiss' cooking. Her cheeks ached from smiling so much. Clearly, those muscles needed the exercise.

The scene in the front room stopped her as soon as she came through the doorway.

Quiss was stirring what looked like enough stew to feed half of Houseldon. Her cheeks were red from heat and exertion; sweat made her hair stick to the sides of her face in streaks. Behind her, servants clattered around the room, setting platters, utensils, and pitchers on the table, bringing pots and tureens and trays from a back kitchen Terisa hadn't seen—and talking to each other loudly through the din. The Domne and Tholden sat together at the end of the table, discussing something intently, raising their voices to make themselves heard. In one corner of the room, a boy perhaps fifteen years old and a girl somewhat younger were arguing hotly; but the only part of their discussion Terisa could make out was the part that went: Did so. Did not. Did so! Did not! Another boy, this one no older than eight or nine, sat near Tholden trying to sharpen a wooden sword with a piece of tile for a whetstone. A third, still-younger boy used a stick the size of a club to experiment with the resonant qualities of a tin washbasin.

For a second, the clamor seemed so intimidating—so at odds with the peace inside her—that Terisa almost turned away. Nothing in her life with her parents, or in her life alone, had prepared her for a home where people acted like this.

But then Quiss raised her head, saw Terisa, and smiled.

Quiss' pleasure changed the meaning of the din altogether. Or changed the way Terisa saw it. All this noise and activity wasn't angry, distressed, or alarmed, didn't represent pain: it was just loud. As soon as Quiss smiled, Terisa knew that Tholden's wife was in her element, flourishing precisely because her family and her household were so busy, so noisy; so full of themselves and each other. And then Terisa understood that the tumult was just another form of peace—hot and hectic, of course; not particularly restful to a novice like herself; but completely without fear.

Smiling back at Quiss, she came forward to meet the noise.

"I understand you spent the afternoon with Minick." Quiss was nearly shouting, but Terisa could hardly hear her. "The whole afternoon? Letting him show you around?"

Terisa nodded.

"Good for you. I knew I liked you as soon as I saw you. He's your friend for life. Most people aren't willing to listen to him that long."

"They ought to give it a try." Terisa tried to speak loudly enough to be audible. "He's nice."

It was Quiss' turn to nod. "Fortunately, his nieces and nephews dote on him." She indicated the children at the other end of the room. "I mean, fortunately for them.

"If his wife weren't so shy, he'd be here tonight. I know it saddens him sometimes that he can't spend more time with us. But I think the poor woman panics every time she sets foot outside her house." Quiss started to laugh, but Terisa couldn't hear what her laughter sounded like through the noise. "They must have had a rousing courtship."

Terisa grinned again, then raised her hands to rub the muscles in her cheeks.

A serving woman appeared in front of her, carrying a foaming tankard on a tray. "Do you like ale? My husband brews for the Domne. You won't find a better ale in the Care."

"Thanks." Terisa didn't know anything about ale, but she knew she was thirsty; she accepted the tankard and sampled it. The serving woman watched her while she discovered that the ale had a bite which wasn't quite sour, wasn't quite bitter, but which seemed to be both. After a second taste, however, the flavor had improved dramatically. Soon it became wonderful. She beamed her approval, and the serving woman went away delighted.

"Terisa!" Tholden gestured to her. She went over to him, and he pulled out a chair for her. "Sit down. I want to tell you what we're doing to get ready. Maybe you can think of something I've forgotten."

The Domne looked a little skeptical; he may have been sensitive to her general bewilderment. Nevertheless he nodded as if he also wanted to hear what she might say. At once, Tholden began to describe his specific arrangements for the possibility of battle.

She couldn't absorb them. In fact, she only heard every third word; the rest of his explanation was lost in a chorus directed at the Domne: Da, it's her fault, No, it's his fault, she did it first, *he* did it first! And she couldn't help noticing that even the Domne appeared more interested in the bickering of the children than in Tholden's preparations. Feeling vaguely irresponsible—but not enough to worry about it—she said once, "Maybe it'll be quieter after supper," then drank her ale and stopped trying to listen.

The chaos of getting supper ready seemed to approach a climax as an inner door burst open and a squall of children blew into the room. They were all about Ruesha's size and age—too many of them too close together in age to belong to any one family. Or any three families. They were all buck naked, full of glee, and glistening with water. And they were followed by Geraden, dripping copiously. He had a couple of towels in his hands, but they were too wet to be much use.

"Come back here, you little monsters!" he roared. "I'm going to towel you until your heads fall off!"

Squealing with delight, small, naked bodies scattered in all directions.

Terisa hadn't seen Geraden for most of the day. She looked at him eagerly, and saw at once that he was still clenched and dour, knotted inside himself. Perhaps for the sake of the children, however, he had pushed his hardness into the background. Or perhaps they elicited that response from him involuntarily: perhaps it was something they did for him, rather than he for them.

It was enough. She could wait for more until they had a better opportunity together. Giving him her best smile, whether he noticed it or not, she relaxed and let the clamor continue to grow on her, like a milling and vociferous form of contentment.

Quiss, Tholden, and the servants snatched up wet children indiscriminately; soon all of Geraden's victims were caught in adult arms. Stifling a laugh, Quiss said to one of the serving women, "Your boys are responsible for this."

"I beg your pardon," the woman protested in tart amusement. "I'm sure Ruesha is the cause. She's the most notorious truant in Houseldon. Ask anyone."

"They're all monsters!" growled Geraden. "They're all going to suffer horribly when I get my hands on them!" Doing his best wild gorilla imitation, he began stalking children.

With the help of three or four servants, he succeeded in herding his fugitives from torture and cleanliness out of the room.

If he hadn't been so busy—and if she hadn't been so comfortably settled with her tankard of ale—Terisa would have gone after him. She felt an unaccountable desire to kiss him far more seriously than she had kissed Minick.

He came back after a while to join his family—and half a dozen men who arrived in the meantime—for supper. These men were the leaders of teams which had been organized to perform various functions during the defense of Houseldon. As soon as the meal was over, and the table had been cleared, the talk turned to the subject that seemed to be uppermost in everyone's mind, except Terisa's: what kind of attack was coming, and when, and how to meet it.

Geraden described a few of the uses of Imagery which Master Eremis had already made against Mordant; and the men quickly lost whatever self-confidence they had brought with them to the Domne's house. Finally, one of them asked almost timidly, "Is there anything you can do?"

He shook his head. "Not until I get a chance to make a mirror."

"But how can such things be fought?" another man inquired. "What can we do?"

"We're already doing it," the Domne said flatly, as if he were sure. "Everything that can be done. We're doing it."

Without looking at her, Geraden added, "Just hope the lady Terisa is wrong. Just hope he gives us a little time. Today we got ready. Tomorrow I'll fire up a furnace and start mixing sand."

To her own surprise as much as anyone else's, Terisa got up and left the room.

She didn't want to hear it, that was all: she just didn't want to hear it. She was too recently come from Orison—from the Castellan's distrust and Eremis' cunning and Gilbur's violence. She hadn't had any sleep except for the short rest which had come over her unexpectedly in the grass below the Closed Fist. And the sense of peace inside her was fragile; it would collapse if she let herself get caught up in the anxiety of Houseldon's defenders, if she let herself get caught up in her own concern for Geraden. Sleep, that was what she needed, not all this talk. In the morning, she would be readier— maybe braver.

Nodding to the servants she encountered along the way, she retreated to Artagel's room.

It was dark. For a moment, she thought about asking someone for help; then she remembered where one of the room's lamps was. On a small table at the head of the bed. She went to it by the light from the open door, picked it up and brought it back to the doorway. Another lamp hung on the wall outside; she used it to light the lamp in her hands. When it was burning brightly, she entered the room again and closed the door.

A second lamp lit from the first helped fill the room with a comforting yellow glow. Amazing how nice Artagel's cot looked in that light. She visited the bathroom, then took off her clothes and doused the lamp she had set across the room. The early spring chill in the air encouraged her to get into bed immediately, cover herself with clean sheets and sweet blankets.

At once, she knew she was right: this was what she needed. As soon as her head reached the pillow, the peace inside her seemed to rise up and swell outward. It reached through the house growing quiet around her; it reached out to Geraden and the men trying to plan Houseldon's survival; it reached up into the deep heavens and across the Care toward Domne's mountains.

Silence and rest spread so far in all directions that they carried her away.

She went to sleep in such sudden contentment that she forgot to extinguish the lamp on the small table at the head of the bed.

That was what saved her from rousing the household and embarrassing herself unnecessarily, that forgotten lamp. In the dark, she might have lost her head; might have screamed.

For the second time in her life, after she had been asleep for a while she felt herself being kissed.

A strong mouth began to nibble on her lips; a tongue slipped between them, searching for hers. A hand just cool enough to call attention to itself found her hip under the blankets, then rose in a long caress across her belly to her breasts. While the tongue probed her mouth more deeply, the hand began to play with her nipples.

Her eyes flew open. In one quick glimpse, she saw the curly hair and intent brown eyes of the man kneeling beside the cot to embrace her; she saw that he wasn't Master Eremis or Castellan Lebbick, wasn't Gilbur or anyone else who terrified her. So she didn't scream. Instead, she swung her arms with all her strength in an effort to fling him away.

One of her elbows caught him squarely on the collarbone.

With a muffled yelp, he fell off her, sprawled to the floor. His arms tried to protect the bandages over his ribs and around his shoulders, but the fall sent a jolt through his fractured bones. For a moment, his back arched in real pain. Then he went limp on the floorboards.

Looking up at her and panting carefully as the pain receded, he murmured, "Terisa," in a wounded tone, "what're you doing? I just want to make love to you. You don't need to hurt me."

Now that she could see his whole face, she couldn't mistake his resemblance to the rest of the Domne's sons. Judging by his bandages, his cracked or broken ribs and collarbone, his crooked features, he must be Stead.

Glaring down at him angrily, she said the first thing that came into her head. "I thought you had too many broken bones to get out of bed."

He gave up sounding wounded and experimented with a smile

instead. "So did I. But that was before I saw you in the hall—outside my door. So I waited until everyone was asleep. Then I gave it a try. I guess a man can stand almost anything if he wants to badly enough."

When she didn't reply, he asked, "Will you help me up? I really am hurt, and the floor is hard."

Fortunately, he was wearing a pair of light cotton sleeping trousers below his bandages. If he had been naked, she might have had trouble keeping her composure. Under the circumstances, however, she was able to look at him squarely and say, "If you try to get up, I'm going to kick you until you wish you hadn't."

But as soon as she said that she nearly started laughing. She had once threatened to kick Geraden. In fact, she *had* kicked him. To make him stop apologizing.

"That isn't kind," Stead protested. His expression was lugubrious for a moment. But then another thought occurred to him, and he grinned. "On the other hand, it might be worth it. You won't be able to get out of that bed to kick me without letting me see what you look like. The way you walk makes me think you must look glorious." His grin sharpened. "I've never been turned down by a woman who let me catch even a glimpse of her breasts."

"In that case"—her desire to laugh was getting stronger—"I won't kick you. I won't get out of bed at all." Stead looked astonishingly like Geraden trying to do an imitation of Master Eremis— with limited success. Keeping herself carefully covered with her blankets, she sat up and indicated the lamp. "I'll just throw burning oil at you."

Stead didn't appear to take this threat very seriously. "No, you won't."

In an effort to stifle her mirth, she glowered back at him. "What makes you think that?"

"You don't really want to hurt me." With no arrogance at all, he explained, "What you really want is a man."

She stared at him. "I do?"

He nodded. "Every woman does. That's what men and women are for. First they want each other. Then they get into bed and enjoy each other."

That sounded dangerously plausible. She countered by asking, "What about Geraden? He's your brother, after all. And I came here with him. Don't you consider him a man?"

"Ah, Geraden." Stead's smile seemed genuinely affectionate.

"Of course I consider him a man. If you want my opinion, he's the best one of us all. Oh, he isn't half the farmer Tholden is. He isn't half the shepherd Wester is. He isn't half the swordsman Artagel is. And he sure doesn't know anything about women. But he's still the best.

"But that's not the point, is it?" he continued rhetorically. It was remarkable how little arrogance he had in him, how little assumption of superiority. He didn't belittle anyone. "The point is, *you* don't consider him a man."

Terisa's mouth fell open. She closed it with an effort. Suddenly, the situation wasn't funny anymore. "*I* don't?"

"You came here with him. He worships every inch of you. If you thought of him as a man, you'd be in his room right now." Nothing in Stead's tone suggested the slightest criticism of Geraden—or of her. His view of the situation was essentially impersonal.

"There must be someone else you want."

Holding her gaze, he began to ease himself up from the floor. Every moment was obviously painful to him, but the pain only accentuated the appeal in his eyes.

"I think you want me," he murmured. "*I* certainly want *you*."

There was something of Master Eremis in the way he looked at her, an intensity of interest which hypnotized. And he had distinct advantages over the Master. He wouldn't demean her. He wouldn't do anything cruel.

"I started wanting you as soon as I saw you," he said as he got his feet under him. "Your lips cry out for kisses. Breasts like yours should be fondled until they give you bliss. The place of passion between your legs aches to be pierced. Terisa, I want you. I want to revel in you until your joy is as great as mine."

Upright despite the way his ribs and collarbone hurt, he moved gently toward her.

He had some of Master Eremis' magnetism. And his desire was less threatening than the Master's.

At the same time, he forced her to think of Geraden.

If you thought of him as a man—

She dropped the blankets. Stead's eyes grew bright, and he reached toward her, but she ignored him. Fending his arms away, she left the bed and crossed the room to her clothes.

"Terisa?"

The shirt and skirt Quiss had given her weren't warm enough

to hold out the chill. They were warm enough for the time being, however; she didn't want to spend time looking for an alternative. And the boots helped.

Stead came up behind her, put his hands on her shoulders. "Terisa?"

She turned to face him. "Take me to Geraden's room."

He frowned in puzzlement. "Geraden's room? Why do you want to go there? He doesn't want you. He thinks he does, but he doesn't really. If he did, he would be here already."

Terisa shook her head; she knew Geraden better than that. "Stead," she said quietly, "I'm not going to threaten you. I'm not going to kick you—or set you on fire. I just don't want you.

"Take me to Geraden's room."

Stead blinked at her. "You don't mean that."

Taking care not to hurt him, she moved around him toward the door. Outside, the lamps had been extinguished. She returned to the table at the head of the bed and took the lamp. "Make yourself comfortable," she said. "You might as well sleep here. I won't be back."

She was out the door and had started to close it before she heard him pant, "Terisa, wait," and come shuffling after her.

His injuries prevented him from walking quickly; he took a moment to catch up with her. Then he braced himself against the door and paused to rest. His expression didn't make sense to her. Behind the strain of movement, he seemed sadder than she'd expected—and happier.

"Quiss always refuses me," he said, breathing carefully. "I don't understand that. I've tried to tell her how much I want her. That's all that matters. But she always refuses.

"I have to admit, though"—by degrees, his happiness took over his face—"she certainly makes me think well of Tholden.

"Geraden's room is that way." Grinning, he pointed down the hall.

Now she found it easy to smile back at him. To help him walk, she slipped her arm through his. That appeared to confuse him—but of course he had no way of knowing how much he was improved by the comparison to Master Eremis. In any case, he let her assist him, and they went down the hall like old friends.

Past two corners and down a long passage, Stead stopped in front of another door. "Here," he murmured softly. Then he put his arm around her waist and hugged her. Touching his mouth to her ear, he whispered, "Are you sure you wouldn't rather come with me? No matter how much he worships you, he can't want you more than I do."

Gently, she disentangled herself. "Go away," she replied as kindly as she could. "This is too important."

He sighed; nodded; shook his head in bafflement. But he didn't argue. A bit morosely, he turned and began to shamble down the hall, holding his arms protectively across his ribs.

She waited until he was out of sight around the corner. Then, before she had a chance to lose her nerve, she lifted the doorlatch and let herself into the room.

By the light of her lamp, she saw that Stead had brought her to the right place. In the wide bed against the far wall, Geraden sprawled among his blankets. Judging by appearances, he had lost a fierce struggle with his covers; now he lay outstretched in defeat, snoring slightly on the battlefield.

Asleep, his face gave up its bitter hardness, the iron of despair. He looked young and vulnerable, and inexpressibly dear. She wanted to go to him immediately and put her arms around him, hold him close to her heart, comfort away everything that hurt him. At the same time, she wanted to let him sleep—let him rest and dream until all his distress was healed. She shut the door behind her gently, so that he wouldn't be disturbed.

But the lamp woke him. He didn't flinch, or jerk himself out of bed; he simply opened his eyes, and yellow light reflected back at her. Without transition, he no longer looked young or vulnerable. He looked poised and deadly, like a wounded predator.

Master Eremis had understood from the beginning how dangerous Geraden was. All at once, the Master's *policy* toward him made sense to her.

"Geraden," she murmured in sudden confusion, "I'm sorry, I didn't mean to wake you. Or I guess I did. I don't know why I came. I couldn't stay away."

Then, mercifully, he sat up, and the change in his position changed the way the light caught his eyes. He relapsed to the Geraden she knew: hard and hurt, closed like a fist around the sources of his pain; but nonetheless human, precious to her.

She took a deep breath to steady herself. "There's so much we need to talk about."

Like Stead, he was dressed only in a pair of sleeping trousers; apparently, he didn't feel the cold as much as she did. He didn't get up from the bed or reach out to her. Yet when he spoke his voice sounded like the voice she remembered: capable of kindness; accessible to pain or hope.

"After supper—after you left—I went to see Minick. I wanted to apologize for yelling at him. People shouldn't yell at him, even though he never gets angry about it.

"Do you know what he said? He said, 'I spent the afternoon with your Terisa. She's nice. If you make her unhappy, you won't be welcome in my house anymore.' Minick said that, my mild brother who never gets angry."

Geraden shrugged. "I didn't tell him that I've already made you unhappy."

"No," she replied at once, "that's not true," reacting too quickly for thought. "How can you say that?"

He watched her impassively. "I look at you, Terisa. I see the way you look at me."

"And what do you see?"

He held her eyes, but he didn't answer.

"I like your family," she protested. "I feel comfortable in Houseldon. Ever since you talked me into leaving my old life, you've done more to make me happy than anyone else I've ever known. How can you—?"

She stopped. It would have been nice if he'd had a fire in his room: she needed an external source of warmth. The darkness beyond the lamplight seemed full of sorrow. Making a special effort to speak calmly, she continued, "Geraden, I think I probably could have made that mirror translate me anywhere. Anywhere I could visualize—anywhere vivid enough in my mind." *And I just came from Stead. He touched my breasts. He wanted to make love to me.* "Why do you think I'm here?"

His eyes didn't waver. "You're here because you think I'm wrong. You think I should have stayed in Orison to fight. You think there are still things I can do against Eremis."

As he said that, she suddenly knew she had to be very careful with him. Maybe it was true that he had become iron. But iron was brittle; he might break. He was blaming himself— She wanted to cry out, *Oh, Geraden, are you blaming yourself? For Eremis and Gilbur? For the Castellan? For Nyle and Quillon? Are you blaming* yourself because some of the best minds around you worked so hard to keep you from understanding your talent? But she couldn't say that to him. He would just turn away. More than ever, she couldn't bear the idea that he would turn away.

Softly, she asked, "Why do you believe I think you're wrong?"

"I told you." The kindness was gone from his voice. "I can see it in your eyes."

"*What* do you see?" she insisted. "*What* do you see in my eyes?"

For a long moment, he hesitated. Then he said roughly, "Pain."

She thought she might feel better if she hit him. She might feel even better if she put her arms around him. Yet she stayed where she was, with her back to the door, holding the only light in the room.

"That's how I know I'm real. Master Eremis says I was created by your mirror, but that can't be true. If I didn't exist, I couldn't be hurt."

"Terisa." He swallowed hard. She had touched him: she thought she could see grief shifting behind the rigid lines of his face. "Nobody says you don't exist. Not even Master Eremis. You're here. You're real. Everything you do has consequences. The question is, were you real before I translated you?"

Automatically, she wanted to ask, Have you changed your mind? Do you still think I was real—back where you found me? But she pushed that question down.

"I must have been," she said. King Joyse had told her to *reason*. "If the place I came from was only created by the mirror you saw me in, then that must be true of every mirror, every Image. So when you look in a flat glass, you don't actually see a real place. You see a created copy of a real place. So when I translated myself into the Image of the Closed Fist, I shouldn't have arrived in a real place. I should have arrived in the copy—a different copy than the one you went to. I should have stopped being real myself until somebody translated me back out again.

"Isn't that right?"

The light of the lamp was imprecise, but she seemed to see a hint of a smile at the corners of his mouth. The shadows there deepened as he listened to her. The sight caused her heart to accelerate a bit.

"That's good," he said. "I wish I'd come up with that argument myself. But I don't think it's enough. Eremis will just say, That's why translations through flat glass produce madness. The only translation that can be done safely is one between the real world and a created Image. Reality is too powerful to tolerate the manipulations of Imagery." In spite of his clenched condition, he began to sound more like his old self as he talked—more like he was interested in the discussion for its own sake. "So the closer a created Image gets to reality, the more dangerous it becomes. And when the Image actually copies reality, reality takes precedence. It rips the translation away from the Image, and the force of that distortion is what causes madness."

She hung on the change in his tone, hoped for it to continue. Almost at once, however, he closed himself again. "Terisa, you didn't come here in the middle of the night to debate the ethics of Imagery."

"Is that right?" Pained to feel the side of him she wanted to nurture slipping away, she made a mistake. "To you it's just a debate. To me it's my life. I can't make sense out of who I am unless I know the truth."

Right away, she knew she'd gone wrong: his gaze dropped from hers; his eyes filled up with shadows. He didn't need to be reminded that other people were suffering: he was already too sensitive to that; he already believed he had made her unhappy. But she refused to back down. She had come too far to retreat. Instead, she changed tactics.

"If I wasn't real until you brought me out of that mirror of yours, how did I become an arch-Imager?"

He didn't lift his head. In a muffled voice, he said, "You know I don't believe that. That's Eremis, not me."

Unexpectedly angry, she retorted, "Wake up. What do you think we're talking about here?" She put the lamp down on a nearby table to free her hands, as if she were getting ready to wrestle with him. "Why do you think who I am and where I come from matters? What he believes is going to affect everything he does to both of us.

"Tell me how I became an arch-Imager."

Now Geraden raised his eyes. Studying her closely—and holding himself completely still, as though he feared what she might do if he moved—he replied, "I created you. When I shaped my glass, I made you." Almost silently, he caught his breath in surprise and recognition; the implications took him aback. "I have the capacity to create arch-Imagers."

"Not just arch-Imagers," she amended for him. "Arch-Imagers

who can shift glass the way you do, arch-Imagers who can work
translations that are irrelevant to what you see in the Image."

"I could create a whole army of them. A whole army of Imagers
as powerful as Vagel. He wouldn't stand a chance." Staring at her—
at the ideas she proposed—Geraden murmured, "No wonder he
wants me dead."

"And that's not all." Gripping her courage, Terisa took the risk.
"How does he know you don't have glass here?"

Geraden jerked his head back, glowered at her in astonishment
or dismay. "What—?"

"How does he know"—she forced herself to complete the
thought, even though Geraden's expression made her feel that she
was accomplishing the opposite of what she wanted—"you aren't
busy creating an army of arch-Imagers right now?"

She horrified him. What a pleasure. All she wanted was to help
him—to comfort or encourage the Geraden who had gotten lost and
become iron—and what did she achieve? Horror. For a moment, he
was so shocked that the lamplight made him look as pale as bone.
Then he sprang off the bed, rushed to her and caught her by the
shoulders, groaned through his teeth as if he were stifling a wail,
"I've got to get out of here."

She stared at him dumbly.

"He'll send everything he's got after me. If he catches me here,
he'll reduce Houseldon to rubble to get at me."

It had to be said. She had gone too far to turn back. And this
was the point, wasn't it? The reason she had brought the subject up
in the first place? Distinctly, she remarked, "He has to try that no
matter what you do."

He stared at her in dismay.

"He knows you're here," she said. "But he won't know it when
you leave. Unless he has a mirror that lets him see you here. If you
run, he won't know it until he's destroyed Houseldon looking for
you.

"*I* did that." For a moment, her eyes filled with tears. She
blinked them back fiercely. "It's *my* doing. When I told him about
seeing the Closed Fist in your mirror, I set you up.

"You didn't know you were coming here. I told him, but I didn't
tell you. You were just trying to escape—and hoping you wouldn't
end up somewhere you couldn't get back from. He has to destroy
Houseldon so that he can stop you, and I set you up for it."

Geraden, it's not your *fault*. None of this is your *fault*.

His face was thrust close to hers, his fingers ground into her arms; but she couldn't seem to read his face. His passion was part of his skull, definitive under his features; yet the flesh over it was so tight and strict that she couldn't distinguish between them.

When he spoke, however, his voice shook her as hard as if he had shoved her against the wall. It was strong, compulsory; it had the power to command her.

"Terisa, people I have known and loved all my life are going to die because I came here."

I swore I was never going to let anybody I loved die ever again.

But there was nothing he could do. Houseldon was already as well prepared to defend itself as possible. He was helpless to save anything or anybody. Because he needed so much from her, she didn't cry or apologize or defend herself or get angry. She faced him squarely and said, "I think I would probably feel better if you hit me."

He looked like he might hit her: he was angry or desperate enough to hit something.

"Why didn't you *tell* me?"

Slowly, she shook her head. At least he wasn't closed anymore. She had achieved that much. And even fury was preferable to his rigid isolation, his mute hurt. "That's not the point," she countered. "It doesn't matter. I just made a mistake, that's all. I didn't know how important all this is." And later on she had been so embarrassed by her submission to Master Eremis that she found it impossible to speak.

"The point is, *I* had a choice." It seemed loony to speak so calmly when he was in such distress. It seemed loony to prefer anyone's anger. "I could have gone anywhere." At the same time, her own misery inexplicably began to become something else, something that bore a crazy and astounding resemblance to joy. She could reach him—she could make him furious. Because of that, everything else was possible. "I *chose* to come here.

"Geraden, listen to me. Why do you suppose I *chose* to come here?"

He was so angry, so frightened for his home and family and friends, that he could hardly refrain from raging. Involuntarily, he bared his teeth. Yet he was still Geraden, still the man who had always done everything he could imagine for her. Panting at the effort he made to restrain himself, he said, "You tell me. Why?"

"No." Again she shook her head. "Come on, think about it. Why did I come here?"

Through his passion, he rasped, "You didn't know where else to go. To escape."

"*No.* Come on, *think.* I could have gone anywhere. Prince Kragen would have been glad to have me. All I had to do was translate myself out of Orison. Anywhere outside the gates."

Now she had him. It was strange how much power she had with him. Her mistakes might result in the complete destruction of his home and family: his reasons for outrage were that good. And yet he felt compelled to try to understand her.

He didn't let go of her, but his fingers stopped grinding into her arms. With less fury, he said, "You wanted to warn me."

"*Yes.*" She didn't smile; yet the inexplicable joy in her started to sing. "I wanted to warn you.

"Why do you suppose I bothered? Why do you suppose I care what happens here? I didn't know your family. I'd never been here before. Why do you suppose I was willing to come here and face you when I knew it was my fault you were in danger—when I knew you had every reason in the world to be angry at me or even hate me and there was nothing I could do to change any of it?"

Oh, she had him. She wanted to shout it out: she *had* him. He wasn't iron now, closed and bitter. His fury had receded. He was scrutinizing her intently: perplexed, almost dumbfounded; fundamentally baffled by her; touched by hope.

"*Think* about it," she murmured to keep herself from crowing aloud.

He opened his mouth, but no words came.

"You idiot. I did it because I love you."

Then she reached her arms around his neck and pulled herself up to kiss him.

He took a moment to recover from the shock. Fortunately, he didn't take too long. Before she could lose the elation singing through her, he clasped her to him and returned her kiss as if his answer came all the way up from the bottom of his soul.

The fabric of his sleeping trousers was so thin that she couldn't mistake the way he felt about her, in spite of her inexperience. She kissed him for a long time while his arms strained around her. Then she eased back from his embrace and began to unbutton her shirt.

His eyes darkened, as if they were on fire with shadows. A bit awkwardly, she kicked off her boots. When she slipped the shirt from her shoulders and dropped her skirt, he caught his breath. Even the hair on his head seemed to burn with desire.

Abruptly, he jerked down his pants and took her to his bed.

He was almost devout in the way he kissed and touched her; torn between wonder and alarm, as if he wanted her so much that he didn't trust himself. As a result, he was tentative when she most wished him to be sure. Master Eremis was right. During the Master's brief stay in the dungeon after the summoning of the Congery's champion, he had said to her, *Whenever you think of another man, you will remember my lips upon your breasts.* That was true: Geraden's touch reminded her of the Imager—of his assurance, his willingness to take possession of her completely.

And yet Geraden conveyed an intensity that moved her deeply. She felt that she had spent most of her life waiting for this time in bed with him. She could do without assurance. They would learn what they needed to know together.

But it went wrong, the way everything went wrong for him. He had discovered his talent for Imagery too late, when he was no longer able to do anything with it. Now he discovered her love for him too late, he held her in his arms too late: he had lost the ability to do anything with her. Maybe his own inexperience made him too anxious. Maybe he couldn't stop worrying about Houseldon and his family. She wasn't sure what the reason was—and in a sense she didn't care. She cared only that he swore under his breath and rolled away from her, lay on his back with his fists clenched at his sides and his muscles knotted, trying to withdraw into iron.

She watched him lock himself away from her, and her joy began to crumble. For a moment, she thought about weeping.

Then she got an idea.

With the tip of one finger, she stroked the hard line of his jaw. "Guess what," she said as if they were engaged in a casual and even bantering conversation. "I've just thought of a reason to believe I'm really real."

"I already believe it," he muttered from the opposite side of the world. "You know that."

"But you don't know why," she returned playfully. "That's the trouble with you. You don't have enough reasons. You just have your 'strongest feelings'—you do everything on faith.

"I'll give you a reason.

"People like Eremis say I was created by Imagery. I came out of you and your talent when you made that mirror. But if that's true, don't you think you would have created a woman you could have an easier time making love with?"

She took him so entirely by surprise that he couldn't stop himself. As unexpectedly as a shout, he burst out laughing.

And once he started to laugh he lost control.

"That's perfect," he gasped between gales of mirth. "I'm so confused I can't figure out my own talent. I can't help my family. Or my King. Or the woman I love. But that's not enough for me. I'm not satisfied with just that."

Briefly, she heard a note of hysteria in his laughter, and she nearly panicked. But the simple act of laughing seemed to clean the sorrow and self-pity out of him; the more he laughed, the more he relaxed.

"No, I'm so confused that when I create a woman to love I make her so perverse she accidentally betrays my whole life. Then she wants to bed me when I'm so scared I can hardly think.

"I don't need enemies. As soon as I stop laughing, I'm going to kill myself.

"Oh, Terisa."

He said her name as if it made him ache. Rolling back to her, he put his hands on the sides of her face to hold her and began kissing her again.

Unquestionably, his kisses lacked Master Eremis' assured passion. But they were sweet and compelling, like the remembered call of horns. And when she remembered horns, the music came back into her.

This time, it went right.

It went right nearly until dawn. When she finally slept, she still clung to him like a promise that she was never going to let him go.

At dawn, the house stirred around them; but she and Geraden continued sleeping.

Fortunately, Houseldon wasn't relying on Terisa and Geraden for vigilance. When the attack came, the men on watch spotted it immediately and raised the alarm.

Shouts echoed like wails among the houses and taverns, the livery stables and granaries. As fast as they could get out of bed, men spilled from their homes, clutching pitchforks and scythes, axes, shepherd's crooks sharpened to resemble pikes, sledgehammers, knives and bucksaws, ordinary clubs, an occasional sword, and more than a few hunting bows. The Domne's six trained bowmen took their command positions around the stockade almost instantly. Shouting for his canes, the Domne himself thrashed out of his twisted bedclothes.

Tholden was ahead of his father. The truth was that he had been too worried for sleep. After trying uselessly to rest until after midnight, he had gotten up, put on his clothes. If Quiss hadn't restrained him, he would have gone to wear himself out pacing around the stockade to no purpose. But she had compelled him—almost by force—to sit down and drink a flagon of wine; she had kneaded the knots in his neck and shoulders and back until her hands ached; she had made love to him. After that, he pretended to sleep until she let down her guard. Then he got out of bed again.

He was in the front room stirring up the fire when he heard the alarm. Roaring in a voice that wasn't made to convey anger or violence, he left the house. For a second, he wheeled, trying to find which direction the alarm came from. Then he set off at a run, his beard lifting in the dawn breeze.

Terisa groped awake, roused more by the way Geraden exploded out of bed than by the shouts. He seemed to jump unerringly into his clothes while she fumbled to follow him, catch up with him; he flung the door open before she had begun to button her shirt.

Nevertheless she did catch up with him. Out in the hall, he collided with Stead and had to stop to lift his injured brother off the floor. Stead clung to him for a moment. "Get me a knife," he panted. "I can't run anywhere. But I can fight here if I have to."

"I'll tell Quiss," Geraden replied as he pulled away.

With Terisa beside him now, he reached the front room, shouted Stead's message to Quiss, then dashed out of the house.

"Where?" he demanded of the first man he met.

The man looked too frightened to have any idea what he was doing. "West."

"West," Geraden muttered, thinking hard. "So it isn't soldiers. Soldiers would come from the north. The northeast."

Terisa saw what he was getting at; but her heart was pounding in her throat, and she couldn't speak.

"Eremis is sending Imagery against us."

She nodded. They ran west among the buildings.

Everyone was running west. Tholden's instructions to Houseldon had been explicit: women and children, stay at home; anyone who was too young or too frail or too sick to fight, stay at home. Unfortunately, the people of Domne had lost the habit of taking orders. The streets were crowded with people who shouldn't have been there. Some of the men who were prepared or equipped or at least determined to fight had difficulty working their way through the throng.

But Tholden had replied to the alarm so quickly that he was ahead of the crowds; he didn't know he was being imperfectly obeyed. He reached the guardpost and climbed onto the platform where the man who had raised the alarm was on watch in time to see the whole attack clearly.

They came in without a sound except for the rush of their paws and the harsh murmur of their breathing: strange wolves with spines bristling down their curved backs, a double row of fangs in each slavering jaw, and something like intelligence in their wild eyes. Only a few dozen of them, Tholden thought when he first spotted them. Enough to ravage a herd of sheep. Or terrorize a farmstead. Not enough to threaten Houseldon. They won't be able to get past the stockade.

Then the leader of the pack sprang at the wall.

The wolf seemed to come straight up at him. Leaping at least eight feet in the air, it got its forelegs over the wall. While its hind legs scrambled for a purchase on the wood, its jaws stretched toward his face.

For an instant more horrible than anything he had imagined, Tholden couldn't move. He was a farmer, not a soldier: he didn't know anything about fighting. Deep down in his heart, he had always believed there was something secretly crazy about people like Artagel, who went into battle with such fierce joy. The men standing on the platform with him had already flinched away. One of the bowmen rushed to bring up his bow. But Tholden just couldn't move.

Then hot slaver splashed into his face as the fangs drew near, and something inside him shifted. Although he never thought about it, he was prodigiously strong, and his strength came to his rescue. He reached out, caught the wolf by the throat, and heaved it backward.

It fell among the pack, breaking the charge, preventing the wolves behind it from gathering themselves to spring. The pack burst into snarls—a raw, red sound, avid for blood. Jaws snapped. Then the wolves swirled around to regain their momentum so that they could leap.

"Bowmen!" the Domne's son cried desperately, "get some arrows into those things! If they get over the wall—!"

Not fast enough. Already three wolves were leaping, four, six. And instead of attacking the guardpost directly, they hurled themselves at a part of the wall where there were no immediate defenders.

He was appalled by the realization that these beasts knew what they were doing. They were at their most vulnerable while they tried to cross the top of the wall—so they moved out of reach.

But an arrow thudded into the chest of the nearest wolf. It fell away, coughing blood. While the bowman snatched up another shaft, someone below the platform threw a hatchet that buried itself between a pair of glaring, wild eyes. Someone else tried to use a pitchfork as if it were a javelin; the tines missed, but the wolf was forced to drop back.

Three down.

The other three got over the wall.

Tholden saw a farmer swing an axe and miss—saw him go down with his throat torn out by an effortless toss of the wolf's head. Luckily, the next man struck a solid blow with a club, and the wolf wobbled. While the beast was still unsteady on its legs, one long sweep of a scythe disemboweled it.

Defenders arrived as quickly as the narrow streets and the crowds permitted. The second wolf over the wall ducked between two hostlers—who nearly brained each other trying to hit it—ripped open the best baker in Houseldon before he could raise his hands, then flung itself at a knot of young boys who had escaped from their mothers. But it went down when an ancient sword in the hands of an old man who remembered the wars struck between the spines protecting its back.

The third wolf took an arrow in its hindquarters from a terrified young apprentice bowman. As if it thrived on pain, it killed the young man, bit off another man's hand at the wrist when the man tried to stab the creature with a knife, then raced down an alley toward the heart of Houseldon.

At the same time, more wolves sprang to the attack.

Only a few dozen of them, Tholden thought. He wanted to tear his hair.

A second bowman ran up from the guardpost where he had been stationed. Like his comrade, he began picking wolves off the top of the wall as fast as he could nock arrows to the string. But they were only two. Every time one of them reached for a new shaft, three or four beasts got into Houseldon.

Calling frantically for help, Tholden leaped off the platform.

The other bowmen were on their way, but hampered by the crowds. And the defenders at the scene of attack didn't know how to fight an enemy like this; they got in each other's way. In a sense, the wolves were losing. They would all be killed eventually. But if enough of them ran loose in the streets, they would do terrible carnage before they were hunted down.

And if they killed the bowmen—

Maybe the wolves wouldn't lose.

Tholden snatched an axe from a man who obviously didn't know how to use it effectively. Planting himself in the path of the wolves, he hewed at them as if they were nothing more than a stand of timber. He had no idea what else to do.

So he didn't see what happened to the beasts that got past him. He didn't see the arrival of the remaining bowmen, or the efforts they made to thin out the attack; he didn't see the wall of defenders behind him crumble and fail as people panicked and fled and even men who knew how to wield their weapons went down.

On the other hand, he was one of the few people in a position to see that the wolves were only the vanguard of the attack.

No one else guessed that. No one else thought about it. The wolves were trouble enough. Cursing the folly which had taken them outside, women rushed back to their homes, hauling their children along behind them. Men dove into hiding. Flocks of chickens fled in a squall of feathers and fright, running crazily in all directions or battering their way heavily up to the rooftops. The whole west side of Houseldon was in disarray, instructions and defenses forgotten.

Suddenly, the street in front of Terisa and Geraden cleared, and they found themselves facing a beast with blood on its jaws and an arrow sticking out of its hindquarters.

The spines along its back made it look like a hedgehog of monstrous size. The double row of its fangs made it look like a great shark.

Terisa was reminded of riders with red fur and too many arms.

The wolf stopped, scented the air. Its eyes seemed to burn with the possibility of intelligence.

"It's hunting us," she said. At any rate, she thought she said that; she couldn't tell whether she spoke aloud.

"When I push you," Geraden whispered, "go for that house." He nudged her slightly toward the nearest building. "Get inside. Close the door. Try to bolt it."

The wolf began to snarl deep in his chest—a sound like a distant rumble of thunder.

"What're you going to do?"

She must have spoken aloud. Otherwise he wouldn't have answered.

"Same thing in the opposite direction."

Automatically, she nodded, too frightened to do anything else.

As if her nod were a signal, the wolf sprang at them, slavering murderously.

Geraden hit her shoulder so hard that she stumbled and fell.

At least she fell out of the way of the beast's charge. Trying frantically to bounce up from the ground, she jammed her legs under her, pounded up onto the porch of the house—

—whirled to see what was happening to Geraden.

He hadn't made any attempt to do what she was doing. After pushing her aside, he had simply ducked. By the time the wolf checked its spring, landed, and came back at him, he was on his feet facing the creature, poised as if he intended to kick its brains out.

"Geraden!"

"Get in the house!"

So fast that she hardly saw it happen, he jumped sideways. The wolf flashed past him. She heard the savage click as jaws strong enough to crush bone tried to close on him. The sleeve of his jerkin burst into tatters.

But there was no blood. Yet.

Faster this time because its second charge had been less head-long, the wolf turned and went for him again.

If he had tripped, if he had missed his footing or misjudged the assault, he would have died. No one could do what he was doing, not for long. The arrow in the wolf's hindquarters wasn't enough of a handicap. Nevertheless he dodged a third time—ripped himself out of the way, ducked and rolled, came to his feet to face the wolf again just before it sprang.

Blindly, stupidly, Terisa started back into the street to help him.

At that instant, a woman came out of the house in mortal terror. So scared that she could hardly control her limbs, she thrust a pitch-fork into Terisa's hands. Then she slammed the door behind her, slammed a bar into place against the door.

Terisa took the pitchfork without thinking. Wailing like a mad-woman to distract the wolf, she leaped off the porch and did her utter best to spear the beast on the tines.

She missed. The wolf was too fast, too smart for her inexpert onslaught. When it came around at her, however, she was able to fend it off, almost by accident; it shied away from impaling itself on the pitchfork.

As if out of nowhere, the head of a cane whizzed through the air and cracked the wolf across the base of its skull.

Coughing a howl, the beast spun and hurled itself on the Domne.

Geraden yelped a helpless warning. Terisa froze, holding her weapon as if she had forgotten its existence.

The Domne couldn't run or dodge. With his bad leg, he could scarcely hobble. But he had a cane in his other hand as well, and when the beast leaped at him he rammed the end of that stick down its throat.

At the same time, Geraden went past Terisa, tearing the pitch-fork from her hands in one motion and hammering it into the wolf's back with all his strength.

Spiked to the ground, the beast writhed for a moment, snarling horribly and spitting blood on the Domne's boots. Then it lay still.

"Thank you, Father," panted Geraden. "Glass and splinters! that was close. You shouldn't take chances like that."

The Domne balanced unsteadily on his feet. His face was white. Yet he contrived to speak calmly. "Someday," he remarked, "you're going to call me 'Da.' I think you'll like it."

Geraden shook his head as if he had lost his voice.

With one cane, the Domne prodded the body at his feet. "How many of them are there?"

"Enough to get past Tholden," croaked Geraden.

Terisa had the vivid impression that she was about to faint. Fortunately, Geraden turned and caught her before her knees folded.

As the last wolf came over the stockade with an arrow in its heart, the bowman on the guardpost platform yelled, almost shrieked, "*Tholden!*" and Tholden gasped a curse because there was nothing else he could say while he retched for breath.

Half the pack had been slaughtered in front of him. Carcasses lay along the bottom of the wall, in piles on both sides of him, among the dead bodies of his people at his back. His axe was covered with blood; his hands and arms ran red; blood dripped from his beard and soaked his shirt. His eyes held a wildness of their own which bore no resemblance to the feral intelligence of the wolves. How many of them had gotten past him? He didn't know. He didn't know what the people of Houseldon were doing to defend themselves. He only knew that the bowman on the platform sounded frantic.

There was more. The wolves were only the vanguard.

Forcing himself into motion, he staggered to the guardpost, heaved his bulk up the ladder to the platform.

When he looked over the top of the stockade and saw what the bowman was pointing at, his first reaction was one of deflation, almost of disappointment.

Oh, is *that* all?

He was gazing across a hundred yards of open ground at a cat.

Just a cat. One cat. Nothing more.

The realization came to him slowly, however, that this cat was bigger than he was. It was at least as big as a horse. At least—

Then he noticed that wherever the cat put its paws the new grass and old leaves caught fire. It had already left a smoldering trail away into the distance, where the wolfpack had come from. And it was approaching—not rapidly, but without any hesitation—advancing as steadily and inevitably as a stormfront.

"Tholden," the bowman murmured like a prayer, "what *is* it?"

This was foolishness, really. Who was he to pretend that he could fill his father's boots, that he could succeed as the next Domne? He didn't understand anything about Imagery. The only real accomplishment of his life, from his point of view, was to figure out the best time of year and the best conditions to fertilize apricot trees. Unless he counted marrying Quiss, or having five children: his family was also an accomplishment that gave him pride.

"How many arrows do you have left?" he asked the bowman.

"None." It was a question the man understood. "I'll have to get them from the wolves."

"Don't bother. Go." Tholden pushed him gently. "Get men for the watertubs. If that thing doesn't just break the stockade, it'll burn it down."

The bowman clattered off the ladder, sped away. Tholden turned to the other bowmen, actually turned his back on the advancing firecat. "If you're out of arrows," he said as if he were speaking to a small circle of friends on an occasion of no great importance, "go rally Houseldon. We need help.

"If you've still got some left, come up here."

No more than fifty yards away, the firecat brushed past a discarded corn shock. At once, the shock sprang into flame and withered to crisp ash.

The platform wobbled as two bowmen clambered up to join Tholden. Nodding toward the firecat, he said, "Aim for the eyes."

"Will that kill it?" asked one of the men huskily.

"Who knows? You got any better ideas?"

The man shook his head. His face was taut with fear, but he didn't back away.

The bowmen nocked their shafts, strained their bows. Almost simultaneously, they let fly.

The firecat flicked its head aside negligently. The arrows caught fire and became charcoal before their heads could pierce the cat's hide.

"I think we need a better idea," the second bowman muttered as he and his comrade readied more shafts.

As if he were losing his mind, Tholden turned again and shouted, "Geraden? Where's *Geraden?*"

The first of his reinforcements had begun to arrive: men who hadn't encountered the wolves; others who grasped that a greater danger was coming; some who were so frightened that the bowmen had to goad them along. No one had seen Geraden. A few of the defenders stared at Tholden as if he were speaking an alien tongue.

"All right," he rasped. "We'll do it ourselves." The wildness in his eyes was getting worse. Suddenly furious, he roared, "Don't just stand there! Get those watertubs up onto the banquette!"

Galvanized by the incongruous desperation in his high, kind voice, the men below him started hurrying.

The bowmen exhausted their shafts—to no purpose—and jumped out of the way of the watertubs. The firecat was so close now that Tholden thought he could feel its heat. Or maybe that was just the sun. The sky was clear and gorgeous to the horizons, and the air was growing warm. With blood running from his face like sweat, he helped several men boost a watertub into position.

Just in time—barely in time. The cat reached the stockade, paused, tested the wood with its nose. Instant flames swept upward, building swiftly from a small flicker to a savage blaze. The hands and arms supporting the watertubs were scorched. Tholden lost his beard and eyebrows; he nearly lost his eyes.

Then two half hogsheads went over the wall almost simultaneously, and water hit the flames and the heat with a roar like an explosion.

The fire in the timbers went out. But the concussion as that much water erupted into steam blasted the men off the platform, off the banquette.

Tholden landed on his shoulder and spent a stunned and useless moment staring paralyzed at the sky while all his muscles locked up around the jolt. It was possible that his shoulder was broken. It seemed possible to him that he would never breathe again. The hard, hot steam disappeared into the air almost immediately, leaving the heavens blue and perfect, untouched.

After a momentary delay, the wet wood of the stockade began to smolder.

Wrenching air into his lungs, Tholden rolled sideways, got his legs under him.

His shoulder was numb. He couldn't move that arm.

Flames licked between the timbers. The lashings that held the timbers began to snap.

With a howl of heat, the wall caught fire again and blazed up like the blast of a furnace.

Tholden and his men staggered backward, stared as the timbers flamed—and the firecat thrust its way between the beams as if they were nothing more than charcoal twigs.

"*Tholden!*" people screamed.

"Help!"

"Tell us what to do!"

"We don't know what to do!"

"Run," he coughed weakly. He had never felt such intense fire in his life, never seen anything that terrified him as much as this firecat did. "Run." The heat drew tears from his eyes as if he were weeping. Houseldon was built of wood. The whole place would burn. "Get out of the way."

Automatically, without thought, he retreated to keep the heat at a distance. The firecat ambled after him with an indirect, even nonchalant gait, as if he were an especially tasty and helpless mouse.

Moving like a madman, he led the firecat in among the buildings.

The cat moved to the side of the lane while it followed him. Fire swept up the wall of a granary; then, with a detonation like a thunderclap, the grain itself took flame. Fire and smoke and blazing grain swirled a hundred feet into the air.

The merchant who owned the granary lived in a house beside it. He was an old man with a vast quantity of fat and no reputation whatsoever for valor; yet he ran raging out onto his porch and flung a washbasin full of water at the cat.

The cat didn't notice his attack.

Almost instantly, the fire consumed him.

Tholden retreated as slowly as he could bear, bringing Houseldon's destruction with him.

He nearly missed what had happened when the firecat abruptly let out a roar of vexation—perhaps even of pain—and flinched to the side. A bit of flame clung to the pads of one forepaw. The beast hunched over and licked its paw clean; its tail switched malevolently. When it started moving again, it appeared angrier, more determined; it looked like it intended to pounce on him without further delay.

Tholden gaped dumbly, transfixed by the incomprehensible fact that the creature had hurt itself by stepping in a small pile of sheepdung.

As if this information were too much for him, his eyes rolled in his head; his scorched and naked face stretched into a wail; his numb arm flapped against his side.

Awkwardly, he turned and dashed out of the firecat's path, fled between the nearest houses as if he had vultures beating around his head. The people who saw him go believed that his mind had snapped.

The cat didn't pursue him. It was after other prey.

Setting homes and shops ablaze almost casually as it went, it continued its malign stroll into the heart of Houseldon.

Toward Terisa and Geraden.

Terisa and Geraden and the Domne heard the screams; they saw fire and smoke blasting into the sky. "Glass and splinters!" Geraden hissed between his teeth. "What's *that?*"

"Not wolves, I'm afraid," muttered the Domne. He nudged the carcass at his feet. "Even wolves like that don't set fires."

Alarm cleared the giddiness out of Terisa's head. She took her weight on her legs and tried to think.

"Where's Tholden?"

Geraden glanced at her. He and the Domne didn't look at each other.

One of the bowmen led the rout down the street. Waving people past him, he stopped in front of the Domne. "My lord," he gasped, urgent for breath, "the wall is breached. Houses are burning."

"I can see that," replied the Domne with uncharacteristic asperity. "How did it happen?"

"A creature of Imagery. A cat as big as a steer. It sets fire to everything.

"It's coming this way."

Terisa felt a cold hand close around her heart. Sets fire to everything. "Castellan Lebbick told me about a cat like that. It killed his guards." He sent out fifty men, and it killed them. "When they were trying to capture the Congery's champion."

Geraden nodded grimly. "Eremis hasn't got enough men. Or enough men to spare. Or he can't translate enough of them here without making them mad. So he's using Imagery to attack us. Trying to slaughter us wholesale instead of murdering us individually."

The fires came closer. A warehouse tossed flames in all directions as kegs of oil exploded. The destruction of Houseldon already seemed to be raging out of control.

The Domne watched his people flee past him as if the sight made him want to throw up. He kept his voice quiet, however.

"You're the only Imager in the family, Geraden. How do we defend ourselves?"

"With mirrors," Geraden snarled. Terisa thought he looked exactly like his father at that moment—so hard and horrified that he wanted to throw up. "Which we haven't got."

Then she caught her first glimpse of the firecat. Involuntarily, she took a step backward.

"Where's Tholden?" she asked again. She was suddenly afraid that he was already dead.

Tholden was running for his life.

His shoulder wasn't broken. If it were broken, it would have started to hurt before this. Nevertheless it remained numb; he still couldn't use it. It hampered his balance, his gait. Because of it, he ran like a hunchback.

Ran between the houses and along the lanes of Houseldon as if he were terrified.

He had forgotten the wolves—forgotten them completely. His desperation didn't hold room for any other danger. One of the houses he passed had had its door torn off the hinges, but he didn't notice that. He didn't hear the dying whimpers from inside, didn't see the beast munching flesh in the doorway. He had no idea what was happening when the wolf left the infant it was eating and leaped at his head.

Because of his lurching gait, it missed his head. Yet its claws raked his back as it went by him.

That pain got his attention. He and the wolf wheeled to meet each other; as fierce as the beast, he faced its charge.

Slobbering blood, it sprang again.

He had no time for fear or forethought. In fact, he had no time for the wolf. Striding forward as the beast leaped, he kicked it in the ribcage so hard that he ruptured its heart.

Then he ran on.

His back bled as if it were on fire. Coughing for help, he ran toward the nearest wastepit where Houseldon accumulated fertilizer for the orchards and fields.

He didn't have much time. The people fleeing along the street had scattered; Terisa, Geraden, and the Domne could see the firecat clearly now.

And it could see them: that was obvious. Its eyes were fixed on them as if at last it had recognized its true prey.

Well, of course. Stunned with fright and helplessness, Terisa had been reduced to talking to herself. Eremis wouldn't trust random violence to kill them. And he must be able to talk to that thing. Otherwise how could he get it to do what he wanted? It might have attacked the champion instead of the Castellan's guards. He probably gave it a description of the people it was supposed to kill.

Uselessly, she wondered what kind of description the firecat would understand. Could Eremis really talk to it?

"Terisa." Geraden had a hand on her arm; he shook her. "Terisa, listen to me. If that creature is after me, you can get away. You've got to get away. Get out of here—get out of Houseldon. Go north. To the Termigan. Maybe he's got some glass you can use. At least you can warn him. He'll protect you.

"I'll try to give you as much time as I can."

"Thanks." What was she talking about? She had no idea. "I appreciate that." Words seem to come out of her mouth without passing through her consciousness first. "What if it's after me? How are *you* going to get away?"

"An interesting question," the Domne put in dryly. "Let's discuss it later, shall we? Start running, both of you. If it's engrossed in destroying Houseldon, you might both get away." Abruptly, he started to shout, cracking his command at them like a whip. "I said *start running!*"

Both Terisa and Geraden nodded.

Neither of them moved.

She began to feel the heat of the fire on her face. The firecat was so close now that she could have hit it with a rock. It wasn't in any hurry—but it was definitely coming straight for them. Its eyes stared malice; its tail lashed the dust.

She and Geraden and the Domne stood their ground as if they had lost their minds.

And the firecat stopped. It regarded them warily. They acted like they weren't afraid of it. Why was that? Terisa had the odd impression that she knew exactly what the cat was thinking. Why were they standing there as if fire and fangs couldn't hurt them? What kind of danger did they represent?

Beyond question, she had lost her mind, even if the men with her were still sane. While the firecat studied them all, she waved her hand at it and said, "Scat. Go away." She could feel her hair growing crisp in the heat. "We won't hurt you. If you go away."

Good. Brilliant. Instead of retreating, the creature crouched to spring.

Unexpectedly, Minick arrived at the Domne's side. In spite of his apparent haste, he didn't seem to be breathing hard—didn't seem to be breathing at all.

Each of his strong, brown hands carried a large wooden bucket.

Water, Terisa thought. Good idea. Too bad it won't work. The firecat certainly hadn't been hindered by the snow when it had attacked Castellan Lebbick's men.

Precisely, as if he were following an elaborate set of instructions, Minick set the buckets down beside him.

Gasping and blowing as though his chest were about to burst, Tholden came into the street. He nearly ran up against the firecat's flank; the heat must have been tremendous.

He held one of the watertubs hugged in his arms.

Full of water, it must have been far too heavy for any one man to lift. Nevertheless he supported it alone, staggered out into the open without help; there he let the tub thud into the dirt.

That dull, hard sound distracted the creature. Dancing aside as daintily as a kitten, it turned to see what he was doing.

"Now!" Tholden croaked hoarsely.

Reaching into his watertub with both hands, he scooped a load of sheepdung into the firecat's face.

The hard pellets hit the cat's whiskers, cheeks, jaws, eyes.

Hit and stuck.

They were fuel: they burned hotly. But they didn't fall away, as water and wood and even iron fell away. They clung to the creature's fur and flesh.

With a scream, the firecat did a complete backflip. Immediately, it began to scrub at its face, trying to dislodge the fiery pellets.

In an instant, its forepaws were covered with fire.

Minick was a little slow; even in an emergency, he couldn't act without his usual care. On this occasion, however, he was quick enough. Before the cat could turn, he stepped forward and splashed its back with the contents of his first bucket.

More sheepdung.

This time, the creature's scream seemed to come from the marrow of its bones. It wrenched itself around in a circle and rammed its burning side into the dirt to extinguish the fire of the pellets.

Abruptly, five or six more men rushed into the street, carrying buckets and baskets and pots of sheepdung; they hurled more fuel into the cat's flames. Stooping to his tub, Tholden shoveled up great handfuls of pellets. Minick emptied his second bucket at the mounting conflagration.

Then all the men had to stop, had to draw back. The creature had begun to burn so hotly that they couldn't get near it. Terisa put up her hands to protect her face.

With a sizzling noise like the shriek of meat on a griddle, of hot iron in oil, the firecat died horribly, consumed by its own blaze.

Tholden staggered, stumbled to his knees; his scorched and beardless face gaped at the charred carcass.

Slowly, the Domne limped around the circle of heat to his eldest son. Minick, Geraden, and Terisa followed; they were there when the Domne put his arms around Tholden's bloody back.

"As I said," the Domne murmured in a voice congested with pride and pain. "The right man for the job."

Before Terisa could think of it, Geraden left to go get Quiss.

Quiss took care of her husband grimly. Like the Domne's, her emotions were too strong—and too mixed—to let her be calm about Tholden's condition.

Standing in the street with his canes propped under his hands, the Domne rallied his bowmen and put them in charge of the hunt for the remaining wolves.

Gently, Minick helped Stead out of the Domne's house. Together, the brothers set about organizing the evacuation of Houseldon.

The firecat's blaze was too well established to be fought. Even without the distraction and damage of the wolves, with nothing on their minds except the safety of their homes, the Domne's people might not have been able to beat this fire. But the truth was that they were seriously distracted, badly hurt. And there might be more attacks— When Minick suggested fighting the flames, the Domne forbade him flatly.

Instead of trying uselessly to save Houseldon, every man, woman, and child who could move himself, lift weight, or accept responsibility was put to work getting supplies and possessions, horses and livestock, infants and invalids out of the stockade.

Geraden ignored all this activity. Taking Terisa with him, he put together a breakfast for the two of them, then found a quiet corner in his father's house where they could eat in peace.

Baffled, she asked him what he thought he was doing.

"Saving time," he muttered through a cold chicken sandwich. "We've got to eat sometime. Better now than later."

That didn't shed any light. She tried again. "What's going to happen?"

"They'll go up to the Closed Fist and dig in. With all the stuff they have to carry, they won't get there for two or three days. But I don't think that matters. If Eremis had anything else ready to attack with, he would have used it by now. I think the first danger is over. And once they're entrenched in those caves and rocks, he'll need an army to root them out."

Terisa didn't understand him at all. Dimly, it occurred to her that the Closed Fist would be an impossible place in which to work glass. "You keep saying 'they.' Aren't you going with them?"

He shook his head and tried to hide the gleam in his eyes.

She studied him as if she had become stupid. His home was in flames around him. Soon Houseldon would be reduced to ashes and cinders. The survivors were being forced into hiding. One of his brothers had been seriously hurt. People he had known all his life were dead. Really, it was astonishing how much his mood had improved.

He was hard and strong, she could see that; but the grim iron was gone, the bitterness. Last night, he had remembered how to laugh. The shine in his gaze promised that he would be able to laugh again.

Looking at him, the numbness which too much fear and destruction had imposed on her heart began to fade. Almost smiling, as if she already knew the answer, she asked, "Why not?"

He shrugged cheerfully. "I've been looking at everything backward. My usual instinct for mishap. In a sense, what happened today is good news. What Eremis did today is good news. It means he's afraid of us—too afraid to wait until he can strike intelligently and be sure of killing us. He thinks there's something we can do to hurt him.

"If he thinks that, he's probably right. He's too smart to scare himself over nothing. All we have to do is find it."

Incongruously, while Houseldon burned, Terisa felt some of the past night's joy come back. "Maybe his plans aren't ready," she said. "Maybe we still have time to warn Orison."

"Right. And along the way we can try to warn some of the lords. When they know what's going on, maybe the Fayle or even the Termigan can be persuaded to do something against him."

She couldn't help herself; she jumped up and kissed him, hugged him so hard she thought her arms would break.

"Come on, mooncalves," Stead snorted from the doorway. "The fire's already on the other side of the lane. This house is going next."

In response, both Terisa and Geraden started to laugh.

They left Houseldon holding hands.

By midmorning, the Domne's seat was little more than a smoldering husk.

From his stretcher, Tholden watched the ruin and wept as if he had failed; but his father would have none of it. "Don't be silly, boy. You saved all our lives. Houses can be built again. You saved your *people*. I call it a great victory. Nobody else could have done it."

"That's right, Da," Quiss said because her husband was too emotional to reply. "He'll agree with you when he's had a little rest. If he knows what's good for him."

Ignoring embarrassment, Geraden kissed all three of them. Quiss and the Domne kissed Terisa. Then Terisa and Geraden went to their horses, the bay and the appaloosa which had brought them down from the Closed Fist.

"Now it's your turn, Geraden," the Domne announced in front of all the inhabitants of Houseldon. "Make us proud of you. Make what we're doing worthwhile." Then he added, "And, in the name of sanity, remember to call me 'Da.'"

Helplessly, Geraden colored.

Terisa wanted to laugh again. "Don't worry, Da. I won't let him forget."

When the Domne's people began cheering, she and Geraden rode away to meet Mordant's need.

THIRTY-FOUR:
FRUSTRATED
STATES

oward the end of the first day of the siege—the day which eventually led to Master Quillon's murder and Terisa's escape—Prince Kragen indicated his ruined catapults and asked the lady Elega what she thought he should do.

"Attack," she replied at once. "Attack and attack."

Raising one eyebrow, he waited for an explanation.

"I am no Imager—but everyone knows that Imagery requires strength and concentration. Translations are exhausting. And in this"—she gestured at the catapults—"you have only one opponent. Only one Master can use the glass which frustrates you. He must be weary by now. Perhaps he has already worn out his endurance.

"If you apply enough pressure, he must fail. Then you will be able to bring down that curtain-wall. Orison will be opened to you."

Despite his confident demeanor, his air of assurance, Prince Kragen couldn't restrain a scowl. "My lady," he asked softly, harshly, "how many siege engines do you think I have? They are difficult to move. If we had brought them from Alend, we would be on the road yet—and Cadwal's victory would be unchallenged. We were forced to rely on what we could appropriate from the Armigite." Thinking about the Armigite always made Kragen want to spit. "It seems likely to me that we will run out of catapults before that cursed Imager is exhausted.

"Then, my lady"—almost involuntarily, he wrapped his fingers around her arm and squeezed to get her attention, make her hear the things he didn't say—"our first, quickest, and best hope will be lost."

"Then what do you mean to do, my lord Prince?" demanded Elega. Apparently, she didn't hear him. Perhaps she couldn't. "Are you prepared to simply *wait* here until the High King arrives to crush you?"

Prince Kragen lifted his head. Too many of his people were watching. By an act of will, he smoothed his scowl, put on a sharp smile.

"I am prepared to do what I must."

Bowing to conceal the grimness in his eyes, he walked away.

That night, covered by the dark, he sent a squadron of sappers to try to dig the keystones out of the curtain-wall.

Another failure. Scant moments after his men set to work, Orison's defenders poured oil down the face of the wall and fired it. The flames forced the sappers back—and gave enough light for Lebbick's archers. Less than half the squadron escaped.

The next morning, when he had had time to absorb the latest news, Prince Kragen announced that he would take no more risks.

He didn't withdraw from his position. He spent all his time projecting confidence to his forces, or designing contingency plans with his captains, or consulting with the Alend Monarch. But he took no chances, incurred no losses. He might have been waiting for High King Festten to join him in some elaborate and harmless wargame.

Elega understood why he did this. He told her why, publicly and privately. And his explanations made sense. Nevertheless his passivity drove her to distraction. At times, she couldn't face him under the eyes of his troops; at times, she could hardly bring herself to be civil to him in bed. She wanted *action*—wanted the wall down, the battle joined; she wanted King Joyse deposed, and Prince Kragen in his place.

She wanted the fact that she had betrayed her own father to mean something. While the Alend forces spent their time in training or leisure—enjoying the suddenly beautiful spring—instead of in bringing Orison to its knees, everything she had done was pointless.

She kept track of the days; nearly kept track of the hours, gnawing them like a dry bone. It was late in the evening of the fifth day

of Kragen's inactivity, the sixth day of the siege, while she waited in
her tent for the Prince to finish discussing his day and his plans with
Margonal, that a soldier from one of the sentry posts brought her a
visitor.

"Forgive the intrusion, my lady." The soldier was a wary old
veteran, and he appeared unsure that he was doing the right thing.
"Wouldn't trouble you with her, but she wasn't trying to sneak into
camp. Walked right up to the sentry and asked to see you. Isn't
carrying any weapons—not even a knife. I said I would take her to
the Prince. Or at least the sentry captain. She said she didn't think
that was a good idea. Said if I brought her here you could decide
what to do with her."

Elega made an effort to be patient with all this explanation.
"Who is she?"

The soldier shifted his weight uncomfortably. "Says she's your
sister."

Elega blinked at him while the blood seemed to drain out of
her heart.

Carefully, so that her voice wouldn't betray her, she replied,
"You did well. You can leave her with me. I'll decide what to do
with her when I hear what she has to say."

The soldier lifted his shoulders in a small shrug. Pushing the
tentflap aside, he ushered Myste into Elega's presence.

The two sisters stood as if they were stunned and stared at each
other. The soldier left them alone, closed the tentflap behind him;
they stood and stared at each other.

Physically, Elega was in her element. She was wrapped in a gauzy
robe the Prince liked. Lamps and candlelight brought out the lustre
of her short, blond hair, the beauty of her pale skin, the vividness
of her violet eyes. In contrast, Myste needed sunshine to look her
best. Indoors, by the light of fires, she tended to appear sullen or
dreamy, and her gaze had a faraway quality that gave the impression
she was immersed in her own thoughts—less interested in events
around her than Elega was; therefore less important. Her thick cloak
had seen hard use.

Yet Myste had changed—Elega saw that at once. Her carriage
had become straighter; the set of her shoulders and the lift of her
chin made her look like a woman who had lost her doubts. A scar
that looked like a healed burn ran from her cheekbone to her ear
on the right side; instead of marring her beauty, however, it had the

effect of increasing her air of conviction. She had earned whatever certainty she felt. For the first time in their lives, Myste's simple presence caused Elega to feel smaller in some way, less sure of herself.

A quick intuition told her that Myste had done something that would make her own efforts to shape Mordant's fate appear trivial by comparison.

Myste met Elega's regard for a long moment. Then, slowly, she began to smile.

It was too much, that smile; it was the way their father used to smile, back in the days when he was still himself; a smile like a sunrise. She couldn't bear it: her eyes filled with tears.

"Oh, Myste," she breathed. "You scared me to death, disappearing like that. I thought you were dead long ago."

Helplessly, she opened her arms and caught her sister in a tight hug.

"I am sorry," Myste whispered while they clung to each other. "I know you were scared. I had no wish to do it that way. I had no other choice."

Awkwardly, Elega stepped back, wiped her eyes, found a handkerchief and blew her nose. "You rotten child," she said, smiling gamely.

Myste smiled back and borrowed the handkerchief when Elega was done with it.

"Do you remember?" Elega murmured. "I used to call you that. When we were little. When I did something forbidden and got into trouble, I used to try to blame it on you. Even when you were so small you could hardly walk, I used to try to convince Mother you tricked me into—whatever it was. I told her you were a rotten child."

Lightly, Myste laughed. "No, I do not remember. I was too young. Anyway, I can hardly believe you ever tried to pass responsibility off on anyone else." She sighed as if the sight of her sister gave her great pleasure. "And now after all these years I have proved that you were right."

"Yes, you have." Elega wanted to joke, and laugh, and yell at Myste, all at the same time. "Completely despicable." She tried to pull some organization into her head, keep her thoughts from spinning out of control. "Sit down. Have some wine." She pointed toward a pair of canvas camp chairs beside a small, brass table. "I really am delighted to see you. I have been so alone—" But she couldn't do it; Myste's unexpected appearance made her brain reel. "Oh, Myste, *where have you been?*"

A hint of self-consciousness touched Myste's gaze. No, Elega realized almost at once, it was more than self-consciousness. It was caution. Slowly, Myste's smile faded.

"That is a long story," she replied quietly. "I have come to you because I must make a number of decisions. Among them is whether I should tell you where I have been and what I have been doing."

More than self-consciousness. More than caution.

Distrust.

Elega felt like crying again.

At the same time, however, her own instinct for caution sprang awake. The Alend camp was a dangerous place in more ways than one; it was especially dangerous for a daughter of King Joyse who hadn't demonstrated her loyalty to Prince Kragen.

"What is the difficulty?" she asked carefully. "I am your sister. Why should you not tell me?"

Whose side are you on?

"Thank you." Myste's manner was firm, unflawed. "I will have wine. As you see"—she dropped her cloak, revealing a battered leather jacket and pants which apparently had nothing in the world to do with lovers and bedchambers—"amenities have been few in my life for some time."

But Elega couldn't respond. She was too busy fighting down an impulse to demand, *Whose side are you on?*

"Elega," sighed Myste, "I cannot tell you my story because I do not know why you are here. I do not know how an Alend army came to besiege Orison. I do not know"—for an instant, she blinked back tears of her own—"if our father still lives, or still holds his throne. Or still seems mad.

"I can decide nothing wisely without the answers to such questions.

"I knew that you were here," she explained. "I saw you ride with Prince Kragen to meet Castellan Lebbick on the day Orison was invested. The distance was considerable," she admitted, "but I was sure I saw you. It has taken me this long, however, to per-suade"—she faltered oddly—"persuade myself to approach you."

Obviously trying to defuse Elega's tension, she asked pleadingly, "*May* I have some wine?"

"Of course. Surely." Jerking herself out of her paralysis, Elega went to the brass table. It held a jug and two goblets. Despite the possibility that she might eventually have to explain to the Prince how his goblet came to be used in his absence, she poured wine for herself and Myste, then sat down and urged Myste to do the same.

Myste accepted the chair and the wine. Over the goblet's rim as she drank, another sun dawned in her eyes. When she lowered the goblet, she grinned longingly past Elega's shoulder. "That is good. I wish I could take a hogshead of it with me."

A few swallows of wine helped restore Elega's composure. With a better grasp on herself, she asked, "Why do you speak of going? You have only just arrived. And"—she attempted her best smile— "you have not yet said anything I can understand about why you came in the first place."

Myste drank again, then held the goblet in both palms and gazed into its depths. "I came to ask the answers to questions, so that I can make my decisions with some hope that they will lead to good rather than ill."

"In other words"—Elega kept her voice steady—"you wish me to trust you enough to help you decide whether you can trust me." Her question refused to be stifled. "Myste, who has your allegiance now? Whom do you serve?"

Myste's eyes darkened. All at once, the distance in them seemed poignant to Elega. Myste was the youngest of the King's daughters, and in some ways the least respected; alone in her romantic dreams, her strange notion that there were no real limits to the lives of ordinary men and women. Only her father had ever listened to her with anything except kind contempt or outright mockery—and now his kingdom was in ruins, and the fault for it was his alone.

Yet here she was, clad more completely in her own courage than in the worn leather on her body. It was quite possible that she was out of her mind. How else to explain the fact that she was here, that she considered it reasonable to simply walk into the Alend camp and ask for answers? Even if she were sane, she had become something Elega didn't know how to evaluate or touch.

On the other hand, what harm could she do, one brave, foolish daughter of a failed King? Was it conceivable that she had somehow gone over to Cadwal? No. The High King's army was too far away— and the Perdon's forces still intervened. Then what harm could she do?

Why, none.

She made no attempt to answer Elega's question. After a long moment, Elega let it drop. Feeling an unexpected sympathy—and a hint of nameless admiration—toward her lonely sister, she decided suddenly, irrationally, to gamble. "Very well," she said. After all, risks came to her more naturally than caution. Prince Kragen's inaction had her at her wit's end. "Ask me something specific."

Her words lit a spark in Myste's gaze.

Myste raised an unself-conscious hand to her cheek. "Again, thank you," she murmured. "It will be a great service to me."

Almost at once, she inquired, "Is Father well? Is he"—she swallowed quickly—"still alive?"

"To the best of my knowledge." As soon as she heard the question, Elega's throat went dry. "It has been some days since I spoke to him." Now that she had decided to gamble, she realized that her own story would be hard to tell. Myste's fundamental assumptions were so different. "Nevertheless emissaries and messengers such as the Castellan and Master Quillon make reference to him without hesitation. He remains King in his own castle, even though his rule over Mordant has collapsed."

Myste let a breath of relief between her lips. "I am glad," she said, nodding to herself.

"And Terisa? How is she?"

Elega muffled her discomfort with asperity. "I fear that the lady Terisa has fallen victim to Geraden's instinct for mishap."

"How so?" Myste's tone conveyed a suggestion of alarm.

Remembering the reservoir, Elega drawled, "She has learned to make the same mistakes he does."

Again, Myste nodded; she clearly didn't understand what Elega meant—and didn't want to pursue it. She thought for a moment, then asked slowly, as if she wanted better words, "Elega, *why* are you here? If our father still rules in Orison, how have you come to take the part of his enemies?"

There it was: the place where all their common ground fell away, the point on which they would never comprehend each other. If the truth hit Myste too hard, Elega might be forced to summon guards and have her sister delivered to Prince Kragen.

Nevertheless she was faithful to the risk she'd chosen. Dryly, she replied, "That is the wrong question, Myste. You should ask why the Prince and his forces are here. My reasons hinge on theirs."

Myste studied her intently. "I suspected as much. That is why

I feared for Father. I thought the Alends might have come because he was dead. But I had no wish to offend you by leaping to erroneous conclusions.

"When I left Orison, Prince Kragen had been insulted in the hall of audiences. Yet the fact that he remained made me think that he had not given up hope for peace.

"Why *is* he here, attempting to pull the King from his Seat?"

"Because," Elega answered, bracing herself for Myste's reaction, "I persuaded him to do it."

In a sense, Myste didn't react at all; she simply went still, like an animal in hiding. The change was so unlike her, however, that it seemed as vehement as a shout. Where had she learned so much self-possession—and so much caution?

"I made his acquaintance after his audience with the King." Elega struggled to keep a defensive tone out of her voice. "He taught me to believe him when he said that Margonal's desire for peace was sincere. Yet Alend faced a dilemma he must resolve. Cadwal has no desire for peace—and the King's strength had become plainly in-adequate to keep the Congery out of Festten's hands. Alend must take some action, so that the High King would not gain all Imagery for himself.

"First I required of the Prince some indication of his good faith. He replied with the promise that if Orison fell to him he would make the Perdon King of Mordant—that Alend would keep nothing for itself if the Congery was made safe from Cadwal.

"Then I persuaded him that a siege was his best hope."

"But, Elega," Myste protested, "that is untrue. Father is the only man who has ever taken Orison by storm. A siege may well last for seasons. And High King Festten surely will not allow seasons to pass before he comes to prevent the Alend Monarch from claiming the Congery."

"It *is* true," insisted Elega. Honesty, however, forced her to admit, "Or it *was*. Two things made it so. First, the curtain-wall is fragile at best—and no one could have foreseen that one of the Masters would conceive a way to defend it.

"And second—"

Involuntarily, she wavered. This lay at the heart of her ache for action, her desire to see the siege succeed. It was her doing: she had convinced Kragen to attempt it.

If he held her to blame for her failure, he gave no sign of it.

Perhaps he had accepted the hazards of what he did, and felt no recrimination. Or perhaps he found a new hope in the reasons for his present inaction. In either case, she blamed herself enough for both of them. Sure of herself, determined to save her world, she had taken Mordant's fate in her own hands.

And she had dropped it.

"Second?" Myste prompted.

"Second," said Elega, more harshly than she intended, "I promised to deliver Orison to him with little or no bloodshed."

Myste sat completely still; not a muscle in her face shifted. Yet her eyes seemed to burn with outrage.

"How?"

Elega's knuckles tightened on her goblet. "By poisoning the reservoir. Not fatally. But enough to indispose the defense until the castle could be taken."

Without a flicker of expression, almost without moving her mouth, Myste said, "That should have sufficed. What went wrong?"

Deliberately, Elega permitted herself an obscenity which she knew Myste particularly disliked. Then she said, "Geraden and Terisa caught me. They were unable to stop me—or indeed capture me. But they warned the Castellan. No one was indisposed because no one drank the water. The defense holds—and I was forced to flee."

Unable to contain her self-disgust, she concluded, "Does that answer your questions? Can you make your decisions wisely now?"

Gradually, Myste let herself move. Her gaze left Elega's face; she lifted her goblet and drained it. Automatically, far away in her thoughts, she poured more wine and drank again.

"Ah, Elega. How terrible that must be for you—to attempt the betrayal of your own home and family, and to fail."

"It is worse," retorted Elega fiercely, "to do *nothing*—to let every good thing in the world go to ruin because the man who created it cannot be bothered to defend it."

Still slowly, still peering into the distance, Myste nodded. "Perhaps. That is one of the decisions I must make.

"Please tell me. Why does the Prince 'do nothing'? Since the first day of the siege, he has taken no action I can see. To all appearances, he is simply waiting for High King Festten to come and destroy him."

Abruptly, as if a stunned part of her mind had just been kicked,

Elega realized that Prince Kragen was overdue. Usually, he finished discussing the day with his father and came to her tent before this.

If he caught Myste here, he would have no real choice but to make her a prisoner. Her potential value as King Joyse's daughter was too great to be ignored. But Myste was also Elega's sister—and Elega wasn't sure yet what her own decision would be. The only thing she was sure of was that Myste wouldn't reveal any of her secrets as Prince Kragen's prisoner.

Muttering, "Wait here," Elega jumped up and hurried past the curtains into the back of the tent.

There she roused the Alend girl who served as her maid. "Hurry, child," she hissed. "Find the Prince. He may still be with his father, or on his way here. Beg him to forgive me. Tell him I feel unwell. Tell him I am half blind with headache—but it will pass if I am allowed to sleep.

"Go quickly."

She hustled the girl out into the night, paused to quiet the hammering of her heart, then returned to Myste.

Myste looked at her inquiringly. Elega explained what she had done—and was more relieved than she considered reasonable when she saw that Myste believed her. So Myste's new caution, her distrust, had its limits. Despite the things Elega had already done, Myste didn't expect her sister to betray her.

In the back of her mind, Elega began to wonder whose side she herself was on.

She sat down again, poured more wine. Myste was still waiting for an explanation of Prince Kragen's inaction. Elega took a deep breath because for the first time what she was about to say might be interpreted as evidence of disloyalty. Then she asked, "Do you remember the day we first met Terisa? The day the Perdon came storming into Orison, demanding help, and King Joyse refused him?"

"Yes." Once again, Myste's sober gaze was fixed on Elega's face.

"I think I told you about it." Elega remembered the Perdon's rage vividly. *You tell him* this, *my lady,* he had roared at her. *Every man of mine who falls or dies defending him in his blind inaction, I will send* here. "Well, he is doing what he said he would. In small groups and squadrons, injured or dead men and their families arrive almost daily from the Care of Perdon, sent to the purported safety of Orison—and as a reproach to King Joyse.

"They are Alend prisoners now—although it would be more

just to say that they are under the care of the army's physicians, and not permitted to leave. Being hurt, exhausted, or bereaved, few of them have the will to refuse when they are questioned."

Myste watched Elega's face and said nothing.

"From them," Elega sighed, "we have learned that the High King's army is not coming here."

At that, Myste's eyes widened. "Not?" she whispered as if she couldn't believe what she was hearing. "Not?"

Elega nodded. "Not directly, in any case. That much is certain. Festten's forces move with what speed they can manage through the hills of Perdon—through the Perdon's resistance. But all recent reports agree that the High King's movement brings him no nearer Orison.

"That is why Prince Kragen believes he can afford to wait."

At last, Myste sounded like her self-control might slip. "Then where is High King Festten going?"

"South and west," Elega answered. "Into the Care of Tor.

"The Perdon's survivors say that the Cadwal army moves along the best route it can find toward Marshalt, the Tor's seat."

"But *why?*" demanded Myste. "Why go *there?* The Congery is *here.*"

Elega had no idea. "I have heard it rumored," she said for the sake of hearing how Myste would reply, "that the Castellan considers the Tor a traitor."

Myste's head twitched. "The Tor? Nonsense." She thought for a moment, then continued, "And if he *is* a traitor, that would be even less reason for High King Festten to invade Tor. It makes no sense.

"What is the Perdon doing?"

To preserve her composure, Elega put on a hard front. "Apparently, he is more dedicated to Mordant's service than his King deserves." The truth was that every thought of the Perdon made her chest ache—made her want to scream because there was nothing she could do. "Festten appears uninterested in Orison. But rather than taking this opportunity to flee—perhaps here, perhaps toward a dubious alliance with the Armigite, or a stronger one with the Fayle— the Perdon shifts his forces so that they are always in Cadwal's way. He began with scarcely three thousand men against at least twenty thousand. If the reports are true, he has less than two thousand now, and every day he is whittled down. And yet he continues fighting.

He spends every life in his command merely to hinder Festten's approach to whatever it is the High King wants.

"Clearly, he is engaged in a personal struggle against Cadwal. If King Joyse had not abandoned him long ago, he would have saved himself—and aided Orison—by coming here.

"Does *that* answer your questions?"

While Elega spoke, Myste's expression changed. Her gaze turned toward Orison; her eyes filled with tears. "Oh, Father," she murmured thickly. "How have you been brought to this? How do you bear it?"

Elega's urge to scream intensified. "If it does," she snapped, "perhaps you will consent to answer mine. I have told you enough to get myself beheaded if I were not in the Prince's favor. I would like some return for my risk."

"Yes." Suddenly, Myste rose to her feet, facing through the wall of the tent toward Orison as though Elega weren't present. "I can make my decisions now. Thank you.

"I must go."

Without a glance at her sister, she started toward the tentflap.

For an instant, Elega was stuck, caught between contradictory reactions. She was full of outrage; she wanted to make scathing demands which would rip Myste's reticence aside. At the same time, the thought that her sister was about to leave her—without trusting her, without *trusting* her—went into her heart like a spike.

She was about to shout for a soldier when a new thought flashed through her like a bolt of illumination.

Before her sister reached the tentflap, she said, "Father sent me a message, Myste."

Myste stopped immediately; she turned, came back toward Elega. As if involuntarily, she asked, "What was it?"

Too absorbed in Myste's importance to be self-conscious, Elega answered, "Castellan Lebbick brought it. According to him, father said, 'I am sure that my daughter Elega has acted for the best reasons. She carries my pride with her wherever she goes. For her sake, as well as for my own, I hope that the best reasons will also produce the best results.'"

Unexpectedly, Myste closed her eyes. Tears spread under her lashes and down her cheeks, but for a long moment she didn't move or speak. Then she looked radiantly at her sister, smiling like a new day.

"Of course," she breathed. "Why did I not see it for myself?"

At once, she returned to her chair. Smiling so beautifully that she wrung Elega's heart, she said, "Very well. Ask me something specific."

Elega gaped at her—gaped like a fish until Myste started laughing.

Elega couldn't help herself; she was suddenly so full of joy and relief and confusion that she laughed herself.

After a while, Myste subsided. "Ah, Elega, we have not done that together since we were girls."

Mocking her own dignity, Elega replied primly, "Do not be arrogant, child. You are hardly old enough yet to be called a woman."

Myste chuckled happily. For a moment, the only thing that prevented her from looking like the Myste Elega remembered—romantic and dear, vaguely foolish, not to be taken seriously—was the scar on her cheek.

But that scar changed everything. It made the new Myste impossible to ignore or forget. She inspired a rush of confusion in Elega.

"Myste, where *were* you? Where did you go? *Why* did you go? And those *clothes*. What have you been doing all this time?"

"Elega," Myste protested humorously, "I said, 'Ask me something *specific*.'" But then she sighed, and slowly the laughter faded from her face. "Well, I will tell you." Her expression became one Elega didn't know how to interpret: sober and contemplative; a little sad; a little excited. "If you do not take it well, however, there will be trouble for us all.

"I left Orison to search for the Congery's champion."

Elega was so surprised that she cried, "You did *what?*" before she could catch herself.

The Myste Elega used to know would have flinched or blushed; she might have hung her head or sounded defensive. The new Myste did none of these things. She only raised her head slightly, squared her jaw a bit, and repeated, "I left Orison to search for the Congery's champion."

A moment later, she added, "Terisa helped me."

Take it well. Elega didn't want to make a fool of herself, so she stared at her sister and said nothing.

"I went from her rooms through the secret passages down to the breach he made in the wall. It was not very well guarded then, so I was able to escape without being seen. From there, I followed his trail in the snow."

Elega stared, waiting for Myste to say or do something that made sense.

"Eventually," Myste continued, "I caught up with him. He was hurt, not able to move quickly. In fact, he was down in the snow, bleeding his life into his armor.

"I startled him—he thought he was being attacked again." Myste's tone remained mild and firm. "He fired at me." She touched her cheek. "Fortunately, he did little harm. Then he saw that I was a woman, and dropped his weapon. I was able to approach him."

Elega forced herself to blink her eyes, clear her throat, shake some of the astonishment out of her head. Carefully, she said, "Go back to the beginning. Tell me why."

"Why?" Myste's gaze drifted into the distance. "Why not? There were so many reasons. There was Father's strange decline, his impulse of destruction—and our helplessness, which I enjoyed no more than you did. There was Terisa, who faced a world she did not know or understand with more courage and resourcefulness than I could find in myself. And there was the dishonesty of the Congery's action."

"'Dishonesty'?" objected Elega. "The Masters were trying to defend Mordant. The translation of their champion was the only action they could have taken that might have aided us."

"No." Myste was certain. "I will not speak of the ethical question—whether it is ever permissible to impose an involuntary translation on any living thing. But the Masters were not honest with themselves. They claim that they translated their champion in response to Mordant's need, trying to find the hope of their auguries—but how did they expect him to react to what they did? He was injured—he and all his men were embattled for their lives—and suddenly he found himself in another world." Her voice took on a hint of passion. "What could he think? Surely he could think nothing except that this change was yet another attack by his enemies.

"If the Masters had been honest, they would have admitted that the only way such a champion could ever become an ally of theirs was if they approached him peacefully, unthreateningly, rather than playing upon his instinct for violence."

In some ways, Elega found Myste's argument as surprising as her previous revelations. What she said seemed perfectly clear, eminently logical. Elega wasn't accustomed to hearing her sister reason in such terms.

"I never thought of it that way," she admitted. Then she added almost accusingly, "But you did. And you decided to do something about it."

Myste shrugged as if to dismiss the suggestion that she had shown bravery or initiative. "The Fayle attempted to warn Father of the Masters' intention. When Father permitted that translation to take place, I realized that if I remained where I was and did nothing I would begin to hate him. And when I conceived the idea of trying to help the champion, my heart lifted."

Speaking dryly to control herself, Elega said, "So you put on your warm clothes and went out into a hard winter for the sake of a warrior who might kill you as soon as he saw you. For no reason, really, except that you felt sorry for him."

A small smile touched Myste's lips.

"And you found him and helped him. How was that possible? Was he a man inside his armor?"

"Oh, yes. Different in little ways—but very much like us. Like us in everything that matters."

To Elega's renewed amazement, Myste blushed. Myste hurried on promptly, however.

"Like Terisa, he speaks our language—perhaps because of the translation. His name is Darsint," she commented by the way. "His instructions enabled me to get him from his armor and tend his wound. His weapon made a fire for us easily, and I had food.

"Since then, we have been together, hiding when we can, fleeing when we must. Shelter and even food have been simple to find in abandoned villages and farms—"

"And since the army's arrival," Elega interrupted, speaking in a rush to catch up with the implications of what her sister revealed, "you have been watching us. *Together*—you and the Congery's champion. You said it took you several days to persuade yourself to come to me. It was not *you* you had to persuade, it was *him*. You are his knowledge, his guide."

Inspired by the fire of ideas in her head, she paused to say, "His lover." The mind which aims the weapon. Then she sped on.

"*That* is the decision you have had to make. You are companion to the mightiest man in any of the kingdoms. He loves you—he is dependent on you. And you must decide how to use his power."

Now it was Myste's turn to stare. Unable to contain her sudden, urgent hope, Elega swept out of her chair to confront her sister. "Myste, you must help us.

"All that force, all that strength, only waiting to be used. Oh, my sister, why have you delayed? You can bring this siege to an end almost without effort. Do you not understand what must be done? We must take Orison. We must put an end to the King's foolish resistance, so that the battle against Mordant's true enemies can begin while the realm and the Congery remain intact."

"No, Elega." Myste came to her own feet swiftly, met Elega's passion face to face. "It is you who do not understand." Her scar made her look fiery and unanswerable. "The question I have sought to resolve is not whether I should help you, but whether I should help Orison against you.

"The Alend forces are too large for even a man with Darsint's weapons to combat alone. Also his strength goes from him with every use. The word he uses is 'recharged.' His weapons cannot be 'recharged' in this world. For that reason, we must be cautious. Nevertheless I have been thinking long and hard about the damage he could do to the Alend Monarch's army. The truth is that I have only held back because of your presence—and because of Prince Kragen's inaction."

Elega started to protest, but Myste cut her off.

"I must warn you, Elega. I am more certain now than ever that I must fight for Father and Mordant. If you require Darsint's guns to be used, they will be used against you."

"Myste," Elega gasped in dismay, "are you *mad?*"

"Only if it is madness to trust our father."

"Yes, that *is* madness! You said so yourself—you spoke of his 'strange decline, his impulse to destruction.' Were you not listening to yourself? You would not have left Orison and gone to help this Darsint if you *trusted* our father."

"Yes." Without warning, Myste's intensity broke into a grin. She seemed at once sheepish and secure. "And no. I have spent days laboring through high snow. I have tended the wounds of an alien warrior and held him in my arms. And I have heard Father's message to you. Fear and exhaustion teach many things. So does love. I have learned to think differently.

"It is hard to say that I trust his decline. But I have come to trust the fact that he allowed the Congery to work this translation.

I have even come to think that he did it for me—in the same way
that he insulted Prince Kragen for you. Do you not see how he has
made us powerful? I can guide Darsint's choices. I can ask his help.
And you are in a place to affect the actions of Alend's entire army."

*I am sure that my daughter Elega has acted for the best reasons. For
her sake, as well as for my own, I hope that the best reasons will also
produce the best results.*

"Elega, we are doing what he intended us to do. He has plans
for us. Perhaps his decline itself is only a goad to make us do what
we can."

Elega floundered in her sister's smile. This optimistic interpretation of the King's behavior was insane. "Myste, you are a fool,"
she muttered as if she were speaking to herself. "A fool." King Joyse
had driven his own wife away rather than make the effort to defend
his kingdom. Or to explain himself. Piece by piece, he had chipped
the hope and trust out of Elega's heart. "Are you not hurt? Do the
things he has done not cause you any pain?"

"Of course they do." Myste's smile became fond and sad at the
same time. "I only say that there is another way to look at what he
has done. We ask ourselves whether he deserves our faith. But we
do not have his burdens. *He* is the King. We should ask, I think,
whether we deserve his faith.

"It appears to me that he has tried to let us know that he trusts
us.

"Elega, do you never ask yourself what kind of man he must
be, to place his trust in the people he has most hurt? Between us,
we have the might to destroy him. Darsint's weapons and the Prince's
army could accomplish that. And our father has pushed us into this
position.

"Either his lunacy is complete, or his need for us is so desperate
that he cannot explain what he wants without making what he wants
impossible."

Groping, Elega asked, "What do you mean? What can you possibly mean?"

Myste shrugged. "Oh, I mean nothing. I only speculate. But
suppose"—her gaze came into focus on her sister—"it is in some
way vital to Father's defense of Mordant that you are trusted by the
Prince. How can a trust like that be achieved between two such old
and mortal enemies? Any attempt to trick or mislead the Prince
would almost surely fail. You are—pardon me for saying this—not

much of a liar. You could not persuade the Prince to believe anything you did not believe yourself."

"No." Elega shook her head, not in denial, but in exasperation. "You suppose too much too quickly. How can it possibly be 'vital' to Father that Prince Kragen trusts me?"

"Elega, *think.* You have already come so close to your own answer. What did Father accomplish by refusing to reinforce the Perdon, when the Perdon came to Orison and demanded help?"

"What did he *accomplish?*"

"Or put it another way. What would have happened when Cadwal marched if the Perdon had been supported by several thousand guards? As you have observed, the Perdon would have retreated *here,* to preserve his forces and defend his King. And High King Festten could not have permitted an enemy that strong to disengage, to maneuver freely. He would have been forced to follow.

"By refusing to reinforce the Perdon, Father made it possible that the Cadwals would not come here directly.

"Do you still not understand, Elega?"

"Time," Elega breathed. At last, she seemed to be catching up. "Since Cadwal is not here, Alend can afford to wait. By refusing to support the Perdon, he gained time."

"Yes!" Myste whispered.

"And by pushing us where we are, he also gained time. He made it possible that I might use my influence with the Prince to encourage inaction. But primarily"—Elega was amazed by how convincing she found this—"he pushed us to be where we are so that if the Prince attacked fiercely you would defend Orison—and so the Alend attack would be frustrated—and because you and I are sisters we might find a way to keep the violence between our forces to a minimum."

"Yes," repeated Myste. Her manner began to relax.

"But *why?*" Elega didn't know whether to laugh or shriek. "*Why* does he need time? What is he *doing?* What is his plan? How can he believe that Mordant will be saved by the things he has done to destroy it?"

Apparently, Myste felt no need to shriek. Chuckling softly, she said, "If I knew *that*—if I could so much as make an intelligent guess—I would tell it to Prince Kragen myself."

Unexpectedly, Elega also began chuckling. "So this is all talk? You can think of no reason why Father might need time—therefore no reason to believe he actually does need time—therefore no reason to trust any of your speculations?"

Myste shook her head cheerfully. "None."

"Except," Elega murmured after a moment, "for the fact that it all seems too tidy to be accidental."

Myste's smile was so complete that it made even the burn on her cheek look like a mark of beauty.

Elega sighed. Slowly, her inexplicable humor faded. "I must say, Myste," she commented, "that I have a powerful wish to make you tell all this to Prince Kragen anyway. Unfortunately, he would make you a prisoner. He would want to use you as a lever against Father— or against your champion."

"In that case," Myste replied, "Darsint would come for me. I doubt that he would be inclined to let me be used as a lever."

"And Alends would be killed," added Elega. "And the force in his weapons might be exhausted. And nothing would be gained."

"That"—Myste grinned sharply, like a woman who had learned to enjoy risks—"is the reasoning I used to persuade him to let me come to you."

As a final surprise in an evening full of surprises, Elega found that she had never liked her sister as much as she did at this moment. "In that case," she drawled, "it behooves me, I think, to help you leave the camp before any word of your visit reaches Prince Kragen. Come, get your cloak. We will take a few skins of this wine with us and go out the back."

Before they left, she and Myste shared a hug as if they had recognized each other for the first time.

The next morning, after he had received the night's reports from his captains, Prince Kragen called Elega out of her tent.

She had never seen him so angry. Even his moustache seemed to have been waxed with outrage.

"My lady," he said, "last night a woman entered the camp. She claimed to be your sister. She was taken to your tent."

Elega faced him boldly, hiding the fright in her heart. "Yes, my lord Prince. My sister Myste."

"The one who disappeared after the Imagers translated their champion." That may have been all he knew about her. "Where is she now?"

Remembering that she was a bad liar, Elega held his gaze and replied, "We talked for a long time. Then I helped her to depart without bothering the sentries."

"King Joyse's daughter. One of the most valuable women in Mordant. You 'helped her to depart.'" The Prince's tone made every soldier within earshot avert his head. "Why?"

Elega did her best to smile the way Myste had smiled, as if she enjoyed risks. "Come into my tent, my lord Prince. I have a story to tell you that will make you doubt your reason."

That was why she loved him. Despite the fact that she was the daughter of his enemy—that she had betrayed her own father and might therefore be capable of betraying anyone—that she had helped another of the King's daughters escape—Prince Kragen went into her tent and heard her story.

At roughly the same hour, Artagel was given permission to leave his bed for the first time. His side was healing well, and he had been free of fever long enough to reassure his physician. In addition, ever since his delirious visit to the dungeons he had been a model patient. So he was advised to get out of bed for a little mild, repeat, *mild* exercise.

He smiled at his physician's severe manner. He smiled at the gap-toothed kitchen maid who brought his meals. He smiled at the sweep who cleaned his rooms. But he didn't actually try to stand and dress himself and walk until he was sure he wouldn't be interrupted.

He didn't want any witnesses while he tested himself to see how weak he was.

The effort of putting on a loose shirt and trousers made him sweat. Bending over to shove his feet into his boots made him light-headed. Simply lifting the weight of his longsword made him tremble. With every movement, his injury pulled as if it were about to tear open.

Grinning unsteady defiance, he left his rooms—mild exercise, *mild*—and went to see Castellan Lebbick.

He had a number of reasons for wanting to talk to the Castellan. One was that Lebbick had tried to see *him* a few days ago, and had been turned away because of his fever. Another was that—if he could be persuaded to talk—the Castellan was the best available source of information about several subjects which interested Artagel keenly: the siege; King Joyse's plans; the Congery's preparations; the search for Geraden.

Thanks to the fact that most of his friends were guards, a number of whom had come to see him while he was ill, he knew that the siege had been passive since the first day. But that could mean almost anything; he wanted to know what it *did* mean. Of course, Master Eremis' solution to the water problem was common knowledge. In addition, Artagel had heard that Master Quillon was dead, that Master Barsonage had resumed his place as mediator of the Congery. He had heard that Terisa was gone. He had even heard that there was a connection between Quillon's death and Terisa's disappearance. And just once someone—probably Artagel's physician himself—had mentioned that questions were still being asked about Underwell.

Curiosity about such things might have been enough to make Artagel visit the Castellan. He and Lebbick were old friends, after all—to the extent that the Castellan could be said to have friends. In fact, he had been Artagel's teacher and commander until Artagel had reached the point where it was no longer reasonable for anyone to tell him what to do. Because of this, he was widely believed—at least among the castle's active defenders—to be the only man in Orison who could go to the Castellan and ask him questions and actually get answers.

As it happened, however, Artagel had two additional reasons for wanting a conversation with the Castellan, reasons more compelling than any of the others.

First, he had thought long and searchingly—not his favorite form of exertion—about his last conversation with the lady Terisa, and he didn't like any of the conclusions he reached.

Second, he had heard from no less than six reliable friends that early in the morning after Terisa's disappearance Castellan Lebbick had returned to his quarters and found a woman in his bed.

Terisa's former maid, Saddith.

He had beaten her nearly to death.

Even now—what was it, five days later?—her physician wasn't sure she would ever use her hands again. And as for her face— Well, no one wanted to describe her disfigurement.

Since then, the Castellan hadn't been out of his rooms. He directed the defense of Orison entirely through an intermediary— through the one man he had chosen to bring him information and carry his instructions.

By a coincidence so odd that it made Artagel's guts knot, the man Castellan Lebbick had chosen was Ribuld, the scarred veteran who had occasionally helped protect Terisa as a favor to Geraden, and who had lost his best friend, Argus, in a failed attempt to trap Prince Kragen.

Why *Ribuld,* of all people? Lebbick had never put him in a position of responsibility before. In fact, Ribuld would have said that the Castellan never noticed him except when he did something wrong.

Even though the effort of walking made his heart labor and his bones ache, Artagel was determined to confront Castellan Lebbick and get some answers.

He didn't like remembering the way Terisa had cried at him, *Are you out of your mind? Geraden is your brother.* At the time, he hadn't understood her. Well, he had been delirious, emotionally and morally sick at what had been done to Nyle. But now her words stuck in him like an accusation.

When he arrived at Lebbick's quarters, he was a little surprised to find the door guarded. The Castellan had never felt the need for protection in his own rooms before. Nevertheless Artagel didn't hesitate. He went up to the guard on duty, a man he had known for years, and asked, "He still refusing to see anybody?"

The man nodded. Despite his evident pleasure that Artagel was out of bed at last, he commented, "And he isn't going to make an exception in your case, either."

Artagel smiled. It was probably a good thing he hadn't tried to bring his sword. He would have looked like a fool pulling it out— and then letting its weight stretch him flat on the floor. As if he'd never been ill, however, he said, "I want to go in there. You aren't really going to stand in my way."

"You're going to get past me?" the guard snorted. "In *your* condition?" But then he put up his hands. "Well, since you force me— Somebody's got to get sense out of him. Might as well be you. After what he did to that woman— If he doesn't answer for it soon, we're going to have trouble on our hands. Too many people who don't have anything better to do are getting ugly about it.

"If he hits you, give a croak, and I'll carry you back to your rooms."

Artagel faked a bow with one arm. "Thanks ever so much. It always feels good to have a man like you behind me."

"I know," the guard replied. "As far behind you as possible."

Chuckling, he opened the door.

Convinced that he really wasn't going to be able to stay on his feet much longer, Artagel entered the Castellan's quarters.

The front room was ill-lit, unswept, and undecorated—which hadn't been the case when Artagel was last here, some time before Lebbick's wife died. Although he wasn't given to luxury, the Castellan had claimed an extensive suite for himself and his wife; he had insisted for decades that they meant to have children, regardless of the damage she had suffered as an Alend prisoner. And she had humored him by keeping up their quarters like a home where children would be welcome. But since her death he had stripped the walls and floor to the bare stone; he had moved a hard cot into the front room and sealed the rest of the doors—even in Orison's overcrowded state, those rooms stood empty. And since Terisa's disappearance he had obviously given up all pretense of housekeeping. The one lamp on the table beside his cot gave just enough light to show that the room was filthy.

So was he: he hadn't shaved, or washed, or changed his clothes for days. His eyes were red with exhaustion and malice—or grief— and his hands curled in front of him as if he badly needed a sword.

Facing Artagel from the edge of his cot, he rasped distinctly, "I'm going to disembowel the man who let *you* in here."

The air was foul with dirt, rancid sweat, food gone to maggots. Artagel stifled an impulse to gag. Pretending that his nauseated expression was a smile, he replied, "No, you won't." Deliberately, he found a chair and sat down. "If you want to get him, you'll have to get me first. And you won't do that. You won't dare. I'm the most popular man in Orison."

"Hog-puke." The Castellan blinked malevolently. "Eremis is the most popular man in Orison." In spite of his tone, however, he didn't leave the bed. "You're just an invalid who's still alive because he got lucky the last time he met Gart.

"That's probably why they sent you. They think I won't hurt a man who's so weak a woman could knock him over."

Feigning nonchalance, Artagel inquired, "'They'?"

"*They.* The Tor. King Joyse. Half the rutting dogs in this stink-hole. The bastard who let you in. The ones who think Eremis is the best thing since King Joyse invented sunshine. The ones who think I ought to be castrated because I slapped that rank whore a couple of times. *They.*

"They want me to come out so they can jump me. They want you to make me come out."

"Sorry." Artagel loathed dealing with Lebbick like this; he would have preferred to meet the High King's Monomach without a sword. As a result, he sounded incongruously happy, as if he were having a wonderful time. "I hate to contradict you when you're in such a good mood. But the truth is, I don't have any idea what you're talking about. I just came to tell you Geraden didn't kill Nyle."

"*I* know *that*," snapped Lebbick. "Don't tell *me*. Tell *them*."

"Wait a minute." Artagel would have been less startled if the Castellan had started foaming at the mouth. "Wait. What do you mean, you know that? *How* do you know?"

"I know"—Castellan Lebbick glared at his visitor as if Artagel were hideous—"because that piss-drinking slut was in my bed. *In my bed.*"

Now it was Artagel's turn to blink. "Wait a minute," he repeated. "Wait."

Lebbick didn't wait. "I came right through that door"—he pointed fiercely at the door—"and she was in my *bed*." He pounded the cot. "Naked as shit. *Smiling* at me. Wagging her tits. Of *course* Geraden didn't kill Nyle."

Then his ferocity dimmed. "I would have believed anybody except that woman."

Artagel held his breath and said nothing.

"She made me think about it over and over again. She kept making me go back to the beginning. But when she was wrong about that secret passage— I was *sure*. And I saw her escaping, I *saw* her. With Quillon. King Joyse's friend. Then I found his body. I caught up with her. She was with Gilbur. I was *sure*. Gilbur *told* me they were allies. Of course I was sure. Of course Geraden killed Nyle. She must have escaped with Gilbur, not Quillon. She was a traitor, a murderer. That proved Geraden was guilty.

"Isn't that what *they* told you?"

"No," Artagel murmured. "They haven't told me a thing."

"Well, they will," Lebbick snarled. "Give them a chance. They're all talking about me. They whisper behind my back." A wild grin stretched his mouth. "Eremis is a hero. Everything that woman said about him is a lie. Geraden killed Nyle. She put him up to it. She helped him escape. Then Gilbur helped her escape. They killed Quillon. I'm a monster. Nobody understands why King Joyse hasn't had me gutted.

"Eremis is a hero."

Groping for some measure of sanity in the conversation, Artagel drawled, "I doubt it. Terisa must have told you Nyle is still alive. She certainly tried to tell me.

"I didn't believe her," he admitted, "but I've been kicking myself for that ever since." Generally, he wasn't much inclined to regret; nevertheless he regretted intensely the things he had said to Terisa. He should have looked at that body more closely. "I finally figured out what must have happened." *Geraden is your brother. You've known him all his life.* "They must have switched the bodies. Underwell and Nyle. That's why they used Imagery—why they let creatures feed on the bodies. To disfigure them. So we would think Underwell was Nyle.

"Geraden wouldn't do a thing like that. It's impossible. I know him better than that."

As if he were discussing the weather, Artagel added, "If *he* didn't do it, that just leaves Eremis. We don't have anybody else to blame it on."

"I *know* that." Grief twisted Castellan Lebbick's features. Softly, he repeated, "I *know* that. Why do you think I hit her so hard? Why do you think I kept hitting her? I was trying to get her to tell me the truth.

"It *was* Quillon who helped that woman escape. That's the truth. He did it because King Joyse told him to. To get her away from me. He ordered me to do my job, and then he tried to sneak her away from me. That's why he leaves me alone now. He hasn't sent for me in days. He knows I was just following orders.

"He wants to break me. He wants me to hide down here until I rot. Because he doesn't trust me."

Artagel felt frantically that he was getting nowhere. He was tempted to back out of the room, put some distance between himself and the Castellan's lunacy. But his regret was stronger than his alarm. He had already let both Terisa and Geraden down.

Instead of retreating, he tried a different approach.

"Well, he must trust you some." Artagel made an effort to sound hearty, without much success. "You're still in command, aren't you? You're still the Castellan."

Lebbick nodded as if he hadn't heard the question.

"Speaking of things you're in command of, how's the defense going?" continued Artagel. "I heard a rumor that Kragen hasn't so much as thrown a rock at us since the first day. Is that true?"

The Castellan nodded again. "Margonal's whoreson," he growled, "is just sitting out there staring at us."

"Why? What makes him think he can get away with that? Isn't he afraid of Cadwal?"

"I can only think of two explanations." As if by accident, some of the tension in Lebbick's face loosened. On some level, Artagel had distracted him. "He knows Festten isn't coming—for some reason—and we don't because he doesn't let the news get to us. Or Alend and Cadwal have made an alliance."

There: that was an improvement. Castellan Lebbick still had some lucidity left in him. Carefully, Artagel said, "Then I guess Cadwal isn't coming. If Festten and Margonal had an alliance, Kragen wouldn't have tried to attack us alone."

"That's probably true," agreed the Castellan morosely. "Festten wouldn't have made an alliance unless he could be sure Margonal wouldn't get to the Congery ahead of him."

Artagel nodded. After a moment, he went on, "Speaking of the Congery—"

Lebbick interrupted him balefully. "Were we?"

Artagel frowned. "Were we what?"

"Speaking of the Congery. Or were you just prying?"

"I was prying." Artagel grinned. "And I'm going to keep prying until you say three sentences in a row that make sense. If you don't pull yourself together, you *will* rot.

"Speaking of the Congery, what're they doing about poor Master Quillon?"

Castellan Lebbick studied his visitor as if at last he had begun to wonder why Artagel was here. "Nothing," he articulated. "As far as I can tell, the only thing they do all day is sit around wiping each other's bums. By which I mean to say, of course"—he began to sound like he was quoting scornfully—"that they are dedicating all their efforts night and day toward discovering how Gilbur and Geraden and that woman are able to use flat glass without going mad.

"That blind lump Barsonage has suddenly"—Lebbick's tone was savage—"figured out King Joyse is right. He's gone all virtuous and noble about it. Mirrors don't create their own Images. The places they show are real. So we don't have the right to take anything that can tell the difference out of them. Which is a dogshit way of saying they aren't going to help defend us. They refuse to touch the only things that might do us some good."

The Castellan barked humorlessly. "It's actually funny. They discovered purity just when King Joyse gave it up. The only real reason we haven't been overrun already is, Kragen can't use his catapults. Whenever he tries, Havelock destroys them with some kind of smoke-bird from one of his mirrors."

Artagel began to hope that he was on the right track. Castellan Lebbick seemed to be recovering his self-command. Maybe it was time to risk—

Because he was the sort of man who took chances, Artagel said conversationally, "That's better. You're doing much better. Any minute now, you're going to be your old self again. There's just one thing I still want to know.

"Castellan"—he took a deep breath—"what in the name of sanity is the connection between Saddith and Nyle? Why does the fact that she showed up in your bed prove Geraden didn't kill him?"

For a long moment, the Castellan glowered as if he meant to explode. A muscle in his cheek twitched. His gaze burned red, drawing the darkness of the room around him; his expression was full of doom.

Like a man chewing iron pellets, he said, "Not Saddith and Nyle. Saddith and Eremis. She's his whore."

Artagel waited.

"He sent her. That's what I was trying to get her to admit. That's why I kept hitting her. Why I didn't stop."

Still Artagel waited.

"He did that to me." Without warning, Lebbick's eyes began to spill tears. They ran down into his dirty beard, leaving streaks through the grime on his cheeks. "I was already so close to the edge. That woman was trying to tell me the truth, and I didn't know how to believe her. And he did that to me. He sent his whore to give me the last push. Because I'm the only one King Joyse has left. Even though he doesn't trust me.

"Master fornicating Eremis," the Castellan said through his loss, "wouldn't have sent his whore to my bed if everything that woman said about him wasn't true. He was trying to distract me."

With difficulty, Artagel resisted the temptation to whistle through his teeth. This time, he found the Castellan's reasoning comprehensible. He had always appreciated Saddith's frank lust; but at the moment he wasn't thinking about her. He was thinking that her appearance in Lebbick's bed was the worst thing Eremis could have done to the Castellan.

It was almost as if Eremis and King Joyse were conspiring together to destroy him.

Gruffly, Artagel said, "That makes sense." Words seemed to stick in his throat; he had to force them out. "What did Terisa actually tell you about our hero, Eremis?"

The Castellan scrubbed his face with his hands, grinding his tears into the dirt. "The same thing you did." On the cot beside him, he found a rank piece of rag and used it to blow his nose. "They must have switched the bodies. If Underwell really wanted Nyle dead, he could have made it happen without the stupid risk of all that bloodshed. But if Geraden was innocent, Underwell must have discovered right away that Nyle wasn't hurt. So Underwell had to be killed. To protect Eremis.

"Nyle is probably still alive. Unless Eremis doesn't need him anymore.

"Eremis is busy acting like the hero of Orison because his plans aren't ready. Cadwal isn't ready to attack. That's obvious—Cadwal isn't even *here*. Or he's waiting for something else to happen. He doesn't want Kragen to get the Congery."

Artagel was right on the edge of asking, So why don't you stop him? Go cut his heart out. Instead of holing up here like a beaten dog? Fortunately, he stopped himself in time. As soon as the question occurred to him, he caught a glimpse of how Castellan Lebbick would react to it. *They want me to come out so they can jump me. He wants to break me. He doesn't trust me.*

Artagel liked to live dangerously, but he wasn't willing to risk pushing Lebbick back into turmoil.

He couldn't grasp what King Joyse was doing. But that wasn't his problem: someone else would have to figure it out. Eremis was another matter, however. Artagel was very sure that he wanted to oppose or hinder the Master in any way possible.

Gazing around the room in search of inspiration, he grabbed the first idea that came to him.

"You know, Castellan, if your wife saw this pigsty she'd spit granite."

Artagel was probably the only man in Orison who would have dared mention Lebbick's wife to his face.

By luck or intuition, however, Artagel had found the right approach. Instead of erupting, the Castellan looked chagrined. "I know," he muttered. "I'm going to clean it up. I'll get around to it soon."

The sorrow in his face wrung Artagel's heart. Without premeditation or forethought, he said quietly, "Don't bother. Leave it. I've got an extra room. I've even got an extra bed. Come stay with me."

Castellan Lebbick stared dumbly. His mouth worked as if Artagel had asked him to give up his link to the only thing that held him in one piece.

"She's dead," Artagel said as gently as he could. "It can't be helped. She doesn't need you anymore.

"*We're* the ones who need you."

Roughly, fighting collapse, the Castellan rasped, "'We'? Who is 'we'?"

"Me." Artagel didn't hesitate. "Geraden. Terisa. Anybody who thinks King Joyse is still worth trying to save, even though he does act like he's got his head stuck up his ass."

Lebbick thought for a long time, gazing away into the gloom around him. He looked like a man lost in memories—lost in love, in old instances of violence; a man who might never find his way back. But then his shoulders sagged, and he sighed.

"All right."

"Good." Artagel sighed as well, let the suspense exhale from him so hard that the release made him shudder. "It's time."

Without suspense and sorrow to keep him tight, however, his muscles went slack, and his limbs turned to rubber. Ruefully, he added, "You can start by helping me get back there. I'm afraid I overdid it coming here."

"Idiot," Lebbick growled. Slowly, he got to his feet. "You're supposed to be resting. I've seen shrubbery with better sense than you've got."

"That's easy." Artagel made a determined effort not to fall out of his chair. "I've seen shrubbery with better sense than any of us.

"Just tell me one more thing." He paused to collect his fraying thoughts. "Why Ribuld? I didn't know you had such a good opinion of him."

Almost gently, Castellan Lebbick helped Artagel to his feet. Supporting Artagel with his shoulder, he started toward the door.

"I need somebody I can trust. He likes Geraden. That's all I've got to work with."

Artagel couldn't help himself: he had to ask, "Are you really in that much trouble? Just because of Eremis and Saddith?"

The muscles along Lebbick's jaw knotted. His eyes were full of gloom. "Wait and see."

On the way back to his rooms, Artagel found himself positively aching with the intensity of his desire to see Geraden again. He wanted somebody to tell him what was going on.

THIRTY-FIVE:
AN OLD ALLY OF
THE KING

hat same day, Terisa and Geraden rode out of the south-western hills of the Care of Termigan and began to approach Sternwall, the Termigan's seat and his Care's principal city.

The relatively direct road from Houseldon—and the lack of rain, atypical at this time of year—had made the journey an easy one, at least for Geraden. He was accustomed to horses, acquainted with roadside comfort, experienced at camping. And he seemed to have become sure of himself. For the first time in his life, he knew exactly what he was doing. The only thing that reduced his eagerness to get where he was going was the pleasure he had with Terisa along the way.

Terisa's eagerness to reach Sternwall was completely different. In a visceral sense, she had lost interest in Orison—in Master Eremis and King Joyse. Her concerns were more immediate. She was aching in every joint, bone-weary, sick of horses. She wanted a hot bath and clean sheets. Thanks to the otherwise-much-desired way Geraden used his weight at night, the hard ground had given her bruises from her shoulder blades to her tailbone. At times, she felt she would have killed for a pillow under her hips. After a day or two in the saddle, every jolt of the bay's gait seemed to grind her bones together. After another day or two, she could hardly keep from groaning whenever Geraden embraced her.

Nevertheless she hugged him back as hard and as often as possible; she locked her legs over his and held him on top of her despite the pain. She was so full of love that she could hardly take her eyes off him, hardly bear to let her skin be out of contact with his. If necessary, she could endure a few bruises.

She had to admit, however, that she had learned to hate horses. Any culture which couldn't devise a better way to travel than *this* really ought to let itself die out. When Geraden announced that they were within reach of Sternwall, she said, "Thank God!" with such sincerity that he burst out laughing.

"You think it's funny," she groused. "I've never been so miserable in my entire life, and you think it's hilarious. I swear I don't know what I see in you.

"Of course," she added considerately, "if I *did* know I'd probably want to put my eyes out."

"Be careful, my lady," he replied in an aggrieved tone. "I have a sensitive nature. If you give me any excuse—*any excuse at all*—I'll have to start apologizing."

"Oh, great," she growled, trying to sound bitter even though she was grinning with her whole body. "The last time you did that, we didn't get to sleep until after midnight."

She made him laugh again. Then he leaned out of his saddle and kissed her dramatically. "Ah, Terisa," he sighed when he had subsided, "you do me good. I wouldn't have believed it was possible. After all those years serving the Congery and failing—after making the wrong choice and stopping Nyle instead of concentrating on Prince Kragen—after botching our chance to stop Elega—after being made to look like my own brother's murderer, and then having to just hurl myself into a mirror without any idea what would happen—" His list of disasters was really quite impressive when he toted it up like that. "I wouldn't have believed it was actually possible to feel this good."

"How much farther do we have to go?" she asked because she didn't have anything better to say. "I want a bed."

Geraden grinned and gave her the best answer he had.

This was their fourth day on the road, and since they had left behind the smoking ruins of Houseldon they hadn't seen the slightest indication that Mordant was at war. Heading almost directly northeast, they had crossed the Broadwine on its way east-northeast toward the Demesne, and had followed the road in the direction of the Care of Termigan. "The Termigan will help us," Geraden had said confidently. "He's an old ally of the King's. There's a story that he saved King Joyse's life in the last of the big battles against Alend—roughly thirty years ago."

Terisa had nodded without taking her eyes off the surrounding landscape. She had met the Termigan: she had the impression that he was a man who could be trusted absolutely—but only on his own terms.

North and east of Houseldon, the Care of Domne seemed to be composed almost entirely of the kind of fertile hills which made cultivation difficult, but which provided abundant rich grass for sheep. Toward the south and the west, mountains remained visible, but they became steadily harder to descry as the road wound out of the Care. Geraden explained that the border of Domne stretched from the eastmost point of the spur of mountains on the north—a point called Pestil's Mouth because there the Pestil River came out of the spur—along a relatively straight line toward a distinctive peak in the southern range, a mighty and unmistakable head of rock named, for no known reason, Kelendumble. That line divided Domne from both the Care of Termigan to the north of the Broadwine and the Care of Tor to the south.

Although the border was purely theoretical, the countryside did appear to change after Terisa and Geraden entered Termigan. The edges of the landscape became flintier; the grasses and shrubs, the wildflowers and stands of trees all had an air of toughness, as if they endured in ungiving dirt against unkind weather. "The soil is good for grapes," Geraden explained, "and not bad for hops. But it isn't much use for corn, or wheat, or worren." Worren was one of the few grains—in fact, one of the few foods—that she found strange in this world. "In Domne, they joke that everybody who lives here develops a permanent case of dyspepsia from eating the food—and then from trying to feel better by drinking too much.

"On the other hand, I've heard it said that High King Festen won't drink anything except Termigan wine."

As the soil changed, so did the hills: they began to look less rumbled, more ragged, as if they had been cut by erosion rather than raised by the ground's underlying bones. The road twisted through ravines and gullies rather than along shallow vales and hollows. In contrast, however, the weather turned increasingly springlike—

warm in the sun despite the cool nights and shadows; full of green
and flowering scents; hinting at moisture.

Terisa wanted a bath so badly that the mere idea made her scalp
itch.

Forcing herself to think about other things, she occasionally
reflected that ravines and gullies were ideal places for ambushes.
Such things seemed entirely unreal, however. After all, Alend had
sent its strength to the siege of Orison. And the forces of Cadwal
were on the far side of Mordant to the east. So the only real danger
came from Imagery. And any attack that struck by Imagery wouldn't
need to rely on ravines and gullies for success.

She reasoned that Master Eremis probably didn't know where
they were. He couldn't know, unless they happened to pass through
a place that showed in one of his mirrors—and he happened to look
during the brief time they were visible.

She couldn't bring herself to worry about the possibility.

In fact, she didn't even remember what the Termigan had said
about trouble in his Care until Geraden brought her in sight of Sternwall itself, late in the afternoon of their fourth day on the road.

The sight made her wonder how she could have forgotten.

Pits of fire in the ground, the Termigan had said.

Sternwall was a fortified stone city. It had a buttressed wall built
of quarried granite; and within the wall all the houses and other
edifices were of stone. From this distance, the basic style of construction seemed to be mud-plaster pointed with cement. The Termigan's people could have laughed at the attack which had destroyed
Houseldon.

Nevertheless Terisa was sure they weren't laughing.

Even from several hundred yards away, she could sense the heat
of the glowing liquid rock which seethed and bubbled in long pools
outside the walls. There were half a dozen of them, all set in higher
ground which sloped down toward the city, all shaped as if they were
flowing slowly, inexorably toward the walls. Eremis had said, *Pits of
fire appear in the ground of Termigan—almost within the fortifications
of Sternwall.* He must have had a hard time restraining his mirth. Fed
by translation, the pits melted the earth between them and the city.
She didn't know how long this had been going on, but she guessed
that it wouldn't continue much longer. Already, the granite wall had
begun to slump like heated wax at four different points; wide sections
of the city's outward face reflected the magma redly, as if they were

slick with sweat. The people of Sternwall were eventually going to be burned out of their homes. Orange-red glared into the sky like a presage of sunset.

Geraden scowled at the sight bitterly. "Glass and splinters!" he murmured. "Oh, Eremis. No wonder the Termigan doesn't trust Imagers."

"I don't understand." Terisa had to swallow hard to make her throat work. "Why? I mean, why do it this way? Why not put this—this lava?—why not translate this lava right into the city and be done with it?"

"It's more fun this way," grated Geraden. Then he shook his head. "No, that's not it. Sternwall itself probably isn't in the Image. The mirror they're using probably shows a place up the hill somewhere. This is as far as they can adjust the focus."

Guards paced the wall without getting too close to the heat. Terisa saw two men stop, point toward her and Geraden; one of them left the wall. She supposed that under the circumstances Sternwall didn't get many visitors. Trying to force down the taste of bile, she nudged her horse into motion.

Grimly, she and Geraden rode past the pits toward the gate on the far side of the city.

Near the lava, she could hear it seething, a deep, almost inaudible rumble that seemed to echo in the marrow of her bones; the sound of the earth being eaten away.

As quiet as that noise was, however, it seemed to deafen her. She hardly heard the lonely cry of a bugle rising from the walls of the city. She hardly heard Geraden say, "Looks like the Termigan is sending men out to meet us. Maybe he doesn't want to risk letting us in until he knows who we are."

She should have been ready. She was near an Image: she should have understood that she and Geraden were in danger of being spotted. Unfortunately, she wasn't thinking that clearly. She was too full of Sternwall's plight to think clearly.

She was taken completely by surprise when *a touch of cold as thin as a feather and as sharp as steel slid straight through the center of her abdomen.*

Yet the surprise itself may have been what saved her. She had no time to be frightened, paralyzed. Instead, she yelped a warning and flung herself to the side, out of the saddle, out of the way.

The fangs missed her. They came so close, however, that they snagged her shirt at the shoulder, nearly tore it off her body.

She hit the ground awkwardly, wrenched her knee, fell flat on her face. Desperately, she scrabbled her legs under her and pitched to her feet—

—just in time to see a gnarled black spot the size of a puppy get up on its limbs and come scrambling toward her. Its savage jaws took up more than half its body: they stretched for her, ravening.

At her yell, Geraden had wheeled his mount. Bounding from an invisible perch on the other side of a translation, a black, round shape flipped past him. With all four limbs, it caught the Appaloosa by the head.

Its jaws ripped the horse's skull apart. Fountaining blood, the Appaloosa went down as if it had crashed into a wall. Geraden landed hard: he was momentarily stunned. Before he could recover, his mount's convulsions rolled the horse over onto his legs.

Munching brains and bone, the black creature began to eat its way through the horse toward him.

Another fierce shape appeared out of nowhere—and another—struck the ground—rolled to a stop—

One of them went for Geraden. The other rushed at Terisa.

She had no choice, no time: when the nearest creature sprang at her, she ducked, flinched aside. Geraden had given her a knife—for cooking, he had said, teasing her because he did all the cooking—and she groped for it while she dodged; she jerked it from its sheath, hacked blindly at her assailant.

Her blow caught nothing but air. Off balance, barely able to support her weight with her twisted knee, she stumbled directly into the path of the second attacking shape.

Its fangs were curved and jagged, made for rending. In a mirror, she had seen a creature like this tear a man's heart out. It was going to rip her to tatters. And there was another one turning to jump her from behind.

Geraden had a few more seconds to live than she did. The red meat of his horse had distracted both of his attackers: they were feeding voraciously. He was safe until they reached his trapped legs.

Wildly, he struggled to open his mount's saddlebags.

The blade he had given Terisa was little more than a filleting knife; a hunter might have used it to skin a rabbit. It was the only thing she had to fight with, however; she didn't question it. Since she was off balance anyway, she thrust her weight in the direction she was falling, so that her arm and the knife came around in a wide, sweeping slash.

Somehow, this blow found the creature before the creature reached her face. The black shape tumbled to the side, spattering green blood everywhere.

She tried to catch herself, but her knee gave out. She toppled with a cry just as the second attacker leaped at her back.

Geraden's assailants were working on the Appaloosa's shoulders.

From the nearest saddlebag, he pulled out a sackful of corn meal and flung it.

The sack burst open on the first creature's teeth.

With a sound like thick fabric being shredded, the shape sneezed.

Like its jaws and its appetite, its sneeze was too big for its body. The blast knocked it backward, off the dead horse; tucking its legs around itself, it rolled away.

Another sneeze: another roll.

Geraden searched frantically for something else to throw.

Terisa was down. She couldn't get back up. Her legs shoved at the ground as if her back were broken, but she couldn't bring them under her.

One of the black shapes moved toward her.

As if sensing her helplessness, it stopped hurrying: its steps were almost dainty as it approached. Its huge jaws opened delicately. Each one of its teeth was sharp for her flesh.

Then the quarrel from a crossbow struck the creature so hard that it skipped off the ground and sailed through the air as though it had been kicked by a giant. A few drops of its green blood splashed into her hair as it flew past.

Like a spike driven by a sledgehammer, another quarrel nailed the feeding beast to the Appaloosa's carcass. Without a sound, the creature gaped and died, gushing rank fluids around its fangs.

One of the Termigan's men pounded the last black shape into a pulp under the shod hooves of his mount.

A moment later, the three men halted in front of Terisa and Geraden. They peered down from their high seats. Snarling, one of them demanded, "What in the name of goatshit and fornication *are* those things?"

Geraden didn't seem to notice that he had been rescued. He continued thrashing through the saddlebag, hunting uselessly for a weapon. "That bastard," he panted between his teeth. "That bastard. If I had a mirror—" His whole face was wet with sweat or tears. "If I just had a mirror—"

Terisa still couldn't get her legs under her. Her knee felt numb, dead. She wanted to say, insist, Help me, is he all right, did you kill them all? The only thing her throat and stomach agreed to do, however, was retch. She had green blood in her hair, and it *stank*—it smelled like corpses rotting in sewage. The head and most of the shoulders of Geraden's horse had been chewed away, devoured— Like the Castellan's two guards and Underwell. She kept gagging, but nothing came up.

Maybe Mordant wasn't at war. But she and Geraden were.

Oh, yes.

The Termigan's men dismounted. Two of them heaved the Appaloosa's carcass off Geraden; the third lifted Terisa to her feet. They were hard men with grim mouths and red eyes: they had spent too much time staring into the destruction of Sternwall, watching it boil closer. "All right," one of them said harshly, "you're safe. We've saved you. Who are you? What're those things?"

"Imagery," Geraden gasped. He still seemed unaware of the men. His attention was on Terisa. "There could be more. He could translate them right now. We've got to get out of range."

The men wanted answers—but they also understood Geraden. Just for a second, they glanced at each other, hesitating. Then the man who had helped Terisa off the ground picked her up and leaped for his horse.

The other two mounted instantly; one of them pulled Geraden up behind him. The horses stretched into a gallop back toward the city's gates, putting as much distance as possible between the riders and the point of translation.

Terisa still had her knife clenched in her fist. Her hand and the knife were covered with foul, green blood.

"Relax!" the man holding her gritted into her ear. "We can keep your balance better if you relax."

She couldn't relax. She couldn't stop trying to retch.

"How far?" one of the other men asked Geraden. "How far do we have to go to be safe?"

At last, Geraden began to respond to his rescuers. "Can't be sure." The pounding of hooves muffled his voice. "Depends on the size of the mirror. And how far the focus was adjusted to reach us." A moment later, he added, "A hundred yards should be enough."

"Right!"

The Termigans drove their mounts up to the gates of Sternwall. There they risked stopping.

Terisa didn't feel anything sharp or cold in her stomach. She didn't feel anything except nausea. No more of the gnarled, black shapes jumped out of the air.

Now instead of wanting to throw up she began to think it would be nice to faint.

She didn't get the chance. The man carrying her dropped her to the ground, then slid down beside her. The pressure of his grip made it clear he had no intention of letting her go. One of the other men held onto Geraden as he dismounted.

There was sunset in the air now, as well as the glare of lava. The heavy timbers of the gate were tinged crimson; red ran in streaks along the edges of the buildings. The faces of the men hinted at bloodshed.

"All right," one of them repeated. "Now tell us who you are. Before we decide to close the gate and leave you outside."

Terisa could still hear the deep, visceral boiling of the lava. That noise seemed to undermine everything around her; it made the Termigans sound malign, full of coiled malice.

But Geraden nodded to them. "We've just come from Domne," he panted. "I'm Geraden, the Domne's son. One of his sons, anyway. Houseldon has been burned to the ground."

The men stood motionless, caught between who he was and what he said. A crowd began to gather in the gate: more of the Termigan's men, hostlers to take care of the horses, merchants, passersby. They all had the same red light in their eyes.

After a moment, one of the men said noncommittally, "You better tell us who the woman is. And why you were attacked."

Instinctively, Terisa put a hand on Geraden's arm, reaching out for protection against a threat she couldn't identify.

He also seemed to feel the menace. His arm was tight; he held himself poised. His gaze searched the faces around him. Carefully, he said, "My father has been a good and loyal neighbor to the Termigan all his life. The last time I was here, I slept in the Termigan's house as a welcome guest."

No one wavered; no eyes dropped. The man who appeared to be the leader of the guards rested a hand deliberately on his sword. "I'm sure that's true," he growled. "You'll probably be a guest there tonight again. But not until you tell me who she is and why you were attacked."

The man's tone nettled Geraden. He straightened his shoulders; his voice gave off hints of authority, as if he were accustomed to command respect. "She is the lady Terisa of Morgan, arch-Imager and augured champion. For that reason, the foes of Mordant wish to destroy—"

He didn't get any further. Or if he did she didn't hear him. Somebody hit her on the back of the neck so hard that the ground seemed to flip over and rush away into the sky.

As she lost consciousness, she grasped that the Termigan was also at war.

Later, the war seemed to be taking place somewhere between the back of her neck and the front of her skull. There was a contest of pain going on. Her forehead hurt as if someone on the inside belabored it with a cudgel; the back of her neck ached stiffly. But which was winning? She didn't want to think about it.

Then she remembered Geraden.

Groaning, she tried to roll out of bed.

At once, both sides of the war joined forces against her. Every movement anywhere in her body took on a dimension of agony.

She sat up anyway and pushed her feet over the edge of the bed.

Her knee commemorated the occasion with a throb as sharp as a howl. She gave an inarticulate gasp. For a moment, she had to sit without moving, hold herself stationary while she tried to regain some measure of control.

She still had the smell of green blood in her hair. It was still nauseating.

Geraden, she thought.

Who hit me?

Despite the pain, she forced her eyes into focus.

She was sitting on the edge of the bed in a large but rather austere bedchamber. A number of candles lit the stone walls and wooden ceiling, the mats of woven reeds on the floor; the massive chairs, so heavy that they might have been designed to accommodate the Tor; the dark planks of the door. Compared to the places she had slept recently, the bed was luxurious.

She wasn't alone.

A man sat across the room from her, in a chair beside the door. He wore a plain brown shirt and breeches, simple boots; he had no weapons that she could see. His eyes were flat; his hair seemed to have no color. The lines of his face and the edges of his features were rough, crudely shaped. His arms were folded across his chest as if he were prepared to wait for her indefinitely.

She recognized him.

The Termigan. The lord of the Care.

"So," he said after scrutinizing her for a while. "You turn up unexpectedly, my lady."

She stared back, trying to fight down the pain so that she could think.

"The last time I saw you," he went on, "you were there for no good reason except to demonstrate that things went wrong when the Congery tried to obey King Joyse. We were supposed to believe you were just an accident, a nothing—only a woman. Now you're here, and Geraden says you're an arch-Imager.

"I want an explanation."

His posture suggested that he would never let her leave this room until she satisfied him.

Terisa made an effort to clear her throat. "Where's Geraden?"

The Termigan shrugged slightly. "Next door. My men didn't have the nerve to hit a son of the Domne, so he's been struggling and shouting ever since I had you taken away from him. But he's bolted in, and he won't get out until I decide to let him see you."

"When is that going to happen?"

The lord shrugged again. His flat gaze didn't shift from Terisa's face. "I'll make up my mind when I hear what you're going to tell me."

She couldn't keep her voice from shaking. "Your men didn't hit Geraden. Why did they hit *me?* Do you beat up women as a matter of general policy, or have I done something personally to offend you?"

Sarcasm had no effect on the Termigan. "My men," he explained evenly, "didn't know I knew you. They just heard Geraden say you're an Imager. I don't like Imagers, my lady. When my father was killed in the wars, and I became the Termigan, I fought beside King Joyse for years because I don't like Imagers. All my life, most of the people I value have been killed by Imagers. Or Alends. I've never let Havelock inside these walls. Even when he wasn't crazy.

"Now we're under attack by Imagery. Sternwall is going to fall soon, and there's nothing we can do to defend ourselves. My men have standing orders to make any Imager who comes here helpless first and ask questions later.

"My lady, how did you become an Imager? Or how did you convince Eremis and Gilbur you weren't an Imager? Or"—his tone sharpened—"why did they lie to us about you?"

The Termigan was definitely at war.

She looked away. Searching for the means to control her anger and pain—and her nausea at the stink in her hair—she scanned the room. *I don't like Imagers.* Almost immediately, she spotted a decanter of wine and a pair of goblets on a table near the bed, beside a tray that held what appeared to be a cold collation. Carefully, moving her head and neck as little as possible, she stood up, limped to the table, poured some wine. *Helpless first and ask questions later.* On the other hand, he didn't mean to starve her. Tremors ran down her arms from her shoulders, but she was able to keep most of the wine in the goblet. Lifting it with both hands, she drained it.

Just for a second, her stomach heaved and her head pounded; she thought she'd made an idiotic mistake. Then, however, she began to feel a little better.

Deliberately, she faced the Termigan. In effect, he had taken Geraden prisoner. Geraden was probably worried sick about her. And he, too, was an Imager. What would the Termigan do if he knew that the son of the Domne was also an Imager? He might keep them locked up for the rest of the war—until Sternwall fell, and Mordant was destroyed, and Master Eremis had slaughtered everybody who stood in his way. Anger gave her the strength she needed.

"My lord, they were lying to both of us. Practically everything they said to us was a lie."

The Termigan didn't move; he hardly blinked. "Why would they lie to *you?* You're one of *them.*"

She gaped at him. Her brain was sluggish; a moment passed before she was able to say, "No, I'm not.

"I didn't even find out I've got a talent until"—she counted backward quickly—"five days ago. How could I be 'one of *them*'? They didn't want me to know I had any talent. That's why they were lying to me. That's why they've been trying to kill me. That's why Houseldon got burned. They were trying to kill us. They think I'm some kind of threat to them."

"What kind of threat?"

"I don't know," she admitted bitterly. She wanted Geraden with her. She didn't like the risk of talking to the Termigan by herself. "But we're trying to find out. In the meantime, we want to make as much trouble for Eremis and Gilbur as we can. That's why we're here."

Abruptly, the lord nodded. "Now I'm beginning to believe you. They want to kill you. You want to cause trouble for them. All this"—his manner referred to more than just the pits of fire outside Sternwall—"is just another contest between Imagers. We're the victims"—now he meant the people of his Care—"but we aren't really the point.

"The point is *power*."

He had misunderstood her. She made an effort to explain. "That isn't what I meant. We're trying to defend Mordant. It's King Joyse that Eremis and Gilbur want to destroy. We're secondary—Geraden and I are in the way, that's all. It's King Joyse who needs your help."

Without a flicker of expression or inflection, the Termigan replied, "Pigslime."

Terisa stopped and studied him, trying to see past his face into his mind. But he was as closed as a piece of flint. In an effort to pull herself together, she poured more wine for herself, then returned to the bed and sat down again.

Slowly, she said, "You don't like Imagers. Is that it?"

"Joyse needs my help, I'm sure of that," he retorted, "but not because you ask it. You don't care about him. You want me to do something that will help you against Eremis and Gilbur. If that helps the King today, it will help destroy him tomorrow."

"Is it because I'm an Imager?" Terisa asked, speaking mostly to herself. "It must be. Everybody who knows the Domne trusts his sons."

"The one thing you all want is to get rid of *him*. That's the one thing you're all united on. He's the only man who's ever succeeded at *controlling* you."

"I see." Terisa had learned a lot from Castellan Lebbick: she had learned how to speak harshly to angry men. "You think an Imager can't be honest. You think that talent—an accident of birth—precludes loyalty. Or compassion. Or even ethics."

Still the Termigan didn't shift in his seat; he didn't raise his head or his voice. "In the end," he articulated flatly, "no Imager is loyal to anyone but himself. That's the nature of power. It seduces—it requires. An Imager can appear loyal only as long as his power and his loyalty don't come into conflict. The only thing"—now just for a moment he did raise his voice—"my lady, the *only* thing which has saved us for the past ten years is Havelock's madness. If Vagel hadn't cost him his mind, he would have gotten rid of Joyse as soon as the Congery was complete. He would have established a tyranny in Mordant to make the atrocities of Margonal and Festten look like boys pulling wings off butterflies."

The virulence, not of his tone, but of his belief, shocked her. "You think that? Even though Havelock was the King's friend and counselor for—what was it?—more than forty years? Even though he gave up his *sanity* for his King?" Pain and the aftereffects of nearly being killed made her savage. "What would he have to do to make you trust him? Slaughter every Imager ever born? Exterminate talent from the world?"

With a small flick of his hand, the lord dismissed her protest. "Even that wouldn't be enough. The Imager I trust is the one who kills himself.

"If you're telling me the truth—which is always possible, I suppose—you haven't known about your talent very long. You've only had a few days to discover what it does to you. My lady, I'll tell you what it does.

"It teaches you—no, it *forces* you to believe you're more important than other people. Because you can *do* more. If you're smart enough, and strong enough, and nobody gets in your way, you can change the outcome of the world. You can remake Mordant in your own image. So how can you let anybody stand in your way? How can you let anybody tell you what to do? How can you submit to any kind of control?

"You can't, my lady. You'll find out that you can't.

"And when you find that out, you'll learn Joyse is your enemy. *I'm* your enemy. Even if you think you're honest now, and loyal, and trustworthy, you'll learn you want us all dead. You'll learn it's better to translate pits of fire to roast us out of our homes than to take the risk that we might get in your way."

Terisa was more than shocked: she was appalled. *How can you let anybody stand in your way?* The Termigan was right: she knew Imagers who met his description. And more than that: she knew people who would meet his description if they became Imagers. Her father was one of them.

If she was her father's daughter, she might be one of them herself.

"Now, my lady," the Termigan said like a sharp stone, "tell me what you think I can do to help my King."

Fortunately, she didn't get a chance to answer. A knock at the door saved her from babbling incoherently. The Termigan turned his head, rasped, "Enter," and one of his soldiers came into the room.

"My lord," the man said in a pale voice. His face was ashen, but his eyes still held the red glow of lava. "It's getting worse."

"'Worse'?" the lord demanded without moving.

The soldier jerked a nod. "They're translating more lava. We can see it pouring out of the air. It's building up against us faster. Two of the pits ran together." He hesitated, then said, "Part of the wall just gave way."

A sting of alarm went through Terisa. Half involuntarily, she said, "That's because we're here. We're too dangerous."

And because they were approaching the crisis—the point where Master Quillon said Eremis would be vulnerable. *So that he would attack here.* The point at which King Joyse intended to strike back. If in fact he had ever had the *policy* Quillon ascribed to him—or if he were still King enough to carry it out. Eremis needed to kill or paralyze the King's allies before that moment, so that King Joyse wouldn't have any force with which to strike.

It was probably true—although the thought made her sick— that Eremis wouldn't try so hard to kill her and Geraden if she hadn't convinced the Master that King Joyse knew what he was doing, that the King's choices were deliberate, purposive, rather than passive or accidental.

"'We'?" asked the Termigan. He sounded fatal—too calm for the extremity of his outrage and dismay. "One new Imager and a failed Apt? I don't believe it."

"You should." Terisa couldn't bear it. Sternwall was going to be destroyed. Like Houseldon. Because of her and Geraden. "He's an Imager, too. He's even more powerful than I am. Let him make a mirror, and he'll get rid of that lava for you.

"Eremis wants us dead. He can't take the chance we'll talk you into helping us."

Then she closed her eyes, trying to rest her head from this prolonged struggle against pain; trying to believe that she hadn't condemned Geraden and herself to spend the rest of their short lives in the Termigan's dungeons.

She expected the lord to do something vehement: spring to his feet, storm around the room, perhaps have her locked in irons. He did none of those things, however. He murmured to his soldier, and the man left the room. Then he sat still, studying Terisa flatly; his gaze was so unreadable that when she finally met it it made her want to scream.

A few moments later, the soldier returned, ushering Geraden into the Termigan's presence.

After that, the man left.

Geraden looked at her, at the lord. He said, "My lord Termigan," roughly, his only concession to politeness. He was already hurrying toward Terisa.

"Are you all right?" he asked in a low voice. "You were hit so hard, I thought they broke your neck."

She managed a crooked smile, a stiff nod. Putting her hand in his, she pulled herself to her feet. "The lava's getting worse," she said, speaking carefully so that she wouldn't start to yell. "I think it's another way of attacking us." She faced the Termigan although she spoke to Geraden, held Geraden's hand; with all her strength, she willed the lord not to harm Geraden. "And I think Eremis is afraid of the Termigan. There must be something he can do to fight back." Because she wanted the lord to understand that she was threatening him, she concluded to Geraden, "I told him you're an Imager."

And Geraden—without hesitation, almost without trepidation—supported her even though he probably had no idea what he was getting into. "That's right," he said. "If you've got any sand here, any kind of furnace or kiln, I might be able to make a mirror. I could translate that fire away."

Terisa squeezed his hand hard and held her breath.

For the first time, she saw the Termigan react plainly. A muscle twitched in his cheek; his brows knotted into a hurt scowl. The emotion she felt wash from him wasn't anger or even disgust; it was grief.

In a ragged voice, he said, "No. Even if you're telling the truth. I won't have it. I won't have Imagery here."

His own severity cost him this hope.

Geraden blew a sigh; but he still didn't hesitate. "Then, my lord," he said clearly, "there's only one thing you can do for your people." Terisa marveled at him—at the strength in his voice, at the certainty with which he met a dilemma that confounded her. "Evacuate Sternwall. Get your men together. Go fight for King Joyse. Before it's too late."

It didn't work. "'Evacuate Sternwall'?" the Termigan spat as if he had discovered a piece of glass in his food. "Leave my people? Abandon my Care?" Softly, but so intensely that it sounded like a cry from his heart, he demanded, "*For what?*"

"For Mordant," answered Geraden. "For peace."

The Termigan didn't respond, so Geraden went on, "Orison is under siege. Prince Kragen brought the Alend army against us—at least ten thousand men. And Cadwal is marching. The High King's army is even bigger—I don't know how long the Perdon can hold out against it. Right now, the Alend Monarch may be in the strange position of defending Orison from Cadwal.

"I don't think you can do anything about that. I don't think you've got enough men.

"But you could attack Eremis directly." He released Terisa's hand so that he could move closer to the Termigan, face the lord more squarely. "He's in league with High King Festten. But Cadwal has to fight Alend and Orison. So the place where Eremis keeps his mirrors is vulnerable—the place where he does translations like this one, the one destroying Sternwall. The place where he and Gilbur and Vagel hid to do their plotting and shape their mirrors.

"You could attack him there. In the Care of Tor. In his home. Esmerel."

Esmerel? Terisa was surprised. That didn't make sense. "What about his father—his brothers?" she asked stupidly. They would have betrayed him long ago. "He couldn't use Esmerel."

Geraden turned to her. Frowning at the distraction, he said, "Eremis doesn't have any family. They all died in a fire years ago. Some of his servants in Orison are people who used to serve his father. I've heard them talk about it."

So that also was a lie, just another of Eremis' attempts to manipulate her. She ground her teeth. Suddenly, she felt a fierce desire to do what Geraden was proposing: ride into the Care of Tor, ride to Esmerel, attack— Get even with that bastard.

But the Termigan wasn't moved. "Will that save Sternwall?" he asked Geraden in a voice like a winter wind.

"Probably not," Geraden admitted. "It'll take too long. Sternwall is probably doomed—unless something good happens for a change. Unless something happens to distract Eremis or Gilbur so they can't keep translating that lava."

"Then I repeat," gritted the lord. *"For what?"*

This time, Geraden said simply, "You might be able to save King Joyse."

The Termigan chewed on that for a while. Then he said harshly, "So you think there's something worth saving? You think Joyse hasn't just gone passive or anile?" He'd been pushed too far: he was losing his calm, his inhuman self-restraint. "You think there's some *reason* why he let those shit-eating Imagers do this to my Care?"

"Yes," Terisa said at once, before the lord's sorrow and distress became too much for her. "I don't like it very well. I don't think it's good enough. But there *is* a reason."

In a few stiff sentences, while the Termigan stared at her as if she were lice-ridden, she told him what Master Quillon had told her about King Joyse's reasons.

The lord surged to his feet; almost before she was done, he snapped, "Is that *all?* He turned his back on us, left his realm to rot, let Imagers do whatever they wanted to his people—just so Mordant would be attacked, instead of Alend or Cadwal?"

His passion stopped Terisa's voice. She nodded dumbly.

Without warning, the Termigan let out a snarl of laughter. Candlelight reflected in his eyes like an echo of lava. "Brilliant. Destroy your friends to save your enemies. Completely brilliant."

"He needs the help anyway, my lord," murmured Geraden. "No matter how slim it is, the possibility that he knows what he's doing is the only hope we have left. You might be able to do him some good by striking against Esmerel."

For a moment, the lord remained motionless, holding himself as though a gale were gathering inside him. Then, abruptly, he lifted his fists and roared, *"No!*

"He decided to sacrifice Sternwall without consulting me! Let him pay for the rest of his reasons himself!"

When he left the room, he slammed the door so hard that splinters jumped from the latch and one of the crossmembers cracked.

Geraden looked at Terisa with trouble in his eyes. "Well," he said finally, "at least I haven't lost my talent for mishap."

She went to him and hugged him. "Wait and see," she muttered dryly. "If he doesn't tie us up and throw us in the lava, you got more out of him than I did."

That enabled him to chuckle a little. "Do you mean," he asked, "that if we simply survive this experience I'm supposed to consider it a success?"

"Wait and see," she repeated. She didn't know what else to offer him.

They waited.

Eventually, a servant brought them hot water, so Geraden braced a chair against the door, and they bathed each other. They drank the wine and ate the food; they took advantage of the bed. They even got some sleep.

The next morning, they answered a knock at their door, and another servant came into the room carrying their breakfast.

A soldier visited them as well. Brusquely, as if he had no time for this, he asked Terisa and Geraden what they needed for their journey.

They were surprised—but not so surprised that Geraden couldn't think of a list. After all, the Termigan had a reputation for fidelity. He may have hated Imagers and lost confidence in his King, but apparently he couldn't forget his lifelong loyalties. To the Domne, for instance. And Geraden and Terisa had lost their horses and supplies outside Sternwall; they needed anything the lord was willing to give them. So Geraden talked to the soldier for several minutes; and by the time he and Terisa had finished their breakfast the man returned to report that their new horses and fresh supplies were ready to go.

In fact, the Termigan sent them on their way better equipped than they had been when they entered his Care. In addition to the horses, he gave them plenty of food, full wineskins, cooking utensils, a short sword for each of them, and bedding that seemed luxurious compared to the thin blankets with which they had left Houseldon. He even provided a rough map which showed a direct route across country toward the Care of Fayle and Romish.

But he didn't do anything to help King Joyse.

THIRTY-SIX:
GATHERING
SUPPORT

ccording to the map, Romish was situated near the southeast point of the Care of Fayle, where the border between Fayle and Armigite met the border between Termigan and Fayle.

Terisa and Geraden wanted to hurry. From one perspective, the attack on Sternwall was a good sign: it implied that Master Eremis was still waiting for his plans to mature, still vulnerable. In every other way, however, the Termigan's plight was cause for alarm. So far, Houseldon had been burned down; Sternwall was falling into a pit of fire. The Armigite had made an agreement with Prince Kragen. The Perdon was alone against all of High King Festten's power. What came next? If this process continued much longer, Mordant would soon have nothing left to save.

Terisa and Geraden had reason to hurry.

Unfortunately, the terrain didn't let them.

They made good progress for a day after they left Sternwall, but that was only because they were able to remain on the road which led eventually to the Demesne and Orison. The second day, their route required them to angle away from the road, heading more to the north as the road shifted east. And this part of Termigan was the roughest land she had yet seen in Mordant.

"Now if this were Armigite—" Geraden panted as he tugged his horse, a rangy gray with a head like a mallet, up an interminable hillside that was too flinty and steep for safe riding. "Armigite in spring is worth seeing. The soil is so sweet they say you only have to wave a few squash seeds at the ground and you'll be up to your hips in vines. The early hay should be just coming up—it smells so fresh you want to take up dancing. And the women—" He glanced at Terisa and grinned. "All that rich soil and relaxed countryside makes their work so easy they really don't have anything better to do than sit around and become gorgeous."

Terisa snorted softly. At the moment, she would have been delighted to be in Armigite. Let the women there become as gorgeous as they pleased. As far as she was concerned, the only thing worse than riding a horse was trying to haul it by main force up a hill it didn't want to climb, when her knee still pained her. Generally, she was willing to put up with the mount the Termigan had provided for her—a roan gelding with a decent gait and no malice. In the present circumstances, however, she would cheerfully have dropped the beast into one of Eremis' fiery pits.

Nevertheless she didn't suggest that she and Geraden forget about the Fayle; that they return to the road and head straight for Orison. The Fayle was the only lord left whom they might bring to the King's support.

And Queen Madin lived in Fayle, in Romish. Myste had mentioned a manor just outside Romish.

Terisa felt a strong, if rather irrational, conviction that Queen Madin had a right to know what her husband was doing. Otherwise the Queen might go to her grave believing that King Joyse had lost his interest in life, his commitment to Mordant; his love for her.

It was typical of Terisa's mood—her soul shocked by Sternwall's danger, her thoughts troubled by the ramifications of what Master Eremis was doing, and yet her heart full of Geraden—that she considered Queen Madin's feelings at least as important as King Joyse's need for help.

So she wrestled her roan up the hillsides, rode it gingerly down the gullies, and trotted it inexpertly across the flats, not precisely without complaint, but without significant self-pity.

The Care of Termigan, as Geraden explained, wasn't heavily populated. And most of the towns and villages were spread out along the Broadwine River, away from the Pestil and Alend. After the second day, the two riders seemed alone in the stringent landscape.

Terisa began to think that Termigan had already lost everything it had ever contained worth fighting for.

For three days, dark clouds locked the sky, threatening rain. Water and mud would have perfected the pleasure of her journey; nevertheless she wished for rain. Orison could always use water. And mud would make the movements of armies more difficult.

Despite the fierce way they glowered down at the earth, however, the clouds were only able to spit a few brief sprinkles before they blew away. The weather itself seemed to have Master Eremis' best interests at heart.

On the other hand, as the clouds drifted off, the terrain improved, as if sunlight had an ameliorating effect on the slopes and soil. Trees became more common: soon the errant and bedraggled copses of the rest of Termigan began to accumulate into long stands of elder and sycamore, ash and wattle. "We're getting closer," commented Geraden. "Fayle is known for its wood.

"Actually, that's one reason Alend traditionally attacks through Termigan or Armigite rather than Fayle. And it's why the Fayle was King Joyse's second ally, after the Tor. You could make yourself old trying to run a military campaign through the forests of Fayle. The Care has more history of resistance—or maybe I should say of successful resistance—than most of the rest of Mordant.

"That probably explains," he concluded humorously, "where the Fayle got his loyalty—and Queen Madin got her stubbornness."

Terisa felt that if she never saw another hillside covered with gorse and nettles again she could die happy. "How much farther?"

He consulted the map. "Two days, if we're lucky. It's easy to get lost in woods and forests. And I've never been in Fayle before. Actually, Batten in Armigite is the closest I've ever been to Romish.

"But the good news"—he looked around—"is that we ought to start seeing people again soon. According to the map, we'll go right through several villages. Technically, some of them will still be Termigan. But for all practical purposes we're coming into the Care of Fayle right now."

Simply because he said those words, she took a harder look ahead—and spotted what appeared to be a smudge against the horizon.

Frowning, she tried to squint her vision into better focus.

Geraden noticed the direction of her gaze. "What do you see?"

"I don't know. Smoke?"

He squinted as well, then shook his head. "I can't tell." Terisa didn't need to say anything; he had the same memories she did. After scanning the map again, he added, "That might actually be the first village. A place called Aperyte. Unless I'm wrong about where we are. If it has a smithy, the forge will smoke."

"Let's find out," she said under her breath.

Self-consciously, he loosened his sword in its scabbard. Then he tightened his grip on the reins and urged his gray into a canter.

Her gelding followed. She was getting better at telling it what to do.

Between the trees, the ground was covered with clumps of dull grass and bracken. The first hint of evening was in the air, but she didn't notice it; she was concentrating ahead, trying to see past a number of intervening wattle thickets. The wattle had bright yellow flowers that grew in sprays like mimosa blooms. The ground was rising: if she had turned in her saddle, she could have seen a panorama unrolled behind her. But she had watched Houseldon burn; she didn't have any attention to spare for flowers and vistas.

The distance was greater than she expected. She began to think that the smudge she had seen was a trick of the light.

Then, abruptly, a knot of copses stood back from a clearing.

A corral with a split-rail fence filled most of the clearing. It wasn't as big as it first appeared; but it was plainly big enough for ten or fifteen horses. Terisa—who felt that she was becoming an expert on horse manure—was sure that the corral had been full of horses.

Recently.

But not now.

Geraden stopped. He studied the clearing. "That's odd."

"What's odd?"

"The gate's closed."

He was right: the gate wasn't just closed; it was tied shut.

"Why?" he muttered softly. "Why take all your horses out and then tie the gate?"

She lowered her voice. "Why not?"

"Why bother?" he returned.

Terisa had no idea.

After a moment, he breathed, "Come on," and slipped out of his saddle. "Let's go see what we're getting into."

When she had dismounted, he led the gray and her gelding away until they were hidden among the copses, out of sight of the clearing. There he tied the reins to a tree; but he didn't uncinch the girths or drop the saddlebags.

Taking Terisa's hand, he moved quietly toward the village.

Because she was trying so hard to look ahead, peer between the trees, she had trouble with her footing. Geraden, on the other hand, didn't trip or stumble. For a moment, she couldn't figure out how he knew where he was going. Then she realized that he was following worn lines in the dirt—marks made by people and animals that had reason to go in every conceivable direction from their homes.

He brought her to the back of a daub-and-wattle shed. Actually, it was little more than a shelter intended to protect straw for the horses from the weather.

Beyond it lay the village.

At a glance, Terisa could see perhaps a dozen huts, all built of daub-and-wattle, all with roofs made from what appeared to be bundles of banana leaves. Among them stood an open-sided structure that might have served as a meeting hall. The size of the cleared space gave the impression that there were more houses and buildings out of sight behind the ones nearby.

From somewhere among them rose a stream of thin, dirty smoke.

The village was disturbingly quiet. No people shouting to each other. No people at all. No dogs. No chickens scratching the dirt. No children whimpering or playing in the distance. The breeze raised a little furl of dust along the hard ground between the huts, but it didn't make any noise.

"Oh, shit," Geraden growled softly.

"Maybe they're all at work," she murmured. "In the fields or something."

He shook his head. "A village like this is never empty. Not like this."

"Evacuation? Maybe the Fayle got them all away?"

He thought for a moment. "I like that idea better." Then he said, "As long as we're whispering, let's go see if they really are gone."

Together, they crept into the village.

Its inhabitants really were gone.

So were all its animals and fowl; beasts of burden; pets. Terisa had the impression that even the vermin had disappeared.

Shadows lengthened across the bare ground. Dusk seemed to gather in the huts and peek out from their gaping doorways, their eyeless windows. The breeze brought the taste of something cold, a hint of something rotten.

She was afraid to ask Geraden if he recognized it.

The village did in fact contain a smithy, but the forge was cold. The smoke came from somewhere else.

Shortly, she and Geraden discovered its source. At the northern edge of the village, three huts in a cluster were on fire.

They had been burning for some time—had nearly burned themselves out. Only their blackened frames still stood. Small flames licked in and out of the fallen remains of the roofs; the smoke drifting upward had a bitter smell.

All three were full of corpses.

Terisa gagged when she saw the stumps of charred arms and legs, the lumps of heads protruding from the ash. "Is that all of them?" she choked thickly. "*All* of them?"

"No." Geraden was having trouble breathing. "Probably just a few families. The whole village wouldn't fit. These are the ones who didn't get away."

Inspired by nausea—and by the strange scent on the breeze, which didn't have anything to do with burned wattle and charred bodies—Terisa muttered, "Or they're the ones who did."

He gave her a look like a whiplash.

She heard a faint, rustling noise—bare feet scuttling across the dirt. She looked around; her peripheral vision seemed to catch a glimpse of something as it slipped into the evening shadows. Then it was gone. She couldn't be sure that she had actually seen anything.

Yet a chill went down her back as she remembered what Master Eremis had told the lords of the Cares. *All Mordant is already assailed. Strange wolves have slaughtered the Tor's son. Devouring lizards swarm the storehouses of the Demesne. Pits of fire appear in the ground of Termigan.*

But that wasn't all. Now she remembered it precisely.

Ghouls harry the villages of Fayle.

"Geraden—" She was barely able to clear her throat. "Let's get out of here."

He was still staring at the huts; he hadn't heard what she heard. But he nodded roughly.

For no apparent reason, he pulled out his sword as he started back toward the horses.

She hoped he didn't have a reason. Nevertheless she was glad that he was armed—and that he was determined, if not skilled. She stayed close to his shoulder all the way through the village and past the corral.

Their boots made too much noise on the hard ground: she wouldn't have been able to hear any soft rustling sounds. But twice she thought she saw movement in the heart of a shadow, the depths of a hut, as if the dark were coming to life.

She was irrationally relieved to find the horses where she and Geraden had left them—and to find them alive. They were both uneasy: the gray bobbed its head fretfully; the roan kept rolling its eyes. Maybe they smelled the same scent that made her so nervous. They were difficult to manage at first, until they realized that they were no longer tied to the tree.

Respecting the uneasiness of the horses—and his own distress—Geraden led Terisa in a wide circuit beyond the empty village before returning to the route marked on the Termigan's map.

Until nightfall forced them to stop, they put as much distance as they could between themselves and Aperyte. She didn't want to stop at all; but of course they couldn't find their way safely in the dark. A flashlight would have come in handy. A *big* flashlight. Sure, she muttered to herself sourly. And while she was at it, why not an armored car to ride in? Or even an airplane to drop a few strategic bombs on Esmerel? On High King Festten's army?

All Geraden needed was a mirror.

He could do it, if he could get to his glass—the one which had brought her here.

Sure.

When they made camp, she helped him build the biggest fire they could. She hunted as far as she dared, collecting firewood. Then, while they ate supper, she commented morosely, "I don't know what made me say that."

Geraden looked at her across the stewpot out of which he was eating.

"You said they were the ones who didn't get away. I said they were the ones who did. I don't know why I said that."

He tried without much success to smile. "Let's hope you just have a morbid imagination." The firelight on his face reminded her of the Termigan.

She couldn't smile, either. "Why is it," she went on, trying to exorcise images which haunted her, "everything that comes here by translation is so destructive? Why is it so easy to find terrible things in mirrors? Is the universe really so malign?"

"I certainly hope not." In a transparent effort to reassure her, Geraden grimaced lugubriously. Then he set himself to give her an answer.

"It's probably true that every world has predators. But even if a world didn't contain any violence at all, its creatures or powers might still be destructive if they were translated—if they were taken out of their natural place. There's nothing immoral about a pit of fire—as long as you leave it where it belongs. What's really destructive is the man who translates it somewhere else.

"Would you call a fox destructive? After all, it hunts chickens. And people need those chickens. Even so, there's nothing wrong with the fox.

"For all we know, the firecat that burned Houseldon might be the same thing as a fox in its own world. It might be anything. It might even be an administer of charity."

An administer of charity. Just for a moment, she took the idea seriously. Someone who ran a mission, for example. Then, however, she was struck by the thought of Reverend Thatcher going around setting towns on fire. On his own terms, that would please him. But *literally* setting towns on fire—

Involuntarily, she grinned. When Geraden rolled his eyes at her, she started laughing.

She felt like a fool—like she was losing her mind. But she went on laughing, and after a while she felt better.

Nevertheless she didn't sleep very well that night. She kept expecting the horses to snort and shy—kept expecting to smell something cold and slightly rotten in the dark. And for some reason Geraden spent most of the night snoring like a bandsaw. When she nudged him awake in the early gray of dawn, so that they could be on their way, she felt cold herself and vaguely stupid, as if the matter inside her skull had begun to turn rancid.

The day began well. The air was clear and crisp, and the horses moved easily along the increasingly traveled paths. And before noon she and Geraden came upon a village that had nothing wrong with it.

Nothing, that is, except anxiety. When the people of the village heard what Terisa and Geraden had found in Aperyte, they muttered nervously and scanned the woods around their homes and began to talk about leaving.

"Ghouls," a woman pronounced, confirming Terisa's guess. "Don't know what else to call them. Never seen one—but the lord sent men to warn us. Attack at dusk or dawn. Little critters, almost like children. Green and smelly.

"Eat every kind of flesh. Don't even leave the grease and bones. That's what the lord's men said."

Geraden scowled as if he were in pain. "That's why the gate was closed," he muttered. "The horses never got out. They were eaten right there in the corral."

Terisa was thinking, *They're the ones who did.* They escaped into their huts and somehow sealed the doors. And then they were incinerated in their own homes.

Eremis.

She was beginning to understand why King Joyse had fought for twenty years to strip Alend and Cadwal of Imagers and create the Congery. He wanted to prevent creatures like ghouls from being translated into the world.

Through a haze of nausea and anger, she asked one of the villagers, "What're you going to do?"

"What the lord's men told us," came the reply. "If we heard any rumor of ghouls around here, saw any sign. Get to Romish as fast as we can."

"*Good*," said Geraden fiercely.

He and Terisa rode on.

She still felt like the meat of her brain was going bad. Even though those villagers were safe, she couldn't rid herself of the impression that the day was getting worse. How many ghouls had Eremis already translated into the Care of Fayle? How much of the Fayle's strength had already been eaten away?

How could he help King Joyse and defend his own people at the same time?

She practiced saying *oh, shit* to herself until it began to feel more natural.

"Here's some more good news," Geraden remarked the next

time he studied the map. "At the rate we're going, we're due to reach another village just about sunset. A place called Naybel."

Oh, shit.

Grimly, she made an effort to think. "Maybe we should stay away from it. Maybe those things are following us."

He glared at her. "You *do* have a morbid imagination." After a moment, he added, "If we're being followed, we've got to warn the village. We can't lead ghouls past Naybel and expect them to leave it alone."

The day was definitely going downhill.

The afternoon wore on, as miserable and prolonged as a toothache. Eventually, Terisa concluded that there were after all worse things than spending so much of the day on horseback. She couldn't get that *smell* out of her mind—

Without making an explicit decision to hurry, she and Geraden began to urge their horses faster. They wanted to reach Naybel before dusk.

Mishap continued to dog them. Because they were hurrying, they rode into the village precisely as the sun began to dip into the horizon. At a slower pace, they wouldn't have arrived until full dark.

The decision to ride straight into the village was also one which they hadn't made explicitly: they did it simply because the need to warn Naybel's people blanketed other considerations. As a result, they were already among the huts, on their way in toward the center of the village, when they realized that Naybel was as empty as Aperyte.

Geraden slowed the gray's canter. The beast's head went up and down like a hammer, fighting the reins. Terisa's gelding had its ears back. Where the sunlight came through the trees, the shadows of the huts were as sharp as blades.

"Geraden," she whispered, "we're too late. Let's get *out* of here."

Geraden hesitated, turned his head to fling a look around him—and lost control of his mount. The gray caught its bit between its teeth and bolted.

Terisa couldn't stop her roan from following.

Almost at once, she heard the squeal of a pig. Geraden nearly lost his seat as the gray wrenched itself aside to avoid collision with a fat porker. Immediately, his horse blundered into a squall of chickens. Terisa followed him through feathers and shadows.

Into the center of the village.

Like Aperyte, Naybel had an open-sided meeting hall among
its houses.

In the hall stood a group of men—six or eight of them. They
wore heavy boots and battle-leathers; they were armed with swords,
pikes, longbows.

As soon as they saw Geraden and Terisa, they began to yell,
waving their arms wildly.

"Fools!"

"Fornication!"

"Get away!"

"Stop!"

Several of them apparently wanted to chase the horses off. Fortunately, one man had a different idea. Or he realized that the gray
was a runaway. With the practiced ease of someone who had worked
with horses all his life, he jumped at the gray's head and caught the
reins. The gray wheeled to a halt so hard that Geraden was nearly
snapped out of the saddle.

More to avoid hitting the gray than because of anything Terisa
did, the gelding also blundered to a stop.

"Fools!" a man shouted. "You're going to be killed!"

Terisa tried to hold herself still, but the whole village seemed
to be spinning. A shadow as distinct as a cut lay across the roan's
head. The men from the meeting hall shifted in and out of shadows;
their weapons disappeared, caught the sun, disappeared again. Geraden had nearly run into a pig. And chickens. Naybel wasn't empty,
not like Aperyte.

Then what—?

It was true: she could smell something cold, something that had
begun to rot; something like the exhalation from a neglected tomb.

Out of a hut beyond the meeting hall came a little boy. She
thought he was a little boy, oddly naked. A grin split his face, leaving
a wide, empty place. He didn't leave the shadows; because of the
dim illumination, a moment passed before she noticed that he had
a chicken in his hands.

The chicken was melting. It slumped over his fingers like heated
wax. But none of it dripped to the ground. Instead, as it oozed it
was absorbed into his flesh.

Now she realized that his whole body was covered with slime.
Maybe the shadows were playing tricks on her eyes. The boy looked
green—

A hoarse cry broke from the men. Two of them already had their longbows up, arrows nocked. Bows like that could have flung their yards straight through the walls of one of these huts. The two arrows that hit the little boy spiked him to the dirt.

Terisa distinctly heard a popping noise, a sound of rupture; she heard a brief wail claw the air.

Instantly, three more green children appeared in the shadow beside the little boy. They grinned as they began to feed.

Somewhere out of sight, the pig squealed—a shriek of porcine agony. The gelding took this occasion to pitch Terisa off its back. With a whinny like a scream, it rushed out of the village.

Terisa landed heavily, knocking the air out of her chest. In the distance, Geraden yelled her name, but she couldn't react to it. The jolt of impact stunned her. A streak of sunlight fell over her face: she looked up and saw one of ghouls standing in shadow no more than four or five feet away. She could *smell* the child—

In fact, the odor wasn't particularly strong. It was insidious, however, and its subtlety seemed to make it more nauseating, more corrosive, than a stronger stench would have been. Smelling it, staring at the small girl who grinned at her as if she were an especially tasty snack, Terisa decided that the slime on the ghoul's skin was acid. It rendered flesh down to a tallow the creature could take in through its pores. And when someone tried to escape by barring the door of a hut, the acid probably set the wood on fire.

The ghoul was so hungry that she started out of the shadow into the light that covered Terisa's face.

Geraden leaped over her and swept the girl's head off with a long swing of his sword.

The popping noise, the sound of rupture; a high, thin cry.

Two, three, no, at least six more ghouls came at once to feed on their fallen sister.

Around the meeting hall, a weird battle raged. Superficially, it was an uneven struggle: the men slaughtered the ghouls with relative ease. Swords, pikes, arrows, even stones thrown hard—everything worked. Panting, raging, the men hacked down, sliced up, or spitted the ghouls as fast as possible. They were only children, as simple to kill as children.

But they were so many—

No, they weren't as many as all that. The truth was more complex. As soon as one of them got enough to eat, the creature split

apart, became two. And whenever one of them died, the body provided enough food for three or four other ghouls to multiply.

And with every death wail, more creatures swarmed out of the
shadows.

In addition, the weapons of the men didn't last long. Every
arrow that struck home caught fire; every blade that cut came back
pitted and weakened, streaked with ruin; every pike that pierced a
ghoul lost its head.

Geraden tried to wrestle Terisa toward the meeting hall, into
the relative center of the battle, where the men watched each other's
backs. She thought she ought to help him, but she couldn't get her
legs under her; the fall from her horse seemed to have broken the
connection between what her brain suggested and what her muscles
did. She wanted to say, Water. Try water. Maybe the acid could be
washed away. Or diluted. Unfortunately, all that came between her
lips was a hoarse gasp for air.

And the air was full of wails and death; the stench of rot; men
cursing for their lives; sunset.

Then, so suddenly that the sound of it almost relaxed her chest
enough to let her breathe, she heard a trumpet.

That high penetrating call seemed to change everything.

At its signal, twenty or thirty men charged through the village
on horseback.

They knew what they were doing: they didn't risk any of their
mounts in an attempt to trample the ghouls. Instead, they carried
lights of every description—torches, lanterns, blazing fagots, even
oil lamps. Shining like a host of glory, the riders swept into Naybel
at dusk.

Obliquely, Terisa noticed that one of them was the Fayle himself. She recognized him by his age, his leanness, his long, heavy jaw.

She didn't have the strength to wonder what he was doing here.
She was too busy watching.

The light seemed to hurt the ghouls worse than death did: it
paralyzed them. They lost their grins, their hunger, the power of
movement. And when they couldn't move, they couldn't feed on
each other; they couldn't multiply.

Clearly, the Fayle's men knew this would happen. At once, they
took advantage of it.

In grim concentration, as if they had never been able to reconcile themselves to killing creatures that looked like children, they began hacking the ghouls apart and setting the pieces to the torch.

They used cast-iron tongs and shovels to pile the dismembered corpses together so that the flames fed on each other. Before long, the bonfire beside the meeting hall of Naybel grew so large that its flames seemed to reach the darkening heavens. After the last of the sun went down, there was no other light in the village except fire.

Hot fire and acrid smoke slowly took the cold, rotting odor out of the air. A gust of wind carried smoke into Terisa's eyes; tears ran down her cheeks as if she were weeping. But she was able to breathe again, able to get air all the way down into the bottom of her lungs, able to move her shoulder. So that was why, she thought deliberately, distracting herself from the slaughter she had just witnessed so it wouldn't overwhelm her, that was why the bodies in those burned huts in Aperyte hadn't been consumed, when every other form of flesh in the village was gone. Once the acid had set fire to the wood, the flames had cast enough light to keep the ghouls away.

After a minute or two, she became aware that Geraden still had his arms around her. Like her, he had taken a faceful of smoke; like her, he appeared to be weeping. The light of burning children reflected in his eyes.

She hugged him, held him; clung to him. She didn't know how much more she could bear.

Trying to recover his composure, he muttered, "I'm never going to tell Quiss about this. Never as long as I live."

Terisa coughed at the smoke, cleared her throat. Remembering the way he had kept her sane when the Congery's champion had brought the ceiling of the hall down on her, she made an effort to return the favor. "That's probably a good idea. If I hadn't seen it myself, I wouldn't want you to tell me about it."

In the same tone, as if he were talking about the same thing, he said, "If I ever get my hands on Master Eremis, I swear I'm going to kill him."

Distinctly, so that there would be no mistake about it, she replied, "You'll have to get to him before I do."

Geraden studied her through the dusk and firelight. Then, just for a moment, he grinned. "If he knew we're this angry at him, he would break into a sweat."

He made it possible for her to smile as well. "You know," she murmured close to his ear, "until I met you, it never once occurred to me that someday I would be able to make my enemies sweat."

"Your enemies, my lady?" Geraden gave her an extra hug. "You make *me* sweat."

When she saw the Fayle riding toward her, she realized that she felt able to face him now.

He dismounted carefully and gave her an old man's brittle bow. "My lady Terisa," he said in a voice like dry leaves, "you astonish me. When last we met, I believed that Master Eremis was the source of my surprise, but now I can see that I was mistaken. The surprise is in you.

"This trap was set for ghouls, my lady. It was never my intention to ensnare you—to endanger you."

"Of course not, my lord Fayle." She didn't know what kind of bow to give him. Fortunately, he didn't seem to expect one. "We were just—" She caught herself, made an effort to take one thing at a time. "My lord, this is Geraden."

The Fayle looked at Geraden. "Son of the Domne," he murmured. "Translator of the lady Terisa of Morgan. A prominent figure in the Congery's augury of Mordant's need." Again, he bowed. "You are welcome in the Care of Fayle."

Geraden returned the bow. Terisa wondered whether he— whether she herself—would still be welcome if the lord knew of their talents; but she wasn't given a chance to explore the issue. Without pausing, the Fayle went on, "I must get out of this smoke. Our camp is a mile from here. There we can offer you hot food and a safe bed. If you will consent to accompany me, we will hear your story in better comfort.

"In the morning, the villagers will return to cleanse their homes, and we will ride to attempt this tactic again elsewhere. You will be welcome to accompany us then, also, if you wish."

"Thanks, my lord," Geraden answered promptly. "We'll be glad to go with you—at least for tonight. We've got a lot to tell you."

"I am sure you do," said the Fayle. "Perhaps you will be able to tell me whether Master Eremis is honest—whether I was wrong to betray his intentions to Castellan Lebbick.

"Come."

As if all his joints ached, he climbed back onto his horse.

All his joints probably did ache. Terisa would have thought that he was too old for ambushes and battles. Privately, she wondered what drove him to it.

She also wondered how much it would be safe to tell him. She and Geraden had come close to disaster by telling the Termigan too much.

Before she had time to wonder what had become of the roan gelding, one of the Fayle's men returned it to her; he had found it in the woods. Soon she and Geraden were riding among the Fayle's companions toward his camp.

After the turmoil and fright of the battle, the ride seemed re-assuring and peaceful, too brief. In a short time, she found herself dismounted before a bright fire near the center of a clearing. Around her were servants and supply wains, bedrolls set out on the ground, more men, extra horses; a few of Naybel's people had come to hear what had happened to their village. A steward brought a flagon of heated wine for the Fayle, then hurried away to get more for the lord's unexpected guests. The way the men looked at her reminded Terisa that she hadn't had a decent bath for days. Her hair probably looked like a rat's nest, and her clothes were filthy. Unfortunately, there was nothing she could do about those things at the moment. Instead, she attempted to ignore the stares of the Fayle's men.

A campstool was brought for the lord, and he seated himself near the fire as if he were chilled. Almost at once, more stools appeared for Terisa and Geraden. They sat down, accepted warm flagons of wine. Terisa took a sip, then forgot her self-consciousness—forgot that at least thirty people were watching her—long enough to give a grateful sigh. The wine was full of cinnamon and oranges, a blissful antidote for the smell of ghouls. If she had enough to drink, she might be able to get that reek completely out of her mind.

She wanted to spend a while savoring the sensation that she was safe.

But Geraden was already eager to talk. "My lord Fayle," he said before she was ready, "we've come a long way to tell you Master Eremis isn't honest. He's the one who translates these ghouls into your Care—he and Master Gilbur, and probably the arch-Imager Vagel.

"We came to tell you King Joyse needs help. If he doesn't get it, Master Eremis may destroy him."

By force of habit, the Fayle sat upright on his stool. His eyes were keenly blue; his gaze was precise. Looking at him, Terisa was struck by the odd thought that he would never have been able to do what King Joyse had done—make himself appear weak and foolish for years. No one who met the Fayle's gaze would doubt that he knew what he was doing.

"It is comforting to know," he muttered dryly, "that Master Eremis deserved to be thwarted. We will discuss that further. Nevertheless his dishonesty does little to explain how you came to fall into a trap which I had set for ghouls."

"Actually, it explains a lot, my lord," countered Geraden. "The rest is just details." For reasons Terisa understood perfectly, he was being cautious. "We rode here from Sternwall. The Termigan wasn't especially glad to see us.

"Like yours, his Care is being badly hurt by one of Eremis' translations. We told him the same thing I just told you. King Joyse needs help. He didn't seem to care about that. I think we were lucky he let us leave.

"My lord, I don't want that to happen again. The lady Terisa and I are going to fight for the King. Even if we have to do it alone, we're going to do it. If you stand in our way, we'll have to fight you, too.

"I'd rather cut off my hands."

All the men around the camp were listening. Some of them pretended to be busy with their weapons or their bedding, but they were listening. A focused hush covered everything except the snorts and rustling of the horses.

The Fayle gazed at Geraden steadily. "You must have told the Termigan something he especially did not wish to hear."

Geraden nodded.

"What was it?" asked the Fayle. "What could you have said to him that would make a loyal and trustworthy ally of the King suspicious of you?"

Geraden referred the question to Terisa.

Simply because the lord's eyes were so blue, so exact, she assented to the risk.

"We told him the truth," Geraden answered the Fayle. "We've both become Imagers. Terisa is an arch-Imager. The ghouls have started getting worse, haven't they? Just recently?"

It was the lord's turn to nod.

"That's because of us. Eremis knew we were coming here. Or

he figured it out. We were at Houseldon first. Then we were in Sternwall. Where else would we be going?

"He wants to kill us before we find a way to hurt him."

"And have you found a way?" the Fayle inquired dryly.

"We've been trying. That's why we went to Sternwall—why we came here. We've been trying to gather support for the King." Geraden took a deep breath. "And if we can't do that, we want to find somebody who can help me make a mirror."

"You have no glass?" The Fayle's gaze was sharp.

Geraden straightened his shoulders, and Terisa thought she heard a distant echo of strength in his voice, a strange menace. "My lord," he said, "a number of things would be different if we had as much as one small mirror between us. For one, we would have helped you fight those ghouls." He was speaking through his teeth. "That's what our talents are good for."

After a moment, however, the menace faded from his tone. "Unfortunately, we're helpless. So far."

The Fayle considered Geraden and Terisa for a while. He turned away to request food and more wine. Then he commented, "Perhaps you should tell me your story now. While we eat."

Geraden glanced at Terisa again. She nodded without hesitation. She was remembering the way the old lord had left the meeting Master Eremis had arranged between the lords and Prince Kragen. *Queen Madin is a formidable woman,* he had explained in an apologetic and even vaguely foolish tone. *Whatever choice I make here, I must justify to her.* His peaked shoulders and elongated head should have made him look silly as he walked out on Eremis' plotting. And yet he hadn't looked silly at all. His clear loyalty had made him admirable.

Under the circumstances, she didn't know what to expect from the Fayle. She was willing to trust him anyway.

Apparently, Geraden felt the same. As soon as the decision to speak freely had been taken, he began to relax.

He didn't try to include everything, however. He still wanted an answer from the Fayle. So he only described the broad outlines of what he and Terisa had learned, what they had done. The Fayle flinched at the news of what had happened to Houseldon, what was happening to Sternwall; but Geraden kept on talking. Whenever the lord stopped him with a question, however, he replied in more detail.

Most of the men were listening openly now. A few of them

fingered their weapons in anger or fear. But because their attention wasn't on Terisa she was able to ignore them.

While Geraden and the lord spoke, she drank her wine, ate the food placed in front of her, and did a little calculating backward. That brought her to the unexpected realization that thirteen days had passed, *thirteen,* since her translation from Orison. In thirteen days, anything could have happened, anything at all. Prince Kragen could have taken the castle—and the Congery. High King Festten could have taken the castle and the Congery *and* Prince Kragen. On the other hand, Castellan Lebbick could have stuck a quiet knife in Master Eremis' back.

"The problem is," she put in when Geraden paused, "we've been away from Orison too long." Abruptly, she became the focus of attention. Swallowing a rush of self-consciousness, she forced herself to say, "Thirteen days for me. Fourteen for him.

"We don't have any way of knowing what's happened in the meantime."

"So perhaps," the Fayle murmured slowly, "this strange *policy* of the King's has already come to its crisis. Perhaps he is already victorious. Or perhaps he has already been defeated and killed."

"We can't know," she agreed. "All we have to go on is that when we left Orison Eremis was still working hard to look innocent. And since then he's been working hard to get us killed. He's still afraid we can hurt him somehow." She shrugged. "It isn't much. But as long as he's afraid of us, we have something to hope for."

"That's something else we might be able to do if we had a mirror," Geraden added. "Get an Image of Orison. See what's going on."

The Fayle faced Geraden acutely. He looked at Terisa, searched her. After a moment, he spread his hands. The gesture was small, but it seemed full of resignation.

"I have no glass, and no way to make it. I have no Imagers— what use do I have for mirrors? Every product or tool of Imagery which has ever been found in the Care of Fayle, I have given to King Joyse and Adept Havelock."

By degrees, his gaze drifted away toward the fire. "Without Imagers, my Care is helpless against these ghouls. You have been away from Orison for thirteen or fourteen days. I have not seen Romish since the day I returned from Master Eremis' meeting. I have been in the saddle, in the villages of my Care—fighting—"

Terisa had never heard him sound so old.

"I cannot win this struggle. In the end, I must fail." He wasn't looking at his men. His men didn't look at him. None of them contradicted him. "You saw that I have failed Aperyte. It is only one among many villages dead, gutted—

"These ghouls are too many. I have hardly enough trained horsemen for four bands such as this one. I must fail."

"Then, my lord," Geraden said softly, formally, hinting at authority, "fight another way. Gather your men. Strike at Eremis in Esmerel. While any hope at all remains."

The old lord studied the heart of the fire. His erect posture didn't shift, didn't sag, but his hands hung between his knees as if they were useless. After a while, he whispered, "No."

"My lord—" Geraden began.

"No," breathed the Fayle. "Joyse is my King—and the husband of my daughter. I love him. I do not understand this *policy*. I do not like it. Yet I love him.

"But he has *never*"—one hand came up into a fist, fell again— "in all his years of warfare against Cadwal and Alend and Imagery, he has *never* asked a lord for aid when that lord's Care was under attack. He came to *me*, freed *my* people. He did not ask me for any help until my Care was safe.

"He will not ask me now. He has no wish to break my heart."

Geraden tried again. "My lord—"

"No." The Fayle didn't sound angry: he sounded sad. "Today we saved Naybel. You were witness. Tomorrow—or in five days— or in *fifty* days"—now both hands were fists, beating the rhythm of his words against each other—"we will spring another trap, and it will succeed. People will live who would die if I left them to the mercy of these ghouls.

"Do you hear me, Geraden? Did your father ride away from his Care? Did the Termigan?

"I will not leave my people to die undefended."

"I understand, my lord." Geraden's voice was as soft and sad as the lord's, but there was no bitterness in it. "It doesn't matter how desperate King Joyse is. He wouldn't want you to abandon your own Care. He didn't create Mordant or the Congery because he was desperate. He created them because he believes the same things you do."

The Fayle stared into the fire, nodded several times. In a voice like a winter breeze, he sighed, "Thank you."

Geraden hesitated momentarily, then ventured to say, "Unfortunately, that doesn't change our problem. Is there anything you can do to help Terisa and me?"

With a shift of his head, the lord brought his blue gaze to Geraden's face. For an instant, Terisa thought he was angry. Then, however, she saw a suggestion of a smile touch his old mouth. "That is true, Geraden," he said. "My stubbornness does nothing to change your problem. You and the lady Terisa are Imagers, and the evil of Imagery must be met and answered by Imagers. That is your 'Care,' in a manner of speaking.

"I will give you supplies. If you need it, I will give you a map. And I will give you two men to ride with you as far as you choose— to Orison, even to Esmerel. They will be useless against Imagers, but they will know how to use their swords to guard your backs and clear your road."

Before Geraden could reply, Terisa asked, "Can they take us to the Queen?"

Geraden was surprised: apparently, he hadn't given much thought to Queen Madin. The Fayle raised an eyebrow; but this time his smile was plain. "A good thought, my lady," he murmured. "It would have come to me in a moment. My men can certainly take you to the Queen. She has a clear right to know what her husband has been doing." His smile faded at the memory. "After all, she has been deeply hurt by his *policy*. And it is possible that she may want to do something about it."

In response, Terisa swallowed hard and said, "Thanks. I appreciate that." The force of her relief took her aback. She had known that she wanted to meet the Queen, but she hadn't realized before just how terrible she would feel if she and Geraden came all this way and then left without taking the time to share what they knew with King Joyse's wife.

Geraden stared at her, but he didn't argue; he didn't say, That's a delay we don't need, a day we could spend better on the way to Orison. Luckily, his instinct to trust her was still intact. After a moment, he let the matter drop and concentrated on eating his supper.

Later that night, however, when she and Geraden were in their bedding together, a short distance away from the Fayle's men, he said under his breath, "I didn't know you wanted to meet Queen Madin. Or is it Torrent you're so interested in?"

Terisa didn't answer directly. After musing for a while, she murmured, "Do you remember what the Castellan said to Elega—the message he said King Joyse sent to her?" In case he didn't remember, she reminded him: "'I am sure that my daughter Elega has acted for the best reasons. She carries my pride with her wherever she goes. For her sake, as well as for my own, I hope that the best reasons will also produce the best results.'"

"Yes," returned Geraden. "It still doesn't make sense. It still doesn't fit with what Master Quillon told you."

"Wait a minute," she said to keep him quiet. "Do you remember that talk I had with Adept Havelock, while you and Artagel were on the other side of the pillar—after he rescued us from those insects?"

Obediently, Geraden nodded.

"He talked about Myste," she whispered, "and the Congery's champion. He said he had cast an augury about King Joyse, and one of the Images showed Myste and the champion together."

Obediently, Geraden didn't interrupt.

"I've always wondered why he told us that. If it wasn't just because he's crazy. And I've always wondered why King Joyse got so upset when I lied to him about Myste—when I said she went back to her mother. Why he was relieved when I told him I helped her go after the champion."

In silence, Geraden waited patiently. At last, he suggested, "Why don't you tell me what you think?"

"I think—" Terisa held her breath, then forged ahead. "I think there's more to King Joyse's plans than Master Quillon told us. I think his daughters are important—I think his whole family is important somehow. I think he wanted to throw Elega and Prince Kragen together. I think he wanted Myste to go after the champion."

"You think he wanted us to go talk to Queen Madin and Torrent? Isn't that a little farfetched? After all, he didn't know either one of us had any talent. There was no way he could have predicted we would ever be here."

That was true. And it made everything more dangerous. Nevertheless Terisa persisted. "I think," she said, "*I* want to go talk to Queen Madin and Torrent. Just in case." After a moment, she added, "He had reason to think we *might* have talent."

She could feel Geraden grinning in the dark. "My lady, you've got a remarkably subtle mind. Or indigestion—I can't figure out which."

She got a hand under his jerkin and poked him in the ribs until he apologized.

Then she poked him for apologizing.

With so many potential spectators nearby, she and Geraden actually got more sleep than usual. And the next day two of the Fayle's men guided them to Romish.

The lord's seat was situated on a fertile plain uncharacteristically—for this Care—devoid of trees. The land for a mile or two in each direction had been cleared to make room for the fields which fed the city. But Terisa saw no more of Romish itself than the earthwork wall around it. As Myste had said, Queen Madin and Torrent lived in a manor outside the city.

The manor, Vale House, which a former Cadwal prince had raised to shelter his poor relations while he ruled Fayle, was tucked into a fold among small hills perhaps half a mile upstream along the small Kolted River which provided most of the water for Romish and the fields. As a defensive position—Terisa surprised herself by thinking about such things—the location of Vale House left a lot to be desired: in full daylight, a rider could probably get within twenty yards of the building unnoticed. On the other hand, the House was so easily reached from Romish, and so stoutly constructed, that it was probably in no danger most of the time. Its walls were of stone—strong against ghouls—and the timbers of its doors were banded with iron.

Through the long dusk of the plain, the Fayle's men guided Terisa and Geraden among the hills to Vale House. They dismounted before the high doors. The Fayle's men told the emerging servants to fetch torches for light, grooms for the horses; also the lady Queen Madin. The windows of the House filled up with brightness as lamps and lanterns were lit inside. In a short time, a woman came across the porch to the steps with a blaze of illumination behind her, as regal as if she ruled the world.

The Fayle's men bowed and stepped back.

"My lady Queen." Geraden bowed as well, bending so low that he nearly fell over. There was a suggestion of tears in his voice. Madin was a sovereign to him, after all—and the wife of the King he loved. "It does my heart good to see you again."

"Geraden." Queen Madin's tone conveyed the immediate impression that she knew how to make up her mind. "This is quite a surprise. But a good one—so far." She didn't sound harsh, and certainly not cold; she only sounded quick to choose. Decisiveness was a power she wielded without noticing it. "I am glad to see a friendly face from home. And I will be glad to hear your news, whatever it is." A moment later, she added, "But if that old fool Joyse sent you here to plead his case, you can forget about it and go back. I will not have it."

"My lady Queen," repeated Geraden. He bowed again, this time to cover a smile. "This is the lady Terisa of Morgan."

"Ah." Queen Madin turned toward Terisa, but Terisa still couldn't see her face; dark against the glow from the house, her features were undecipherable. "The lady Terisa. My father mentioned you, after his return from Orison.

"My lady—Geraden—you are welcome in Vale House. Please enter."

She turned and walked back into the light.

Geraden touched Terisa's shoulder, nudged her toward the steps and the porch. The light shone on his face, and she was filled for a moment with the unexpected conviction that they had done the right thing by coming here. He had never looked taller; his gaze had never seemed keener. This was the way he might have appeared when he stood in front of King Joyse—if his King hadn't been so studiously dedicated to breaking his loyalty.

She slipped her arm through his and hugged it so that they went up to the porch and entered the high doorway of Vale House together.

They followed the Queen's back and a bowing servant along an entryway hall with tapestries and portraits on the walls, several doors on each side, and a wide stair at the end. Queen Madin chose a door on the left; the servant held it open for Terisa and Geraden, and they found themselves in what looked like a large sitting room. A blazing fireplace dominated the outer wall, and two deep couches and four or five plush armchairs were semicircled before the hearth with their backs to the paneling in the rest of the room. Queen Madin sent the servant for some wine, then gestured her guests toward the chairs; but she remained standing beside the fireplace.

Neither Terisa nor Geraden sat. He may have stayed upright out of courtesy, but her thoughts were elsewhere. At last, she could see Queen Madin clearly, and what she saw kept her on her feet.

Until that moment, she hadn't realized how much she was expecting the Queen to resemble Elega. From Terisa's point of view, Myste favored her father: Myste's laugh was so much like King Joyse's smile that the resemblance seemed more important than any differences. Simply on that basis, because the contrast between Myste and Elega was so pronounced, Terisa had assumed that Queen Madin would prove to be the parent Elega favored.

It was clear now, however, in the light of the fire and the bright chandelier and the surrounding lamps, that Terisa's assumptions were mistaken. One good look at the Queen made it plain that both Elega and Myste in fact resembled their father. Madin was still a luminous woman, despite her years; her gaze was strong, and the years hadn't cost her manner any discernible loss of firmness. But her features were at once too blunt and too forthright to be the model for Myste's and Elega's faces.

What kept Terisa on her feet, however, wasn't the Queen's appearance, but rather her bearing: she stood the way a queen should stand, as if not just her authority but her wise use of it as well came to her so naturally that both were beyond question. She was the Fayle's daughter in more ways than one; she even conveyed a suggestion of the same sorrow which harried the old lord. Nevertheless, perhaps because her frame was more solidly constructed than his, she projected more force of personality, more of both the ability and the willingness to make other people do what she wanted.

Her failure to make King Joyse put down his passivity and become a decent ruler for Mordant again must have been more galling to her than any other wound she had suffered in her life.

But she was obviously not a woman who felt much self-pity, and she wasn't feeling sorry for herself at the moment. She was studying both Terisa and Geraden with keen interest. And she seemed to find him especially intriguing, even though Terisa was the one who had come to Mordant from an alien world. After a moment, she explained her attention by saying, "Geraden, you have changed."

Terisa's immediate reaction was, No, he hasn't. From her perspective, he had come back to his essential self from iron and despair. Queen Madin's observation made her think again, however. In fact, he *had* changed. He hadn't simply lost his clumsiness: he had lost his puppyish look, his appearance of being a boy hidden inside a man. His back was straight and strong, and she had a hard time imagining him making a mistake.

As if to demonstrate the change, he smiled almost without embarrassment. "It's Terisa's influence, my lady Queen. She made me stop apologizing."

"No," Queen Madin replied firmly. "The difference is that you are more at peace within yourself." She was sure of her own judgment. "You have become an Imager."

In response, he shrugged self-deprecatingly; but he held her gaze. "I didn't know it shows."

"Oh, it shows, Geraden," the Queen affirmed, "it shows. No one would mistake you now for the oldest failed Apt ever to serve the Congery.

"As for you, my lady," she went on, turning to Terisa, "you are less clear to me. Your surprises are better concealed, I think. You both have a great deal to tell me."

"That's true, my lady Queen," Geraden said at once. His awareness of how hard that job would be showed in the way he asked, "But what of yourself? Won't you first tell us how you are? And Torrent?"

The Queen shook her head. "What I tell you of myself will depend entirely on whether you were sent here by that old dodderer the King. I have asked you that once, but you did not answer clearly."

For a moment, Geraden measured his reply. Then he said flatly, "King Joyse didn't send us. I think he would be *astonished* if he knew we were here."

Queen Madin appeared to receive this information as if it inflicted a deep hurt which she had no intention of showing. As she spoke, however, she couldn't muffle the roughness in her voice. "In that case, Geraden—Torrent and I are well. But not as well as we would be if our family were whole again. The King's aberrations exact a price from us all.

"Will you not be seated?" she continued, shaking herself out of her thoughts. "Here is wine." The servant had reentered the room carrying a silver tray. "And Torrent will be with us soon, I am sure."

"Ah," the Queen concluded as the door opened again, "here she is now."

Terisa turned in time to see King Joyse and Queen Madin's second daughter close the door behind her and approach the fire.

Torrent's carriage and downcast eyes and demure gown conveyed two impressions almost simultaneously: first, she was so shy
that she made Myste and Elega seem as extroverted as mountebanks;
and second, despite her shyness, she was nearly the image of her
mother. She could have been Queen Madin's shadow: they were as
alike as reflections of each other. Only her mother's decisiveness was
missing, her mother's assurance.

"Torrent," the Queen said, "here are Geraden and the lady
Terisa of Morgan. They have a great deal to tell us. She has done
something all the Masters of the Congery together could not do. She
has made him an Imager."

Torrent paused among the chairs. The gaze which she raised
beneath her lashes was at once so hesitant and so full of wonder that
Terisa blushed involuntarily.

"Under the circumstances," Geraden muttered humorously—
perhaps for Torrent's benefit, perhaps for Terisa's—"I don't think
that's much of a compliment. The only benefit I've gotten from the
change is that now people want to kill me.

"My lady Torrent," he went on, "I'm glad to see you. When
you and the Queen left Orison, I didn't think I'd ever have that
privilege again."

"Oh, 'privilege,' Geraden." Torrent spoke as if she, too, were
blushing; yet her cheeks remained pale, untouched. "You're making
fun of me."

Before he could reply—perhaps so that he wouldn't have a
chance to reply—she came abruptly toward Terisa. Facing Terisa as
if holding her chin up were an act of courage, she said, "I'm sure
Mother has made you welcome, my lady, but let me welcome you
also. Grandfather—the Fayle—told us everything he knew about
you, but it only made us more curious. I'm afraid we'll exhaust you
with questions."

"Please." Terisa had no idea why she was blushing. She made
a special effort to speak calmly, comfortably, to put Torrent at ease.
"Call me Terisa. Both Myste and Elega do."

That brought a smile to Torrent's face, a lift of self-confidence.
"Do you know Myste and Elega? I suppose you must, since you've
been in Orison. Are you friends? How are they?" After an instant
of hesitation, a quick glance at Queen Madin, she asked, "And Father? How is he?"

"Torrent," the Queen said both kindly and firmly, "we must sit down. If we do not, Geraden and the lady Terisa will remain standing all night."

In a convincing imitation of a woman with no will of her own, Torrent immediately sat down in the nearest chair.

Queen Madin took an armchair near the fire. Geraden and Terisa seated themselves on a couch between the Queen and her daughter. Promptly, the servant brought around goblets of wine on a tray, then set the wine down near Torrent and withdrew.

"You are tired from your journey," Queen Madin said after she had tasted her wine. "We will bathe and feed you shortly. You will be given all the rest you can allow yourselves. But you must understand that we are hungry for news. In Vale House, we do not hear even rumors from Romish, not to mention truth from Orison. How *are* Elega and Myste?" Just for an instant, her throat closed. "How is the King?"

Now Geraden hesitated; the change Queen Madin had observed seemed to desert him momentarily. Which made perfect sense to Terisa. Her heart was suddenly thick, and she felt an ache gathering around her. It was possible that the Queen and Torrent would take the news of King Joyse gladly: possible, but very unlikely.

"This is difficult," Geraden murmured awkwardly. "I can't really tell you anything without telling you everything—and I don't know where to start. I can't think of any way to say this that won't be hurtful."

Torrent studied her hands, but Terisa could see that she was breathing deeply to steady herself. Queen Madin, on the other hand, faced Geraden's uncertainty without blinking.

"Tell us the truth," she said bluntly. "Speculation will be more hurtful to us than any news."

Still Geraden faltered.

Grimly, because the only thing worse than knowledge was ignorance, Terisa said, "The King knows what he's doing. He's doing it on purpose."

Torrent didn't raise her eyes; she seemed to freeze in her seat.

"'On purpose,'" Queen Madin echoed slowly. "My lady, you must explain that observation."

"Unfortunately, it's true," Geraden rushed in. "Terisa knows more about King Joyse's reasons and intentions than anybody else. She's had several talks with him—he answered questions for her. He's gone out of his way to give her explanations. I think it's because of the way she came to Orison. An impossible translation—or we all thought it was impossible until I realized I can do it anytime I want. She was so obviously important. She's involved in the Congery's augury. We didn't know what her talent is, but it was obvious she had to have some kind of unprecedented power."

Abruptly, he made himself stop. Speaking distinctly, he said, "The last we heard, Elega is fine. We don't know about Myste."

"It's a trap, my lady Queen," Terisa tried to explain. "He's setting a trap for his enemies, for Mordant's enemies. They were too powerful—and he didn't know who they were. And he was afraid that they would keep getting stronger—that they might swallow Alend or Cadwal or both—and leave him alone while they got stronger and stronger, until they were too strong for him, too strong for anyone. He was afraid that if he didn't find out who his enemies were and stop them he would lose everything."

"That was true," the Queen put in crisply. "Any fool could see it."

"So," Terisa went on with an inward groan, "he made himself weak."

Queen Madin stared at her. "I do not believe you. What nonsense! What good is weakness? How is it used against Imagers and armies?"

She might have said more, but Geraden intervened. The unexpected authority in the way he raised his hand stopped her. "Listen to us, my lady Queen," he breathed gently. "Please listen."

"I'm sorry," Terisa murmured. "It's the truth. It's all we have.

"He paralyzed his own strength. He made it impossible for the Congery to do anything effectively. He undercut the Castellan. He abandoned the Perdon without reinforcements. He insulted Prince Kragen—the Fayle probably told you that. He made himself look like a fool. He"—her voice caught briefly—"he did his best to drive his family away." She thought she ought to mention the Tor's son, but she didn't have the heart for it. "He practically punished people like Geraden for being loyal."

Queen Madin sat without moving a muscle, listened without any reaction except a slow reddening of her cheeks. Torrent was breathing so hard she was almost panting.

"My lady Queen, he made himself a *target*. So that his enemies would attack *him*, instead of chewing Alend and Cadwal and Mordant up slowly until they were too strong to be beaten. It was all a ruse, a trick to make his enemies try to destroy him before they became strong enough to be safe."

The Domne had put his finger on it. King Joyse wanted to save the world. He hurt all the people he loved best because saving the world was more important to him than anything else.

That was a terrible burden for him to bear.

On the other hand, it wasn't exactly easy for the people he loved.

Without warning—and almost without transition, as if she had been secretly standing all along—Queen Madin swept to her feet. "Why?" she demanded in a voice that made Terisa want to hide under the couch. "If this is true, why did he not tell me?" She didn't shout, but her tone had the impact of a yell. "Did he not trust me? Did he believe that I would not understand?—that I would not *approve?*"

Geraden stood to face her. "My lady Queen," he asked softly, intently, "what would you have done if he told you?"

"I would not have *come here.*" The Queen might as well have been shouting. "I would have stood by him, instead of allowing all the world to think that I have lost my love for him and his ideals and the realm."

Geraden gave Terisa a look full of pain and sorrow, a look that brought her to her feet at his side, but he didn't back down. "That's the problem, my lady Queen. You would have stood by him. And as long as you were there, no one would believe he was collapsing. Not really. Or if they did believe it, they would know you were there to make decisions for him, Queen Madin, daughter of the Fayle, the most formidable woman in Orison. His trap would have failed. No one would fall into it.

"And if he had asked you to leave?" Geraden went on. "If he had explained his trap and asked you to cooperate by abandoning him? Could you have borne it? Could you have sat on your hands here for—what is it, two years now?—while he risked his life and everything you both believe in?"

He was right: this was hurtful with a vengeance. Nevertheless Terisa was certain these things had to be said. She was just grateful that she wasn't the one saying them.

And Queen Madin was hurt: that was unmistakable. She had been dealt a blow which shook her to the bone.

"My lady Queen," Geraden concluded in a voice thick with regret, "if this policy is to succeed—if there's any chance to save Mordant—what else could he have done?"

"Oh, Father." Torrent was so distressed that she watched Geraden's face openly, without shyness, without self-consciousness. "What have I done? I should have stayed with you. Like Myste and Elega."

"No, Torrent." Queen Madin tried to speak as if she had no tears spilling down her cheeks, no grief in her chest. "We would have broken his heart. It was a hard thing for him to drive us away. It would have been terrible to try to drive us away and fail—and so lose the chance to save his kingdom."

"But he's caused all this pain"—sitting, Torrent looked small and helpless, too little to understand or be consoled—"and we left him to endure it alone. I left him. He has no wish to cause pain. His heart is broken already, or he wouldn't have done something so desperate—"

Despite her own hurt, the Queen gave her daughter a comforting response. "Hush, child. Do not be in a hurry to call him desperate. Your father has always been given to risks. We must not believe the worst until it is proven."

Then she wiped her eyes and faced Geraden and Terisa squarely. "Now," she said in a tone of barely concealed ferocity, "you must tell us what the outcome of the King's weakness has been."

Geraden nodded. Terisa murmured, "Yes."

In pieces back and forth as details and developments occurred to them, they told their story as coherently as they could.

And while they told it, Queen Madin became another woman before their eyes. She seemed to find sustenance in the events they described, the implications they discussed. She knew, of course, about the disaster of the Congery's champion, and about Master Eremis' strange attempt to make an alliance of the lords of the Cares, Prince Kragen, and the Congery: reminders of that information had no effect on her now. But the presence—and the freedom—of the High King's Monomach in Orison made her straighten her shoulders. King Joyse's treatment of the Perdon and Prince Kragen seemed to strengthen her bones. Myste's foolish and gallant pursuit of the champion caused her eyes to glow. And Elega's plot with Nyle and Prince Kragen to betray Orison—which Geraden explained with considerable difficulty because it, too, must be hurtful—seemed to bring a flush of youth to the Queen's cheeks. "Brave Elega," she murmured as if she would have done the same thing in her daughter's place. But when she heard that Orison was besieged, she snapped like a soldier, "Then why are you *here?* Why are you not *there,* fighting for King Joyse and Mordant?"

"My lady Queen," replied Geraden, "we still have a lot to tell you."

Just for a second, the Queen paused—not hesitating, but simply allowing the forces inside her time to come together. Then, surprisingly, she said, "Let it wait. Until dinner, perhaps. I have no time for it now."

At once, she clapped her hands twice, summoning a servant.

Almost immediately, the servant who had brought the wine came into the room. Without a glance at her guests, she commanded, "Please conduct Geraden and the lady Terisa to their rooms. Supply them with bathwater and clean clothes. Announce dinner for them in an hour. Then bring the Fayle's men to me.

"Come, Torrent. We must prepare."

As the servant bowed, Queen Madin swept toward the door as regally as if she had an entire procession behind her.

With a flustered look, Torrent jumped up and hurried after her mother.

Geraden met Terisa's gaze in quick apprehension; then he mustered his temerity to ask, demand, "My lady Queen, what're you going to do?"

Queen Madin paused in the doorway. "'Do,' Geraden? My husband and my home are besieged. One of my daughters has allied herself with Alends. Another—if she still lives—is embarked on a mad quest after a champion from another world. I will not be left out of such events. I am going to Orison.

"I intend to be there in three days."

She left the room with Torrent nearly gasping in her wake.

For a long moment, Terisa and Geraden stood where they were as if they expected the ceiling to collapse on them. Then she took hold of herself, made an effort to shake the surprise out of her head. To break the shock, she murmured, "Well, at least she's going to let us have time for a bath and some food."

He snorted. "I should have guessed something like this would happen. I've known her long enough.

"The truth is"—he shrugged rather helplessly—"I've always liked her."

Terisa was quietly disturbed to find herself thinking of her own mother, who hadn't resembled Queen Madin in any meaningful way.

And she, Terisa, could so easily have become her mother's image: passive and wan, all her passion kept secret. If Geraden hadn't come for her—

Slipping her arm like a promise through his, she accompanied him out of the sitting room.

Dinner at the long table in the formal dining room of Vale House was an odd experience.

An abundance of candles made the ornaments and paneling glitter. There was a deep rug underfoot, thick cushions on the chairs. The food was good, better than anything Terisa and Geraden had eaten for quite a while; the wine was almost equal to the food. And the sensation of being clean again from head to toe, of being wrapped in clean clothes, of having a clean bed to look forward to, was so luxurious that it seemed practically indecent.

In addition, Torrent was fascinated by the personal side of Terisa and Geraden's story. Before she finished her soup, she was so caught up in what she heard that she forgot to be shy. She was indignant at Master Eremis' manipulations, horrified by Master Quillon's murder. Terisa's repeated rescues from Gart thrilled her. She grieved for Castellan Lebbick, and yet couldn't refrain from shuddering at the things the Castellan had done to Terisa. Artagel's injuries and Nyle's unhappiness touched her heart. The discovery of talent in her guests filled her with wonder. She heard about the destruction of Houseldon and the danger to Sternwall with parted lips and flushed cheeks.

Unwittingly, unself-consciously, she helped make the meal as pleasant as possible for her guests.

It was Queen Madin who provided the occasion with its oddness. She didn't appear to hear a word either Terisa or Geraden said.

She wasn't vague or befuddled: she was simply absent. Her attention was so sharply focused elsewhere that she had none to spare for such comparative details as Master Eremis' mendacity or Castellan Lebbick's accumulated distress.

As a result, neither Geraden nor Terisa was able to relax. Unexpectedly, she found herself thinking that the Queen was rather an old woman to attempt something as arduous as a wild ride to Orison. So she resolved to speak to Torrent privately after supper, to ask whether there was anything Torrent could do to dissuade the Queen.

Unfortunately, when Queen Madin announced the end of dinner she took Torrent with her at once. Instead of saying good night, she informed her guests that the men who had brought them here would procure a team of horses from Romish, "So that we need not stop too often on the road. We will depart as soon as the mounts are able to see their footing." Then she led Torrent away.

Terisa returned with Geraden to her room, troubled by the sense that this visit to the Queen wasn't producing the results she had intended. Whatever those were.

When they were alone, she asked him, "Is this a good idea?"

"What?" he replied disingenuously, "this rush to reach Orison in only three days?"

She poked his shoulder to get his attention. "Of course, you idiot. What else did you think I was talking about? Isn't she a little old to try something like that?"

He snickered. "*You* tell her she's too old—if you've got the nerve." Before Terisa could poke him again, however, he tried to give her a serious answer. "It isn't the ride I'm worried about. Either she can do it or she can't. Either way, it's out of our hands. What I'm worried about is the siege. Prince Kragen and his ten thousand Alends. Or, worse yet, High King Festten and twice that many Cadwals.

"How does she propose to get past them into Orison? Assuming it hasn't already been taken. When they find out who she is, they aren't exactly going to step aside for her. She's the perfect hostage. King Joyse may have been able to turn his back on the Perdon. He may have been able to swallow what happened to the Tor's son. He may even have been able to let Myste and Elega go. But he is not"— Geraden said the words distinctly, like drum beats—"going to be able to sit still when someone like the High King threatens his wife.

"She's the only weapon Alend or Cadwal needs to beat him."

At the thought, Terisa's stomach turned over. "Oh, good," she muttered. "I'm so glad you told me that."

"Sleep well," he replied with a malicious grin and rolled away from her.

She had to poke him several times to get him back where he belonged.

For a variety of reasons, neither of them slept much. Long before dawn, they got up, got dressed, and went to help with the preparations for the road.

Outside the protective stone of the manor, the air seemed colder than it had for several days. Even in the gray light before the sun came up, the day had an almost prescient clarity, a dimension of visual precision which made Terisa shiver. She hugged the half cloak the Termigan had given her around her shoulders and tried not to think about how tired she was.

The boards of the porch creaked under her feet.

From the porch of Vale House, the hills which enfolded the Kolted River appeared to bulk larger than they had the previous evening. They were dark in the dim forecasting of dawn, deep with potential; the whole world lay beyond them, completely hidden. They reminded her that Vale House would be easy to ambush.

On the other hand, an ambush didn't seem very likely at the moment. Even self-respecting villains and traitors were still in bed at this hour. And the Fayle's two men were already there, along with a groom they had brought from Romish to care for the horses and a servant to look after the needs of the ladies Queen Madin and Torrent. As for the horses—

There must have been sixteen or seventeen of them, filling the hollow between the manor and the river. Terisa's and Geraden's mounts. Horses for the four men and the two ladies. A pack animal to carry supplies. And a second mount for everyone, so that the horses could be rested while the Queen kept moving.

They shuffled their hooves, shook their manes; two or three of them snorted disconsolately. Their tack jangled softly, muffled by leather. The groom moved among them, settling the saddles of the ones that would be ridden first, cinching up their girths. Queen Madin's servant was busy checking the contents of his packs again.

Because she was cold and had to do something, Terisa asked Geraden, "Do you think we should try to stop her?"

He shrugged; the dimness hid his expression. "I'll try. But don't get your hopes up."

The sky spanning the hills grew to the color of mother-of-pearl, but without that nacreous flatness: it was at once deep and impenetrable. If anything, the approach of dawn made the hills darker; they clenched themselves around the river and Vale House, brooding. Nevertheless a stretch of water near the bend of the hills caught the air's reflection and gleamed silver.

Terisa wished that she could stop shivering.

After a moment, Queen Madin came out onto the porch with

Torrent beside her. The light was improving: Terisa saw that both
ladies were wrapped in warm cloaks; riding boots protected their
feet and calves; they had scarves bound around their heads to keep
their hair out of their faces.

"Are we ready?" the Queen asked anyone who could answer
her. "Can we go?"

"In a moment, my lady Queen," replied the groom. He was
busy inspecting the hooves of the horses.

Geraden cleared his throat. "My lady Queen, are you sure this
is wise? I have qualms about it."

"Geraden"—Queen Madin wasn't looking at him; her gaze was
fixed on the sharp outline of the hills—"you underestimate me if
you think that any 'qualms' of yours will stand between me and my
husband."

He let a little sharpness into his voice. "Maybe *you* underestimate *me,* my lady Queen. You don't know what my qualms are."

"Do I not?" She still didn't look at him. "You are concerned
that I may fall hostage to the forces besieging Orison."

"Yes," he admitted. His tone told Terisa that he felt rather
foolish.

"That is an important concern. I have no intention of allowing
any Alend or Cadwal to use me against the King." She paused, then
said, "It will be your duty to help me insure that the difficulty does
not arise."

"Yes, my lady Queen," Geraden murmured glumly.

Terisa put her hand on his arm and gave him a small squeeze
of consolation.

"Now, my lady Queen," the groom announced over the champ-
ing and rustling of the horses. "You can mount whenever you wish."

Torrent gave a stifled gasp. "A moment," she said quickly. "I
have forgotten something." Before anyone could react, she hurried
back into the manor.

Softly, so that no one except Terisa and Geraden heard her,
the Queen breathed, "Probably one of her dolls. She does not like
to sleep without her dolls." Her tone was affectionate, but it suggested that she didn't know how she had managed to produce a
daughter like Torrent.

It was astonishing how distinct everything was to Terisa. Every
one of the hills across the river had a particular shape, an individual
character. Each of the mounts was facing in a different direction,

stubbornly determined to see life from its own angle. Geraden held his head up as if he had caught some of the Queen's mood. Queen Madin herself was a knot of controlled impatience. The groom and the servant waited. The Fayle's men had begun to move toward the porch in order to help the ladies mount.

And *a touch of cold as thin as a feather and as sharp as steel slid straight through the center of her abdomen.*

"*Geraden!*" she shouted, almost wailed because her desperation was so sudden. "There's a translation coming!"

As if she and Geraden had the same mind, the same will, they grabbed Queen Madin by her arms, one on each side, and practically flung her off the porch, down the steps, out among the abruptly milling horses.

Terisa had time to hear one of the men curse as if a horse had kicked him. She registered the Queen's quick gasp of surprise, her swift self-command. She felt rather than saw the tethered mounts twist their heavy bodies around her, blunder against each other, stumble, start to panic.

Then she turned in time to see a fall of rock appear out of the empty sky and crash down on the roof of Vale House.

A fall of rock as massive as an avalanche. A few heavy, bounding stones hit, followed instantly by rushing thunder, the side of a mountain coming down.

The slates and beams of the roof couldn't hold, couldn't begin to think of holding. Almost without transition, the whole attic storey of the manor buckled and collapsed, plunging down into the level where the bedrooms were.

"Torrent!" cried Queen Madin. Without thinking, she twisted against Terisa and Geraden's grasp, tried to run back into the house. "*Torrent!*"

Terisa helped Geraden drag the Queen backward.

A frightened horse hit them with its hindquarters and knocked them all off balance.

The rockfall went on with a sound as if the hills themselves had begun to rumble and break. The bedroom level of the manor held until too many tons of rubble piled into it; then, one room at a time, it crumbled toward the ground floor.

Bouncing like balls, huge rocks came off the pile into the hollow. A horse screamed horribly; others squealed, wheeling in wild circles. They were tethered, had no way to escape. Behind Terisa, the groom was trampled to death. She didn't know how any of the stones missed her. The rockfall and the horses made so much noise that she couldn't hear any of the stones splash into the river; couldn't hear any cries, commands, any warnings.

Slowly, almost one stone at a time, the avalanche thinned. The rush of rock turned to scree and gravel, loose dirt.

Terisa stared in shock as the thunder subsided and huge clouds of dust swelled into the dawn.

The fact that she wasn't moving nearly got her killed.

There were men on horseback in the middle of the chaos, at least half a dozen of them. They lashed their beasts among the tethered mounts.

One of them clubbed Geraden to the ground; he never knew they were coming. Another knocked Terisa into a swirl of panic-stricken hooves.

And yet somehow, before she covered her head and curled into a ball to protect herself from being stamped on and broken, she had time to see three men leap from their mounts and snatch up the Queen.

She had time to see that they were armed and armored just like the men of Prince Kragen's army.

They were Alends.

Then hooves danced on all sides of her, thudded the dirt, hammered at her life, and she couldn't do anything except cling to herself and clench her eyes shut until the horses either killed her or backed away.

They backed away. Geraden was on his feet: he yelled at the horses, slapped at them until they retreated. At once, he reached down and pulled her to her feet.

"The Queen!" he panted as if he had broken something in his chest. "What happened to the Queen?"

At the same time, another woman cried from the bottom of her heart, "Mother? Mother!"

Staggering, Terisa turned; she dragged Geraden with her.

Torrent stood amid the ruins of the porch as if she had never been touched. Her arms were locked and rigid at her sides; one of her hands clutched a knife. She didn't look down into the hollow, at the horses, down at Terisa and Geraden; her face was lifted to the sky.

"Mother!"

Terisa stumbled in that direction, out of the confusion of horses, trying to reach the Queen's daughter before Torrent went mad. With Geraden behind her, she clambered among the splintered and canting remains of the porch.

"She wasn't killed!" she answered Torrent's wail, shouting to make herself heard over the memory of thunder. "They took her! She's been kidnapped!"

Master Eremis had sprung another of his imponderable traps. But this one changed everything. Alends—! He was in league with Alends? As well as Gart and the High King? What in the name of heaven was going *on?*

Terisa's shout snapped Torrent's head down, brought her frantic gaze out of the sky to Terisa's face.

"What?"

And Geraden demanded fiercely, "What? Kidnapped?"

"Soldiers came." Terisa could hardly distinguish between her own voice and the long, deep rumble echoing inside her. "Alend soldiers. They took her. That's why this happened. So they would have a chance to take her."

"*Alend* soldiers?" Geraden began to snarl uncharacteristic obscenities, ones Terisa had never heard him use before.

"Why?" Torrent asked softly, as if she were being split apart.

"Because she's so important!" Geraden rasped at once. "King Joyse will do anything to save her. He'll surrender Orison and the Congery and every one of us to save her."

Slowly, Torrent raised her knife, stared at it. "It's my fault." Terisa was amazed that Torrent wasn't weeping. The Queen's daughter sounded like she was weeping. "I wanted to take a knife. So I could help defend us. Elega would have been ready for that. Myste would have been ready. But I forgot. I ran to the kitchen." She turned the blade from side to side as if she had the idea of stabbing herself. "If I'd been with her—if I hadn't forgotten—I could have saved her. I could have tried to save her."

There was no doubt about it in Terisa's mind: Torrent was going mad.

If she had gone to her bedroom, as her mother had expected, instead of to the kitchen, she would have been killed almost instantly.

"No!" Terisa replied as loudly as she could, trying to convey conviction through her mounting sense of horror. "None of us could have saved her. They took us by surprise. The horses caused too much confusion. The men—"

Abruptly, she pivoted away to see what had happened to the groom, the servant, the Fayle's men.

The dawn was brighter now: it didn't raise much color, but it showed everything clearly.

A hoof had crushed the groom's head: he lay in the dirt as if he were abasing himself. One of the Fayle's men clutched at an incapacitating wound in his left shoulder; the other had been hacked to death. Dead and dying horses sprawled everywhere, some of them still quivering. Perhaps ten of the beasts remained alive, but of those at least half showed injuries of one kind or another.

In the middle of the carnage, Queen Madin's servant knelt beside his mount, whimpering for his life.

Swallowing nausea, Terisa whipped herself back to face Torrent. "None of us could have saved her," she repeated hoarsely.

"Then"—Torrent's voice shook wildly, but she drew herself up as if she had become a different woman—"we must rescue her."

Terisa stared at her, shocked by the strange sensation that she could see King Joyse in Torrent's eyes.

"How?" With a visible effort, Geraden forced himself to speak gently, reasonably. "We don't have any weapons—and there aren't enough of us. By the time we get help from Romish, they'll be long gone. They'll have plenty of time to hide their trail."

Torrent shook her head. "Not Romish." She took several deep breaths as if she were hyperventilating, with the result that she was then able to control the wobble in her voice. "You must get help from Orison."

Both Geraden and Terisa gaped at her.

"They will not hide their trail from me. I will follow and make a new one behind them. I am helpless for everything else, but that I can do. He"—she indicated the man with the badly cut shoulder—"will get support for me from Romish. But you must ride to Orison. You must warn Father."

She had lost her mind. There was no question about it.

Torrent couldn't entirely stifle her rising hysteria. "Do you not understand? It is his only hope!"

Terisa and Geraden stared at her, gaped, held their breath—and suddenly he gasped, "She's right!" He grabbed at Terisa's arm, wheeling toward the horses. "Come on! We've got to get out of here!"

Terisa froze: she couldn't move at all. Get out of here. Of course. Why didn't I think of that? Ride like crazy people halfway across Mordant to Orison, while she goes after those Alends and her mother *alone*. You've done this once before. Don't you remember? You sent Argus after Prince Kragen, and he got killed. And stopping Nyle didn't do us any good.

"*Terisa*," he demanded. "I tell you, she's *right*. It's his only hope."

"What—?" She couldn't make her throat work. An avalanche had come *this close* to falling on her. Like the collapse of the Congery's meeting hall. "What're you talking about?"

In response, Geraden made one of his supreme and unselfish efforts to control himself for her sake. Intensely, he said, "His only hope is if he finds out what happened to her before the people who took her know he knows. Before they can tell him. Before they start trying to use her against him. During that gap—if we can give him a gap—between when he knows and when they know he knows— he can still act. He can do something to save her. Or himself."

"Yes," Torrent breathed. "It is the only thing I can do."

Abruptly, she climbed out of the ruin of the porch, heading toward the horses. Her knife was still gripped in her fist.

As if she were her mother, she commanded the injured man, "Take a horse, ride to Romish. You'll be tended there. Tell them what happened. Tell them I require help. I'll leave a trail for them." Then her tone softened. "You're badly hurt, I know. There's nothing I can do for you. I must attempt to save the Queen—and my father's realm."

As if she were accustomed to extreme decisions—not to mention horses—she chose a horse, untethered it, and swung up into the saddle.

Terisa would have tried to stop her, but Geraden's acquiescence held her. "Geraden—" she murmured, pleading with him. "Geraden—"

"Terisa," he replied, so full of certainty that she couldn't argue with him, "she's right. I've got the strongest feeling she's right."

"Farewell, Geraden," Torrent broke in. "Farewell, my lady Terisa. Save the King.

"Do that, and together we will rescue Queen Madin."

Geraden turned to give the King's daughter a formal bow. "Farewell also, my lady Torrent. This story will fill King Joyse with pride, whatever comes of it." A moment later, he added, "And both Myste and Elega are going to be *impressed*."

That almost made Torrent smile.

Alone, she rode out of the hollow on the trail of Queen Madin's abductors.

Terisa put the best tourniquet she could manage on the wounded man's shoulder. Gritting his teeth, Geraden slapped a measure of sense into the Queen's whimpering servant, then instructed him to make sure the Fayle's man reached Romish.

After that, they selected the two best horses, packed a third to carry their supplies, and started toward the Demesne and Orison.

THIRTY-SEVEN:
POISED FOR
VICTORY

T he Alend army didn't move.

It hadn't moved for days.

Oh, Prince Kragen kept his men busy enough: he was determined to be ready for anything. But he didn't waste another catapult; didn't risk any kind of sortie, much less a massed assault; didn't make anything more than covert efforts to spy on the castle. In fact, the only thing he apparently did to advance his siege was to completely prevent anyone from getting into or out of Orison: he cut King Joyse off from any conceivable source of news. Other than that, he and his forces might as well have been engaged in training exercises.

He was busy in other ways, of course. For instance, he had quite a number of men out at all times, furtively searching for some sign of the Congery's champion. Knowing what the champion had done to Orison, Prince Kragen felt a positive dislike for the prospect of being attacked from behind by that lone fighter. In addition, he spent quite a bit of time, both alone and with his father, trying to fathom King Joyse's daughters.

But King Joyse's warnings haunted him—and Master Quillon's. He took no direct action to hasten the fall of Orison.

That changed during the night which Terisa and Geraden had spent with Queen Madin.

Naturally, Prince Kragen had no way of knowing where Terisa

and Geraden were. He couldn't know that they had ever left Orison—or that Mordant's need was coming to a crisis around him.

On the other hand, he was alert to every outward sign of what was happening in the castle.

When the men who had the duty of watching the ramparts more closely after dark reported to him that they heard shouts and turmoil, saw lights in the vicinity of the curtain-wall, he didn't hesitate: he sent half a dozen hand-picked scouts to creep as near to the wall as possible, climb it if necessary, and find out what was going on.

The news they brought back tightened excitement or dread around his heart.

There was a riot taking place on the other side of the curtain-wall.

Apparently, the overcrowded and raw-nerved populace of Orison was breaking into active rebellion against Castellan Lebbick.

After a while, the noise receded, as if the riot were moving into the main body of the castle. But light continued to show at the rim of the wall, blazing up in gusts like a fire out of control. And when dawn came the Prince saw dirty plumes of smoke curling upward from the wound in Orison's side, giving the castle a look of death it hadn't had since the day the champion had first injured it.

Again, Prince Kragen didn't hesitate: he had spent the night preparing his response. At his signal, fifty men carrying a battering ram in a protective frame ran forward to try the gates. The walls and roof which received the arrows of the defenders made the ram look as unwieldy as a shed; but the use of the frame could be an effective tactic, as long as the gate failed before the defenders had time to ready a counterattack—or as long as they were distracted by trouble elsewhere.

As a distraction, Prince Kragen sent several hundred soldiers with storming ladders and grappling hooks to assail the curtain-wall.

Unfortunately, Orison's guards proved equal to the occasion. A tub of lamp oil and a burning fagot turned the ram's protective frame into a charnal. And the Castellan—or whoever had taken command after the riot—had obviously expected the attack on the curtain-wall; so the defense there had been reinforced.

When Prince Kragen saw that his men were taking more than their share of losses and getting nowhere, he chewed his moustache, swore, and shook his fists at the sky—all inwardly, in the privacy of his thoughts, so that no one witnessed his frustration. Then he ordered a withdrawal.

Rather tentatively, as if sensing the Prince's state, one of his captains commented, "Well, they have to run out of oil *some*time."

Prince Kragen swore again—out loud, this time. Then he instructed the captain to begin raiding the surrounding villages and trees for wood: he wanted more battering rams, more protective frames. And while that raid was underway, he set about using up the rams and frames he already had.

If the defenders had left any of the battering rams he now sent against them alone, they would have soon learned that none of the rams had enough men with it to actually threaten the gates. This time, however—for once!—his tactics succeeded. The defenders faithfully burned every ram and frame to charcoal.

The Prince grinned grimly under his moustache. Apparently, Castellan Lebbick—or whoever had replaced him after the riot—was still human enough to be outwitted once in a while.

The riot which had taken place in Orison that night was an ugly one.

It had a number of excuses. The castle was indeed overcrowded, badly so—a detail which became increasingly onerous for everyone as the siege wore on. And of course the siege had come at the end of a hard winter, before spring could do anybody any good; so supplies were relatively short, and everything from food and water to blankets and space was strictly—a swelling number of people said *harshly*—rationed. By Castellan Lebbick, naturally. Despite Master Eremis' heroic replenishment of the reservoir.

And Orison's surplus population had nothing to do. Nobody really had anything to do. As long as the Alend army just sat there with all their heads crammed up the Prince's ass—as one tired old guard put it—nobody had any outlet for long days of pent-up fear.

Why didn't Prince Kragen *do* something?

Where was High King Festten?

For that matter, where was the Perdon?

How much longer was this going to go on?

Tempers grew ragged; hostility fed on frustration and uselessness; grievances multiplied in all directions. Orison's sewers kept backing up because the drainfields weren't adequate to the population. And the leaders of Orison, the men in command—King Joyse, Castellan Lebbick, Master Barsonage—did nothing to ease the pressure. They all went about their lives in isolation, as if the burgeoning misery sealed within these walls were immaterial to them. Even the castle's most comfortable inhabitants—men of position, women of privilege—were in an ugly mood; and the ugliness was spreading.

But even ugliness couldn't function in a vacuum: it needed a focus, a target.

It needed the Castellan.

He would have been a likely candidate in any case. After all, the responsibility for deciding and implementing Orison's distress was on his shoulders. Merchants and farmers had time to become bitter about the confiscation of their goods. Mothers with sick children had cause to complain about the rationing of medicines. People with a normal need for activity—and privacy—didn't have anyone else to blame for the lack of those necessities.

The guards, however, were loyal to their commander. Most of them had had years to become familiar with his loyalties—to them as well as to King Joyse. And they were accustomed to taking his orders. One way or another, they worked to control the pressure building against the Castellan.

As a result, there was no riot—no outbreak of resentment—until someone threw a spark into the tinder of Orison's mood.

That someone was Saddith.

She was on her feet now, able to get around. Despite the loss of a few teeth, and the rather dramatic damage done to the rest of her face, she was able to talk. And that was what she had been doing ever since she had healed enough to climb out of her sickbed: getting around; talking.

She had started with every man in Orison who had ever visited between her legs—or had let her know he'd like to visit. She had told those men what the Castellan had done to her, and why: she had gone to his bed out of simple pity for his loneliness, out of compassion for the pressure he was under; and he had hurt her *here*, and *here*, and *here*. But as her strength returned she broadened her range. She carried her injuries everywhere in public: her left hand broken and useless, the right nearly so; her face so badly battered that it would never regain its shape, one cheek crushed, one eye unable to close properly, scars in all directions. If anything, she wore her blouses unbuttoned farther than before, enabling the world to see what Lebbick had done to her there.

And everywhere she went, her message was the same.

You sods were quick enough for fornication when I had my beauty. If you were men now, you'd hoist Castellan Lebbick's balls on a stick.

His violence had no reason and no justification: it was as senseless as it was brutal. As senseless as all the other little brutalities he committed throughout the castle.

How long would it be before some other helpless woman received the same treatment? How long would it be before brutality became the governing principle in Orison?

How much longer will you sods and sheepfuckers permit this to go on?

Of course, when she spoke to women—which she did often, more every day—her words were different. Her message, however, remained the same.

Her disfigurement, as well as her intensity, made her impossible to look away from. She compelled stares and pity; nausea and indignation. It was impossible to look at her and not feel fear.

Because of the way she talked, and the way the men who had once reveled in her talked, and the way the women who were terrified of the same fate talked, this fear took the form of a call for justice, a thinly concealed demand for retribution. With Alend just outside, rape and murder were on everybody's mind.

At the time, few people had any notion of how this demand came to be translated into action. One day, people were growling to each other, muttering vague threats which they had no actual intention of acting on: the next, rumors seemed to filter everywhere that voices would be raised, justice insisted upon; action taken. Come to the disused ballroom this evening, the great hall where King Joyse and Queen Madin were married, and where the peace of Mordant had been celebrated.

Oh, yes? Whose idea was this?

No one knew.

We're besieged. Is it really a good idea to challenge the Castellan at a time like this?

Perhaps not. But it's gone too far to be stopped. Better to support it, make sure it succeeds, than take the chance he'll be able to crush it—the chance he'll be left alone to do something worse the next time.

Yes. All right.

So that evening the crowd began to gather in the high, vast, dusty ballroom. At first, it was plainly a crowd rather than a mob, despite the fact that its numbers quickly swelled to several hundred: the fear threatening to become violence was counterbalanced by uncertainty; by habits of mind learned during many years of King Joyse's peaceful rule; by the perfectly reasonable idea that it was dangerous to weaken Orison during a siege; by the manifest presence of Castellan Lebbick's guards all around the hall. Nevertheless, as darkness deepened outside the windows, the only light came from torches which someone had thought to provide, and the erratic illumination of the flames had a disturbing effect on faces and rationality. People began to look garish to each other, wild and strange; the air was full of grotesque shadows; the atmosphere seemed to flicker. And through the shadows and the orange-yellow light Saddith appeared, around and around in the ballroom, displaying her wounds, speaking of outrage. The seething murmur of several hundred voices took shape in fits and bursts as more and more people found occasion to say the name *Lebbick.*

Lebbick.

And the guard captain who had been detailed to preserve order made a mistake.

He was a tough old fighter with bottomless determination and not much intelligence; and during one of King Joyse's battles the Castellan had saved his entire family from being cut down when they were caught in the path of an Alend raid. He heard all these whimpering shitholes—they were practically puking with self-pity—start to mutter *Lebbick, Lebbick,* as if they had the right, and he decided that the crowd had to be dispersed.

Even though the odds were against him, he might have succeeded if he had been able to drive people out of the ballroom back into the public halls and passages. Unfortunately, he failed to do that. Someone with more presence of mind—or maybe just a nastier sense of humor—than the rest of the mob went to the entryway which led to the laborium and called everyone else to follow.

Fear of the Castellan and fear of Imagers formed a powerful combination. Several hundred people surged in that direction as if they had lost the capacity to think.

Somehow, they forced the guards back. Somehow, they were swept into the laborium, where the great majority of them had never set foot in their lives. Somehow, they found themselves packed into the ruined hall where the Congery had held meetings until the champion had blasted one wall open to the world.

Men closed the doors against the guards, shot the bolts. Torches ringed the stumps of pillars which used to hold up the ceiling. Because the curtain-wall didn't completely seal the hole in Orison's side, the hall was theoretically exposed to the guards defending the wall. The wall, however, had been built to protect against siege rather than against riot: its defensive positions faced outward rather than back down into the hall below. Only the archers could have taken any action. And even Lebbick's staunchest supporters knew better than to begin slaughtering Orison's inhabitants.

Lebbick. Men and women shouted back and forth, made threats. *Lebbick.* Their mood grew uglier by the moment. They started demanding blood.

Lebbick. Lebbick!

Back against the wall near one of the doors stood a tall man who wasn't shouting, didn't make any demands. Wrapped in his jet cloak, he was nearly invisible among the shadows. But the hood of his cloak couldn't hide the way his eyes caught the reflection of the torches, or the way his teeth gleamed when he grinned.

"Very good so far," he said in a conversational tone because absolutely no one could hear him. "Now the time has come. Do what I told you."

Around him, the confusion began to change. Something caught the attention of the mob, focused it.

Amid the torches, Saddith stood on the dais of the Masters.

She was just tall enough to be seen over the heads of the people nearest her.

"Listen to me!" There was nothing left of her beauty: it had all become disfigurement and rage. Her voice rang off the stones, rang through the mob. "Look at me!"

She raised her hands into the light.

"Look at me!"

The mob snarled.

She shook her hair away from her face.

"Look at me!"

The mob hissed.

She stripped open her blouse, exposing her maimed breasts.

"Look at me!"

The mob shouted.

"Lebbick did this! He did this to me!"

The mob roared.

"Yes, my sweet little slut," the man in the jet cloak commented. "And you deserved it. Perhaps that will teach you the folly of betraying my secrets."

"Now he has threatened you," Saddith went on, as fierce as her nakedness, "for no reason except that you think this should not have been done to me!"

Lebbick! Lebbick!

"I went to him because I pitied him!" she shouted. "I went to offer him my love when I was beautiful and all men desired me! This is the result!"

"No," said the man in the jet cloak, entirely unheard. "You went to him because you were ambitious. And you went when I told you to go. I understood his need far better than you did."

Her voice seemed to turn the torchlight the color of blood. *"He must pay!"*

Lebbick! Pay! Lebbick!

"Think about this gambit, Joyse." The man in the jet cloak was no longer grinning. "Save him if you can. Stop me if you can. You thought to play this game against me, but you are outmatched."

Then he cocked an eyebrow in mild surprise and peered over the heads of the crowd as a figure wrapped in a brown robe stepped unexpectedly up onto the dais beside Saddith.

Lit by torches and looking like an image out of a dream, the figure turned sharply; the robe seemed to swirl through the air and float away, thrown off as the man revealed himself.

Castellan Lebbick.

He wore the purple sash of his authority over his mail, the purple band of his position knotted around his short, gray hair. He had a longsword in a scabbard on his hip, but he didn't touch it; he didn't appear to need it. His familiar scowl answered the torches blackly. The lift of his head, the thrust of his jaw, the movements of his arms and shoulders were tight with passion and command. He wasn't tall, yet he made himself felt everywhere in the hall.

He had never looked more like a man who beat up women.

"All right." His voice carried; it promised violence, like a hammer knocking chips from stone. "This has gone on long enough. Get out of here. Go back to your rooms. The Masters don't like having their precious laborium invaded. If they decide to defend it themselves, they might translate the whole lice-ridden lot of you out of existence."

An interesting threat, thought the man in the jet cloak—plainly hollow, but interesting. Nevertheless everyone stared at the Castellan. He had clapped a hush over the mob. Surprise and old respect and inbred alarm did more for him than fifty guards.

Saddith ignored his threats. She ignored his appearance, his proven capacity for harm. After what he had cost her, she had nothing left to lose, no more reason to be afraid. And she hated him—oh, she hated him. Her face was a scabbed and deformed clench of hate as she spat his name:

Lebbick."

Despite his authority and fury, he turned to look at her as though she had the power to compel him.

"What do you wish here?" she asked thickly. "Have you come to gloat? Have you come to lay claim to your handiwork? Are you proud of it?"

"No." His voice was quiet, yet it could be heard throughout the hall. "I was wrong."

"'Wrong'?" she cried.

"It wasn't your fault. It probably wasn't even your idea. I shouldn't have taken it out on you."

At a calmer moment, the crowd might have been utterly astounded to hear Castellan Lebbick say something that sounded so much like an apology, almost a self-abasement. But the people weren't thinking as individuals: they were feeling like a mob, ugly and extreme. *Lebbick,* someone murmured—and another, *Lebbick*—a chant began, far back in the throat, through the teeth, a hunting growl, *Lebbick, Lebbick.*

"'Wrong'?" repeated Saddith. She was breathing hard, trying to get enough air for her vituperation. "You admit that you were *wrong?*" Her damaged breasts shone with sweat. "Do you think that *heals* me? Do you think that one small piece of my pain is made less, or one small scar is removed?" Her arms beat time to her respiration, *Lebbick, Lebbick,* the snarl of the mob. "I tell you, you will pay with *blood!*

"Blood!" she howled, matching the rhythm in the hall: "*Blood!*"

And the mob responded, "Lebbick! *Lebbick!*"

The man in the jet cloak grinned with undisguised relish.

Nevertheless Castellan Lebbick wasn't daunted. Maybe he

wasn't even afraid. "Oh, stop it!" he snapped over the heavy shout as if the people surrounding him were nothing more than bad children and he had no time for their misbehavior. "Do you think all this surprises me? I knew it was going to happen. I've been ready for *days*."

His voice wielded enough of the whip to slash through the beat of his name, the outrage. Men and women faltered, began to listen.

"I had you driven in here so I could do what I wanted with you. You didn't know I was here. You don't know how many of my men are here. Well, I'll tell you. Ninety-four. All disguised. All pretending to be one of you. The person standing next to you shouting *Lebbick, Lebbick* like a dog with the mange is probably one of my men. If anyone raises a hand at me, he'll be cut down where he stands. And the rest of you will be *remembered!*"

It was a remarkable ploy. The man in the jet cloak was virtually certain that it was in fact a ploy, that the Castellan was in fact undefended, as vulnerable as he would ever be; but that changed nothing. It worked. Like water on hot coals, it transformed the fury of the mob back into fear.

All the shouting stopped. Men and women glanced at each other, tried to edge away from each other. When the Castellan barked, "Now get out of here. Open the doors and get out of here. You've all been stupid enough for one night," the people near the doors undid the bolts, and the crowd began to move.

This was too much for Saddith—as the man in the jet cloak knew it would be. Of course, he was as surprised as anyone by Castellan Lebbick's appearance in the hall; and more vexed than most, although he didn't show it. From the beginning, however, he had been prepared for the possibility that she might fail—that the crowd might refuse to gather, that it might not become a mob, that the mob might not rise to bloodshed. And then she would break. The hate inside her would refuse to be contained.

That was why he had given her a knife.

She had it in her hand now, and she wailed in a high, shrill voice as she flung herself at Lebbick.

Maybe he wasn't as ready as he pretended to be. Or maybe something had distracted him. Or maybe this was what he had had in mind all along. Whatever the reason, he was slow turning, slow with his hands; too slow to prevent Saddith from driving her blade through his throat.

Nevertheless she didn't so much as scratch him.

While she swung, Ribuld came up onto the dais in a headlong charge and spitted her on his longsword, ran her through so hard that they both crashed into the throng on the far side and fell to the floor.

Just for a second, the Castellan's features seemed to crumple as if he were disappointed. Almost immediately, however, he swept out his own sword and went to stand over Ribuld so that no one would try to strike at the guard who had saved his life.

The man in the jet cloak was mildly entertained to hear Castellan Lebbick rasp at Ribuld, "Next time don't be in such a hurry."

The time had come to go with the crowd. If the man in the jet cloak lingered, he might get pulled along when the crowd's departure became flight, people hurrying and then running to get away from the Castellan and trouble. With a shrug, he eased out of the hall.

The next morning, however, he was gratified to hear that some of Saddith's supporters had been sincere enough in their outrage to burn everything flammable they could find before guards arrived to drive them out of the laborium. She deserved at least that much recognition. She had become too ugly to go on living, of course; but while she lasted she had been worth the risk of knowing her. Although he wasn't exactly grieved by her loss, he admired the aesthetic judgment of the man or men who had tried to commemorate her death by doing a little trivial damage to the laborium.

On the other hand, he was both surprised and rather amused that the better part of the day passed before anyone discovered that during the riot someone had broken into the warren of rooms where the Congery's mirrors were kept and had shattered several of them.

Treachery was everywhere, it seemed. What a shame.

Chew on that, Joyse, you old goat. I hope it chokes you.

The next morning, with Orison full of news which he might be presumed to have come by honestly, Master Eremis went to visit the mediator of the Congery.

He had a number of matters that he wanted to pursue with Master Barsonage. He had been putting them off for days, partly because he hadn't wished to call attention to himself, partly because he'd been busy elsewhere. But the time was ripe for a little probing. Perhaps he would be able to learn something useful—and sow a hint or two of uncertainty in the process.

Twirling the ends of his chasuble, he walked through the tower which held King Joyse's private quarters. In fact, he made a point of passing that way often, whatever his destination might be. If anyone had asked him why he occasionally walked a considerable unnecessary distance in order to cross the waiting room in front of the stairs up to the King's rooms, he would have replied that he always hoped to overhear something—any gossip or rumor which might ·reveal where he stood with his sovereign.

After all, King Joyse had said exactly nothing to him, either in person or by message, after his solution to the problem of Orison's water supply. Since what he had done was so obviously the kind of thing which King Joyse had always demanded from his Imagers, he, Master Eremis, might be forgiven for drawing worrisome inferences from the King's silence. Was Eremis not trusted? Were his enemies speaking against him? Had he offended against King Joyse's apparent desire to bring about the collapse of the realm? Or was it true that the King's insistence upon an ethical use of Imagery had never been sincere?

Surely Master Eremis' interest in any news which might somehow emanate from the King was understandable? Under the circumstances, how could he be confident that his life wasn't in danger, even though he had saved Orison from terrible suffering and inevitable defeat?

This explanation—although Master Eremis would have supplied it with perfect assurance—was no more than a by-blow of the truth.

The truth was that he had come this way by accident several days ago, and had chanced to find the Tor in the waiting room.

The old lord was alone, of course. The waiting room was almost always empty, now that King Joyse had made plain his disinclination to respond intelligently—if at all—to the petitions of his subjects. It was possible that the Tor had been alone there for hours—and would be alone for hours more.

He was asleep on the floor, with his face pressed into the corner between the floor and wall; his fat made a quivering mountain, and he snored like a sawmill; he was so drunk that Master Eremis might have been unable to awaken him with a trumpet. The stink exhaling from him was so strong that simply breathing it made Master Eremis feel tipsy and arrogant.

While the old lord's thick flesh shook from his raucous snoring,

Master Eremis paused to think. He considered taking this opportunity to slip an unobtrusive knife between the Tor's ribs. That might
be helpful—not at the moment, naturally, but later on. Vagel would
do it without hesitation; Gilbur, with glee. On the other hand, it
would be almost no fun at all. Eremis wanted to humiliate the Tor
before killing him.

In addition, there was only one lord whom Master Eremis feared
less, and that was the Armigite, who had already sold his Care to
Prince Kragen to purchase a temporary safety for himself and his
women and his fresh boys. Upon reflection, Eremis let the chance
for murder pass.

But he didn't forget it.

If the Tor was occasionally to be found in the waiting room
alone and drunk and asleep, then it was possible that he might also
occasionally be found there alone and drunk and awake. Awake
enough to talk—and too drunk to be cautious.

Master Eremis believed that opportunities were like women:
they came to men who knew how to court them.

As a rule, he was given more to flashes of inspiration than to
steady labor. That was why he—and Vagel as well—needed Master
Gilbur. Nevertheless he began courting this opportunity assiduously.
He made sure that he passed through the waiting room more often
than any other man in Orison.

Today, on his way to talk with Master Barsonage, his diligence
reaped its just reward. The Tor was sitting on one of the deserted
benches, so drunk that he could hardly find his head with both hands.
His eyes were red and miserable, self-abused, and he exuded a sour
smell of old sweat and acid vomit. What was left of his hair straggled
into his face.

Clearly, the long, strange wait while Prince Kragen sat outside
Orison and did nothing had begun to bear fruit. A riot against Castellan Lebbick, what a shame. Mirrors broken in the laborium. And
the King's oldest friend reduced to this, drinking himself to death
in full view of anyone who bothered to notice.

It was odd and wonderful that the man who bothered to notice
wasn't the King at all, wasn't the one at whom this display was directed. Instead he was Master Eremis.

"My lord Tor," the Master said amiably, "this is fortuitous."

Slowly, as if he were bringing long forgotten muscles into service, the Tor raised his head; he peered at Eremis through a haze of drink. With no discernible self-awareness, he belched.

Then he said in a surprisingly clear voice, "Got any wine?"

Master Eremis smiled across his teeth. "I have wished to speak with you, my lord. Great events transpire in Orison."

The old lord considered this assertion soddenly. After a moment, he dropped his head; it lolled on his neck. Nevertheless when he spoke every word was as distinct as a piece of glass: broken and precise, like augury.

"Too far to get. Too many stairs."

He belched again, aimlessly.

"We have had a riot against the good Castellan," explained Master Eremis. "And it may have been premeditated. While the guards were distracted by the riot, several of the Congery's mirrors were destroyed."

The Tor's head continued rolling back and forth, back and forth, as if he were rocking himself to sleep.

"And now, like a man who knows what happens within our walls, Prince Kragen attacks at last—although I must confess that I am less impressed by the audacity of his assault than by its circumspection."

And may the attacks continue, the Master wished, daring fate to deny him. They are an admirable distraction.

Simply because he was so willing to pursue his aims even if everything went against him, he felt confident that fate would in fact heed his desires.

The Tor met Master Eremis' remarks with a snort; he might have been starting into a snore. A quiver ran through him then, however, and he blinked his bloodshot eyes. "Wine," he pronounced, as if he expected a cask to appear magically before him.

Master Eremis had difficulty restraining a laugh. True, some of King Joyse's supporters were proving to be more resourceful than Eremis could have predicted. Others, however, only saved themselves from appearing pathetic by being ridiculous.

"What do you make of it all, my lord Tor?" he asked in kind good humor. "Where are the forces of Cadwal? Where is the Perdon? How has Prince Kragen dared to let us endure against him so long?"

Without looking up, the Tor countered absentmindedly, "Did I tell you my son was killed?"

"It seems clear, does it not"—at the moment, Eremis was delighted that he hadn't knifed the old lord—"that the Prince and his illustrious father know something we do not." This conversation was too much fun to be missed. "They would not have wasted so much as a day in hesitation, unless they had reason to believe that High King Festten would not arrive against them. What conclusions do you draw, my lord?"

The Tor appeared to suffer from the delusion that he was actually participating in the discussion. "Did I tell you," he replied, "that he gave Lebbick permission to torture her?"

That was an interesting revelation; but Master Eremis could guess its import too easily to pursue it. Instead, he inquired, "What conclusions can you draw? There are only two. The first is that Festten and Margonal are in alliance—and Festten trusts Margonal enough to give him time to capture the Congery for himself. And if you are able to believe that, I fear we have nothing more to say to each other."

"*Torture* her," repeated the Tor, "despite her obvious decency—and her proven desire to help him."

"The second," continued Master Eremis, grinning, "is that the Prince has cut us off from information which he himself possesses— from the knowledge that we are not indeed threatened by Cadwal at all. High King Festten has other intentions. He has mustered his army, not against us and Alend, but to wage another war entirely. And if you are able to believe *that,* I fear you have nothing left to say to anyone."

"I begged her." Fat tears rolled down the old lord's aggrieved cheeks. "I should have begged him, of course, but he was past hearing me. I begged her. Betray Geraden. So that he would not be responsible for what Lebbick would do. So that he would not have her on his conscience." He seemed unaware that he was weeping. His ability to speak so exactly when he was barely sober enough to keep his eyes from crossing was delightful, even entertaining, like a trick done by a mountebank. "But she has the only loyal heart left in Mordant. She would not betray Geraden, even to save herself from Lebbick."

Master Eremis was so pleased that he could hardly contain his relish. Because his exuberance absolutely had to have some outlet, he spun the ends of his chasuble like pinwheels.

"My lord Tor," he asked nonchalantly, coming at last to the point, "what has he been doing all this time, while his people riot, and mirrors are shattered, and women are maimed and murdered? What has good King Joyse been doing?"

As if the word had been surprised out of him, the Tor replied, "Practicing."

"Practicing?" A brief giggle burst from the Master: he couldn't hold it down. "What, hop-board? Still? Has he not given up that folly yet?"

The old lord shook his head, as morose as cold potatoes and congealed gravy.

"Swordsmanship."

That stopped Master Eremis' mirth: it made him stare involuntarily, as if the Tor had somehow, miraculously, opened a pit of vipers at his feet—or had told him a joke so funny that he couldn't believe it, couldn't laugh at it until he had thought about it for a while. *Swordsmanship?* At *his* age? Was he strong enough to do as much as *lift* a longsword?

"My lord Tor," Eremis said casually to conceal the intensity of his attention, "you jest with me. Our brave King cannot swing a sword. He can barely *stand* without assistance."

Abruptly, with an effort that seemed to make his whole body gurgle, the Tor heaved himself to his feet. He hadn't looked at Master Eremis since the start of the conversation. Dully, as if he were losing his gift for enunciation, he announced, "Got to have wine."

With his hams rolling unsteadily under him, he lurched away.

Master Eremis was about to spring after him, pull him back, wrench an explanation out of him, when the true point of the joke struck home. King Joyse intended to fight—and he was years or even decades past the time when he was strong enough to do so. That shed a new light on everything—on every sign that the King knew what he was doing, that he did what he did out of deliberate policy rather than petulant foolishness. He intended to fight because he didn't know or couldn't admit he no longer had the strength. He wasn't self-destructive or apathetic: he was just blind to age and time. He risked his kingdom in an effort to prove himself still capable of saving it.

That was a rich jest, too rich for any coarse display of mirth. Instead of laughing aloud, Eremis whistled cheerfully through his teeth as he continued on his way to see Master Barsonage.

The mediator answered his door wearing only a towel knotted around his middle—a style of dress which emphasized his girth at the expense of his dignity. Water glistened on his pine-colored skin, his bald pate: apparently, Master Eremis had caught him bathing, and his servants were out. His flesh didn't sag on him as the Tor's did, however; his bulk was solid, tightly packed over muscle and bone. He didn't seem especially embarrassed to receive Master Eremis in this damp, disrobed condition.

In fact, he sounded almost friendly as he said, "Master Eremis, good day to you. Come in, come in." He stood back from the door, waved a dripping arm. "It is an honor to be visited by the man who saved Orison. Let us hope that you have saved us permanently. Have you recovered from your ordeal? You look well."

Master Eremis laughed lightly at Barsonage's uncharacteristic gush. "And a good day to you, Master Barsonage. I have clearly come at an inopportune moment. I can return later."

"Nonsense." The mediator touched the sleeve of Eremis' cloak, urged him into the room. "Orison is under siege. In one sense, all times are inopportune. In another, the present moment is always better than any other. Some wine?"

Thinking of the Tor, Master Eremis said deliberately, "With pleasure."

He accepted a goblet of a very mediocre Armigite vintage, then seated himself in the chair Master Barsonage indicated. He had visited the mediator's rooms on any number of occasions—disputes privately arbitrated at one extreme, formal feasts welcoming new Masters at the other—but whenever he came here he always took a moment to admire the furniture.

It had all been made by Master Barsonage himself.

Eremis did him the justice of admitting that the mediator was a competent Imager. In particular, the preparation for and execution of the Congery's most important augury had been deftly done. On the other hand, he was much more than competent with wood: he was an artist. It was universally acknowledged around the Congery that his frames were better than anyone else's: better made, better fitted; altogether finer. And his furniture could have graced the finest salon in Orison—or in Carmag, for that matter. The expanse of his table had been so well shaped and polished that it seemed to glow from within; the arms of his chairs flowed so naturally with the grain of the wood that it was surprising to find them comfortable.

Secretly, Eremis laughed at Master Barsonage for dedicating

himself to his lesser talents—for wasting his time with Imagery when
he could have contributed some real beauty to the world in another
way.

And he wanted to laugh more now. Instead of leaving the room
to put on at least a robe, Barsonage sat down as he was, drank off
his wine in a gulp, wiped the water out of his stiff eyebrows, and
began to prattle.

"You are much admired now, Master Eremis. Of course, you
have always been admired. But it will not surprise you to hear that
you have not always been liked. You are too able, too quick. And
you mock people. You have not made yourself easy to like.

"Ah, but now— The refilling of the reservoir was a clever action
as well as a courageous one. No, do not deny it," he said although
Eremis hadn't moved a muscle. "The exhaustion of so much prolonged translation. If I had made that attempt, my heart would have
failed me. Yet you did not hesitate to risk complete prostration. And,
as I say, it was clever. Your reputation has not been the only ben-
eficiary of your action. Your heroism and Master Quillon's foul murder have combined to raise the esteem in which all the Congery is
held.

"Shall I give you an example? My servants no longer sneer at
me when I put them to work."

Grinning, Master Eremis raised his hands to ward off the babble.
"Master Barsonage, please. I did not come to you for flattery. I am
precisely aware of my own virtues, and they do not merit this praise."

"Really?" the mediator returned. "I think you are too modest."
His eyes were as bland as bits of glass. "But if praise is offensive I
will cease. Of course you did not come for flattery. How may I serve
you?"

"I am well rested now, as you see," Eremis answered. "And
another matter which required my attention has come to an end. It
is no secret that the maid Saddith was my lover." He spoke with
admirable sincerity. "After I recovered my strength, I spent much
of my time with her. She needed friends—"

He grimaced. "Sadly, she would not give up her hatred of our
good Castellan. There was nothing I could do with her." Grief wasn't
his best pose, but he projected as much of it as possible. As if he
were putting Saddith and her death behind him by an act of will, he
said, "Master Barsonage, I am ready."

The mediator raised an eyebrow. As his skin dried, it looked more and more like cut pine. "'Ready'?"

"I have heard that the Masters are busy—that since Quillon's death you have rediscovered your sense of purpose. I am ready to rejoin the work of the Congery."

"Our work?" Master Barsonage's features reflected nothing. "What work do you mean?"

Master Eremis had difficulty suppressing a smile. The mediator was almost ludicrously transparent. Fixing him with a glittering gaze which was intended to express indignation as well as penetration, Eremis replied slowly, "So it is true. I am still not trusted. That is the reason I have not been summoned to any of your meetings—to any of your labors. I have saved Orison from a quick fall to Alend. I did everything any man could do to keep Nyle alive—and I was the only man here who so much as made the attempt. I have been striving with unmatched diligence to find some means to avert Mordant's fate. It was not *I* who disbanded the Congery. And I am *still* not trusted. That murderous puppy, Geraden, casts a few groundless aspersions on my good name, and suddenly nothing I can do is enough to redeem it."

"Oh, no, Master Eremis." Barsonage put up a thick hand in protest. "You misunderstand me. You misunderstand us all." In a tone as bland as his expression, he explained, "You fail to grasp, I think, how high your standing has become. The man who refilled the reservoir—the man who did so much to save Nyle—is not someone who can be 'summoned' to meetings like an Apt. He cannot be put to labor like a packhorse. You have been much involved in your own concerns—and you have earned the right to be. The Congery does not distrust you. We only respect your high standing—and your privacy."

Firmly, Eremis resisted a giddy temptation to snort, During a *siege?* With Orison's fall tied like a noose around your neck, and no hope anywhere? Can you truly believe me silly enough to swallow that lie? The mediator, however, didn't look like a man who had an opinion about Master Eremis' silliness, one way or the other. He looked—his blandness itself betrayed him—like a man who had spent some time preparing for this encounter.

Master Eremis sat forward in his chair; his relish for the conversation sharpened.

"Perhaps," he said in a skeptical drawl. "You will forgive me if I reserve judgment on that point.

"It remains true, does it not, that there have been meetings to which I have not been invited? That there is work in progress which I have not been asked to share? That the Congery has rediscovered its purpose?"

Master Barsonage nodded. "Indeed." Something about him—perhaps it was the way his eyebrow bristled—suggested an intensification which his mild gaze contradicted. "I am glad to say that is the case."

"Am I permitted to ask how it came about?"

"Certainly. At last we are able to see clearly that the lady Terisa is an Imager."

Eremis scowled to conceal the fact that he didn't like what he heard. "Master Barsonage, that is an answer which explains nothing."

"Well, perhaps not." Apparently, the mediator had prepared himself quite well for this encounter. "A man of your assurance and ability may have difficulty understanding men whose chief talent lies in their capacity for doubt.

"Nevertheless in practice—as distinct from theory—the great stumbling block for the Congery has been the question of the lady Terisa. What does she signify? What does her presence among us indicate? Is there a *reason* for her unexpected appearance, or was Geraden merely the agent of a monumental accident?

"If she is an accident, then all Imagery is accidental in the end, and our research, like our morality, is only foolishness. Geraden's role in the augury has no meaning."

Master Eremis nodded as if the truth were obvious to him.

"But if," the mediator continued, "there is a *reason,* then two conclusions are inescapable. So inescapable," he commented without discernible sarcasm or humor, "that even our most contentious members have accepted them. First, the responsibility she represents falls upon us. Imagery is our demesne. Second, since the problem she represents exists it must have a solution. What one Imager can do, another can understand and counter.

"It has been demonstrated," he concluded, "that there *is* a reason. She is an Imager. We can regret that she has chosen to ally herself with Master Gilbur and arch-Imager Vagel, but we cannot shirk either the responsibility or the hope which that knowledge implies."

"Yes, very well." Master Eremis made an impatient gesture. "That is all reasonable as far as it goes, but you have not yet explained it. How do you know she is an Imager? What evidence has she given? Lebbick reports that Gilbur freed her from her cell. He killed Quillon. He took her to the room where Havelock's mirrors are kept. Lebbick found them there. After Gilbur felled Lebbick, he and she disappeared from Orison. What does that demonstrate? Gilbur's ability to come and go is as well established as Gart's—and as unexplained. There is no reason to attribute Imagery to her."

Master Barsonage shrugged, scratched his chest. As if to compensate for his baldness, his chest was matted with yellow hair. Water clung to it like beads of sap. "That is true," he replied without hurry or hesitation. "On the other side, it could be argued that Master Gilbur and the arch-Imager would have no reason to free her—just as the High King's Monomach would have no reason to kill her—if she were *not* an Imager. Speaking only for myself, I have examined that argument and found it persuasive. In fact, it persuaded me to accept the position of the Congery's mediator once again.

"Since then, however, we have been given evidence instead of argument, the kind of evidence you and several of the other Masters require."

Maddeningly, he halted and gazed at Eremis as if he had said enough.

Master Eremis forced himself to take a deep breath, relax, stop grinding his teeth. When he had recovered his nonchalance, he said, "You say that you do not distrust me. Do you trust me enough to tell me what that evidence is?"

Once again, Master Barsonage replied, "Of course.

"The Castellan is a hard man, hard to defeat. He was already coming back to consciousness when the lady Terisa and Master Gilbur left the storeroom of Adept Havelock's mirrors. He saw that they did not depart together.

"The lady Terisa vanished into a glass. Master Gilbur was too far from her to have translated her. He left the room the same way he entered it, along the corridor."

The mediator favored Master Eremis with a smile as bland as milk.

Eremis prided himself on his restraint. Nevertheless he betrayed some surprise as he protested, "That is not the story Lebbick tells."

He was surprised because he hadn't expected Barsonage to know so much. And a man who knew more than he was expected to might also *do* more than he was expected to.

And if he really didn't trust Eremis, as his manner made clear, why was he revealing what he knew?

"No"—the mediator corrected his visitor amicably—"it is not the story Castellan Lebbick has told in public. I gather from what I have heard that at first he was too full of fury and desperation to grasp the significance of what he had seen. And since then he has chosen to keep his thoughts to himself. But he did speak to Artagel. And Artagel brought the story to me. He believed—quite rightly— that his information was vital to the Congery."

In a tone that made him sound like a simpleton, Master Barsonage said, "It has enabled me to unite the Masters for the first time since the Congery was created."

Master Eremis drank more wine to conceal the fact that all these surprises were beginning to affect him. Lebbick told Artagel. Artagel told Barsonage. But Gilbur had sworn that Lebbick was still out cold when he left. Was he just trying to cover up a mistake? Or was Barsonage lying—*Barsonage,* of all people? Was he playing some kind of game?

Eremis grinned around the rim of his goblet. This was better than he had anticipated, more fun. He liked opponents who were capable of surprises. He had grown almost fond of King Joyse. Even Lebbick had his good side. Geraden was almost likable. And as for Terisa—

That made their destruction especially exciting.

Unite the Masters, was that it? Then they would have to be un-united.

He twirled his goblet in his long fingers. "Thank you, Master Barsonage," he said happily. "I understand you now.

"What work is the Congery doing with its rediscovered purpose?"

Again the mediator shrugged. A trickle of water ran out of his chest hair across his belly. "It will not surprise you. We labor to learn how it is that men such as the High King's Monomach, who is no Imager, and Master Gilbur, whose talents are known to us, can be translated in and out of Orison at no cost to their sanity. Translation through flat glass drives men mad. That has been true since the dawn of Imagery. Why, then, are our enemies not destroyed by the very weapons they use against us?"

Ah. That was a subject which Master Eremis had come prepared to discuss. With a small, inward sigh—relief, perhaps, or disappointment—he said, "There I may be able to help you. I have an idea that may shed some light."

For the first time since the conversation began, Master Barsonage looked interested. "Please explain it," he said at once. "You know that the matter is urgent."

"Certainly." Matching the blandness of Master Barsonage's tone, Eremis explained. "To the best of our understanding, as you know, the peril of flat glass arises from the translation itself, not from the simple movement from place to place within our world. Put crudely, translation is too strong for simple movement. The power which makes passage possible between entirely separate Images turns against the man translated because it is not needed."

Barsonage nodded.

"On the assumption that our understanding is accurate," Master Eremis went on, "my idea is this. Suppose that two mirrors were made—one flat, showing, say, an unused chamber in Orison, the other normal, showing a barren, deserted plain. Suppose then that the flat glass is now translated into the other, so that it stands upon the plain in the Image, and the focus of the Image is adjusted so that the flat mirror fills the glass. Is it not conceivable that the Imager who shaped those mirrors could now step straight through them, performing in effect two safe translations rather than one which would make him mad?"

The mediator was listening intently; he seemed to soak up Eremis' words through his pores. Softly, as if he were astonished, he breathed, "It is conceivable."

"Of course," Master Eremis continued, simply marking time while he watched the mediator's reaction, "the difficulty is that if the Imager stepped through himself he would not be able to step back. And to send and then retrieve someone else by such a method, he would need to be able to perform both translations simultaneously. We have no way of knowing whether such a thing is possible." Like most of his lies, this one bore an insidious resemblance to the truth. "There Vagel is ahead of us. He may have spent fifteen years perfecting simultaneous translations.

"But surely we can attempt it? We can learn for ourselves whether this idea is indeed possible as well as conceivable?"

"Yes." Master Barsonage had lost his air of studied mildness, of deliberate simplicity. His eyes shone. "We can."

Abruptly, he surged to his feet like a breaker off the sea. "We can and we will. Today. Give me an hour to gather the Masters. Come to the laborium. We will begin experimenting." Almost in the same breath, he added, "It is a brilliant idea. Two mirrors—simultaneous translations. Even if it fails, it remains brilliant. Brilliant."

Having hooked his fish, Master Eremis proceeded to act as if he were letting the mediator go. He agreed to everything, stood up, started to leave, then paused at the door. As if he were innocent of all malice, he said, "Oh, Master Barsonage, one other matter—in case I forget it later. There is a rumor that some of our mirrors have been broken. Can that be true?"

Master Barsonage turned immediately grim: apparently, he was shocked by what had happened. "During the riot against Castellan Lebbick," he admitted. "Five mirrors." He shook his head. "It is plain that someone hates us. But why only five? Why those five? If you were insane enough to deprive us of the means to defend Orison and ourselves, would you not break every glass you found?"

"Certainly." Master Eremis made a sincere effort to look shocked himself. "Unfortunately, insane actions are by their very nature insane. Which mirrors were broken?"

The mediator replied promptly: once again, he was prepared. "The glass with which you refilled the reservoir. That was an attack on Orison. And Geraden's mirror, the one that brought the lady Terisa here. Either he or she is stranded now, wherever they are— as is our lost champion. That was an attack on one of the three of them. But the third was a flat mirror of Quillon's, showing a field of Termigan grapes. The fourth was the one with the Image of the starless sky. The fifth, the one where that gigantic slug-beast can be seen—one of the mirrors King Joyse captured in his wars. An attack on wine? On the heavens? An attack on monsters? It makes no sense.

"Geraden and the lady Terisa and our champion—if he still lives—may have been stranded entirely at random, by someone who had no idea what he did."

Trying to sound disturbed, perhaps even grim, Eremis said, "My glass. Then we must depend on the weather for water. I cannot save us again."

"That is true," replied Barsonage. "Prince Kragen's position is now much stronger. We must hope he does not know it."

Master Eremis swallowed a final smile and made his way out of the mediator's quarters. He wanted to reach his own rooms quickly, where he could afford to laugh out loud.

He realized, of course, that he was in a tricky situation. But it was a situation of his own devising. Thanks to the seeds he had just planted, Barsonage and the other Masters might spend the rest of their time until they died trying to work a simultaneous translation because they didn't know it was impossible. Or, rather, it was trivial. The trick was not in the translation, but in the glass.

For all practical purposes, he had neutralized the Congery— the only force in Orison still capable of fighting him.

On the other hand, he would have to be very careful. Lebbick had said something to Artagel, who had told it to Barsonage. Not something about Terisa: something about Eremis himself. The mediator had lied to him.

For him, the trick would be to determine exactly what that lie was.

Thinking about things like this made him look like he was about to burst with good humor.

THIRTY-EIGHT: CONFLICT AT THE GATES

he trick," Geraden said the first time they rested the horses, "is not to get stopped."

They had ridden hard for most of the morning: the road from Romish was easy going, and he was in a hurry. But the horses couldn't sustain a pace like that indefinitely.

"Oh, really?" Terisa didn't realize how sourly she spoke. She was still thinking about Torrent: the idea of the King's shy daughter riding away alone in a foolish and dangerous effort to rescue Queen Madin clung to her mind like a splash of acid. "We're going back to Orison. Where Master Eremis wants us. Why would anybody try to stop us?"

Geraden looked at her sharply; for a moment, he seemed unsure how to respond. As if he had missed the point, he said, "We've been riding so long—and it feels so good to be with you—I keep thinking you know Mordant better than you do. Would you like to look at the map again?"

She shook her head. She didn't care about the map. She didn't care about being stopped. At the moment, she didn't even care about having to face Eremis again.

Geraden, that's how Argus got killed.

"Well," he explained, still missing the point, "there's really only one fast way to get from Romish to Orison, and that's along this road—the main road through Armigite. Which just happens to be the route Prince Kragen used. It's his link to Alend—his supply line, his line of retreat. It'll be crawling with his men.

"On top of that, even the Armigite can't be as stupid as people think. He's got to have scouts and spies everywhere, especially along the road. He needs to know what's happening. And right now he probably wants an Imager or two more than anything in the world. If his men get their hands on us, they aren't going to let us go just because we smile and say please."

Terisa stared into the trees without saying anything.

"And on top of *that*"—Geraden's tone became slowly harsher—"I assume Orison is still under siege. I *assume* it hasn't already fallen, or there wouldn't be any reason to kidnap Queen Madin. If we're going to get in to see King Joyse, we'll have to get past the whole Alend army.

"The men who took the Queen were Alends. It looks like this is some plot of Prince Kragen's. So he's the one we have to worry about. And he won't let us in to Orison until he's ready—until his trap is ready."

He surprised her, and she winced. "Do you really think that's true? Do you really think Prince Kragen is responsible for kidnapping the Queen?"

"Don't you? You said those men were Alends. They took her toward Alend."

The acid in her mind was turning to nausea. "But if he's responsible—" Until now, she hadn't considered the question closely. "That means he's working with Master Eremis. Where else would he get an Imager who could translate an avalanche?"

Geraden watched her and waited.

"But if that's true, why did Eremis refill the reservoir? Why didn't he just let Prince Kragen into Orison?"

"An interesting question," Geraden murmured past his teeth.

She tried to imagine an explanation; but almost at once another aspect of the situation struck her. "If the Prince did it, he must have done it behind Elega's back. She'd never approve of something like that."

Geraden nodded once, roughly.

The implications brought Terisa to a halt. "Elega's being betrayed herself." She faced Geraden squarely, showed him her distress. "What're we going to do?"

The way he met her gaze gave the impression that he had accomplished his goal: he had shifted the direction of her thoughts. "We'll stay on the road until we get close to Batten," he replied. "That's where the Alends will pick it up. And it turns south there to meet the road from Sternwall. We can go straight southeast toward Orison. We'll save some miles—and maybe we won't lose much time."

"When we reach the siege, we'll try to get to Elega before the Prince realizes what we're doing." Abruptly, he grinned—a sharp smile with no humor in it. "If she knows what happened to her mother—if she allowed it to happen, if she approves of it—I'm going to be *very* disappointed in her."

"And if she doesn't know," Terisa completed for him, trying to reassure herself, "she might be willing to help us."

He nodded again.

After a while, they mounted their horses and went on.

They rode out of the last hills of Fayle onto one of Armigite's many fertile flatlands at what felt like a breakneck pace. Leaving the woods behind increased Terisa's anxiety: Armigite appeared to be almost unnaturally open, as if everything that moved through it were somehow exposed. Perhaps that was why the Armigite had become what he was: perhaps his personality had been distorted by the pressure of being so exposed. But actually there were quite a few trees around, even in lowlands which had obviously been under cultivation before Prince Kragen and his army crossed the Pestil. Concealment was scarce, but shade was available. Partly for that reason, and partly because of the soil's richness, the flats of Armigite bore no resemblance to the arid spaces of Termigan.

Terisa and Geraden made good progress, despite the lack of fresh mounts. He studied the map repeatedly—they were still crossing a part of Mordant where he had never been before—and assured her that their progress was good. He may have been trying to shore up her spirits. For some reason, his own didn't appear to need support: his keenness suggested that he liked this rush across the landscape, this clear and urgent sense of purpose; that he was eager to return to Orison. By the time nightfall forced them to halt and make camp, they were well on their way toward making the journey to Orison as Queen Madin had intended it, in three days.

The more he looked ahead, however, the more her attention turned backward. Torrent had touched her unexpectedly, made her aware of her own inadequacies. In their separate ways, each of the

King's daughters had daunted her. They had inherited more courage than she seemed to possess. Her determination to oppose Master Eremis was little more than a pretense, after all—a pretense that she could somehow transcend her past.

As she gazed across the campfire into the open dark of Armigite, she murmured, "Geraden, there's something I don't understand."

"Just 'something'?" he returned, making a transparent effort to jolly her out of her mood. "Then you are marvelous to me, my lady. *My* lack of understanding doesn't stop at 'something.' It's as vast as the world."

She looked over at him. His face was as dear as ever. And if anything he had become more handsome; the excitement he had felt since Torrent left brought out the best in his eyes, in the lines of his features. He didn't deserve her gloom. For his sake, she made an effort to smile.

"That's probably true. But I'll bet you know the answer to this one."

He met her eyes and smiled back. "Try me." The dancing light of the campfire created the impression that his smile went all the way to the bone.

Almost at once, she found that the weight pushing down on her spirit wasn't quite as heavy as she had thought.

"I think I will," she said. "But first I want you to explain something."

The gleam in his eyes grew brighter as he waited for her to continue.

"That avalanche," she said. "They must have used two mirrors. Isn't that right? One to translate it away from wherever they found it. One to translate it *to* Vale House."

"Yes," Geraden replied at once. "But that's been true of everything we've seen. Those pits of fire outside Sternwall. The ghouls in Fayle. Even the creatures that attacked Houseldon." A shadow which might have been grief or rage darkened his gaze briefly. "They all needed two mirrors. That must be Eremis' secret. It must be how he's able to attack so many different places in Mordant without actually going to them. And it must be how he's able to move people in and out of Orison without costing them their minds.

"We've talked about that before," he added.

"I remember. It's the only explanation I've heard that seems to make sense. Two mirrors. One shows a scene with a lot of landslides.

The other is a flat glass with Vale House in the Image. That means"— her heart tightened as she came to the point—"Eremis could have seen us in the Image. He *must* have seen us. I know I was in the Image. Otherwise I wouldn't have felt the translation.

"That means he knows where we are.

"And it means we're responsible for what happened to Queen Madin. She was taken because of us."

"No." Geraden rejected the idea without hesitation. "That can't be true. It wasn't because of us."

"Why not?"

"It's too complicated. He had men ready for that attack. They must have been on their way before we ever got near Fayle. If we had anything to do with it, he must have known we were going there—and not to Romish—long before we did. And his men wouldn't have ignored us. He would have been glad for a chance to capture us.

"That attack was aimed at the Queen herself. Even the timing was just a coincidence. Eremis couldn't control the avalanches in his mirror. He had to be ready to act whenever the opportunity came along."

Involuntarily, Terisa shook her head. She didn't like what she was thinking. "No. He probably *can* control the avalanches. I mean he can cause one whenever he wants. All he has to do is focus his mirror on the right kind of mountainside. Then, when he wants a landslide, all he has to do is translate away the rock supporting the mountainside."

Geraden stared at her, his eyes glittering flames. "You're right. I never thought of that."

"The attack wasn't aimed at us," she assented. "But he knows we *were* there. He could have seen that we survived. He could have seen us ride away. He could guess where we're going.

"That means we can't warn King Joyse. It won't do any good. There won't be any gap between when he knows what happened to the Queen and when Eremis knows he knows. He won't have a chance to act. What we're trying to do doesn't make any sense."

She stopped and watched Geraden's face, holding her breath as if she feared his reaction.

She was relieved to see that he wasn't discouraged. His expression became intently thoughtful, but he didn't look especially alarmed; he certainly didn't look horrified. Softly, he commented,

"I've said it before. You have a morbid imagination. No wonder you've been so depressed all day.

"This time," he said after a moment, "I think you're wrong."

Quietly, she let the air sigh out of her lungs.

"If Eremis saw us," he asked by way of explanation, "where's Gart?"

Terisa's mouth fell open. She wasn't the only one with a morbid imagination.

"While we were talking with Torrent," Geraden continued, "while we were trying to help the Fayle's man, while we were packing our horses—that was the best chance Gart's ever had to kill us both. We were defenseless. Why didn't Eremis get rid of us while he had the chance?

"I don't think he saw us.

"He *could* have seen us, of course. We found that out outside Sternwall. But this time I don't think he did.

"I'm sure he didn't before the avalanche. We were on the porch, under the roof, and his mirror was focused in the air over the house. After all, he didn't want to kill Queen Madin. She wouldn't have done him any good dead. But that's not really the point. The point is, if you're translating several hundred tons of rock out of one glass into another, what do you do with it while it's between translations? If you make even the tiniest mistake, all that rock will shatter the second mirror, and you'll have the entire avalanche in your lap."

In spite of herself, Terisa let out a slightly hysterical giggle. That would have been perfect justice, if the landslide Eremis had planned for Vale House had come down on his own head.

Geraden flashed her a grin. "The solution," he said, "is the one we talked about—a hundred years ago or so in Orison, when we didn't know we were two of the most powerful people alive. Translate the second glass into the first. In effect, the rock goes straight into the flat mirror.

"But." He held up a hand to forestall interruption. "This is what saved us. When you do a translation like that—when you put the second mirror into the first before you start—what can you see? You can see the mountainside. You can see the rock. But you can't see the Image in the second mirror. The *back* of the flat mirror faces you, so the front can translate the rock.

"And once you start a process like that you have to keep it going until the dust clears and you're sure you're safe. If you stop while there's *any* chance one or two boulders are still hopping down the mountainside, the flat glass could be crushed, and the boulders could end up in your face. So you can't be in a hurry to translate the second mirror back out of the first and turn it around and refocus it.

"That's why we had time to get away."

Listening to him, Terisa felt a knot inside her loosen at last. He was right. It was possible that Eremis hadn't seen them. If he had, surely he would have sent an attack after them—wolves or a firecat, if not Gart himself. There was still hope for the wild scheme Torrent and Geraden had conceived.

That night, she experienced some of the benefits of Geraden's keenness. She began to feel a bit keener herself.

At about the same time, when the embers had died down, and clouds covered the moon, Prince Kragen sent men to clear the charred remains of his battering rams and their protective shells away from Orison's gates. He wanted the new rams and shells being hammered together to have an unimpeded approach.

And the next morning, he pressed his attack.

Well, they have to run out of oil some*time.*

It seemed a rather thin tactic on which to hinge Alend's hopes for survival, never mind victory. Nevertheless he persisted. He simply didn't have any better ideas. With enough time, he could have sat where he was in perfect safety, discussing governance with his father, or with the lady Elega, training his forces—and waiting for Orison to starve itself into submission. That was the way sieges were supposed to go. But nothing that had anything to do with King Joyse ever went the way it was supposed to go. And as for High King Festten—

If the Prince could use up Orison's supplies of lamp oil, cooking oil, flammable grease, he might be able to bring his battering rams to bear on the gates more effectively. All he needed was to get the gates open.

He knew he had enough men to overwhelm the castle, if he could just get the gates open.

Around midafternoon that day, while the fifth of Prince Kragen's makeshift rams burned like a bonfire, Terisa and Geraden sighted Batten and left the road to work eastward around the city.

This was one of the tricky parts, Geraden explained. Here they had to cross Alend's supply route. The danger of encountering Alend soldiers was now severe. And the Armigite's scouts or spies would almost certainly be concentrated along the lines where Alend forces were expected. Geraden and Terisa slowed their pace almost to a walk; and he spent long moments on the crest of every rise, straining his eyes toward the horizons. From time to time, he found a tree and climbed it to study the terrain from that vantage.

For no good reason except that she saw nothing—not even the walls of the city, once she and Geraden had left the road—she began to think these pauses for caution were unnecessary. They crossed the unmistakable swath of ground which had brought the Alend army to the road—unmistakable because the soil still held the cut of wheels, the gouge of hooves, the pressure of boots—but they didn't see any sign of Alend supply wains or Armigite spotters. She would have preferred the risk of speed to the frustration of delay.

She changed her mind, however, when he came down out of a tree so fast that he nearly fell like the fumblefoot he had once been. Hissing instructions rapidly, he dragged the mounts into a nearby thicket; with her help, he forced the beasts to lie down, then did his best to muffle their noses, prevent them from whickering as the other horses came near.

A small band of riders with grime-caked clothes and eyes made evil by fear passed so close that Terisa could have hit them with a stone.

"Mercenaries," Geraden grated under his breath after the riders were gone. "Men like that— If they were in a hurry, they might cut your throat *before* they raped you.

"I thought every mercenary in the world worked for Cadwal."

Terisa was having trouble with her pulse. "Then what're they doing here?"

He shrugged stiffly, as if all his muscles were in knots. "Working for somebody else. Or spying for the High King. If the Lieges send Prince Kragen reinforcements, Festten will want to know about it. He may have men all over this part of Mordant by now."

Oh, good, Terisa muttered to herself. Just what we need.

She and Geraden had to hide twice more before the end of the day, but both times they were able to avoid discovery with relative ease. The scouts or mercenaries expected many things, but they clearly didn't expect to encounter a man and a woman with three horses cutting across open ground around Batten.

In a fireless camp that night in a small gully, she remarked, "I can't live this way."

"What, sneaking around like this? Surrounded by people who would gut us unless they had the good sense to take us prisoner if they only knew we were here? You aren't having fun?" Geraden snorted softly. "Terisa, I'm surprised at you."

Actually, she was surprised at herself. Without warning, she was filled with a sense of how strange her circumstances were. Wasn't she Terisa Morgan, the passive girl who had typed sad letters for Reverend Thatcher until she had lost faith in him and his mission? Wasn't she the lonely woman who had decorated her apartment in mirrors because she didn't know any other way to prove she existed? So what was she doing *here?*—surrounded, as Geraden observed, by enemies; struggling across country on horseback in a nearly crazy effort to warn King Joyse that his wife had been abducted; so angry at Master Eremis that she couldn't think about it without trembling. What was she *doing?*

"So am I," she murmured; but Geraden had been teasing her, and she was serious. The night on all sides felt at once vast and subtle, too big to be faced, too cunning to be escaped. And the stars— She knew in her bones that the city where her apartment was had nowhere near this many stars watching it. "Right now, it seems like there isn't another place in the universe farther away from where I used to live than this."

"Are you afraid?" he asked gently. "We still have a long way to go."

He wasn't talking about the distance to Orison.

"That's the funny part," she mused. "When I stop and take my pulse, I get the impression I've never been so scared in all my life. But when I think about where I came from"—my apartment, my job, my parents—"I think I've never been so brave."

After a while, he said, "It makes an amazing difference when you have good, clear reasons for what you're doing. I think I used to have so many accidents because I was confused. In conflict with myself."

She agreed, but she didn't say so. Instead, she said, "Don't get cocky. I saw you almost fall out of that tree."

That made him laugh. And his laughter always made her feel better.

Prince Kragen also had reasons for his actions.

What he was doing was unprecedented. Despite the darkness—despite the fact that his men couldn't see Orison's counterattacks in time to defend themselves very well—he was belaboring the gates with the heaviest battering ram he had.

He had two reasons for risking the blood of his army so lavishly, one immediate, the other alarming.

His immediate reason was that just before sunset the defenders had stopped pouring oil on the shells of his rams. The particular ram spared by this forbearance wasn't especially impressive: its shell protected only enough men to move it, not enough to seriously threaten the gates. Nevertheless the forbearance itself was significant. Without hesitation, the Prince called back that ram and sent out a bigger one, fully manned.

This one, also, was allowed to do its work without being set afire.

Two interpretations immediately suggested themselves. Orison was out of oil. Or Orison was trying to conserve oil—was trusting the dark for protection.

Under other circumstances, this chance to hit the gates wouldn't have been worth the risk. At night, protected by darkness from archers, the castle's defenders would be able to swing down from the walls on ropes and strike at the ram in a matter of minutes. But the Prince was too worried to miss any opportunity, however costly it might prove.

He was alarmed because during the afternoon his scouts had intercepted two hacked and dying men who were apparently the last survivors the Perdon would ever send to Orison.

They weren't actually sure of their lord's fate. When he sent them away, he still had several hundred men around him, was still fighting. But he knew he was finished. He sent these two soldiers to warn King Joyse.

They were too badly hurt to last the night; but Prince Kragen pieced their story together from their confused and feverish babblings. What had apparently happened was that High King Festten had suddenly changed his tactics. He had halted his unexplained march into the Care of Tor: for a while, he had even stopped striking at the Perdon. Instead, he had camped his huge army as if he had gained his goal, as if his only real purpose had been to capture the ground where he now stood—a relatively uninhabited region of complex hills and thin rivers no closer to Marshalt than to Orison.

And then, while the Perdon was still trying to figure out what Festten was doing, the High King had sent out nearly five thousand soldiers to encircle and trap the lord. In the end, only the terrain had enabled these two wounded men to escape. They had hidden in a tree-clogged ravine until darkness allowed them to creep away northward.

How many days ago? Prince Kragen wanted to know. How far exactly? In fact, he wanted to know so badly that out of raw frustration he was tempted to resort to some of the harsher forms of questioning. But it was obvious that the Perdon's men, in effect, had already been tortured past the point where they were able to think or speak coherently. Prince Kragen was left with very little idea when they had left their lord, or where Festten was.

So he attacked Orison's gates at night, despite the losses he knew he was going to incur. He was afraid: he could feel a kind of doom stalking him through the dark. An enemy who would march at least twenty thousand men that far into the middle of nowhere—in this case, the middle of the Care of Tor—for no discernible purpose except to *make camp* was capable of anything.

Through the hours of darkness, Kragen listened to the flat, dull booming of the ram against the gates, to the shouts of the defenders and the cries of his own forces—listened, and ground his teeth to restrain his rage at a war he couldn't either avoid or understand.

Castellan Lebbick appeared to be in a completely different mood. If he felt any desire to rage, he didn't show it. From the battlements above the gate, he watched the massive Alend ram at work with a twisted expression on his face, as if something inside him were being torn; yet he didn't so much as raise his voice or curse. He didn't even grin. For no very clear reason, he muttered in disgust words that sounded to the guards around him like, "fool woman." Then he called for ropes and began mustering men to fight for the gates.

He didn't stay to watch the struggle, however. A number of his captains knew what to do in a situation like this. Wandering away like a shadow of the man he used to be, he went to spend as much of the night as possible drinking with Artagel.

Unfortunately, ale—even in that quantity—did nothing to quench the hot, dry sensation in his mind. He was full of foreboding; his brain chewed anticipations of disaster. So he was grimly amazed when he woke up the next morning and learned that something good was happening.

It was raining.

A hard rain, so thick that it blinded the castle and turned the dirt of the courtyard into immediate soup; what the people where Lebbick had grown up called a real gully-washer. And long overdue: Mordant expected rain like this in the spring.

Of course, it made Orison impossible to defend. The guards above the gates wouldn't have known if the entire Alend army had come within a stone's throw of their noses.

On the other hand, the rain also made attack impossible.

The Alends had no footing. They could bring up battering rams until they broke their hearts; but they couldn't swing them effectively. The gates would stand forever against any pounding they might receive in this rain. And other siege engines were equally useless.

The rain didn't cheer Castellan Lebbick up. He was past the point where anything could have cheered him. But it did give him a breathing space, a bit of time in which to get a better grip on himself.

It also helped Terisa and Geraden.

That surprised her. She got so wet and so cold so quickly that she felt defeated before the day had well begun. She soon realized, however, that she and Geraden were in next to no danger of being spotted or captured through this downpour. If she had let him get more than ten feet away, she wouldn't have been able to spot him herself.

Now the trick had nothing to do with being stopped. The trick was to know where they were going.

"How do you know we're not lost?" she shouted into the deluge.

"The rain!" Despite the water streaming down his face, he grinned. "At this time of year, it always comes from the west! We're going south, so all we have to do is cut across the wind!"

She would have been impressed if her whole body hadn't felt so miserable.

Nevertheless she kept going; she and Geraden kept each other going. While their enemies were blinded was the best time for them to go forward. The rain might make it impossible for Torrent to follow her mother; but Terisa was too cold and soaked to worry about something that far out of her control. She concentrated solely on Geraden and motion until the storm finally blew away an hour or two before sunset, and he had an opportunity to find his bearings.

"Tomorrow." There was relief in his voice; yet she had never heard him sound so tired. "We'll be in the Demesne tomorrow morning. Tomorrow afternoon or evening we'll reach Orison."

Just for something to say, she muttered, "If Prince Kragen doesn't give me some dry clothes, I'm going to spit right in his face."

Geraden nodded his approval. "Just don't kick him. I've heard princes tend to get cranky when they're kicked."

"I don't care," she retorted. "I've been on a horse for as long as I can remember, and my whole body hurts. I'm going to kick anybody I want."

Again, he nodded. "You may have to." It was obvious that his thoughts were elsewhere. "We've been carrying a lot of questions around for a long time. Tomorrow we'll start getting answers. You may have to kick everybody we meet."

Terisa refused to worry about that. All she wanted at the moment was to be warm and dry.

The inhabitants of Orison had the opposite reaction: they prayed for more rain.

Unluckily, they didn't get it. By the next morning, the ground was dry enough for Prince Kragen to resume his attack.

The mud was still thick: a sea of it surrounded Orison. But decades or centuries of use had packed the roadbed hard; it gave the Alends enough footing to put some heft into the swing of their ram.

Protected by shields and shells, nearly a thousand men edged close to the walls to ward the ram as it hammered the gates. Every blow seemed to carry through the stone to the tops of the towers, the bottoms of the dungeons.

In response, Castellan Lebbick's guards cranked up mangonels powerful enough to dent iron and splinter wood. The mangonels shattered Alend shields almost effortlessly, reduced the flesh under the shields to pulp and crushed bone. Lebbick didn't have many of the ponderous crossbows, however. And his men had to fire scores of lead bolts in order to damage the shell protecting the ram.

Slowly, inevitably, one blow at a time, the gates began to fail.

The wood started to compress and crack; stress showed along the iron strutwork; mortar sifted from between the stones which held the gates in the wall; bolts began to work loose.

At the moment, Prince Kragen was paying for this success with dozens and then hundreds of his men. Inside the castle, Orison's defenders suffered no losses. But that imbalance would shift as soon as the gates broke.

"Tomorrow," Lebbick muttered, inspecting their timbers with an expert eye. "Those shitlickers'll be in here tomorrow. We've got that long to live."

He didn't sound upset. He didn't even sound angry.

He sounded satisfied.

Dutifully, he sent a report to King Joyse. Then he reduced Orison's defenders to a minimum. Every guard who could be spared he ordered away to spend as much time as possible with whatever friends or family the man had left.

His wife would have approved of that.

Amiably, Artagel asked him, "What do you suppose King Joyse will do to save us?"

Entirely without warning, Castellan Lebbick recovered his rage. "The way our luck's going"—he was clenching his teeth so hard his forehead felt like it might crack—"he'll challenge Prince fornicating Kragen to a *duel*."

With fury crackling in every muscle, he left the gates and the courtyard. While he was angry, at least, he couldn't bear to watch what was happening.

Like the Prince, he had no way of knowing that Terisa and Geraden were already in the Demesne.

Late that afternoon, they rode as if they were fearless straight up to the first Alend patrol they met and demanded to be taken to the lady Elega.

Swords and distrust surrounded them promptly. Terisa's mount showed a distressing inclination to shy in all directions; she had to fight to keep the beast under control. She was conscious that the weather had turned chilly since the previous day's rain. Alends? she wondered. Not Cadwals? Does that mean Orison is still standing? But she had no intention of asking those questions aloud. After all, these soldiers were dressed and armored just like the men who had taken Queen Madin.

The leader of the patrol snapped, "What makes pigslop like you two think you've got a reason to see the Prince's lady?"

Geraden's mouth smiled, but his eyes were hard. "We're servants," he answered with a hint of danger in his voice. "Our parents have served her family since before we were born. We grew up with her.

"We've come from Romish. The Queen sent us to see her."

The Alend leader snarled a curse. "The Queen? Madin, that shithole Joyse's wife?"

The effort of controlling her horse disguised Terisa's face as effectively as a mask. Geraden's expression was positively serene: only his eyes threatened to betray him. "So you've heard of her," he said blandly. "Good. Then you'll understand that the lady Elega won't take it kindly if you prevent us from delivering our messages."

"Queen Madin?" the Alend repeated in a voice congested with hostility. "You've got messages from Queen Madin?"

Geraden's mouth smiled again. "My, you *are* quick." Then, softly, he said, "Take us to see the lady Elega."

A little thrill touched Terisa's heart as she heard the authority in his tone.

The leader of the patrol hesitated; he was taken aback—a fact which seemed to surprise him. To compensate, he growled an obscenity. Then he said, "I think the Prince is going to want to hear your messages."

"As long as we get to talk to her," replied Geraden, "I don't care who else hears us. Take us to see them both.

"Just do it."

To his own obvious astonishment, the Alend leader turned and organized his men to escort Geraden and Terisa toward the encampment. A pair of the Alends galloped ahead; the rest formed a knot around the travelers.

Suddenly giddy with relief—perhaps because her horse had stopped shying—she took the risk of giving Geraden a wink. He pretended not to notice it.

They were closer to the siege than she had realized. In only a short time, they came in sight of the Alend army and Orison.

She was surprised by how small the castle looked under these circumstances, invested by ten thousand soldiers, half a hundred siege engines, and an uncounted number of servants and camp followers. Orison's bluff gray stone, which should have appeared impregnable, bore an unexpected resemblance to cardboard; tiny flags fluttering from the towers gave the place the air of a child's plaything.

At the same time, the breach partially covered by the curtain-wall seemed to gape unnaturally wide, as if it were bigger than it used to be, darker; a fatal wound.

The men who had ridden ahead had already caused a commotion: Terisa could see the army and its adherents shifting to receive her and Geraden. People ran forward to stare; questions were called which the Alend leader either ignored or shouted down. The attack on the gates used only a fraction of Prince Kragen's forces; the rest had nothing to do at the moment except wait and worry. Some of the soldiers only wanted news. But others offered jokes and insults that turned Geraden's eyes as sharp as bits of glass. He preserved his expression of serenity, however, and followed the patrol in through the camp.

They passed an area of tattered and scruffy tents where the poorest of the camp followers lived, ankle-deep in the overflow of their own squalor. Then the order and cleanliness of the encampment began to improve, according to the increasing status of its occupants. In minutes, the patrol brought Terisa and Geraden to an open area like an imitation of a courtyard, around which were pitched several tents so large and luxurious that she felt sure she and Geraden had reached their goal.

Their immediate goal, at any rate. In order to enter Orison, they first had to get past Prince Kragen.

He came out of one of the tents into the evening shadows before anyone had a chance to dismount. He moved as if he intended to approach the riders directly; but as soon as he saw them he stopped. He planted his fists on his hips when Terisa met his gaze; his black eyes flashed as if she had given him a slap. For a moment, forcing himself to be thorough, he turned his head and considered Geraden; then he faced Terisa again.

"'Servants of the Queen'?" he demanded of his men in a tone that might have been jesting or bitter. "They said that, and you believed them? Did not one of you louts think to ask them their *names?*"

He didn't give the leader of the patrol a chance to respond, however. "Oh, let it pass. They would have lied about their names as well, and then you would have been worse fooled than before.

"At least have the common sense to disarm them. Then go."

Stung, the leader of the patrol snatched away Terisa's and Geraden's weapons, the swords the Termigan had given them. Then the men withdrew.

Prince Kragen gave the impression that the patrol had already ceased to exist as far as he was concerned. He was concentrating exclusively on Terisa.

"My lady Terisa of Morgan." He spoke slowly, drawling in a way which suggested humor or scorn. "You astonish me entirely. And your companion must be the infamous Apt Geraden, the butt alike of mirth and augury. I can think of no other possibility.

"However, you may amaze me there as well. Since you are *out here*"—he released one fist from his hip to gesture at the ground between the tents—"when it is obvious that you ought to be *in there*"—he indicated Orison—"I conclude that you have a remarkable story to tell me.

"You will tell it"—gradually, his tone convinced Terisa that he wasn't in a happy mood—"now."

"My lord Prince," Geraden put in steadily, as if he weren't interrupting the Alend Contender, "where is the lady Elega?"

"I am here, Geraden."

Terisa turned in her saddle and saw the King's daughter.

Elega stood between the flaps of one of the tents. A streak of sunset caught her face, so that her usual paleness was covered with an orange-gold blush, and light muffled the vividness of her eyes. In that way, she looked like she had become an entirely different woman since Terisa had last seen her.

"So it is true, my lady Terisa," she said clearly, lifting up her voice as though this were a formal occasion. "It was always true. You are an Imager."

Prince Kragen's mouth moved under his moustache, swearing. When he spoke, however, he kept his tone neutral. "How do you reach that conclusion, my lady Elega?"

Elega's gaze didn't shift from Terisa; she studied Terisa through the failing beams of the sun. "As you said, my lord Prince, they are not in Orison. It is doubtful that they were able to creep out through your siege. Therefore they must have removed themselves by Imagery."

"Or someone else removed us," Geraden put in acerbically.

"Don't forget that possibility. You don't think Gart does his own translations, do you?"

An unexpected silence fell over the tents. Elega half raised a hand to her mouth, then dropped it. A glint of white teeth showed between Prince Kragen's lips. From somewhere in the distance, Terisa heard a methodical booming, a deep thud at once so hard and so far away that it seemed to come through the ground rather than the air. Men shouted faintly. Her presence there, and Geraden's, must have come as a complete surprise to Elega and the Prince. Now the idea Geraden suggested appeared to shock them further, as if it made the whole situation incomprehensible.

Well, Terisa thought, this was better than being tied up—or cut down. She felt an off-center, almost loony desire to give Geraden a round of applause. The men who had taken Queen Madin were Alends. And Terisa and Geraden had so many questions— And they wanted to get into Orison. If Kragen really had ordered the Queen's abduction, their only hope was to keep him off balance and pray for something unexpected to happen.

Trying to make a contribution, she asked, "My lord Prince, may we get down? I've been on this horse ever since I can remember."

A small shudder seemed to pass through Prince Kragen, a brief convulsion of will. At once, he became calmer, as if his self-possession had been tightened a notch.

"Of course, my lady Terisa." He moved toward her. "Where other matters are concerned, I have said that the debts between us are settled. Yet you are a friend of the lady Elega's, and so you are welcome among us. Permit me to offer you the Alend Monarch's hospitality."

He reached up his hands to help her dismount.

That was a courtesy to which she wasn't accustomed, but she did her best to let him assist her. Geraden swung down and came to her side; at once, he bowed formally to Prince Kragen.

"My lord Prince, I haven't been properly presented, but you've named me. I'm Geraden, the seventh son of the Domne, an Apt of the Congery of Imagers.

"As you say, we have a remarkable story to tell." Somehow, he contrived to sound like he couldn't think of a single reason to distrust the Prince. "And there must be a lot you could tell us, if we can persuade you to do it."

"Geraden." Elega had come forward while Terisa was focused

on Prince Kragen. Her face and form were in shadow now, with the paradoxical result that she looked brighter, keener; more capable. "What does this mean?" she demanded. "Why are you here? And *how?* Surely you will not ask us to believe that this is nothing more than another of your colossal mishaps?"

"No," Geraden replied. "On the other hand, I do expect you to believe that it's hard for me to trust you enough to tell you anything."

There: he had given the first hint of his loyalties; therefore of his intentions. Terisa held her breath, afraid that he might be risking too much too soon.

Fortunately, Kragen wasn't surprised enough to react badly. He knew what had happened to Nyle's attempt to reach the Perdon: he was probably able to take Geraden's loyalties for granted. Before Elega could respond to Geraden's gibe, Prince Kragen stepped between them and took Terisa's arm.

"We will discuss such things thoroughly, I assure you," he remarked, "but I can see no reason why we should not discuss them in comfort—and in private." With his hand on her arm, he urged Terisa into motion, steering her toward the largest of the surrounding tents. "In addition, I have offered you the Alend Monarch's hospitality, and he does not like to be refused." As if she weren't already moving—as if she had a choice—he asked, "Will you come with me?"

Terisa nodded. But she didn't let out her breath until she saw that both Geraden and Elega were following.

The Prince took her into what she realized after a moment was a fore-tent. It was lit only by the braziers which warmed it, with the result that its furnishings were obscure, vaguely ominous; the chairs seemed to crouch in the dimness, as unpredictable as beasts. Prince Kragen clapped his hands, however, and called for lamps as well as wine. The servants responded almost instantly; soon warm yellow light filled the fore-tent, and the danger crept away, hiding in the darkness at the tops of the tentpoles, or in the shadows behind the chairs.

"The Alend Monarch has gone to his bed," Prince Kragen said casually. "Otherwise he would welcome you himself. This tent serves as his council chamber, and I doubt"—he smiled—"that there is a man in all the camp who would dare eavesdrop on what is said here. We will speak freely."

Briskly, he got Terisa, Geraden, and Elega seated. When the

wine had been served, he took a chair himself. Terisa drank a gulp of the fine vintage, trying to control her nervousness; but Elega watched her and Geraden, while Geraden faced the Prince.

Prince Kragen toyed with his goblet. "My lady Terisa, Geraden, these are complex times. I suspect that all stories are remarkable. Nevertheless your arrival here suggests questions to which I must have answers."

"Forgive me, my lord Prince," Geraden put it as if he hadn't heard Kragen. "So much has happened— The last we knew, Cadwal was marching. A vast army. Where *is* it? What's happened to the Perdon? How has Orison been able to hold you back so long?"

"Geraden, I am in command of this siege." The Prince's voice became a soft purr, a threat. "This army is mine. I wish to understand how you come to be here."

"Of course"—Geraden allowed himself a slight, suggestive pause—"my lord Prince. On the other hand, I wish to be able to measure the consequences of what I tell you. I'm talking to an honorable enemy and a dishonorable friend." He ignored the way Elega stiffened, the violet flare of her gaze. "Knowledge is power. I don't want to place a weapon in the wrong hands."

"You will not." Prince Kragen might have been a cat pretending that he wasn't about to spring. "You will place it in *my* hands."

Geraden didn't blink. "Or else?"

The Prince shrugged delicately. "There is no 'or else.' I simply state a fact. You *will* tell me your remarkable story."

His tone left Terisa's stomach in knots. When she looked in her goblet, she found that it was already empty.

"Geraden," Elega put in, "why did you come here? You have never been stupid. You knew that this situation would arise. You knew that both the Prince and I desire the defeat of Orison. And you knew"—she seemed to falter, but only for an instant—"that we cannot afford to let you keep your knowledge secret. We are too much at risk. My life is perhaps a little thing, but the Prince is responsible for the whole Alend army. In the end, he is responsible for the survival of all his father's realm.

"And for that," Elega added firmly, "I have my own responsibility. Like the King, I have brought us to this place.

"Why did you put yourself and the lady Terisa in our hands, if you do not intend to tell us what you know?"

"Because we are unable to reenter Orison without your consent." Geraden didn't elaborate.

"That is what you want?" demanded Prince Kragen softly. "You wish to be allowed to enter Orison, so that you can tell King Joyse the story you mean to withhold from me?"

Geraden contemplated this view of the situation. "That's essentially true, my lord Prince."

"I suspected as much." The Prince held his hands together on his thighs, the tips of his fingers touching each other lightly as if his self-command had become perfect. "My mind is not like my lady Elega's. When you entered my camp, I did not say, Here are Imagers. I said, Here are scouts who wish to report to their lord.

"If you believe that I will let you pass my siege in order to take assistance or information of any kind to King Joyse, you are seriously deranged."

Geraden shrugged. Judging by the blandness of his expression, he had no idea how seriously he was being threatened.

Terisa was too full of anxiety to sit still. Without asking permission, she stood up and went to the wine decanter. "Why don't we trade?" she said impulsively. Fatigue and the first effects of the wine might have been speaking for her. She had played the game of trading information with King Joyse: she knew it was dangerous. But it was the best she had to offer. Her goblet full, she returned to her seat. "You tell us something. We'll tell you something. Fair exchange. That way we don't have to trust each other."

"Who will speak first?" asked Elega in a carefully neutral tone.

"You will." Terisa didn't hesitate. "We're in your power. You can do anything you want to us anytime you want. What have you got to lose?"

She sat down.

Geraden kept his reaction hidden. The lady Elega looked at Prince Kragen.

The Prince thought for a while; he didn't appear to be aware that he was chewing his moustache. Two of his fingertips tapped soundlessly against each other, measuring the menace in the foretent. Then he said with steady nonchalance, "I think not.

"My lady Elega," he continued before Terisa was sure that she had heard him right, "you have not heard the details of our guests' arrival. You will be interested, I am sure.

"Geraden and the lady Terisa made no attempt at stealth. They confronted one of my patrols"—he paused ominously—"but they did not request an audience with me. They did not request permission to approach Orison. No, my lady, they demanded the right to speak with you."

Involuntarily, Elega caught her breath.

While she stared at Geraden and Terisa, Prince Kragen added, "It is clear that whatever device or policy they have prepared to get them into Orison is directed at you. They believe that they have the means to persuade you." Again, he paused; then he remarked cryptically, "It is even conceivable that they are aware of the existence of a precedent."

In response, Elega's eyes widened with pain and anger. "That is unfair, my lord." Almost instantly, however, she seemed to catch the implications of what he said. In a rush, she asked, "Geraden, have you seen—?"

So suddenly, so loudly that the sound made Terisa's heart lurch, Prince Kragen slapped his hands together, interrupting Elega; stopping her.

"My lady," he articulated, "I have said that I do not wish to trade stories with them. When they have told us what they know, I will decide what they may hear."

Elega held her tongue; yet her face showed the difficulty of restraint. Abruptly, Terisa became aware that she wanted to hear Elega's story: the Elega she remembered wouldn't have suffered a command to *shut up* so compliantly. What had happened to change the lady, to make her acquiescent? What kind of contest was going on between her and the Prince? Was it just a question of blame because her attack on the reservoir had misfired? Or had she done something else to earn Kragen's distrust?

Because her heart was still racing and she wanted to be calm, Terisa went to get some more wine.

As if they were being polite, the other people in the fore-tent waited until she had seated herself again. She had the impression that they were all watching her.

"You serve a heady wine, my lord Prince," Geraden murmured softly. "I haven't tasted anything like it for a long time."

In Terisa's opinion, that was an odd thing to say at a time like this.

Apparently, Prince Kragen agreed with her. He ignored Geraden's comment. Still speaking to Elega as if she were the true subject of his scrutiny, he said, "In any case, my lady, I have not yet told you everything you must hear. When Geraden and the lady Terisa demanded to speak to you, they gave a most interesting explanation. They said that they had messages for you from Queen Madin, your mother."

At once, Elega was on her feet. "The Queen?" She didn't appear to realize that she was standing. "You have spoken with the Queen? She sent messages for me?" Her eyes shone with excitement and anguish; her voice held a visceral tremor. "Doubtless you told her of my part in the siege. What does my mother wish to say to me now?"

Terisa was bemused to find that she had slipped down in her chair. The wine seemed to have made her top-heavy.

Pushing herself upright, she said, "We can tell you who the traitors are inside Orison. Who the renegade Imagers are. We can tell you how they planned all this with Cadwal. Together, we might be able to guess what kind of trap they plan to spring."

Prince Kragen's gaze burned darkly at her. For no particular reason, she added, "If you want to trade, we can even tell you what Domne and Termigan and Fayle are going to do about it."

As far as she could tell, Geraden and Elega and Kragen were all speaking at once. Geraden asked, "Do you know what you're doing? You look like you've had too much wine." He sounded like a man who had lost his sense of humor.

At the same time, Elega protested, "No! I will hear my mother's messages!"

Prince Kragen was saying, "Continue, my lady Terisa." Despite his self-control, he looked eager. "I am sure that we will be able to achieve an equitable exchange when you are done."

Grinning, Terisa wagged her finger at him. "Oh, no, my lord Prince." She actually wagged her finger at him. "Be fair. That isn't the way the game is played."

Geraden stood facing Elega; his voice was pitched to cover Terisa's. His tone didn't hold any authority, however. It didn't even convey confidence. Instead, it hinted at hysteria.

"The fact is," he said, "we don't have any messages from the Queen. She didn't have time to give us any. She was planning to come here herself. She wanted to stand beside the King. But she didn't get the chance."

In spite of the pressure to speak, he faltered. Elega's gaze was fastened to his face; her whole body concentrated toward him.

"Go on," she said with her throat clenched.

"Continue, my lady!" Prince Kragen snapped, apparently trying to startle words out of Terisa.

Just in time, Terisa put her finger to her lips and made a shushing noise.

"Elega, I'm sorry," Geraden said miserably. "While we were there, the Queen was taken. Ambushed. Imagery and soldiers. She was abducted."

Slowly, as if she could barely lift them, Elega raised her hands to her mouth.

"We know who the Imager was."

Her breath came hard, straining between her teeth.

"The soldiers were Alends."

Prince Kragen was so startled that he sprang to his feet and barked, "You lie!" before he could stop himself.

Terisa studied the three of them. "No." It was wonderful how clearly she could speak, despite the weight in her head. "He's not lying. We were there. That's why we want to go into Orison. That's what we want to tell King Joyse. Your men kidnapped Queen Madin."

From Terisa's perspective, the lady Elega went up like a candleflame. Without moving, she seemed to burst into passion; it swept through her toward the ceiling, hot enough to scorch. Confronting the Prince as if Terisa and Geraden were forgotten, she whispered like a cry, "What have you done?"

Kragen's face twisted; his teeth showed under his moustache. "They lie. I tell you, it is a lie."

She didn't flicker. "Geraden has never told a lie in his life— never one of such hurt. *What have you done?*"

"Nothing!" he shouted at her, trying to drive back her fury. "Geraden does not lie? Perhaps not. *I* do not lift my hand against lonely and harmless women! Never in my life."

Perhaps she didn't hear him: perhaps she couldn't. Her hands clenched into fists against her cheeks; blazing, she lifted her voice into a wail.

"Where is my mother? What have you done to my mother?"

In that outcry, she burned up too brightly to sustain herself.

She was too vulnerable: her strength failed, and she fainted. Delicately, like heated wax, she slumped toward the floor.

Geraden caught her.

Holding her in his arms, he faced the Prince. Now he was the one breathing hard, panting for air as if he had caught fire from her. Her distress made him savage, heedless. Prince Kragen came to him in dismay, tried to take her from him. He wrenched her away as if he didn't care that the Prince could have him killed.

"There are only two possibilities. My lord Prince. Isn't that right? Either you did it. So you're going to tie me and Terisa up and start torturing us. Or it was done to you. So you're going to let us go see the King.

"Which is it?"

But Prince Kragen wasn't listening. "Release her, Geraden," he murmured, almost pleading. "She is only your friend. I love her. If all of Cadwal and the wide sea itself come between us, I will wed her before I die. Give her to me."

He held out his arms.

Terisa saw Geraden burning the way Elega had burned; she saw him on the verge of hurling something he wouldn't be able to retract into the teeth of the Prince's regret. Fortunately, she was already on her feet, pulled erect by his fury. Otherwise she couldn't have reached him in time. She put a hand on his shoulder, then slipped her arm around his neck and hugged him.

"I believe him," she said softly. "You called him an honorable enemy. He wouldn't do something like that. And if he did, he would have done it long ago.

"He's going to let us into Orison."

She felt Geraden's muscles pull tight, as rigid as Elega's cry.

After a moment, she felt them relax.

Gently, he shifted Elega into Prince Kragen's embrace.

At once, Kragen sank to the floor, holding Elega close while he checked her pulse and respiration, made her comfortable. He bowed his head over her, ignoring Terisa and Geraden.

They stood near him and waited. The sides of the fore-tent were lined with servants and soldiers, summoned by the lady Elega's wail. They had no instructions, however, and didn't move.

Then Elega's eyes fluttered open. When she saw where she was, a slight smile curved her mouth. Gently, as if she didn't want to hurt him, she put up her hand to touch the Prince's cheek.

He let out a stiff sigh and raised his head.

His voice had to struggle out of his chest. "Why am I going to let you into Orison?"

Geraden cleared his throat. Constricted with emotion, he rasped, "Because if the men who took Queen Madin were Cadwals or mercenaries disguised as Alends, the attack is aimed at you as well as King Joyse. Part of the point is to keep anybody from trusting you. And part of it is to keep you and King Joyse from trusting each other, from forming an alliance.

"You're being manipulated. By High King Festten. And the traitors. And the only way you can save yourself is to let us talk to the King."

"And if I do not let them into Orison"—the Prince was speaking to Elega—"you will believe that I am responsible for your mother's abduction."

Elega didn't nod or shake her head. The small smile stayed on her lips; her hand cupped Kragen's cheek. "You want an alliance, my lord. You have always wanted an alliance, not this misconceived and aimless siege. Perhaps that is possible now. Perhaps it would be worth the attempt."

Prince Kragen made a harsh noise like an attempted laugh. "The last time I proposed that, he humiliated me. He went to considerable lengths to humiliate me."

"He didn't—" Terisa began. Her legs were unsteady, however, and she had to support herself on Geraden's shoulder. For a moment, she forgot what she was saying.

Then she remembered.

"He was testing you. He thought you were his enemy. He didn't know who the traitor was. He didn't know what alliances had already been made. Now we can tell him."

Prince Kragen's head turned; his eyes held an obsidian smolder which would have frightened her if she had been able to concentrate on it. Softly, he commanded, "Tell me."

Geraden took a deep breath, straightened his back. "I'll tell you this much, my lord. The traitor is Master Eremis. We can guess how he does the translations that let him attack anywhere in Mordant— that let him and Gart and Master Gilbur move through flat glass without losing their minds. And we know where his power is located, where he keeps his mirrors."

With an intensity Terisa didn't quite understand, Prince Kragen demanded, "Where is that?"

When Geraden had described Esmerel and its location, the Prince lowered his head.

"My lady," he asked Elega, "can you stand?"

She nodded.

A flick of his fingers brought two servants running forward. They eased the lady out of his arms, assisted her to her feet. At once, Prince Kragen surged upright. He kept his face averted, so that Terisa and Geraden couldn't see his expression. Under his breath, he murmured, "I must speak to the Alend Monarch."

Without offering an explanation or waiting for an answer, he entered the darkness of the main tent and closed the flap behind him.

While Geraden and Elega studied each other with uncertainty and some embarrassment, Terisa went to refill her goblet.

She was stretched out on the floor, sound asleep and snoring gently, when the Alend Contender returned.

In a subtle way, his manner had changed. He looked less angry, less sick to the teeth with frustration; the prospect of immediate battle or danger came as a palpable relief to him. Despite his efforts to sound neutral, his voice was several shades lighter as he announced, "The Alend Monarch has decided that you will be allowed to enter Orison tomorrow morning."

When he said that, Elega's face shone at him.

Geraden let the air out of his tight chest with a burst like a laugh. "Thanks, my lord Prince. I'm glad we were right about you. And I'm glad you don't hold a grudge against me for stopping Nyle." He glanced affectionately at Terisa. "She'll be glad, too—when she wakes up."

The Prince nodded brusquely and continued, "I will accompany you, both to demonstrate my good faith and to pursue the Alend Monarch's desire for an alliance."

"Good idea," Geraden remarked.

"The lady Elega will remain here to ensure that King Joyse does not abuse my good faith."

Elega dropped her eyes, but didn't try to argue.

"In the meantime," Prince Kragen concluded, commanding the attention of his soldiers with a gesture, "it might be advisable to discontinue our assault on the gates." He looked at one of his men. "Give the order."

The man saluted and left. The rest of the servants and soldiers also filed out of the fore-tent.

To his own surprise, Geraden found that he felt suddenly giddy, in the mood for jokes and foolishness. "With your permission, my lord," he said, "I'll have some more of that strong wine. Then, if you're interested in the trade Terisa mentioned, I'll tell you a story that will curl your hair."

Grinning like a predator, the Prince refilled Geraden's goblet himself.

THIRTY-NINE:
THE FINAL PIECE
OF BAIT

y midnight, Prince Kragen and the lady Elega knew most of Geraden's secrets.

The Alend Contender was an honorable man, however, and he kept his word.

While Terisa and Geraden slept the heavy sleep of too much wine, servants carried them to another tent, and put them to bed. At dawn more servants awakened them, offered them baths and food and clean clothes. According to the servants, Prince Kragen wished his guests to take full advantage of his hospitality. When they were entirely ready, he would approach the castle with them.

Terisa felt loggy with sleep, thick-headed with the wine's aftereffects. She wanted a bath so badly that she could hardly contain herself.

She was also considerably embarrassed.

When she realized that she couldn't quite meet Geraden's eyes, she asked awkwardly, "Are you still speaking to me?"

"Of course." There was a watchful air behind his smile, but no discernible irritation. "If you want me to stop speaking to you, you're going to have to do something worse than that."

At least he didn't pretend he didn't know what she was talking about. She covered her face with her hands. "Did I make a complete idiot out of myself?"

He chuckled easily. "That's the amazing part. You scared me, all right. I thought you were going to get us in terrible trouble. But everything you did turned out fine. Even drinking as much as you did may have helped. It made you believable. I don't think I could have handled either Elega or the Prince without you."

She pulled down her hands. Deliberately, she glared at him. "Stop being so nice to me. I was irresponsible. You ought to be furious."

Geraden gaped like a clown. "You're right. I'm sorry. Oh, I'm sorry, I'm sorry. Please forgive me. I'm so ashamed."

She made a grim but halfhearted effort to kick his shins.

Laughing, he caught hold of her, held her, hugged her. After a while, a strange desire to weep came over her, and she found herself clinging to him hard. Fortunately, the desire only lasted a moment. As soon as it faded, she felt better.

She had to let go of him to wipe her nose. "Thanks," she said softly. "Someday I'll do something nice for you."

It surprised her to see that he was leering. "If we had time, I'd get you to do it right now."

That brought a smile out of her. "No, you wouldn't." She was definitely feeling better. "I stink like a pig. I think I've got cock-roaches living in my hair."

He stuck out his tongue in mock-nausea.

She went to take a bath.

When they were clean, and dressed in the new clothes Prince Kragen had provided for them—comfortable traveling clothes sewn of leather as supple as kidskin—they ate breakfast. The impression that they were keeping the Alend Contender waiting nagged at the back of Terisa's mind; nevertheless she let him wait so that she would have a last chance to talk to Geraden. She had to prepare herself for Orison.

"We're aren't likely to get much of a welcome, you know," she said between bites of honeyed bread and souffléed eggs—an un-expectedly rich sample of the Alend Monarch's hospitality. "I tried to make the Castellan think I might be innocent, but Master Gilbur did a pretty good job of wiping that out." She didn't mention Artagel. "Everybody there has spent the whole time thinking you killed Nyle and I'm in league with the arch-Imager."

Geraden nodded. "It won't be much fun. But I'm not too worried. We'll have Prince Kragen with us. We'll be under a flag of truce.

No matter what Lebbick and everybody else thinks of us, they'll leave us alone."

He chewed for a moment in silence, then added, "What *I'm* worried about is that mirror—the one that attacked the Perdon when he came here to get King Joyse's help."

Suddenly, Terisa found a sick taste in her mouth. "Didn't Eremis change all that? He used those creatures to try to kill us outside Sternwall. He may have used them to kill Underwell. What can he still do?"

"Well, he must have switched flat mirrors in the Image of the world where those creatures come from. Otherwise he couldn't have attacked us. But he's had plenty of time since then. He could have switched the mirrors back.

"In any case, the point is that he has a glass that shows the approach to Orison, the road. He'll be able to see us go in. He'll be forewarned."

She thought about that while the taste in her mouth changed to an old, settled anger. Then she muttered, "At least he'll be surprised. He won't have any idea how we managed to talk Prince Kragen into this."

It did her good to be angry. Facing down Castellan Lebbick— or the Tor and Artagel, who had turned against her—would be hard enough. But confronting Master Eremis would be worse. The more she loved Geraden, the more her skin crawled at the memory of the things Master Eremis had done to her.

She could see Geraden's eagerness in his eyes, in the way he moved: he was starting to hurry. She had never been as confident or as clear as he was; but she, too, felt a need for haste. By tacit agreement, they left the remains of their meal. They had nothing to pack, nothing to carry. They kissed each other once, like a promise; then they went out of the tent.

Prince Kragen was waiting for them. They caught him in the act of pacing back and forth across the open area among the luxurious tents.

He was dressed in his ceremonial garb: a black silk doublet and pantaloons covered by a brass breastplate with a high polish; a sword in a gleaming brass scabbard on his hip; a spiked brass helmet on his curling hair. The sheen of the metal emphasized his swarthy skin; it made his black eyes glitter and his moustache shine. And his impatience only increased the self-assertion of his bearing, emphasizing his habit of command.

Three horses were held ready beyond the tents. They, too, were dressed for show, with satin and silk streaming from their saddles and tack, gilt cords knotted into their manes and tails. Around them, an honor guard was already mounted: ten men to carry the Prince's pennon, and his dignity.

Terisa didn't see Elega anywhere.

Prince Kragen nodded to Geraden, bowed to Terisa. In a tightly reined voice, he explained, "The lady Elega sends her goodwill to you—and to her father—but she cannot bid you farewell. She has already been placed under guard. The Alend Monarch intends to assure that no mistakes are made with us, and the lady Elega is his only means to that end. Even I do not know where she is held. Therefore I cannot enable the King's men—or his Imagers—to find her."

Terisa swallowed hard. The sun was up, but it didn't seem to be enjoying its work. The light over the encampment and against the walls of Orison was thin, unconvincing; the air had a cold taste, more like a residue of winter than a part of spring. The castle's battlements looked bleak, as if they had been abandoned. If anything happened to her and Geraden there—but especially if anything happened to Prince Kragen—Elega would be in serious trouble.

"My lord Prince"—Geraden changed the subject awkwardly—"you must have heard about the mirror that attacked the Perdon. If he didn't tell you about it himself, surely Elega did?"

"Yes." A subtle shift in his expression suggested that Prince Kragen was glad to discuss something other than Elega. "But I must confess that I am baffled. Our siege engines have no approach to the gates, except along the road. Our rams must pass through the Image which struck at the Perdon. Yet nothing has been translated against us.

"You have told me that Master Eremis is in league with Cadwal to destroy Mordant—and Alend as well. For that reason, his power has been used to defend Orison against us. Yet we are now within hours—within a day at most—of breaking down the gates, and he has done nothing to hinder us."

Breaking down the gates. Terisa's stomach twisted. So it was now or never. If she and Geraden couldn't get King Joyse to accept an alliance, Orison would fall almost immediately.

The muscles along Geraden's jaw bunched; but if he was worried about Orison's vulnerability to Prince Kragen he didn't admit it. "He probably hasn't given you trouble," he said, "because you haven't been attacking very hard. If you're about to break in, and he still isn't using Imagery, I'd guess his trap is just about ready to spring."

Prince Kragen nodded darkly. Without a word, he beckoned for the horses and his honor guard.

In a moment, Terisa found herself being offered a charger so big that she couldn't see over its back. Oh, shit, she muttered to herself. That was one thing she had learned in Mordant, anyway: after some practice, she was now able to say *oh, shit* without sounding like she expected to have her mouth washed out with soap. If she fell off that beast, she might take days to hit the ground.

Unfortunately, Prince Kragen had already mounted; Geraden was swinging up into the saddle of his horse. This probably wouldn't be a good time to ask for something smaller.

Somehow, she climbed onto the charger's back.

The reins carried so many streamers that they looked like the lines of a maypole. She was afraid to move them: they might make her horse shy. But Prince Kragen and Geraden weren't having any trouble. Apparently, these beasts were trained for ceremonial occasions. Nothing embarrassing happened as she guided her mount to Geraden's side.

"Simply as a precaution," the Prince announced, "we will avoid the road. We will ride to the walls directly, and around them to the gates."

Geraden seemed to think that made sense.

Prince Kragen nodded to his honor guard. His standard-bearer raised the green-and-red pennon of Alend, then affixed a flag of truce below it. The soldiers took their formal positions around their Prince and his companions.

In formation, the riders left the encampment.

The charger's strides made the distance shorter than it had any right to be. Before she had time to accustom herself to the beast's gait, Terisa found herself moving into what looked like arrow-range of the castle. She could see men on the walls now, watching, pointing; some of them hurried from place to place. She tried to stifle the fear that they would ignore the flag of truce and start firing, but it refused to go away.

Luckily, there was still some common sense left in Orison. None of the men on the battlements bent their bows. None of them made any threatening gestures.

Instead, the castle's trumpeter winded his horn, sending a forlorn call like a wail of defiance into the skeptical sunlight. As the riders rounded the corner of Orison and neared the entrance, they heard the great winches squeal against the strain of raising the battered and deformed gates up into the architrave.

Terisa felt nothing to indicate that a translation had ever taken place near here.

In formation, Prince Kragen and his company crossed the bare ground to the road in front of the gates.

Castellan Lebbick and ten of his men came out on horseback to meet them.

Seeing the Castellan filled Terisa's stomach with a watery panic. His men were nervous; the horses fretted because they hadn't had enough exercise. In contrast, he looked too obsessed and single-minded for nervousness. His eyes were red and raw, dangerously aggrieved; he moved as if the violence coiled in his muscles might burst out at any moment. His features were sharp with anticipation—almost with yearning.

"My lord Prince." He bared his teeth: maybe he was trying to smile. "You've got strange friends. A fratricide and a traitor. I never thought I was going to see either of *them* again."

"Castellan Lebbick." Prince Kragen lacked Lebbick's air of madness, but he matched the Castellan's tone. "Geraden and the lady Terisa accompany me under a flag of truce. I have no interest in your opinion of them. You will respect the flag."

"Oh, of course. They're as safe as babies. Especially since they're with *you*. You're the man who intends to break down my gates. I wouldn't lift a finger against any of you."

Prince Kragen clenched his jaws. Before he could speak, however, Geraden said hotly, "Castellan, I didn't kill my brother." His face was flushed; anger glinted from his eyes. Hints of authority echoed in his voice. "Terisa isn't a traitor. It's time for you to start believing us. You're doomed if you don't."

The Castellan actually laughed—a rough sound like a piece of stone being crushed. "Believe you? *I* believe you. I don't need you to tell me I'm doomed. That's not the problem."

Prince Kragen contained himself. "What *is* the problem, Castellan?"

"The problem, my lord Prince," retorted Lebbick fiercely, "is that I'm the only one. Nobody else here cares enough. Nobody else is *desperate* enough."

Terisa recoiled from his vehemence. She didn't want to know what he was talking about: she wanted to get away from him. Geraden leaned forward in his saddle, however; he was almost panting. "Did I hear you right, Castellan?" he demanded. "Did I just hear you admit Terisa and I are innocent?"

"No." The Castellan bared his teeth again. "You heard me say I believe you. They all think I'm insane. If I said the sun is shining today, the people in there"—he indicated Orison with a twitch of his head—"would run to get out of the rain.

"Nobody cares what a crazy man believes. Besides"—he shrugged maliciously—"I might be wrong."

"Castellan Lebbick." Prince Kragen spoke harshly, trying to gain control of the situation. "We will discuss the question of your sanity at another time. As you may guess, Geraden and the lady Terisa have traveled widely since they departed Orison. They bring news. I must have an audience with King Joyse."

"An audience?" Lebbick snapped back at once, "you? The Alend Contender? Any news you want King Joyse to hear is either false or dangerous. They're going to scream for your heart's blood when I let you in. Of course you can have an audience."

Wheeling his horse as if the matter were settled, he faced his men. Counting off four of them, he ordered, "Tell King Joyse. I'm going to take Kragen and these two to the hall of audiences. Tell him there are going to be riots unless he backs me up. We'll have to kill people to keep the Prince and his friends alive if King Joyse doesn't come to the hall."

At once, Prince Kragen put in grimly, "And tell him also that the lady Elega is being kept hostage. Until now, she has been an honored guest and friend of the Alend Monarch. To ensure my safety, however, she has been deprived of her freedom." He spoke as if he intended to make someone pay for the necessity which compelled him to let Elega be used in this way. "If any harm comes to me, or to my companions, she will be hurt as well.

"Tell King Joyse *that*."

"Oh, of course, my lord Prince," the Castellan grated without looking at Kragen. "I burn to do everything you command. My men will keep you alive. Somehow."

His four guards rode back into the courtyard. Terisa saw them dismount, saw them head at a run for one of the inner doorways.

"Come on," added Lebbick. He might have been speaking to the wall stretching high above his head over the gates. "Or ride back to Margonal and admit you haven't got the bare courage to do whatever it is you've got in mind."

With his remaining men, he reentered the mouth of Orison.

Prince Kragen stared at the Castellan's back. He made no effort to lower his voice. "That man has lost his mind."

Still aching inside, Terisa murmured, "King Joyse cut the ground out from under him. His wife died, and he didn't have anything else to live for except his loyalty, and the King made him look like a fool for being loyal."

"A pitiful tale," rasped the Prince. Obviously, he had no patience for Lebbick's problems. "Sadly, it does not tell us whether or not he can be trusted. Will he not have us killed as soon as we cross that threshold?"

"Suit yourself." Abruptly, Geraden jerked up his charger's head. "I trust him. I'm going in."

Breaking formation, he started for the gates.

Prince Kragen swore at him, ordered him back. Terisa was already following him, however, urging her mount almost onto his horse's heels. The Prince and his guard had no choice but to enter Orison behind Geraden and Terisa.

As she passed through the thick stone wall into the protected rectangle of the courtyard, her pulse went up a beat. In spite of her numerous anxieties—or perhaps because of them—she had the strange sensation that she was coming home.

The interior faces of the castle loomed above her, crowded with spectators, punctuated with clotheslines. Castellan Lebbick had dismounted in the mud. When the Alend party approached him, he saluted with withering sarcasm. At once, his guards took the heads of the horses and held them so that Prince Kragen and his people could dismount in an orderly fashion.

Pulling her leg hesitantly off the back of the charger, Terisa found herself caught and lifted down in Artagel's grasp.

He embraced her as if she were dear to him.

"Artagel!" He had hurt her once, badly. On the other hand, he was Geraden's brother; she knew most of his family. And his hug was as eloquent as an apology. Instinctively, she flung her arms around his neck.

After a moment, he pushed her away and gave her a lopsided, rather embarrassed grin. "Be careful, my lady." He rolled his eyes at Geraden. "We don't want to make him jealous."

"*Artagel.*" Geraden practically jumped on his brother; he grabbed Artagel, shook him, hugged him, thumped his back. "How are you, how's your side, are you all right, what's going on here, what's the matter with Lebbick?" Geraden's face shone with joy. "Do you realize how long it's been since I saw you *well?* I can tell you, the Domne had some stern things to say about letting yourself get hurt like that."

"'Da,'" Terisa put in happily. "You promised to call him 'Da.'" Artagel's smile told her everything she needed to know. Now she was just glad that she had never told Geraden about Artagel's distrust.

Nevertheless Artagel's next words reassured her further. Instead of trying to answer Geraden's questions, he commented half casually, "I heard what he said." He nodded toward the Castellan. "We all heard him. Actually, he isn't the *only* one who believes you. But I have to admit we're in the minority."

Terisa beamed with pleasure and relief.

"Don't worry about it," said Geraden. "We'll get that straightened out as soon as we see King Joyse. Tell me something important. *How's your side?*"

Artagel laughed easily. "Terrible. All this rest is giving me the twitches." Humorously, he whispered, "If I don't get to fight somebody soon, I'm going to end up like Lebbick."

"My lady Terisa. Geraden." Prince Kragen addressed them coldly, but his expression was one of bemusement rather than irritation. "It might be wise to conduct this reunion later. The present circumstances are less than cordial. We must meet with King Joyse promptly."

Artagel laughed again. "He's right. First things first. I'll follow you to the hall. When you're done there, we'll talk."

Waving his hand cheerfully, he retreated among the horses and guards.

When Terisa looked at Geraden, she saw that his eyes were full of tears.

He was happy: she knew he was happy. He loved Artagel. For that reason, she was surprised by the pain on his face.

Until she noticed Geraden's pain, she didn't absorb the fact that Artagel moved with a slight limp, as if he had an unhealed stiffness in his side.

And he wasn't carrying a sword.

Oh, Artagel!

Had Gart hurt him that badly? Or had his long sequence of overexertions and relapses aggravated the damage enough to cripple him? A swordsman of Artagel's prowess didn't have to be maimed or broken to be crippled. A few muscles which didn't heal properly in his side could do it.

"It's too much, Terisa," Geraden gritted between his teeth. "Too many people have been hurt. Too much harm has been done. This has got to stop. We've got to stop him."

She put her arm through his and squeezed it: she knew whom he was talking about.

Unfortunately, she couldn't get the feeling out of her stomach that a lot more people were going to be hurt soon.

"Come on," she murmured so that Prince Kragen wouldn't summon them again. "If we're going to stop him, this is the way to do it."

Geraden nodded; he scrubbed the expression of sorrow off his face.

Together, he and Terisa joined the Prince and Castellan Lebbick.

Lebbick considered them balefully. He didn't look like a man who believed them. He also didn't sound like a man who believed them. Without preamble, he asserted, "You'll leave your men here, my lord Prince."

Prince Kragen stiffened. "What an odd idea, Castellan. Why would I do such a thing?"

The Castellan's mouth twisted. "I understand your problem. You don't think you're safe here. Well, I have a problem, too. I could be wrong about you. You could be plotting treachery.

"If you're honest, I can tell you one thing for certain. I'll die before you do. But if you aren't—" He shrugged. "You'll leave your men in the courtyard."

Prince Kragen's fingers stroked the hilt of his sword lightly. His demeanor was unruffled, but Terisa could sense his ire. Softly, he asked, "Are you so unconcerned about the lady Elega's position, Castellan?"

Castellan Lebbick returned a snort. "She isn't *my* daughter. I don't care what happens to her. I'm in command of Orison. If you make me cut you down, King Joyse will never know the difference. I'll report it any way I like."

He faced the Prince, daring the Alend Contender to doubt him.

The darkness in Prince Kragen's eyes scared Terisa. She thought she ought to do something, intervene somehow. But Geraden was holding her arm now; he kept her still.

After a moment, the Prince said, "If you had come to me, Castellan, you would have received better treatment."

"Swineswater," remarked Lebbick succinctly.

Prince Kragen's jaws bunched; blood deepened the hue of his skin. After a moment, however, he nodded.

"My guard will wait outside the gates. If we do not return in an hour, they will ride to the Alend Monarch. The lady Elega will be killed. Tell King Joyse what you will."

Castellan Lebbick gave another of his crushed-rock laughs. "Let the Alends wait outside the gates," he told one of his men. "Be civil about it. Keep the gates open."

Without waiting for a reply, he headed toward the nearest doorway.

Prince Kragen glanced at Terisa, at Geraden. She chewed her lip; but Geraden assented promptly. "It's the best chance we've got. He's never stabbed anybody in the back."

"You are a bad influence," murmured Prince Kragen, "both of you. You urge me to accept horrifying risks as if they were entirely plausible. If I am ever crowned the Alend Monarch, I will have to become more cautious."

Smiling ominously, he led Terisa and Geraden after the Castellan.

Inside the castle, past the guards at the door, the halls were deserted. The spectators who packed the inner windows and balconies were nowhere to be seen; every indication of Orison's overcrowding was gone. "Curfew," Castellan Lebbick explained as he strode along the echoing passage. "I thought you were going to break through the gates today. I ordered everybody out of the way. Nobody's allowed to use the halls except the King's guard."

He may have intended his explanation to be reassuring. Nevertheless the unnatural silence of the place plucked at Terisa's nerves. She seemed to feel vast numbers of people crouched out of sight, waiting—

Rumors would travel fast in a besieged castle. When enough people heard that Nyle's murderer and Master Quillon's murderer and the Alend Contender were in Orison, the curfew wouldn't hold. No curfew would hold.

And when it broke, what would Lebbick do?

King Joyse had to listen to them. That was all there was to it. He had to listen. He had to believe them.

Otherwise she and Geraden and even Prince Kragen might not live long enough to find out what Master Eremis' trap actually was.

They were obviously being watched. She didn't see anybody, but she could hear voices. Just a murmur at first, an impression of whispering which filled the corridors with hints of menace. Then the voices grew louder, bolder. One of them said, "Killer." Another called out clearly, "Butcher!"

Castellan Lebbick didn't glance aside. He didn't seem to hear the voices. Or maybe he approved of them. He waited until they faded behind him. Then, to no one in particular, he commented, "They don't mean you. They mean me."

The way he walked was so tightly controlled that it made his whole body appear brittle.

He took Terisa, Geraden, and Prince Kragen directly to the audience hall.

Across a high, formal space marked with windows and pennons, they approached a set of peaked doors. Like the ones to the courtyard, those doors were guarded. Terisa took that as a good sign. She held Geraden's arm and tried to keep her respiration steady as the guards opened the doors into the hall of audiences.

She remembered it vividly—its cathedrallike height and length; the walls covered by carved wooden screens, their finials reaching twenty or thirty feet toward the vaulted ceiling; the two narrow windows high in the far wall. Working on short notice, a flustered old servant hurried along the rows of candles, past the batteries of lamps, trying to light them all as fast as he could. He still had a long way to go; yet he—and the windows—already gave enough illumination to show King Joyse's ornate mahogany throne on its pediment. A run of rich carpet led from the doors to the pediment; the rest of the wide area in front of the throne was open, surrounded by benches like pews. From each side of the pediment, a row of chairs reached toward the benches.

Because the light was so dim, the balcony surrounding the hall above the screens was shrouded in darkness. Terisa could see well enough, however, to note that the Castellan already had guards in position. Archers ranged there along the walls of the hall, four on each side.

Two pikemen closed the doors and stood to hold them. Four more were at attention beside the King's seat. She counted them again: fourteen guards. Sourly, she supposed that Lebbick's refusal to permit the attendance of Prince Kragen's honor guard made sense. If the Castellan could only produce fourteen guards, Kragen's ten soldiers might have been sufficient to protect him from the consequences of treachery.

Then, as the old servant continued to do his job, and the light improved, she realized that the benches and chairs weren't empty.

The gathering was small, compared to the one which had greeted Prince Kragen's first visit. Terisa suspected, however, that the people here were the ones who mattered. No courtiers were present, no lords or ladies whose sole claim to significance arose from birth or wealth. Around the benches were several more guards, each wearing the insignia of a captain: Lebbick's seconds-in-command. Artagel sat among them, grinning encouragement. She saw some of King Joyse's counselors, men she had met only once before: the Lord of Commerce, for example; the Home Ambassador; the Lord of the Privy Purse. And in the chairs—

To the right of the throne sat the Tor, sprawling his bulk over at least two chairs. To all appearances, he hadn't changed his robe since Terisa had last seen him: it was crumpled and filthy, so badly stained that it looked like it would never come clean. The dull red in his eyes and the way his flesh sagged from the bones of his face gave the impression that he was drunk. If he recognized either Terisa or Geraden, he didn't show it.

As if to avoid him—as if he stank or had lost continence—everyone else was seated on the left.

The men there were Masters. Terisa knew Barsonage, of course: the mediator was scowling at her as if she had betrayed everything he valued. And most of the Imagers with him she had seen before. But at least one of them looked so unfamiliar—and so young—that she thought he must be an Apt who had just recently earned his chasuble.

Two of the three of them were breathing hard. They must have come at a run. After all, the Castellan's men hadn't had much time to summon people to this audience.

The reason for the attendance of the Masters was obvious. King Joyse had threatened to defend Orison with Imagery. To do that, he needed the support of the Congery.

The Imagers made her think of Master Quillon, and her heart twisted.

Then she realized that Adept Havelock was missing. The High King's Dastard wasn't in the hall anywhere.

Neither was Master Eremis, however. That was a relief.

Soundless on the carpet, Castellan Lebbick strode toward the chairs on the right and sat down a few places away from the Tor, leaving Prince Kragen, Geraden, and Terisa in the open space before the throne. Inconsequently, she noticed the burned spot on the rug, where Havelock had once dropped his censer. No one had bothered to mend it. King Joyse hadn't had much use for his audience hall in recent years.

He didn't have much use for it now, apparently. He wasn't present.

Prince Kragen surveyed the hall; he scanned the balconies. The corner of his moustache lifted as if he were sneering. When he had completed his study of the King's defenses, he said clearly, "Remarkable. Is this the best audience King Joyse can produce? If an ambassador came to the Alend Monarch, at least a hundred nobles would commemorate the occasion, regardless of the hour—or the urgency." A moment later, however, he remarked politely, "Most impressive, Castellan. For the first time, I truly believe that you do not intend to harm us. You would not need so many men—and so many witnesses—to procure our deaths.

"What *do* you intend? Where is King Joyse?"

Castellan Lebbick remained sitting. In a voice which resembled his laugh, he barked, "Norge!"

Slowly, almost casually, one of the captains stood and came to attention. He saluted the Castellan calmly. In fact, everything about him seemed calm. He sounded like he was talking in his sleep.

"My lord Castellan?"

"Norge, where is King Joyse?" demanded Lebbick.

Norge shrugged comfortably. "I spoke to him myself, my lord Castellan. I told him what you said. I even told him what the Prince said. He said, 'Then you'd better get the audience hall ready.'"

Apparently, the captain didn't think any other comment was necessary. He sat down.

Terisa heard a door open and close as the servant left, his job done.

Castellan Lebbick faced the Prince. "Now," he said, "you know as much as I do. Are you satisfied?"

"No, Castellan," put in King Joyse. "I doubt that he knows as much as you do. And I'm sure he isn't satisfied."

Somehow, Terisa had missed the King's arrival. He must have entered from a door hidden behind his seat: she jumped to that conclusion because he was beside the pediment now, with one hand braced on the base of the throne as if he were about to go up the four or five steps and sit down. Nevertheless she hadn't seen him come in. For all she knew, he had appeared by Imagery.

He was wearing what she took to be his formal attire: a robe of purple velvet, not especially clean; a circlet of gold to keep his white hair off his forehead. And from a brocade strap over his right shoulder hung a tooled sheath which held a longsword with a jeweled pommel. His blue eyes were as watery and vague as she remembered them; his hands appeared arthritic, swollen and inflexible. The way he moved conveyed the impression that he was frail under his robe, barely able to support his own weight; too frail for dignity or decision.

Only his beard had changed. It had been trimmed short and neatly combed. Under his white whiskers, his cheeks showed a flush of exertion or wine.

At once, everyone stood. A bit too slowly for decorum, Lebbick stood also and bowed. "Attend," he drawled by way of announcement. "This audience is granted to Prince Kragen, the Alend Contender, by Joyse, Lord of the Demesne and King of Mordant. It's a private audience. Everyone here is commanded to speak freely—and to say nothing when they have left the hall. To speak outside of what is said here is treason."

Bitterly, as if he had no use for the King's permission, he sat down.

No one else sat. Even Lebbick's captains remained on their feet while King Joyse looked up and down the hall as if he were making a mental note of everyone present. Meeting Terisa's gaze, and Geraden's, he scowled so dramatically that she was tempted to think he didn't mean it; tempted to think he was scowling to conceal a leap of joy. She had no way of knowing the truth, however. Instead of addressing her or Geraden—or the audience generally—he turned abruptly and ascended his seat, dragging his sword upward like a millstone. When he reached his throne, he collapsed into it; he had to pause and breathe deeply for a moment before he was able to tell the gathering to sit.

The assembled captains and counselors and Imagers obeyed.

Of course, Prince Kragen, Terisa, and Geraden had to remain standing.

Her reaction to the sight of King Joyse was more complex than she had expected: she was at once gladder and more distressed. He had a strange power which always surprised her, an attraction of personality that made her want to believe he was still as strong and idealistic and dedicated and, yes, heroic as he had ever been. That was why his appearance upset her. He was simply too weak. There on his throne, with Mordant in shambles, and Eremis poised to strike the last, crushing blow, he was too close to his grave—the burial ground as much of his spirit as of his decaying frame. She understood why Geraden loved him. Oh, she *understood*. Everything in her chest ached because he wasn't equal to the love people gave him anymore.

Somebody else would have to save Orison and Mordant.

He seemed to share her opinion. In a dry, querulous tone that made him sound nearly decrepit, he said without preamble, "You first, Kragen. And be quick about it. I don't have much patience for men who threaten my daughters."

Prince Kragen's fists knotted on his anger; he held his voice steady. "Then you must have no patience at all for yourself, my lord King. I have come because I have news which you must hear. Thanks in part to Apt Geraden and the lady Terisa—and in part to other sources of knowledge—I have an astonishing range of threats to lay before you. But they are all of your own making, not mine. Even the lady Elega is entirely safe—unless you have lost even the small honesty necessary to respect a flag of truce."

Unexpectedly, the Tor let out a snorting noise like a snore. His eyes seemed to be falling closed; his head began to loll on his thick neck.

"Whoreslime," commented Castellan Lebbick unceremoniously. "You must have noticed that we're besieged. Maybe you've even noticed that you're the one besieging us."

When King Joyse didn't intervene to silence the Castellan, Terisa's heart sank. The King had to listen, *had* to. He had to understand. Nevertheless he didn't look capable of understanding—and he didn't seem to be listening. He only stared at Prince Kragen as if the Alend Contender's presence were no more pleasant—and no more interesting—than a bad smell.

"No, my lord King." Prince Kragen did what he could, under the circumstances: he treated Lebbick's words as if they came from King Joyse. "Even that threat you have brought upon yourself. When I first came to you seeking an alliance, you humiliated me deliberately. And since that time your only ambition has been to destroy your realm before you die. You forget that Alend also is bound up in Mordant's need. You created the Congery, my lord King, and now you must face the consequences. If the power of all Imagery falls to High King Festten, our ruin is certain. We must fight for our survival. Even dogs will do as much. If you are determined to let the Congery fall to Cadwal, then we have no choice but to prevent you as best we can."

The Prince had moved a step closer to King Joyse. Terisa and Geraden were on either side of him, a bit behind. Across Prince Kragen's back, she whispered to Geraden, "This isn't going to work. We've got to do something."

A clenched glitter filled Geraden's gaze. "My lord King—" he murmured as if the words stuck in his throat. "My lord King, please. Give us a chance."

King Joyse paid no attention to him.

"No, my lord Prince." Master Barsonage glared from under his shrubbery eyebrows. He didn't stand. On the other hand, he did speak courteously. "Your view of the situation is persuasive, but not entirely fair. You forget that the Congery is composed of Imagers—and Imagers are also men. Like yourself, we must fight for our survival. Unlike you, however, we are men who have accepted the King's ideals, the King's purposes. Oh, there are some among us who serve the Congery only because they dislike the alternatives available to them. But they are few, my lord Prince—only a minority. The rest of us value what we are.

"Do you think we will calmly resign ourselves to High King Festten when Mordant collapses?

"You say you must keep the Congery from falling into Cadwal's hands, and that is a worthy endeavor, I am sure. But the assumption on which your actions are based is that the Congery is a thing, not men—that we do not choose, or believe, or have worth as men.

"Why do you believe you have the right to determine our survival—and our allegiance—for us?"

Prince Kragen received this argument with a closed face. Once again, he treated what was said as if it came from King Joyse. Only the sweat at his temples betrayed the pressure he felt.

"A fascinating debate, my lord King," he said grimly, "but irrelevant. We cannot leave Alend's future in the hands of men who are so confused—either by Imagery itself, or by the necessity of achieving decisions through debate—that they believed the translation of an uncontrollable battle-champion to be a sensible action.

"No, my lord King. Your people will defend you, as they must. Nevertheless the responsibility for this siege is yours."

King Joyse shrugged. At least he was listening well enough to know that Prince Kragen had paused. He gave the Prince a chance to go on, then said abruptly, "I know all this. Tell me something I don't know. Tell me about your 'astonishing range of threats.'"

The Tor snorted again, softly, and opened one eye. "So Terisa and Geraden are traitors after all," he rumbled. He was lost in a world of wine. "How sad." At once, he closed his eye again, dismissing whatever happened around him.

"In any case, my lord Prince," the Castellan grated as if King Joyse hadn't spoken, "you do have choices. We've already told you what they are. Withdraw to a safe position. Wait and see what happens. If you do that, King Joyse is willing to meet Margonal under a flag of truce and discuss an alliance."

When she heard that, a small flame of hope leaped up in Terisa.

And was quenched immediately. Before Prince Kragen could reply, King Joyse muttered shakily, "No, Castellan. It's too late for that. It's too late for anything.

"It's time for the truth."

His swollen hands gripped the arms of his seat; he had trouble holding himself upright. Almost whining, he said to the Prince, "Tell me about your threats. Tell me what Terisa and Geraden know. Tell me why you stopped beating on my gates." Under his whining, however, lay an iron blade, too well whetted and keen to be mistaken. All the light in the hall seemed to shine on him. "Tell me now."

A tight silence closed around the onlookers. Terisa couldn't bear to look at King Joyse any longer. She glanced at Geraden, saw him chewing the inside of his cheek; his eyes were wide and white, as if he were thinking desperately. Because Prince Kragen stood closer to the throne than she did, she couldn't see most of his face; but she could see a twitch run down the long muscle of his jaw, a bead of sweat trail from his temple across his cheekbone. Ignoring the proprieties of a royal audience, she turned her head and caught Artagel's eye; she was looking for inspiration. He didn't have any to give her, however. He looked stretched and pale, as if he were stifling nausea.

Still avoiding the King, she faced Master Barsonage. You're wrong about us. That was what she ought to say to him. All the assumptions here are wrong. Geraden didn't kill Nyle. I didn't kill Master Quillon.

But she didn't say anything. The silence held her.

Why were Geraden and Prince Kragen sweating? Surely the air was cooler than that?

Prince Kragen's fist sprang involuntarily from his side; he forced it down again. "No," he said through his teeth, "I will not."

A grin split Castellan Lebbick's face. He was going to laugh. Or wail. "Why not, Prince? Why else did you come?"

Kragen ignored the Castellan. "I will not suffer this senseless treatment. I will not trade my only hopes to a King so contemptible that he respects no one else." Despite his efforts to speak quietly, his voice grew thick with passion until he was nearly shouting. "The lady Elega persuaded me to come. Apt Geraden and the lady Terisa persuaded me. They are all deluded by the idea that their lord remains possessed of some vestige of wisdom—or of courage—or of bare decency."

To Terisa, every word sounded like a nail being driven into the lid of Mordant's coffin.

"Do you hear me, Joyse?" Prince Kragen raged. "You are deaf to everything else. You are deaf to the misery of your people, locked in a useless siege—caught in Cadwal's path—slaughtered by renegade Imagers. You are deaf to the simplest requirements of kingship, the wisdom and the *necessity* of dealing fairly with other monarchs. You are deaf to love, deaf to the loyalty which destroys your friends and family."

"Enough, my lord Prince." King Joyse raised one hand. "I have heard you." Now he didn't sound querulous. And he didn't sound angry. He sounded oddly like a man who was experiencing a personal vindication. "You have said enough."

But Prince Kragen had gone too far to stop. For a second, he let his fists pound the air. "By the stars, Joyse, it is not enough. You will not pull Alend down in Mordant's ruin. I will not allow it.

"I will tell you *nothing!*"

Abruptly, he wheeled away from the throne.

Catching hold of Terisa and Geraden, he pulled them with him toward the doors.

Instinctively, she wrenched her arm out of his grasp.

She hadn't made a conscious decision, either against him or for King Joyse. She was simply so torn, so hurt by the difference between what was needed and what was happening, so urgent for another outcome that she couldn't bear to give up.

Geraden was clearer. He, too, jerked free of Prince Kragen. Swinging toward the throne, he cried out like a trumpet, "My lord King—! Houseldon is destroyed. Sternwall is falling. The people of Fayle are butchered by ghouls. *Your* people, my lord King, everywhere!"

King Joyse was on his feet. Terisa hadn't seen him stand: she only saw him standing now, towering over her on the pediment with his beard thrust forward and his hair full of light.

"*And?*" he demanded. "*And?*"

As if he left her no choice, she replied, "And the Queen is gone. She's been abducted."

Then her stomach knotted as if she were about to be sick.

The idea that he would crumple now, that she had hurt the King hard enough to break him, was too much for her. Prince Kragen was shouting, "You fools! He will have me killed!" Too late. She turned her back on King Joyse, hugged her arms over her belly.

A movement on the balcony caught her eye. She cast a glance upward in time to see one of the archers fold to the floor.

Hands grabbed her, spun her. King Joyse had come down from his seat so fast that she didn't have time to think, to react; he clenched his fists in her soft shirt. Shouting the King's name, Geraden tried to intervene. King Joyse thrust him away.

"Who took her?" The king seemed to swell over Terisa. His eyes were blue fire; his teeth flashed; he shook her as if her heart were an empty sack. "I'll have that man's head! *Who took her?*"

Terisa struggled to turn her head, look back up at the balcony. But King Joyse was shaking her too hard; she couldn't get her gaze into focus.

"Alends!" cried Geraden. "She was taken by Alends!"

So suddenly that Terisa nearly fell, King Joyse dropped her. His sword came into his hands swiftly, catching the light like a whip of fire.

She stumbled around to scan the balcony.

Three of the archers were down.

The rest were so engrossed in the scene below them that they hadn't realized what was happening.

King Joyse and Prince Kragen confronted each other. The Prince had drawn his own blade: the tips of their swords danced at each other in the glow of the lamps and candles.

"Where is she?" demanded the King.

Wildly, Geraden pushed himself between the blades. "They were dressed like Alends!" he panted. "We think it's a trick! Prince Kragen came here to prove his good faith!" Before his King could cut him down, he added, "Torrent went after her. She's going to leave a trail for help to follow."

"The balcony," Terisa said. She was hardly able to hear herself.

Shielded by Geraden, Prince Kragen lowered his sword. Facing King Joyse regally over Geraden's shoulder, he avowed, "My lord King, I spit on the men who did this to you. And I spit on the cheap ploy which made them appear Alend. I would rather die than become a man who can only gain his ends by violence against women."

He was too late: the blow which felled him was already in motion. Too quickly for any reaction—even from King Joyse—Artagel reared up behind the Prince and chopped him so hard across the back of the neck that he went down as if he had been hit with an axe.

At the same time, Castellan Lebbick cried like a howl of glee, *"Gart!"*

Terisa could see the High King's Monomach now. As the fourth archer went down, Gart rounded the balcony to attack those on the other side. He was black and swift, a slash of midnight, and his sword seemed to splash blood in all directions.

The remaining archers had their bows ready to protect King Joyse from Prince Kragen. Instantly, they shifted their aim toward Gart and let fly.

Unfortunately, he wasn't alone. He had a number of his Apts with him. Swooping like shadows, they caught the archers from behind, hacking the guards down, spoiling their aim. Only one of the arrows went true.

Gart knocked the shaft aside with the flat of his blade.

His return stroke beheaded the nearest archer. The head flopped lopsidedly over the balcony railing and fell among the benches with a thud.

Men yelled everywhere. Castellan Lebbick roared, "I'm coming, you bastard! *I'm coming!*" and sprinted toward a door hidden behind one of the screens. Most of the Imagers started to flee. Master Barsonage lashed them back to his side with curses.

Geraden cried at Artagel uselessly, "You idiot!"

"I didn't know!" retorted Artagel. Looking frantic and self-disgusted, he flung a glance up at the balcony, at Gart, then scanned the hall; he couldn't decide what to do. In spite of his uncertainty, however, he didn't hesitate to help himself to Prince Kragen's sword.

Laconic in the tumult, Norge demanded reinforcements. Two of the captains headed out of the hall to rally Orison; the rest of Lebbick's men followed him toward the stairwell to the balcony.

The noise awakened the Tor. He opened his eyes with a snuffle and gazed around blearily.

Terisa felt that she was still watching the severed head flop off the balcony and fall. The sound when it hit the bench was unmistakable: she would remember it for the rest of her life. She had to get out of the way, but for some reason she couldn't move. Geraden turned toward the Masters: she thought she heard him ask, "Can you fight? Have you got mirrors with you?" The strain around Artagel's eyes was clear as he hefted the Prince's blade; he moved stiffly. She knew as if he had explained his dilemma at length that he yearned to go after Gart—that he feared to go because he was no match for the High King's Monomach. Distinctly, she heard a Master snap, "We brought none. How could we know that mirrors would be needed in the audience hall?" She really ought to get moving. Before Gart or his Apts had a chance to come after her.

Instead of moving, she waited until she felt *a touch of cold as thin as a feather and as sharp as steel slide straight through the center of her abdomen.*

Then she flipped forward, dove to the floor, rolled away. When she got her feet under her again, she ran toward Geraden and the Masters.

Out of the air where she had been standing stepped Master Gilbur and Master Eremis.

Master Gilbur gripped his dagger in one fist. The hunch of his back and the thickness of his arms made his hands look as powerful as battering rams.

Master Eremis carried a sword in a scabbard belted around his jet cloak. His chief weapon was already in his hands, however.

A mirror the size and shape of a roofing tile.

With a precision that seemed like lunacy, she noticed that both men still wore their chasubles.

Immediately, Master Gilbur leaped to attack Prince Kragen.

Grinning happily, Master Eremis came toward Terisa and Geraden.

There were no guards to oppose them. Norge's reinforcements hadn't arrived. And the rest of the men had followed Castellan Lebbick.

Lebbick burst out onto the balcony with his sword in both hands, snarling for blood. And he almost caught Gart. Unfamiliar with the stairwell, Gart couldn't know where it opened; out of ignorance, he had placed himself in an awkward position. Nevertheless he countered Lebbick's first cut, blocked it against the railing so hard that chips flew. Retreating nimbly, he countered the backstroke.

That gave him all the time he needed to recover his balance.

Behind the Castellan, six guards and as many captains led by Norge rushed from the stairwell one at a time to engage the Monomach's Apts.

Gart had only four men with him: they were badly outnumbered. But the balcony was too narrow for any two men to stand and fight abreast. Gart blocked Lebbick on one side; on the other, an Apt battled the first pikeman to come at him. The rest of the defenders were caught in the middle, helpless.

Gart struck furiously, trying to jam his opponents against each other; he almost succeeded at driving the Castellan backward. Lebbick slipped one blow, blocked a second which hit hard enough to jar his joints and leave a notch on his blade. But he was happy at last, nearly ecstatic at the chance to fight without restraint. Savage joy lit his face as he held Gart's attack.

"Bastard!" he panted. "I'll teach you to think you can do what you want in my castle!"

Behind him, unfortunately, the first pikeman didn't fare as well. The guard probably hadn't had a fraction of the training given to Gart's Apts. He stumbled; and his black-armored opponent gutted him almost without effort, then used the moment of surprise while he fell to cut halfway through the nearest captain's chest.

Norge stooped, snatched up one of the bows. So placidly that he didn't seem to be hurrying, he flipped a shaft into the Apt's throat.

Across the hall, one of Gart's men recklessly flung a dagger. It should have missed from that distance: its target should have seen it coming. Unluckily, he didn't. The guard went down with the blade buried in his left eye.

Norge shot the Apt cleanly in the chest.

Gart's gaze swept the balcony. He took in the positions of the people below him. Instead of ripping Castellan Lebbick's parries aside, the High King's Monomach began to give ground.

Artagel watched what was happening above him for one more moment, then turned his attention to Master Gilbur.

Plainly, Gilbur intended to kill the Alend Contender.

It was also plain that he wasn't going to succeed. Artagel's side was sore and tight; in some sense, he was a cripple. Nevertheless he could have handled a lone Imager armed with only a dagger in his sleep.

"Guard the Prince!" shouted the Tor for no discernible reason. He was on his feet, his legs splayed, swaying under the influence of too much wine.

Smiling pleasantly, Artagel aimed Prince Kragen's sword—and barely saved himself when Master Gilbur turned suddenly, picked up one of the benches, and hurled it at his head.

A corner of the bench punched his shoulder, and he went down; he hit the floor heavily, lost his direction. The Master's strength was prodigious. How was it possible to fight somebody who could throw benches around with one hand? Shock numbed Artagel's shoulder, but he ignored it. He ignored his side. Suppressing any kind of pain, he surged upright again as smoothly as he could—

Facing in the wrong direction.

He wheeled back to the Prince's sprawling body just in time to block Master Gilbur's dagger.

Roaring, Gilbur hit Artagel's blade so hard that Artagel nearly dropped it.

Nearly: not quite.

Mustering his balance, his poise, his old skill, Artagel pointed his sword at the base of Master Gilbur's throat and dared the Imager to move again.

The struggle over Prince Kragen apparently held no interest for Master Eremis. He approached Geraden and Terisa and the knot of Masters as if he were on the verge of an epiphany. His smile was so keen it seemed to cut the air. When Geraden cried in frustration, "Doesn't anyone have a mirror?" Eremis began to laugh.

He tightened his fingers, murmured something Terisa couldn't hear.

Instantly, a creature the size and shape of a fruit-bat swept out of the glass, flapped forward, and fastened itself to the nearest Imager's cheek.

The man toppled backward, screaming.

"Eremis!" Geraden yelled as if that were the worst obscenity he knew. From under his jerkin, he produced a knife—an eating utensil he must have appropriated at breakfast—and threw it with all his strength.

For once in his life, he did something right. He had never trained with a knife; but by chance his blade shattered the glass in Eremis' hand as neatly as if that was what he had intended all along. Splinters sprayed out of Eremis' grasp, glittering like jewels in the light.

The Master's laugh turned to a snarl.

While he ripped out his sword, the doors of the hall slammed open and twenty guards charged inward.

Norge's reinforcements.

The guards were too late to save Geraden or Terisa. Their backs were to the wallscreens: they had no escape from the easy action of Eremis' blade. He plainly knew what to do with a sword. It seemed to flex like a live thing in his hands.

In contrast, Artagel didn't need any help. This was the work he had been born to do. First he slapped the dagger out of Master Gilbur's fist. Then he began to make small, delicate cuts in the Imager's thick neck, as if he were marking the spot at which Gilbur's head would be hacked away. All his movements were taut and precise.

Up on the balcony, Gart lost another Apt. Gart himself hadn't killed anyone: Lebbick kept him back. Lebbick's fury appeared almost equal to Gart's skill. The Apts had accounted for five of the defenders. Surveying the situation, Gart judged that one more pikeman would die before his last student fell. He prepared himself to dispatch Lebbick, perhaps eviscerate him; then he glanced downward, saw the arrival of the reinforcements, and changed his mind.

Before anyone could grasp his intent, he sprang away from Castellan Lebbick and vaulted over the railing.

A drop like that could have killed him; it should have snapped his legs. But he had been jumping from high places ever since he began his training under the previous Monomach: he knew how to do it.

When he hit the rug, he collapsed into himself and rolled to absorb the impact. Then, despite the fact that his feet and legs had gone numb as if his spine were broken, he launched himself at Artagel's back.

The only warning Artagel got was the thump when Gart landed. He turned just in time to keep the Monomach's sword out of his ribs.

Swiftly, he launched a second parry, a counterstroke. He knew he couldn't beat Gart, but in the rush of action, the heady flow of battle, he didn't care.

Unfortunately, he never finished his riposte. Gilbur's quickness was like his strength: prodigious. In an instant, he sprang after Artagel and clubbed him to the floor with both fists.

Prince Kragen was still unconscious. He could have been killed almost without effort.

Now, however, Master Gilbur and the High King's Monomach had other priorities. The charging guards had already covered half the distance from the doors: Master Eremis' allies only had a few seconds left.

Behind them, Castellan Lebbick came down on the rug with a smashing impact. He had tried Gart's jump, had landed badly. Pain ripped a gasp out of him; it muffled the sound of breaking bones.

Together, Gilbur and Gart raced to help Eremis.

He was fighting for his life.

No one had opposed his advance on the Masters, on Terisa and Geraden. The Masters were as useless and cowardly as he had always believed them to be; they wouldn't be worth the trouble of killing. Even Master Barsonage wasn't worth killing.

Geraden, on the other hand—

But at the last moment, Master Eremis had paused. He saw something in Geraden's eyes—an unexpected threat; some kind of fatal promise.

It caused the Master to check his swing.

Terisa didn't look dangerous. She didn't even look desirable. She had turned inward with her back against the wall as if she were trying to faint.

Eremis raised his sword to fend Geraden away while he grabbed at her.

Suddenly, a mountain of flesh slapped against him with such force that he nearly went sprawling.

The Tor—! Eremis got his blade up just in time to keep the fat, old lord from splitting his head open.

Considering the Tor's skill and age and drunkenness, his sword might as well have been a cudgel. Nevertheless it had *weight* behind it, and a mad, blubbering fury. Master Eremis parried as hard as he could, and again, and *again;* yet he was driven backward. He would have to disembowel that old slob to stop him.

"My lord!" Geraden yelled. "Look out!"

The Tor didn't seem to hear the warning. He was still swinging his sword like a club when Gart kicked him in the stomach hard enough to rupture his guts.

Retching, he collapsed to his knees and presented his exposed neck to Gart's blade.

Geraden jumped at Eremis.

Gilbur intercepted him, however, and flung him aside like a handful of rags. Like Prince Kragen, Geraden wasn't important enough to risk death over. Terisa was the one who mattered. Eremis closed a hand around her arm. Gart braced himself for the quick satisfaction of beheading the Tor.

Fuming curses and agony, one knee crushed, an ankle cracked, Castellan Lebbick came up behind the High King's Monomach. He was barely able to stand; every movement ground splinters of bone against each other. His sword hung in his hands, too heavy to lift through the pain.

Yet he kept Gart from killing the Tor.

To save himself, Gart whirled and drove his sword straight through the Castellan's heart.

Lebbick's eyes flew wide, as if he had just seen an astonishing sight. Blood burst from his mouth, gushed down the front of his mail. He dropped his weapon. For a moment, his hands clutched at Gart's blade as if he wanted to wrench it out of his chest. Then, like a man who had decided to let go, he released the iron.

"Bastard," he breathed between gouts of blood as if he were talking to someone else, not Gart at all. "Now I'm free. You can't hurt me anymore."

Slowly, as if performing at last the only graceful action of his life, he slid backward off Gart's sword.

In that way, Lebbick finished mourning for his wife.

Full of horror, Terisa tried to break Master Eremis' grip; but she couldn't do it. She had never been strong enough with him. Geraden lay on the floor without moving. Helplessly, she watched as Eremis made a strange, familiar gesture, a signal she had seen once before.

Only a heartbeat ahead of the charging guards, she and Eremis, Gilbur and Gart were translated out of the hall.

In the resulting confusion, a long time passed before anyone noticed that King Joyse had also disappeared.

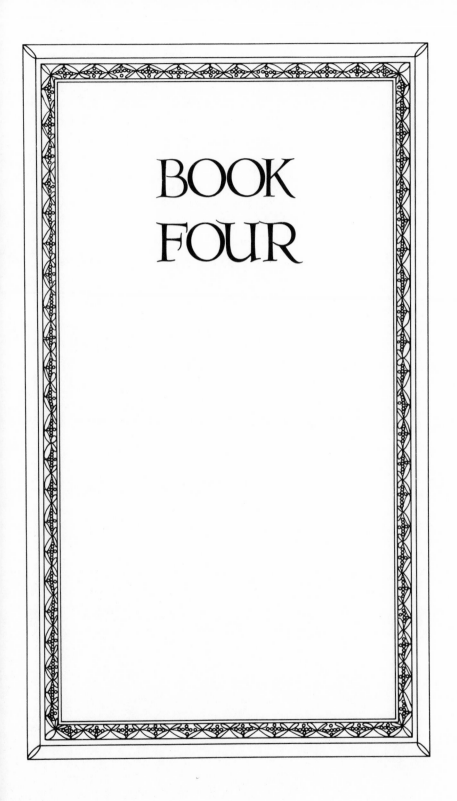

BOOK
FOUR

FORTY: THE
LORD OF LAST
RESORT

orge ordered everyone to stay in the hall; but he was already too late. Most of King Joyse's counselors had scattered, fled like their lord. And the Imagers were no better. Even Master Barsonage, who might in a reasonable world have been expected to set a good example—even the mediator of the Congery was gone. Apparently, he had taken Geraden with him. The only Master left was the man Eremis had killed; the creature which had actually slain him was still chewing on his head, oblivious to everything except food.

"Perfect," Norge muttered generally. This was as close as he ever came to despair. All those Imagers and old men who could hardly hold their water for fear, already loose in Orison; already spreading panic. They would tell their friends, their wives, their children, their servants; some of them would tell total strangers. And when the story got out—when people heard that King Joyse was gone, and Lebbick was dead, and the "hero of Orison," Eremis, was in league with Cadwal— Norge sighed to think about it. Orison was going to come apart at the joints.

The siege was going to succeed after all.

Doing what he could, he sent one of the captains to take command of the gates, control the courtyard; make sure nobody did anything wild. That was the crucial place, the point at which panic could spill outward—the point at which Alend could be made aware that Orison was in chaos.

He ordered two more men to dispatch Eremis' vicious fruitbat. He detailed guards to locate the counselors and the Masters, so that decisions could be made. For no particular reason except thoroughness, he organized a search for the King. He made sure that Prince Kragen and Artagel were still alive.

Then he went to help the Tor get up.

The old lord was on his hands and knees, staring at Castellan Lebbick's face.

The Tor was in terrible pain. No, that wasn't true: he was *going* to be in terrible pain; he knew he was going to be in terrible pain as soon as the shock of Gart's kick faded a bit. At the moment, however, he was still stunned, protected from agony by surprise and wine.

He wanted to raise his head, but the effort was too much for him. He couldn't do anything except stare at Lebbick's ruined and happy face.

People looked like that, he thought, when their kings betrayed them. When they let something as simple and fallible as an ordinary human monarch cut the strings which held their lives together, the cords of purpose. When they drank too much— And then were lucky enough to die without having to watch everything else come apart around them.

It would be better to die. Better to think Gart's boot had torn something vital inside him and surrender to excruciation in advance. Better to let wine and loss carry him away. The alternatives—

The alternatives were distinctly unpleasant.

Unfortunately, the expression on Lebbick's face wouldn't let him go. Lebbick's blood wouldn't let him go. The first twinge of pain rumbled through his guts, and he nearly groaned aloud, Oh, Castellan. Mordant and Orison and you, he betrayed us all, abandoned us all—and you fought for him to the end. What did he ever do to deserve such service?

As soon as the Tor asked the question, however, he found that he knew the answer. Despite his tears, he could see it in Lebbick's twisted face, his wounds and blood. What King Joyse had done was to create something larger than any one man, something which deserved loyalty and service no matter how fallible and even treacherous the King himself proved to be.

Mordant. A buffer between the constant, bloody warring of Cadwal and Alend.

The Congery. An end to the ravages of Imagery when mirrors were used for nothing but power.

Pain pushed against the back of the Tor's throat, and his stomach knotted; but he clung to the cold stone with his hands and knees, kept his balance. When that captain, what was his name? Norge, when Norge came to him and tried to help him erect, he managed somehow to knot his fat fist in the captain's mail and pull him down, so that Norge had to meet him face-to-face.

"The King—" he gasped. His voice was a sick whisper, lost in the hurt clench of his abdomen.

"Gone, my lord Tor. I've sent men to look for him, but I don't expect any results."

"Why not?"

Norge shrugged. "Men who vanish like that usually don't want to be found."

His immunity to distress was remarkable. Peering into the captain's face, the Tor began to remember him better. It was possible that Castellan Lebbick had promoted Norge simply because Norge was the only man under him who never flinched.

A man like that was hard to talk to. What did he care about? What were his convictions, his commitments?

"Help me up." The Tor made no effort to move. The pain squeezed his voice to a husk. "I will take his place."

The Tor wasn't trying to stand, and Norge didn't try to lift him. Instead, the captain asked calmly, "You, my lord?"

"Me." For all the strength the Tor could muster, he might as well have been whispering deliberately. Maybe Gart really had ruptured something vital. "Who else? I am the King's oldest friend. Apart from Adept Havelock—and you will not offer him the rule of Orison and Mordant."

No question about it: the hurt in his bowels was going to be stupendous. Already it seemed to cut off his supply of air. Sweat or tears ran from him as if he were a sodden towel being twisted. There were too many candles glaring in his eyes. Yet he kept his grip on the captain.

"And I am the only lord here. King Joyse suffered me to remain when the others rode away. I have acted as his chancellor and advisor. Something must be done about the panic. Power must be assumed by someone who will be believed. Who else would you have?

"Who else is there?"

Norge blinked at this question as if he didn't think it was worth answering.

"I have no hereditary claim, no official standing." The Tor wanted to wail or weep, but he couldn't get that much voice past the pain. "But if you support me in this, Castellan Lebbick's second, a man with the King's guard behind him—" A gasp came up from his kneecaps, nearly blinding him. "If you support me, I will be accepted."

"My lord Tor," the captain remarked dispassionately, "even if I support you, you'll scarcely be able to stand." After a moment, he added, "If I can say so without offense, my lord, you aren't the king I would have chosen."

"A fat old man sodden with wine and unable to stand." It was embarrassing to be in tears at a time like this, but the Tor's hurt had to have some outlet. "I understand. Do you?"

"My lord"—Norge's calm was maddening, really—"you need a physician. Let people in better condition worry about Orison."

"Fool," the lord moaned. "You do not understand." Pulling on Norge's mail, heaving against the pain, he got one leg under him; that enabled him to shift his other hand from the floor to Norge's shoulder. He felt like he had Eremis' fruitbat gnawing on his guts. Nevertheless he panted through his tears and sweat, "Someone must take command. Orison must be led. And I am *here*. Prince Kragen is *here*. For the first time, we know our enemies. We must not miss this opportunity."

"Opportunity?" Norge asked noncommittally.

Oh, for the strength to scream! The Tor's stomach and throat seemed to be filling up with blood. "An alliance with Alend," he croaked out. "Against Cadwal. A chance to end this siege and fight."

The captain said nothing; his reaction was unreadable.

"Norge." Peering through a blur of pain, the lord leaned closer to whisper straight into the captain's face. "If I can make an alliance with Prince Kragen, will you support me?"

Norge spent an astonishing amount of time lost in thought. He took forever to arrive at a decision. Or maybe he just seemed to take forever.

Then he said, "All right, my lord Tor," as if he had never hesitated in his life.

The Tor groaned thickly—relief and anguish. A desire to lie down and hug his belly nearly overwhelmed him. Somehow, however, he forced himself to ask, "How is the Prince?"

Norge glanced away, then answered, "Rousing."

Hoarse with stress, the Tor breathed, "Reports. I need reports. I must know what is happening."

Ponderously, as if Norge weren't carrying most of his weight, the old lord struggled to his feet.

For a moment, pain rose like vomit into his mouth. He couldn't see, couldn't breathe; if Norge hadn't held him, he would have fallen. But that was intolerable. So much weakness was intolerable. If he let himself fail now, Castellan Lebbick would probably get up from the dead and go do his job for him.

With a gasp that went through him like a blade, he pulled air into his chest.

Almost at once, his vision cleared.

Prince Kragen was rousing, no question about it. Artagel still sprawled on the floor as if Master Gilbur had broken his neck; but the Prince was crawling stupidly toward his sword.

A guard who didn't know any better and probably hated Alends stepped forward to kick the sword out of Kragen's reach.

"Stop," coughed the Tor.

Norge ordered the guard to stop.

Still barely conscious, Prince Kragen got a hand on his sword and at once began climbing to his feet.

Each movement helped bring him back to himself; the weight of his weapon seemed to make him stronger. By degrees, he came upright, planted his legs, clenched both fists on the hilt of his longsword. His eyes lost their glazed dullness and began to smolder with a murderous rage.

Instinctively, he sank into a fighter's crouch. The tip of his blade searched for the nearest enemy. He was going to swing— The Tor nearly wept at the thought that Prince Kragen might do something which would force the guards to kill him.

But the Prince didn't swing. Slowly, he turned toward the doors; he saw that men blocked his way. "Dastards!" he spat as he wheeled back.

"Who struck me?" he demanded softly. "Where is King Joyse?"

"My lord Prince." Trembling, the Tor released one of his hands from Norge, then the other. Alone, he took two tottering steps toward Prince Kragen, as if he were presenting his belly to the Prince's blade. Fire seemed to run like water out of his guts and down the nerves of his legs; nevertheless he kept his head up. "Forgive my weakness. I am unwell.

"You were struck by Artagel." He nodded toward Artagel's supine form. "You see the outcome.

"King Joyse is gone. He disappeared shortly after you fell— when Gart attacked."

"Gart?" Prince Kragen's eyes widened; his rage receded slightly. His mind was beginning to function. He shifted his grip on his sword. "The High King's Monomach was here?"

The Tor nodded, conserving his strength.

At once, Prince Kragen scanned the hall, plainly searching for confirmation. He noticed the archers and pikemen dead on the balcony, the slain Apts; he absorbed the absence of the King's counselors, the absence of the Masters. He saw Castellan Lebbick stretched out behind the Tor, and his mouth twisted under his moustache as if he were suddenly sick.

"My lord Tor," he said in a bitter snarl, "where are my companions, Geraden and the lady Terisa? They also were *protected* under a flag of truce."

Still whispering because he didn't have any choice, the old lord replied, "Gart had allies. Master Eremis. Master Gilbur." He saw from Prince Kragen's face that the Prince wasn't particularly surprised by the names he mentioned.

"They took the lady Terisa, my lord Prince," Norge put in casually. "As for Geraden, he went with Master Barsonage. Or maybe it would be more accurate to say the mediator carried him off."

Took the lady Terisa. The Tor blinked stupidly. He hadn't seen her go, hadn't known— But he couldn't afford to think about that now. He had to deal with Kragen.

"So you see," he said as well as he could, "we have nowhere else to turn for answers. My lord Prince, I think you should tell us the things you came to tell King Joyse."

"*Why?*" Prince Kragen's question cut the air. "Your King accused me of an atrocity. Although I was protected under a flag of truce, I was struck down before I could defend myself." He bit into the words to control his passion. "Apparently, it is amazing that I am still alive. Even your King's *audiences* are not safe. And now he has 'disappeared.'

"Why should I say one word to you, my lord Tor?"

The Tor had to suppress a yearning for sleep. "*Because* King Joyse has disappeared, my lord Prince." The damage to his stomach dragged at him. If he were horizontal, it might hurt less. And if he were asleep, it might stop hurting entirely.

On the other hand, Orison had been kicked in the gut as well. He was needed. He had to do whatever he was capable of doing.

"He is gone. And the Castellan is dead. He died saving my life when Gart was ready to kill me. There is no power left in Orison.

"None except Captain Norge, Lebbick's second. And Master Barsonage, the mediator of the Congery. And me.

"Master Barsonage is not present, but I will speak for him. If you deal openly with us, we are prepared to offer you an alliance. Orison's strength, and the Congery's, against Cadwal."

That brought Prince Kragen's fury up short. He stared for a moment; his mouth hung open. Then, in a tone of fierce care, he asked, "Do I understand you, my lord Tor? Have you just proclaimed yourself King of Mordant? Have you murdered Joyse? Have you and Norge been plotting revolt?"

"Of course not," the Tor groaned. "I claim only the position of a chancellor." Really, this was too much. How could he possibly be expected to stand here and argue when he was probably bleeding to death inside? "If I were a younger man, I would teach you to regret that accusation." If Lebbick hadn't saved his life, he would have given up the whole business and let himself collapse. "The King is only gone, not deposed. Not murdered. In his absence—and in his name—and with Captain Norge's support," he added, hoping that Norge wouldn't contradict him, "I will make decisions.

"We are prepared to offer you an alliance," he repeated. "If you will deal openly with us."

Prince Kragen continued to hesitate, caught—the Tor supposed—between suspicion, curiosity, need. And he probably didn't trust the wine-soaked old lord in front of him. Who would? A guard came into the hall and crossed toward Norge, but the Tor ignored him. In addition, Artagel began to fumble toward consciousness. The Tor ignored that as well. He concentrated on Prince Kragen's silence.

"Come, my lord Prince," he wheezed. "I am not well. I will not be on my feet long. You have said that you desire an alliance. And your desire is demonstrably sincere. With the rupture"—poor choice of words—"of Orison's gates nearly accomplished, you desisted when Terisa and Geraden came into your hands. But you did not keep them and their knowledge for yourself. You brought them here, risking them and your own person for the sake of what you hoped to gain.

"The blow which struck you down under a flag of truce was a mistake. Artagel will admit as much." The Tor saw no reason to refrain from extravagant promises. "Will you sacrifice your own needs and desires merely to punish us for a mistake?

"My lord Prince, tell us the things you came to say to King Joyse."

Artagel levered himself off the floor, lurched to his feet; one hand clasped the back of his neck, trying too late to protect it from Gilbur's attack. When he saw Prince Kragen facing him, sword poised, he took a step backward and looked around urgently, searching to comprehend what had happened.

"A report, my lord Tor," Norge announced tranquilly. "You asked for reports.

"There's panic in Orison, and it's spreading, but we've been able to keep it out of the courtyard—away from the gates. The Prince's honor guard is waiting as patiently as possible. No sign of King Joyse. Geraden is definitely with Master Barsonage. The mediator's quarters.

"Two of the duty guards say they saw Adept Havelock's brown cloud lift off the King's tower." Nonchalantly, Norge avoided Prince Kragen's sharp gaze. "If they're right, it didn't attack the encampment. It just floated out of sight."

The Tor suffered this interruption as well as he could, but he hardly heard what Norge was saying. At the moment, all he really wanted in life was the ability to cry out; scream his pain at the ceiling. And not just the pain of his brutalized abdomen. He had other hurts as well. Lebbick's death. King Joyse's abandonment, when he, the Tor, had staked his heart on the belief that Joyse still deserved trust. And the humiliation of being distrusted because he had drunk too much wine.

His eyes ran again. Stupid, stupid. Through the blur, he croaked, "Artagel."

"Is this certain?" Prince Kragen snapped at Norge. "The report is to be trusted? The King's Dastard has not attacked us?"

"Lebbick?" Artagel demanded like a man who still wasn't entirely conscious. "Lebbick?"

"You struck Prince Kragen under a flag of truce. That was a mistake. Tell him you know it was a mistake."

Both Prince Kragen and Norge stared at the Tor as if the old lord had lost his mind.

"*Lebbick!*" Artagel cried through a clenched throat. "What have they done to you?"

The Tor tried again. "Artagel."

"Terisa? Geraden?" Artagel jerked his head from side to side, scanning the hall, the guards, the bodies. "Where are they?" A flush of blood and pain filled his face. "Did Gart get them? Somebody give me a sword! *Where are they?*"

"Artagel!" Norge put an inflection of command into his easy tone. "Eremis and Gart took the lady. Geraden is all right. Pay attention. The Tor gave you an order."

"Gave me a *what?*" Artagel rasped as if he were about to begin howling. But then, abruptly, he froze; his eyes widened. Almost matching Norge's casualness, he asked, "Where is King Joyse?"

"That," said Prince Kragen in heavy sarcasm, "is a question we would all like answered."

Slowly, Artagel's jaw dropped.

The Tor made one more effort. "Artagel, you struck Prince Kragen under a flag of truce. I want you to apologize."

Then, deliberately, the old lord closed his eyes and held his breath.

He didn't look or breathe again until he heard Artagel say, "My lord Prince, I was wrong."

Artagel was smiling like a whetted axe. His voice held an edge he might have used against Gart. And yet—

And yet he did what the Tor needed.

"It's inexcusable to violate a flag of truce. And you saved my life once—you and the Perdon. I just didn't have time to think. I was afraid of what King Joyse might do. Everybody in Orison knows he's been practicing his swordsmanship. The Castellan said he was probably going to challenge you to a duel. I thought he was crazy enough to try it."

Prince Kragen couldn't hide his surprise at this information, but the Tor clung to his pain and let everything else pass over his head.

Unexpectedly, his spirits lifted a bit. There was good reason why everybody in Orison liked Artagel.

"I've seen you fight," Artagel concluded. "King Joyse didn't stand a chance. I was just trying to save him."

Artagel had the Prince's attention now. Kragen thought intently for a moment, then said, "Artagel, you have the reputation of a fighter. You understand warfare. What is your opinion? Who has the most to gain from an alliance, Orison or Alend?"

Without hesitation, Artagel answered, "You do, my lord Prince. We've got the Congery."

The Tor couldn't be sure of what he saw any longer. His eyes kept running, and the damage to his stomach seemed to throb up into his head; his brain felt like a balloon about to burst. Nevertheless he had the impression that the Prince was sagging, letting go of his fury.

"My lord Tor"—Prince Kragen's voice came from somewhere on the other side of a veil of pressure—"Geraden and the lady Terisa approached me from the Care of Fayle, where they had witnessed Queen Madin's abduction. But that was by no means their only news. Among a number of other things, they informed me of Master Eremis' treachery.

"Simply for that—to warn King Joyse of his enemies—I might have been willing to risk myself here. But I have other information as well, knowledge which both confirms and worsens the things Geraden and the lady Terisa revealed.

"I know where High King Festten's army is."

The Tor felt himself about to fall. Really, somebody ought to teach Gart to treat old men with more respect. Nevertheless he was determined to do what he could.

"Norge, announce in Orison that I have taken command during the King's absence. You are appointed Castellan. Make it heard. It is our only defense against panic. The people must believe that we still stand, regardless of treachery."

Norge saluted equably, but the Tor ignored him. "My lord Prince," he wheezed as if his wounds were going to kill him, "we must leave this hall before Master Eremis sees fit to attack again. Come with me to King Joyse's rooms. We have much to discuss.

"I must discuss it sitting down."

FORTY-ONE:
THE USES
OF TALENT

hen Geraden actually recovered consciousness, he was sitting in one of Master Barsonage's handmade chair.

He had opened his eyes before the mediator got him out of the hall of audiences; he had forced his legs under him, despite their awkward tendency to flop in all directions, and had carried most of his own weight during the walk from the hall to Master Barsonage's private quarters; he had received the news of Terisa's capture as if he understood it. Nevertheless he had no effective idea of where he was or what he was doing until Barsonage shut the door on Orison's problems, positioned him in a sturdy armchair, and handed him a flagon of ale.

This room was familiar. And almost comfortable, like a restoration of old relationships, old truths. Master Barsonage was the mediator of the Congery. Geraden was an Apt—part servant, part student. That made everything simple. He had no worries, no responsibilities, unless the mediator assigned them to him. Unless the mediator explained them to him.

Simple.

Moving slowly because of the way his head throbbed, he accepted an automatic swallow from the flagon; then he drank deeply.

And then he remembered so hard that he nearly gasped.

Terisa. Eremis had *Terisa.*

"We've got to help her."

Perhaps he wasn't entirely conscious after all. He wasn't aware that he had spoken aloud; he certainly didn't realize that he had dropped his flagon on the floor. He only knew that he was trying to get out of the chair, trying with all his strength, and Master Barsonage held him back. Braced over him, the mediator's bulk was implacable: he couldn't shift it.

Terisa!

"Let me go. We've got to help her."

"How?" demanded the Master bluntly. "How will you help her?"

"The mirror I made." Geraden wanted to fret like a child, slap at Barsonage's hands, wail; somehow, he restrained himself. "The one like Gilbur's—the one I used to bring her here. I can shift it. I made it take me to Domne."

"What will that accomplish?" The mediator continued to block Geraden's escape from the chair. "Surely she was not taken to Domne?"

"No." Geraden found it almost impossible not to yell or weep. "He took her to Esmerel. That's where he's been working all this time. I've seen Esmerel. I can make my mirror show that Image. I can use it to look for her. If I find her, I can translate her back."

Let me go!

"No. Forgive me." Suddenly, the mediator didn't sound firm or implacable. He sounded grieved, almost wounded. "That will be impossible."

Maybe Master Barsonage had stepped back. Or maybe Geraden felt authority rise in him like fire, giving him strength no one could oppose. He was no Apt, not anymore. Eremis' enmity had transformed him.

Don't you understand? He's going to rape her. She's an arch-Imager. He's going to find some way to rape her talent.

Almost without effort, Geraden surged to his feet, pushed the older man back, cleared his own way to the door.

Yet the change in the mediator's tone stopped him; it had more effect on him than a shout of rage or protest. Now that he could have left, he stayed where he was, caught.

"What do you mean? Why is it impossible?"

"Geraden, forgive me," Barsonage repeated. His grief was plain on his face. "In this, I have failed you badly."

Just for an instant, Geraden hung on the verge of an explosion:

he was going to spit outrage, batter the mediator into talking sense, do something violent. Almost at once, however, he pulled himself back from the edge. "Apologize later," he said between his teeth. "Just tell me what's wrong."

"The truth was obvious." Master Barsonage wasn't able to meet his hot gaze. "A child could have seen it. Of course you were able to work wonders with that glass. You brought the lady Terisa among us. You escaped into it, leaving no trace of yourself. We all knew of your talent at last—

"But I did not think of your talent. I thought only of your guilt—or your innocence. And so I missed the obvious implication of the obvious truth. There I failed you."

Geraden beat his fists against his thighs to keep himself from shouting, Get to the point!

"I did not see," the mediator explained sadly, "that your mirror required special protection, either to keep it from you if you were guilty, or to preserve it for you if you were innocent." At last, he forced himself to look into Geraden's face. "Some days ago, a riot took place. It appeared to be an outbreak against the Castellan— but by an astonishing series of coincidences its worst violence occurred in the laborium. During the tumult, several mirrors were shattered.

"The only one of importance was yours."

Distinctly, as if the admission were an act of valor, Master Barsonage concluded, "I have cost you the means to help the lady Terisa. You have no glass with which to search for her."

Geraden found himself staring at nothing. For some reason, the mediator no longer seemed present in the room. Which was nonsense, of course, he was right there, with his chasuble hanging down his vast chest, with his face twisted in difficult honesty. Nevertheless the older man was gone in some way, erased from Geraden's attention.

A riot had taken place. In the laborium. Against Castellan Lebbick. And mirrors had been destroyed. The only whole, perfect mirror which he, Geraden, had ever made—

He would need at least a day to make another glass. Eremis had Terisa. At least a day.

A riot against Castellan Lebbick?

"You must understand how confused matters were to us in your absence." Master Barsonage was speaking earnestly, trying to explain. Maybe he thought an explanation would help. "First you were accused of Nyle's murder. Then Nyle's body was mutilated by means of Imagery, and the physician Underwell disappeared. Then Master Quillon was killed. That was clear evidence of the lady Terisa's guilt—evidence which demonstrated your own guilt by association. The Castellan himself witnessed her power, as well as her alliance with Master Gilbur."

No, this wasn't working. Geraden didn't need an explanation. Or he didn't need *this* explanation. At least a day. Eremis had Terisa. If he could somehow have focused his attention on the mediator, he would have demanded, A riot against *Castellan Lebbick?*

"And then," Barsonage was saying, "the Castellan himself began to insist on your innocence—on the lady Terisa's innocence. Plainly, he had lost his reason. The King's madness had at last driven Lebbick mad. And yet he insisted, when all Orison except the guard had turned against him. He insisted—but privately, privately, so that few could hear him—upon accusing Master Eremis, who had single-handedly saved us from an Alend victory by thirst.

"What were we to think? Without doubt, the lady Terisa's talent—and your own—gave us back our purpose. The meaning of the Congery had been restored. But what were we to do? Had she come to save us, or destroy us? Had you in fact murdered your brother, or were you innocent? Such questions consumed us. We were not concerned for the safety of our mirrors. Men who covet the power of Imagery do not destroy mirrors."

Geraden had the impression that if he moved—if he so much as opened his mouth to breathe—he would at once fall into a pit of blackness. It filled the room all around him, lurking behind the illusory images of Master Barsonage and the furniture. Everything he had ever done had gone wrong. Wasn't that true? For all practical purposes, he had brought Terisa here simply so that Master Eremis could have her at the peak of his power, at the moment of her greatest vulnerability. What a triumph. The climax of a brilliant life. Everything had gone wrong since the day his mother had died, and he had sworn, *sworn,* that he was never again going to let that happen to anyone he loved.

Nevertheless he couldn't stop trying. The bare idea of surrendering to Eremis made him sick. There had to be something he could do—

A riot against *Castellan Lebbick?*

Deliberately, he opened his mouth. Gritting his teeth, he forced himself to take a deep breath, focus his eyes on the mediator.

"Why Lebbick?" That wasn't exactly the question he wanted to ask, but it was close enough. "Why did they turn against Lebbick?"

Master Barsonage shrugged his massive shoulders. "The maid Saddith." This subject was considerably less personal for him. "He beat her—beat her nearly to death. She was maimed by it.

"She incited the riot to gain revenge."

Suddenly, as if Barsonage had murmured the words and made the gestures to perform a translation, Geraden's weakness was gone, banished. There wasn't any pit of blackness around him: there was only a room he knew fairly well; a room which on this occasion didn't have enough lamps lit, with the result that the corners were obscure, like hiding places.

"Master Barsonage"—Geraden was mildly astonished by his own calm—"why did he beat her? That's where it started—the 'series of coincidences.' What did she do?"

Geraden's interest obviously took the mediator aback. He hesitated for a moment, as if he thought he ought to steer the discussion in a more useful direction. Whatever he saw in Geraden's face, however, persuaded him to answer.

"The story is that she went to his bed, the night after the lady Terisa's disappearance. She said that she grieved for him in his distress and wished to comfort him. Those who were willing to doubt her—and they were few after the extent of her injuries became known—said that she offered herself to him so that he would elevate her above the position of a chambermaid."

Again, Geraden wanted to explode. "And *that* didn't warn you?" he snapped. "It didn't make you suspicious at all? Didn't you remember she was Eremis' lover? I told you that. I *told* you he's been using her. Didn't it ever occur to you that he might have sent her to Lebbick? What have you done with your *mind?*"

"Geraden." Master Barsonage's face turned hard; his eyes glittered. "You are no longer an Apt. No one could deny that you have become an Imager. Yet I remain the mediator of the Congery. I expect your respect.

"I have admitted my fault. I did not foresee the danger to your glass. In other matters, however, I have not earned your anger."

With difficulty, Geraden restrained himself. "I'm sorry," he gritted, unable to unclench his jaws. "I didn't mean to offend you. I'm just terrified for Terisa." At once, he went on, "Do you mean you *were* suspicious of Eremis? What did you do?"

The mediator studied Geraden for a moment, then apparently decided to let himself be mollified. Shrugging again, he replied, "The relationship between Master Eremis and the maid was of interest to me, naturally. But it was a matter of inference only—hardly a demonstration of treachery. And his public display of loyalty was impressive. I might," he admitted wryly, "have dismissed my suspicions, inevitable though they were.

"However, your brother Artagel came to speak with me—"

Geraden held himself still, waiting.

"After the lady Terisa's show of talent," Master Barsonage explained, "the Congery at last went to work with a will, showing the kind of dedication King Joyse has always wanted. Respecting the strictures he had placed upon us from the first, we began to search for tools of defense, ways in which we might preserve Orison, or even Mordant—methods to oppose or assist you and the lady Terisa when we learned the truth about you."

Half-smiling, the mediator digressed to say, "Prince Kragen seemed on the verge of breaking Orison's gates when you distracted him. I can assure you, however, that he would not have been able to enter this castle without my consent."

Then he resumed, "In this work, Master Eremis at first took no part. He was assumed to be resting after the exertion of refilling the reservoir."

Geraden held his breath.

"The day after the riot, however, he came to me to announce that he was ready to take up his duties among the Congery.

"He could not know that I had had a long conversation with Artagel several days previously.

"Artagel informed me that—despite his own evidence—Castellan Lebbick was now convinced of your innocence. He was convinced of Master Eremis' guilt. And his reasoning was persuasive. From Artagel, it was very persuasive."

Master Barsonage sighed. "Unfortunately, Geraden, there was no proof. There was no basis on which Master Eremis could be accused, no way it could be shown that the man who had saved us from Alend had done so for Cadwal's benefit rather than our own.

"Therefore I could not turn against him. I could not so much as deny him his place in the Congery, for fear that he would be alerted to my distrust. And yet I also could not further expose the Congery to his betrayal.

"Geraden, I have not served you well—but I have served the King better. I concealed the Congery's true work from Master Eremis. I lied to him about it. I allowed him to see no sign of it, play no part in it. He does not know how well prepared we are to assist in the defense of Orison."

Geraden cleared his lungs slowly. His head was clear, and a number of things seemed to be growing clearer around him. After all, there was really no way Master Barsonage could have predicted that Eremis would use Saddith to start a riot in order to cover up an attack on his, Geraden's mirror. But to keep the Congery's work secret—to do practical labor on Orison's behalf without allowing the knowledge to fall into Eremis' hands— That was well done.

And Artagel trusted him, trusted Terisa. Even Castellan Lebbick had trusted both of them, despite Master Eremis' manipulations.

There was hope. He didn't know what it was yet, but he had the strongest feeling—

"What did you tell him?" he asked the mediator softly. "What kind of lie did he believe?"

Unexpectedly, Master Barsonage smiled—a grin so sharp it seemed almost bloodthirsty. "I told him that we have dedicated all our resources to discovering how our enemies are able to make use of flat mirrors without going mad."

A muscle twitched in Geraden's cheek. Yes, that was a lie which would be believed by anyone who was convinced of the Congery's fundamental ineffectuality. "Wasn't that true?" he asked.

The lift of the mediator's shoulders was like his grin. "There was truth in it. I have asked two of the Masters to concentrate on that question. The rest of us, however, have been laboring for more immediate results."

Geraden felt his courage coming back to him, his hope growing stronger. "Good," he pronounced.

"How did Eremis react?"

"He offered his help." As he spoke, Barsonage lost his look of fierceness; it faded into a more familiar bafflement. "In fact, he proposed the most plausible theory I have ever heard. He suggested that the translations are done, not with one mirror, but with two. A flat glass is placed in the Image of another mirror, and then both translations are enacted simultaneously, so that the flat mirror functions like a curved one and therefore doesn't exact the usual penalty."

"He told you *that?*" Geraden was startled; his still-fragile self-confidence flinched. "Then it must be wrong." His own theory must be wrong.

"It is," sighed Master Barsonage. "Did you know that translation pulverizes glass? I did not. Yet it is true. We have attempted Master Eremis' suggestion three times, and each time the flat mirror was reduced to powder as it passed into the Image of the curved mirror."

"Glass and splinters!" Geraden groaned. This was too much: he was wrong again; everything he thought he understood was wrong; Eremis was too far ahead of him. Hope was nonsense. He couldn't hold his head up, face the older Imager. There was nothing he could do to save Terisa.

"This surprises you," observed the mediator thoughtfully. "Not Master Eremis' suggestion, but rather its failure surprises you. Geraden, you amaze me. You had already considered this idea for yourself, when no other member of the Congery had so much as imagined it."

Eremis was playing with him, playing with all of them, using them in an elaborate and insidious game they couldn't win, a game from which they couldn't even escape because they didn't know the rules. Like Prince Kragen in his audience with King Joyse, forced to play hop-board. At the mercy of his opponent.

But Master Barsonage was still speaking. "You have disguised yourself for years as Geraden fumblefoot," he said in a tone of admiration, "and now at last I learn that your talent is prodigious. You are able to do translations which diverge from the Image in your mirror. Ideas which astonish us are familiar to you.

"Is there more, Geraden? Does your talent encompass other wonders as well?"

Geraden hardly heard the mediator. He was thinking, Oh, prodigious. Absolutely. They tremble when I walk into the room.

He was thinking, A riot against Castellan Lebbick.

Eremis wanted to preserve Orison for Cadwal. And no man could defend the castle better than Lebbick. And yet Eremis had sent his own lover to get beaten nearly to death, simply to generate a grievance against Lebbick, simply to make a riot possible, simply to make it possible for a riot to enter the laborium, so that Geraden's mirror could be destroyed. All that risk for nothing except to dispose of Geraden's only weapon.

Were Eremis and Gilbur and Vagel really that badly afraid of him?

It sounded ridiculous. But—

He took hold of himself, did his best to steady his heart.

But they knew his talent better than he did. Why else had they gone to such lengths to distract him, confuse him, demean him, kill him? Master Gilbur had guided—and studied—every moment of his mirror-making.

They knew his talent better than he did.

They feared it for reasons he didn't yet understand.

The same kind of argument had helped move him into action while Houseldon burned—and yet he had made no progress toward understanding it. Why had Eremis needed to attack Houseldon? Or Sternwall, for that matter? Why wasn't the destruction of Geraden's only mirror enough?

Suddenly—so suddenly that he couldn't pretend he had been listening to the mediator—Geraden said, "Havelock."

Master Barsonage blinked. "Havelock?"

"He's got all those mirrors." Geraden was already on his way toward the door. "Come on."

Mirrors which had helped Terisa escape from Gilbur. Mirrors which didn't belong to any Imager except the Adept—mirrors Geraden could take chances with.

Outside the mediator's quarters, he began to hurry; in a moment, he was almost running. Nevertheless Master Barsonage caught him, got a heavy hand on his arm and slowed him to a fast walk.

"What do you hope to accomplish with the Adept's mirrors? Will he permit you to touch them?"

A manic laugh burst from Geraden. "Oh, he'll let me touch them. He is certainly going to let me touch them."

Moving as rapidly as he could with Master Barsonage clasped on his arm, and refusing to answer the mediator's first question, refusing even to think about it for fear that the possibilities would evaporate if he did, he headed toward the lower levels of Orison, down toward the only entrance he knew of to Adept Havelock's personal domain.

During his one previous visit there, the circumstances had been very different. For one thing, Orison's extra inhabitants hadn't arrived yet; the depths of the castle had been deserted. And for another, he hadn't been paying particularly close attention: most of his mind had been focused on Artagel, suffering from a chestful of corrosive black vapor. As a result, he was momentarily flustered by the realization that he now didn't know how to get where he was going.

Fortunately, Master Barsonage knew.

At least some of the Adept's secrets had been exposed when Castellan Lebbick had followed Master Gilbur and Terisa into the room where Havelock kept his mirrors. As a matter of course, the Castellan's discovery had eventually been reported to the mediator of the Congery. And Master Barsonage had gone so far as to visit that room full of mirrors himself, in part to see it with his own eyes, in part to make one more painful and ultimately futile effort to communicate with the Adept—specifically, to persuade Havelock that the Congery as a whole should be given access to these mirrors.

The memory caused Master Barsonage to shudder whenever he thought of it. Adept Havelock had responded with a gracious bow, had taken his hand as if to congratulate him, had kissed each of his fingers like a lover—and while Barsonage was distracted by this odd performance, Havelock had urinated on his feet.

Occasionally, Master Barsonage dreamed of beating the Adept senseless. Although he would never have admitted having them, he enjoyed those dreams.

Nevertheless he didn't hesitate to take Geraden to the Adept's quarters.

He and Geraden approached through the storeroom full of empty crates—crates, apparently, in which Havelock's mirrors had been brought to Orison. A door in a niche at the back of the room let them into a short passage. Unexpectedly, Geraden stopped.

Pointing at the impressive array of bolts and bars inside the door, he asked, "Doesn't he ever lock this place? Does he let people just walk in whenever they want?"

Master Barsonage sniffed in distaste. "I cannot say. I have come here three times. Twice the door was sealed, and he would not open it to me. Perhaps he did not hear me. The third time, the door was open. I found him snoring in his bed. And when I roused him, he was"—Barsonage grimaced—"unpleasant."

After a moment, he added, "For my own peace of mind, however, I have insisted on guards in the outer hall. Men dressed as ordinary merchants and farmers marked us before we entered the storeroom. If you had not been in my company—or if you had not been recognized—you would have been halted."

Geraden was scowling. "Does Havelock know anything about that?"

"Perhaps. Who can say what the Adept knows? Perhaps he neither knows nor cares."

Geraden was thinking about Terisa. Maybe she could have been saved—maybe everything would have been different—if guards had been placed outside the storeroom earlier. If Adept Havelock had had any idea what he was doing.

Snarling to himself, Geraden headed down the passage.

Almost immediately, he and Barsonage reached the room where Havelock's mirrors were kept.

It had been dramatically changed.

The difference was unmistakable: the room was tidy. Someone had dusted the tables and floor, the mirrors; swept the broken glass from the stone; arranged the full-length mirrors around the walls, displaying them as well as possible in the relatively constricted space. Someone had set up the small and medium-sized mirrors on the tables and adjusted them so that they caught the light of the few lamps and gleamed like promises.

That someone must have been Adept Havelock. Geraden and the mediator spotted him as soon as they entered the room: he was in one corner with a featherduster, crooning over a glass which had been restored to pristine clarity after decades of neglect.

He had made the chamber into a shrine. Or a mausoleum.

Just for a moment while Geraden and Master Barsonage stared at him, he failed to acknowledge their arrival. Then, however, he wheeled to give them a bow, flourishing his duster as though it were a scepter. His eyes gaped in different directions; his fat lips leered. "Barsonage!" he cackled. "You honor me. What a thrill. Who's the puppy with you?"

Simply because he couldn't resist staring, Geraden noticed a detail which might have escaped him otherwise: Havelock's surcoat was clean. In fact, it had been scrubbed spotless. Havelock wore it as if he were dressed for a celebration.

Master Barsonage kept his distance. "Adept Havelock," he said with formal distaste, "I am certain that you remember Apt Geraden. He is an Imager now, and has an urgent interest in your mirrors."

As if to tease the mediator, Havelock advanced toward him, smiling maliciously. "What, 'Apt Geraden'?" he cried in mock protest. "This boy? How has that figure of augury and power been reduced to such doggishness? No, you're mistaken, it's impossible."

Swooping suddenly away from Barsonage, he pounced on Geraden. With his hands clapped to Geraden's cheeks, he shook Geraden's head from side to side.

"Impossible, I tell you. Look, Barsonage. He's alive. He came back alive. Without her. She risked everything for him, and he came back without her." Bitterly, the Adept began to laugh. "Oh, no, Barsonage, you can't fool me. Geraden would never have done such a thing."

Geraden seemed to hear the Adept through an abrupt roaring in his ears, a tumult of anger and distress. The suggestion that he might have come back without Terisa by choice, that he had turned his back on her in some way, was more than he could bear.

Harshly, struggling to control his passion, he demanded, "Let me go, Havelock. I need your mirrors."

As if he had been stung, the Adept let out a wail.

He dropped his hands, plunged himself to the floor; before Geraden could react, he kissed the toes of Geraden's boots. Then he scuttled backward. When he hit the leg of a table, he bounded to his feet.

Crouching in the intense stance of a man about to do battle, he commented casually, almost playfully, "If you ever talk to Joyse like that, he'll cut your heart out. Or force you to marry all his daughters. With him it's hard to tell the difference."

Shocked and disconcerted, Geraden turned a plea for help toward Master Barsonage.

Grimly, the mediator nodded. Swallowing to hold down a bellyful of uneasiness, he stepped forward, edged his bulk a bit between the Adept and Geraden.

Geraden took that opportunity to turn his back on both of them.

Deliberately, he placed himself before the first full-length flat mirror he could find.

It was an especially elegant piece of work: he noticed its beauty in spite of his concentration on other things, because he loved mirrors. Its rosewood frame was nearly as tall as he was, and the wood had a deep, burnished glow which only long hours of care and polish could produce. The surface of the glass was meticulous, both in its flatness and in its craftsmanship. The glass itself held an evanescent suggestion of pink—a color which now appeared to complement the frame, although of course the frame had actually been chosen to suit the glass.

And the Image—

Bare sand. Nothing else.

Wind had whipped the sand into a dune with a keen, curled edge, like a breaker frozen in motion; but there was no wind now. The color of the sky was a dry, dusty blue that he associated almost automatically with Cadwal.

In some ways, this landscape was the purest he had ever seen, too clean even for bleached bones. No one and nothing alive had ever set foot on that dune.

Only urgency kept him from studying every inch of the mirror, simply to understand the Image—and to appreciate the workmanship.

He had no idea how Terisa worked with flat glass. And he had no particular reason to believe he could do the same thing. In fact, he hardly knew how he had contrived to translate himself from the laborium to the Closed Fist. He certainly hadn't done anything to prove himself an arch-Imager.

Nevertheless he didn't hestitate.

He came back alive. Without her. Geraden would never have done such a thing.

Facing the glass, he closed his eyes; he swept his thoughts clear. Master Barsonage and Adept Havelock were watching him, and Terisa was lost, and he had never tried anything like this before. Yet he had the strongest feeling— He pulled his concentration together, firmly wiped panic and confusion and anguish out of his heart.

In the mirror of his mind, he began to construct an Image of Esmerel.

Still trying to intervene between Geraden and Havelock, the mediator asked the Adept carefully, "You mentioned King Joyse. Do you know where he is?"

"He has flown," spat back Havelock, his mouth full of vitriol. "Like a bird, ha-ha. You think he has abandoned you, but it is a lie, a lie, a lie. When everything else is lost, he breaks my heart and gives me nothing."

Geraden ignored both of them.

He found it easy to ignore distractions now. Something luminous was taking place. He had no training in Image-building; no Imager practiced that skill. He was working with an entirely new concept: that the Image of a mirror could be chosen; that translations could be done which ignored the apparent Image of a mirror. As new to the world as Terisa herself. And yet the process of creating the Image he wanted in his mind excited him; it enabled him to close his attention to anything which interfered.

Line by line, feature by feature, he put together a picture of Eremis' "ancestral Seat."

He had only seen it once, of course—and only from the outside. He had no notion what it looked like inside. But that didn't worry him. He believed that the scenes and landscapes in mirrors were real, that Images were reflections rather than inventions. So if he could induce the glass to show Esmerel from the outside, the manor's true interior would be included automatically.

"What do you mean," asked Master Barsonage, "'flown'?" He didn't seem to expect an answer, however. He may not have been listening to himself at all.

Esmerel was a relatively low building in a deep, wedge-shaped valley with a brook bubbling picturesquely over its stones and out-croppings of rock like ramparts all along the walls—not low because of any lack of sweep or grace in its design, but because it was con-structed on only one rambling, aboveground level. According to rumor, some of the best features of the house were belowground, dug down into the rock of the valley: an enviable wine cellar; a gallery for weavings, paintings, and small sculptures; a vast library; several research halls. But naturally Geraden knew nothing about those things. He knew, however, that a portico defined the entrance—a portico with massive redwood pillars for columns. The entrance, as he remembered it, was plain, only one lamp in a leaded glass frame on either side, no carving on the panels of the doors. The house's walls were layered planks—waxed rather than painted against Tor's weather—but all the corners and intersections were stone, with the result that Esmerel's face had a pleasingly varied texture.

Unless something had happened since he had seen it—or unless his memory or his imagination had gone wrong—Master Eremis' home looked precisely like *that*.

Master Barsonage let out a stifled gasp. His respiration was labored, as if he had stuffed his fist into his mouth and was trying to breathe around it.

To commemorate the occasion, Adept Havelock began whistling thinly through his teeth.

Geraden opened his eyes.

The mirror in front of him showed a sand dune under a calm sky, almost certainly somewhere in Cadwal.

The pang of his disappointment was so acute that he nearly groaned aloud.

"I would not have believed it," whispered Barsonage. "When I was first told that such things could happen, I did not believe it."

"Are you out of your mind?" inquired the Adept politely. "That's how I know this isn't Apt Geraden. Even if he did talk to me that way. A man who can do this wouldn't have to come back without her."

Geraden blinked hard, shook his head. No, he wasn't going blind. The Image he was staring at hadn't changed at all.

Distressed and baffled, he turned toward Master Barsonage—

—and saw Esmerel, as clear as sunlight, exactly as he had envisioned it, in the curved mirror standing beside the flat glass he had chosen to work with.

"By the pure sand of dreams," he murmured, "that's incredible." A curved mirror, a curved mirror. Excitement leaped up in him; he could hardly restrain a yell. "I wouldn't have believed it myself." A curved mirror, of *course!* Flat glass was Terisa's talent, not his. If he had tried to translate himself through a flat glass, he would have gone mad. Like Havelock.

"Don't flatter yourself," Havelock advised sententiously. "If you think I'm going to kiss your boots again, just because you can do a little trick like that, you're full of shit."

But *curved* glass—! Like the only mirror he had ever been able to make for himself, the mirror which had reached Terisa behind the Image of the champion. He could shift the Images in curved mirrors.

Quickly, before he had time to be overwhelmed by his discovery, he approached the glass and began to adjust the focus.

"Now I'll find her." The pressure of hope and need cramped his lungs. "I'll get her away from you, you bastard. If I find you, I'll even get *you.* Just try to stop me. Just try."

Fighting the tremors in his hands, the long shivers which made his fingers twitch, he tipped the mirror's frame to bring the Image of Esmerel closer.

Distance was the problem, distance. He knew that—and tried to keep it out of his mind, tried not to let it terrify him. If the focus of the Image was too far from the place where Terisa was being held, he wouldn't be able to adjust the mirror enough to reach her. Every glass had a limited range: it couldn't be focused more than a certain distance from its natural Image. If he couldn't reach Terisa, he would have to start over again from the beginning: based on what he learned now, he would have to build the Image of Esmerel again, re-create it in his mind—but closer this time, closer.

In his present turmoil, that kind of concentration might be impossible.

No, don't fail, he exhorted the glass, don't fail now, you've never done anything right in your life except love her, she's all there is for you and Orison and Mordant and even Alend, *don't fail now.*

With a jerk because his hand was unsteady, the Image moved to a near view of the entrance under the portico.

Another jerk.

The Image moved into the forehall of the manor.

Geraden stopped breathing.

Like the exterior walls, the floor was formed of fitted planks anchored with stone. Years of use and wax made the boards gleam, but couldn't conceal the fact that men who didn't care what damage they did had been there in nailed boots—had been there recently. Mud, footprints, gouged spots, splinters: they were all distinct in the Image.

Nevertheless the forehall was empty.

Sweat streamed into Geraden's eyes. He scrubbed at it with the back of his hand. Dimly, he was aware that both Master Barsonage and Adept Havelock were standing over him, watching his search; but he had no attention to spare for them.

More smoothly, he moved the Image into the first room which opened off the forehall.

A large sitting room: the kind of room in which formal guests sipped sweet wines before dinner. Tracked with mud and bootmarks.

Bloodstains.

Deserted.

"Why is no one there?" asked the mediator softly. "Where is Master Eremis? Where are his mirrors—his power?"

Geraden's heart constricted. Nausea rose in his throat as he moved the Image through the house.

A cavernous dining room. More mud and bootmarks, more bloodstains. The edges of the table were ragged with swordcuts.

Deserted.

Oh, Terisa, please, where are you?

Geraden scanned two more fouled rooms, both empty, then located a wide staircase sweeping downward.

"The cellars," mumured Master Barsonage. "That is where they would imprison her."

Of course. The cellars. Esmerel's equivalent of a dungeon. Eremis wouldn't keep his mirrors or his apparatus or any of his secrets where passersby or even tradesmen might catch sight of them. Everything would be belowground.

Who was responsible for all this mud, all these bootmarks?

Geraden nudged the Image downward.

For the first few steps, he was so absorbed in what he was doing—so caught up in the focus of the glass, the search for Terisa, the need to succeed—that he didn't understand what was about to happen to him, didn't realize the truth at all, even though it was perfectly plain in front of him, so obvious that any farmer or stonemason, any ordinary man or woman, would have grasped it automatically.

But then the Image began to dim, began to grow palpably dim in the glass, and Master Barsonage croaked, "Light."

Light.

Geraden's hands froze on the frame. His whole body lost movement, as if the breath and blood had been swept out of him. The stairs loomed below him darkly, treads descending into an immeasurable black.

There was no light. No lamps or lanterns or torches or candles. They had been extinguished.

The Image still existed, of course; but without light there was nothing to see.

He had no answer to that defense. By that one stroke, any attempt to rescue Terisa was instantly and effectively prevented. He couldn't help her if he couldn't find her—and how could he find her if he couldn't see her?

"Maybe—" The air seemed to thicken in his lungs; he felt like he was suffocating. "Maybe there's light farther down. Maybe only the stairs are dark."

At once, Master Barsonage clamped a warning hand onto his

shoulder. "Geraden," he hissed as if the former Apt were far away, lost in urgency, almost out of reach, "how will you find it? If there *is* light, how will you find it? You cannot focus an Image you cannot *see*. You may shift it into the foundations of the house, where no light will ever reach."

"I've got to try." Geraden was choking. The mediator's hand on his shoulder was choking him. "Don't you understand? I've got to find her."

"No!" Master Barsonage insisted. Geraden's passion appeared to affect him like anguish. *"You cannot focus an Image you cannot see."*

That was true. Of course. Any idiot could have told him that. Even a failed Apt who had never done anything right in his life could recognize the truth. Darkness made all the mirrors blind—and all Imagers.

Somehow, Geraden stepped back against the pressure of Barsonage's grip. Facing the Image as it blurred into the obscure depths, he said harshly, "Then I'll have to go myself."

With a look of iron on his face, and no hope in his heart, he made the mental adjustment of translation and stepped into the glass.

As his face crossed into the Image, he cried out, "Terisa!"

Master Barsonage wrenched him back so hard that he sprawled among the tables.

Before he could regain his feet—or curse or fight—Adept Havelock sat down on his chest, straddling his neck.

"Listen to me," the Adept snarled, savage with strain. "I can't do this for long." His eyes rolled as if he were going into a seizure. "You can make us let you go. Just use that voice. We'll obey. But we won't be able to get you back."

Geraden bucked against the Adept, tried to pitch Havelock off him. Havelock braced his legs on either side, clutched at Geraden's jerkin with both hands, hung on.

"*Listen* to me, you fool! Your power sustains the shift! When you translate yourself, that glass will revert to its natural Image. You'll be cut off!—you and the lady Terisa both! You'll *both* be lost!"

It was too much. Geraden flung Adept Havelock aside. He surged to his feet. With all his strength, he punched Master Barsonage in the chest—a blow which nearly made the massive Imager take a step backward.

Then he faced the mirror and began to howl.

"Eremis! Don't touch her!"

FORTY-TWO:
UNEXPECTED
TRANSLATIONS

remis was touching her. He was certainly touching her.
She had never been strong enough against him.
Her concentration had never been strong enough.
While he had approached her in the audience hall, while
he had threatened Geraden, while he had fought with the Tor, she
had attempted something she didn't know how to do, something she
had never heard of before: wild with anger and desperation, she had
tried to reach out to the mirror which had brought him here and
change it.

On some level, she knew that was impossible. She was on the
wrong side of the glass, the side of the Image, not the side of the
Imager. But the knowledge meant nothing to her. If she could feel
a translation taking place, surely that gave her a link, a channel? And
she didn't have any other way to fight. Her need was that extreme:
she didn't care that what she was trying was probably insane. Her
strange and unmeasured talent was her only weapon. If she could
fade, if she could go far enough away to reach his mirror—

His hands made that impossible. They forced her to the surface
of herself when she most needed to sink away.

First there was his grip on her arm. He flung her toward the
translation point as if it were a wall against which he intended to
break her bones. But he didn't let her go.

Then there was the bottomless instant of translation, the eternal dissolution.

Then there was a completely different kind of light.

It was orange and hot, part furnace, part torches—and full of smoke, rankly scented. Another man was there, someone she hadn't seen before, a blur as Eremis impelled her past him, kept her spinning. Gilbur and Gart were right behind her, as blurred as everything else.

And Eremis was shouting, "The lights! Put out the lights!"

Before she could get her eyes into focus, see anything clearly, the torches dove into buckets of sand; a clang closed the door of the furnace. Darkness slammed against her like a wave of heat.

"What went wrong?" someone demanded in a rattling voice.

"Geraden," snapped Master Eremis. "He remains alive. We must not let him see this place."

"I tried to kill him," Gilbur snarled. "I hit him hard. But that puppy is stronger than he appears."

"*She* must not see it," continued Eremis. "She is his creation. Who knows what bonds exist between them? Perhaps they are able to share Images in their minds."

The first voice, the man she didn't know, made an assenting noise. "Then it is good that we were prepared for this eventuality. If we were in the Image-room—" A moment later, he added, "It would be interesting to learn what he does when he regains consciousness."

"As long as he cannot find us," muttered Master Gilbur.

"In the dark?" Master Eremis laughed. "Have no fear of that." He sounded exultant, almost happy. His grip on Terisa shifted; with one hand, he held both her arms behind her back. "She is mine now—and they are ours. No matter that Geraden still lives, and Kragen. That will only add spice to the sauce. They will do exactly what we wish."

"And Joyse?" asked the rattling voice.

"You saw," rasped Gilbur. "He fled when we appeared. No doubt he is cowering in some hidey-hole, hoping for mad Havelock to save him."

The tone of Eremis' laughter suggested that he doubted Gilbur's assessment. He didn't argue, however. Instead, he said, "It will be safe to renew the lights when the door is closed."

Firmly, irresistibly, he pushed Terisa ahead of him into the dark.

And all the time, she was still trying to concentrate, still trying to fade.

Now, of course, she wasn't reaching toward the glass Eremis had used; she was struggling to find Adept Havelock's supply of mirrors, striving to feel the potential for translation across the distance. She could sense translations as they occurred. She was sensitive to the opening of the gap between places. That must mean *something*. There must be some way she could use it.

But Eremis' grasp made everything impossible.

He held her too roughly, so that her arms hurt; he pushed her too far ahead of him into the blind dark. Through a doorway, along a lightless passage, through another door: the visceral fear of running into something kept her from being able to pull her heart and mind away. The way he chuckled between his teeth filled her with rage and despair.

I'm not yours. Never. I'll find some way to kill you. No matter what happens. I swear it.

It was impossible to fade while she was so full of fury.

And then the way he held her changed.

Through the second doorway and across a rough floor, he suddenly thrust her down. She couldn't catch herself because he didn't free her arms: she landed heavily on a pillow, a bed. Deftly, he turned her so that she lay on her back, with her wrists now clamped above her head by one of his hands. Then he clasped something iron around her left wrist; she heard a click, a faint rattle of chain. In spite of the fetter, however, he continued to hold her arms pinned.

He went on chuckling while his other hand undid the hooks of her soft, leather shirt, exposing her breasts, her vulnerable belly.

"I must chain you," he murmured pleasantly, "a small precaution against your strange talents—and Geraden's. But it will not prevent me from satisfying my claim on you. You will find that I am not easily satisfied. On the other hand, we have plenty of time.

"If you are compliant, I will keep you bound as little as possible."

In the dark, she struggled; she wanted to smash his face, wanted to feel his blood on her hands. He pinned her easily, however; he knew how to keep women from getting away from him. When she paused to gather her strength so that she wouldn't weep, he curled his tongue like a lick of wet fire around each of her nipples, and his hand slipped aside the sash of her trousers.

Gasping on the verge of tears, she tried to twist out of his hold; failed.

Abruptly, she stilled herself, let the resistance sag out of her muscles. She wasn't accomplishing anything; she was just contributing to her own defeat by making herself wild. She couldn't concentrate— Let him think her stillness was a form of surrender. If he was that arrogant.

"You will accept my manhood completely," he murmured. "I will take possession of you in all ways. And I will not be satisfied until you beg me to enter you wherever and whenever I desire."

His mouth clung to her nipples, teasing them involuntarily erect, caressing and probing them. At the same time, his hand moved down into her open trousers to the place between her legs which only Geraden knew. His fingers stroked her there as if he believed that she was being seduced.

Far away in her mind, she was imagining his death.

When he began to pull her trousers off her hips, however, she returned to defend herself. Her eyes were starting to adjust—and this room wasn't absolutely lightless. Hints of illumination filtered into the air from what may have been an imperfectly sealed window in the wall above her. Eremis' head was a shape of deeper blackness poised to make her breasts ache. She couldn't fight him physically. But she could still fight.

Taking advantage of the fact that he had left her mouth free, she said, "Gilbur thinks King Joyse is a coward, but you don't agree." Her tone should have warned him: it wasn't unsteady enough, frightened enough, to indicate surrender. "Why is that?"

"Because, my sweet lady"—he was too full of victory to refuse to answer her—"you betrayed him to me."

She could feel him grinning over her in the dark.

"I might have believed that he was a fool, or a coward, or a madman. But you came to me while Lebbick had me in his dungeon, and you opened my eyes. At a time when I might have remained innocent of the knowledge, you showed me that King Joyse understood his own actions—that he did what he did deliberately."

Terisa's spirit squirmed at the thought; but she kept her body passive.

"This revelation enabled me to adjust my plans to accommodate the possibility that he may have been setting traps of his own. If I had been forced to wait until Quillon finally exposed himself and

Joyse by rescuing you, I might have found myself in difficulty. But you"—Eremis entered her maliciously with his fingers, making her flinch—"gave me time to prepare a more personal snare—time to arrange for Queen Madin's abduction, to cut the ground out from under Joyse at precisely the moment when I might be most exposed to counterattack.

"You made that possible, my lady." His head was turned toward her now, momentarily sparing her breasts. He was gloating, hardly able to contain his triumph. At that moment, he might have been willing to tell her anything. "You allowed me to perfect my plans against an opponent who may have proved worthier than he appeared."

As he spoke, her mind turned cold and sick. It was true: she had given King Joyse to his enemies.

"You deserve Saddith's fate for attempting to thwart me. But because I am grateful I will use only as much force as you require."

He laughed again—a snort of pleasure and contempt. Her senses were full of him. He smelled of sweat and confidence. "Gart wished to kill you when you left Vale House, but I did not allow it. Doubtless your death and Geraden's would have been to our benefit. But then who would have taken the news of the Queen to King Joyse? How else could I arrange to master both you and Joyse at the same time, except by letting you live?

"You have served me perfectly, despite your opposition." His fingers continued to work between her legs. "My only regret is that I do not yet have Geraden in my power. That will come, however. I have said that I must think of something truly special to reward him for his interference, his dunderheaded enmity, and I will do it.

"If you are compliant, my lady, you will live a life which many women would envy. But *him*"—Eremis' fingers hurt her, nearly made her gasp—"him I will destroy."

"I doubt it," she said, breathing hard to diffuse the pain. She was going to kill him. All she had to do was stay alive long enough. "He can do translations you don't understand. Translations you didn't even know were possible until he brought me to Orison."

For a moment, Eremis' laugh sounded more like a snarl. "That is true. And it offends me. But again I have been abundantly fore-warned. The Congery's augury made me suspicious of Geraden. And Gilbur learned much while teaching him to shape his mirror. That allowed me to set in motion all the dangers and distractions which prevented both him and you from exploring your talents, learning what they were. And it allowed me to preserve the disregard in which he was held by the Masters, so that the Congery did not try to help you.

"In that way, we gained a great deal of necessary time.

"And now, of course, he is helpless. You cannot threaten me with his power. He can translate nothing he cannot see."

"I know that," Terisa replied harshly—too harshly. She hadn't intended to let so much of her fury show. "But you can't see, either. You need light sometime—unless you're planning to give up on Orison and Mordant and Alend, and spend the rest of your life just raping me." She felt him grin over her. "And when you go out into the light"—she did her best to lodge each word like a knife in his vitals—"you'll find that he knows too much about you. He knows how you use flat mirrors without going mad."

Eremis' reaction was stronger than she was expecting. He stiffened; his breath hissed between his teeth; his hand raked across her belly as if to hurt her breasts or strike her face.

"How is that, my lady?"

Lying still, expressing defiance with her voice alone, she said, "You put the flat glass inside a curved one and work both translations at the same time."

As quickly as she had gained it, she lost her advantage. The Master relaxed tangibly; his fingers stroked her nipples while the tension ran out of him. "That is quite accurate," he commented. "And I must say that I am impressed by Geraden's ability to reason his way so near the truth. By now, however, Barsonage has discovered that the technique you describe is impossible. Glass translated through glass only shatters.

"The true secret, my lady, lies in the oxidate which prepares the curved mirror. That is *my* discovery, the result of *my* sweat and study. *I* learned how to make a mirror into which other mirrors could be translated."

At the moment, her determination to kill him was all that kept her from despair. There simply wasn't room in her for so much anger *and* the horror of seeing her last hope collapse.

"Most of my fellow Masters," Eremis continued, "would laugh themselves sick if they knew how I have spent my years as an Imager. And yet on my small discovery the world hinges. When I am done, all Mordant and Alend and Cadwal will be at my service, and even High King Festten will acknowledge me supreme."

The prospect filled him with passion. He began kissing Terisa again, and this time she could feel his hunger in the way his mouth nipped and sucked her nipples, the way his tongue thrust against them. His free hand was back inside her trousers, pulling them down, making her ready for him.

If he had let her arms go—just for a second—she would have done her best to put his eyes out. In spite of his triumph, however, he didn't shift the grip that kept her under control.

She had no way to make him stop.

She didn't need to make him stop. Out of the dark, the unfamiliar, rattling voice said sourly, "Festten wants you."

Nearly choking with anger, Master Eremis sprang to his feet and wheeled away from Terisa. "Am I to be interrupted with her forever? She is *mine,* I tell you, and I have earned her. Festten does not command *me!*"

The other voice conveyed a shrug. "He has twenty thousand men who believe otherwise. And he desires a report."

Her arms were free. She pulled them down, swung her legs off the bed, sat up; she tested the chain. It wasn't long enough to let her reach Eremis. The cold cuff on her wrist held.

"Report to him yourself," Eremis countered. "Send Gilbur to report. Send *Gart.* I do not come and go to suit the High King."

"Eremis," the rattling voice warned, "think. The High King trusts me. He has always trusted me. But he does not trust you. He accepts your leadership—he does as you wish—only because you obtain results which please him. You bring him nearer to victory than he has ever been.

"But now you have risked a foray into the heart of Orison itself, and have accomplished nothing except Lebbick's death and her capture. High King Festten considers that so far all his actions under your guidance have come to nothing. His only satisfaction has been the annihilation of the Perdon.

"He desires a report."

"That sheepfucker," growled Eremis in disgust. "A man who has lost his interest in women—a man who can only find pleasure in animals—is not fit for kingship."

Nevertheless his tone expressed acquiescence. Despite his

anger and frustration, the Master left Terisa alone. Muttering obscenities to himself, he strode away through the dark.

Because she wasn't done—because she had never been further from surrender and wanted to know her enemy—she demanded after him sharply, "Why are you doing this?"

He must have paused. His tone was at once hard and light; malign; jubilant.

"Because I can."

Almost at once, she was sure that he was gone.

For what felt like a long moment, she didn't move. She had given King Joyse to his enemies. Queen Madin's abduction was her fault. She had gone to Eremis in the dungeon and told him what he needed to know and let him command her to betray Geraden and *how could she have been so stupid?* And Geraden didn't know the secret of the oxidate. He couldn't fight the Master. He couldn't find her in the dark.

Hope was out of the question, really.

Never mind that. She probably didn't have room for hope anyway. Her yearning for Eremis' blood was too big: it squeezed out everything else. It made the kind of concentration she needed impossible. She was powerless precisely because her ache for power was so intense.

The chain left her room to move around the bed. Grimly, she pulled up her trousers, tied the sash tightly, and began to rebutton her shirt.

"Unfortunate," the rattling voice muttered.

She froze.

How many people were watching her—people she couldn't see?

"I see well without light. Darkness conceals no secrets from me. But opportunities to witness such nakedness have been rare in recent years." The speaker's voice sounded like pebbles on glass. "A woman with such proud breasts, and yet so full of fear. A tantalizing combination. And there is time. Eremis will be away for some little while. Festten will question him narrowly before allowing him to go ahead with his plans."

Terisa wanted to finish buttoning her shirt, but she couldn't make her fingers work. How many people—? Until now, she had only been afraid of Eremis, not of the dark itself, not of the place where he had left her.

"Sadly, however, Eremis does not like used meat. And I do not like any meat enough to risk my alliance with him. Hide your breasts—or flaunt them—as you choose." She heard relish as well as scorn in the rattle. "They will not sway me."

As if she had been waiting for his permission, she fumbled at the fastenings of the shirt.

At last, her eyes were adjusting to the dark. When she peered hard, she was able to discern the outlines of a figure near where she guessed the doorway to be. The voice came from that direction.

Clenching her teeth for courage, she stood up and tested the chain.

She was able to swing her arms before she came to its limit. Following it to its anchor, she found that it was stapled into the wall at the head of the bed—nearly ten feet of it, enough to let her perform almost any conceivable gymnastic feat on the bed, but not enough to let her evade the dim figure in the doorway. Nevertheless she was comforted to have that much range of motion. If everything else failed, she would at least have a chance to hit Master Eremis before he touched her again.

Deliberately, she wrapped some of the chain around her fist to give it weight. She placed her back against the wall. Then she faced the figure with the rattling voice.

"You're Vagel." She didn't need confirmation: she was sure. "The famous arch-Imager. The man who drove Havelock mad. Why do you do it?"

"Do what?"

"Put up with him. You call it an alliance, but he probably treats you like a servant. You're *the* arch-Imager. The most powerful man anybody has ever heard of. Why are you serving him? Why isn't it the other way around?"

The outlines of the figure suggested a shrug. "Power," he said like stones scattering against a mirror, "is more often a matter of position than of talent. He told you the truth, in a way. The whole world hinges on the little discovery which enables him to translate glass through glass. But that is not his real power."

"Really?" She couldn't stifle her impulse to goad Vagel. She was too frightened and furious for any other approach. Apparently, Vagel had been listening—*watching*—while Eremis had her naked. "What *is*?"

"His real power," rattled the arch-Imager, "is that he is irre- placeable to all his allies—because of his talents, of course, but also because of his position, in the Congery, in Orison. What access do I have to his resources, his freedoms? Gilbur, I grant you, has also been favorably placed. But there it is his talent which is replaceable. He is only swift—uncommonly swift—rather than brilliant. And he hates everyone too much to form bonds—everyone except Eremis.

"No, Eremis' real power is that he can have his way with anyone.

"He has his way with me, although my Imagery far surpasses his—and although I am the link which allowed him to begin his dealings with Festten, years ago when he rescued me from renegade destitution among the Alend Lieges. He will have his way with Festten, despite the High King's taste for absolute authority. He will have his way with you"—Vagel let out a malign chuckle—"until the only thing which prevents you from begging for death is that he does not let you speak.

"He will even have his way with King Joyse in the end." Now Vagel's tone suggested hard things—broken things with sharp edges. "For that reason I do not care how utterly I serve him."

Unexpectedly, Terisa had stopped listening. The Alend Lieges. The way he said those words triggered a small leap of intuition, fitted on odd, minor detail into place. In surprise, she said, "Carrier pigeons."

Vagel was silent, as if she had startled him.

"You're the one who brought carrier pigeons here. You gave them to the Alend Lieges."

"Those mucky barons," growled the arch-Imager. "Their squalor and their petty ambitions nearly drove me mad. They demanded—*demanded*—Power. Imagery. I had to satisfy them to keep myself alive, *me,* the greatest Imager they had ever known. And yet they were *satisfied* with birds that could carry messages. I would have destroyed them long ago—I would have *required* that of Eremis—if they weren't such *little* men.

"For that also, for the humiliation they cost me, Joyse will suffer."

"Revenge," Terisa muttered. Her attention shifted back to Vagel. "He and Havelock beat you back when you thought you were about to become the master of the world, and you can't live with it. Now you don't care who has the power. You don't care how much *Eremis* humiliates you. All you care about is hurting the people who showed you you were wrong about yourself.

"What Eremis is doing to you is worse than anything King Joyse ever did."

"Is it?" Vagel's voice purred like a fall of small stones. "How strangely you think. Your defeat becomes less and less surprising, despite all the nearly unguessable implications of your talent.

"Eremis' manner is demeaning, but the rewards he offers are not. Do you believe that either Joyse or Havelock proved themselves better men than I am—more able or deserving, more powerful? No. They only proved that they were more treacherous. And you have seen in the decline of Mordant and the collapse of Orison that there exists *nothing* so desirable, worthy, or powerful that it cannot be betrayed. I was beaten, not by a good Imager or a good king, but by a good *spy*."

She expected the arch-Imager to advance, but he didn't. "Do not despise revenge. Unless I am much mistaken"—he was sneering at her—"you yourself have no other passion.

"In your case, however, revenge must fail. You do not *serve* any man who can make glass from the blood-soaked sand of your desires. Eremis will have his way with you, and then the truth of you will be proven absolutely."

"It's the same for you," she retorted, fighting back so that what he said wouldn't crush her. "He's using you—having his way with you. And when he's done, he'll just discard you. You won't get your revenge after all. He wants all the fun for himself."

Vagel made a sharp, hissing noise. After that, there was a long silence. Terisa tightened her grip on the chain, although the vague figure hadn't moved.

"No," he said at last, as if she had provoked him to candor. "All his allies must fear the same thing—but he will not discard *me*. Festten trusts me. Eremis' plotting would have come to nothing, if I had not stood with him before the High King. He needs Cadwal too much to risk that alliance by discarding me.

"And without me all the force of Imagery at his disposal will become a blunt instrument—able to strike hard, but unable to strike at will. Useless. I am the arch-Imager, as you have observed. The procedures by which we shape mirrors that show the Images we desire are mine. Did you believe that our successes could have been achieved randomly? That Gilbur for all his speed could have made the glass we need simply by mixing accidental combinations of tinct and oxidate, sand and surface? I tell you, he could have sweated until his heart burst without ever producing a mirror which gave us access to Vale House—or one which showed the audience hall of Orison. That victory is *mine*.

"Alone, I have overturned the tenets of Imagery, and no one on Joyse's foolish Congery can compare with me."

Vagel's voice intensified. "Eremis cannot do without me. His need for glass which only I can provide will never end. And because of that"—he seemed to be controlling an impulse to shout—"*before I am done I will roast Joyse's guts over a slow fire.* I will hear him *howl* until his mind goes, or by the stars! I will take my satisfaction from Eremis himself."

A visceral tremor started up in Terisa's guts, so hard that she couldn't speak.

Abruptly, the arch-Imager turned to leave. "Remember that," he snapped while his voice faded. "Perhaps it will inspire you to surrender to him prematurely, and then his pleasure in you will be made that much less."

He left her with the chain wrapped around her fist and no one to strike.

She didn't trust his departure. Her senses strained into the dark, searching for evidence that she wasn't alone. But she heard nothing, felt nothing. As for sight— She could discern a hint of the doorway, but the corners of the room were as obscure as pits. When she turned her eyes to the wall behind the bed, however, she was able to make out the source of the scant illumination. Her first guess had been right: the light came from a window not quite perfectly sealed.

Dropping the chain to increase her range of motion, she climbed onto the bed and reached for the window. From that position, she could get her hands on the boards nailed over the frame. Unfortunately, her fingers found no purchase, either at the edges or in the cracks. She tried until her fingertips tore and her self-control threatened to crumble; then, so that she wouldn't start sobbing, she got down from the bed.

Calm. It was essential to remain calm. To preserve a semblance of calm until it became the real thing. So that she could concentrate *although of course it was impossible to translate herself out of here with a chain on her wrist* no, don't think about things like that, do not. Be calm. Concentrate.

Fade.

Pressing her hands over her face, she sat on the edge of the bed and tried to fade.

She couldn't do it: she was too angry and scared, deprived of hope. She had the shakes so badly that her heart itself quivered. She had betrayed King Joyse, and Vagel was going to make him *howl*— Geraden had no way to find her, rescue her. Too many people might still be watching her, concealed behind spyholes, hidden in the corners—

Eremis would come back as soon as he finished with High King Festten.

She needed time to pull herself together.

Searching for calm, she decided to explore the room as far as the chain allowed. What else could she do? Maybe if she failed to find anything she would recover some self-possession.

Shaking badly, and too angry to care whether she looked foolish to a spectator, she moved to the staple holding her chain and from there started to grope her way toward the corner, searching the cold, crude stone with her fingers.

When her hand touched iron in the wall, she nearly flinched.

Iron: another staple.

A short chain fixed to the staple. A manacle.

A wrist in the fetter.

That did make her flinch. She recoiled to the bed, sat down facing the dark. Her breath came in hard gasps.

She had felt a wrist. Skin. A hand that flexed away from her touch.

Another prisoner. Someone was chained in the corner.

Eremis had intended to rape her before witnesses.

Who are you? she panted. For a moment, the words refused to come out of her throat. Almost gagging, she forced them.

"Who are you?"

No answer. Maybe because she was breathing so hard herself, she couldn't hear any sigh or rustle of life.

"Are you hurt?" That was another possibility. Who could tell what Eremis or Vagel or Gilbur—or Gart—might do to their enemies? If she hadn't felt skin and movement, she would have been tempted to imagine a skeleton. Or a corpse.

"Can you hear me?" She got off the bed and started along the wall again, slowly, *slowly,* trying to control her alarm with caution. "Are you all right?"

She found the staple, the short chain. The hand in the manacle tried to avoid her touch. Nevertheless she shifted from the fettered wrist to an arm. It was draped with loose cloth—the sleeve of a cloak? The fabric was rough and warm; worsted, perhaps.

She found a covered shoulder, a bare neck. The shoulder and neck twisted hard, but they couldn't get away; the other arm must be chained as well. Curse this dark. The prisoner was only a little taller than she was. Although she was near the limit of her own chain, she had no difficulty touching an unshaven face that strained away from her; terrified of her.

"Are you hurt?" she whispered. "Who are you?"

Roughly, he wrenched his head up and sucked a strangled breath through his teeth.

"All right. You've found me. They told me not to make a sound, not to let you know I'm here, but this isn't my fault."

His voice was familiar to her. His bitterness was familiar.

Nyle. Geraden's "murdered" brother.

For a moment, she was so glad to find him alive that she could hardly stand. So it *was* Underwell who had been killed, disfigured; Eremis' plotting was just as vile as she had believed it must be.

And Nyle was *here;* had been kept prisoner for how long now?— held in case he were ever needed again against his brother.

"Oh, Nyle," she whispered in relief and quick nausea, "I'm so sorry. What have they done to you?"

"Same thing they're going to do to you." His bitterness was worse than anger; he had gone too far beyond hope. "A kind of rape. I'm just lucky Eremis still wants me alive. Gilbur likes what they call 'male meat,' but he has a tendency to kill his toys, so Eremis makes him leave me alone. Most of the time.

"They need me to make sure Geraden doesn't do something unpredictable. Or King Joyse either, for that matter."

Oh, Nyle.

She couldn't stay on her feet. Nausea crowded all the relief out of her. Without thinking, she retreated to the bed, sat down again. For some reason, she wasn't trembling anymore. But she was going to be so sick— If she let go, she was going to puke her heart out.

"It's the same reason they've got you." Now that Nyle had begun to talk, he seemed intent on continuing. "Only the details are different. We're hostages. And bait. We're here to make sure Geraden and King Joyse do what Eremis wants.

"I actually thought somebody would try to rescue me." His tone made her want to throw up. Gilbur liked *male meat.* "But I was wrong. Maybe they'll forget about you, too. That's your only hope now—that Eremis made a mistake bringing you here."

Fighting down bile, she forced herself to say, "Nobody in Orison knew you needed rescuing. Don't you know what they did? They killed that physician, Underwell. They let monsters eat his face"—don't think about it, don't *think* about it—"they dressed him up to look like you. Everybody thought you were dead." Because it had to be said, she concluded, "They thought Geraden killed you. You accomplished that, anyway."

"I know all that." Nyle coughed thinly, as if he were too weak and beaten to curse. "They sent Gart and a couple of his Apts into the room to knock the guards and Underwell out. So there wouldn't be any noise. They translated me here. Then they sent some of their creatures to feed on the bodies. They told me all about it.

"Do you think that's what I wanted? Do you think I had a choice?"

No, it was cruel to accuse him, cruel, he had been Eremis' prisoner and Gilbur's for a long time now, and the decisions he had made which had put him here had all been based on King Joyse's policy of foolish passivity, it wasn't fair to include him in her anger. Nevertheless she said, "Everybody has a choice."

She had a choice, didn't she? She was chained to the wall in the dark, and Eremis intended to use her for his pleasure until her spirit broke, and there was no way she could possibly be rescued, and she still had a choice. Only dead people didn't make choices.

He coughed again, like a man whose lungs were full of dry rot. She could picture him in his fetters, with his mouth hanging open in his dirty beard and no strength. "You're wrong," he murmured when he was finished coughing. "You're like Elega. You don't know. I haven't had a choice about anything since Geraden hit me with that club."

Oh, great. Terisa barely swallowed a snarl. Now he was going to start blaming Geraden. Her stomach tried to come up; she had to force it down. She had already been harsher than she wanted to be. Instead of pursuing what Nyle said, she asked thickly, "Do you know where we are? Do you know this place?"

"All I wanted to do was save Orison and Mordant." Maybe he hadn't heard her. "You can't say I deserve this. You can think I was wrong, but you can't say I was being malicious. I wasn't going to get anything out of it for myself. Not even Elega— Even if I was right, my family was still going to hate me. I was never going to be able to go home again. They all believed in King Joyse personally, not in the ideas that made him a good king—not in the Congery and Orison and Mordant. They were never going to forgive me for *betraying* their hero, even if everything I did turned out right.

"I didn't do it for myself."

"Oh, Nyle," she breathed softly. "You don't understand. Of course they'll forgive you. They've already forgiven you."

But maybe he wasn't able to hear her. Maybe he had spent too much time helpless, caught in an everlasting reiteration of what he had done and why—and what it had cost—without any way to break out. Instead of reacting to what she said, he continued explaining himself.

Trying to justify himself against the dark.

"But Geraden destroyed me. I know that wasn't what he wanted, but he set me up for all this. When he came after me, instead of concentrating on Prince Kragen— If he weren't so determined to have accidents—

"He got me locked up. Like an assassin. Like I was dangerous to all the decent people around me. If I were a farmer who went berserk and started slaughtering his friends and family with an axe, I would have been locked up, but I wouldn't have been sneered at. I wouldn't have been despised.

"Don't you understand? *I* love King Joyse, too. I always loved him, even though he didn't let me serve him—even though he didn't want me around. But some loves are more important than others. He wasn't interested in my loyalty—and that hurt, because he was so obviously interested in my brothers. Artagel. Geraden. But I could still love his victories, his ideals, his beliefs.

"What do you think I should have done?" For a moment, Nyle's voice brought a touch of passion into the dark. "Abandon everything that made Mordant valuable for the sake of a failing old man who didn't care whether I lived or died?

"Then Geraden stopped me, and they threw me in the dungeon. Do you know what that means?" A coughing fit came over him, draining his intensity away. "You should.

"It means I couldn't get away.

"Artagel came and flaunted his wounds at me. I couldn't get

away. Castellan Lebbick practiced his obscenities on me for quite a while. I couldn't get away.

"And then Master Eremis came—"

"Nyle, stop." Terisa didn't want to hear it. She knew what was coming, and she didn't want to hear it. "This doesn't help. You're just tormenting yourself." All she wanted was some way to contain the horror surging at the back of her throat so that she could concentrate, bring her fury and her dread and her ache for blood into focus. "Do you know where we are?"

"Just like that," Nyle went on as if she hadn't spoken. "He just walked into the dungeon. He just unlocked my cell and took me out. I couldn't get away." His tone frayed at the edges, worn ragged by bitterness and fatigue and coughing, by anger that didn't have anywhere else to go. "He took me down the passage a little way. Then he made some kind of gesture, and we were translated here. Into his personal laborium. I couldn't get away from him.

"Do you know what he did to me?"

"Yes!" Fighting for a defense against pain, Terisa jumped to her feet. "I *know*." When she moved, her chain rang lightly against the wall. Quickly, she caught the chain in her fist and swung it harder, made the stone clang. "I know what he *did* to you."

Of course, she didn't truly *know:* she hadn't suffered the same experience. But she knew enough—more than she could stomach. Fiercely, she rushed on:

"He showed you a mirror with Houseldon in the Image." She swung the chain. "And he showed you other mirrors." The iron links chimed on the wall. "Mirrors with firecats. Mirrors with corrupt wolves. Mirrors with avalanches—mirrors with ghouls." Each time, she swung the chain harder. "And he made you believe he could bring them all down on your home and family without any warning of any kind if you didn't do what he wanted. If you didn't help him turn the Congery against Geraden."

Panting, gasping, she stood still.

Nyle's silence was all the acknowledgment she needed.

"So you agreed because you thought you were saving most of the people you loved. And you figured somebody was bound to notice *eventually* that you weren't actually dead—which would save Geraden and recoil on Eremis. And somehow you managed to avoid the simple deduction that Eremis knew as much about the flaws in his plans as you did.

"Nyle, you made a *choice*. Geraden didn't do this to you. You did it to yourself."

There. Now she had begun attacking people who were manacled to walls, accusing them of bad logic as well as weak moral fiber. As if they had caused the things their enemies did to them. What was she going to do next? Start beating up cripples?

And yet in her own case she had no one to blame but herself for the fact that she had been so slow to distrust Master Eremis, so poor at opposing him.

Out of the dark, Nyle asked in old pain, "What choice did I have? What could I have done?"

Oh, shit. She forced her fingers to release the chain. "You could have refused."

"Weren't you listening to yourself?" He had some anger left in him after all. "If I did that, he would have destroyed Houseldon. He would have killed my whole family—everybody I grew up with— my home, all of it."

"No, Nyle," she sighed. By degrees, she wrestled down her nausea, her racing pulse, her desire to hurt something. He was going to be hurt badly enough already. She didn't need to increase the force of the blow. "You're the one who isn't listening. *He destroyed Houseldon anyway.* He burned it to the ground while Geraden and I were there, trying to kill us. Your cooperation didn't make any difference. You gave yourself away for nothing."

There. It was said.

Far away from her, Nyle groaned softly, as if she had just slipped a knife between his ribs—as if she had just cut down the defenses, the self-justifications, which kept him alive in his fetters.

She went to him, feeling at once as brutal as a child molester and as vulnerable as a molested child. "Nyle, I'm sorry." Trying to comfort him, she stroked his face. Her hand came back wet with tears. "We'll get out of here somehow. Sometime. I've talked to your whole family. I know they understand. They know *you*. They know you wouldn't betray Geraden unless you were trying to protect them. And it would have worked, if he hadn't escaped—if he and I hadn't gone to Houseldon."

Then, aching like a prayer that no one could overhear her, use what she was about to say against her, she put her mouth close to his ear and whispered, "They're safe. They all got away. They went to the Closed Fist and dug in. To defend themselves.

"Eremis doesn't know that."

Trembling at the risk she had taken, she stepped back to the bed and waited.

Nyle didn't react. She had no way of knowing whether or not he heard her. But she had done what she could for him. She had needs of her own to take into account. After a while, she returned to her first question—the only one of her questions which he might be in any condition to answer.

"Nyle, do you know where we are?"

After a moment, he took a shuddering breath; he seemed to be raising his head. "Esmerel, I guess. I don't know. I never saw this place until he brought me here—translated me. But he said it was Esmerel."

"Nyle"—the casual threat in Master Eremis' voice was unmistakable—"I told you not to speak to her."

Stung and urgent, almost panicking, Terisa whirled to face the Master.

But not panicking: she was too angry and hurt and focused for panic.

"Why?" she demanded before she had time to think, time to falter. The Imager's shape, as vague as Vagel's, approached her out of the doorway's deeper black. "You've got everything else you want. Why are you doing this to him? He can't do you any harm."

"What, my lady?" Eremis drawled. "Questions? Challenges? That is a poor start to our lovemaking." He sounded confident, immaculately sure of himself—and sharper than he had earlier, as if he had spent his absence enduring petty vexations. "I am surprised that you do not require to know what the High King and I said to each other."

Terisa brushed his words away. "I don't care about the High King. I'm talking about Nyle. Why do you need him? Why don't you let him go?"

Why have you got us chained here together? Why do you want him to know everything you do to me?

Focus. Concentration.

A blank space in the dark, a gap of existence.

Anger and blood.

"For the same reason I need you, my lady." The Master's tone was full of mirth and scorn. "To perfect my triumph. Your capture will require my enemies to march against me. They must attempt to rescue the lady Terisa of Morgan and her strange talents. They will form an alliance, or they will not. They will destroy each other, or they will not. Whatever happens, they must come to Esmerel in the end.

"Then I will release Nyle. I am not as harsh as you think me— I do not torment him gratuitously. He will witness what becomes of you while we await your rescuers." The raw-edged pleasure in his voice went through her like a chill. "And when I am ready, I will send him out to tell them what I have done to you.

"Then Geraden will begin to understand what a burden he has undertaken by opposing me."

No. Never. Never.

Concentration. Focus.

"You bastard."

He was near enough to touch her now. He could have hit her. She felt his presence, the pressure he emanated; she thought she could smell his lust. Yet he didn't hit her. "Come, my lady," he said as if he were sure of her. "Is that how you speak to the man who will master you?" His hand reached out; one finger stroked the line of her cheek. When she didn't flinch, he cupped his hand around the base of her neck inside her shirt. Slowly, his grip tightened. "Must I use force to teach you humility?"

A blank space; a gap between them. She was vanishing into the darkness, groping farther and farther away from him; groping— Her mind was full of Images, all of them insubstantial; wishful thinking.

"No," she said from so far away that he would never be able to possess her. "Take my chain off. Let me show you what I've learned from Geraden."

She made no effort to sound seductive or helpless, to conceal her distance from him.

The trap she set for him was like the one he had prepared for his enemies. Obvious. And irresistible. How could he doubt that he was more than a match for her? that he could control her, coerce her, defeat her whenever he chose? Resistance would only make her final submission the more appalling to her.

Chuckling, he took hold of her arm and clicked the fetter off her wrist.

Because she was so far away, she did nothing to betray herself. And because she was so full of anger, she didn't hesitate.

Before he could secure his grip, she swung her leg with all her strength and kicked him in the crotch.

He gasped as much in surprise as in pain; recoiled violently from her.

Almost at once, he caught his balance, recovered from the shock and hurt. She wanted to hear him cursing in agony, frothing at the mouth; but he didn't oblige her. The oath he spat at her was simply vindictive, a promise that she had pushed him too far and was going to suffer for what she did.

Quickly, he jumped forward to capture her, punish her.

But not quickly enough. While he was still on his way toward her, she touched a moment of eternity.

It was hardly longer than the space between one frightened heartbeat and another—yet it was enough. Images coalesced, took on light and shape: dozens of them; chaos and fragments everywhere. She only needed one, however, the sharpest Image, the one with details so precise and unalienable that they might have been acid-cut on her mind.

A sand dune poised in the timeless gap between high winds and nonexistence.

She had no idea where she might have seen that Image before. She didn't care. As soon as she saw it, she knew it was hers—

—and a touch of cold as thin as a feather and as sharp as steel slid straight through the center of her abdomen.

Eremis was grappling for her, trying to catch her by the shoulders and strike her at the same time. Only an intuitive reflexive leap enabled him to pull himself out of danger as she faded from him and fell backward into the wall.

Into the light of lamps; onto the floor so heavily that she knocked the breath out of herself.

For a long moment, she couldn't speak. She couldn't do anything except gape back up at Adept Havelock, Master Barsonage, and Geraden, who were staring at her as if she had tumbled out of a coffin.

FORTY-THREE: THE ONLY REASONABLE THING TO DO

he light was extraordinary, as life-giving as sunshine. While she waited to breathe, she was content to simply lie where she was and accept the glow of her escape.

Then Geraden let out a whoop and seemed to pounce on her. Oblivious to the fact that she couldn't inhale, he swept her up into his arms and began to whirl her, crying and laughing, "Terisa! *Terisa!*" spinning her into a dance of wild joy. His happiness burned so brightly that she clung to his neck and didn't care whether she was able to breathe or not. If Master Barsonage hadn't immediately clamped a massive hug around both of them, forced Geraden to stop, he would have carried her careening into the mirrors, shattering glass in all directions.

"Stop," the mediator panted. "Are you mad? Stop." He sounded half-delirious himself.

For a moment, her relief and exaltation turned into a convulsive retch for air.

At once, Geraden halted, put her down, held her tightly. "Are you all right? Terisa, are you all right? I couldn't find you. I couldn't reach you. I changed a mirror to go looking for you, but I couldn't find you. I was afraid he had you for good. Oh, love, are you all right?"

She did her best to nod while the knot in her chest loosened enough to let air leak past it. Then she returned his hug, gasping in his ear, clasping him almost savagely because she was still full of impossible translations and promises of murder. After her encounter with Master Eremis, Geraden was so dear to her that she held him as if her heart depended on it.

Geraden. Help me.

He was going to rape me. Just for the fun of it. And to hurt you.

Geraden.

I'm going to kill him.

"My lady," Adept Havelock said judiciously, as if he had become a completely different person, "that was a very pretty trick. If you can truly do such things, then every action he has taken against you is plainly justified. In his place, I would have done the same."

"Proof," murmured Master Barsonage now that he no longer had to protect the Adept's mirrors. "I would not have believed it. *Proof.*" He seemed lost in the wonder of his thoughts. "Images *are* real, independent of their mirrors—independent of Imagery itself. King Joyse has been right all along."

"Fornicate that uxorious bastard," replied Havelock, relapsing to normalcy. "A fine time to go kiting off. He should have seen this."

I'm going to—

Nyle!

"Geraden." Terisa jerked back, pulled away far enough to meet Geraden's gaze. He moved to kiss her; the look on her face stopped him. Quickly, so that he would understand, she said, "He's got Nyle."

He frowned, instantly sympathetic to her urgency. "We knew that," he muttered. "Or we guessed it—"

"I've *seen* him." Well, not *seen,* exactly; but she was in too much of a hurry to explain. "I've talked to him. Eremis has him prisoner. The same place he took me. In Esmerel." Eremis wanted him to watch what he did to me. So you would be hurt as much as possible. "We've got to get him out of there. He's—"

She almost said, He's being destroyed. Eremis is breaking his spirit.

"She changed the Image," Master Barsonage went on, caught in a kind of rapture. "Across that distance, she took a glass with an Image which did not contain her, and she shifted it until the Image *did* contain her. Geraden could not have done it. Flat mirrors are not his talent. And she could not have done such a thing if she were not independently real. It is inconceivable that a woman created in a mirror could have power greater than the mirror—and the Image— that created her."

"Who cares?" retorted the Adept happily. "She's female. That's the point. We can't trust her. We can't trust *him*." He sounded like a doting uncle. "Look at him. He's as bad as Joyse. He's ready to die for her. If things get dangerous, he'll save her instead of us."

She and Geraden weren't listening. As she caught herself, they both turned automatically to look at the mirror which had brought her back to Adept Havelock's rooms.

Its Image was dark, almost impenetrably black. Maybe she could have discerned a shape or two—the bed? the doorway?—if she had been given time; but before she could study the Image it began to melt away. Light bled into the darkness; the potential for obscure shapes became mounded sand. In a moment, the glass had resumed its natural scene, the desertscape for which it had been formed. A breeze was starting to blow, lifting delicate curls of sand from the rim of the dune.

"Nyle!" A new pain shot through her, a loss she hadn't anticipated. "He was there. In that room. We could have reached him— rescued him—"

Holding himself steady, Geraden murmured, "It takes effort to make that shift. As soon as you relaxed, as soon as you let go, the fundamental Image came back."

"That must have been what happened the second day you were here, when you saw the Closed Fist in a flat glass." It was obvious now that he was talking simply to help her, give her something to think about until she grew calmer. "You were so surprised to find the Closed Fist in my glass that you instinctively recreated the Image in the nearest flat mirror. But as soon as Eremis and I distracted you, you let go, and the fundamental Image came back."

Came back. She remembered, in spite of her distress. That Image had come back in time to let her see the Perdon's men being attacked by rapacious black spots which chewed their hearts out.

And Vagel had said that so far High King Festten's *only satisfaction has been the annihilation of the Perdon.*

Curse them all. Damn every one of them.

"A simple matter," commented Havelock. He sounded as lunatic as ever, but somehow he clung to a pragmatic grasp on the situation. "Restore the change. You've been in that room. Bring the Image back, and we'll rescue Nyle."

He's chained, Terisa protested inwardly. They aren't going to just stand there and let us cut him loose.

Nevertheless she faced the flat glass at once, tried to push panic and doubt and urgency out of her mind, tried to recapture the particular dark where Eremis had held her prisoner—

She couldn't do it. She was too frantic; her concentration was too badly frayed. She couldn't so much as remember what the bed was like, how far away the doorway was, where the staples which had held her chain and Nyle's were in relation to each other. And without a precise Image in her mind—

Geraden put an arm around her. "It isn't your fault. It's just impossible." His tone was soft, soothing; it had an undercurrent of misery and yearning, which he suppressed. He must have been through horror of his own while she was away—he must be frantic to rescue Nyle—but he put himself aside for her sake. "That's why he keeps the important parts of Esmerel dark. That's why I wasn't able to come after you. If you shift the mirror now, you won't know if you've got exactly the right piece of darkness. And if you're wrong we might all be killed. You might produce an Image that's actually inside a mountain somewhere, and as soon as you do any kind of translation we'll have a few million tons of rock to deal with. You need light."

Hugging her, he repeated, "It isn't your fault. We'll get him out some other way."

There was no authority in his voice, no unexpected strength. All he was trying to do at the moment was comfort her. And yet she found that she believed him. *We'll get him out some other way.* He meant it, the same way she meant, I'm going to kill him.

Slowly, the panic in her muscles receded, and she slumped against him, mutely asking him to hold her until she had time to recover.

"Geraden is right, I think." Apparently, Master Barsonage had returned from his exaltation. "Master Eremis is cunning. Darkness is a ploy to which no Imager has ever found an answer. Even the crudest translations require light. Do not blame yourself, my lady. Already your achievements seem quite miraculous."

All right. All right. She could never fight if she let herself collapse like this. She couldn't reach Nyle: all right. She could still think. Eremis had violated her with his hands. *Think.* He had come close to doing much worse things—but she got away. It was possible to think; choose; act. Just start somewhere. Geraden still held her. The way his arms supported her was more miraculous than any translation. He had no more intention of abandoning Nyle than she did. All right.

Start somewhere.

She took a shuddering breath. "I don't understand. How did I do it? I was on the wrong side of the glass. I didn't think it was possible for something in an Image to translate itself out."

Geraden tightened his hug. It was the mediator who answered, however.

"The Adept did that, my lady. The idea was Geraden's, but he can do nothing with flat glass.

"You are right. We know of no way for what is in an Image to translate itself out. Even for us—for Imagers of talent who have shaped the mirrors—entering a glass is nearly effortless, but bringing what is in the Image out requires gestures, invocations—a particular way of concentrating the Imager's talent. After all, the mirror itself is *here*, not where you were.

"Yet when the Image in this glass shifted from sand to darkness, we could hardly fail to notice the fact. And Geraden guessed that the shift was your doing. And Havelock is an Adept. We are fortunate"—Barsonage smiled sourly—"that he is in a mood which allows him to react to events reasonably. After Geraden had made himself understood, the Adept performed the translation which rescued you."

With startling clarity, Terisa felt Master Eremis springing toward her through the dark, remembered his attack. As if she were panicking, she broke away from Geraden. But she wasn't panicking; she may have lost the capacity for panic altogether.

Before Havelock could try to avoid her, she caught her arms around his neck and kissed him.

Just for a second, the mad old Imager's eyes came together; he grinned at her like an ecstatic boy. It was amazing, really, how easily she was able to forgive him for failing to help her against Master Gilbur.

Almost at once, however, his gaze split again; his nose jutted fiercely, like a promise of violence. Fortunately, he didn't try to say anything.

He didn't try to stop her when she turned back to Geraden.

Geraden was watching her hungrily. For the first time, she realized that he had tears streaming down his face.

This clear sight of him made her stop. He had known the danger she was in. While she was Eremis' prisoner, he had been here—cut off— She could picture him desperately trying to bridge the gap—

Abruptly, she locked an embrace around him. "Oh, love," she

breathed, aching for him. "You changed a mirror. You must have gone crazy trying to reach me."

Geraden held her hard; but again it was Master Barsonage who answered. "Our Geraden has proved to be nearly as great a source of wonders as you are, my lady." He sounded steady, but behind his self-control she could hear a tremor of pride and vindication. "Of course, we knew of his ability to perform astonishing things with his own glass. For that reason, in some sense we were not surprised when Orison's enemies contrived the destruction of his mirror."

In shock, Terisa stiffened. *The destruction—?* Her link with her home was gone.

Then how—?

"Without his glass," the mediator continued, "we believed he would be helpless. But he has shown himself an Adept in his own right, at least where normal mirrors are concerned." Barsonage indicated a curved glass beside the flat desertscape. "He imposed an Image of Esmerel there and used it to search for you. Only the ploy of darkness prevented him from reaching you."

As she absorbed the mediator's words, her dismay lifted. "You can do that?" She was so pleased that she pushed back again to look into Geraden's anguish. "You're an Adept as well as an Imager? That's wonderful!" Suddenly, she was so furious that it felt like ecstasy. "Heaven help that bastard. *We'll tear him to pieces.*"

Her passion seemed to give him what he needed. She could see him shrug away his failure to rescue her, his helplessness to rescue Nyle. The lines of his face grew sharper; his eyes cast hints of fire.

"It won't be easy. Esmerel is two days away on a good horse. Prince Kragen thinks High King Festten has at least twenty thousand men. Not to mention all the abominations Eremis can translate. They can still use flat glass whenever they want—and we don't know how they do it." He wasn't trying to daunt her. He was simply bringing up problems in order to solve them.

"I don't care about any of that," she replied in the same spirit. "They've got Nyle. They've got the Queen. High King Festten is there. Eremis talked to him this morning. They've destroyed the Perdon. *Annihilated* is the word Vagel used. They're destroying Sternwall and Fayle. And it's just going to get worse." Tersely, she explained what the arch-Imager and Master Eremis had revealed about the speed, precision, and flexibility they had achieved with mirrors. While Geraden scowled at the information, and Master Barsonage blinked in consternation, she concluded, "We've got to stop him before he goes any further."

The mediator started to ask a question, then subsided. But Geraden accepted her explanation without wincing. When she was done, he said, "There's one more thing. King Joyse is gone."

Gone—?

"I mean really gone. Adept Havelock says he flew away." Geraden glanced dubiously at the mad old Imager. "I don't know what that means. But the last we heard no one's been able to find him."

"Then who's in charge?" Orison without King Joyse: the concept was strangely appalling. His absence was a pit yawning at her feet. "This whole thing was his idea. *He* wanted to fight Eremis this way. Who's giving the orders now?"

Geraden didn't flinch: he had regained his feet; felt as combative as she did. "We don't know. We've been down here most of the time. Probably nobody knows where to find us." He hesitated, then said, "With King Joyse gone and Castellan Lebbick dead, the whole place may be collapsing." Another flicker of hesitation. "They may have turned on the Prince."

That was true. Terisa imagined riots storming through the upper levels of the castle; panic and bloodshed. It was conceivable that Orison might destroy itself.

She wheeled on Adept Havelock.

"Where is he? This was *his* idea. *Your* idea. Curse that old man, we need him."

A sick feeling rose in her stomach as she saw Havelock hunch forward with conspiratorial glee; his eyes nearly gyrated in opposite directions, rapacious and loony. He crooked a finger at her, summoning her near, as if he wanted to tell her a secret.

She didn't move; nevertheless he reacted as if she had come closer to hear him.

"I have seen an Image," he whispered, "an Image, an Image. In which the women are peculiar. Their tits are on their backs. Because of this, they look very strange. But it must be delightful to embrace them."

Grinning, he concluded, "He came to me and commanded. *Commanded.* What could I do? I don't know how to beg." His manner didn't change, yet without transition his tone turned fierce. "I have said it and said it. Hop-board pieces are *men.* Women make everything impossible."

Terisa wanted to swear at him—and give him a hug as if he

needed comforting. Torn between anger and pity, she faced Geraden and Master Barsonage again. She included the mediator in what she was saying, but all of her attention and intensity were focused on Geraden.

"We've got to find out what's going on."

Both men nodded, Barsonage willingly, Geraden in passion and approval.

"Somebody has got to figure out what King Joyse intended to do now and make sure it gets done."

Master Barsonage hesitated. Geraden nodded again.

To the Master, she said, "We'll explain as soon as we get the chance. King Joyse set this all up. It's all deliberate." Then she took hold of Geraden's arm.

Clasping each other hard, they strode away into the passage which led to the storeroom, out of Adept Havelock's quarters.

Master Barsonage followed them quickly. The bristling of his eyebrows and the frown of his concentration gave him a look of unfamiliar certainty.

Behind them, Havelock picked up his featherduster and went back to cleaning his already immaculate mirrors. The particular glass he chose to work on now happened to show the Image in which he had found the flying brown cloud that he had used against Prince Kragen's catapults.

Like Castellan Lebbick, he had been abandoned.

He didn't seem to be aware that he was weeping like a child.

Terisa, Geraden, and Master Barsonage heard weeping, especially in the lower levels of the castle, where most of Orison's newer occupants had been crowded: small children; frightened women; helpless oldsters and invalids. They heard shouts of alarm and fear, cries of protest and distrust. They heard blows. Once they saw several guards raise the butts of their pikes to strike at men who wanted to break out of a closed corridor. The men cursed and pleaded as they were forced back; the rumor of Gart's attack had reached them, and they wanted to clear a path for their families out of Orison before Cadwal's army arrived from nowhere to butcher them all.

But there was no sign of a riot.

Instead of rioting, the castle was full of guards. They were everywhere, blocking the movement of people and panic, controlling access to crucial passages or stairs or doors, facing down farmers and

merchants and servants and stonemasons who wanted to attack or
flee with their loved ones because Orison had been penetrated.

"Who is in command?" Master Barsonage demanded of the
guards. "Where is King Joyse?"

The answer was, Pissed if I know. Or the equivalent.

"Where did you get your orders?" asked Geraden.

That was easier. Norge. Castellan Lebbick's second.

For the moment, the fact that Norge was actually only one of
the Castellan's seconds-in-command seemed unimportant. The point
was that power still existed in Orison. It was being held together by
someone from whom the guards were willing to take orders. Someone with enough credibility to be obeyed during an emergency.

Norge himself? What gave him precedence over the other captains? *Who* gave him precedence?

A Master of the Congery? Impossible. Never in the mediator's
absence.

One of King Joyse's counselors? One of Orison's lords?
Unlikely.

Prince Kragen himself? Inconceivable.

Artagel?

Was the situation so bad that no one could be found to take
charge except Geraden's independent-minded and slightly crippled
brother?

Terisa wanted to run. She would have run if Geraden hadn't
held her back.

As she and her companions left the castle's lower levels, however, Orison's mood improved. Here the halls were under better
control; less frightened by the possibility of an attack by Imagery.
Soon a guard appeared who saluted the mediator. "Master Barsonage," he panted. Apparently, he had come running from the Imager's
quarters. "Geraden. The lady Terisa?" He knew enough about the
day's events to be surprised. "You're wanted in the King's rooms."

The King's rooms? Terisa and Geraden and Master Barsonage
stopped in their tracks.

"The audience hall is no longer safe," explained the guard.

"*Who* wants us?" demanded Barsonage instantly.

Breathing hard, the guard replied, "My lord Tor. He says he's
taken command. In the King's absence. He and Norge. Norge is the
new Castellan."

The *Tor*. Terisa felt a surge of energy. Bless that old man!

"What about Prince Kragen?" she asked.

The guard hesitated as if he were unsure of how much he should say. After a moment, however, he answered, "It's just a rumor. I was told my lord Tor offered him an alliance."

Geraden let out a fierce cheer.

Together, he and Terisa started into a run.

Master Barsonage took time to pursue the question. "What was the Prince's reply?"

The guard said, "I don't know."

Barsonage did his best to catch up with Terisa and Geraden.

In the King's tower, more guards joined them, escorted them upward. Guards swept the King's doors open; Terisa, Geraden, and the mediator went in. For the sake of dignity—not to mention caution—they slowed their pace as they entered.

The King's formal apartment was just the way she remembered it—richly appointed, paneled blond, carpeted in blue and red. She hardly noticed the furnishings, however. Although there were only eight or ten men—most of them captains—in the room, it seemed crowded; too full of anxiety and passion, conflict.

Before the door closed, she heard Prince Kragen's voice blare like a trumpet, "*I will not do it!*"

Her chest tightened. She found suddenly that she was breathing harder than she had realized. The Prince's shout seemed to throb around her, and the hope she had felt at the idea of an alliance began to curdle.

On one side of Prince Kragen stood Artagel, close enough to react to what the Prince did, far enough away to dissociate himself from the Alend Contender. On the other side was a captain Terisa didn't know. Norge?

All three of them had their backs to the doors. Each in his separate way, they confronted the chair where King Joyse used to sit when he played hop-board.

There sat the Tor, slumping over his great belly as if he were barely able to keep himself from oozing out of the position he had assumed.

"The alternatives you propose," the old lord was saying as if he were in a kind of pain which had nothing to do with Prince Kragen, "are intolerable." He had a hand over his face. "I will not permit you to occupy Orison, making us little more than a hostage population. I do not call that an *alliance*."

"And I do not call it an *alliance* to wait outside in danger while you sit here in safety," retorted the Prince hotly. "If—no, *when* High

King Festten marches against us—we will be helpless while you remain secure, watching the outcome. *We must be allowed to enter Orison.* I *will not* remain where I am, waiting for King Joyse to return—if he ever does return—and tell me his pleasure—if his pleasure involves anything more productive than a game of hop-board."

The Tor didn't look strong enough to raise his head. "I understand your dilemma, my lord Prince. Of course I do. But you cannot believe that Orison's people—or Orison's defenders—will sit quietly on their hams while *Alend* takes power over them. I have already said that I will open the gates to you if you—"

"No!" Prince Kragen barked. "Do you take me for a fool? I have no intention of making Orison's people hostage. I will grant them precisely as much freedom and respect as the necessary crowding of so many bodies permits. But I will *not* submit my forces to your authority."

Orison's captains muttered restively. Some of them were viscerally incensed at the idea of an alliance with Alend. And some of them had noticed Geraden and Master Barsonage—had noticed Terisa—

"My lords!" Geraden cut in sharply. His voice carried potential authority across the room; and a thrill prickled suddenly down Terisa's back. "There's no need to argue about *waiting*. We're done *waiting*. It's time to march!"

The Tor snatched his hand down from his face, peered bleary pain and desire at Terisa and Geraden. Artagel wheeled with joy already catching fire across his features. Norge turned more cautiously; but Prince Kragen spun like Artagel, his swarthy face congested with conflicting needs.

"Terisa! My lady!" Artagel crowed. "Geraden! By the stars, you did it!" As if he had never been injured in his life, he caught Geraden in an exuberant bearhug, lifted him off his feet, then dropped him to snatch up Terisa's hand and kiss it hugely. "Everytime I see you, you're even more wonderful!"

She wanted to hug him, but she was distracted; there were too many other things going on. The captains were shouting encouragement to each other, or demanding silence. And the Tor had risen to his feet. Unsteadily, almost inaudibly, he murmured her name, Geraden's. "You are indeed wondrous." He spoke huskily, as if he were dragging his voice along the bottom of a cave. "There must be hope for us after all, if such blows can be struck against our enemies."

Prince Kragen was right behind Artagel; he grabbed Geraden

by the shoulders when Artagel dropped him. "How did you do it?" the Prince demanded. "How did you rescue her? What has changed? Where is King Joyse? Did you say *march?*"

Somehow, Norge made himself heard through the hubbub. His laconic tone sounded so incongruous that it had to be heeded.

"You got away, my lady. What did you learn from him?

"What did you do to him?"

In the stark silence which followed, a moment passed before she understood the point of his question.

With her chin jutting unconsciously, she met the hot and eager and worried stares of the men around her. "I didn't do anything to him." I didn't kill him. I didn't even hurt him. "But I learned enough."

Too quickly for anyone to interrupt her, she added, "Before Gilbur killed him, I had a long talk with Master Quillon. He told me what King Joyse has been doing all this time. Why he's been acting like a passive fool. What he wanted to accomplish. Geraden is right. It's time to march."

In response, the room burst into tumult. Only Prince Kragen had been given any hint of the things she knew; and he had only heard pieces of the story from Geraden under the influence of too much wine, not from her. For a man like the Tor, who had spent so many miserable days praying that his besotted and stubborn loyalty would prove valuable in the end, her words must have struck as heavily as a blow. Norge and Prince Kragen and Artagel were surprised; Master Barsonage and the captains, astonished. But the Tor's cheeks turned the color of wet flour, and he sank down in King Joyse's chair as if his heart were being torn out.

Urgently, Terisa pushed between Artagel and Prince Kragen, hurried to the lord. "Get him some wine!" she called. "Oh, shit. He's having a heart attack.

"My lord Tor. Are you all right?"

His hands fluttered against the arms of the chair. For a moment, he gagged as if he were choking; under his lowered eyelids, his eyes rolled wildly. Then, however, he took a breath that made all his fat quiver. He raised one hand to his chest, knotted it in his robe; and his head lifted as if he were pulling it up by main strength.

"Do not be alarmed, my lady," he wheezed thinly. "The difficulty is only that I have pawned all I am for him. I have made myself contemptible for the belief that my King would at last prove worthy of service." With remarkable celerity, one of the captains brought forward a flagon of wine. Then Tor accepted it and gulped a drink.

Then torment clenched his features. "Did you truly mean to suggest that he has been acting according to a plan—that the things he has done have had a purpose?"

"Yes," she avowed at once, despite the fact that at the moment she would cheerfully have wrung King Joyse's neck. "He didn't know you would come here. You heard him say you defy prediction." The explanation Master Quillon had given her wasn't good enough to justify the cost King Joyse had exacted from men like Castellan Lebbick and the Tor, from his daughters, from Geraden and everybody else who loved him. "His plans didn't include you. He didn't mean to hurt you." For the time being, she supported the King, not because she approved of what he had done, but because he had left her no alternative.

"All this time, he's been working to save Mordant."

Until now. That thought was enough to turn the edges of her vision black with bitterness. King Joyse put his people through the anguish of the doomed. And just when events arrived at the point when he could have safely explained his policy, safely given at least that much meaning or justification to the people he had hurt, he chose to disappear. *To go kiting off*, as Adept Havelock had said.

Nevertheless she took his side as if she had never doubted him.

"He didn't know who the renegades were—the Imagers who were willing to translate abominations against people who couldn't defend themselves. He didn't know where they made their mirrors, where they built their power."

When she began, she was speaking to the Tor alone; she hadn't intended to address the entire gathering. But King Joyse's intentions carried her further than her own. As she spoke, her voice rose, and she turned partly away from the Tor to include everyone in the room.

"He knew they needed soldiers to back up their Imagery. Imagery can destroy, but *rule* requires manpower. But he didn't know what alliances they might have made, with Cadwal or Alend. There was only one thing he could be sure of. As long as he was the strongest ruler here—as long as Mordant was strong enough to fight back both Cadwal and Alend—the renegades would leave him alone. They would chip away at the Alend Lieges, or find a way to swallow Cadwal—but they would leave him alone. Until they were too strong to be stopped."

She had to raise her voice more, until she was nearly.shouting. That was the only way she could control her frustration and grief.

He had smiled at her so gloriously that she would have done anything for him. And he had caused so much pain—

"The only way he could find out who they were, how they worked, where their power was before they grew too strong—the only way he could bring them out into the open—was to make himself weak. He had to convince everybody, *everybody,* that he had lost his will, his sense, his determination. He had to make himself the only reasonable target.

"*So that they would attack here.*

"So that he would have a chance to stop them. A chance to surprise them by turning their own traps against them."

She had ruined that, of course. She had warned Eremis. Her bitterness included herself: she hadn't earned the right to be self-righteous. Yet her culpability only made her more determined.

"That's what we have to do. I don't know why he isn't here. He's been working toward this moment for years. I don't know why he's abandoned us now." If he went to rescue Queen Madin— That was understandable, but it didn't help. At that distance, he wouldn't be able to return until long after the battle was decided. Terisa made an effort to steady herself, calm her raw anger. "It doesn't matter. We're still here. We still have to save Orison and Mordant.

"We don't have any choice. He hasn't left us any choice. The only thing we can do is what he would do if he were here. We've got to march."

The room was still; the men around her listened with all their senses, avidly. Geraden's face shone as if nothing could stop him now. Artagel nodded to himself happily. Prince Kragen's eyes were dark with dismay and calculation—and with something else, which might have been eagerness. Master Barsonage gaped, his mouth hanging open; he gave the impression that he was reeling inside.

"March," muttered the Tor, struggling to straighten his spine against the back of his chair. "'So that they would attack here.' My old friend. How I must have hurt you."

Finally, however, it was Norge who asked the obvious question. "March where, my lady?"

She was so full of pressure that she could hardly articulate the word:

"Esmerel."

At once, Geraden supported her. "That's Eremis' family Seat. Apparently, that's where he has his laborium. That's where he and

Gilbur took her. And Vagel is there. Gart is there. *Cadwal* is there. Eremis consulted with the High King there this morning.

"That's where we need to strike."

Terisa was thinking, In the Care of Tor. Where those riders with the red fur and the hate-filled eyes had come from to attack her and Geraden. No wonder they had been mounted on horses with tack from the Tor's Care.

The old lord's mind was running in a completely different direction, however. "That explains it, then," he rumbled.

He braced himself upright with an arm on one side, an elbow on the other. Canted in this posture as if his weight were about to overturn the chair, he muttered, "That is why he told Lebbick to do whatever he wanted to her. He had to appear weak—had to seem like he had lost his reason. He had to persuade *me*. If I had failed to believe him, I could have betrayed him to Eremis.

"At the same time, he sent Master Quillon to remove her from the dungeon, so that no one would suffer from his feigned weakness—so that Lebbick would not have a crime on his heart—so that she would not be harmed.

"At last I understand."

The Tor looked like a man whose hands had just been released from thumbscrews.

"And we have another reason to march now," Geraden went on in a tone which Terisa would have found impossible to refuse. "In Esmerel, the lady Terisa discovered Nyle alive."

That announcement snatched most of the eyes in the room to him. Something in Artagel leaped up: his expression was as keen as a honed blade.

"I didn't kill him." Geraden spoke through his teeth, restraining outrage. Now he didn't need the strange authority which sometimes came to him: his bone-bred passion was enough. "I never lifted a hand against him. Eremis forced his help by threatening my family. *Our* family," he said to the sharpness in Artagel's face. "Nyle pretended I stabbed him. Then Eremis carried him off. He called for the physician Underwell, who was almost exactly Nyle's size and coloring. He had Underwell butchered by creatures of Imagery. Then he dressed Underwell in Nyle's clothes to make it look like I came back to finish what I started."

This was news to the Tor, as well as to the captains. They stared at Geraden in undisguised astonishment.

"But Nyle is still alive. Eremis has him chained to a wall in Esmerel. To use against me if I ever try to fight him.

"I'm a son of the Domne." Geraden held himself powerfully still. "My family have been dear and loyal friends to King Joyse and Mordant from the beginning, and I want my brother rescued!"

Yes! Terisa said with the way she lifted her head, the way she carried herself. *Yes*.

"It's a simple question, really," Artagel drawled into the silence when Geraden was finished. His nonchalant manner contrasted dramatically with the flame of combat in his eyes. "As my lady Terisa says, we don't have any choice. We've already let the Perdon be destroyed." His stance was casual, but his hands curled as if they ached to hold a sword. "If we don't return to King Joyse's policy of supporting his lords—and do it soon—we'll lose everything that holds Mordant together, whether Eremis and Festten beat us or not. Everything that made Mordant worthwhile will be gone."

Terisa smiled at him. She was trying to express thanks, gratitude; but the tension in her muscles made her grin too fierce for that.

The Tor took a deep breath, then gasped. The flagon dropped from his hand, spilling wine across the rug; but he didn't notice it. He looked at Norge, nearly squinting to get his eyes into focus; he looked at Prince Kragen.

"I am content." His voice was flat, curiously unresonant. Apparently, Gart's kick still pained him. "Let us call the matter settled. Tomorrow we will march against Master Eremis in Esmerel."

Terisa wanted to applaud until she heard Prince Kragen rasp, "No."

"My lord Prince?" A fine dew of sweat covered the Tor's forehead.

"I am not *content*." Kragen chewed the words under his moustache as if they were gristle and gall. "I do not call the matter settled. You have proposed an *alliance*—on which we have been utterly unable to agree. Now you announce your intention to march away on a fool's mission. Is it your intention that Alend should march with you?" His tone sounded oddly conflicted to Terisa, at once furious and hungry, as if his passion had another name than the one he chose to give it. "Is that what an *alliance* means to you now? Do you believe that the Alend Monarch will be *content* to let all his strength commit suicide beside you, for no other reason than because you have decided to die insanely?"

Artagel started to retort; Geraden stopped him.

"You have a better idea, my lord Prince?" Geraden asked. His voice made Terisa shiver: it was thick with hinted promises or threats.

"Of course!" the Prince snapped. "An alliance *here*. In Orison. Let the High King come against us *here* and do his worst. Together, we will withstand him."

"What about Nyle?" demanded Artagel, unable to restrain himself.

Geraden ignored his brother. "I don't think so," he answered Prince Kragen. "Eremis doesn't need to come here. He can attack us anywhere by Imagery. While we stay in one place, *any* place, we're powerless, vulnerable. Without risking one Cadwal, he can fill Orison with enough horrors to leave even you screaming, my lord Prince. The only reason he hasn't done it so far is that he isn't ready. *Wasn't* ready. All he needed is time. He's ready now. If we don't carry the fight to him *now,* High King Festten and his twenty thousand men won't have to do anything except come here at their leisure and clean out the ruins. We'll all be dead or scattered."

As well as she could, Terisa controlled her frustration at Prince Kragen, her fear of the things she remembered. "Eremis—" she said, then swallowed hard to steady herself. "Eremis knows how to use flat glass safely. He's discovered an oxidate which lets him translate a flat glass into a curved one, so that whatever is in the curved Image can be translated straight to whatever is in the flat Image."

Master Barsonage and Geraden had had time to absorb this information. They didn't flinch. And they didn't interrupt her.

"Didn't Geraden tell you?" she asked the Prince. "Eremis dropped an *avalanche* out of nowhere onto Vale House. That's how he was able to kidnap Queen Madin. And he has a flat mirror with *the audience hall* in the Image. He could bring an avalanche in there right now if he wanted to. And we know he has at least two other mirrors that show parts of Orison. His rooms. That place in the lower levels—near the dungeons. Maybe he has more.

"But that's not all. Vagel—the *arch-Imager* Vagel—has devised a system that allows him to create specific Images deliberately, instead of by trial and error."

Despite the fact that she had already told Master Barsonage this, the mediator looked like he was on the brink of apoplexy.

"And Gilbur has the talent to make mirrors quickly," Terisa continued. "Together, they can shape enough Images to attack Orison anywhere, anytime.

"Eremis is ready now. It isn't suicide to march. It's suicide to stay here."

A murmur rose from the captains—agreement, worry, caution.

"Perhaps." For a moment, Prince Kragen's eagerness seemed to outweigh his outrage. "Perhaps in that, you are right." As if by an act of will, however, he brought back his indignation. "Yet if it is madness to remain here, it is not therefore sane to march against Esmerel."

He glanced at the Tor. Briefly, he appeared to consider addressing his challenge to Terisa. But at last he turned to Geraden and Artagel, drawn to them by the blood-claim of Nyle's imprisonment—and by Geraden's new stature.

Dangerously calm, he inquired, "You have some acquaintance with Esmerel, I suppose?"

Artagel nodded without hesitation. Geraden said distinctly, "Some."

"I have heard reports of the terrain. Who will be favored in a battle there?"

"Good question," Norge observed equably.

Artagel grinned. "Whoever gets there first. The entrenched forces can pick their ground. It's a trap for whoever arrives second."

Geraden shook his head, dismissing the issue. "Why do you think Eremis chose that place, my lord Prince? You didn't think it was an accident. You didn't think High King Festten drove twenty thousand men there just for the pleasure of *annihilating* the Perdon."

"No, Geraden"—Prince Kragen allowed himself a snarl of sarcasm—"I did not think it was an accident. It is *your* thinking I question, not my own. Did you not hear Artagel use the word *trap?* You say that Nyle is intended as a hostage against you. Is he not also intended as *bait?* A march to Esmerel is precisely the action Eremis wishes us to take."

"Of course," Geraden retorted.

"That's one reason I was captured," commented Terisa. "More bait. Eremis wanted to have me where I couldn't hurt him." He wanted to rape me. He wanted to break Geraden. "But he also wanted to make sure you went to Esmerel. All of you."

"Everything he's ever done us to us is a trap," Geraden continued. "that's his great strength—and his great weakness."

"And you still believe we should go?" Prince Kragen's protest was an inextricable mixture of excitement and fury. "*Knowing* he has set this trap to destroy us, you believe that we should accommodate him—that we should rush to put our necks in his noose for him? Geraden, you *are* mad." Wheeling toward the Tor, he unleashed a shout. "My lord, *this is madness!*"

The Tor sat in his chair like a lump of stale dough and waited for Geraden's answer.

To Terisa's surprise, Geraden started laughing.

His laughter was like Artagel's grin: bloody-minded; ready for battle.

"That's King Joyse's method. His policy. Don't you understand? He sets his traps inside Eremis'. If he were here to spring them himself, it would make your head reel. But he isn't here, so we've got to do it for him. We've got to put our necks in Eremis' noose— and then take it away from him. We've got to walk into his trap and turn it against him."

Prince Kragen stared as if Geraden were breaking out in boils. So flabbergasted that his sarcasm deserted him, he asked, "How—? How do you think we can do that? He has at least twenty thousand men. He has Imagery. He has the terrain. He has at least one hostage. How can we possibly turn his trap against him?"

No longer laughing, Geraden replied, "By being stronger than he expects."

When Geraden said that, Terisa permitted herself a sigh of relief. Master Barsonage jerked up his head, listening intently. The Tor brushed a hand through the sweat on his forehead, then rubbed his fingers on his robe.

"How?" Prince Kragen pursued, nearly whispering. "In what way are we stronger than he expects?"

Geraden shrugged. "For one thing, there's no way he could have planned for Terisa's talent—or mine either. That's why he's worked so hard to distract us, confuse us, keep us guessing. He didn't know what he was up against—and he didn't want us to find out what we can do. He couldn't possibly know I'm an Adept, of a certain kind. I can shift the Images in normal mirrors, whether I made them or not."

"That is true," Master Barsonage averred. "I have witnessed it."

"And Terisa is even more powerful," Geraden went on. "What I do with curved glass, she can do with flat mirrors. *And* she's an arch-Imager. She can pass through flat glass without losing her mind. *And* she can use her talent across incredible distances. That's how she escaped. From as far away as Esmerel, she shifted a mirror *here* until she was in the Image. Then Adept Havelock translated her out of danger."

"That also is true." The mediator of the Congery seemed to be taking bulk with every passing moment, growing larger or more substantial as the tenets of Imagery were altered. "I have witnessed it.

"And I am another way in which we are stronger than Master Eremis expects."

Prince Kragen swung to face Master Barsonage. Geraden and Artagel turned. Terisa studied the Tor to be sure he was holding himself together, then directed her attention to the mediator.

"I mean that the Congery is stronger," Barsonage amended as if his own certainty surprised him. "We have not been held in much esteem. Why should we be? Generally, we are little more than a body of discontented ditherers. And all our actions in defense of Mordant—and of ourselves—went awry. Oh, the augury we cast for Mordant's future was well done. On the other hand, the summoning of our champion was a disaster. Why should anyone esteem us? We did not esteem ourselves enough to preserve our own usefulness after we saw how badly we had gone wrong with our champion.

"But then we learned of Geraden's talent—and of the lady Terisa's. That restored us immeasurably. We did not know whether these new talents would be used to harm or benefit us. No, Artagel," he digressed, "even after your explanations, we still had room for doubt. But we knew now that our work was vital—that we had unleashed forces which only we could support or oppose—that the Congery had at last come into its own significance.

"Therefore we set to work as we had never worked before.

"And now we have been vindicated." That was the linchpin of Master Barsonage's new sureness. "We have been given proof that King Joyse was always in the right—that Images possess their own full independent reality, that the things we see in mirrors are not created by Imagery. The Congery's establishment has been justified." He was elevated by clarity; his face shone. "the translations of Master Eremis and Master Gilbur and the arch-Imager Vagel are not merely evil in their *consequences,* but also in their *means.*"

"The point," growled Prince Kragen. "Come to the point."

"My lord Prince," the mediator announced, "my lord Tor, Master Eremis is ready. That is evident. The Congery is ready also. In the name of King Joyse—and of Mordant's need—we are prepared to do battle at your side against Esmerel."

"How?" The Prince had an unflagging interest in that question. "What can you do?"

Master Barsonage's smile bore an unfamiliar resemblance to a smirk. "My lord Prince, you have not agreed to an alliance. For that reason, I will not discuss our weapons with you. But two things I will tell you. First, our weapons violate none of the strictures which King Joyse has placed upon the Congery. And second"—he paused for a moment of frank self-congratulation—"until weapons are necessary, we can *supply* the march to Esmerel."

Prince Kragen's mouth formed the word *supply* without a sound.

"We cannot translate men, of course," the mediator explained, "but we are prepared to move food, swords, bedding, or tents in whatever quantity you require. You will be able to travel without supply-wains, without the vast entourage of camp followers and porters which slows you. You will be able to reach Esmerel more swiftly than Master Eremis can possibly guess.

"My lord Prince, does that not make us stronger?"

"And then there's the matter of an alliance," Geraden put in before Prince Kragen could recover from his surprise. "Eremis must know it's a possibility, but he can't *expect* it. What do you have, my lord Prince? Roughly ten thousand men?"

The Prince nodded dumbly.

"And what about us, Castellan Norge?"

Norge consulted the ceiling. "Near eight thousand altogether. We can put six thousand on the road and still leave enough here to keep the defenses going for a while."

"My lord Prince"—Geraden spoke carefully, controlling his emotion—"Eremis doesn't expect to face an army of sixteen thousand. High King Festten doesn't expect it. They don't want to fight us. They want to overwhelm us." He didn't need to say the word, *annihilate:* it was implicit in his tone. "And they don't have the strength to overwhelm sixteen thousand men."

For a few moments, Prince Kragen didn't answer; he chewed his moustache and glowered at his thoughts. Geraden kept himself still. Terisa held her breath. Norge appeared to be wondering whether this might be an opportune time for a nap. In contrast, Artagel was barely able to refrain from hopping from foot to foot like an excited boy. The Tor clamped both arms over his belly as if he feared that something inside him might burst.

Abruptly, the Prince turned to face the old lord.

He cocked his fists on his hips. Terisa couldn't tell which took precedence in him, his eagerness or his anger; but he didn't prolong the suspense.

"My lord Tor," he said clearly, "you ask too much."

The Tor raised an inquiring hand, lifted an eyebrow. The effort brought sweat rolling down the bridge of his nose.

"If this alliance you propose fails," Kragen articulated, "you can retreat to Orison. You have two thousand men for a final defense. I have nothing. *All* the Alend Monarch's might will be destroyed, and my people will have no defense left between the Pestil River and the mountains. I can *not* risk my father's entire monarchy on this business of necks and nooses.

"I will not go. I advise you not to go."

Terisa wanted to yell at him; she wanted to hit him with her fists. *Don't you understand? We've got to try.* She contained herself, however, because Geraden was clenched still, unprotesting, and Artagel had gone ominously quiet.

In a dull rumble, the Tor asked, "What *do* you advise, my lord Prince?"

"Fight for Orison as long as you can," replied the Prince. "Then join me across the Pestil. Bring the Fayle and the Termigan—bring the Armigite, if you can bear him—and add your forces to mine. With the Alend Lieges behind us, we will make Eremis and Festten pay dearly for every foot of ground they take."

To himself, the Tor made a muttering noise, as if he were considering the idea. But before Terisa could panic—before Geraden could intervene—he heaved himself to his feet.

He tottered. Afraid he might fall, she reached out to support him. What was left of his hair straggled with sweat; his skin had a gray underhue, as if his heart pumped ashes rather than blood; his eyes were glazed, nearly opaque.

Nevertheless he spoke as if no one could doubt that he would be obeyed.

"Castellan Norge, do you hear me?"

"I hear you, my lord Tor." Norge sounded vaguely somnolent: detached; impervious to argument.

"Escort my lord Prince out of Orison. I want him returned safely to his father. Safely and politely. Do you hear me?"

"I hear you, my lord Tor."

"We march against Esmerel at dawn. Be ready. Confer with the Congery on the matter of supplies."

Master Barsonage nodded assent.

"Yes, my lord Tor." This time, there was a small bite in Norge's tone, a touch of grim happiness.

Prince Kragen threw up his hands.

"Wait a minute." Artagel wore his battle grin. He was unarmed, but at the moment he didn't look like he needed a weapon. "You're talking about marching into the teeth of the siege. Is that wise, my lord Tor? Shouldn't we keep Prince Kragen with us? A hostage of our own? If we let him go, he can cut us down as soon as we ride out of here."

"No," the Tor said at once. The flatness in his tone was turning to nausea. "*That* the Alend Contender will not do. He knows where we go, and why. He may well resume his attack on Orison when we are gone. For that reason, we will leave two thousand men behind us, and someone reliable to lead them. But he will not harm or hinder us."

Terisa wanted to ask, Are you sure? The mix of emotions on Prince Kragen's face was too complex to give her much confidence. Maybe that was what he planned: a killing attack as soon as the guard left Orison? Unexpectedly, however, the Prince's excitement seemed to gain the upper hand for a moment.

"Thank you, my lord Tor." He spoke softly; yet his voice carried a hint of trumpets. "Rely on my respect. If my father's friends were as honorable as King Joyse's, Alend would have no need of Contenders to win the Seat."

Kragen turned to go. Norge sent two captains to accompany him until more guards could be mustered. Nevertheless Terisa didn't see his departure. She was busy trying to catch the Tor's great weight as it tumbled to the floor.

The old lord had fainted.

FORTY-FOUR:
MEN GO FORTH

erisa and Geraden wanted to talk to Artagel—they wanted to know in detail what had happened in Orison during their absence—but for most of the day he had no time. He was busy with Norge, supporting the new Castellan's authority, and the Tor's, against anyone who doubted it, distrusted it. Of course, he had no official standing, no authority of his own. That, however, only increased his credibility. He was Artagel, the best swordsman in Mordant—and a son of the Domne. Since King Joyse's decline, he was the closest thing Orison had to a popular hero. And he wasn't actually a member of the guard—wasn't actually under Norge's command. His word, his simple presence at Norge's side, threw more weight than half a dozen catapults.

Failing Artagel, Terisa and Geraden would have been content with Master Barsonage. But the mediator was busy as well. He had to ready the Congery for battle. And he had to make all the arrangements for supplying the guard. In practice, this meant determining with Norge's seconds what supplies were necessary, in what quantities, and then issuing explicit instructions for the placement of those supplies in manageable piles in the vast disused ballroom outside the laborium.

Since the Congery had rediscovered its sense of purpose, the Masters had been busy. Working from the formula Barsonage had used to create the mirror of his augury, one of them had chanced to shape a flat glass which showed the ballroom. With as much haste as possible, two other Masters had succeeded at duplicating that new mirror; one glass alone would have been too slow—and would have placed too much strain on the Master who had made it. Along with its other weapons, the Congery intended to carry these mirrors on the march. Then the supplies which had been piled in the ballroom could be translated to Orison's army at need.

Because the mediator had to put these plans into effect, Terisa and Geraden were left with no comfortable source of information.

Ribuld was almost gleefully glad to see them. Especially after Lebbick's death—which he had been unable to prevent—the scarred veteran was eager to assign himself the job of protecting them. And he was happy to talk. From him, they heard about Saddith's fate. On the other hand, he couldn't answer the pertinent questions—couldn't explain, for instance, how the maid had come to serve as a diversion for the breaking of Geraden's mirror. He didn't know the things Terisa and Geraden most wanted to hear.

For most of the day—what was left of it, at any rate—they had to rely on each other's company.

This didn't particularly distress them.

They had given the Tor over into the care of a physician, who had assured them that the old lord had the constitution of a stoat and would almost certainly recover as soon as he began to consume a diet more nourishing than wine alone—with the proviso, of course, that Gart's kick hadn't produced any interior bleeding. After the physician had reassured them, Terisa and Geraden went to her former rooms in the tower, the peacock rooms.

They explained to Ribuld that they were waiting to talk to either Artagel or Master Barsonage; and Ribuld promised to hound Artagel and the mediator with reminders. Then they closed the door and bolted it.

Suddenly giddy with relief and suppressed hysteria, they wedged a chair into the wardrobe—where her clothes still hung—to block the entrance from the passage inside the wall. "Anybody who tries to sneak in here," he said, "is going to crack his shins."

Laughing so that they wouldn't weep, they welcomed each other back as if they had been apart for months.

"Ah, love," he murmured some time later, when he had become calm, "I came so close to reaching you. That was worse than being helpless, I think. There I was, doing something so amazing that it turns everything we know about Imagery upside down, and Eremis made it all useless just by putting out the lights." He paused, then admitted, "Havelock had to sit on me to keep me from going after you anyway."

"But you weren't really helpless, were you." This was important to her.

As always, what she said was more interesting to him than his own pain. "What do you mean?"

"You couldn't reach me," she explained, "you couldn't rescue me directly. But with that power there must have been dozens of things you could have done. You could have translated guards into Esmerel to look for me. Hundreds of them."

He peered at her in a way that made her want to hug him again because he so obviously wasn't hurt, didn't interpret what she said as criticism. All he said was, "I didn't have time."

"I know that, you idiot." Instead of hugging him, she tickled his ribs. "That's not the point."

He caught her hand by the wrist and punished her attack by nibbling gently on the tips of her fingers. Between nips, he asked, "What *is* the point?"

"The point is"—it was amazing, really, just how much difficulty she had concentrating while he sucked her fingers—"You weren't helpless. If I hadn't done that shift, you could have found a way to strike back. You would have found a way." Determined to be serious, she repeated, "You weren't helpless."

"Of course I'm helpless," he replied around her fingers. "I'm completely at your mercy."

"Idiot," she said again.

But she didn't have any trouble thinking of something to do for him while he was at her mercy.

Still later, when her own sense of postponed fright had receded, she murmured softly into his shoulder, "What would we have done?"

He analyzed that for a while before he remarked, "I have no idea what you're talking about."

"If the Tor hadn't agreed with us," she explained. "If Norge hadn't agreed with him. If they hadn't put themselves in charge of Orison. What would we have done?"

He stared up at one of the peacock-feather decorations on the wall. "Well, *somebody* had to take command. We would have persuaded *him*."

"And what if he turned us down?"

Geraden considered the question. "I guess we would have left with Prince Kragen. We would have tried to persuade him—or Elega—or maybe even Margonal himself—to back us up.

"I know," he added when she started to object, "Prince Kragen is the one who wants to stay here. But that's only because the Tor wants to go. If he didn't have any hope of an alliance with Orison— if he knew he couldn't get in here without spending all the lives that would take, making himself that much weaker—he might have been persuaded to march. If Elega took our side. If he thought he didn't have anything else to try."

"And what," she continued, "if we couldn't persuade him."

He shrugged under her head. "Then we probably would have to get back into Orison. We'd have to get anybody who agreed with us—Artagel, maybe some of the Masters, maybe some friends of Ribuld's—and use one of Adept Havelock's mirrors to translate our-selves to Esmerel. Try a surprise raid."

She reached across his chest to hug him. "So we wouldn't have given up."

He held her hard. Through his teeth, he muttered, "You suit yourself. I wouldn't give up if I had to walk there alone and take Esmerel apart with my fingernails."

That was what she wanted to hear. Feeling at once more relaxed and readier for battle, she asked casually, "Has it occurred to you that we're luckier than we look?"

"'Luckier'?" he inquired.

"Or King Joyse is. If it weren't for Elega, we probably wouldn't have been able to talk our way in here. If it weren't for the Cas-tellan"—she felt a pang whenever she remembered Lebbick—"Gart would probably have killed you and Artagel and Prince Kragen and the Tor. If it weren't for the Tor, Orison might be in chaos by now. Eremis hasn't won yet. We're still able to lay here and make love and talk about fighting." Geraden kissed her, but she didn't stop. "We've been *lucky*."

In an unexpectedly somber tone, he returned, "Or King Joyse is better at this game than anybody realizes."

She nodded. After a moment, she said, "I wonder why he can't beat Havelock at hop-board."

Geraden looked at her sharply. "That's an interesting question. Do you suppose it's just because Havelock is out of his mind most of the time?"

That sounded plausible. Terisa started to say, I guess so. But then, unaccountably, she remembered the time Adept Havelock had come to her rooms—had sneaked in through the secret passage and taken her to Master Quillon, so that Quillon could give her the raw materials with which to think about Mordant's need. He hadn't exactly been in one of his lucid phases. And yet he had said—

She groped for the memory momentarily; then it came to her, as clear as the note of a well-made chime.

No one understands hop-board. The King tries to protect his pieces.

King Joyse had protected her, protected Geraden. Had tried to protect the Tor. At some personal cost, he had done what he could to protect his wife and daughters. It was even conceivable that he had tried to protect Castellan Lebbick.

Individuals. What good are they? Worthless. It's all strategy. Sacrifice the right men to trap your opponent.

Maybe that was the truth. Maybe King Joyse couldn't outplay the Adept because he couldn't match Havelock's ruthlessness.

Maybe that was why he was gone now. Maybe he was out on a mad chase after Torrent and Queen Madin, driven by a need to protect individuals without regard to his overall strategy

Did that fundamental flaw cripple everything? Was his policy fatally marred by his inability to sacrifice individuals for the sake of something larger?

Geraden must have felt her shivering: he tightened his arms around her suddenly. "Terisa," he murmured, "love. What's the matter?"

She couldn't explain, not directly; the idea scaring her was too elusive, almost metaphysical. Instead, she said, "Do you remember the time King Joyse asked me to find a way out of a stalemate? It was the day after Master Gilbur translated his champion." That memory did little to improve her morale. "You rescued me from the Castellan by persuading the Tor to send for me in King Joyse's name."

Geraden nodded. "I remember."

"After you got me to the King's rooms," she continued for her own sake rather than for his, strengthening her grip on what she meant, "he showed me a hop-board problem. A stalemate. He said Havelock set it up for him. He said there was a way out, but he couldn't find it."

Her shivers mounted. "So I tipped all the men off the board. No more stalemate."

"I remember," Geraden repeated, trying to steady her.

"I think I almost made him sick. He was almost in tears."

He had said, *To you, it's just a game. To me, it's the difference between life and ruin.*

And he had said, *I suggest that you give the matter more consideration before you once again attempt to end a stalemate by tilting the board.*

"Geraden, what if that's what we're doing? Tilting the board?"

Instead of doing what King Joyse wants. Protecting his pieces. Or what Havelock wants. Sacrificing the right men.

"Do you think we should go alone?" Geraden countered. "Against Eremis and Gilbur and Vagel and terrible Imagery and twenty thousand men?"

Abruptly, her trembling stopped; it fell away from her like an old panic fading into the dark.

"No," she said distinctly. That would be sacrificing men for no reason. "We wouldn't stand a chance. Even if we could fight all that Imagery, we couldn't stop High King Festten.

"It's just that I agree with King Joyse. Somehow, he persuaded me he's right by leaving us in the lurch. At first, I was angry. But now I think I'm starting to understand."

Geraden studied her face. "Terisa, you aren't making any sense."

"I know." She mustered another indirect effort to explain herself. "Did I ever tell you about Reverend Thatcher?"

"The man who ran the 'mission' where you served before I came to you."

She kissed Geraden's nose quickly. "I probably told you he was futile. Sad—hopeless. He must have felt that way. But he taught me something— Something I didn't understand for a long time.

"He was trying to help the most miserable people in the city. Indigents. Street people. Crazies. Drunks. Trying to give them food and clothing and maybe shelter. And that was hard because nobody wanted to pay for it. If you feed and clothe and shelter them today, what have you accomplished? All you've done is save their lives, so they'll need more food and clothing and shelter tomorrow. So if you have money and want to do some good, giving it to that mission is like throwing it away. There must be hundreds of things you can use your money for that would do more good for the city as a whole."

"Yes, but—" began Geraden.

"Yes, but," she agreed. "Doing good for the city as a whole wouldn't make those poor people go away. It wouldn't make their

misery go away. And Reverend Thatcher couldn't stop caring about
them. If you gave him a choice between"—she searched for an example—"I don't know, between free education for the whole city
and helping one drunk get through another day with a hot meal, he'd
choose to help the drunk. Not because he didn't think education is
important, but because he couldn't help caring about the drunk.

"Maybe that's sad. Maybe it's even stupid. It's certainly
hopeless.

"But it's also wonderful."

She stopped as if she had made herself clear.

Geraden had to struggle for a couple of minutes, but eventually
he reached the conclusion she hadn't been able to articulate. "King
Joyse," he said slowly, "persuaded you he was right by abandoning
us. You think he went after Torrent—after Queen Madin. When
somebody he loves is in danger, he forgets all about Mordant—all
about his plans for saving his kingdom. He leaves that to us. Not
because he doesn't think Mordant is important, but because he can't
help caring about her."

Terisa's spirit lifted. "He isn't an idealist—not really. If anyone
here is an idealist, it's Havelock. King Joyse didn't create Mordant
and the Congery out of an abstract set of beliefs. He did it because
people he knew and cared about were being hurt in the wars—hurt
by Imagery. He wanted to save the world, a world made up of individual farmers and merchants and children who couldn't defend
themselves.

"Don't forget that he risked a lot to protect *us*. Treating us the
way he did, he confused us—even hurt us. But that gave Eremis a
reason not to kill us. And we were left free to make our own choices.
Just to keep us alive, King Joyse took the risk that we might go
against him completely. Just to protect our lives and our choices.

"And," she concluded, "he trusts us to do the same thing for
him. He trusts us to defend Mordant for him while he's out trying
to rescue his wife."

As if a knot of tension had been released in him, Geraden collapsed back on the bed. Happily, he said, "I knew there was *some*
good reason why I love that old man."

"Besides," she went on, now that she was sure of herself; "we
aren't the ones who want to tilt the board. That's what Eremis is
doing. What we're doing may not be right, but we aren't making that
mistake."

"No," he assented. Eagerness brightened his eyes and animated his features, making him inexpressibly precious to her. "We aren't making *that* mistake."

For the time being, she was content.

Just when it seemed, however, that she had reached the point where she no longer worried about what anybody else in Orison did, Master Barsonage arrived in answer to Ribuld's messages. She and Geraden kept the mediator waiting only long enough to put on some clothes; then they admitted him to her sitting room.

"Sleeping all day while Orison bustles, I see," the Imager commented pleasantly while he closed the door. He looked happier than she had ever seen him: activity and a clear sense of purpose agreed with him. "Well, doubtless you need the rest. I can only imagine the exertions and perils which you have endured.

"Since my imagination has not been all it should be, as you know"—he seated himself, frowned into the empty wine decanter, then shrugged his thick shoulders—"I am eager to hear what has happened to the rest of Mordant. The siege has cut us off completely," he explained. "We know nothing but what we have learned from you and Prince Kragen."

Terisa blew a sigh. "That's going to take a while," she said; and Geraden went to the door, chuckling. Outside, he asked Ribuld for wine and food.

Ribuld made some retort she didn't catch; then Geraden returned. "Ribuld says we can have anything we want, if we don't mind waiting. Apparently, there's no end of servants available, but the kitchens are in chaos, trying to get supplies"—he glowered humorously at Master Barsonage—"ready for tomorrow."

"That is true," replied the mediator with a nod. "An appalling situation, in fact. No one knows what to do. Norge or one of his captains has to make every decision. It seems that Castellan Lebbick established plans and procedures for every conceivable eventuality—except a march.

"And, of course, every man who carries a sack of meal or a keg of water or a bale of hay to the ballroom goes in terror of his life, expecting to be translated away into madness at any moment." Master Barsonage permitted himself a growl of disgust. "If Norge were not so phlegmatic—and if Artagel were less supportive—we would be in worse danger of riots now than at any other time today."

Terisa and Geraden glanced at each other. "As Terisa says," Geraden remarked to the mediator, "our story is going to take a while. Why don't we wait for supper?" He set two chairs facing Master Barsonage and sat down in one of them; following his example, Terisa took the other. "Maybe by then Artagel will join us, and we won't have to go over the same things twice.

"In the meantime, you can tell us how the preparations are going."

Just for a moment, the Imager looked doubtfully at Geraden's proposal; he seemed to think Geraden intended to avoid answering him. Almost at once, however, he inhaled deeply, shook his head as if to rearrange his thoughts, and smiled in acquiescence.

While Terisa and Geraden listened intently, storing up information they might need, Master Barsonage described how the Congery planned to transport their mirrors—no simple problem, considering that the mirrors would have to be moved over hard road and uneven ground by horse cart. With deliberate frankness—perhaps reproaching Geraden's evasion—he discussed the chief weapon the Masters had devised, as well as the secondary actions they were equipped to take. That brought a shine to Geraden's eyes, made Terisa grip herself hard to keep her excitement in perspective; but neither of them interrupted as the mediator went on to explain the arrangements he had designed for the supplies in the ballroom, so that Orison's people could replenish the piles of stores without any risk of being inadvertently taken by a translation.

When he was done with his particular responsibilities, he gave the best report he could on the state of the castle. So far, the Tor's authority and Norge's were being accepted without much resistance: eagerly by most of the guard, men who favored almost any change which promised action; and eagerly as well by the servants, for whom the departure of six thousand guards would mean that much less work; more stoically by Orison's visiting population, people who felt King Joyse's absence keenly in theory, but in practice found Artagel's assurances persuasive; with ill grace and no little suspicion by many of King Joyse's minor lords and functionaries—excise-tax assessors, for example, or storeroom accountants, or secretaries to the Home Ambassador—men whose entire existence depended on the King, on his style of kingship. And without any active opposition to the Tor or Norge, most of Orison's social machinery continued to function. Meals were cooked, despite the chaos Ribuld had described. Halls were patrolled, guarding against unrest—and against attacks of Imagery. Duty rosters were maintained, the walls and gates manned.

In short, thanks to the Tor's quick assumption of authority, and to Norge's demonstrated acceptance, and to Artagel's grinning support, Orison remained almost miraculously intact after King Joyse's disappearance.

"Thank the stars," Geraden breathed when Master Barsonage was done. "You're right, Terisa. We're luckier than we look." Then his eyes narrowed, and his lips pulled tight over his teeth. "I wonder how many times Eremis has thought he could get away with laughing at the Tor. If he can see us now, he isn't laughing anymore."

"And he isn't laughing at the Congery," Terisa put in, partly to please Master Barsonage, and partly because the mediator had impressed her. "Or he won't be, when he finds out what he's up against."

"Thank you, my lady," Barsonage replied quietly. "We have been useless for a long time, while we distrusted both our King and ourselves. It is a pleasure to think that we will be effective at last."

"If only Prince Kragen had listened to us," Geraden mused.

"Or if he changes his mind—" added Terisa, remembering the strange conflict she had seen in the Prince's face.

Master Barsonage looked back and forth between them. Geraden knotted his fists as if to control an irrational hope.

Terisa started to say something about Elega and Margonal, then stopped because she heard voices at the door.

Someone—Ribuld?—guffawed at an unexpected joke.

Without knocking, Artagel swung the door open and entered the room.

He was grinning; his eyes flashed steel fire. If there hadn't been a thin sheen of sweat on his forehead, or a slight pallor of old pain in his cheeks, or a barely discernible hitch in his stride, he would have looked ready and able to carry the whole castle on his shoulders into battle. He was primed for action, packed full of necessity by long days of recuperation, by emotional stresses he couldn't relieve, by betrayals and self-doubt and grief. As soon as she saw him, Terisa knew that he wouldn't hesitate to tackle an entire platoon of Gart's Apts.

The mere sight of him did her good.

And it scared her. It reminded her that if eagerness went too far it could become a form of suicide.

For some reason, she noticed that the sunlight slanting in through her windows was tinged with red, approaching dusk.

Leaving the door for Ribuld to close, Artagel approached Geraden. Geraden surged upright, and Artagel clasped him in a hug which gave no sign of weakness or injury. Then Artagel came to Terisa and dropped to his knees, actually dropped to his knees, in order to capture both her hands and kiss them. Before she could protest or respond, however, he retreated to his feet again, glared at the empty wine decanter, humorously muttered a soldier's obscenity, then dropped himself half-sprawling into the nearest chair.

"Mirrors preserve us," he drawled in a joking tone. "Seeing you two makes me weak in the head. I don't think I can do much more of this dance between hope and despair. First you're gone forever. Then you show up—with Prince Kragen, may his skull ache for the rest of his life. Then he provokes a fight with King Joyse, and Gart appears, and the King disappears, and you're abducted"—he indicated Terisa—"and you"—Geraden—"run off with the mediator. Then the Tor tries to make an alliance with Prince Kragen, and it looks like the only reason that isn't going to work is because I hit him. And suddenly you both come back, and everything starts to go right, and I don't *care* what that pig-brained Alend decides to do about it. I don't even care where King Joyse is. I'm sure it'll all make sense eventually.

"Incidentally, I haven't exactly been cautious in the things I've said to keep people from worrying." By *worrying* he obviously meant *questioning Norge and the Tor.* "What scares them most is the idea of translations into Orison. Terrible Imagery, monsters, fire, a few hundred thousand Cadwals—that kind of thing." He faced Terisa frankly. "I've been telling everybody you can solve that problem. I've been saying you can shift Eremis' mirrors so they won't translate here. If that's not true, you might want to keep it to yourself."

Shift Eremis' mirrors, Terisa thought while her stomach twisted. Oh, shit.

"Just tell me one thing." Artagel hauled himself erect, nearly laughing. "What in the name of sanity *is* going on here?"

"I'll be glad to explain it," Geraden replied, grinning like his brother's reflection. "All you have to do is *shut up.*"

With a gleam of joy, Artagel collapsed back into his sprawled posture.

At once, however, he jerked his spine straight, squared his shoulders. "No," he said, and all the mirth fell out of him. His expression turned to sweat and pallor. "Tell me what happened at home. You said Houseldon was destroyed."

Geraden made a warding gesture, warning his brother back from an explosion.

As if on summons, there was a knock at the door.

Ribuld pushed the door open, and two servingmen entered, carrying trays loaded with food and wine.

Artagel contained himself; but his eyes burned like fuses while the servingmen set out the food, poured the wine, handed around goblets. Master Barsonage accepted his goblet gratefully, emptied it in one long pull, and held it out to be refilled. Geraden and Artagel gripped their goblets without drinking, without looking anywhere except at each other.

Until one of the servingmen knelt to light a fire in the hearth, Terisa didn't realize that the air was turning cooler.

"No lamps tonight," Ribuld commented generally. "No oil. We used up what we had protecting the gates. There's just enough left to keep King Joyse's quarters and the public halls lit for a few more days. Don't let your fire go out."

Ushering the servingmen out of the room, he paused to add, "The Tor wants to talk to you. Before we march. The Castellan will send somebody to get you in the morning. Early."

On that cheerful note, he closed the door.

At once, Master Barsonage articulated, "You said, 'Houseldon is destroyed,'" speaking steadily so that Artagel wouldn't have to shout. "'Sternwall is falling. The people of Fayle are butchered by ghouls.' Everyone who heard you wants an explanation, Geraden."

Geraden didn't hesitate; he had had time to marshall a reply. "The Domne is all right," he said promptly. "At least he was when we left. Our family is safe. Most of the people we know survived. Under the circumstances, our losses were small."

"But Houseldon was burned to the ground."

Holding his hands together because he didn't have a sword, Artagel listened to every word as if he were studying his enemies to learn how to fight them.

Grimly, Geraden described the salient features of his arrival at the Closed Fist, and Terisa's; he described the consequences for Houseldon. Then he explained, "That's what made Nyle do it. That's why he cooperated with Eremis. The threat of an attack like that.

"But when we left, the Domne and all our people were going to dig themselves into the Closed Fist. If Eremis tries the same threat again, our father wants us to ignore it."

At the moment, Terisa didn't care that Geraden had promised to call the Domne *Da.*

Slowly, Artagel sighed, letting violence out of his lungs. "Tholden must be a lot tougher than he thinks."

"So is the Tor," Geraden muttered.

"But you did not return to Orison by translation," prompted
Master Barsonage. "I gather the lady Terisa did not know then that
her talent could reach across such distances."

Terisa nodded; and Geraden said, "But it might not have helped,
even if she *had* known. She can translate herself through flat glass.
If she translated me, I'd lose my mind."

"I understand," said the mediator. "For that reason, you were
required to cross Mordant on horseback. And you chose a road which
took you to Sternwall and Romish."

"Yes," Geraden replied. "That's how we happened to be at Vale
House when the Queen was taken. We were trying to gather support
for King Joyse—trying to get the Termigan and the Fayle to ride
against Eremis."

As briefly as possible, he told the story of the journey back to
Orison, controlling his outrage at Eremis' tactics as well as he could.
Terisa listened to him for a while; gradually, however, her attention
drifted. The room was growing darker as the sun set. A few hints
of crimson still clung to the plumage on the walls, but most of the
light was gone. Darkness accumulated against Orison. She didn't
want to remember pits of fire in the ground, or ghouls. She wanted
to remember the Fayle.

The evening after the battle to save Naybel, sitting with her
and Geraden in his camp, Queen Madin's father had talked about
King Joyse. With one hand clenched into a fist he couldn't sustain,
he had said, *In all his years of warfare against Cadwal and Alend and
Imagery, he has never asked a lord for aid when that lord's Care was
under attack. He came to me, freed my people. He did not ask me for any
help until my Care was safe.*

He will not ask me now. He has no wish to break my heart.

Terisa understood the Fayle better now. She grieved for him—
for his losses, his inadequacy in the face of the ghouls—but she
understood him. And she wanted to believe that he and the Termigan
were doing the right thing by not riding to King Joyse's support. By
protecting their pieces.

I will not leave my people to die undefended.

She also wanted to believe that King Joyse wasn't making a
horrible mistake.

Then Geraden was done. He drank some of his wine and began to pick at his food as if his story had left a bad taste in his mouth.

"Well," Master Barsonage muttered morosely. "Well. You have worked wonders to bring us this news, Geraden—my lady. But I am like other men in Orison, I suppose. I must admit that I had hoped to hear a more encouraging tale. We have all dreamed of the Perdon in vain. *Annihilated,* you said." The mediator scowled. "And now we learn that any dreams we may have had of the Termigan or the Fayle are also in vain.

"King Joyse has chosen a bad time to disappear."

"He didn't choose it," Artagel countered. "There aren't any good times to have your wife abducted."

"Do you believe," Master Barsonage asked carefully, "that is where the King has gone? To rescue Queen Madin?"

Artagel's confidence was greater than Terisa's or Geraden's. He said, "Of course."

The mediator considered that for a moment. Then he said, "I hope you are right. I hope he is not simply cowering somewhere, overwhelmed by the consequences of his actions. To pursue the Queen at such a time may be foolish, but it is certainly understandable."

Without waiting to debate the point, Barsonage rose to his feet. "I will leave you to your supper. I have no urgent need of food"— he slapped his girth—"and many other things to do. With your permission, Geraden, I will tell your story to the Congery." Geraden nodded. "And to Castellan Norge." Geraden nodded again. "And to the Tor. It will do us no good to march with false expectations of help."

Geraden shrugged his assent.

"One other small matter," the Master added before he reached the door. "Do you want a chasuble, Geraden? Do you, my lady? I am prepared to initiate you to the Congery whenever you wish."

The proposal seemed curiously irrelevant to Terisa. When Geraden heard it, however, his face turned as crimson as the sunset. Master Barsonage had just offered him his life's dream. The fact that he had tears in his eyes embarrassed him acutely.

"Later—" he murmured. "Maybe later." Roughly, he rubbed his hands into his eyes; then he met the mediator's gaze. "All I want right now is to stop Eremis."

Master Barsonage accepted that answer. "My lady?"

Terisa shook her head. She had no desire to become a member of the Congery.

Still, she was glad to see that the mediator didn't take her refusal as a reproach. He had too many other things on his mind. Saying only, "As you wish. We will see each other in the morning," he let himself out of the room.

Terisa and Geraden and Artagel looked at each other.

She was starting to feel hungry, but that could wait a little longer. Reflections from the hearth continued to cast a red hue into Geraden's face. Rising to her feet, she moved around behind his chair and put her hands on his shoulders. His muscles were hard, knotted like iron. A chasuble: his life's dream. And now it didn't make any difference. He didn't need it. Deliberately, she dug her fingers into the knots, trying to massage them loose.

Artagel opened his mouth like a man who intended to say something facetious, perhaps at the mediator's expense; but his brother forestalled him. "Now it's your turn," Geraden said, still struggling to regain his composure. "I want you to tell us *everything* that happened while we were away."

"'Everything'?"

Terisa felt a tremor under her hands which wasn't audible in Geraden's voice. Acerbically, he returned, "Leave out the part where you refused to eat all your vegetables and drank too much wine. And terrorized the serving girls. Tell us the rest."

For a moment, Artagel chuckled, but there was no mirth in him now. Drawling to soften his tone, he warned, "You aren't going to like it."

"I know that already." Slowly, Geraden's trembling eased. "If I thought I was going to like it, I'd eat first. But I don't think I can stand it on a full stomach."

Terisa rumpled his hair, kissed the top of his head. Then she went back to her chair.

"Castellan Lebbick," she said, as if she had the strength to mention his name without panic or outrage; without sorrow. "Tell us what happened to him."

Artagel nodded stiffly in the gloom. He refilled his goblet as if he needed courage; however, he didn't drink.

As well as he could, he told Lebbick's story.

Along the way, of course, he mentioned Saddith. He discussed his own efforts to persuade Master Barsonage that Eremis was a traitor. He sketched the extent of Eremis' popularity after the refilling of the reservoir. He described the Tor's long drunkenness, as well as King Joyse's sudden interest in swordsmanship. He detailed the progress of the siege—and of the defense of Orison, by Adept Havelock as well as by the guard.

But mostly he talked about Castellan Lebbick. From his perspective, Orison's story had become the tale of Lebbick's wild and doomed struggle against disintegration. The Castellan had been driven to such desperation, and at last to such lorn heroism—the heroism, not of fighting Gart, but of keeping at least some grasp on sanity—by the fact that he stood almost alone for the castle and its people against Master Eremis' betrayals. And against King Joyse's abdication of responsibility.

And Artagel, who valued heroism, had watched Lebbick's story unfold, and had tried to affect its outcome. Now he didn't know whether he had helped or failed.

Listening to him, Terisa found her anger at King Joyse returning. To cut a man like Lebbick adrift, merely for the sake of a stratagem—merely because the Castellan had no duplicity in him and couldn't be trusted to tell lies—

Maybe the King wasn't particularly interested in preserving his pieces after all. Maybe Master Quillon's account of his actions was false. Maybe his disappearance—and everything else he did—had a completely different meaning.

Terisa wondered how Artagel had been able to retain his faith in King Joyse.

Geraden's thoughts, however, had taken a different turn. When Artagel was finished, Geraden muttered into the inaccurate light of the flames, "It's hard to feel sorry for him. After what he did to Saddith. What he meant to do to Terisa."

"No," Terisa said at once, "it's easy. His wife died. She and Orison and King Joyse were his reasons for living." Curse that old man anyway, *curse* him. "King Joyse would have been kinder to cut him off at the knees."

"I know what you mean," murmured Artagel, while Geraden studied Terisa bleakly. "It was hard to watch. I just couldn't get him to look at things the way I did."

"How did you look at them?" Geraden asked.

Artagel shifted in his chair, a bit embarrassed. "Well, take you two, for example." Terisa supposed he was thinking of the bad days during which he had believed the worst of his brother. "All the evidence was against you. Eremis did a good job of making you look terrible. We only had two things to go on. Lebbick saw you"—he faced Terisa—"disappear into a mirror *without* Master Gilbur. Whatever you did together, you escaped separately. And it was easy to guess Saddith got the idea of going to Lebbick's bed from Eremis. But that was enough. Because we *knew* you. We knew you weren't the kind of people Eremis made you look like. We didn't need much to make us question the whole situation.

"So I tried to tell him"—Artagel swallowed at the emotion in his throat—"to look at King Joyse the same way. We *knew* the King. We *knew* he wasn't what he looked like. All we needed was some reason to believe in him."

"What reason?" Geraden demanded. He sounded hungry.

"You two," repeated Artagel. "Why was Eremis afraid of your talent, my lady? Why was he afraid of yours, Geraden? Well, why else? He knew you were his enemies. He knew you were loyal to King Joyse.

"*Why* were you loyal? *We* didn't know. But you must have had a reason. I was sure of that. And it was enough. You know me. You know I don't exactly have a towering mind. There are probably lots of things I'll never understand. But *you* had a reason." He made a sweeping gesture, at once vague and vehement in the dim light. "That was enough for me.

"But Lebbick couldn't do it. I think he took it all too personally. The hurt"—Artagel stumbled over the word—"went too deep. I know he tried. He held himself together because he didn't have anything else to hope for. But in the end—" Abruptly, Artagel shrugged; he picked up his goblet and drank it dry. "In the end I guess he was glad to find a way to get killed."

After a while, Terisa breathed to Geraden, "You see? It's easy."

Geraden nodded once, roughly. His gaze burned back at the embers of the fire.

The unexpected cold in the air made her pull her chair closer to the hearth.

Artagel stayed and talked for some time after supper. He wanted detailed news from Domne: he wanted to know about the Domne's health, and how tall Ruesha was now, and if Tholden and Quiss were likely to have more children; he wanted to know whether any irate husbands had succeeded at beating sense into Stead, or whether Minick's wife had lost any of her shyness. And talking about things like that did Geraden good. It eased Terisa, bringing back to her memories she treasured, memories which reminded her what the battles ahead would be fought *for,* as well as what they would be fought *against.* Nevertheless the day had been long—not to mention difficult. At last, she grew too tired to stifle her yawns.

Artagel took the hint, such as it was. Promising to see them early the next morning, he left her and Geraden alone.

They didn't have any trouble persuading each other that they needed to go to bed.

She felt safe in the peacock rooms. If Eremis had the means to attack here, he might hesitate, concerned by the impossibility of estimating what she or Geraden could do in retaliation. And she seemed to have left panic a long way behind her.

As soon as she was sure that Geraden was drowsy enough to sleep—that he wouldn't get out of bed to sit up and brood all night—she let herself slide away into dreams.

At first they were easy dreams, full of rest: in them, she watched herself sleep soundly. But gradually they took on rhythm—the slow labor of blow and rebound, repeated again and again. The rhythm grew faster. Out of the dark, she kicked at Eremis as hard as she could, felt her foot strike; then she recoiled, plunged backward to get away from his fury, backward against the wall, through the mirror. This time, however, there was no mirror, no translation. Her heart was too full of rage for fading, and the wall admitted nothing, allowed nothing; it only held her where he could reach her. So she kicked again, recoiled again; and he sprang at her again and again, violent, ultimately irresistible, a man who knew how to have his way with anyone; and horror rose in her throat like sobs because there was nothing she could do to fight him, no way she could beat him—

—until Geraden shook her shoulder, hissed, "Terisa! You're having a nightmare!" and she heard the flat, wooden sound she made when she kicked against the blankets, the knock which seemed to pitch her back into the mattress.

The knock—

Abruptly, she locked herself still, sweating in runnels; and the sound went on, a wooden sound, not her feet belaboring the bed.

Someone was pounding on the door hidden inside one of the wardrobes. She could feel her pulse hammer against the bones of her skull.

She jerked upright.

At once, the sweat seemed to freeze on her skin.

The dim glow from the embers in the hearth lit Geraden as he leaped past her. He grabbed his underclothes and breeches, pulled them on; tossed a couple of logs into the fire. Then he went into the sitting room, unbolted the door, warned the guard outside.

The knocking was steadier than the rhythm of her heart.

A small crackle of flame caught at the new wood. As if that small sound, that little jump of light, released her, she swung her legs out of bed.

Luckily, her robe was in the other wardrobe, the safe one. Shivering as if her limbs were crusted with ice, she snatched out the garment, got her arms into the sleeves, sashed the velvet around her.

The knocking went on. Whoever was in the secret passage was apparently determined to pound there all night if necessary.

"You all right?" Geraden whispered.

She nodded. "Just a bad dream." She faced the wardrobe. "Let's open it."

The door of the wardrobe was already slightly ajar. Geraden swung it out of the way, then reached in and unblocked the chair from the hidden entrance.

As the secret door opened, light filtered through the clothes like sunshine through a forest.

Adept Havelock.

The light came from his hand-sized mirror, his piece of translated sun—the same mirror he had used to incinerate the red-furred creature which had attacked Geraden.

Seeing the Adept, Geraden let out a slow breath. At once, he turned away, left the bedroom. Terisa heard him tell the guard to relax, heard him bolt the door.

Havelock held his light with an unsteady hand. Its shifting illumination, and the dance of the flames in the hearth, cast wild shadows across his features—winks and leers; deathmasks; contortions of sorrow. His insanity looked irreparable.

"Take off your clothes," he commanded her, grinning like a dog. "I haven't seen a good pair of teats for a long time. Don't ask me any questions."

Don't ask— To herself, she groaned bitterly.

Just to be on the safe side, she clenched one hand in the v of her robe, holding it closed.

Then Geraden rejoined her. "You heard," she said, afraid that any question might upset the Adept.

"I heard," Geraden muttered. "No questions. This is going to be such fun."

"Have you been rutting?" demanded Havelock. He was incensed for a moment, full of righteous indignation. "Naked as animals? Avid as goats?" Without transition, his self-righteousness became self-pity. "Why didn't you invite me?"

Terisa hardly noticed what he said. She was watching the way his light weaved and wavered—the way it moved through the illumination from the hearth; the darkness across the back of his hand. Until she saw black drops spatter to the floor, she didn't understand that his hand was bleeding.

Knocking on the door inside the wardrobe, he had damaged his knuckles.

"Havelock—" She faltered momentarily, then took hold of herself, straightened her shoulders. "You had a reason for coming here. It was a good reason. You hurt yourself to make us notice you. Tell us what it was."

"A *reason?*" he cackled, laughing instantly. "A madman like me?" And just as quickly, his mirth vanished. He extinguished his light, put his mirror away in a pocket somewhere, then raised his hand to his mouth to lick the blood. Red smeared his lips, his chin; a spot of blood appeared on his fierce nose.

Between licks, he said casually, "Trust me."

Terisa stared at him, waiting for him to explain. When he didn't say anything else, she shook her head. The air was *cold*—too cold for the time of year. Even the stones under her bare feet were warmer. And she was angry.

"I went to you for help. Master Gilbur was after me, and I didn't have anywhere else to go. You refused.

"Tell me how to trust you."

To her chagrin, his eyes suddenly filled with tears, and his face twisted until he looked like a damaged schoolboy. His voice ached and cracked.

"I know it's hard. I'm crazy, aren't I? Vagel took my mind away. He showed me how to understand everything. Most of the time, I can't tell shit from shallots.

"But Joyse does it." Trying to rub the tears from his eyes, he wiped blood across his face. "Joyse does it."

"Tell us—" Geraden put in softly, carefully, "tell us where he is."

One of Havelock's eyes turned toward Geraden; the other seemed to plead with Terisa. "He told me not to."

"Havelock—" Terisa was never able to sustain her anger against him. His dilemma moved her. As far as she was concerned, there was no real reason why she hadn't emerged in a condition like this from the closet where her parents had locked her. And maybe a certain kind of madness was required to play hop-board successfully with human beings as pieces.

"Havelock, you killed that creature in the dungeon." Behind bars, helpless; burned down to tallow and stink. "The one that attacked Geraden. With your mirror. But when Gart tried to kill me, you let him live. You didn't even damage him. You just blinded him temporarily.

"I want to trust you. He was trying to kill me. Tell me why you didn't even damage him."

Geraden drew a breath between his teeth, held it hard.

"Oh, *that*." Somehow, the Adept passed from distress to scorn without any discernible effort. "You disappoint me. You should have figured that out long ago. How many times has Joyse told you to *think?*"

Terisa clamped her mouth shut and waited.

"It's obvious." Havelock fluttered his hands as if he meant to start dancing. "If I hurt him—if I really blinded him—he would have been caught. We'd lose the chance that he might lead us to his allies. If I killed him, we'd have the same problem, only worse." Sharply, the Adept giggled. "If you think things are bad *now,* try to guess how much trouble you'd be in if Gart hadn't accidentally betrayed Eremis by charging in here.

"*And,*" he went on, "if I killed him, everybody would think *you* did it. Try to guess how long they would have let you live if they thought"—he giggled again—"thought you were Imager enough to charcoal the High King's Monomach.

"No, you're being stupid." From scorn and humor, he lapsed into vexation. "You're wasting my time. If you aren't going to let me fondle your female beauties, at least learn something *useful.*"

In a rough voice, Geraden demanded, "Tell us what you want us to know."

For a moment, the Adept faced Geraden as if he couldn't bring the younger man into focus with either eye; then he muttered, "Idiot. It's not that simple," and headed back into the wardrobe.

Desperately, Terisa called after him, "You said you saw the King's daughters in an augury," because she didn't have any better ideas. "Tell us what Elega was doing."

Slapping at clothes, with a gown wrapped over his head and

both fists full of fabric, he replied, "Spreading her legs for Prince Kragen."

That shocked Terisa; for a moment, it paralyzed her brain. Helplessly, she echoed Geraden. "Tell us what you want."

The Adept ripped the gown off his head. With both arms, he flung a bundle of clothes to the floor.

"I want you to trust me!"

Banging the hidden door after him, he vanished into the darkness of the passage.

She stared after him, dumbfounded.

Spreading her legs. For Prince Kragen.

So King Joyse had known. Before the Prince ever came to Orison as the Alend Monarch's ambassador, King Joyse had known that the Contender and his eldest daughter would become lovers. And he had let it happen. He had practically driven Elega into Kragen's arms.

Suddenly, the test King Joyse had arranged for Prince Kragen, the strange game of checkers in the audience hall, became poignant to her—poignant and awful. By that test, King Joyse had learned that his daughter would betray him.

By that test, he had forced her to betray him.

Now his last message to her made sense. *She carries my pride with her wherever she goes.* He had chosen to put her where she was. And Terisa's nagging sense that Elega had a vital role to play in his plans was confirmed.

And yet, despite what she had just learned, she knew she had missed the point of Havelock's visit.

Left weak by what had happened, what she was thinking, she murmured, "What was *that* all about?"

Glowering darkly, Geraden thought for a moment. Then, to her surprise, his expression lightened, and he smiled like a son of the Domne.

"I think he wants us to trust him."

Trust him. The man who advocates sacrificing pieces to win the game.

Oh, shit.

Really, she needed to increase her range of expletives. Thinking *oh, shit* over and over again just wasn't an adequate way to express herself.

Eventually, she and Geraden went back to bed.

The summons of the guard came much too early.

When Geraden stumbled into the sitting room to answer the door, the guard handed him a breakfast tray and said, "The Tor wants you in an hour. In the King's rooms."

Outside, the sky was still dark, too full of night to give any hint of dawn.

Today, the march would begin.

The air was unconscionably cold.

Blearily, Terisa asked, "Is there any chance we can get some bathwater?"

"Use all the water you want, my lady." She didn't recognize the guard's voice: he must have come during the night to relieve Ribuld. "No rationing this morning. But you'll have to heat it yourself. Nobody has time to do it for you."

"Thanks," muttered Geraden.

After he had closed the door and put down the tray, he came into the bedroom. "I'll put a bucket on the hearth," he offered. "We don't have time to let it get hot, but at least we won't freeze to death."

Pulling a blanket around her, she forced her tired limbs out of bed. Off the rugs, the floorstones were still warmer than the air. On her way to help put more wood on the fires, she asked, "What's happened to the weather?"

Geraden's tone conveyed a shrug. "We had an early thaw. Now it looks like we're having a late freeze."

Good. Perfect. I love being cold.

When she had put three more logs on the coals in the bedroom fireplace, she nearly climbed into the hearth in an effort to absorb some of the new heat.

Once the logs had begun to burn warmly, however, she went to look for some clothes.

Apparently undaunted by the cold—or maybe simply saving as much warmer water for her as he could—Geraden splashed around in the bathroom for a while; he came out toweling himself urgently. Still wrapped in her blanket, with a pile of the clothes Mindlin had made for her nearby, she set out the breakfast and began to gulp down hot tea, warm porridge. Then, when she and Geraden were done eating, she took the bucket from the hearth and retreated into the bathroom.

She didn't notice until she had given herself the best sponge bath she could manage, and had started to get dressed, that all her clothes carried a faint smell of blood.

Every garment she had—everything she could possibly wear on horseback, on a march—was stained with a few drops or a small smear of Havelock's blood.

For a moment, she wanted to break down and cry. The night seemed to have taken the courage out of her, cost her her immunity to panic. But the Adept's visit meant *some*thing. He wanted to be trusted. Or he had promised that he could be trusted. And King Joyse had known all along that Elega and Prince Kragen would become lovers.

Roughly, Terisa washed the fear off her face with the coldest water available. Then she put on a sturdy twill riding habit over some of Myste's silk undergarments.

Havelock's vehemence had left a crescent smear on the fabric over the curve of her left breast; but there wasn't anything she could do about that. As soon as she stopped thinking about it, the smell of blood receded.

Geraden grinned as she emerged from the bathroom. He had found her sheepskin coat and boots.

"What're you going to wear?" she asked.

He wasn't worried. "I'll get something from the guards."

Sooner than she was expecting, someone knocked on the door again. This time, it was Ribuld. He brought with him a mail shirt and a longsword in a shoulder scabbard for Geraden, in addition to a winter cloak. Something about the way he avoided looking at Terisa made her wonder why he hadn't brought any protection or weapons for her; but he started talking about the march, and she forgot her question.

"Six thousand men," he said as he pulled the mail over Geraden's head. "Two thousand horse. Four thousand foot. Castellan says we can make it to Esmerel in three days. Only sixty miles across the Broadwine, and the terrain isn't bad. But we couldn't do it carting supplies. If this translation business works, it's going to be the biggest thing in warfare since crossbows. Traveling light and fast."

"Is the guard ready?" asked Geraden.

Ribuld nodded. "But that isn't the hard part. Armies march on food. If we had to wait for it, we wouldn't get out of here for two or three more days. That's another way we save time, having our supplies translated. Orison can keep cooking for us long after we're gone."

Getting as much information as he could, Geraden inquired, "How's the Tor?"

"His physician says he should stay in bed. But he's got more guts than the rest of us put together." Ribuld chuckled. "He's up yelling at everybody."

A sudden thought alarmed Terisa. "He's staying here, isn't he? Somebody has to defend Orison. And he's in no condition to ride a horse."

Deliberately, Ribuld continued not meeting her gaze. "*You* tell him that, my lady. Ever since Lebbick took my hide off for saving you from Gart without orders, I've given up arguing with lords and Castellans."

Geraden's features seemed to grow sharper. "Who's he going to leave in command?"

Ribuld shrugged. "Better ask him yourself. That way, he'll end up yelling at you instead of me."

Geraden looked at Terisa hard. "I don't think I like the way this is starting to sound."

"Come on." She moved toward the door. "Let's go see him."

Geraden followed her with his sword dangling against his hip as if he had no idea what it was for.

Ribuld brought up the rear, brandishing his scar cheerfully.

Outside the peacock rooms, four more guards joined them, an escort to protect them from Master Eremis' unpredictable resources—creatures of Imagery, the High King's Monomach, flat mirrors. Terisa found, however, that she wasn't particularly concerned about a surprise attack here. If that was what Eremis wanted, he could have done it at any time. She felt sure that his real intentions were considerably nastier.

And she was worried about the Tor—

When she and Geraden reached the King's formal apartment, she noticed the fire blazing in the hearth. Apparently, the lord of Tor felt the cold as badly as she did.

There were four men already in the room: the Tor himself, Castellan Norge, Master Barsonage, and Artagel. Norge stood with his back to one wall, casually at attention: he looked like a man who never needed sleep because he was always napping. In contrast, Master Barsonage seemed to be actually wringing his hands; he faced the Tor and Artagel alternately with a discomfited expression, as if he wanted to intervene but didn't know what to say.

The Tor and Artagel confronted each other like combatants. The old lord thrust his belly forward assertively; his cheeks were red with wine or exertion. Artagel stood in a fighter's balanced stance, his hands ready to go for either his longsword or his dagger.

As Terisa and Geraden entered the room, Artagel turned toward them. His grin twisted her stomach. He looked primed for battle, as fatal as his weapons—and yet in some way lost, like a man who needed help he wasn't going to get against impossible odds.

"Just in time," he said, denying the Tor the bare courtesy of a chance to speak first. "My lord Tor is a bit confused this morning. He doesn't realize I'm your bodyguard. You better tell him. I'm your *personal* bodyguard."

Master Barsonage cast an unhappy look at Terisa and Geraden, then retreated to give them room in front of the Tor and Artagel.

"Artagel," the Tor rumbled to them as if he were on the verge of an outburst, "refuses a direct command. He refuses to obey me."

Terisa looked at Geraden, baffled by the hostility in the room and the knot in her stomach. Geraden's gaze shifted to Artagel, then back to the Tor. "Don't tell me, my lord Tor," he said with a bitterness of his own. "Let me guess. You want him to stay here."

"I want him"—the Tor contained himself with difficulty—"to rule Orison in my absence."

Rule Orison—?

Artagel snarled an obscenity. "It comes to the same thing. He thinks I'm a cripple."

Terisa stared at him, at the Tor; she was simultaneously surprised, relieved, and appalled. The idea of putting Artagel in charge of Orison had never occurred to her.

"No!" the Tor retorted, almost retching, "it does not come to the same thing. I do not ask you to remain behind because you are unfit to go. I command you to stay here because you are needed!

"I must leave Orison with less than two thousand men to defend it. And I have no alliance with the Alend Monarch. He will let us depart, of that I am sure. But when we are gone, he will not hesitate to renew his siege. Prince Kragen considers this castle to be the best safety available.

"If Orison is not defended—*well* defended—it will be lost."

Artagel was in no condition for fighting. And yet the cost of having to stay behind—the price he would pay for remaining in Orison while Mordant's fate was decided without him—would be severe.

"After King Joyse," the Tor concluded, "you are the only man who can hope to hold these walls against the Alend army."

"How?" Artagel snapped back. "I don't have any authority. I don't even belong to the guard. I've never been able to take orders. How do you expect me to give them?"

"By being who you are," the Tor answered heavily. "The best-liked man in Orison."

The old lord was right, Terisa thought. The guards would fight to the death for Artagel, of course. But so would half the population of the castle. He was the best swordsman in Mordant; his feats were legendary. And he was a son of the Domne. By simple likability, he might be able to rule Orison even more effectively than Castellan Lebbick.

Cursing, Artagel returned to his brother. "Tell him," he demanded. "I'm going with you. You need me. When you go up against Eremis, you'll need somebody to watch your back. I want—"

The look on Geraden's face stopped him.

"You want to try Gart again," Geraden said softly, "is that it?"

Anger and distress pulled Artagel's expression in several directions at once.

"With muscles in your side that haven't finished healing?" Geraden continued: soft; relentless. "You want to tackle a man who's already beaten you twice, when you can't even lift that sword without a twinge?"

Artagel flinched in helpless fury or frustration; he took a step backward. "I'm coming with you somehow," he said between his teeth. "I won't stay here."

"Yes, you will," rasped the Tor. "You may succeed in refusing to obey me, but I assure you that you will stay here."

Artagel flung a glare like a challenge at the old lord. "Are you going to make me, my lord Tor?"

"No, Artagel. *I* will not 'make' you. Norge will do that. He will support me in this."

From his place against the wall, the new Castellan nodded amiably. His bland calm was more convincing than a shout.

"Your choices," the Tor finished, "are to remain in command of Orison—or to remain in the dungeon."

Artagel studied the Tor and Norge; he directed a last appeal at Geraden.

In response, Geraden muttered miserably, "Don't you understand, you halfwit? You're too valuable to waste on a senseless contest with Gart. The Tor wants you to do the hardest job there is. King Joyse needs someplace to come back to. If everything else fails, he needs a castle and some men for the last defense of Mordant. He needs someone to give him that. He can't do it for himself. He needs someone like you, who can make old men and serving girls and children fight for him just by smiling at them."

For a moment, Terisa feared that Artagel would break out in protest, do something wild. He was a fighter, by temperament and training unsuited to sit still for sieges. But then his face took on a smile she had never seen before—a grimace bloodier and more bitter than his fighting grin; a look that chilled her heart.

To Norge, he said, "I want Lebbick's mail—I want all the things he was wearing when Gart got him. I want his insignia—his sash and that headband. The more blood on them, the better. Anybody who looks at me is *by the stars* going to know what I stand for."

Norge glanced at the Tor. The Tor nodded; his eyes were glazed with pain. Phlegmatically, Norge said, "Come," and left the wall.

Artagel didn't look at either Geraden or Terisa as he followed the new Castellan out of the room.

Simply because she hated to see Artagel hurt like that, she groaned to herself. But what was the use of being upset? The Tor had found a better answer to Orison's problem—and to Artagel's— than she had been able to imagine for herself. Geraden had told his brother the truth. She could understand how Artagel felt—but so what? He—

"You also, my lady," the Tor said as if he had boulders rolling around in his gut, "will remain here."

What—?

She looked around her. Geraden was gaping at the old lord, frankly dumbfounded. Master Barsonage's expression was white with consternation.

She had heard right. The Tor intended to leave her in Orison.

Which was why Ribuld hadn't brought any protective clothing or weapons for her. And why he had evaded her eyes, her inquiries. Of course.

Unexpectedly calm, she faced the lord. Her gaze was steady; even her pulse didn't flutter. Geraden started to speak for her; but when he noticed her demeanor, he bit his mouth closed. "My lord Tor," she said gently, as if he were as mad as Havelock, unable to be questioned, "you don't want me to go with you."

The tone of her reaction seemed to weaken his resolve. Speaking loudly in an apparent effort to shore up his position, he retorted, "You are a woman."

Because he had raised his voice, she lowered hers. "And that makes a difference to you."

"I am the lord of the Care of Tor." His face grew redder, goaded toward passion by the fact that she wasn't yelling at him. "And I am the King's chancellor in Orison. His honor is in my hands, as is my own. You are a *woman*."

Deliberately rejecting sarcasm, she replied quietly, "Please be plain, my lord Tor. I want to understand you."

As if she were driving him to distraction, he shouted, "By the heavens, my lady, *I do not take women into battle!*"

In spite of her determination to be kind, Terisa smiled. "Then don't think of me as a woman, my lord. Think of me as an Imager. Ask Master Barsonage. He offered to make me a Master. I'm not going with you. I'm going with the Congery."

The Tor took a deep breath, preparing to bellow.

At once, Master Barsonage put in, "My lady Terisa is quite correct, my lord Tor," speaking in the most placating voice he could manage. "You have not forgotten that she is an Imager—in effect, a member of the Congery. It is possible that she is the most powerful Imager we have ever known. I do not believe that we can confront Master Eremis and Master Gilbur and the arch-Imager Vagel without her."

Livid with anger—or perhaps with the pain of holding his damaged belly upright—the Tor demanded, *"Do you defy me, mediator?"*

Master Barsonage spread his hands. "Of course not, my lord Tor. I merely observe that the lady Terisa is a question which belongs to the Congery. Regardless of the role we assign to her in the support of Orison and Mordant, she casts no aspersion on your honor—or the King's."

Carefully, Geraden commented, "And King Joyse doesn't hesitate to use women when he needs them. Adept Havelock told us last night that King Joyse knew years ago the lady Elega and Prince Kragen would become lovers. He consented to his own betrayal— he practically drove her into the Prince's arms. I don't think the Prince would ever have let Terisa and me into Orison if she hadn't been there. And she may do other things for us yet.

"My lord Tor, we need Terisa with us."

The Tor looked back and forth between Master Barsonage and Geraden, his eyes swollen and baleful as a pig's. His face was crimson with stress.

Nevertheless he acquiesced.

Slowly, he slumped into a chair; his hands made weak gestures of dismissal. Terisa had to remind herself that she wasn't his only— or even his primary—reason for appearing so defeated. "Leave me," he muttered. "We march at full dawn. I must have a moment's peace."

She felt that somebody ought to stay with him. He seemed to be in need of comforting. He had suffered so long, and to so little purpose. From the day when he had arrived in Orison with his eldest son dead in his arms until now, he had been groping like a doomed man, struggling against his own heart and King Joyse's machinations for some way to heal his grief. Surely there were things he needed more than "a moment's peace."

But Master Barsonage moved to leave, and Geraden put a hand on her arm, urging her toward the door. "Come on," he breathed, "before he changes his mind."

Dumbly, she accompanied Geraden and the mediator.

Outside, trying to articulate her own sorrow, she said, "Gart must have hurt him pretty badly. He doesn't look like he can stay on his feet much longer."

Away from the Tor, Geraden's expression turned bleak, unconsoled. "That doesn't matter. King Joyse hurt him worse than Gart did." To Master Barsonage, he explained, "Artagel told us the Tor spent most of the time we were away blind drunk."

The mediator nodded grimly.

"What's holding him together," Geraden continued, "is feeling needed. As long as he knows he's necessary, he can stand being kicked. That's why it hurts him so much when we argue with him— even when he's wrong. He hasn't got the strength or the resolution or the *hope* left to survive doubting himself."

Terisa hugged Geraden's hand where it held her arm; she was grateful that he understood.

Master Barsonage thought for a while as they descended from the King's tower. Then, speaking wryly as if to distance himself from what he felt, he said, "I, on the other hand, have a passion for doubt. I cannot resist it. That is why I try to surround myself with so much solidity." He made a mocking reference to his girth. "Is he right, do you think? Are you certain of what we do? Are we on the path King Joyse would have chosen for us, if he were here?"

"And if we are," Geraden growled, at least partially serious, "did King Joyse know what he was doing? Did he ever know what he was doing? Do any of us have even the vaguest conception of the consequences of our actions?

"No, I'm sorry, Master Barsonage. I don't have any wisdom for you. We're doing the only thing that makes sense to me."

Terisa nodded once, grimly.

The mediator sighed. "We must be content with that, I suppose."

More quickly than the circumstances required, they moved downward. The air took on a sharper edge as they neared one of the main public exits to the courtyard. No question about it, Mordant was having a late freeze. Terisa's breath began steaming well before she reached the high doorway. She could feel cold prickling along her scalp like an omen of some kind.

The halls of Orison had been nearly deserted; but there was nothing deserted about the courtyard. She could hear shouts and movement, hundreds—no, thousands—of boots hurrying in different directions. And from the doorway she saw a dark, torchlit seething of men and horses, as troubled in the early gloom as the contents of a witch's cauldron, brewed for destruction and bloodshed. From the cavernous stables under Orison, horses by the score had been led into the courtyard and readied for mounting. And more torches lit the passage which led like a throat down to the stables; in the passage more horses crowded, with more behind them. Most of the mounts were already tended by the men who would ride them, the men whose lives might depend on them.

And around the inner walls of the castle, around Orison's benighted inward face, the guards who would travel on foot were gathering in squads and platoons; ordinary individuals uprooted from their lives in order to endure a forced march for three days so that they could be hurled against an army which outnumbered them nearly four-to-one. And for what? Well, Terisa knew the answer to that. So that men like Master Eremis and High King Festten wouldn't have their way with the innocent of Mordant. To say such things, however, she had to believe that what the Congery and the guard, what she and Geraden were doing might work.

Failure meant *annihilation*. For all these people.

Clutching her coat against the cold, she followed Master Barsonage and Geraden, with Ribuld behind her, across the ice-crusted mud among the horses to the place near Orison's gates where the Congery assembled with its beasts and wagons.

The Masters nodded and muttered to the mediator. Some of them greeted Geraden with salutations or smiles which seemed sincere in the erratic light of the torches; others were too embarrassed by their old scorn for him to say anything; one or two of them made it clear that they still didn't believe what they had heard about his demonstrations of power. They all, however, acknowledged Terisa with as much courtesy as the circumstances allowed. Then they went back to the job of securing their cargo in the wagons.

She counted nine large bundles as big as crates: the Congery's mirrors. Each glass had been wrapped in blankets, then lashed into a protective wooden frame, then wrapped in more blankets and tied tightly before being bound to the side of the wagon. And the wagons themselves were unusual: a new bed had been built to fit on padded supports inside each of the original ones, so that over particularly rough terrain the new bed holding the mirrors could be lifted out and carried by men on foot.

Wiggling her toes against the cold that seeped into her boots, Terisa looked up at the sky.

It was gray with dawn, and cloudless, at once translucent and obscure, like a mirror on which cobwebs and dust had accumulated for years.

The march would begin soon.

Curse this freeze. Yesterday she was ready to set out on a moment's notice. But today, in the cold— She wondered if anyone was ever truly ready.

More men. More horses. Shouts rang hoarsely off the walls: questions; commands; messages. The bazaar was crowded with guards and their mounts. Gart had attacked her there once; Prince Kragen had used the bazaar to cover his meetings with Nyle. Now, at least temporarily, the whole place was unfit for business. But of course it had probably been unfit for days, cut off by the siege from any way to replenish its wares.

Grooms led horses forward for Terisa and Geraden. She glared suspiciously at the colorless old nag assigned to her, a beast clearly too decrepit for any rider except one who didn't know what she was doing. Geraden's mount, in contrast, was a spirited gelding with an odd white spot like a target on either side of its barrel.

Seeing her expression, he asked teasingly, "Want to trade?"

"This thing's almost dead already," she snorted. "After what we've already been through, I think I could ride a firecat."

Ribuld grinned around his scar.

But she didn't want to trade. She had an instinctive sense that she was in danger of overestimating her abilities.

As full dawn approached, and the level of noise in the courtyard increased, lights began to show in the windows around Orison's inner face—children dragging their parents out of bed to see what was happening; lords or ladies rousing themselves to witness events; wives and children and loved ones wanting some way to say good-bye to the guards.

By stages Terisa couldn't measure, the turmoil of men and horses seemed to resolve itself. More and more guards climbed onto their beasts. The Masters began to mount—except for those who intended to drive the wagons, or to ride on them to watch over the mirrors. The frost from the horses' nostrils was gray now, as pearly as mist, lit by the dawn rather than by torches. Geraden nudged Terisa's arm, indicated the horses; but she didn't move until she saw the Tor emerge from one of the main doors and waddle toward his charger.

She mounted when he did.

Slowly, accompanied by his personal guard—the men who had come with him from his Care—as well as by the Castellan Norge and Artagel, he rode to the gates so that when they were raised he would be the first to face the Alend army, the first to face the march. For some reason, his black cloak and hood—the mourning garb which he had worn to bring his son to Orison—made him appear smaller. Or maybe her horseback perspective deemphasized his bulk. He didn't look large enough to take King Joyse's place, imposing enough to threaten King Joyse's enemies.

Yet when he lifted his voice he lifted her heart as well, like the remembered call of horns.

"It is a dangerous thing we do." Somehow, the old lord made his words carry across the courtyard, made them echo around the face of Orison. "Barely six thousand of us go to meet Cadwal and vile Imagery on the ground they have chosen for battle. And we will have the Alend army at our backs—if I cannot persuade the Alend Monarch to see reason at last. An attempt may be made to take Orison in our absence. King Joyse is not with us, and the power against us is staggering.

"It is a *dangerous* thing we do.

"*But it is the best we can.*

"The Congery rides with us. We have powers which our enemies cannot suspect. Artagel will preserve Orison for us—and High King Festten is weaker than he knows, helpless to supply his forces by any means which cannot be cut off. King Joyse has planned and labored for years to reach this moment. It will not fail.

"It is a dangerous and *desirable* thing we do. I am proud to take part in it."

The Tor signalled with one hand. At once, the castle's trumpeter blew a fanfare which echoed against the walls, rang into the sky. Groaning, the great winches began to crank the gate open.

While the gate went up, the Tor pulled his charger around to face the opening and the future as if he had never been afraid in his life.

Artagel withdrew. Castellan Norge called the guard to order.

When the gate was up, the trumpeter sounded another fanfare.

With the Congery and six thousand men behind him, the Tor rode out of Orison.

FORTY-FIVE: THE ALEND MONARCH'S GAMBLE

ut in the dawn, the Alend army waited.

Prince Kragen had withdrawn all his forces—his patrols and scouts, his siege engines, his battering rams—to the great circle of his encampment. Beyond the gates, none of his men came closer than the tree-lined roads from Tor and Perdon and Armigite. But his foot soldiers stood ready, holding their weapons. His mounted troops were on their horses. Past the intervening guards, past the Tor and Norge, Terisa could see the Alend strength among the trees like a black wall wrapped around the castle.

One of the riders who held the roads was a standard-bearer with the Alend Monarch's green-and-red pennon.

A cold wind came up out of the south, out of Tor, making the pennon flutter and snap like a challenge.

The standard-bearer held no flag of truce.

As always, however, Prince Kragen's men avoided the intersection where the roads came together. This created a gap in the Alend line, as if Kragen intended to let Orison's guard through.

The Tor spoke to Norge; Norge muttered a command Terisa didn't hear. At the head of the guard, King Joyse's plain purple insignia was raised.

Maybe Prince Kragen would think the King had returned.

Maybe he would reconsider.

Terisa gripped her reins with icy hands and prepared to nudge her nag into motion. Geraden held his head up as though he were waiting for sunrise. Ribuld scratched at his scar as if it itched in the chill, an old wound remembering pain.

Snorting steam, shaking their heads, rattling their tack, crunching the crusted mud, the horses began to follow the Tor and Castellan Norge.

Artagel still had his back to the Alends. By holding his mount stationary, he sifted through the vanguard until he was directly in front of Terisa and Geraden—until he came between them, forcing them to stop. As she had feared, he was wearing Lebbick's old, bloody mail over his shirt and leggings, Lebbick's purple sash and headband. The sword belted to his hip looked so dark and grim that it must have belonged to the dead Castellan.

When he was dressed like that, she was afraid of what he might do.

At the moment, however, he didn't do anything fearful. He clasped his brother's shoulder; without quite managing to smile, he said, "Take care of yourself. Take care of her. Rescue Nyle. This family has already suffered enough."

Geraden replied with a grin that looked like it belonged to Artagel.

Artagel turned to Terisa. Striving to appear ready and whole—perhaps for her benefit, perhaps for his own—he said stiffly, "Don't make a liar out of me now, my lady."

"A liar—" she repeated as if the cold numbed her mouth. She had no idea what he was talking about.

"I've told half the men and women in Orison you can shift Eremis' mirrors so they won't translate here." He watched her, studied her, like a man who didn't want to get caught pleading. "The Tor is heading straight for the place where the Perdon and his men were attacked."

Terisa thought her heart was going to stop.

The mirror which had brought those ravening black spots down on the Perdon and his men out of nowhere— Shapes no bigger than puppies, and yet as fatal as wolves—

She had forgotten it. Forgotten, forgotten.

Geraden winced. "Terisa—" he started to say. "Terisa—"

"Stop him," she said, gasping gouts of steam. "*Stop him.* I need time to think."

Instantly, Artagel wheeled his mount and plunged through the press of horses, chasing after the Tor.

—gnarled, round shapes with four limbs outstretched like grappling hooks and terrible jaws that occupied more than half the body—

The idea shocked her to the marrow, revolted her. The same creatures had attacked her and Geraden outside Sternwall—but that was different; then they had attacked completely by surprise, without time for panic or nausea. This time— The Tor and Castellan Norge were effectively defenseless. If they met Prince Kragen in the intersection, all the leaders of the armies could be struck at once. How had she *forgotten?*

Artagel had told everyone that she could *shift Eremis' mirrors.*

Outside the gates, Artagel caught up with the Tor and Norge, spoke to them urgently. Master Barsonage brought his horse up between Terisa and Geraden. "What is amiss?" he asked. "I was unable to hear."

Geraden overrode the mediator. "Why hasn't he used it already? If he still has that mirror set up—if it's ready—why hasn't he used it before this? He could bring anything through. Even if he didn't hurt us, he could cripple the Alends, maybe even kill Prince Kragen—or the Alend Monarch."

"Because he didn't need it then." Terisa wasn't thinking about what she said; the words seemed to come out by themselves, reasoned into clarity by a separate part of her mind. "He needed time to set his traps, time to spring them. He needed time to get Festten's army in position, time to get rid of the Perdon, time to make all his mirrors." The rest of her brain blundered helplessly around the edges of the promise Artagel had made in her name. "But we let him do all that safely. Prince Kragen held off—he *held off* from trying to take Orison. Nobody interfered with what Eremis was doing. So he didn't need to use this mirror. He could afford to leave Alend alone."

Geraden nodded harshly. "I understand. *Now* it's time. *Now* he needs it. We're moving. His traps are ready. He's got everything he wanted except you. He can't beat us with just one mirror. Even a few hundred of those black spots can't beat an army this size. An avalanche can't. Firecats can't. But if he can hurt us now—if he can kill the Tor, or Norge, or Prince Kragen—he can damage us terribly."

"Then we will foil him simply," put in Master Barsonage. "We will turn from the road. We will pass outside his mirror's range of focus."

Geraden nodded again, rose up in his stirrups to shout to Artagel. But Terisa said at once, "No!"

Master Barsonage and Geraden stared at her.

No. Oh, curse it. What was she *thinking?* This was insane.

"Artagel told everyone I can shift Eremis' mirrors." But that wasn't what she meant to say, that wasn't the point. She tried again. "This is a trap. We need to stick our heads in it. We need to spring it the other way. Isn't that why we're marching in the first place? Isn't that what we decided?"

Ahead of the guard, the Tor and Norge had stopped. Artagel had finished explaining what was on his mind. In the gray dawn, the Tor looked strangely sunken, irresolute, as if he were torn between the desire to flee and the necessity of marching. Kicking his mount, Artagel started back toward Terisa and Geraden.

"Eremis wants to scare us," she said while her thoughts throbbed like her heart. "He wants to make us doubt ourselves.

"We should try doing the same thing to him."

"What do you mean, my lady?" asked Master Barsonage, nearly whispering.

"She means," Geraden snarled back as though she appalled him, "she thinks she ought to do it. Stick her head in the trap." He had to swallow fiercely to clear his throat. "Shift Eremis' mirror so he can't use it."

"Impossible," protested the mediator. "Is it not true that she has never seen the mirror which shows the place where those fatal creatures are found? And how can we be sure that Master Eremis does not intend to translate some other evil against us? And—?"

"Not that mirror," Geraden snapped, controlling his alarm with anger. "The flat one. The one that shows the intersection.

"No." Now he was speaking to Terisa, speaking so intensely that his words seemed to burn. "What makes it impossible is the vantage, the direction. We know what the Image is, but we don't know what side it's seen from, what the perspective is. You can't shift an Image if you can't identify it first, see it exactly in your mind."

He was saying, Don't do this, *don't do this.*

"I've got to try." As if that were an explanation, she said, "Artagel promised." But the stricken look on Geraden's face demanded better. She made another effort. "I don't really know how far my talent goes. I haven't had very many chances to explore it. We're counting on the idea that I have power we can use, but we don't really know what we're counting on. And the closer we get to Esmerel, the more dangerous everything is. I've got to try."

Geraden clearly wanted to argue, shout. Deliberately, she went on, "We're staking everything on the hope that King Joyse didn't abandon us. He *trusted* us—he *trusts* us to make his plans work while he's away." She had the distinct impression that she was completely out of her mind. "If we aren't going to at least make the attempt, we might as well stay here."

For one painful moment, Geraden's expression turned to bleak, bitter iron. But then his lips pulled back into a fighting grimace. "I'm coming with you."

"No, you aren't," Terisa countered before Master Barsonage could object. "We can't afford to risk both of us."

"If you think I'm going to let you do this alone—" Geraden began.

She wasn't listening to him: she had already hauled on her reins, dug her heels into the nag's sides. As if she were unaware of her own quickness and had never considered the possibility that she wouldn't be obeyed, she commanded, "Stop him, Ribuld. Keep him here," and started to forge among the riders toward Artagel, the Tor, and Castellan Norge.

Ribuld caught Geraden by the strap of his swordbelt and neatly plucked him off his horse. While Geraden sputtered in outrage, Ribuld wrestled with him. Geraden was tougher than he appeared, nearly frantic as well: he managed to unseat Ribuld. They fell together into the mud. But Geraden couldn't break away.

Terisa reached Artagel.

"I need protection," she panted; her own strange audacity took her breath away. "Eremis won't miss a chance to attack when he sees me in his mirror. Somebody's got to keep me alive so I can work."

Artagel's excitement shone as brightly as Geraden's frenzy. Calling men after him, he wheeled his mount and began clearing a path for her.

They reached the Tor and Norge and rode past with six more guards behind them, hurrying now so that she wouldn't have time to lose her nerve—so that she wouldn't be infected by the Tor's slumped irresolution.

While she rushed toward the intersection, she tried to clear her mind, make herself ready.

This decisive urgency was different than the rage which sometimes blocked her. It was full of fear—and fear lead to fading—and fading led to translation. The first thing she needed was an alternative Image, a place she could shift Eremis' glass *to*. As soon as she recognized that necessity, however, her mind filled up with scenes which couldn't bear attack: the Closed Fist; rooms and halls in Orison; Sternwall; Vale House. She had to thrust them away, get them out of her thoughts before she did something terrible unintentionally. If only she had seen any part of Esmerel accurately, she could have used it—or tried to use it—to hurl Eremis' attack back against him.

He had cleverly avoided that danger.

Was his foresight really that good? Was he ready for her now?

A squad of Alend horse rode into the intersection, intending either to meet or to stop her. Artagel stretched his mount a few strides ahead and began yelling at the Alends, warning them away. She caught a glimpse of Prince Kragen, saw him react without hesitation, shout his men back.

Around her, the trees seemed to skid into focus past the bare ground leading from Orison. She had only been here on one previous occasion: the day Geraden had caught Nyle, dooming him to Master Eremis. And the ground then had been still covered with snow, the trees still black, leafless. And beyond the intersection had been cold, ice-caked snow, not an army of Alends.

Sawing inexpertly on the reins, she brought her horse to a halt. At once, Artagel and his companions formed a defensive cordon around her; instinctively, they faced the Alends with their swords drawn, as if the danger came from Prince Kragen's soldiers.

Her pulse straining and her head giddy, she did her best to ignore the men, the horses, the swords. A number of the Alends sat their mounts with their spears levelled—*ignore* that. She needed *time*, time to see the place vividly as it was now, time to consider it from as many different angles as possible; time to prepare herself for the Image which had to be shifted.

Unfortunately, her enemies weren't stupid. And her disappearance from Eremis' cell had given them at least a hint of her true talents. Either she had effected her escape herself, or she possessed some kind of link with Geraden which had enabled him to locate and translate her in the dark. In either case, she was a dangerous opponent.

Before she had a chance to calm herself, before she finished turning wildly, trying to see the intersection from every side at once, before she knew what she was going to do, *a touch of cold as thin as a feather and as sharp as steel slid straight through the center of her abdomen*—

—and a black shape full of teeth came down on the shoulders of one of the guards.

With a single, tearing bite, it ripped out the base of his neck.

By the time his body toppled to the ground, the creature had already gobbled its way into his chest.

More shapes: five, ten, fifteen. Shouts hit the trees. Swords flared in the cold sunrise. Prince Kragen and a dozen Alends charged into the fray. Artagel seemed to be dancing on the back of his mount, pirouetting, as he slashed an attacker out of the air above Terisa's head. Then he dove at her, carried her off her horse to the ground where he could control her movements, keep his sword between her and the creatures.

And still through the chaos of whirling vision, whirling blades, of horses and teeth and blood, she felt that *touch of cold* as the mirror stayed open, the translation continued, launching black raveners at her as fast as they could come.

She tried to use the sensation, cling to it, make it lead her to its Image; she had to see that Image in her mind before she could change it. But it eluded her.

Geraden was right. It was impossible.

Another guard went down. All the guards seemed to be down, with gnarled shapes no bigger than puppies feasting on them. But some of them must have been Alends, because she had guards around her yet, protecting her like Artagel, hacking their swords madly at the open air.

Artagel had to fling her aside, had to use both hands on his sword in order to cut away three beasts at once. The catch in his side slowed him, nearly cost him his life. With a wrench of effort and pain, he hauled his blade around.

She sprawled toward the hooves of a panicked horse. That *touch of cold* was driven through the center of her belly like a spike, nailing her to the ground. She was so afraid that she forgot everything— forgot to dodge the horse, the creatures, forgot to ward herself—

forgot everything except the feather-and-steel sensation of Eremis' glass.

There she found it: on the edge of fading, the verge of the blind dark. *Above* her—higher than her own vantage. That was how it had eluded her: she hadn't taken into account the way the black shapes came *down* onto her defenders.

As if she were leaping up inside herself, carrying the cold of translation with her, she looked into its moment of temporary eternity, its flat abyss, and saw the Image.

She saw the bloodied ground from nearly fifteen feet in the air, saw the frantic and squealing horses, saw her defenders, the corpses, the dead or feeding creatures—

Fast and hard, desperately, like slamming a door, she turned what she saw opaque, gave it an Image as blank as frosted glass.

Inside her, the *touch of cold* snapped and vanished as if she had shattered something.

At the same instant, the rush of gnarled bodies and teeth was cut off. In fact, it was cut off in midcreature. Two of the beasts flopped to the ground without the rest of their bodies: they had been sliced in half as neatly as with a cleaver.

The attack was over.

"Terisa," Artagel gasped, "my lady." He got his hands under her arms, lifted her to her feet. "Are you all right?"

"I think I broke it." She couldn't find a point of balance anywhere in the intersection. The ground tilted; men veered from side to side; Artagel's face swam in and out of view. She had no idea how she was able to speak, when it was obvious that she had lost the ability to breathe or think or hold up her head. "The mirror. I think we're safe."

Prince Kragen appeared: he seemed to heave over the horizon from somewhere far away. "You like risks, my lady," he said through his teeth. "I have lost seven men."

"And Eremis lost a mirror," Artagel retorted over his shoulder, panting and angry. "Maybe *you* don't like the trade, but *he's* going to think hard before he tries it again. My lord Prince."

Terisa had no attention to spare for Kragen. Clinging to Artagel, she asked, "How many did we lose?"

He looked around. "Three."

Three. Ten men altogether. Ten men dead because she took a risk she didn't know how to handle, *ten.* And if she hadn't finally shifted the mirror when she did, the carnage would have been worse. Maybe much worse. Because she took the risk—

Trembling like a child, she sank to the ground and clamped her hands over her face to shut out the sight of death.

Artagel stood over her and glared at Prince Kragen as if daring the Prince to blame her for anything. When Kragen shrugged and withdrew, Artagel sent his guards back to Orison. "Tell my lord Tor the intersection is safe. And tell Geraden she's all right. She broke the mirror."

Terisa didn't hear the men leave.

"My lady," Artagel said thickly, "you did the right thing. If we only lose ten men for every mirror Eremis has, he doesn't stand a chance."

She couldn't raise her head, even for Artagel.

What about High King Festten and his twenty thousand Cadwals?

The Tor and Norge and their escort were the first riders to arrive from Orison. The Tor didn't dismount—maybe he couldn't, and still be sure of being able to get back up on his horse. But he addressed her in a voice she remembered, a voice with cunning and resolution hidden in its subterranean rumble.

"My lady Terisa of Morgan, it would have been a grave mistake if I had required you to remain behind."

She tried to nod without looking up. Apparently, he had recovered some measure of assurance. She had accomplished that, if nothing else: she had given the old lord a bit of hope by demonstrating that it was possible to fight Eremis' Imagery.

Then Geraden reached her. Muddy and bedraggled, almost delirious with anger and relief, he flung himself off his mount in front of her as if he meant to snatch her from the ground. Instead of picking her up, however, he hunkered down to her, gripped her shoulders hard, shook her gently. "Don't ever do that to me again," he demanded. "Don't you *dare*. Can't you get it through your thick skull that I love you? We're *together* in this. I'd rather walk through fire until I drop than be a spectator while you live or die."

Oh, Geraden.

She put out her arms to him, and he caught her in a fierce hug. "Together," she murmured so that he wouldn't let her go. "I promise."

After a while, he helped her to her feet.

Until she wiped her eyes and looked around, she didn't realize that all the forces of Orison and Alend were waiting for her.

Prince Kragen was there, mounted before the Tor, with a new squad of men behind him. Artagel had gone back to his duty in Orison; but Castellan Norge and his escort supported the Tor, with a road full of guards issuing from the castle at his back. The old lord faced Prince Kragen squarely; however, the Prince didn't speak until Terisa met his gaze.

To her surprise, she saw unmistakably that some conflict in him had been resolved. The clenched bitterness, the suggestion of savagery, was gone from his expression; his black eyes shone with excitement. She had no idea what decision he had achieved—but she could see beyond question that he liked it.

After holding her gaze for a moment, he turned to the Tor.

"Should I conclude from this display of force, my lord Tor," he asked acerbically, "that your intention to march against High King Festten and Master Eremis in Esmerel is unchanged?"

"Assuredly, my lord Prince," the Tor replied in a corresponding tone. "If I had the slightest desire to do battle with you, I would not go about it in this fashion."

Kragen indicated the purple pennon. "Has King Joyse returned?"

"He has not."

"In that case"—Prince Kragen straightened his shoulders—"the Alend Monarch wishes to speak with you. He asks you to accept the hospitality of his tent, with Geraden, the lady Terisa, and Master Barsonage—and Castellan Norge, of course."

Terisa and Geraden stared. Norge clenched his jaws as if he were stifling a yawn. The Tor's eyes showed an undisguised gleam of hope. Nevertheless he didn't ask what Margonal wanted to talk about. Instead, he inquired firmly, "What guarantee of safety does the Alend Monarch offer us? As his guests, we will be deeply honored—and completely vulnerable."

Prince Kragen shrugged slightly. "My lord Tor, the Alend Monarch is a man of honor. He neither insults nor betrays his guests. On this occasion, however, he is prepared to match your vulnerability with his own. You may bring with you a hundred horsemen, who will be permitted to surround his tent. Surely no treachery on our part will succeed at killing a hundred men before they can threaten or kill the Alend Monarch himself."

"A remarkable gesture," Master Barsonage whispered to Terisa and Geraden. "The Alend Monarch is not notoriously complaisant about hazards to his person. Perhaps there is hope for an alliance yet."

Terisa and Geraden didn't reply. They were waiting to hear what the Tor would say.

"My lord Prince," drawled the old lord as if nothing surprised him, "the Alend Monarch is unexpectedly considerate. I am prepared to rely on his honor entirely. I will accompany you at once, with Master Geraden and the lady Terisa of Morgan."

The Tor held up his hand to forestall movement. "Castellan Norge will remain among his men—as will the mediator of the Congery. They will keep their strength ready to march at the earliest possible moment."

Norge nodded amiably. Master Barsonage started to object, but subsided at once. The point of the Tor's decision was obvious: if the old lord was betrayed, most of Orison's fighting force would remain intact.

Prince Kragen permitted himself a bleak smile. "As you wish, my lord Tor." With a look toward Terisa and Geraden, he asked, "Will you mount and join us?"

Trying not to hurry—trying not to look like people who desperately wanted an alliance—Terisa and Geraden found their horses, swung themselves up, and rode to the Tor's side.

Without discernible anxiety, Castellan Norge withdrew his escort; he retreated a short distance down the road and immediately sorted his men into a defensive shield around the Congery and its wagons. At his orders, what remained of the mounted guard emerged from Orison, fanning out into a formation ready either to commence battle or to resume marching. Then Norge followed the men on foot, while Master Barsonage told the other Masters what had happened and prepared them for the possibility that they might have to defend themselves.

At the same time, Terisa and Geraden—with Ribuld trailing after them as if he thought no one would notice him—rode beside the Tor and Prince Kragen toward the tent where they had talked with the Prince and Elega less than two days ago.

As they moved, Geraden tried discreetly to wipe some of the mud off his clothing.

Terisa was distantly surprised to discover that her own clothes weren't especially dirty. The mud in the intersection had been frozen hard. And somehow she had escaped all that blood— Even the gnarled creatures had died without marking her.

In the open area surrounded by luxurious living tents, the riders dismounted. Refusing the Prince's offer of help, the Tor got down by himself; but he had to hold his breath and hug his gut until his face turned black in order to do it. Gasping thinly, with his legs wedged to keep him upright, he murmured as an explanation, "My lord Prince, I hope the Alend Monarch does not require his guests to be in good health. The blow I received from the High King's Monomach troubles me"—his face twisted—"considerably."

"My lord Tor," replied the Prince evenly, "the Alend Monarch will require only that you be seated comfortably, that you enjoy a flagon of wine"—Kragen bowed his guests toward the most sumptuous of the tents—"and that you consent to see him without light."

Allowing Terisa, Geraden, and the Tor no opportunity for questions, Prince Kragen approached the tentflaps and told the soldiers on duty to announce him.

Terisa and Geraden glanced at each other; but the Tor ignored both of them. Struggling as if he were up to his thighs in mire, he followed Kragen into the tent.

"Oh, well," Geraden whispered. He had recovered his sense of humor. "If we aren't allowed any light, at least I don't have to worry about appearing before the Alend Monarch looking like a pig wallow."

Terisa wanted to smile for him, but she was too busy trying to control her sense that the defenders of Mordant urgently needed some good to come of this meeting with the Alend Monarch.

They entered the tent behind the Tor.

Ribuld tried to go with them. Kragen's soldiers stopped him.

As on the occasion of their previous visit, the fore-tent was illuminated only by braziers which had been set for warmth: apparently, Margonal suffered from an old man's sensitivity to cold. Now, however, Prince Kragen summoned no lamps to augment the glowing embers. In the gloom, slightly tinged with red, the chairs and furnishings were hard to see—imprecise; vaguely suggestive. Tent poles loomed out of the dark like obstacles.

A moment passed before Terisa realized that she and Geraden, the Tor and Prince Kragen weren't alone. Two soldiers held the tentflaps tightly closed. Servants waited around the walls.

And the dark shape of a man sat in a chair across the expanse of the fore-tent.

"My lord Tor." The voice issuing from the dark shape was old and thin. "I like courtesy, but I will dispense with it today, so that your march will not be delayed. Yet I must take time to give you my thanks for not bringing the hundred men I offered to permit. Even if I meant you ill—which I do not—your decision made you safe with me. A man of Mordant must be valorous to trust the honor of an Alend."

"My lord Monarch," replied the Tor, "I also like courtesy. It would please me to give you the formal salutations and gratitude which custom and humility suggest. Unfortunately, I have been injured. I confess that I am hardly able to stand. Forgive me, my lord— I must sit."

Prince Kragen had moved to stand beside his father. From that position, he made a sharp gesture. At once, a servant hurried forward with a broad stool for the Tor.

Groaning involuntarily, the Tor lowered his weight to the seat.

"You are injured, my lord Tor," said the Alend Monarch, "and yet you propose a hard march of three days in order to confront High King Festten and his new cabal of Imagers. Is that wise?"

Behind the age in Margonal's voice, Terisa heard another quality. Perhaps because the gloom in the tent gave every shape and tone an ominous cast, she thought that the Alend Monarch sounded haunted; harried by doubt.

He had invited—no, *summoned*—her and Geraden and the Tor here in order to test them in some way. Because he was afraid.

"My lord Monarch"—the Tor seemed to lift his voice by main strength off the floor of his belly—"I am sincerely unsure that it is wise. King Joyse would never permit me to do such a thing in his place, if he were here to forbid it. But he is not here, and so I determine the nature of my own service to my King.

"The question is not one of wisdom, my lord. It is one of necessity. I go to fight the High King and his Imagers simply because they must be opposed."

For a moment, no one spoke. Abruptly, Prince Kragen made another gesture. As if a ritual had been correctly completed, servants now came forward with chairs for Terisa and Geraden. Silently, they were urged to seat themselves.

Then a tray was brought around; it held four wine goblets, one each for Terisa, Geraden, and the Tor, one for the Alend Monarch himself. Margonal drank briefly before inviting his guests to do the same.

Prince Kragen abstained as if he were only a servant in his father's presence.

Terisa peered at the Alend Monarch until her temples throbbed, but she couldn't make out any details of his face or posture or clothes. Maybe the braziers weren't intended to warm him after all. He sat as far away from them as possible.

Why did he insist on darkness? What was he hiding—strength or frailty?

"So," he said without preamble. "I have heard rumors of violence and Imagery from the intersection." Strangely, his suddenness didn't convey decision. Speaking quickly only made the note of anxiety in his voice more obvious. "What transpired there this morning, my lord Tor?"

"An unexpected and hopeful thing, my lord Monarch." For reasons of his own, the Tor made no effort to project optimism. "Master Eremis translated vileness against us—and the lady Terisa of Morgan defeated him. Some men were lost defending her," the old lord added. "Prince Kragen gallantly aided her, and so some of the men lost were yours, my lord. Yet the attack was turned against our enemies. Across the miles, Master Eremis' mirror was broken."

The Alend Monarch seemed to be fond of long silences. Eventually, he asked Terisa, "How was that possible, my lady?"

With difficulty, she forced herself to sound steady. "I guess I have a talent for flat glass, my lord. If I can see the mirror's Image— see it in my mind—I can make it change." She spread her hands as if to show the blood on them. "When I saw the Image Eremis was using, I made it go blank.

"Some of his creatures were caught in translation. I think the stress broke the mirror."

"An unprecedented display of power," remarked the Monarch, this time without pausing. "And you, Master Geraden? Do you also have a talent which this Eremis cannot equal?"

Prince Kragen stood at his father's side without moving, without offering Terisa or Geraden or the Tor any help.

Slowly, Geraden replied, "My lord Monarch, I can do roughly the same thing with normal mirrors—make them change their Images. But I haven't tried it across distance. I suspect my talent doesn't go that far. I think I have to have the glass in front of me to work with it."

Again, the Alend Monarch lapsed into silence.

To ease the strain on her vision, Terisa turned her head away, glanced around the tent. Except in the immediate proximity of the braziers, the light was only enough to let her see the servants and soldiers as concentrations of gloom. Like Prince Kragen, they all stood against the walls, waiting for their sovereign's commands—

No. Almost directly behind her, in a corner she couldn't scrutinize without craning her neck ostentatiously—a corner as dark as the spot where Margonal sat—she glimpsed another seated figure. This audience had at least one spectator who was permitted to sit in the Alend Monarch's presence.

"My lord Tor." Margonal seemed to be making an effort to key his voice to a firmer pitch. "We are old enemies—although to my recollection most of your personal warfare has been waged against Cadwal rather than Alend. You know enough of my history to understand my caution where King Joyse is concerned.

"Where is he?"

"My lord Monarch?" asked the Tor as if he didn't understand the question—or hadn't expected it to be stated so bluntly.

"King Joyse." The Monarch's enunciation hinted at anger and fear. "Where is he?"

The Tor lifted his goblet, took what was for him a modest swig. "My lord, I do not know."

Stillness spread out around him. No one moved—and yet Terisa had the impression that every Alend in the tent had gone stiff. Margonal's posture filled the dim air with warnings.

As if the pressure of the silence had become too much for him, the Tor said huskily, "Please believe me, my lord Monarch. He disappeared without consultation, without explanation. If I knew where he is—or why he has gone there—it is unlikely that I would be before you now. I would prefer to await his return, so that he could preside over our saving or destruction as he saw fit. This war is his doing and his duty, my lord, not mine."

"Yet surely you speculate," snapped the Alend Monarch promptly. "You must have some conception of his actions, some guess as to his purpose."

Carefully, the Tor replied, "Does it matter, my lord Monarch?

We must do what we do, regardless of his whereabouts—or his reasons."

"It matters to me." Margonal's voice conveyed the impression that he was sweating profusely. "While I have held my Seat in Scarab, he has twice overturned the order of the world, once for peace and prosperity, for an end to bloodshed and the depredations of Imagery, and once for the ruin of everything he has created. He has *power*, that man, the power to plunge all our lives into chaos as surely as he once raised us to peace.

"Where is he?"

Terisa looked at Geraden. She could see him a little better than anyone else; the red tinge on his features made him appear fervid, a little mad—and a little hopeless.

The Tor sighed painfully. "My lord, my only *guess* is that he has gone somehow in search of Queen Madin."

Terisa thought that the Alend Monarch was going to fall silent again. Almost at once, however, he retorted, "And Queen Madin has been abducted by Alends—or by men who appeared to be Alends. What will he do, my lord Tor, when he has rescued her?" Despite its thinness, his voice gathered passion. "I do not doubt that he will rescue her. That man fails at nothing. And when he has restored her to safety, what will he do?"

As if he were in the presence of an ambush, the Tor answered, "My lord Monarch, I only *guess* at where King Joyse has gone. Years have passed since I felt able to predict his actions."

The Alend Monarch shifted suddenly, straightened himself in his chair. "You have not studied him as I have, my lord Tor. *I* know what he will do. He will fall on me like the hammer of doom!"

Shocked, Terisa peered into the gloom, tried to penetrate it to read Margonal's face. But she could see nothing useful.

"My lord Monarch," Geraden ventured cautiously, "those men weren't Alends. Master Eremis admitted as much to the lady Terisa. King Joyse vanished before we could tell him everything we knew. That's a problem. But surely he'll find out the truth for himself. Surely when he's questioned"—tortured?—"those men, he'll realize why she was taken. To disrupt his plans for Mordant's defense. And drive a wedge between us, so we don't join forces.

"When he comes back— Surely it isn't inevitable that he'll attack you."

"Master Geraden." Slowly, Margonal's voice lost its vehemence.

"I am the Alend Monarch, responsible for all my lands and all my people—as well as for a rather unruly union with the Alend Lieges. In my place, would you be prepared to risk your entire kingdom on the naked hope that an apparent madman will recognize the truth— and respect it?"

The Monarch appeared to be shaking his head. To the Tor, he said, "You wish an alliance. But if I unite my force with yours, I will lose most of my ability to defend myself and my realm. Against King Joyse. And against the possibility that High King Festten will strike behind you when you have left Orison.

"What you wish is impossible."

Now it was the Tor's turn to be quiet for a long time. When he spoke, he sounded disappointed, even sad—but also untouched, as if nothing the Alend Monarch could do would weaken his determination.

"Then there is no more to be said, my lord. I thank you for the courtesy of this audience. With your permission, we will resume our march."

The Tor made a move to rise from his seat.

"Why?" the Alend Monarch demanded suddenly, almost desperately. "Can you deny that King Joyse appears to have gone mad? Can you deny that his purposes and policies have brought you to the verge of destruction? Why do you still serve him?"

For a moment, Terisa thought she sensed a fiery retort rushing up in the old lord, a subterranean blast. When his answer came, it surprised her with its gentleness. He might have been speaking to an old friend.

"My lord, Master Eremis and his Imagery have cost me my eldest son. In time, the High King will cost me all my family. Such men must be opposed."

Prince Kragen didn't change his stance at all. None of the servants or soldiers moved. The figure seated behind Terisa made no sound. Geraden seemed to be holding his breath.

With a rustle of rich fabric, the Alend Monarch slumped back in his chair.

Thinly, he murmured, "You are blessed with several sons, my lord Tor. I have but one. And by no act of mine can I assure his accession to my Seat. I must be careful of my risks."

Then his tone sharpened. "My lord, we would be safe in Orison. At worst, we would be safer than we are now. It is your fixed intention to march against Esmerel. What is to prevent us from taking possession of Orison as soon as you are gone?"

Apparently, the Tor had come prepared for that question. "Adept Havelock," he replied without hesitation—a bolder bluff than Terisa had expected from him. "Artagel and two thousand guards. And several thousand men and women who would rather lose their lives than be taken by Alend."

"I see," breathed the Alend Monarch as if he were sinking to the floor.

Through the dimness, Terisa barely saw him reach out and touch Prince Kragen's arm.

The Prince made a commanding gesture. At once, servants hurried forward to hold the chairs so that the Tor, Terisa, and Geraden could stand.

The audience was over.

The Tor braced a heavy hand on Geraden's shoulder and started toward the tentflaps.

Terisa turned the other way so that she could take a closer look at the person sitting behind her.

The flare of light as the tentflaps were opened confused her vision momentarily, made her squint, filled the corners of the tent with darkness. Before the soldier at the exit ushered her outward, however, she saw the mute figure in the chair clearly enough to recognize her.

The lady Elega.

At the last moment, Elega met Terisa's gaze deliberately and smiled.

Then Terisa found herself blinking in the cold sunshine outside the tent. The Tor and Geraden were already moving toward the horses.

Prince Kragen didn't emerge from his father's presence to accompany them.

Ribuld brought her nag and offered to help her mount. Apparently, no one had troubled him while he waited with the horses. For no clear reason, the fact that he also was smiling disturbed her. When had the scarred veteran learned to enjoy being alone and unprotected in an enemy camp?

She wanted to tell Geraden and the Tor about Elega—especially Geraden, who might be able to imagine what the lady's silent presence in the Alend Monarch's tent meant. Obviously, however, she had to contain herself until she and her companions had rejoined Orison's army.

The forces under Castellan Norge's command readied themselves to move again. Horsemen corrected their formations; guards on foot strode doggedly out of the castle by the dozens, the hundreds. Terisa's news perplexed and fascinated Geraden; but the Tor and Norge and even Master Barsonage didn't seem particularly interested in it. It changed nothing: they had still lost their last hope of an alliance with Alend. At the Tor's side, Castellan Norge gave the order which set the army in motion, then led it toward the intersection—toward the road which branched south in the direction of the Tor's Care.

Before the Tor and Norge, with Terisa and Geraden, Master Barsonage and the Congery behind them, reached the intersection, they began to receive reports which made them hesitate.

On the far side of Orison, the Alends had started to roll back the perimeter of their siege. Mounted soldiers took to their horses; foot soldiers formed squads.

Like King Joyse's guard, the Alend troops were moving.

Men spat obscenities and curses into the cold wind. Trying to match his Castellan's calm, the Tor asked, "What do you suppose this means, Norge?"

Impenetrably phlegmatic, Norge shrugged. "The Prince doesn't want to keep Orison cut off. Not anymore. What's left?

"As soon as we're gone, he's going to hit the gates headlong and drive his whole strength inside as fast as he can."

The Tor nodded once, stiffly. His lips had a blue color in the chill; Terisa saw them trembling. To himself, he murmured, "So the Alend Monarch masters Orison at last. And we must let it happen. My King, forgive me."

Geraden looked like he was chewing a mouthful of glass, but he didn't say anything. Master Barsonage's expression was bleak and grim. Only Ribuld kept grinning, like a man with secret sources of gratification. Terisa didn't have any attention to spare for him, however. She was too busy trying to evaluate the new clarity she had seen in Prince Kragen's face.

Would it make him happy to take Orison?

Would Elega let him be happy about it?

In a mood that resembled defeat, despite Terisa's recent victory, the vanguard of Orison's army passed through the intersection and headed south, toward the Broadwine Ford and the Care of Tor.

Unencumbered by supplies or unnecessary equipment and weapons, they set a brisk pace. Soon the last of the riders were in the intersection; the last of the unmounted guards were emerging from Orison. Southward, the ground rose slightly—not enough to block the sight of the Broadwine from the high towers of the castle, but enough to give the vanguard a view down the length of the army. Now Terisa and everyone with her could see what Prince Kragen's men were doing.

Peeling away from Orison on both sides, they formed themselves into two masses: one larger, which took shape on the road northwest of the intersection; one considerably smaller apparently positioning itself to approach the gates.

The vast number of Alend servants and camp followers had already begun to strike the tents, break down the encampment.

The Prince must have been very sure that he would be settled inside Orison before dark.

Scanning the nausea on the faces of his companions, Ribuld chuckled maliciously.

At the crest of the slow, southward rise, the Tor left Castellan Norge to lead the army. With Terisa, Geraden, Master Barsonage, and a handful of guards, he moved to a vantage off the road from which he could watch the progress of his forces—and the fall of the castle.

"How long can Artagel hold out?" Terisa asked Geraden quietly.

"A lot longer than Prince Kragen thinks," he replied, biting down hard on each word before he released it. "He knows how important this is. If he fails, the Prince can cut off our supplies."

Oh, good, Terisa groaned. Wonderful.

She could feel that her face was red, chafed by the cold. She wished the Tor looked the same, but he didn't. His cheeks were too pale; his mouth and eyes, too blue. He didn't seem to have enough blood left in him to bear what he was about to see.

Or perhaps he did. "Now, Prince Kragen," he muttered as the last of the guard reached the intersection and turned south, "do your worst. Preserve yourself and your father if you can, and remember you were warned that this would never save you."

While the lord and his companions watched, the smaller mass

of the Alend army placed itself across the road in front of Orison's gates, just beyond effective bowshot from the walls.

At the head of the larger body, Prince Kragen rode into the intersection.

With his standard-bearer carrying the Alend Monarch's pennon before him, Prince Kragen led at least six and perhaps seven thousand of his soldiers south along the road Orison's army took.

"You knew about this," Geraden said severely to Ribuld.

Ribuld grinned. "They shouted a lot of orders while I was waiting for you. I didn't have much trouble figuring out what they meant."

"And you didn't think it was worth mentioning to us?" demanded Terisa. She wanted to hit the scarred veteran. She also wanted to shout for joy.

Enjoying his own joke, Ribuld replied piously, "I could have been wrong, my lady. I didn't want to mislead you."

"They were getting this ready while we talked to the Alend Monarch," Geraden muttered with fire rising in his eyes. "The decision was already made." Which explained the excitement Terisa had seen in Prince Kragen. "They were just waiting for a final word from Margonal."

"Then why didn't they tell us?" asked Terisa.

"They don't want an alliance." Geraden sounded wonderfully sure. "They want to be ready to help if they think we're right. Prince Kragen *does* think we're right. But they also want to be free to abandon us—or even turn against us—if we're wrong.

"I told you the Prince is an honorable enemy."

The Tor didn't say anything. While Prince Kragen led his forces up the rise after Orison's army, the old lord sat on his mount with tears in his eyes and a look like a promise on his broad face.

FORTY-SIX:
A PLACE
OF DEATH

he wind continued to blow out of the south—not hard
now, but steadily, and full of cold, rattling through the
trees and along the ground like a rumor of icicles—and
Orison's army marched into the teeth of it. The men
went almost boisterously at first, when the word was passed down
the lines that Prince Kragen and his troops were coming toward
Esmerel instead of attacking the castle; then slowly the guards' mood
turned grimmer, more painful, as the wind wore down hope, drove
both men and horses to duck their heads and brunt a way forward
with the tops of their skulls. The unseasonable chill stung the eyes,
rubbed at the spots where tack or mail galled the skin; it searched
out the gaps in winter cloaks and made the air hurtful for sore lungs
and caused earaches. By the time the Tor and his forces had crossed
Broadwine Ford and halted to make their first camp, they had lost
whatever optimism they had carried with them from the Demesne.
Dispirited and worried, the army turned its back on the wind, hud-
dled into itself, and cursed the cold.

The men already looked beaten.

By Castellan Norge's reckoning, however, they had pulled
nearly four miles ahead of the Alends.

"That disturbs me," muttered the Tor while Master Barsonage
and the other Imagers chose an open patch of ground and began to

unpack their mirrors. "I do not wish to be separated from the Prince—and I do not wish to wait for him."

Norge shrugged as if the movement were a twitch in his sleep. "They're carrying all their food and equipment and bedding and tents—everything they need. They're lucky they can come this close to our pace. If Prince Kragen tries to drive them this fast tomorrow, some of them will start to break."

"And that will benefit no one," fretted the Tor. Abruptly, he called, "Master Barsonage!"

"My lord Tor?" the mediator answered.

"Do I understand correctly? This evening you will translate our necessities from Orison—and tomorrow before we march you will return everything to the castle for the day?"

Master Barsonage nodded. He was impatient to get to work. One of the Congery's three supply-mirrors was his.

The Tor kept him standing for a moment, then said, "I will wager the Alends carry enough food and water to sustain them for eight or ten days. If their supplies were added to ours, could you manage so much translation?"

That got the mediator's attention. "My lord, you propose a vast amount of material to be translated. All Imagery is taxing. And we have only three mirrors."

"I understand," the Tor replied rather sharply. "Can you do it?"

Master Barsonage glared at the ground. "We can make the attempt."

"Good." The old lord turned away. "Castellan Norge."

"My lord Tor?"

"Send a messenger to my lord Prince. Say that I wish to consult with him—that I wish to consult with him *urgently*—on the subject of his supplies."

"Yes, my lord." If Norge had any qualms about the Tor's idea, he didn't show them. Instead, he gave the necessary orders to one of his captains.

Muttering under his breath, Barsonage went back to work.

"He's right, you know," Geraden commented to Terisa as they hugged their coats and watched the Masters prepare. "That's a lot of translation for only three mirrors—three Imagers. It's going to be hard."

Terisa didn't want to think about it. In fact, she didn't want to think. Men had died to keep her alive. That was what war meant: some men died to keep others alive. The bloodshed had hardly begun. Numbly, she asked, "What do you suggest?"

He studied her. "We could help."

She blinked at him. She could see that he was cold, but he didn't seem to feel it as badly as she did. He was still able to be worried about her.

"The practice might be good for us," he said casually. "And you look like it wouldn't hurt you to be reminded that Imagery has a few"—he searched for a description—"less bloody uses."

She grimaced. "I don't think I have the strength."

"Terisa," he said at once, "listen to me. You didn't kill anybody. You were trying to stop the killing."

He touched the sore place in her, the ache of responsibility. Stiffly, she said, "They died protecting me."

"But you didn't *kill* them. Their blood is on Eremis' head, not yours."

"No," she retorted. "Don't you understand? I didn't have to give him the chance to attack me. We could have gone around the intersection. Nobody had to die. *I* made that decision."

Like Lebbick, the men protecting her had died for nothing more than a ploy, a gambit—a move at checkers.

"That's true." Geraden practically smiled at her. "You struck back. You took the risk of striking back—and all risks are dangerous. Next time, you might want to choose your risks more carefully, so nobody has to face them except you. Us.

"But you were right. That's why we're here, *we,* all of us. Including those men who got killed. To strike back. If we aren't going to strike back, we should have stayed in Orison."

Choose your risks more carefully.

"In the meantime," he said as if he knew what her answer would be, "we can make ourselves useful. The Congery has curved mirrors they aren't going to need tonight. I can tackle one of them. And there's probably a flat glass to spare. If there isn't, you can try your hand at a regular translation, where you don't have to shift the Image."

As well as she could, she met his gaze. Sometimes she forgot how handsome he was. He had a boy's eyes, a lover's mouth, a king's forehead; the lines of his face were capable of iron and humor almost simultaneously. He lacked Eremis' magnetism—he was too vulnerable for that kind of attraction—but his vulnerability only made his strength more precious to her, just as his strength made his vulnerability dear. And he was so good at turning his attention to her when she needed it—

With one cold hand, she touched his cheek, ran a fingertip down the length of his nose. "I hope Master Barsonage is in a tolerant mood," she muttered. "I might make some pretty dramatic mistakes."

"Nonsense," scoffed Geraden happily. "After the mistakes I've already made, anything you can do wrong is going to be paltry by comparison."

Chuckling, he led her toward the open ground where the Masters were unpacking their mirrors.

When he explained what he had in mind to the mediator, Master Barsonage's harried look eased noticeably. "This is too good to be true," Barsonage said as he assessed the possibilities. "Something *must* go amiss. If neither of you cracks a glass—and I feel constrained to remind you that nothing of what we have can be replaced—perhaps Prince Kragen's Alends will be overwhelmed by sentiment against Imagery, and will feel compelled to throw a few propitious stones.

"Master Vixix." This was a middle-aged Imager with hair like roofing thatch and a face as bland as a millstone. "We require your glass." To Terisa, the mediator explained, "Master Vixix has shaped a flat mirror which shows a scene lost somewhere in the Fen of Cadwal. We brought it because a fen can be a useful place to drop trash and corpses. As a weapon, however, it has little value. Perhaps it would serve for you?"

Without waiting for an answer, he instructed another Master to unpack one of the Congery's normal mirrors for Geraden.

Soon the ground was cleared, the mirrors were set, and guards stood ready to carry away translated equipment and supplies. Nodding in satisfaction, Master Barsonage approached his own glass and said, "Very well. Let us begin."

Standing more beside the mirror than before it, he gave its focus a last touch, then began to stroke the edge of the frame with one hand while muttering words Terisa couldn't distinguish.

From the Image of Orison's ballroom, two sacks of flour and a side of cured beef flopped to the ground at Master Barsonage's feet.

Another Imager produced a cask of wine, which was greeted

with a rough cheer by the nearby guards. The third began to spill a steady stream of bedrolls through his glass.

"You realize, don't you?" Terisa said to Geraden under her breath, "that I don't have any idea how to do this. I don't know what words to say, or how to move my hands, or anything."

His eyes sparkled as he faced the mirror which the Masters had unpacked for him. It showed an arid landscape under a hot sun, so dry that it seemed incapable of sustaining any kind of life, so hard-baked that the ground was split by a crack as deep as a chasm and wide enough to swallow men and horses. Despite his past, the Congery—or at least Master Barsonage—trusted him with that glass. Touching the convoluted mimosa wood frame delicately with the tips of his fingers, he smiled and said, "This may sound strange, but that isn't exactly a secret. It's one of the first things Apts learn—as soon as the Congery knows them well enough to be sure they're serious. Imagery doesn't depend on waving your hands the right way, or making the right sounds. It depends on talent. The rest—"

Interrupting himself, he came to look at Master Vixix's glass with her. In the gloom of evening, the Fen of Cadwal looked forbidding: dark and wet; unpredictable.

"Here," he said. "Move your left hand on the frame—like this." He showed her. "Gesture with your right hand—like this." He showed her. Then, without allowing her any opportunity for practice, he said, "While you're doing that, mumble these sounds." In her ear, he murmured a complex string of nonsense syllables.

"Most Apts," he commented, "work on things like this for a year, off and on. You ought to be able to handle it"—he gazed at her innocently—"almost immediately."

She stared back at him, unwilling to believe that he was making fun of her—and unable to think of any other interpretation.

"Try it," he urged, as if half a hundred guards and most of the Congery weren't watching her. "Go on."

His smile seemed to promise that nothing would harm her.

Quickly, so that she wouldn't be paralyzed by self-consciousness, she approached the flat mirror.

Move your left hand on the frame—like this. No, more *like this. Gesture with your right*—that was wrong, try again—*with your right hand—like this.* At the same time. And *mumble.*

Working hard to remember the syllables Geraden had told her, she forgot for a moment what she was trying to accomplish.

With a roar like a cataract, rank swampwater began to rush over the edge of the frame onto her feet.

Startled, she jumped back.

Instantly, the translation stopped.

The Masters and most of the guards were laughing; but Geraden's grin was too full of approval to hurt her. "I'm sorry." He chuckled. "I didn't mean to embarrass you. This is just one of those situations where if you know what you're trying to do it gets harder."

Terisa looked down at the muck on her boots. Croaking in hoarse astonishment, a frog hopped away across the hard dirt. Despite the chill, her cheeks and ears were hot from the laughter of the spectators. Balanced between indignation and mirth, she rasped, "I hope you can give me a better explanation than that."

Her tone made him serious at once. "The words and gestures don't have anything to do with translation. They're for your benefit— to help you concentrate in a particular way. When you're first learning, they help by forcing you to think about them instead of translation. And when you've learned, they help—sort of by force of habit. After enough repetition, they put you in the right frame of mind almost automatically.

"But if I told you all that first, you would think about *how* you were concentrating, instead of actually concentrating. It would be harder. Now that you know what the right frame of mind is, you'll have an easier time getting yourself back there."

He made sense. She knew him well enough to know that he wasn't trying to make fun of her. She ought to laugh—

But she had seen men die today. And she had every intention of killing Master Eremis. She was in no mood to laugh at anything.

Deliberately, she went back to the mirror and began to clear her mind so that she could shift the Image, transform the Fen of Cadwal into the ballroom of Orison.

Before long, Prince Kragen arrived in person to discuss the question of his supplies with the Tor. By that time Terisa had already succeeded at bringing a stack of groundsheets through from the ballroom—and no one was laughing. The guards and the Masters were all hard at work, preparing to feed and shelter six thousand men for the night.

Prince Kragen observed that he had no alliance with Mordant. And without an alliance he certainly couldn't entrust his army's supplies—in effect, his army's ability to function—to a group of men who were historically his enemies, in addition to being notoriously crazy.

The Tor observed that if the Alend army continued to carry its own supplies, and continued to try to keep up with the forces of Orison, it would reach Esmerel no better able to function than if it had lost all its supplies.

Prince Kragen observed that it would not hurt Alend to let Orison meet Cadwal first and test the High King's mettle.

The Tor observed that two separate armies of six thousand men each would pose a trivial problem for High King Festten's twenty thousand, compared to a united force of twelve thousand.

Prince Kragen acquiesced. He also accepted the Tor's invitation to supper. Behind his tone of doubt and his dark glower, he looked positively happy.

That night, wrapped in their blankets and an oiled groundsheet, Terisa allowed Geraden to apologize again. "I know you were right," she sighed eventually. "I just don't seem to be very resilient. All those men laughing— That's something else Master Eremis and my father have in common. They like to jeer."

"But you showed them they were wrong," Geraden countered. "None of them has ever seen a woman with talent before. Most of them have never taken a woman seriously before. Until this evening, there was a chance they wouldn't back you up, if you ever needed them.

"Now you've got their attention. The whole camp is talking about you. What you did in the intersection was good. The only problem with it is, it was too abstract to have much impact. Nobody could *see* what you accomplished. Here—" He hugged her. "Here you've got hundreds of witnesses. You're a Master. And the Masters are doing something useful, something vital. For a change.

"Terisa"—in the dark, he sounded like Artagel, eager for battle—"we're going to beat that bastard."

She hoped he was right. But she seemed to have lost the ability to laugh. For that reason, she wasn't sure.

The next morning, she and Geraden, with Master Barsonage and the other two Imagers, worked like mill-slaves to return Orison's equipment and virtually everything the Alend soldiers had carried to the ballroom. Then, guarded by a detachment of fifty horsemen, they had to drive the Congery's wagons furiously to catch up with the armies.

In some ways, that drive was harder than the translation. So much translation was a mind-numbing exertion: it sapped her strength until she felt too weak to stand; it ground her spirit down to the nub. But it wasn't dangerous. All she had to do was maintain the Image-shift, and be sure that none of Orison's inhabitants wandered into the ballroom at a bad time, and keep the glass open while guards pitched bedrolls and food sacks and cooking utensils through it.

On the other hand, the drive to rejoin the armies was distinctly dangerous.

The obvious danger was to the wagons themselves, to the mirrors they carried. From Broadwine Ford, the armies left the relatively smooth Marshalt road to turn west-southwest toward Esmerel, and the way to Esmerel wasn't particularly well maintained because it wasn't particularly well used. As soon as the wagons passed the small, clustered village around the inn which served the Ford (from a sensible distance, to avoid the danger of floods), the roadbed became much rougher.

In addition, the terrain rapidly grew more challenging. According to Geraden, what was in effect the only flatland in the Care of Tor lay along the road toward Marshalt. The rest of the Tor's Care was at best hilly; more often rugged than not; in places nearly mountainous. Despite the best efforts of the drivers, the wagons had to lumber over knobs of exposed rock, along gullies cobbled to jar bones apart, up hillsides barely packed hard enough for the horses' hooves to find purchase. And each jolt against an obstacle, each tilt over a boulder, each thud into a hole threatened the Congery's precious glass.

When the drive first began, Terisa thought that she would rest—and avoid the stiff-jointed gait of her nag—by riding on one of the wagons for a while. She soon found, however, that its ride made her nag's saddle look like a sedan chair by comparison.

If anything, the weather was getting colder. In the ravines and gullies, the wind swirled from all sides, chilling skin and bones like invisible ice; on the rises and crests, it swept straight down off the southern mountains, remorseless and keen. As tired as she was, as empty-hearted as she felt, there didn't seem to be anything Terisa could do to make herself warm.

"What do you suppose," she asked Geraden in an effort to keep her mind occupied, "those twenty thousand Cadwals are doing all this time?"

"*Resting*," Geraden snapped with uncharacteristic bitterness. "Building fortifications. Getting traps ready. Learning how to co-ordinate their movements with whatever Eremis and Gilbur and Vagel plan to do. Resting."

"Looks like we have all the advantages," she murmured. "By the time we get there, we'll be exhausted."

He nodded; then he added, "Which reminds me. We've had so many other things to think about, I forgot to mention it. I've got the strongest feeling this isn't what we're supposed to be doing."

She found that idea so upsetting that she stared at him in spite of her fatigue and the raw cold.

"Say that again."

"I've got the strongest feeling—"

Their road was little more than a dirt track trodden hard by several thousand men. It lurched over a ridge and angled down into an erosion gully. "Do you mean," she interrupted, "we shouldn't be going to Esmerel like this? We shouldn't be sticking our necks in the noose like this? It's all wrong?"

Why didn't you say so before we got started?

"No," he replied at once. "I'm sorry. I'm not being clear. I don't mean the Tor, or the army, or the Congery—or even Prince Kragen. I mean you and me. Personally. There's something else we should be doing."

The advantage of an erosion gully was that the rocks were padded with sand. The disadvantage was that the wheels tended to cut in, making the wagons harder to pull. The teams began to snort and struggle in the traces.

Hardly able to contain herself, Terisa demanded, "Like what?"

Geraden grimaced sheepishly. "I don't have the vaguest notion. That's why we aren't doing it. You know me. I always take these feelings seriously, even when they don't make sense. If I understood it this time, I wouldn't be able to stop myself."

The bed of the gully was wide enough for the wagons and riders. The walls quickly grew sheer, however; the gully became a ravine twisting among heavy hills. With an effort, she resisted a vehement urge to argue with him. Sourly, she muttered, "You and your 'strongest feelings.'"

He spread his hands. "I'm sorry. I shouldn't have brought it up. I just thought you ought to know."

She should have reassured him that he had done no harm—that he was right to tell her what he was feeling. In addition, she should have kicked him for apologizing so often. Unfortunately, she was too frightened.

Like the voice of her fear, a shout rose from one of the guards at the front of the group.

The cry was so consistent with her mood that it didn't seem to need any other explanation. For a moment, she didn't even raise her head to see what was happening.

Then there were more shouts. The walls of the ravine caught the cries and flung them into chaos along the wind. Ahead of the wagons, horsemen snatched out their swords, brandished their pikes. Guards surged past the wagons on both sides, yelling at Terisa and Geraden and the Congery to stay back.

Ribuld spurred after them furiously.

For no reason except instinct, Terisa jammed her heels into the sides of her nag.

"No!" Geraden caught at her reins.

Recovering her balance, she heard a throaty snarl among the shouts as if the ravine itself were growling for blood.

Through the press of riders, she saw a guard plunge off his mount, unseated by a wolf strong enough to leap as high as his chest, big enough to topple him.

At the same time, more wolves came off the edge of the ravine: dozens of them; leaping onto the men and horses below as if they were in no danger of breaking their own legs and backs, or didn't care; wolves with spines jutting down their back's and double rows of fangs in their jaws, and malign eyes.

Those that were close enough launched themselves at the wagons. At Terisa and the Masters.

At Geraden.

The same kind of wolves which had attacked Houseldon. Predators with his spoor in their nostrils and no fear left at all.

Screaming, one horse in the traces pitched to the ground with its shoulder torn open. Its weight pulled its fellow over on top of it, nearly upset the wagon.

A wolf crashed like a hammer into the wagon, hit it so hard that the wagonbed recoiled as if its axles were springs. Despite the tumult of shouts and pain and wolves, Terisa distinctly heard glass shatter.

The wagoner jumped from the bench, scuttled under the wagon for shelter.

Ignoring a Master who yelled at it frantically, flapped his arms at it as if it were nothing more than an tomcat, the wolf lunged off the wagon toward Geraden.

Apparently, Geraden had forgotten his sword. Instead of trying to fight, he wrenched his mount out of the way, drove his horse bucking against Terisa's nag so that both horses stumbled to the wall of the ravine away from the attack.

A guard buried the head of his pike in the wolf's skull—then couldn't work the blade free in time to defend himself from another beast which seemed to sail entirely over the wagons at him. He fell with his fists knotted in the wolf's ruff, straining to keep the fangs from his face.

The fall broke his back before the wolf had a chance to kill him.

From horseback, Master Barsonage jumped awkwardly into the bed of the other wagon. Lashing the leads, the wagoner forced his team over against the wall directly under the wolves. In that position, the leaping wolves carried over the mediator's head toward the wagon with the broken glass.

While Master Vixix and the wagoner cowered on the bench, the mediator blocked the rails with his girth, swinging his fists like mallets at every wolf within reach, using his furnituremaker's strength to batter beasts away from his mirrors.

The guards milled in the ravine, thwarting each other, striking ineffectively; the walls crowded them, blocked them. And a number of them had gone ahead of the wagons to meet the attack, with the result that now most of the wolves were behind them. Nearly shrieking in fright, Terisa cried, *"Protect Geraden! They're after Geraden!"*

Men shouted, raged; blades flashed; horses collided, knocked each other to the dirt. Nevertheless Terisa's shout pierced the confusion. The captain of the company roared orders she couldn't understand through the din.

The nearest riders wheeled back toward the wagons.

A wolf shot past the horses, slavering like a rabid thing. At the same time, two more picked themselves up off the ground behind the wagons, hurtled to the attack. And another sprang from the ravine's rim, hurling itself at the wagon between it and Geraden.

With a demented wail, the Master who had tried to shoo the first wolf away leaped off the wagonbench and attempted to catch this beast in middive.

Its weight and his leap carried the two of them over the rail among the horses.

Now Geraden remembered his sword. Still forcing his mount between Terisa and the wolves, driving her nag against the wall, he fumbled behind him, got a hand on his swordhilt, struggled to wrench the blade out of its scabbard over his shoulder.

The sword seemed to be stuck. Terisa could see a wolf already lifting from the ground as if it could fly. Wildly, almost unseating herself, she reached for Geraden's back and caught hold of the scabbard.

The blade rushed free, split the beast's head open from eye-socket to throat. Geraden was swinging so hard that only the jolt of impact kept him from being pulled off his mount by his own blow.

Out of the chaos, Ribuld's pike took another wolf by the chest and gutted it. That gave Geraden time to recover his balance—but not enough time for his lack of expertise to mislead him. Unable to haul the heavy blade back and swing it again before the next wolf sprang at him, he simply jammed his swordpoint into the beast's maw.

In case the wolf wasn't dead yet, Ribuld hacked its head off.

Without warning, the attack was over.

Men brandished their swords, shouting across the cries of the wounded; horses wheeled and stamped; the captain yelled warnings, instructions. But no more wolves appeared, either in the ravine or along its rim.

Terisa felt that she was about to fall over from holding her breath too long. Why hadn't she felt the translation? "Watch out!" she called with as much strength as she had. Maybe it took place too far away. "Eremis still has the mirror." She had the impression that she was barely audible. Maybe Eremis didn't have exactly the mirror he needed, so he had to simply release his wolves among these hills and let them hunt for Geraden in their own way. The actual translation may have happened miles or hours ago. "He can translate more whenever he wants."

"I doubt it," Geraden muttered, apparently speaking to himself. He held his sword erect in front of him and stared at it as if it appalled him. "Wolves travel in packs." Blood ran down the blade onto his hands, his forearms; the front of his cloak was splashed with red. "And mirrors have a relatively small range. There isn't likely to be another pack living that near this one." As he gripped the hilt, his arms began to shake. "After his attack on Houseldon, Eremis probably had to wait all this time just to get these wolves."

Abruptly, as if every movement hurt him, Geraden wiped the blade on his cloak and drove it back into its scabbard.

"Eremis can drop an avalanche on us whenever we're near one of his flat mirrors. But he can't force a wolf pack on another world into his reach."

The captain nodded grimly, then announced, "We're going to take precautions anyway." He sent five men ahead to catch up with the Tor and report what had happened. Ten more men were assigned scouting duties.

Somehow, Terisa had come through the attack untouched. No blood had marked her. The only stain she bore was the one Adept Havelock had left on her shirt.

This time, no more than six of the people around her were dead. Two horses were dead. Two more had to be put out of their misery. One Master was dead: Cuebard. Until she saw his body, Terisa had never heard his name spoken. The captain counted nineteen dead wolves. "Curse this terrain," he rasped. "On open ground, we could have chopped them into dogmeat—and suffered nothing but scratches."

Trying not to hurry, Barsonage and the rest of the Masters unpacked all the mirrors.

Luckily, only one was broken: Master Vixix's flat glass, with its Image of the Fen of Cadwal.

"Thank the stars." Despite the cold, Master Barsonage was sweating thickly. "We are more fortunate than we deserve."

"It's my fault," said the captain, growling obscenities at himself. "Castellan Norge is going to hang my balls on a stick. I should have had scouts around us right from the beginning."

"Don't worry about it, captain," Ribuld muttered sardonically. "He needs you too much. He won't actually unman you unless we win this war and end up safe in Orison again.

"But if that happens, watch your groin."

Several of the guards laughed, more in reaction to the fight than because they thought Ribuld was funny.

"Are you all right?" Terisa asked Geraden privately.

He shook his head; contradicted himself with a nod; shrugged his shoulders. To the cold wind and the ravine's wall, he said, "I've got another strong feeling."

"Oh, good." She tried to help him by sounding wry rather than troubled. "Somehow, I just know I'm going to love this one."

"I've got the strongest feeling—" The muscles at the corners of his jaw knotted, released. "When the fighting really starts, we'd better be sure we've got somebody with us who handles a sword better than I do."

Terisa assented bleakly. And better than Ribuld, too, she thought to herself, remembering Gart, who had beaten Ribuld and his dead friend Argus simultaneously.

Choose your risks more carefully. She intended to do that. If she could just figure out how.

Well before noon, she and Geraden, with Master Barsonage, the Congery, and the guards, rejoined Orison's army. When the Tor had assured himself that their news was no worse than the report he had received, he rumbled, "Tomorrow you will have five hundred men with you. Master Eremis may strike at you again. And tomorrow there will be a clear danger of encountering High King Festten's scouts and outriders."

That made Terisa feel neither worse nor better. Caution was sensible. On the other hand, she felt sure that Mordant's fate wouldn't be decided by a chance encounter with scouts or outriders. And she had a distinct sense that Eremis wasn't going to attack again. With his enemies so close to him now, he would wait until they came all the way into his trap, put themselves completely in his power. He wasn't interested in anything as relatively straightforward as victory. He wanted to crush and humiliate, to *annihilate* everyone who opposed him. Whatever he did when his enemies reached Esmerel would be intended to hurt them spiritually as much as physically.

When she thought about Nyle, her insides contracted until she could scarcely breathe.

Throughout the afternoon, across the complex and dangerous terrain, Orison's army and Prince Kragen's marched into the unseasonable cold. Impatient and apprehensive young men demanded a return of spring; grizzled veterans with bunions or arthritis predicted snow. Horses stamped restively, pulled against their reins, shied at nothing. Orison and encouragement seemed painfully far away, despite the magic of mirrors. Mile after mile, the defenders of Mordant shortened the distance to Esmerel.

That evening, the men stopped to make camp on the high ground of a cluster of hilltops, where the wind could get at them with all its ice, and where their lights and cooking fires would be visible in all directions—and where it would be almost impossible for enemy troops to surprise them. Prince Kragen's commanders deployed their soldiers; Castellan Norge organized the guard. Master Barsonage and the Congery unpacked the mirrors.

When the mediator uncovered his glass, the first thing he and everyone else saw in the Image was Artagel sitting atop a particularly high pile of bedrolls and groundsheets.

He still wore Lebbick's clothes, Lebbick's blood. His expression was a strange combination of excitement and boredom.

"What is that idiot doing?" demanded the Prince. "Is he not in danger of translation?"

Then: "What has he done with our supplies?"

Kragen was right: none of the Alend supplies which had been translated to Orison that morning were visible in the Image.

Before anyone else could speak, however, Artagel made his purpose clear. With the air of a man repeating an action he had already performed to the point of tedium, he held up a large sheet of parchment and turned it slowly so that it could be seen from all sides around him.

There was writing on the parchment. Across the hillside where the mirror stood, the sun was setting, and the light wasn't especially good. But Artagel was prepared for that difficulty. Around him, the ballroom blazed with torches.

His message was easily read.

What do you want done with Kragen's supplies?

The Prince stiffened; his hand fingered his sword. He watched narrowly as the Tor called for a piece of parchment and a charcoal stylus.

The old lord wrote:

Prince Kragen treats us honorably. Return his supplies.

He showed his message to Prince Kragen, then handed the parchment to Master Barsonage.

Deftly, Barsonage deposited the message in Artagel's lap.

Artagel read it, glanced around him, shrugged. He looked disappointed; nevertheless he didn't balk. He waved his arms, shouted something; and at once men and women—conscripted villagers, apparently—began running stacks and piles of Alend possessions back into the center of the ballroom.

Noticing the congested look on Prince Kragen's face, Terisa gave a small, silent sigh of relief. He would have had little or no trouble believing that he had been betrayed—and then he would have had no choice but to attack the forces of Orison.

Shortly, everything was ready. Saluting the empty air casually, Artagel left the Image so that the process of translation could begin.

While guards and Alends gathered to distribute utensils and food and drink and bedding around the camp, Master Barsonage and his fellow Imagers went to work.

Geraden joined them, using the curved glass he was accustomed to. Terisa, on the other hand, had no contribution to make. Master Vixix's was the only flat glass of any size which the Congery had brought to supplement the three supply-mirrors. So, after watching the work for a while, she went to the most obviously weary of the three Masters—a frail, nearly antique individual named Harpool, who hadn't borne the attack of the wolves especially well—and offered to take his place so that he could rest.

He accepted gratefully and tottered away at once in the direction of a cup of wine and a nap before supper. When she faced his mirror, however, Terisa found to her chagrin that she could do nothing with it. She gestured and mumbled as Geraden had taught her; she reached toward the special frame of mind, the particular concentration, which had become familiar to her the previous evening and this morning. But now nothing happened.

Geraden, Master Barsonage, and the other Imager were unaware of her problem—they were straining like cart-horses over their own translations—but everyone else in the vicinity noticed her difficulty and stopped to observe.

"She's lost it," a guard muttered. "Scared out of her."

"Give her time," snapped Ribuld loyally.

This was too much—*really* too much. Two hard days on the road. Two bloody attacks on her life, or Geraden's. Hours of mind-draining labor at Master Vixix's mirror. And now her talent disappeared as if it had been switched off inside her.

If King Joyse thought she could bear *this* on top of everything else, he was out of his mind.

For no reason except that she absolutely couldn't endure the shame of turning away, of showing off her failure in front of all those men, she tried to shift the Image.

Almost without effort, the ballroom of Orison became the Fen of Cadwal—not because she chose that scene consciously, but because it happened to be present in her thoughts.

Oh. She stared at it. The Fen of Cadwal. Her talent hadn't disappeared.

Then why—?

She touched the frame of the glass; gestured; mumbled. Like a fool, she brought a second gush of swampwater pouring onto her boots. This time, there were no frogs.

Oh.

Then she understood. She couldn't use a mirror unless she shifted the Image. Her power only functioned with Images she had placed in the glass herself.

No, that didn't make any sense. Why had she been able to use Master Vixix's mirror yesterday without shifting it?

Concentrating fiercely now, ignoring the men carrying supplies away, the men watching her, she let Master Harpool's glass resume its natural Image. Then, with the brightly lit ballroom squarely in focus, she tried again to translate a hogshead of water.

This time, it came through the mirror so promptly that she had to jump aside to avoid being crushed.

Perfect. I love this. Who says Imagery is hard?

Grinding her teeth to stifle a yell, Terisa continued translating supplies out of the ballroom until Castellan Norge announced that the Alends and the guard had everything they needed for the night. At once, she stamped away from the mirror, demanded wine from Ribuld, and drank two cups so quickly that they made her head spin.

Nearly staggering with fatigue, Geraden moved to join her. At the moment, she considered it a blessing that he was too tired to notice her knotted state; too tired even to ask how her translations had gone. But later, after a hot supper had restored him somewhat, and they went to bed together, she forced herself to tell him what had happened. She needed an explanation, if he had one to give her.

Her tone made him open his eyes to look at her sharply. He listened hard until she was finished; then he rolled onto his back and stared up at the cold stars.

"Have you got any ideas?" she asked.

He took a long moment to think before he murmured, "I'm not sure.

"This is all unmapped territory. Havelock is the only Adept the Congery has ever had—and he hasn't contributed much to our general knowledge of Imagery in recent years. We don't really understand people who can use mirrors they didn't make. For most of us, the way it usually works—you already know this—is that there's some kind of interaction between an Imager's talent and his mirror while he's shaping it. So no one can use that mirror except the man who made it.

"As an experiment years ago, the Congery took several men who wanted to be Apts, but who obviously had no talent of any kind, and let them try to make mirrors. It didn't work. Something always went wrong. You have to be an Imager to shape a mirror. And you have to be that particular Imager to shape that particular mirror.

"I'm not sure why you couldn't use Master Harpool's glass, and then you could. But we know he has a special relationship with it. No ordinary Imager could use it at all, except him. My guess is, his hold on it was too recent. You had to replace his talent with yours, impose your power on it, and you couldn't do that without shifting it first.

"If I'm right, the reason you didn't have any trouble with Master Vixix's glass is, he hadn't used it recently. In fact, he may never have done any translations with it at all. His interaction with it wasn't fresh enough to get in your way."

Terisa had no way of knowing whether this explanation made sense or not. Softly, she said, "You make it sound like the glass is actually alive."

Geraden kissed her forehead. "I don't know about that. But talent is certainly alive. The relationship between an Imager and his mirror must be alive in some way."

She thought about that for a long time after he went to sleep. *Choose your risks more carefully.* If she wanted to help fight Master Eremis—if she really intended to kill him—she needed to understand her own limitations.

The next morning, before she and the Masters had finished returning supplies to Orison, the wind brought clouds up out of the south.

The rack was thin at first, dull gray rather than oppressive; it cut off the sunlight without making the air noticeably colder. But as the morning and the march wore on, the clouds thickened, turning the sky dull, bleeding away the colors of the landscape. A solid mass covered the Care from horizon to horizon; it weighed on the morale of the armies, pressing expectation into worry, worry into dread.

At the same time, the wind became a few significant degrees warmer.

Apprehensively, Terisa asked Geraden, "You don't think Eremis has the power to translate *weather* against us, do you?"

Geraden snorted. "If he could do translations on that scale, he wouldn't need to fight us at all. He could just send out tornadoes until we collapsed."

That was a relief—of a sort. Eremis, also, had his limits. "In other words, he's just lucky to get a cold spell like this when he needs it most."

"Or we are." Geraden looked at her, grinning with his teeth. "The worse things get, the more we know we're doing what King Joyse wants. At the moment when Eremis looks most unbeatable, that's when he's most vulnerable."

Now it was her turn to snort. "Aren't you the one who accused *me* of having a morbid imagination?"

Geraden laughed, but he didn't sound especially amused.

Shortly after noon, the armies of Orison and Alend began to meet blood on the ground.

Old bloodstains: weatherworn, gone black; some across broad swaths of hard dirt; some in sheltered crannies; some clinging like lichen to rough rocks. They mottled stones and soil like the marks of a disease—infrequent at first; but soon more common, showing in open ravines or accessible hillsides all over the complex terrain, in pieces of earth where men could have fought for their lives.

"The Perdon," Prince Kragen pronounced grimly. "His men fought alone here against High King Festten. They were trapped here, hunted down in this"—he swallowed an obscenity—"this maze, and massacred.

"They could have saved themselves. They could have fled to Orison. If we understand the High King rightly, he never intended to bring his force anywhere but here. But the Perdon did not know that. He knew only that he must fight for Mordant—and that he could not trust his King. So he led Cadwal here, where High King Festten most wished to go.

"He was a valiant man," the Prince rasped, "badly betrayed. I hope that he did not learn the truth before he died. It would have been unutterably bitter."

But there were no bodies.

No remnants of weapons and gear.

No bones.

The entire region had been cleaned.

Carrion eaters might have emptied the mail, picked the iron clean; some of them might have dragged bones away to gnaw. Nevertheless the dead should have left more behind than just their blood.

Scouts brought back no word of Cadwal. Everywhere the men rode, they met old blood. In gullies protected from wind or rain, they found the marks of boots and hooves, running in all directions, trampled everywhere. But none of them encountered any evidence of High King Festten's army anywhere.

The Tor voiced the opinion that this was impossible. Castellan Norge and Prince Kragen sent out more scouts, doubled and tripled the number of men scouring the hillsides, the dry waterbeds, the stands of stubborn thicket. Yet the scouts discovered nothing, learned nothing.

And an hour or two before evening the vanguard of Orison's army and Alend's arrived in sight of Esmerel.

Master Eremis' "ancestral seat" sat at the head of a wedge-shaped valley, almost directly against the sheer defile which brought a brook running into the valley. A bowman on the roof of the manor could have hit the valleysides in three directions. From the defile, however, the valley spread wide until it was more than broad enough to accommodate the armies approaching it. Its brook, and the expanse of its floor, gave the impression that it must be one of the most pleasant places in the Care of Tor.

Its walls, on the other hand, were high and rugged; impassable more than not. Blunt outcroppings of rock supported them like ramparts. And they didn't decline as the wedge spread wider. Instead, they reared their black stones against the sky until they ended abruptly, hooking inward before they stopped as if to constrict the wide foot of the valley.

There was no blood here. Nearly a mile outside the valley, all evidence of the Perdon's life and death disappeared.

The valley itself was empty.

Esmerel was a low building, for reasons which were obvious to the eye: even in this dull, cloud-locked light, the manor's flat-roofed,

rambling profile suited its surroundings, providing enough contrast
to be distinctive, enough self-effacement to be harmonious. Terisa
had heard from Geraden that much of the house was belowground,
anchored in the rock of the valley. Instinctively, she believed that—
although she couldn't forget the sealed window and the faint light
in the room where Eremis had chained her. Maybe Nyle's cell was
on the aboveground level. Certainly the window was. It shouldn't
be hard to locate.

With Prince Kragen and his captains, the Tor and Castellan
Norge, Geraden and Master Barsonage, she studied Esmerel's front
up the length of the valley. From this distance, she couldn't make
out what gave the walls their texture; but she could see the portico
clearly, supported over the main entrance by sturdy pillars.

The door was closed. All the windows were shuttered and dark.
No one moved around the building, or in the neat horseyard on one
side of the house, or along the brook. Under the dark clouds, the
whole place had an air of desertion, as if it had been forgotten a long
time ago.

The ground, however, still held the scars of hundreds of horses,
hundreds of men.

After a while, Prince Kragen asked, "What do you think, my
lord Tor?"

"I think," the Tor muttered as if his confidence were ebbing,
"we must look inside."

"It's a trap, my lord," commented Norge.

"Of course," the Tor sighed. "Is that not why we have come,
Geraden, my lady Terisa?" He glanced at them morosely. "To place
our heads in the trap?"

For some reason, Geraden's mount distrusted the valley and
tried to shy away. Reining his horse uncomfortably, he said, "The
only way we can find out what we're up against is to go look at it,
my lord."

Terisa couldn't take her eyes off Esmerel. It held her as Master
Eremis himself did, full of promises and destruction. She had been
a prisoner there. Had met Vagel; seen Nyle. Eremis had almost had
his way with her—

"Let's go," she said without meaning to speak aloud. "Let's go
look at it."

Castellan Norge shrugged. The Tor blew his nose on the hem
of his cloak.

Prince Kragen gave Terisa a bow which suggested either mockery or respect.

As if no one had actually given any commands, orders began to sift back to the main body of the armies. While the vanguard advanced on Esmerel, the Alend soldiers and the guard followed until they were well within the relative shelter of the valley, nearly halfway to the defile; then, with a company of five hundred horsemen, the vanguard pulled ahead, and the two armies—Alend on one side of the brook, Orison on the other—began to ready themselves for camp or battle. The men closest to the foot of the valley started throwing up a precautionary earthen breastwork from wall to wall.

In silence, the vanguard approached Esmerel.

"Do you know?" Master Barsonage said to no one in particular, talking simply to steady himself, "I had never seen this manor until Geraden made an Image of it in Adept Havelock's glass. I am astonished now to observe how accurately he was able to envision it."

No one in particular listened to the mediator.

The riders continued to advance. Now Terisa could tell that the pillars of the portico were redwood; that the sides of the manor were built of waxed boards supported by stone ribs and columns. A beautiful design—but the place was still vacant. Esmerel's air of abandonment grew deeper as the riders moved farther into the gloom of the valley walls.

All the horses became restive: prancing; stamping; sawing against their reins.

Prince Kragen's standard-bearer winded a call on his battlehorn, a fierce run of notes which nevertheless sounded forlorn and maybe doomed as it echoed back from the ramparts. Nothing shifted in Esmerel. None of the windows winked or opened. Under its portico, the door looked heavy enough to withstand anybody.

Abruptly, Geraden winced; Prince Kragen spat a curse; and all at once Terisa could smell what was disturbing the horses.

The sweet, rank, nauseating reek of blood and old rot, neglected death, flesh gone to carrion.

"What's *in* there?" one of the captains asked as if he had forgotten that everyone could hear him.

"Lucky you," Ribuld muttered in response. "Lucky us. We're going to find out."

As soon as she recognized the stench, however, Terisa lost her fear. She had been expecting something like this. A spiritual attack as much as physical. Adrenaline pumped through her; energy filled her muscles. This was Master Eremis' domain: he was in his element here. Everything that happened now would happen because he intended it.

First she said, "It wasn't like this four days ago. I couldn't smell any of this." Then she said, "This is where I saw Nyle. Inside."

His face twisting, Geraden surged toward the door.

"Geraden!"

The Tor's shout snapped like a whip, jerked Geraden back. Fierce and pale, he wheeled to face the old lord.

"Come on," he whispered. "We've got to find him."

The Tor didn't drop Geraden's gaze. "Castellan Norge," he coughed, "open that door. Secure the rooms inside. We will enter when you signal for us."

Norge saluted. At least three hundred guards rode away to form a protective perimeter around the manor and the vanguard. Some men dismounted to tend the horses. The rest followed Castellan Norge on foot.

In combat formation, swords ready, they approached the door.

It wasn't bolted. When Norge lifted the latch, the door swung inward, opening on darkness.

He and his men entered the house.

Terisa scanned the harsh rims of the valley. For no clear reason, she expected to see men there: Cadwals clutching their weapons; an army moving to surround the forces of Orison and Alend. Esmerel was a trap. But that didn't make any sense. She had been a prisoner here just a few days ago. Master Eremis had his own laborium here, his furnaces and glassworks. He had spoken to High King Festten here. It was inconceivable that he would surrender the Seat of his power to his enemies.

Sure. Of course. So where *was* he?

Where had she gone wrong?

Abruptly, the Castellan reappeared.

The gloom—and the fact that he was a few dozen yards away—confused Terisa's sight. She had the distinct impression that he had gone white. He held his arms stiffly at his sides; he moved as if he carried something breakable in his chest.

"My lord Tor—" His voice caught.

Peering at the portico and the door and Norge, the Tor asked, "Is it safe?"

Norge shook his head, nodded. His throat worked. "You need to see this. They're all here."

No, Terisa thought blindly, don't go in there, don't go, it's too dangerous. But Geraden had already flung himself off his mount, was already running—

The Castellan stopped him, made him wait.

The Tor glanced wearily up at the sky. "The truth is," he rumbled, "that three days in the saddle have done little to heal my belly." The stubborn resolution which had brought him here appeared to be eroding. "I fear that once I dismount I will never get up onto my horse again."

Prince Kragen's gaze shone darkly. "I will go, my lord Tor."

The Tor passed a hand over his face. The skin of his cheeks seemed to pull away from the bones, giving him a skeletal aspect for a moment despite his fat.

"We will all go, my lord Prince," he sighed.

No, Terisa thought as if she were panicking, it's a trap, Eremis is in there, he's already killed all Norge's men. Yet what she felt wasn't panic. Instead of crying out against Norge's pallor, Norge's distress, she swung off her nag and went after Geraden.

"Nyle," he muttered urgently when she joined him—the only explanation she needed.

Heaving against his mortal weight, the Tor got his leg over the saddle, stumbled to the ground. For a moment, he sagged there as if his capacity to support himself were crumbling. But then he called up his fading strength and lumbered into motion.

With Prince Kragen, half a dozen Alend soldiers, Master Barsonage, and Ribuld, the Tor approached Esmerel on foot.

Terisa was right about Norge: his face had turned the color of old ash. He didn't say anything, didn't try to account for himself. When the Tor and Prince Kragen neared him, he pivoted harshly and stalked back into the manor.

They're all here.

Holding Geraden's hand to steady herself—and to restrain him from anything wild—Terisa entered Esmerel behind the old lord and the Prince.

Inside, the smell of blood and rot grew worse. Much worse.

Instead of fainting, Terisa tightened her grip on herself and went ahead.

The forehall was empty except for Castellan Norge and his men.

They lined the walls, pale and grim, mirroring his distress. No one else was there—no one to account for the damage which nailed boots and mud had done to the once-fine floor. Some of the marks in the woodwork looked like swordcuts.

Full of misery, the Tor started for the nearest doorway off the forehall.

"Empty," Norge croaked to stop him. "Damage like this." He gestured at the floor. "And blood. There was a fight here. But there's nobody left."

"It was like this," Geraden breathed. "In the Image I made."

Master Barsonage nodded confirmation. "I saw it."

"What do you want me to see?" the Tor demanded of Norge.

The Castellan pointed toward a wide staircase sweeping downward. His arm shook until he snatched it back to his side.

"The cellars!" Geraden spat.

Norge and the Tor, Prince Kragen and Master Barsonage, Terisa and Geraden followed a line of guards to the stairs.

The staircase blazed with light: the Castellan's men had lit lamps down the walls. From the head of the stairs, the whole descent was visible until it reached bottom and spread out into the complex underground levels of Esmerel.

The stairs were like the floors: marked, stained, scarred. From below rose the reek of death, as palpable as a fist.

On both sides of the passage at the foot of the descent, corpses had been stacked like cordwood.

Under the dried blood, among the stiff, gaping wounds, the bodies wore the armor and insignia of the Perdon's men.

Forgetting caution—forgetting sanity—Geraden sprang down the stairs three at a time. Headlong into a storehouse of the dead, he rushed to find his brother.

Terisa and Ribuld went after him, with Prince Kragen close behind them.

Norge's men were already in the cellars, lighting more lamps, opening new rooms to look for signs of life. Most of them fought grimly against nausea; quite a few had already succumbed, adding a patina of bile to the general stench. Rats ran everywhere, so busy feasting that they hardly noticed the intrusion of light and boots. As soon as she reached the foot of the stairs, Terisa noticed one stack of bodies that obviously hadn't been soldiers. They looked more like servants—the men, women, and children who belonged to Esmerel.

Trying to keep up with Geraden, she hurried on.

Corpses were piled everywhere, neatly, deliberately. High King Festten had *annihilated* the Perdon. And he had brought the Perdon's dead here. Stacked them here, left them to rot. Where the defenders of Mordant might find them.

"Nyle!"

Geraden's yell died without echo in the halls, absorbed by flesh and maggots and rot.

The belowground rooms were much larger than she would have guessed. One had obviously been a library—but all the books were gone. One might have been intended to display artwork—but all the paintings or sculptures were gone. There were workshops without tools, kitchens gutted of equipment. The people who had broken into Esmerel and slaughtered the manor's retainers had stripped it of everything valuable.

Ahead of her, Geraden faced a closed door. "What's in there?"

"Wine cellar," a guard answered as if he had just finished puking. "Doesn't have any lamps, so we left it. Looks empty."

No lamps, Terisa thought. That made sense. Wine needed to be kept cool. Lamps put out heat.

Geraden hauled the heavy door open.

Striding hard behind Terisa, Prince Kragen snapped, "Bring light!"

With her and Ribuld, he followed Geraden into the cellar.

The air was colder here—much colder—therefore less foul. In this unseasonable chill, with no one to care what happened, the temperature had dropped below freezing. She was bitterly sure that Eremis hadn't left any wine behind to be ruined.

Using the reflected illumination from the doorway, Geraden moved among the wineracks.

Guards arrived carrying lamps; they entered the cellar.

When she saw what Eremis *had* left behind here, Terisa stopped to consider the advantages of passing out.

Preserved by the cold, more bodies had been stacked on the wineracks. Judging by the sigils on their mail, they were the Perdon's captains. Here, however, they hadn't been simply piled up like lumber. Instead, the bodies had been arranged in grotesque and degrading postures, as if death had caught them in a devils' dance, abusing themselves, copulating with each other, performing intricate atrocities. The shadows cast by the motion of the lamps gave the impression that the men were still alive, yearning toward a last taste of pleasure or pain.

On the corkage table in the middle of the cellar lay the Perdon himself.

Terisa recognized his bald pate, his red, thick eyebrows, his stained and shaggy moustache, his hairy ears; she recognized the passion in his glazed, staring eyes. It would have been impossible for her to mistake the man who had once helped Prince Kragen and Artagel save her from Gart.

The way he had died sickened her to the bottom of her heart.

His limbs and torso were cross-hatched with cuts, but none of them had caused his death. No, an honest end in battle apparently wasn't satisfactory for an enemy of Cadwal, a man who had pitted himself against High King Festten all his life. The Perdon had been killed by a corkscrew driven between his teeth through the back of his throat into the wooden table, so that he lay pinned there until he drowned on his own blood.

Passing out had advantages, no question about it. Oblivion might give Terisa the comfort she craved, if she could fade into it and never come back.

At the same time, she was so angry that when she bit down her lip to keep herself quiet she drew blood.

White with strain and horror, Geraden wheeled on the nearest guard. "Where's Nyle?"

"Not here," the guard answered thickly. "Unless he's one of the bodies. No one's here." A moment later, he added, "None of the rooms down here was used for a cell."

Then someone bumped Terisa so hard that she stumbled. The Tor brushed past without noticing her, shouldered Prince Kragen aside to approach the corkage table.

For a long moment while everyone watched him, he slumped against the edge of the table; the courage and determination seemed to leak out of him, as if he were sinking in on himself like a deflated bladder.

"Oh, my old friend. My old friend."

In a constricted voice, Geraden muttered, "He was never here. You were never here." Apparently, he was talking to Terisa. "We all made the same assumption, but we were wrong. When High King Festten came here, he had to kill Esmerel's servants and maybe even

Eremis' relatives to get into the house. Eremis hasn't used this place for years."

Abruptly, the Tor raised his head and brought up a wail like the cry of his damaged guts. Terisa was behind him: she couldn't see what he was doing. She didn't realize what he had done until a terrible convulsion shook him from head to foot and then his right fist sprang into the air, brandishing the corkscrew which had killed the Perdon.

As if he had no idea what was going on around him, Geraden muttered, "We've come to the wrong place. This is just a trap. It doesn't even give us a chance to strike back."

With a tearing groan, the Tor lifted the Perdon's rigid corpse. When he turned, Terisa saw that his face was streaked with tears. In the lamplight, he looked as pallid as the dead.

"And you wanted to make an alliance with that monster," he cried to his friend's body. But he didn't expect an answer. Jerking his head at the ceiling, he shouted suddenly, "Are you laughing at him now, Eremis? Does it amuse you to do this to a man who believed you?"

Oh, Eremis was laughing, all right. Terisa was sure of it.

Dumbly, she went to the Tor's side and helped support his quivering arms until Ribuld and some of the other guards came to take the Perdon away.

When she and Geraden went back outside, they found that the weather had turned to snow.

The air was as dark as evening, prematurely dim: the snow fell so thickly that it swallowed the light. Swirling inside the walls of the valley, it blanketed the atmosphere until she couldn't see five feet past the edge of the portico—a snowfall as heavy and thorough as a torrent, and yet composed of delicate, dry flakes, bits of powder so fine they stung the skin. The guards at the door had lit torches which the snow smothered as soon as they left the shelter of the portico. Everyone else in the valley, twelve thousand fighting men, had been erased from sight. Already the white cold accumulating on the ground was two or three inches thick.

Terisa shivered with a chill that felt almost metaphysical. She had dreamed once of snow; and because of that dream she had accepted Geraden's invitation to leave her old life behind.

With Castellan Norge and Master Barsonage, Prince Kragen came out of the house, gusting curses. "By the stars," he growled, "if this snow does not blind our enemies as it does us, we are dead men. As matters stand, we will be hard pressed to locate our own encampment."

Norge struggled to recover his essential equanimity. "I think we should do that right away, my lord Prince. If we don't, we might get stuck here for the night. The armies need us. And I can't ask my guards to stay with that many corpses."

The Prince nodded. "I will instruct men to string lines to keep the horses together." Followed by his soldiers, he strode away into the snowfall and disappeared as if the flakes swept his reality away.

Rather aimlessly, Norge commented, "The Tor is resting. I'll go get him. But I don't think he'll be able to ride."

No one answered. Scowling uncharacteristically, the Castellan went back into the manor.

Master Barsonage cleared his throat. "It was a natural mistake, Geraden. We all made it. What do we know of Master Eremis, but that Esmerel is his ancestral home? What is more reasonable than the assumption that he built his power here—held his prisoners here?"

"Yes, it was reasonable," Geraden said in a bleak tone.

"No, it wasn't." Terisa hadn't intended to speak; she didn't know what she was going to say until she said it. "King Joyse told me to think." Her mind was full of the Perdon and the Tor, and the implications of snow. "Esmerel was too obvious.

"We had to come here. We didn't know where else to go. But we should have known he wouldn't be here."

"And now we're stuck," Geraden finished.

No one argued with him.

Guards brought horses up to the portico. The mounts already had snow caked in their manes, on their withers; the flakes were so thick and cold that the horses' heat turned it to ice as it melted. But the wind kept the hoods and shoulders of the guards clear.

Men began to file out of the house. After a while, Castellan Norge and Ribuld brought the Tor to the portico. Physically, the old lord had never looked worse. His limbs were as frail as a child's; his hands shook as if the chill had already reached his bones; his skin was the color of moldy potatoes.

Nevertheless the glare in his eyes was unquenchable. His outrage at what had been done to the Perdon sustained him when his body and his ordinary courage failed.

As long as she ignored the rest of him and watched only his eyes, Terisa was able to keep her grasp on hope.

Norge was right: the Tor couldn't bear to be mounted again. But Ribuld stayed with him, and the Castellan assigned other guards to his side; shuffling heavily, he moved away into the snow. Like Prince Kragen, he seemed to vanish from the world almost immediately.

At a word from Norge, Terisa, Geraden, and Master Barsonage climbed onto their beasts. Led by guards who were connected with lines to other guards, invisible in the impenetrable snowfall, they rode away from Esmerel to search for their encampment.

Swirling snowflakes burned her eyes. They prickled on her cheeks like bits of premonition; hints sharp enough to cut, cold enough to numb the damage they did.

Despite the caution of the riders, they reached their part of the camp sooner than she would have believed possible. The men of Orison and the Alend soldiers had laid out a protected position for their commanders near Esmerel and the head of the valley, away from the exposed foot of the wedge; so Terisa and Geraden, Master Barsonage and Castellan Norge didn't have as far to go as the rest of the guards. And tents had already been set up for them: Master Harpool and his companion had apparently been at work with their mirrors for some time, translating equipment and supplies from Orison.

Master Barsonage and Geraden hurried to join them.

From horseback, Terisa saw bonfires and torches around her, some of them as much as twenty or thirty feet away. Maybe the snowfall was thinning. Even so, it was at least four or five inches deep. And—unless her sense of time had failed completely—sunset was still an hour or so away. Even if the snowfall *was* thinning, there might be a foot or more on the ground before night.

A guard urged her to dismount and enter a large tent which had been raised for the Tor and Castellan Norge; but she stayed where she was, trying to read the suggestions in the snow, until the Tor himself reached the camp. Then she got down and went with him into shelter.

A servant took his cloak, then brought food and wine, which the old lord rejected with a grimace. Supported by Ribuld and another guard, he lowered himself into a camp chair. He had snow in his eyebrows, snow on his head. His cheeks were the color of worn-out ice. Ribuld knelt in front of him, offered to pull off his boots; he declined that comfort as well. "I must go out again soon," he murmured. "There is no escaping it."

"My lord Tor," Ribuld said in a tone Terisa hadn't heard him use since Argus' death, "you don't need to go out. Prince Kragen and Castellan Norge will come to you."

"Ah, true," sighed the Tor. "But if I remain here, who will give the King's guard my blessing? I must visit every campfire tonight, every squadron, so that every man will know his bravery is valued and his loyalty, precious.

"No, Ribuld, I will wear my boots. I do not mean to take them off again."

Ribuld bowed and withdrew to stand with Terisa. Around his scar, the veteran's face was tight with unexpected grief.

"Ribuld—?" she tried to ask; but she couldn't find the words she wanted. All she knew about him was that he had been Argus' friend; he liked and served Artagel; he seemed to enjoy suggestive conversation. And he had killed Saddith to save Lebbick. He would have saved Lebbick from Gart, if he could.

"My lady," he said, almost snarling to control himself, "my home's in the Care of Tor. Not far from Marshalt. I fought for the Tor—that's how he knows my name—and for the Perdon, too, before I joined the King's guard." He looked at her as if, like her, he couldn't find the right words.

Maybe she understood. "Take good care of him," she replied softly. "He needs you more than Geraden and I do."

The twist of Ribuld's expression could have meant anything.

Terisa left the tent and went to see if Master Harpool required help.

As she and the Masters finished translating the last of the tents and bedrolls, the snowfall abruptly lessened. She felt cold to the bone; her face was wet and numb; her fingertips left trails of moisture down the frame of Master Harpool's glass. Nevertheless the easing of the snow caught at her attention like a call of horns—

—the call for which her heart had always been waiting.

She jerked her back straight, lifted her head, spun around before anyone else noticed the change.

Yes. Blowing down from the head of the valley, the wind parted the snow like curtains, let the gray light of early evening through the clouds. As if without transition, Esmerel and the valley became a winter landscape before twilight, a scene which needed only sunshine to reveal its surprising beauty.

Perhaps the horns—and those who sounded them—were on the far side: the far side of the manor, where the defile brought the brook gamboling over its ice into the valley.

Now Geraden joined her, looked around. Several of the Masters breathed thanks that the snow was stopping. Guards expressed the same sentiment less delicately. None of them could hear the premonition in the air *whetted with cold,* the implication *as penetrating as splinters.*

"Get the Tor," she said as if the horns had lifted her out of herself, despite the fact that she couldn't hear them, could hardly remember them; maybe she had never heard them. "Get Prince Kragen. Tell them to hurry."

"Terisa?" Geraden asked. "Terisa?"

She ignored him. She didn't need reason: intuition was enough. She was fixed on Esmerel and couldn't look away.

Master Barsonage sent Imagers into motion. Someone shouted for the Castellan. Infected by an urgency they couldn't explain, guards began to obey, began to run. She had that much credibility with them, anyway.

Then past the snow-clogged side of the manor *came charging men on horseback. As the horses fought for speed, their nostrils gusted steam, and their legs churned the snow until the dry, light flakes seemed to boil.* The sides of the valley and the snow muffled every sound, but each movement was distinct, *as edged as a shard of glass.*

Three riders with longswords held up in their fists and keen hate in the strides of their fierce mounts. The riders she had seen in the Congery's augury. The riders of her dream.

"Bowmen!" Norge snapped from somewhere nearby. "Be ready! We'll pick them off as soon as they get in range."

"No!" coughed the Tor. He had come out of his tent; he stood with his legs splayed in the snow, supported by Ribuld. "That is a traitor's deed. Let them approach. We kill no one unless we must!"

"Well said, my lord Tor!" Prince Kragen arrived at a run, with his sword in both hands. Using the blade as a pointer, he commanded, "Look more closely!"

The light wasn't good: at first, she couldn't see what the Prince was pointing at. But after a moment she realized that each of the riders had a white cloth tied to the tip of his sword.

Flags of truce.

A *truce*, Eremis? With *you?*

One of the riders was certainly Master Eremis: that was unmistakable. He drove his mount plunging forward with an air of jaunty peril, as if he were in the grip of an exquisite and unutterable joy.

Beside him came Master Gilbur, hunchbacked and murderous.

The third man she didn't know by sight. Nevertheless she was sure of him. The arch-Imager Vagel. A relatively small man, at least compared to Eremis and Gilbur; dwarfed by his charger. Lank gray hair fluttered from his skull. He rode with his toothless mouth open like the entrance to a pit.

The riders of her dream.

"The gall of those bastards," someone whispered. Ribuld? "The *gall.*"

Abruptly, Gilbur and Vagel hauled on their reins, wrenched their horses to a halt. Just beyond reliable bow-range, they wheeled and stamped, waiting.

Master Eremis came forward as if he feared nothing. Intensely nonchalant, he approached his enemies.

There he stopped.

"My lord Prince." His tone was full of secret laughter. "My lord Tor. Master Barsonage. Terisa and Geraden. How fortuitous that you are all here together."

The Tor leaned on Ribuld as if he had lost the power of speech. Geraden scowled intently, concentrating not on anger but on the ramifications of Master Eremis' presence. Terisa faced the tall Imager and felt the blood congeal in her chest.

"We are not patient with traitors," snapped Prince Kragen: he was the Alend Contender, accustomed to authority. "Tell us what you want and be done with it."

Master Eremis paid no attention to that demand. "My companions fear you," he said. "They believe you will kill them if they come near, despite our flags of truce."

Prince Kragen snorted. "That would be an action worthy of you, Eremis. We are not such men."

In response, Master Eremis laughed along the wind, sent mirth and scorn across the snow. "Do you hear?" he called over his shoulder. "The Alend Contender thinks he is not such a man as we are."

"You're lucky Lebbick isn't here," muttered Norge. "He'd castrate you first and worry about honor later." But no one listened to him.

Spurring their horses, Master Gilbur and the arch-Imager came forward to join Master Eremis.

"Tell us what you want," Prince Kragen repeated harshly.

"As I say," gloated Master Eremis, "it is fortuitous that you are all here together. Because you *are* all here, you will be able to give me what I want. I have a requirement for each of you. Each of you except the Congery"—he sneered at Master Barsonage—"which has my permission to go sodomize itself whenever it chooses."

Instead of retorting with threats, the mediator folded his arms on his thick chest and produced a grim smile. "Be careful what you say, Master Eremis," he articulated. "Your insults only betray your fear."

"Fear!" Master Gilbur waggled his sword mockingly. "The day you teach me to fear you, Barsonage, I will walk into this camp naked and let you use me however you wish."

The Tor made a weak gesture, requesting silence. In a thin voice, he said, "You mentioned requirements, Master Eremis."

"Indeed," Eremis replied with a grin. "And if you satisfy me, I am willing to let you all live."

Norge pronounced an obscenity. No one else spoke.

"By now," the tall Imager explained, "even the thickest-headed among you must realize that we have an alliance with High King Festten. By force of Imagery and arms, we are prepared to crush you completely. We will wash the ground with your blood until you beg to share the Perdon's fate."

"Try it," grated Ribuld. Again, no one else spoke.

"As it happens, however," Master Eremis continued humorously, "the High King is not a comfortable ally. He wants to rule the world—and I intend that mastery for myself. Our ambitions are not well mated."

"Doubtless," the Tor sighed. "What are your requirements?"

Master Eremis straightened his legs, raised himself high in his saddle. "My lord Tor, my lord Prince, I require you to surrender."

This time, it was Prince Kragen who laughed—a bloody and mirthless guffaw.

"If you do so," Eremis went on smoothly, "if you will pledge your precious honor and your lives to me, we will turn against Festten. Our Imagery and your arms will break him here, far from his sources of supply, his reinforcements. Then it will be Mordant which rules the world, not Cadwal.

"From the first," he commented while everyone stared at him, "my plans have cut in two directions. We are prepared to *annihilate* you, my lords. You are too paltry—you have no hope against us. At the same time, however, I have maneuvered Festten and his strength into a position of vulnerability—here, my lords, *here*—so that he, too, can be annihilated.

"Your choice is simple. Serve me and live. Refuse me and die."

Geraden held himself still. Terisa glanced at him and saw that he wasn't looking at Master Eremis. He was watching the Tor with a dangerous brightness in his eyes.

Growling curses through his moustache, Prince Kragen also turned toward the Tor.

For a long moment, the Tor said nothing. In fact, the way he stood, his slumped and dependent posture, suggested that he didn't know what was going on. Nevertheless, before the Prince could lose patience with him, the old lord found his voice.

"You mentioned requirements for each of us. Except the Congery. What do you want from Master Geraden and the lady Terisa?"

Terisa caught her breath while the knot of anger and fear inside her pulled tighter.

Master Eremis shrugged, grinning as if only an iron will kept him from laughing his heart out. "A small sacrifice, my lord. It will cost you little. I require them for myself."

Master Gilbur snickered.

No, Terisa ached inside herself. No.

Geraden watched the Tor as if he expected something wonderful or terrible from the old lord.

"As a condition of your surrender," Eremis explained. "When you have pledged your honor to me—and when Terisa and Geraden have been given into my hands—at that moment, High King Festten's doom is assured."

No.

Prince Kragen started to retort; but the Tor stopped him with another weak gesture. "An interesting suggestion, Master Eremis." The old lord's frailty made him sound mild. "Unfortunately, you are a demonstrated traitor. What assurance is there that you can be trusted?"

"You need none," Master Eremis shot back hotly, happily. "Your choice is too simple for assurances. If you do not satisfy me, you will be destroyed."

"My lord Tor," Prince Kragen put in fiercely, "he wants the lady Terisa and Geraden because he fears them. Their power is our assurance that he cannot destroy us."

Again, the Tor gestured for silence, asking Kragen to bear with him.

"Master Eremis, you are overconfident," he said softly, "so sure of your strength and your *superiority* that you insult us. You insult our honor—but that does not surprise us." His voice sank as he spoke—and yet gathered force at the same time, so that his quietness carried like a shout. "No one expects a man of your moral poverty to respect honor.

"You do wrong, however, to insult our intelligence.

"You have no interest in our surrender. You have no intention of turning against High King Festten. I doubt that the arch-Imager would permit such betrayal." For some reason, Vagel shook his head. "Gart certainly would not. Your only interest here, your only purpose in coming, is to take the lady Terisa and Master Geraden from us."

Eremis had heard enough. "My lord Tor," he snapped, "I have not yet begun to insult your intelligence—but now you demonstrate that you are mad. I fear no one. I covet Terisa's female flesh. And I have a score to settle with Geraden. My reasons for coming are exactly as I have explained them."

No! Terisa protested, insisted, *no.*

And the Tor said, "No.

"You are a fool, Master Eremis. In the end, you will die a fool's death. If you had the slightest wish for our service—if you had the slightest intention of turning against the High King"—his passion was too fundamental to be shouted—"*you would have treated the Perdon with more respect.*"

Dismissing Eremis, he moved with Ribuld's support toward his tent.

"My lord Tor." Geraden's face shone; he looked ready now to tackle both Master Eremis and High King Festten single-handedly. He spoke to the old lord's back formally, and his voice seemed to defy the snow and the wind, as if he had the power to command them. "King Joyse has been fortunate in his friends—but never as fortunate as when he won your loyalty."

The Tor stumbled, but Ribuld caught him.

Prince Kragen also turned his back. Glowering bloodshed, he barked at Castellan Norge, "Give these traitors a count of five. Then instruct your bowmen to kill them."

He didn't stay to watch the riders as they lashed their mounts away from Norge's eager call, surged back in the direction of the manor and the defile, strained for speed as if they had been routed. Bowing first to Geraden, then to Terisa, the Prince strode off toward his own camp.

Terisa heard a few bowstrings thrum, a few arrows hiss in the air. Unluckily, none of the riders fell.

As if on signal, more snow came down the valley. Snow closed off the light, swarmed over the tents, drifted onto Terisa's head and shoulders. The riders of her dream—and the Congery's augury. Geraden was right: she belonged here. And King Joyse was fortunate in his friends.

She put her arms around Geraden, hugged him tightly. Holding each other close, they followed the Tor toward the shelter of his tent.

Before the snowfall became thick enough to blind the sky completely, two or three of the guards on sentry duty down at the foot of the valley thought they saw an imprecise puff of smoke overhead, riding against the wind. Then the sight was gone, and snow came down so thickly that it made everything dark.

FORTY-SEVEN:
ON THE VERGE

he Tor's tent was large enough for eight or ten people to stand and shout at each other, but it was ascetically furnished—one bedroll for the lord, one for the guard at the tentflaps, a brazier for warmth, three lanterns hanging around the pole, the Tor's camp chair, a few other stools. Maybe he wanted it that way: maybe he feared that if he ever became comfortable he wouldn't be able to move again. Or maybe he wasn't willing to put any more strain than necessary on the Masters and their translations.

When Terisa and Geraden entered the tent, they found the Tor in his chair, leaning as far back as it would allow. His eyes were dull, and he was panting thinly, as if he needed somehow to get more air past an obstacle which hurt him whenever he inhaled. Ribuld and one of the guards' physicians had removed his cloak, his mail, his shirt. Ribuld was dumb with misery.

For the first time, Terisa saw the place under the lord's ribs where Gart had kicked him.

Involuntarily, she tightened her grip on Geraden.

The Tor's injury was swollen like a tumor, black-purple and angry; it bloated out from his belly as if his skin might burst.

"Oh, my lord," Geraden breathed, nearly groaned. "What are you doing to yourself?"

The Tor had been bleeding inside for days, killing himself with the effort to fill his King's place.

He made a dismissive gesture; he may have wanted Terisa and Geraden to go away. Nevertheless they stayed where they were. After a moment, Geraden asked the physician, "How is he?"

"As you see," the man muttered. "I told him this would happen. We all told him." He mixed some herbs in a goblet and handed it to the Tor. "He's too old. He drinks too much wine. He shouldn't be alive."

For some reason, Ribuld shot out his arm, knotted his fist in the physician's cloak, jerked the man silent. Almost at once, however, he seemed to realize the uselessness of his anger. Releasing the physician, he muttered an apology, then moved away to get a stool for the Tor's legs.

With his legs supported, the lord was able to sink down until he could rest his head on the back of the chair. His eyes were closed now, and a bit of the strain went out of his breathing; apparently, the physician's herbs did him some good. He looked like he might sleep.

He didn't, however. Without opening his eyes, he murmured, "Where?"

The physician stopped to listen.

"'Where,' my lord?" asked Ribuld.

The Tor's fat lips tightened around a spasm of pain. For a moment, he couldn't breathe. Then, tightly, he asked, "Where is Nyle?"

Where is Nyle. Where are Eremis and Gilbur and Vagel. Where is their laborium. Where is the High King. Terisa resisted an impulse to curse herself.

Geraden squeezed her, then left her to approach the old lord. Controlling himself grimly, he said, "We've been wrong, my lord. Terisa and I. He was never here. We just assumed he would use Esmerel." Geraden glanced at Terisa. "I guess Nyle made the same assumption. He told Terisa Eremis was here. But he wasn't."

Clenching his courage, Geraden concluded, "We've brought you into a trap we can't get out of."

The Tor inhaled weakly around his hemorrhage. "Where?" he repeated.

"Somewhere close." Geraden seemed to be speaking to Terisa as well as to the lord. "Close enough for High King Festten to attack us. Close enough for Eremis and Vagel and Gilbur to find their way here through the snow. If I had to guess, I'd say the first thing Eremis did after he decided he wanted to rule the world—maybe even before he found Vagel—was build a secret stronghold for himself. Somewhere in these hills." Somewhere in this maze. "But it could be anywhere. Even if it's just on the other side of the valley rim, we can't get to it."

The Tor exhaled thinly, a constricted sigh. "What will you do?"

"About what?"

"What will you do"—the Tor made an effort to be clear—"when Master Eremis decides to use Nyle against you?"

Terisa was glad that the old lord couldn't see the flush of distress in Geraden's face, the flinch around his eyes.

"I don't know," Geraden murmured.

"Maybe," she said without thinking, "maybe we can find them. The snow will cover us. It's almost night. Maybe we can sneak out through that ravine and find them."

Geraden shook his head. "Snow and night will cover him, too. They'll cover his guards. If we don't get lost and freeze to death, we'll probably be captured."

All right. All right. It wasn't a good idea. But we've got to do *some*thing. We can't just sit here and watch—watch—

Watching the lord's struggle to breathe made Terisa feel sick and wild.

At that moment, she heard voices outside the tent: a bark of command, a muffled acknowledgment.

The tentflaps were swept aside, and King Joyse strode in.

He startled Terisa so badly that she nearly stumbled to her knees.

He was filthy. Clots of mud clung to his battle gear—his breastplate and mail leggings, the protective iron pallettes on his shoulders, the brassards strapped to his arms. His mail had been cut, hacked at by swords. Blows dented his breastplate. Blood stained his thick cloak and the leather under his armor; black streaks marked the tooled scabbard which held his longsword. Grime filled his beard, caked his hair to his scalp.

Nevertheless he entered the tent like a much younger man. He strode forward with strength in his legs, authority in his arms; and his eyes flashed a blue so deep that it was almost purple.

When he saw Terisa and Geraden, he grinned like a boy.

"Well met. Better to come late than not to come at all, I always say."

"My lord King," Geraden breathed, gaping. He was too surprised to bow, almost too surprised to speak. "Are you hurt?"

"A few scratches." The King's grin broadened into the smile Terisa remembered, the smile of innocence and pleasure, the sunrise which lit all his features and made him the kind of man for whom people were willing to die. "Nothing my enemies can pride themselves for."

He might have gone on, but the Tor stopped him.

Hearing King Joyse's voice, the old lord jerked up his head, snatched open his eyes. Urgently, almost frantically, he hauled his legs off the stool and blundered to his feet like a surfacing grampus. Around the vivid bulge of his hemorrhage, his bare skin looked as pale as disease, tarnished with frailty and need.

Tottering, he caught a hand on Ribuld's shoulder. "Prince Kragen," he gasped. "Summon the Prince."

Then he plunged to his knees as if the ground had been cut out from under him.

Ribuld started to help the lord, but King Joyse's presence daunted him.

Bowing his face to the canvas, retching for breath, the Tor panted, "My lord King, I beg you."

King Joyse's smile turned to ashes on his face.

"I beg you. I have brought your guard and your Congery and all your friends to destruction. Tell me I have not betrayed you."

"*Betrayed* me?" The passion in the King's face was wonderful and dire. As if he had no arthritis and no years, no weakness of any kind to hamper him, he caught hold of the Tor's arms and raised him to his feet by main strength. "My old friend! If you have put all I love and all my force in the path of ruin, you have not betrayed me. If you have sold my kingdom to the Alend Contender, so that I have nothing left to rule, you have not betrayed me. You are here— *here*, where the fate of the world hinges." Tears trailed through the grime on his cheeks. "My lord Tor, I have used you abominably. I considered you an obstacle, your loyalty a stumbling block. And you have served me better than my best hope."

Hardly able to bear what he heard, the Tor clamped his hands over his face and shuddered as if he were sobbing.

King Joyse glanced up and down the Tor's frame; at once, his expression darkened. To the astonished physician, he snapped, "How was he injured? How severe is his hurt?"

"A kick, my lord King," the physician fumbled out quickly. "The High King's Monomach. He bleeds inwardly." The man faltered, then forced himself to say, "If he does not rest, he will die. And even if he does rest, I cannot vouch for his life. He has used himself"—the physician seemed unaware that he was aping the King's words—"abominably."

"Then he will rest," King Joyse replied in a tone which no one could have ignored. "You will give him your best care. If he dies, you will justify yourself to *me*."

Without waiting for an answer, he eased the Tor back into his camp chair. The Tor collapsed against the chair back weakly.

Geraden put a hand on Ribuld's arm. "Prince Kragen." He spoke in a whisper; but his tone was like the King's, irrefusable. "And Master Barsonage."

Ribuld went out of the tent in a daze.

"Now." King Joyse faced Terisa and Geraden. He stood slightly poised, as if he were ready to spring, and his eyes blazed blue. "You have a great deal to tell me. Before Prince Kragen comes. Begin from Gart's attack in the hall of audiences.

"Where is Castellan Lebbick?"

His intensity was so compelling that Terisa almost started to answer. Geraden, however, had other ideas. He shifted a bit away from her, a bit ahead of her, placing himself between her and danger. Folding his arms on his chest, he said firmly—so firmly that Terisa was simultaneously amazed and proud and frightened—"You've been fighting your enemies, my lord King. I can decide better what to tell you if you'll tell me who gave you your 'scratches.'"

The King's eyes narrowed. "Geraden," he said harshly, "do you remember who I am?"

Geraden didn't flinch. "Yes, my lord King. You're the man who abandoned the throne of Mordant when we needed you most. You're the man who brought us all to the edge of ruin without *once*"—his anger stung the air—"having the decency to tell us the truth."

Instead of retorting, King Joyse studied Geraden as if the younger man had become someone he didn't know, a completely different person. A moment later, he shrugged, and the peril in his gaze eased.

"Your father, the Domne," he said evenly, "has given me many gifts, both of friendship and of service. His greatest gift to me, however, is the loyalty of his sons. I trust you, Geraden. I have trusted you for a long time. And I have given you little reason to trust me. You will answer me when you are ready.

"I have been fighting, as you see"—he indicated his battle gear—"to rescue Queen Madin."

Rescue Queen Madin. Rescue the Queen. Terisa didn't understand how that was possible—the distances were too great, the time too short—but his mere statement filled her with so much relief that she could hardly keep her legs under her.

"Doubtless," King Joyse explained, "you have been told of the strange shapeless cloud of Imagery with which Havelock broke Prince Kragen's catapults. That shape is a creature, a being—a being with which Havelock has contrived an improbable friendship.

"I must confess that when you told me of the Queen's abduction I became"—he pursed his lips wryly—"a trifle unreasonable. It was always my intention to lead whatever forces Orison could muster myself. I meant to beg or intimidate an alliance out of Margonal. I could coerce the Congery somehow. For that reason, my old friend"—he nodded toward the sprawling Tor—"had no place in my plans. I did not know that I would need him."

"That's my fault," Terisa said abruptly, unexpectedly. Geraden had placed himself between her and the King for a reason, a reason she ought to respect. Nevertheless she couldn't keep still. "You were doing what you had to do. You hurt the Tor and Castellan Lebbick and Elega and everyone else so they wouldn't realize your weakness was only a ploy. So they wouldn't betray you. But I already betrayed you. I told Eremis"—the thought of her own folly choked her—"told Eremis you knew what you were doing. That's why he took the Queen."

King Joyse looked at her hard, so hard that she blushed in chagrin. Yet his gaze held no recrimination. After a brief pause, he said, "My lady, you were provoked," and returned his attention to Geraden.

"As I say," he continued, "I became unreasonable. I abandoned you. Though he pleaded with me to reconsider, I forced Havelock to translate his strange friend for me, and that shape bore me to the Care of Fayle as swift as wings. At the debris of Vale House, I found the trail of a motley collection of the Fayle's old servants and soldiers attempting to pursue Torrent and the Queen. That trail led me eventually to Torrent's—eventually, I say, or I would have returned to you a day or more sooner—and so to Torrent herself and the Queen.

"At the cost of much hardship and privation and danger"—his eyes hinted at pride—"my demure and retiring daughter saved her mother. She enabled me to find the Queen and set her free.

"Her abductors defended themselves as well as they could— well enough to prevent the Fayle's men and me from capturing or questioning them—but at last they fell." The state of his gear testified that the battle hadn't been easy. "When I had taken Queen Madin and Torrent to safety in Romish, Havelock's friend brought me here as quickly as possible."

Geraden absorbed this account without obvious surprise or appreciation. When King Joyse had finished, Geraden asked noncommittally, "And you didn't stop in Orison? You don't have any news from there?"

The King was losing patience. "Do I look like a man who has spent time on social amenities and conversation? I knew that if I did not find you here I could return to Orison at my leisure. But if I had stopped there first and failed to find you, the delay might have made me too late to join you. I have learned nothing, heard nothing, since the moment I left the hall of audiences.

"Geraden," he concluded warningly, "I must know what has happened in my absence. I must hear the tale you brought to Orison with Prince Kragen. I cannot go into battle without that knowledge."

"My lord King," Geraden responded as if he were immune to Joyse's impatience, "Eremis is holding my brother Nyle hostage somewhere near here—a stronghold of some kind, probably. Eremis is going to use him against us. Against me. And it's my doing. If I hadn't been so determined to stop him from betraying you for Elega and Prince Kragen, he never would have been vulnerable to Eremis. He wouldn't have been locked up where Eremis could get at him.

"But it's your doing, too. You've always been such a friend of the Domne. You welcomed Artagel. You went out of your way to draw me to you. And yet you always ignored Nyle.

"His yearning was as great as mine. He has plenty of ability. And he was raised from the beginning on Artagel's stories about you, the Domne's stories. He would have been willing to kill for you by the time he was *six*."

"Geraden," King Joyse growled.

Nevertheless Geraden went on, "Why didn't you value him at

all? Why didn't you give him something to save him while he was still young enough to save?"

"You exceed yourself," snapped the King. "I have not come all this way to answer such questions."

"But you're going to answer this one," Geraden replied as if he were sure—as if he had the capacity to make King Joyse do what he wanted. The hint of authority in his voice was so subtle that Terisa scarcely heard it. He meant to wrest some kind of truth from his King.

And the King did answer. To her astonishment, he retreated visibly, with a crestfallen air, a look of embarrassment; Geraden had touched an odd shame. "Yes," he muttered, "all right. You are right. I always did ignore him. There was always a quality in his dumb need which I disliked. He pitied himself before I could pity him—and so I had no desire to pity him.

"But that is not the reason.

"Artagel was another matter altogether. His talent with the sword was obvious. Anyone would have welcomed him. But you, Geraden—" The King's gaze was angry and hurt at once, as if his own sense of culpability baffled him. "I did not choose you out of a desire to give you precedence over Nyle. I would not have done that to the son of a friend. No, I drew you to me because I had already seen your importance in Havelock's augury."

Geraden hissed a breath; but King Joyse didn't stop.

"The glass which he broke when I was an infant showed you exactly as you appear in the Congery's augury"—for a moment, the King's voice sounded as raw as splintered wood—"surrounded entirely by mirrors in which Images of violence reflected against you. How could I let you be? I had to save you, if that were possible. And if it were not, I had to give you the chance to save me.

"Geraden," King Joyse admitted in frank pain, "on your father's love, I swear to you that I slighted Nyle's yearning only because I was not wise enough to see where it would lead him. The Domne has given me nothing but love and loyalty. In the matter of his son Nyle I failed him."

For a long moment, Geraden didn't speak. When he did, his throat was tight with emotion. "We all failed, my lord King. For my part—I swear to you on my father's love that I'll save you if I can. No matter how many people you've hurt. You haven't been honest with us for a long time, and I *hate* that. But you're still my King. Nobody can fill that place but you."

Terisa couldn't keep quiet any longer. "Castellan Lebbick is dead," she put in cruelly to get the King's attention. She needed answers of her own. "Gart killed him. All he managed to do before he died was save the Tor."

That made Geraden turn toward her, made King Joyse face her again.

The two men looked unexpectedly like a match for each other, suited to meet each other's demands.

"I defended you," she said with Lebbick's body vivid in her mind, and the Perdon's; with the Tor's hurt displayed under the light of the lanterns. "I stood up in front of everybody and told them what Master Quillon told me. You made yourself the only reasonable target. So the enemies you hadn't been able to identify would attack you instead of someone else, somewhere else. I told them. That's why we're all here. We decided to trust you even after you abandoned us.

"But Master Quillon is dead. Castellan Lebbick is dead. The *Perdon* is dead. The Tor is dying." Her distress accumulated as she spoke. She thought that she would never be reconciled to all the different kinds of pain King Joyse had exacted from his friends. "Nyle is a hostage, and Houseldon has been burned to the ground, and Sternwall is sinking in lava, and the Fayle doesn't even have enough men left to rescue his own daughter, and now we're probably going to be slaughtered because we don't know where Eremis' stronghold is," oh, curse you, curse you, you crazy old man, "and I want to know how you stand it. How do you live with yourself? How do you expect us to trust you?

"You can't help us now!" Overwhelmed by unpremeditated bitterness, Terisa cried, "You can't even beat Havelock at *hop-board!*"

Despite her outburst, however, King Joyse faced her gently. Her accusation hurt him less than Geraden's had: maybe he was readier for it. His face softened while she protested against him; his gaze was blurred by compassion. He waited until she was finished. Then, incongruously, he pulled an old handkerchief out of the seam of his breastplate and handed it to her so that she could wipe her eyes.

Geraden stood now at the King's shoulder as if he had been

won over. "Terisa—" he began; but King Joyse touched his arm, stopped him.

"No, Geraden. I must answer her.

"My lady, I have already proved myself to you, after a fashion. You have seen atrocities in Mordant. Yet it was not I who perpetrated them. If I had not, as you say, made myself a target, if I had not risked those I love most in the name of my weakness, those atrocities would be everywhere. Without the lure of my weakness, Eremis might have had great difficulty forging an alliance with High King Festten—and so he would have had no choice except to afflict Cadwal and Mordant and Alend with vile Imagery until all things were destroyed. At the cost of Quillon's life, and Lebbick's, and the Perdon's—at the cost, yes, of my own wife's indignation, my own daughter's betrayal, I have procured my enemy's name as well as his attention, so that for Cadwal and Mordant and Alend there is still hope. I have given us the opportunity to fight for our world.

"But that is not what you wish to know, is it?"

His voice searched her, and his eyes seemed to probe her bitterness. When he looked at her like that, she felt an unaccountable desire to tell him about being locked in the closet, as if it were his fault in some way, as if there were something he could have done about it. Until this moment, he had cut himself off from her—as her father had cut himself off. What made King Joyse a better man than her father?

"You dislike what I have done," the King said, "but you are able to grasp the necessity of it. Otherwise you would not have supported me. No, my lady, what you want from me is a more immediate hope. You wish me to be greater than you can imagine. You wish me to justify myself with power. You wish me to tell you that I have the means to save you."

Involuntarily, she ducked her head, unable to meet his steady blue scrutiny.

"Terisa," he said softly, "my lady, I cannot save you. I do not have the means.

"You know that already," he continued at once. "As you have observed, I cannot so much as defeat the Adept at hop-board. It is only a game, of course, a mere exercise—but I cannot forget that the pieces live and breathe, with names and spouses, children and bravery and fear. I am an *unreasonable* man. When Quillon told me that Myste went to you before her disappearance, I risked myself and all my plans in order to challenge you, even though Havelock's augury had given me reason to think I knew where she had gone. When my wife is threatened, I do not ask whether any larger need should outweigh her peril in my mind. I lack Havelock's particular sanity.

"And the same unreason weakens me everywhere. Shall I tell you a thing which shames me? When I learned that you had fled to Havelock after Quillon's death, that you had gone to him for rescue with Master Gilbur hot behind you, and that he had refused you— My lady, Havelock is my oldest friend. It was he who put me on the path to become what I am. But when I learned that he had refused you, I struck him—"

Geraden's eyes widened at that revelation; but he said nothing.

"Nevertheless," the King went on as if mere shame couldn't hold him back, "I am here. When Quillon was killed—Quillon, who had served me so long with such courage and cunning—I knew that this battle was mine to wage, rather than only to command. The blood must be on my hands. I will not have my pieces so contemptuously used. I will not allow Master Eremis to tilt the board, to remake the world in his own image." Terisa could have sworn that he was growing taller, rising to power in front of her. "Do you believe I care nothing for Lebbick's suffering, or the Tor's? Do you believe I have not felt your distress—or Geraden's—or Elega's?"

"My lady, you have not seen me fight."

Curse you. Oh, curse you completely. I'll do anything you want. Just tell me what it is.

"I *have* seen you fight, however," put in Prince Kragen as he came between the tentflaps. "Though it galls me to say so, my lord King, I am glad that you have come."

The Prince had Ribuld with him, and Castellan Norge. Master Barsonage entered the tent on the Castellan's heels. And with them came a slim figure cloaked from head to foot in dark satin, face and shape and even hands hidden. As Prince Kragen strode forward to confront the King, as both Master Barsonage and Norge stopped and stared as if they couldn't believe their eyes, the cloaked figure slipped back along the tent wall, trying to remain as unobtrusive as possible.

"My lord Prince." King Joyse swung away from Terisa and Geraden; the keenness in his stance intensified. "Master Barsonage." He looked ready to leap in any direction, haul out his sword at a moment's notice. "Captain Norge.

"I have said it before, but I will gladly say it again. We are well met."

"My lord King." The Tor tried to reach his feet against the physician's restraining hands. His voice sounded as thin as a light breeze in cornshucks. "I must speak."

At once, King Joyse turned toward the Tor; but he kept his back to the tent wall, away from Prince Kragen. "Speak sitting, my lord," he commanded. "And speak as little as possible. Your life is precious to me."

Muffling a groan, the Tor sagged.

"If we are here wrongly, the fault is mine alone," he said in a deathbed whisper. "Master Geraden and the lady Terisa have discovered their talents. Already they have worked miracles of Imagery. Norge has become your Castellan, at my command. He leads the forces of Orison."

With a visceral shiver, Terisa realized that the Tor was struggling to prepare King Joyse for his encounter with the Prince.

"Master Barsonage and the Congery have devised means of supply and defense, in accordance with your strictures. We would not have come so far without them.

"Prince Kragen is here with six thousand Alend soldiers because he is an honorable man."

King Joyse put a hand on the Tor's naked shoulder, mutely urging the old lord to conserve his strength. "'An honorable man,'" he echoed distinctly, as if he had doubts on that point. Almost without transition, he appeared to become someone different—a figure of barely suppressed anger, spoiling for conflict. Facing the Prince again, and speaking mildly, but with a bright threat in his eyes, he asked, "Does my old friend mean that he and the Alend Monarch have formed an alliance?"

"No." Prince Kragen studied the King warily. The excitement which had brought him here was alloyed with a long-standing distrust; but his posture made it clear that he wouldn't back down from his own desires. "He means that he has explained to the Alend Monarch his intention to place his head on Eremis' cutting-block and die rather than submit to a war of attrition he cannot win. And the Alend Monarch sent me to accompany him with the bulk of our force because we have no other way to determine whether the Tor's intention is mad or brilliant. My instructions from my sovereign are to join the Tor or to flee, according to the things I learn here."

"Margonal is crafty," commented King Joyse with deceptive nonchalance, "and apparently he has grown in courage. Well, now you are here, my lord Prince. What have you learned?"

Prince Kragen allowed himself a noncommittal shrug. "I have learned that we are indeed trapped. All our heads are on the cutting-block, and Alend will stand or fall with Mordant, regardless of my instructions."

"I think not," King Joyse retorted with the air of a man pouncing. "I think you will turn against us at the last and join Cadwal, to preserve your father's true cowardice."

At that, Kragen's head jerked back; a flush of fury darkened his cheeks; he closed his fist on his swordhilt.

In response, both Ribuld and Norge braced themselves to draw their blades. The cloaked figure against the tent wall started forward, then retreated. Geraden edged closer to Terisa, moving to protect her from the danger of swords.

No, she thought urgently, you don't understand, Prince Kragen is here *with* us, *with* us.

The Tor repeated hoarsely, "He is honorable. Honorable."

"My lord King," the Prince said between his teeth, "because you *are* the King, and because I have been told at length why I must trust you, I will assume you have *reason* to accuse me of such a betrayal."

"I have *reason*," snapped King Joyse. "During my absence, I saved Queen Madin from her abductors. It will not surprise you to hear that when at last I found her she was across the Pestil. In Alend, my lord Prince. Her abductors were Alends, and she was being taken by the most direct route toward Scarab."

Prince Kragen's mouth tightened under his moustache. His dark eyes burned with old enmity, with decades of violence, generations of bloodshed. He looked willing to gut King Joyse on the spot.

Yet he contained his outrage. And he didn't draw his sword. "And you persist," he demanded, "in the mad belief that I am capable of such a vile act?"

"No!" Terisa protested. "Eremis did it. He told me so." What was the matter with King Joyse? How could he suddenly be so wrong-headed? "It's just a trick to keep you and the Prince from joining forces."

Before she could go on, King Joyse pointed a forbidding finger at her. "That proves nothing." The command in his stance forced her to be still. "Master Eremis has a pact with Cadwal. Why not with Alend?"

"Because," the cloaked figure cried, "*he is honorable!*"

"You do not trust him." Elega swept the hood back from her head as she advanced, and her vivid eyes flashed in the lantern-light. "Is the Tor wrong? Are Terisa and Geraden?" She called every gaze to herself, a cynosure of indignation and passion. Bright as a flame, she challenged her father. "He held Orison in the palm of his siege for days and *days*. He could have taken you apart stone from stone. Yet he withheld. Does that mean nothing to you? He allowed you *time* to prove yourself. And you *dare* accuse him of dishonor? *You dare that to my face?*"

King Joyse looked at her as if he were stunned.

"No, Father!" she raged. "The only dishonor in this tent is *yours!* It was *you* who refused to support the Perdon, *you* who refused to hear the Fayle. It was *you* who humiliated Prince Kragen in the hall of audiences, *you* who allowed Terisa's attacker to roam Orison freely, *you* who drove Myste away. You have no *right* to doubt the Prince. There is no alliance between Alend and Mordant because no one is able to trust *you!*"

Emotions throbbed under the King's old skin: outrage; alarm; disbelief. And vindication? *She carries my pride with her wherever she goes.* For a moment, no one moved; he didn't move. Elega met his stare as if she were prepared to outface the world.

All at once, King Joyse burst out laughing.

"Oh, very well, my lord Prince," he chortled while the people around him stared. "You are honest, and your father is honest, and I must apologize. If I do not, she will take the skin from my bones."

Geraden's mouth hung open. Prince Kragen clenched his jaws as if he didn't dare speak.

"It was not wise to bring her with you," King Joyse went on, "a woman in battle, a useful hostage if Eremis should capture her. But it was *honest.* If you intended treachery, you would have left her with Margonal. And she would not love you if you had such treachery in you. I know that about her.

"My lord Prince, please accept my regrets—and also my thanks. If we can be saved, it will be because of your courage, as well as your honor."

As King Joyse spoke, the excitement came back to Prince Kragen, the strange new eagerness which had led him into risks no Alend had ever hazarded before. His mouth twisted up the tips of his moustache. Slowly, he produced a smile to match Joyse's humor.

"Why do you think the decision was mine? Have *you* ever been able to tell her what to do?"

In response, the King laughed again; kindly, happily. He grinned like a new day. "Tell *her* what to do? *Me?*" Elega glared at him in confusion, but he didn't stop. "I am only her father. Tell her what to *do?* Most of the time, I am hardly allowed to make suggestions."

Then he sobered. "One thing, however, I will tell *you,* my lord Prince. Heed me well. While this war lasts, you will obey my orders." Now his tone admitted no argument: his command was as clear as a shout. "If we do not work together, we are doomed."

Prince Kragen only hesitated for a moment; then, still grinning, he nodded once, briefly.

Still ignoring the surprise and consternation and hope around him, King Joyse turned to Elega.

"As for you, my daughter," he said gladly, "you are pride and joy to me." Taking her hands, he raised them to his mouth and kissed them. "No one could have done better. The Queen herself could not have done better. Alone and without power or position, you have made an alliance where none existed.

"Oh, you please me!" Abruptly, he swept his gaze around the tent, swung his arms expansively. "You all please me! If we cannot save our world now, it will be because I have failed you, not because any one of you has failed Mordant. You have all given me better than I deserve."

In sheer joy, he kept on laughing; and after a moment Geraden joined him. Then, surprising even himself, Prince Kragen began to chuckle. Elega's smile grew softer and easier as it spread.

Master Barsonage shook his head, laughing as well. Terisa squeezed her eyes hard to keep herself from weeping foolishly; but she didn't start to laugh until she realized that the Tor was snoring as if nothing had happened.

They talked together for a long time, King Joyse and Prince Kragen, Terisa and Elega, Geraden and Master Barsonage, with Castellan Norge looking on as if he would have found a good night's sleep far more interesting. Guards brought supper, cleared it away when it was done. Ribuld helped the physician put the snoring Tor to bed. For the most part, King Joyse and Prince Kragen and Elega listened, asking an occasional question, while Terisa and Geraden and the mediator recounted and explained. Little of what was said was news to the Prince or Elega, but King Joyse listened intently, emitting concern and curiosity and approval like benefactions.

His friends and supporters had done well: he said that repeatedly. His unwilling allies had done well. His smile shone on everyone until the tent was full of warmth; he seemed to take every sad or hurtful thing onto himself, so that no one around him felt blamed or criticized for confusion or distrust or failure. The time passed in a glow, and Terisa understood at last why so many people had loved and served him for so long. She no longer wondered why the Perdon had sacrificed himself and all his men for a King who had abandoned him, or why the Tor had come to her in the dungeon to beg her to save herself for the King's sake, or why the Domne was able to view the destruction of Houseldon without recrimination against his old friend, or why Queen Madin's first reaction on hearing of her husband's peril was to rejoin him. Terisa felt that way herself now, would have done those things herself.

She felt that she had come through hate and defeat to something else, to a kind of settled commitment, a mood in which all things were possible. She wasn't exactly eager to face the coming day—but she wasn't afraid of it, either.

For his part, Geraden was eager. His eyes shone at his King, and he took every occasion he could find to look toward Terisa and smile, as if he wanted to say, See, I told you he's worth serving.

He didn't come down from happiness until the talk turned to battle plans.

Master Barsonage described the Congery's resources, and King Joyse gave him instructions for the Masters. The King and Prince Kragen devised chains of command, ways to convey messages; they made the best arrangements they could to treat the injured and feed the well; they deployed in their minds the forces of horse and foot. And gradually Geraden's expression turned somber.

"What troubles you, Geraden?" asked Prince Kragen eventually.

Geraden shook his head, staring at nothing.

"Say it, Geraden," King Joyse urged mildly. "Words will not hurt us."

"I'm sorry, my lord King, my lord Prince." Geraden tried to force a happier look onto his face, without much success. "Nothing's wrong. I just can't get rid of the feeling that Terisa and I don't belong here."

Oh, good, Terisa thought dimly. This again.

"Why?" inquired the King. "Where else should you be?"

Geraden grimaced in exasperation. "I have no idea." Almost at once, however, he added, "But it's obvious we're useless where we are. The Congery doesn't really have mirrors to spare for us. And if we had mirrors, what could we do? We don't know where Eremis' stronghold is. We don't know"—a more crucial point—"what it looks like. We have all this talent—and Eremis presumably thinks we can hurt him, or why would he try so hard to hurt us?—but there doesn't seem to be anything we can *do*."

Prince Kragen frowned studiously; Elega nodded as if she understood the problem. But for some reason King Joyse seemed unable to take Geraden's concern seriously. "Well, Geraden," he said in a tone of confidence, "you can hardly expect advice from *us*. Those talents are yours, not ours. You are the only judge of what you can and cannot do."

"True," put in Master Barsonage. He seemed glad that he wasn't responsible for whatever Geraden and Terisa did.

"You will think of something in good time," concluded the King comfortably.

Before anyone could object, he began to dismiss his companions so that they all could get a few hours of sleep.

Terisa made sure that Geraden came with her when she left the Tor's tent. He wasn't actually reluctant to accompany her: he was simply so caught up in King Joyse that he had trouble tearing himself away. The King insisted, however; and she and Geraden went out into the snow to find their bedroll.

She had no intention of sleeping. In fact, she couldn't imagine sleeping, under the circumstances. She just wanted to have Geraden to herself for a while.

They found their bedroll at the edge of the light cast by the guards' lanterns outside the Tor's tent. The snow was still falling, although less heavily; but the bedroll was wrapped in a waterproof canvas sheet, with one large end propped up by sticks to form a kind of miniature tent, letting air into the bedroll while keeping snow off its occupants. The only trick, Terisa soon discovered, was to get *into* the bedroll without tracking too much snow—

Shivering, she and Geraden swaddled themselves in their blankets and hugged each other for warmth.

"Have you got any ideas?" he asked; his mind was still on King Joyse and battle.

"Yes," she said, "but they don't have anything to do with Imagery."

With her hands and her lips, she persuaded him to think about her instead. She wanted her whole body and her heart to be full of him, as if he were an antidote to Master Eremis and violence.

After that, they found it easier to relax.

Nevertheless they got up a few hours later—a long time before dawn—when King Joyse emerged to begin readying his forces.

The snowfall had stopped. It covered the ground deeply, shrouded the tents and bedrolls of twelve thousand men; it melted off the backs of the horses; it muffled every sound, absorbed even voices, and kept the campfires all across the valley small. King Joyse himself looked small in the face of so much snow and darkness. The way he rubbed his hands together suggested that the cold had brought back his arthritis. Nevertheless his eyes gleamed with blue. Gusting steam into the lantern-light, he demanded of Castellan Norge in feigned vexation, "Where's that slugabed Prince?"

Norge shrugged with so little show of enthusiasm that the King chuckled. "Make an effort to stay awake today, Castellan," he joked. "Our lives may become quite stimulating."

The Castellan allowed himself a wan smile.

Through the light, Prince Kragen appeared with several of his captains and the lady Elega.

Together, he and King Joyse moved away to visit as much of their combined army as possible, ostensibly to explain their plans and reassure their men, but primarily to make King Joyse's presence—and his alliance with Alend—as widely felt as possible; to give every soldier and guard as many reasons for hope as possible.

At the same time, Master Barsonage and the Congery began to unpack mirrors. The Imagers needed time to get into position—and to conceal themselves. Several hundred men went with them to defend them, and their mirrors.

At the tentflaps, Terisa and Geraden learned from Ribuld that the Tor was still sleeping. They left the old lord.

With Elega, they watched the army prepare.

The mediator and his comrades translated more food from Orison. Horsemen delivered supplies throughout the camp and brought bedrolls and tents by the thousands back to the Masters. Huge stacks of hay appeared and were carried away for the mounts. The entire valley seethed with motion—dimly seen by firelight from the higher ground where the Tor's tent had been pitched—as thousands of men visited the brook and the latrines and the cooking fires.

"What do you think our chances are?" Terisa asked to ease the cold anxiety gnawing inside her.

"We're well bottled in this valley," Geraden muttered. "That's bad. On the other hand, it looks like we can only be attacked from one direction. The defile is too narrow. They can't send enough men through it fast enough to hurt us seriously. That's good. So what they'll try to do is drive us toward the walls. If we get too close, they can drop all kinds of things on us."

"If Eremis has a mirror with Esmerel in the Image," Terisa said, "or any part of this valley—"

"Then," Geraden finished for her, "he can attack us any way he wants." Abruptly, he turned and looked at her hard. "But he won't. He won't risk it. He'll be afraid of you. If you shattered his glass, he wouldn't be able to see what's going on. What you did back at the crossroads is going to save us. If you hadn't done that, we'd probably all be dead by now."

She didn't know how true that was. Nevertheless the fact that he said it loosened a knot inside her. "Thanks," she murmured to him privately.

"And there are other hopes," the lady Elega commented. While darkness still filled the valley, her indoor beauty clung to her, and in the lantern-light her eyes seemed luminous with knowledge. "The world is full of strange things, which our enemies do not understand. Master Eremis comprehends only fear and power. He is blinded by his contempt. He does not grasp how far valor may go against him."

Terisa hardly heard the King's daughter. She was thinking, *Choose your risks more carefully.* And she was thinking, *We're useless where we are.* Geraden had the strongest feeling—

Unfortunately, no flash of inspiration came to her.

The sky began to grow pale. Laboring urgently, Master Bar-

sonage and his companions translated unnecessary food and bedding
and encumbrances back to Orison. Scouts were sent to watch the
foot of the valley. Shifting through the gloom, the army moved into
its battle formation: wedged-shaped, like the valley, but reversed, so
that an attack from the foot of the valley would meet the point of
the wedge and split, be forced against the walls itself; a wedge with
mounted troops at the edges for mobility and a core of foot soldiers
for strength.

When the sky grew pale enough to cast the valley rim into stark
relief, everyone saw that during the night siege engines had been
pulled into place.

Catapults: black against the pearl heavens: six, seven—no, nine
of them around the valley, ready to pitch rocks or boulders onto the
heads of Mordant's defenders.

Terisa groaned uselessly.

A murmur rose from the army. At first, she thought it was a
reaction to the catapults. But then she saw King Joyse striding toward
her from among the troops, holding his standard high in his fists.
On the hillside leading up to the Tor's tent, he fixed his plain purple
pennon, drove the butt of the standard into the snow and the ground.

The flag rose and fluttered there as if he had brought it straight
from the Masters' augury.

"Here we stand."

Terisa had the impression that King Joyse wasn't shouting. Yet
his voice carried as if it could reach every corner of the valley.

"Let them come against us if they dare."

No one cheered. No one got the chance.

Without warning, the beat of a wardrum throbbed in the air.
The sound came from far away, down below the foot of the valley;
yet like the King's voice it carried, a flat, fatal pulse so visceral that
Terisa seemed to hear it with her throat and chest rather than her
ears.

And from below the foot of the valley the darkness gathered
into motion.

FORTY-EIGHT:
THE CONGERY
AT WORK

T he beat of the drums didn't waver. It continued to labor up the valley like the march of doom.

During the night, the sky had blown clear. Now as the sun rose, the heavens modulated from pearl to an ineffable purple-blue, transforming to vastness the mere scrap of King Joyse's pennon. Although the valley remained in a clenched gloom, enshadowed by its walls, the effect of clear daylight around the ramparts was to make the catapults look smaller, less imposing. According to the sun, those siege engines were only sticks of wood lashed together, as capable as toys of throwing a few rocks at irregular intervals. And the snow gave the ramparts themselves an aspect of enchantment and play.

Terisa didn't believe it. King Joyse's men were vulnerable to toys which threw rocks.

King Joyse obviously didn't believe it, either. After he had set his standard and cast his defiance, he called together Castellan Norge, his captains, and Prince Kragen, as well as all the Masters who weren't already deployed. Terisa, Geraden, and the lady Elega joined him in time to hear him say, "We are readier to meet the High King than he thinks—thanks to the forces of the Alend Monarch, and to the dedication of the Congery. Nevertheless he has sprung his trap well. We must find a reply to those catapults. Men who must dodge danger from the sky will not fight well on the ground."

"The best thing," Norge observed, "would be to circle around behind them. But we can't do that. I'm willing to wager Festten has the defile sealed."

"Find out," commanded the King.

With a nod, Castellan Norge sent one of his captains to lead a scouting party.

"Do you have any ideas, my lord Prince?" King Joyse asked.

Prince Kragen squinted up at the walls. Slowly, he said, "There are regions of Alend—especially among the Lieges—where the villagers cannot get to market without scaling cliffs as bad as these. I have men who are good with ropes and rock."

"My lord Prince," one of the captains objected, "Cadwal isn't going to leave those catapults unprotected. Anybody who climbs those walls is going to be defenseless on the way up—and outnumbered at the top."

"We must make the attempt in any case," King Joyse pronounced. He wasn't looking at Prince Kragen or the captains. He was looking at the gathered Masters. "Any harm we can do to those catapults will be worth the cost."

Several of the Masters shuffled their feet. Some of them studied the ground. In their robes and chasubles, they seemed decidedly unadventuresome. Without the mediator to lead—or goad—them, they had the air of men who would have preferred to be at home doing research.

After a moment, however, Master Vixix cleared his throat. "My lord King." He rubbed a nervous hand through his thatch of hair. "I have a small glass I shaped as an Apt. It shows little more than a puddle of dank water. But when I translated a bit of that water— purely as an experiment—it ate a hole in my worktable.

"I carry it to defend myself."

King Joyse nodded sharply. "Very good, Master Vixix. Can you climb?"

The Master shrugged, showing as much discomfort as his bland features allowed. "I fear not, my lord King."

"He can be carried," said Prince Kragen.

Vixix faltered for a moment. Then he took a deep breath. After all, he was old enough to remember Joyse's years of glory.

"I will do whatever I can, my lord King."

"Very good," King Joyse repeated, and turned his attention to the other Masters.

Eventually, three more Imagers admitted that they carried personal mirrors which might be useful against a catapult—or a catapult's defenders. With Master Vixix, they were hustled away by one of Prince Kragen's captains.

Geraden met Terisa's gaze and shrugged ruefully.

Elega studied the lower end of the valley as if she expected some kind of alteration to take place when the sun rose high enough, changing the churned and clotted snow until it became a setting for wonders.

The mass of the Cadwal army below the valley was plainly visible now: sunlight blocked from the valley itself caught the standards and armor of High King Festten's forces and made them shine. Twenty thousand men? Terisa wondered. They looked like more than that— more than enough to crush King Joyse's mere twelve thousand. Of course, the High King had had plenty of time to bring up reinforcements during the siege of Orison—

When were the catapults going to start?

Was she going to spend the entire battle trying to run away from falling rocks?

Abruptly, the wardrums ceased.

The absence of the beat snatched at everyone's attention.

After the silence came the hoarse, bleating call of a sackbut.

A rider left the massed front of the Cadwal army. His armor burned with sunlight as if he were clad in gold.

At the end of his spear, he displayed a flag of truce.

"An emissary," observed King Joyse. "The High King wants to speak to us. He means to offer us an opportunity to surrender."

Growling through his moustache, Prince Kragen asked, "Why does he bother?"

"He hopes to see some evidence that we are frightened."

"Will you meet him?"

"*We* will, my lord Prince," the King said; his tone didn't encourage discussion. "It may surprise you to hear this, but in all my years of warfare and contest, I have never had a chance to laugh in High King Festten's face."

Elega's eyes shone at her father as if she were delighted.

The Cadwal emissary was stopped and held at Mordant's front line, and a horseman brought to the King the message that High King Festten did indeed wish to speak to him and Prince Kragen. In reply, Joyse sent back word that he and Kragen were willing to meet Festten midway between the two armies as soon as the High King wished.

Mounted on sturdy chargers which had been trained for combat, King Joyse and Prince Kragen rode down the valley, accompanied only by Castellan Norge. Before them stretched the Cadwal army, as unbreachable as a cliff. And above them on the ramparts, the catapults watched and waited, apparently oblivious to several hundred men with ropes and four Masters who were already attempting to scale the walls at a number of different points.

At the front of their army, the King and the Prince waited until they saw High King Festten emerge from his own forces.

"Watch for treachery," Norge warned, stifling a yawn.

"Treachery?" King Joyse chuckled grimly. "The High King only betrays those he fears. At the moment, I feel quite certain he does not fear us. That is his weakness." At once, he amended, "*One* of his weaknesses."

"My lord King," Prince Kragen said like a salute, "I admire your confidence."

King Joyse gave his ally a fierce grin. "You justify it, my lord Prince."

When they saw the High King leave his guards behind, they rode out alone to meet him, crossing clean, white snow unmarked except by the emissary's passage.

At the agreed spot—a long bowshot from both armies—the three men came together. No one offered to dismount; and High King Festten kept some distance between himself and his enemies, as if he expected them to do something desperate. The stamping of the horses raised gusts of dry snow around the riders.

He was a short man—too short, really, for all the power he wielded. He compensated for his shortness, however, by wearing a golden helmet topped with a long spike and an elaborate plume. Between the cheekplates of his helmet, his eyes were stark, as if he had outlined them with kohl to give them force. His beard as it curled against the gold breastplate of his armor was dark and lustrous, probably dyed; only the lines and wrinkles hidden under his whiskers betrayed that he was older than King Joyse—and dedicated to his pleasures.

Ignoring Prince Kragen, he said, "Well, Joyse," as if he and the King were intimately familiar, despite the fact that they had never met, "after years of success you have come to a sorry end."

"Do you think so?" King Joyse smiled a smile which held no innocence at all. "*I* am rather pleased with myself. At last I have a chance to deal with all my enemies at once. It was only with the greatest reluctance that I allowed the Alend Contender to persuade me to offer you this one last chance for surrender."

If this remark surprised Prince Kragen, he didn't show it.

"'Surrender'?" spat the High King. Clearly, King Joyse had caught him off balance. "You wish *me* to surrender?"

King Joyse shrugged as if only his sense of humor kept him from losing interest in the conversation altogether. "Why not? You cannot win this war. The best you can hope for is the chance to save your life by throwing yourself on my mercy.

"You may be unaware," he went on before High King Festten could sputter a retort, "that your Master Eremis has offered me an alliance against you—which I have accepted."

"That is a lie!" the High King shouted, momentarily apoplectic. Quickly, however, he regained control of himself. In a colder voice, a tone unacquainted with pity, he said, "Master Eremis is mendacious, of course. But I have not trusted him blindly. Gart is with him. And he knows that I have commanded Gart to gut him at the slightest hint of treachery. Also he is aware that I no longer need him. I can *crush* you now"—he knotted his fist in the air—"without Imagery.

"You have no alliance with him. And the strength of Alend is as paltry as your own.

"No, Joyse, it is *you* who must surrender. And you must surrender *now,* or the chance will be lost. You have thwarted me for years, denied me for decades. The rule which is my *right* you have cut apart and dissipated and limited. You have opposed my will, killed my strength—*you have denied me Imagery.* There is no day of my life which you have not made less. If you do not capitulate to me *here,* I will exterminate you and all you have ever loved as easily as I exterminate *rats!*"

At that, King Joyse looked over at Prince Kragen. Mock-seriously, he said, "Come, my lord Prince. This discussion is pointless. The High King insists on jesting with us. In all the world, no one has ever succeeded at exterminating rats."

Casually, he turned his horse away.

His dark eyes gleaming, Prince Kragen did the same.

Together they rode back to their troops. The High King was left so furious that he seemed to froth at the mouth.

That was Joyse's way of laughing in his face.

Behind them, the sackbut blared again—and again. With a palpable thud, the wardrums resumed their labor.

Around the valley rim, all the catapults began to cock their arms.

"Now," said King Joyse to the Prince and Castellan Norge, "If Master Barsonage is ready, we are ready. I do not doubt that High King Festten and Master Eremis have a number of unpleasant surprises in store for us. For the present, however, we will stand or fall according to our success against those engines."

Prince Kragen considered what could be seen of the men climbing the walls. Quite a few of them were out of sight, concealed among the complex rocks. That was a good sign: perhaps the men would also be hard to spot from above.

Grimly, the Prince reported, "Each catapult will be able to throw at least twice before it is threatened."

King Joyse nodded. "Castellan, only the front lines are required for battle—say three thousand men. Unless Master Barsonage miscalculates. Instruct the rest of the men to watch the catapults and protect themselves as best they can.

"Oh, and ready the physicians," he added before Norge could ride off. "Provide horses for litters. Tell them we will use Esmerel as our infirmary. It is unpleasant, but we have no other shelter to offer the injured."

"Yes, my lord King." Castellan Norge spurred away.

The King and Prince Kragen returned to the pennon, where Terisa, Geraden, and Elega waited, fretting.

The massed front of the Cadwal army was in motion, marching to the insistence of the wardrums.

As that army approached the foot of the valley, it took on its attacking formation: a core of horsemen like the shaft and point of an arrow; flanks of foot soldiers on both sides to provide the cutting edges of the arrowhead.

The pulse of the drums quickened slightly. The army increased its pace. All the catapults were cocked; now they took on their loads. Apparently, High King Festten wanted to time his charge so that it coincided with the first throw of the engines.

King Joyse remained on his mount to improve his view down the valley. From horseback, he looked tall and sure, capable of anything. "Sound my call," he said to his standard-bearer, who stood guard at the pennon.

Putting his trumpet to his lips, the standard-bearer raised a blast like a shout into the morning.

The sackbut bleated in response: three hoarse bursts.

With their spears set, the Cadwal horsemen kicked their chargers into a controlled canter, an attacking stride.

The King's forces braced themselves to receive the assault. Castellan Norge had gone to join them, so that his orders wouldn't need to be relayed down the length of the valley.

"Now," King Joyse commented to no one in particular, "we shall see if Master Barsonage is as good as his word."

Terisa's chest hurt as if she were holding her breath. Involuntarily, she clasped Geraden's hand, gripped it hard. He tried to murmur something reassuring, but she didn't hear him; she was focused on the drums and the horses, the coming thunder of hooves.

Over the heads of Mordant's defenders, she saw the Cadwal horse charge into the valley.

At that moment, all the catapults threw.

The brutal sound they made as their arms hit the stops caught at her, jerked her head up.

Boulders this time: nine of them, imponderably graceful as they arced against the sky's blue; stones as big as ponies, just to show what the engines could do.

A chaotic yell went up from the army—shouts of warning, cries of fear, urgent commands. Cadwal responded with a battle howl. The shock as the forces came together resounded from the walls, broke into bloodshed against the ramparts. Only the boulders seemed to make no sound as they hit the snow, scattering men in all directions, splashing white into the air—white streaked with red where the soldiers of Alend and the guards of Orison didn't dodge well enough.

At once, the cocking of the catapults began again.

The King's lines bent under the weight of the Cadwal charge. Men and horses recoiled, retreated, as if they could see Festten's full strength coming at them and knew they had no hope. Spears thrust forward and either hit or failed. Swords flailed against each other, against shields, against armor; a metal clamor among the cries and whinnies of the beasts. Mounts reared, blundered, trampled. Bodies were buried in the snow, marking their own graves with their blood. The Cadwal battle howl took on a note of triumph.

Then the Congery struck.

Hiding themselves as well as they could in the jumbled rocks

542 A MAN RIDES THROUGH

at the ends of the valley walls, the Masters had set two tall mirrors facing each other—exactly facing each other across the foot of the valley. The positioning of the mirrors to face each other exactly was a problem with which the Congery had wrestled for days; but it had been resolved by the simple—if imprecise—expedient of memorizing the Images as they appeared from every side, so that the mirrors could be held at angles which complemented each other. Their alignment across the intervening ground was more easily achieved: from their hiding places, under cover of darkness, the Masters had used lamps to orient themselves.

As the horsemen of Cadwal broke into the valley, they passed between two mirrors which showed the same Image—but the same Image seen from opposite sides, and from positions nearly a hundred yards apart.

The Image of an arid landscape under a hot sun, so dry that it seemed incapable of sustaining any kind of life, so hard-baked that the ground was split by a crack as deep as a chasm and wide enough to swallow men and horses.

Master Barsonage flashed his signal, a strip of blue silk which he waved from a place high among the rocks so that it could be seen over the heads of the charging troops. At once, the two Masters who had shaped the mirrors began their translation.

With a noise like a cataclysm and a violent heave that seemed to crack the bedrock of the valley, a chasm appeared under the hooves of the horses. The ground shook; tremors ran into the distance, pulling loose rock from the ramparts, knocking men and horses off their legs. The sound shocked the valley, stunned the air. Dust sifted from the cleft as if the sky itself had shattered.

Riders slammed headlong into the rent snow and dirt, toppled from the edge; horses dropped screaming with their legs shattered. And more of the charge plunged into the cleft until the Cadwals had time to halt, rear back. Even then, dozens of soldiers were forced over the lip by the uncontrolled press behind them. A few horsemen tried to leap the chasm: a few of those succeeded. The rest were swallowed by the riven ground.

The Cadwals who had already ridden into the valley were cut off from the support of their army.

Instantly, Castellan Norge gave up the appearance of retreat and rallied his forces. His riders parted to let foot soldiers in among their enemies. Three thousand of King Joyse's men turned on scarcely a third that many Cadwals.

Outnumbered, trapped in confusion, with no escape possible except by a wild and unlikely leap across the chasm, High King Festten's soldiers fell without doing much damage.

As if nothing unpropitious had happened, the catapults threw again.

Scattershot this time, for variety; hundreds of fist-sized stones launched into the valley with the force of crossbows.

Smaller stones were more effective than boulders. They were harder to see coming, harder to dodge. And most of the King's army had involuntarily turned to watch the fighting—and the Imagery— at the valley foot. Alends and Mordants died because they weren't watching the sky.

Master Barsonage saw a sudden pocket of carnage appear among the troops as he scrambled down the rocks. Another—another—he couldn't look anymore. Reaching the young Master who held the mirror, he panted, "Hold the translation. As we agreed. If you stop and he"—the Imager at the other mirror—"does not, our own chasm will engulf us."

The young Master nodded without lifting his head from his fixed concentration.

Thank the stars he was young. He would have stamina. The man at the other glass, however—

Urgently, Master Barsonage scrubbed the chilled sweat out of his eyebrows.

They were in a gap like a room hidden among the rocks—a gap in which three or four men could have hacked at each other, as long as they didn't swing their swords too widely—with packed snow underfoot, ragged black boulders for concealment. The mirror was set between two rocks facing the opposite wall; another opening allowed the mediator to see across the valley. He and his companions were a good ten feet above the valley floor, however, and had more rock curving outward to protect them from above.

"Now the true danger begins, as you were warned," he muttered, more to himself than to his companions—the young Imager and Master Harpool. "The High King will turn his attack against us. And we dare not release the chasm, or enough Cadwals will sweep inward to slaughter us, regardless of how we are defended. As matters stand, we can only be attacked over the rocks." Stroking his glass, the flat mirror with the Image of Orison's ballroom, he added, "I hope Artagel received the King's message."

"I saw him pick up the parchment," muttered Master Harpool, not for the first time.

Master Barsonage ignored Harpool. He wasn't talking because he wanted answers—or even reassurance. He was talking so that he wouldn't dither.

He didn't like danger. Philosophically, he didn't approve of it. Imagery was for research and experiment, for understanding and knowledge, not for bloodshed. For that very reason, however, he approved passionately of the creation of the Congery. And the conflicts inherent in his own position had made him an indecisive mediator—a man, as someone had once observed, who couldn't keep his feet out of the shit on either side because he couldn't get the fencepost out of his ass.

Well, he had made decisions at last. He had brought the Congery here, into this mess, because he believed that was the right thing to do. But he still needed to keep talking.

"What I would most like to do at this moment," he continued for no one's benefit except his own, "is design a new couch. I am not altogether satisfied with the backrest of my last attempt."

"Oh, shut up, Barsonage," said Master Harpool; but he obviously didn't expect the mediator to heed him.

The valley had become strangely quiet. The sackbut had called back the Cadwal troops; the wardrums were still. Undoubtedly, High King Festten was conferring with his captains. In the meantime, Castellan Norge had sent half a thousand foot soldiers to pitch the High King's dead into the chasm; get the bodies out of the way. Weapons were collected; uninjured horses were appropriated; wounded men were unceremoniously clubbed senseless and taken to the infirmary. Everything else had to go.

"If you were the High King, Master Harpool," Master Barsonage asked pointlessly, "how much time would you require to get five hundred men into the rocks above us?"

The two Imagers were old friends. "Oh, shut up, Barsonage," Harpool repeated.

Most of the catapults were ready to throw again.

Master Barsonage had a painfully clear view of the engine nearest to him across the valley—a painfully clear view of Prince Kragen's men as they were stripped from the wall by a shower of rocks. As far as he could see, none of them survived the fall.

In contrast, the next catapult—cocked ready to throw—abruptly twisted itself into a wreck and collapsed, as if some of its crucial lashings had been cut or burned away so that it was destroyed by its own force.

Consumed by vexation, the Cadwals around the wrecked engine hurled a number of bodies off the rampart. Master Barsonage distinctly saw a chasuble flutter to the valley floor.

"Vivix," he muttered. "May the stars have mercy on you, Master Eremis, for I will not—if I ever get the chance."

He did his best to tally the next throw, but he wasn't sure of the results: he thought he saw seven boulders thud into the army. One of them smashed a squad of injured Cadwals on its way to the infirmary (no great loss), killing at least one physician (a serious blow).

Seven. Had some of Prince Kragen's climbers succeeded? They must have.

"The difficulty of backrests," he said through his teeth, "is that they must suit such a variety of backs."

The young Master at the mirror was beginning to breathe like a poorly trained runner. Sweat trickled from his beardless chin to the ground at his feet, where it grew slowly into ice. Shaded from the sun, the air in the gap was cold. One of his hands was clenched too tightly on the frame; the other rubbed the mimosa wood too hard, threatening the focus of the Image.

Master Barsonage was absolutely sure that he heard boots and armor among the rocks above him.

The chasm was vital now, vital. The Masters were prepared to release it, if necessary; close it. If, for instance, the Cadwals threw a bridge across the cleft, the chasm could be erased and then replaced, destroying the bridge. Nevertheless for the sake of the mirrors themselves the translation had to remain steady. If the chasm wavered or failed, nothing could stop the Cadwals from shattering the mirrors— or killing the Imagers.

In theory, at least, King Joyse's men—and the Masters—were ready for any attack which came at them over the rocks.

"Gently," the mediator breathed into the young Imager's ear, "gently. You are a Master, a *Master*. Translation has become a simple matter for you, an easy matter. You do not require such effort. Only relax. Hold the translation in your mind. Let your arms rest."

The young Master didn't nod or speak. His eyes were shut in strain. Nevertheless he managed to soften his grip, ease his rubbing; some of the exertion left his shoulders.

"Good," Master Barsonage whispered. "You are doing well. Very well indeed."

He was *sure* he heard boots and armor in the rocks—

He was right. From a hiding place twenty yards away, one of Norge's bowmen loosed a shaft, and a Cadwal with an arrow in his throat dove headfirst down the wall, gurgling audibly as he fell.

Past the young Master's shoulder, Barsonage saw soldiers of all kinds clambering toward the opposite mirror.

"Be ready, Harpool," he breathed. "Cover yourself with your glass. Remember that a mirror open for translation cannot be broken from the front."

For some reason, Master Harpool chose this moment to say, "You know, Barsonage, my wife begged me to stay at home. Said I was too old for such goings-on. If I fail to return, she promised to curse me—" Without warning, his old eyes spilled tears.

"Look out!" yelled a guard. Arrows flew. Cadwals staggered down the rocks, spilling blood everywhere.

"*Cover yourself,* you old fool!" Master Barsonage cried in desperation.

He himself was set to protect the opening through which he watched the valley. The space behind the mirror, the space through which he and his companions had entered the room, was Master Harpool's responsibility. Harpool turned toward it with an old man's fumbling slowness, a teary husband's confusion.

As if from nowhere, a brawny Cadwal appeared. He wore a helmet spiked like a less assertive version of the High King's, a brass breastplate rubbed to resemble gold; the longsword in his hand looked heavy enough to behead cattle. "Here!" he roared when he saw the Masters. "Found 'em!"

So quickly that Master Barsonage had no chance to do anything except flinch, the Cadwal drove his sword straight at Master Harpool's glass.

Master Harpool may have been old and grieved, but he understood translation: he had been doing it for decades. Somehow, he seemed to put himself in the right frame of mind without transition, achieve the right kind of concentration as simply as striking a flint.

The sword passed into the glass.

Carried forward by his own momentum, the Cadwal stumbled into the Image and vanished—

—into the ballroom of Orison, where (the mediator devoutly hoped) Artagel was ready to receive such gifts.

Another Cadwal came after the first. He fell into the mirror with an arrow in his back; already dead.

Master Barsonage was too busy watching Harpool: he missed the rope as it uncoiled across the opening he was supposed to guard. But he heard a grunt of effort from the man on the rope, turned in time.

The swing of the man's descent brought him within reach. The mediator hugged his mirror, muttered his concentration ritual as well as he could. Unfortunately, he couldn't think while the Cadwal released one hand from the rope, pulled out a knife. He didn't have the right kind of nerves to face danger. For one stupid, necessary instant, he shut his eyes.

Another present for Artagel.

There he nearly made a mistake, nearly let his glass close. Luckily, the sudden pressure on the rope warned him. Artagel must have been ready, must have gotten the message Master Harpool sent. Someone in the ballroom had a grip on the rope, was hauling on it fiercely.

If Master Barsonage had stopped his translation, the rope would only have been cut. Or the mirror would have broken. But he kept the glass open—

Abruptly, the three men anchoring the rope in the rocks above were dragged off their perch. They fell screaming past the mediator's vantage.

More arrows: more shouts. From somewhere out of sight came the clash of swords.

Then silence.

The attack was over. Temporarily. Some of the Cadwals were probably hidden among the rocks, marking the mirror's position while they waited for reinforcements; others must have gone back to report. Barsonage risked a look out over the young Master's shoulder and saw men still fighting around the opposite end of the chasm. The forces of Orison and Alend, however, seemed to be winning.

"Harpool," Master Barsonage panted, "I told you to *cover* your-self. You stood beside your mirror *begging* them to cut you down."

Master Harpool didn't say anything. He had his eyes closed. Maybe he was taking a nap. More likely he didn't want to witness his own peril.

From the distance of the pennon, of course, Terisa and Geraden, Elega and King Joyse and Prince Kragen couldn't see the details; but they saw the threat to the mirrors approach, saw it beaten back. Terisa let out a sigh to ease her cramped lungs. "How long can they keep that up?"

"A good question," replied King Joyse calmly. "All translation is arduous. The Masters are already weary. And as his frustration mounts, High King Festten will redouble his attacks.

"As a defense, however, that chasm has already exhausted most of its usefulness. Its chief purpose now is to protect the Masters themselves—and to give us a period of time during which we can try to counter the catapults. When we must, we will muster a charge of our own. The Masters will close the chasm—and while we ride to engage Cadwal outside the valley, they will retreat to prepare another unexpected crevice somewhere else.

"At the moment, we are as effectively besieged as we ever were in Orison. If the High King trusted to that and held back, we would eventually be defeated. But he will not. He wants our blood—and he wants it today. That is another of his weaknesses.

"As for the catapults—"

One party of Prince Kragen's assault on the walls brought back a Master with an arrow in his shoulder. They hadn't been able to find any way upward which wasn't exposed to the defenders of their target; and after the Master with them was hit, they were forced to retreat. So there were still seven engines.

All seven of them were already cocked.

Another series of hard wooden thuds, like the sound of bones being broken: another hail of scattershot. This stone deluge did less harm than the last because the soldiers and guards were more careful. Nevertheless Terisa thought she saw as many as a hundred men go down.

At once, physicians ran with horses and litters to do what they could for the wounded. The procession of injuries toward Esmerel and the infirmary seemed to go on continuously. The dead were left where they lay.

If this onslaught continued, the army would be forced to protect itself by leaving the center of the valley, moving closer to the walls—too close for the catapults to hit. And then the King's men would be vulnerable to rockfalls, avalanches—

"The next move will be Eremis',," Elega said softly to Terisa and Geraden. "We have introduced Imagery to the conflict. He will attempt to counter it."

"How?" asked Geraden anxiously.

The lady looked at him, a faint smile on her lips. Sunlight cost her much of her beauty, but couldn't weaken the color of her eyes. "You know him better than I do. You understand Imagery better. What *can* he do?"

"*I* don't know," Geraden muttered. "I'm willing to bet he has a mirror he can see us in. In fact, if I were him—and if Gilbur and Vagel are as good as they think—I'd have two. One to watch with, one to use. But he has to be careful. Terisa has already shattered one glass for him. If he gives her the chance, she can do it again."

Terisa had no idea whether or not this were true. It seemed irrelevant.

The gaze King Joyse sent toward her and Geraden was curiously bland, like a mask.

The air was warmer than it had been for several days, but it didn't warm her. Clenching herself inside her robe, she shivered and ached. No matter how often she turned to Geraden, no matter how she clung to him, he couldn't help her. Helplessness and watching made her frantic. He had the strongest feeling they were in the wrong place. But what choice did they have? Where else could they be?

For some reason, the Cadwals were massing again outside the valley. The sackbut bleated raucously: the wardrums commenced their labor: horsemen cleared the way. Foot soldiers drew forward, as if High King Festten had decided to drive them into the chasm for their failures.

King Joyse studied them hard, his blue eyes straining to pierce their intentions. Abruptly, he put out a hand to the Prince. "Reinforcements," he snapped. "Where in all this rout is Norge? The Masters must be reinforced."

Prince Kragen had apparently passed the point where he

needed—or even expected—explanations from the King. Wheeling away, he headed for his horse, shouting to his captains as he ran.

When Terisa first heard the distant, throaty rumble, as if the earth were moving, she had no idea what was about to happen.

When the Tor woke up—gasping, as he always did these days, at the great, hot pain in his side—the rumble hadn't started yet. Outside his tent, the valley was strangely quiet. That disconcerted him: he was expecting combat. The relative silence sounded like an omen of disaster, an indication that bloodshed and death had lost their meaning.

Opening his eyes, he saw from the hue of the canvas overhead that day had dawned. He was alone in the tent, except for Ribuld, who dozed against the tentpole with his head nodding on his knees. An experienced veteran, Ribuld could probably sleep on a battlefield, if he were left alone.

Silence outside: only a few shouts from time to time; the mortal sound of catapult arms against their stops. And a few daring or oblivious birds, following their calls among the rocks. The Tor knew all the birds of his Care. He would be able to identify each call, if he listened closely enough. For the sake of his sons, who had grown up in more peaceful times than he had, he had become avid at birding.

But there should have been a battle going on. Strange—

The Congery. Of course. Master Barsonage had promised to translate that crevice somewhere.

Must be quite a sight—clefts in the ground out of nowhere; the fate of Mordant depending on Imagery as well as swords.

"Ribuld," said the old lord, "help me up."

Not loud enough: Ribuld didn't move.

"Ribuld, help me up. I want to see what is happening."

I want to strike a blow for my son and my Care and my King in this war.

Ribuld jerked up his head, blinked the sleep out of his eyes. Alert almost at once, he rose and came to the cot where the Tor sprawled. "My lord," he murmured, "the King says you've got to rest. He *commands* you to rest."

Speaking softly around his pain, the Tor replied, "Ribuld, you know me. Did you believe I would obey such a command?"

The guard shifted his feet uncomfortably. "I'm supposed to make sure you do."

The Tor managed a thin chuckle. "Then let him execute us both when this war is done. We will share the block with Master Eremis for our terrible crimes. Help me up."

Slowly, a grin tightened Ribuld's scar. "As you say, my lord. Disobeying the King is always a terrible crime. Anybody fool enough to do that deserves what he gets."

Bracing himself on the sides of the cot, Ribuld helped the lord roll into a sitting position.

Agony threatened to burst the Tor's side. He took a moment to absorb the pain; then, hoping he didn't look as pale as he felt, he said, "Some wine first, I think. After that, mail and my sword."

May it please the stars that I am able to strike one blow for my son and my Care and my King.

Ribuld produced a flagon from somewhere. The sound of catapults came again, followed by cries and curses, yells for physicians. *May it please the stars—* Some time passed before the Tor realized that he was staring into the flagon without drinking.

Gritting his courage, he swallowed all the wine. Before he could lapse into another stupor, he motioned for his undershirt and mail.

With gruff care, Ribuld helped him to his feet, helped him into his leathers and mail and cloak, helped him belt his ponderous and unusable sword around his girth below the swelling in his side. Several times, the old lord feared that he would lose consciousness and fall; but each time Ribuld supported him until his weakness went away, then continued dressing him as if nothing had happend.

"If I had a daughter," the Tor murmured, "who obeyed me better than the lady Elega obeys her father, I would order her to marry you, Ribuld."

Ribuld laughed shortly. "Be serious, my lord. What would a boozing old wencher like me do with a lord's daughter?"

"Squander her inheritance, of course," retorted the Tor. "That would be the whole point of marrying her to you. To give you that opportunity."

This time, Ribuld's laugh was longer; it sounded happier.

"Now," grunted the lord when Ribuld was done with his belt, "let us go out and have a look at the field of valor."

He managed two steps toward the tentflaps before his knees failed.

"My lord," Ribuld murmured repeatedly, "my lord," while the Tor's head filled up with black water and he lost his vision in the dark, "give this up. You need rest. The King told you to rest. You'll kill yourself."

Precisely what I have in mind, friend Ribuld.

"Nonsense." Somehow, the Tor found his voice and used it to lift his mind above the water. "I only want to watch King Joyse justify the trust we have placed in him. I want to watch him bring High King Festten and Master Eremis to the ruin they deserve.

"A horse to sit on. So I can see better. Nothing more."

Ribuld's eyes were red, and his face seemed congested in some way, as if he understood—and couldn't show it. "Yes, my lord," he said through his teeth. "I'd like to watch that myself."

Carefully, he helped the Tor upright again.

Together, they reached the tentflaps and went out into the shadowed morning.

From the tent, they could see most of the valley, including the slope where King Joyse had planted his pennon. That purple scrap looked especially frail in contrast to the bright sunlight beyond the valley, the massive strength of the ramparts, the active violence of the siege engines. Around the standard stood King Joyse and his daughter, Prince Kragen and Terisa and Geraden. They were all watching the foot of the valley, however, watching unmounted troops mass as if the Congery's chasm could be defeated by swords and spears; they didn't notice the Tor and Ribuld. And neither the Tor nor Ribuld called attention to themselves.

Ribuld moved the Tor a little to the side, a bit out of sight. Then the guard went looking for horses.

The Tor did his best to estimate the damage the catapults had done. As a younger man, he had fought his share of battles. He was accustomed to carnage. But King Joyse possessed a quality he himself had always lacked. Perhaps it was an instinct for risk. In his bones, he counted loss instead of gain. That, really, was why he had given Joyse only two hundred men, all those long years ago, when Joyse was hardly more than a boy, and Mordant was nothing more than a battlefield. Not cowardice. And certainly not deafness to Joyse's bright, hopeful promises. No, he had simply given his future King as many men as he could bear to lose.

The lord fell into reverie, thinking about loss. Friends of many years ago, valiant fighters, precious villagers and farmers and merchants who didn't deserve to be slaughtered. The old Armigite, who hadn't earned a foppish son. And now the Tor's own firstborn. His tough, good comrade, the Perdon. The tormented Castellan, sick and honorable Lebbick. Too many, all of them: the cost was too high.

He shook his head. As if his pain were an anchor, a gift from the High King's Monomach, he used it to steady himself so that he could watch what happened in the valley.

Why was the High King massing his men? An interesting question. Well, obviously he intended to attack something. Someone.

I need a mount.

The Tor looked around for Ribuld.

There, he was coming. He had two horses, his own roan and the Tor's familiar bay. Now all the lord had to do was surmount his hurt one last time—

Distinctly, he heard King Joyse speak.

In that carrying voice which required obedience, the King snapped, "Reinforcements. Where in all this rout is Norge? The Masters must be reinforced."

Frantic with pain, the Tor lunged at the bay and struggled into the saddle.

He could have fainted then; but he was desperate, and his desperation held the darkness back. He was already moving, already kicking the bay into a gallop, when the rumble began.

The sound was a distant, throaty growl, as if by translating their chasm the Masters had given the earth a mouth with which to utter its distress.

But this wasn't the earth protesting, oh, no, the Tor saw that almost immediately as he goaded his horse faster, away from people who wanted to stop him; out of the center of the valley to the less occupied ground closer to the wall. This rumble had another meaning entirely.

As if someone had opened a window in the empty air, rock began to thunder downward. Across the gap between worlds, an avalanche rushed roaring into the chasm.

Broken rock in tons; hundreds and thousands of tons; enough rock to build a castle, a mountain; all slamming down out of the sky directly above the chasm, all howling torrentially into the Masters' crevice.

Enough rock to fill the rift. Plug it. Make it passable.

And behind the translated collapse of the mountainside came High King Festten's men, pressing forward to breach the valley as soon as the rockfall ended.

The avalanche moved along the chasm, distributing rubble as evenly as possible.

Then, while the whole valley watched in shock, the plunge of stone began to thin. Quickly, too quickly, the tons of rock became dirt and pebbles; the dirt and pebbles changed to dust; the dust billowed everywhere, as light and swirling as snow.

Raising their battle howl, High King Festten's men charged.

The crevice wasn't perfectly filled: in some places, the rock piled too high; in others, the dirt sank too low. Nevertheless at least a third of the chasm could be crossed now. Cadwal's troops rushed forward while Castellan Norge and Prince Kragen were still straining to rally their forces.

Within the valley, Festten's men split into two groups, curving around the inside of the chasm to attack the Masters hidden in the ends of the walls.

The Tor saw the Cadwals come as he rode, lashing his horse for more speed than it could give him. He had forgotten his pain: he had forgotten loss. He only knew that he was too late to help break the first shock of the assault. Norge had hundreds of archers and bowmen hidden around the Masters. And the Masters had mirrors. That would have to be enough, until help could come.

It wasn't enough; it was never going to be enough. Already there were a thousand Cadwals in the valley, two thousand. More came as fast as they could cross the chasm.

Forgetting all the things he couldn't do, the Tor unsheathed his longsword.

In the rocks ahead, he saw Master Barsonage. The mediator had climbed to his signalling-place above the mirrors. He looked small and doomed there, his chasuble fluttering. As if he had lost his mind, he yelled through the Cadwal battle howl, waved a blue cloth wildly at the opposite wall.

The Tor didn't understand what happened next until it was over; but somehow, by luck or inspiration, Master Barsonage achieved his aim.

Both Masters ceased their translation at the same moment.

The chasm blinked out of existence.

Now there was solid ground where the avalanche had fallen. Stone and soil occupied the space which the rockfall had filled.

In the convulsion, the Tor's horse stumbled, nearly lost its footing. With a spasm like an eruption, the closed earth spat the entire rockfall straight into the air.

Without transition, the battle howl changed to screams and chaos. Hundreds of Cadwals died in the blast while they tried to cross the vanished chasm; hundreds more were crushed by the rejected rock as it plunged back to the ground, blocking the valley from wall to wall. Granite thunder and groaning swallowed the sound of wardrums.

Unfortunately, the High King still had as many as two thousand men inside the valley—men still charging to kill the Masters, shatter the mirrors. And King Joyse's reinforcements were still too far away.

The Castellan's archers recovered their wits enough to begin shooting. But their arrows were too few, and the Cadwals were well armored. Men with swords swarmed up into the rocks, fighting to reach the Masters.

Master Barsonage had scuttled downward, vanished into a gap the Tor couldn't see. That movement told the Cadwals exactly where their target was. Spared the necessity of searching, they surged ahead.

With Ribuld beside him, the Tor crashed against the rear of the Cadwal force.

His sword was heavy: his whole body was heavy, weighted with pain and bereavement. He hacked at the Cadwals from side to side, once on the left, once on the right, back and forth; and each blow seemed to shear helmets and heads, breastplates and leather. His horse plunged, stumbled, scrambled forward—somehow he kept his balance. His sword was his balance, his life: up and down, side to side, hacking with all its strength, while his belly filled up with blood.

Above him, the Cadwals who reached the Masters' position seemed to be disappearing.

In their gap among the rocks, the Imagers concentrated grimly, working their translations against impossible odds.

That is to say, Master Barsonage concentrated grimly, grinding his courage into focus with such urgency that sweat stood on his skin and a dangerous flush darkened his face. For all the distress Master Harpool showed, he might as well have been performing translations in his sleep. Standing mostly behind his glass, with his eyes closed and an old man's mumble on his lips, he kept his mirror open and simply let everything that came near it fall into the Image—trusting, no doubt, that the haste and frenzy of the Cadwals would spare him from a direct attack on his person.

The young Master wasn't doing anything at all. He had slumped to the snow-packed floor; his glass leaned over him, useless. Something in him, some essential fortitude or will, had snapped. He had kept his translation open for the chasm until Master Barsonage had called for him to let it go; then his eyes had rolled back in his head, and he had crumbled.

The mirrors were vital: the Congery had nothing else to contribute to Mordant's defense. Ignoring the young Imager, Master Barsonage forced himself to translate and translate, on and on, when every nerve in his body wailed to flinch away from the swords and blows and curses coming at him.

Unhappily, from where he stood he could see clearly that reinforcements were still too far away. He could see that the Tor and Ribuld didn't stand a chance.

The Tor went on fighting anyway, long after he had lost his strength and his balance and even his reason. A blow for his son. A blow for his Care. And now a blow for King Joyse. Then back to the beginning again. A blow for everyone he had ever loved, everyone who had ever died.

For some reason, there was a knife stuck in his leg. It was a big knife; really, quite a big knife. He couldn't tell whether it hurt him or not, but it seemed to catch his leg in a way he couldn't escape, so that he had no choice except to fall off his horse.

He dreaded that fall. It was a long way to the ground, and his swollen side couldn't endure an impact like that. Luckily, however, he managed to land on the man who stuck him; that was one less Cadwal to worry about. Now all he had to do was roll onto his back. He knew he didn't have the strength to stand again; but from the ground he would be able to cut at the legs of the men around him.

He rolled onto his back.

Unluckily, he had lost his sword. He didn't have anything left to fight with.

Ribuld stood over him.

Gripping his own blade in both fists, the guard fought for both of them: blows on all sides; spurts and splashes of blood; chips of armor, iron sword-shards. Ribuld's scar burned as if his life were on fire in his face, and his teeth snapped at the air.

Someone shouted, *"My lord Tor! Watch out!"*

The voice was familiar, but the old lord couldn't place it. It was too recent: it belonged to someone he hadn't known long enough to remember.

Then a swordpoint came right through the center of Ribuld's chest, driven like a spear from behind.

Oh, well. The stars had granted the Tor his last wish. And King Joyse had said, *You have not betrayed me.* That was enough.

A moment later, someone slammed a rock down on his head and brought all his losses to an end.

But when Master Barsonage cried, *"My lord Tor! Watch out!"* the young Imager sprang to his feet as if he had been galvanized.

Like Ribuld's, the young Master's home was in the Care of Tor, in Marshalt. In fact, he was distantly related by marriage to the Tor himself. That familiar name—and the mediator's alarm—wrenched him out of his stupor, brought him to his feet crying madly, "The Tor? The Tor? *Oh, my lord!"*

He had no idea what was going on: his eyes held nothing but exhaustion and distress. The broken part of him only made him urgent; it didn't make him sane.

Sobbing, "Save the Tor!" he grabbed up his mirror.

Master Barsonage was too slow. He was watching the Tor, watching the reinforcements; he didn't react in time.

The young Imager was hardly more than a boy, pushed past his limits. Facing his mirror in the general direction of the opposite glass, he began translating his chasm straight into the huge ridge of rock left by the avalanche; the rock which sealed the valley.

But of course the Master holding the other mirror didn't know what was about to happen. In any case, the two mirrors were no longer properly aligned. There was nothing to stop the tremendous and convulsive tremor which split the ridge and the ground and went on until it hit the end of the other wall and tore apart all that old stone, reducing the opposite glass and everyone near it to rubble.

Under the circumstances, it was probably a good thing that the young Master didn't live long. There was no way to tell how much damage his chasm might have done, if the translation had continued unchecked. And there was no way to tell how he would have endured the consequences of his action.

As matters fell out, however, he was saved by a particularly

stubborn Cadwal, who already had his sword up to chop open Master
Harpool's oblivious face when an Alend arrow nailed him between
the shoulder blades. Falling forward, his upraised arms hit the top
of Harpool's mirror. That impact made his fingers release his sword.

As if it had been thrown deliberately, the hilt of the blade
snapped the young Master's neck. He, in turn, fell forward onto his
glass, shattering it completely.

Full of terrible defeat, Master Barsonage hardly noticed that
Master Harpool had somehow contrived to keep his own mirror from
being broken. And the mediator's was undamaged. That was less than
no consolation; it was almost an insult in the face of the general ruin.
Every other glass which the Congery had prepared for this battle was
destroyed.

He half expected another violent recoil as the chasm ceased to
exist for the second time; but that didn't happen. The previous convulsion had been caused by reversing the translation. This translation,
on the other hand, was only stopped, not undone. Vast portions of
the piled ridge were engulfed; most of the end-rock of the opposite
wall disappeared into the new crevice. Then the rending and spitting
of the earth was over.

As a result, the High King's forces once again had access to the
valley—a ragged and constricted access, treacherous to cross, like
the spaces between rotting teeth, but access nonetheless.

When he saw that there were already men riding at full career
in through one of the farther gaps, he covered his face with his hands.

FORTY-NINE:
THE KING'S
LAST HOPES

tanding near the King's pennon with Terisa, Geraden, and her father, the lady Elega didn't know where to look, or what to feel.

She could watch the struggle down at the end of the valley wall, off to her right, where the Tor had fallen, and where Castellan Norge and his men fought to save what they could of the Masters and their mirrors. Or she could watch the breach where the other Masters used to be, the gap which had been made in the piled ridge of the avalanche by translating the Congery's chasm from only one side.

Riders were coming in through that gap, driving their horses hard. And Prince Kragen was there. From this distance, he appeared to be doing everything at once: rallying his men; finishing off the incursion of Cadwals; searching over the new jumble of rocks for survivors. To her eyes, each of his actions seemed as quick as a thrust, as decisive as a sword; the precision with which he used his men made Norge look like a blundering lout by comparison.

He was worthy—oh, he was worthy! Surely King Joyse could see that. Surely her father in this new manifestation could see and appreciate the qualities which made the Alend Contender precious to her. Prince Kragen deserved—

He deserved to be right.

Almost as an act of self-mortification, to humble herself so that she wouldn't hope so hard, fear so much, Elega forced her eyes to stay on the right side of the valley foot, not the left.

The question of what to feel was more difficult. She couldn't resolve it by an act of will.

Pride and panic: vindication and alarm. Suddenly, as much "out of nowhere" as if translation were involved, the King had proved himself. He had made real the interpretations of himself which until now had been only ideas—concepts put forward by people like Terisa and Geraden for reasons of their own. He had shown that he merited the risks she had taken in his name, arguing for him against reason, common sense; he had justified the forbearance she had won from Prince Kragen and the Alend Monarch. In the privacy of her own thoughts, she understood why he had found it necessary to use her like a hop-board piece in his plans, rather than to hazard the truth with her. She was *proud* of him, there beside his standard, blue eyes blazing; as ready as a hawk to strike or defend.

She was proud of him—and afraid that she had failed him.

In a sense, she was playing his own game against him. At her urging, Prince Kragen and the Alend Monarch had made decisions concerning this war on the basis of knowledge and speculation which they hadn't shared with any representative of Orison.

Her purpose—as distinct from Kragen's or Margonal's—had been twofold: to make the forces of Alend *wait*, withhold their siege, long enough for King Joyse's plans to ripen; and to put pressure on the King, pressure which would force him to accept an alliance with Alend. By keeping secrets from her father, she reinforced Prince Kragen's position.

Now, today, here, what she had done came to the test. She would be right, as the Prince deserved—if for no other reason than because he had trusted her. Or she would be wrong.

Mordant itself might stand or fall on the outcome.

She could choose to keep her eyes away from Prince Kragen, away from the riders boiling into the valley on the left; but she couldn't choose to ignore her fear. The more pride she felt in King Joyse and the Prince, the more she dreaded the possibility that she had helped bring them both to ruin.

Maybe that was why she looked her worst in sunlight. The sun couldn't expose her secrets, of course; but it seemed to lay bare the fact that she had them.

Under the circumstances, she considered it fortunate that no one was paying much attention to her.

Unconscious of himself, Geraden muttered, "Get up. Get up." Everyone had seen the Tor go down; no one had seen the old lord regain his feet. For that matter, no one had seen any of the Masters emerge from the rocks. "Get *up*. We need you."

Terisa held his arm with both hands, clung to him. Nevertheless she kept her eyes averted as if she couldn't bear to watch what he was seeing. Facing to the left of the valley's foot, she asked softly, "Who is *that?*"

Geraden apparently had no idea what she meant. And Elega was determined not to look. She needed a way to live with her fear, a way to endure her failure when it came.

Abruptly, it became obvious that Castellan Norge was done with the Cadwals attacking the Masters. Shouts were raised, and some of the men relaxed. Bowmen hurried out of the rocks to retrieve their shafts; riders sped away, some to deliver messages, others to help the Prince. Master Barsonage appeared, holding a glass nearly as tall as himself. Behind him came Master Harpool, doddering painfully. Two guards carried the old Imager's mirror for him.

Together, five or six men picked up the Tor's corpse; as gently as they could, they set it in a rude litter. Then they lifted the litter to other men on horseback. Ribuld's body also was put in a litter to accompany the Tor's. Castellan Norge mounted his horse, placed himself at the head of his riders.

In procession, like a cortege, the Castellan and his men came up the valley toward King Joyse.

"My lord," Geraden sighed—an exhalation with his teeth clenched down on it hard enough to draw blood. "My poor lord."

Terisa shook his arm; maybe she was trying to distract him. "Geraden, look. Who *is* that?"

Involuntarily, the lady Elega turned.

At once, she saw that the horsemen attempting to enter the valley were fighting for their lives—

—fighting for their lives against the forces of Cadwal outside. She had assumed that they, too, were Cadwals; but she was wrong. High King Festten opposed them bitterly: seen through the breaches in the piled ridge, it appeared that he had sent his entire mounted strength to destroy them.

She saw Prince Kragen spur his charger into a gallop, leading several hundred Alends to the defense of the riders; headlong against thousands of Cadwals.

At the same time, King Joyse shouted to the nearest captain,

"Get archers down there! I want bows up in those rockpiles! I want an ambush in each of those gaps! We cannot keep Cadwal out, but we can make the High King cautious. We must not allow him to mass his men inside those piles!"

Cupping his hands on either side of his mouth to make his voice ring, he added, *"Support the Prince!"*

With her jaw hanging down like a madwoman's, Elega saw that one of the riders Prince Kragen was risking himself to help bore the dull grape-on-wheat colors of the Termigan.

The *Termigan?*

What in the name of all sanity was *he* doing here?

"The Termigan!" Geraden breathed to Terisa. "I don't believe it. He came after all."

Elega was too surprised to notice that the catapults were ready to throw again. And she certainly didn't notice that one of them behind her had been reaimed toward King Joyse's pennon. She hardly heard the flat thudding of the arms, or the thin, high scream of scattershot through the air. At the moment, her only concern was that none of the engines could strike at Prince Kragen or the Termigan.

She didn't know how lucky she was when the catapult behind her failed to throw.

Instead of attacking, it leaned forward and toppled crookedly off the rampart, tearing itself to scrap on the rocks as it fell. From the valley rim, a group of Prince Kragen's climbers raised an inaudible cheer, then turned to defend themselves from Cadwals arriving too late to save the engine.

King Joyse, however, seemed to notice that as he noticed everything else. With a glance upward, he said to himself, "Six left. Progress is made, friend Festten. Be warned."

Unfortunately, the siege engines had already cost him hundreds of men, dead or hurt.

Elega held her breath, watching Prince Kragen hurl himself against High King Festten's horsemen. Hadn't Geraden said that the Termigan refused to come? She gnawed the inside of her cheek. Yes, that was what Geraden had said. Yet he was here. She felt a chill, despite the air's relative warmth. What new disaster had he come to report?

Who were those people in the center of his formation, those cloaked figures that didn't fight, that didn't do anything except ride where the Termigan's men took them? One of them seemed ordinary enough. The other was huge—

Echoes brought the sounds of battle to her, the strife of swords and shields. Piled rock hid most of the fighting: Prince Kragen had ventured through the gap and was out of sight behind the debris of the avalanche. He didn't have enough men to oppose that many Cadwals, not nearly enough. Only the speed of his charge could save him, its unexpectedness. But a mixed group of guards and soldiers was almost in position to help him, two hundred horse in the lead, half a thousand foot pelting furiously behind. And when the Termigan had brought all his people into the valley, he wheeled his mount, called most of his strength after him, and returned to aid the Prince.

Together, nearly side-by-side, Prince Kragen and the man who had declared flatly, *I trust no Alend,* fought their way back toward the bulk of King Joyse's army.

The rough mounds close on either side saved them: all that broken stone constricted the Cadwal countercharge; an abundance of scattered rubble where the chasm used to be prevented riders from moving in tight ranks. And when the High King's forces tried to enter the valley again, archers began loosing their shafts from high up among the rocks.

Prince Kragen and the Termigan brought each other to safety as if they had never been anything except comrades.

"Who're those people with him," asked Terisa, "the ones in the cloaks—the ones who didn't fight?"

Elega's heart began to soar. Who dared to speak of failure, where King Joyse and his daughters were at work?

The men bearing the Tor's body, and Ribuld's, arrived at King Joyse's pennon before the Termigan did; and King Joyse met them as if he weren't in the midst of a war, with catapults and unexplained arrivals to worry about; met them as if for that moment at least nothing was more important to him than the burden they carried, his old friend's corpse.

"He saved us," said Master Barsonage. The Imager seemed too weary to dismount; he looked too haggard to say, *my lord King.* "He and Ribuld—" The mediator's voice lapsed into grief.

"That's true, my lord King," Castellan Norge reported without his usual ease. "They were just two, but they hit at the right time. They did just enough damage, caused just enough confusion—" Like

Barsonage, Norge seemed to be losing his voice. "Without them, we wouldn't have saved the mediator. Or Master Harpool, either."

Dully, as if he had said the same thing a dozen times, Master Harpool murmured, "My wife promised to curse me if I don't return. She was that angry—" His nose was running; but he didn't have anything to wipe it with, so he snuffled loudly.

King Joyse looked at the Tor's body; he started to speak. Nevertheless he couldn't: he was breathing too hard. As if the sight of his friend's crushed head hit him harder than he was expecting, dealt him a blow for which he had thought he was braced and now found he wasn't, not braced at all despite the fact that he must have seen this moment coming, his chest began to heave, and he fought for air urgently, in great gasps. To stifle the sound, he clamped his hands over his mouth, against the sides of his nose; but he couldn't restrain his harsh respiration, his labor against grief.

After all, he wasn't young anymore. He had been alone for a long time; comforted—or at least understood—by only mad Havelock and lost Quillon. And the cost of his efforts to save Mordant kept growing. Without the Tor, there would have been no Mordant, no kingdom to defend; no King to be so profligate with the blood of those who loved him.

Fiercely, he pulled his hands down from his face, gripped the side of the Tor's litter. He seemed to want to lift his old friend in his arms, pick the Tor's body up out of death. But of course the corpse was too heavy. Four men were needed simply to support its slack weight.

Involuntarily, King Joyse sank to his knees in the trampled slush.

Terisa and Geraden started toward him without thinking; their desire to console him somehow was obvious in their faces. The lady Elega stopped them, however. She put a finger to her lips. Then, smiling despite the Tor's end and her father's sorrow, she pointed toward the riders approaching the pennon.

Prince Kragen. The Termigan. And the two cloaked figures, with everything about them except their size wrapped and hidden, kept secret.

Prince Kragen had a few battlemarks on him: some blood, plainly not his own; lines like galls across his mail. He looked worthy to Elega, *worthy* beyond question, like a man who had met the consequences of his most hazardous decisions and deserved his victory. The Termigan was in worse condition, gaunt from hard travel, strained and bitter around his eyes. Yet he, too, had an air of worth, almost of triumph, as if he knew now that he had done the right thing. His hard, flinty face held no reproach.

"My lord King," he said, "I've come to help you. I've only got two hundred men—all I could spare. But they're enough."

"Enough and more," put in Prince Kragen, kinder toward the King's grief. "Is it not true that Mordant itself began with only two hundred men?"

"Father." Myste pushed her hood back from her face, raised her strong gaze and her scarred cheek into the sunlight reaching past the valley rim.

"Myste."

Terisa was at once so surprised and so thrilled that she nearly shouted; her whole body seemed tight with pleasure.

"You're all right."

Geraden nearly burst out laughing in delight. Men all around the King's pennon whispered Myste's name as if it were powerful and dangerous.

"With the Termigan's aid," she said, "I have brought your champion."

While the reaction to her appearance spread, the huge figure beside her dropped his cloak, revealing bright, blank armor scorched black in several places, burned open twice, with a flat, impenetrable plate over his face. Strange guns hung on his hips; the rifle with which he had blasted his way out of Orison was strapped to his back.

The circle of guards and soldiers stared. A number of them grabbed at their swords; a few unslung bows.

But the champion didn't make any threatening moves. Slowly, he reached one hand to his head, touched a stud in the side of his helmet. Without a sound, his visor slid up and away, exposing his face.

It was a man's face, ordinary in its details: pale eyes; a large nose, crooked as if it had been broken more than once; tight lips above an assertive jaw. Only the strange way he moved his mouth when he spoke betrayed his origins.

"My lord King," he said in an alien voice, a tone with an incongruous resemblance to birdsong, "I'm lost on this God-rotting planet. Myste says it's not your fault I'm here. Says the only people who might be able to help me are your Imagers. But you can't help me while you're stuck in this mess.

"I'm willing to do what I can. For her. On the off-chance your Imagers can help me."

"So that's what it meant," Terisa breathed, her tone hushed with relief and wonder. But at the moment even Geraden didn't have any attention to spare for her.

Kneeling beside the Tor, King Joyse had jerked his head up at the sound of Myste's voice, had stared at her and the champion with joy dawning in his blue eyes. Now he rose to his feet as if all his courage had come back. At first, however, he didn't speak to her, or to Prince Kragen and the Termigan, or even to the champion. Instead, he addressed Norge briskly.

"Several things, Castellan. Provide for my lord Termigan's men. Get those that need care to the physicians. Those that do not, assign among our horsemen. If I judge rightly"—he glanced toward the foot of the valley—"High King Festten is regrouping. He will attack again shortly. We need riders desperately.

"My dear friend the Tor," he continued without pausing, "must be given an honorable grave outside Esmerel. Command as many men as necessary, bury him well. And the Perdon beside him—two faithful and valorous lords who spent their lives so that we will have a chance to save our world. If we succeed, their names will be praised before any other."

Then, in a rush, he left the Tor's litter, pulled Myste off her mount, and hugged her to his heart.

At once, the champion, Darsint, dismounted; he seemed to think Myste might need his protection. When he had pushed the horses out of his way, however, he stopped, apparently content to leave Myste and the King alone.

Watching her sister and her father, Elega's only regret was that she had never been able to smile the way they did, with that clarity, as if they were able to go through life with their innocence intact.

"Dear child," King Joyse murmured thickly, "my Myste, I'm so glad— Havelock told me to trust you, but I couldn't help being afraid. My little girl, in such danger— I wanted you to be safe. And yet I needed you to do what you did." He tightened his embrace momentarily, then released it and stepped back. "Your mother would break my pate if she knew how I risked you."

"Father," Myste replied like the sun, "all children must be risked. Mother knows that. How else are we to discover ourselves?"

If anything, her smile became warmer, cleaner, as she turned toward Elega.

Elega wanted to say, You have saved us—meant to say, Oh, Myste, you have saved us—but her throat closed suddenly, and her vision ran with tears. Myste's smile still had the power to make everything worthwhile.

Myste came to stand close to her. They didn't embrace: the way they felt was too private for the occasion. Nevertheless Myste said softly, "You did it. Everything I wanted—everything I couldn't say. I'm so proud of you."

Elega looked up at Prince Kragen, still on his horse, and held his gaze happily while Myste went to hug both Terisa and Geraden, then moved back to King Joyse.

"Now that the truth is revealed, my lord King," the Prince said, speaking dryly to cover his pleasure, "I suppose I must admit that the Alend Monarch's motives—and my own—have not been entirely disinterested recently. We withheld the siege of Orison to give you time in which to mature your plans. We kept open the possibility of an alliance, even when we had refused it, so that we might be able to aid you at need. But we also did those things"—he grinned under his moustache—"because the lady Myste threatened to bring the champion's fire down on us otherwise."

There: it was acknowledged in front of everyone that he and Elega had known Myste was alive, known she was with Darsint. The information brought a speculative frown to Geraden's face as he drew inferences; it turned Terisa's cheeks alternately pale and hot—relief at Myste's safety, anger that Myste's safety had been kept secret.

King Joyse wasn't offended, however. "In other words, my lord Prince," he retorted, suppressing a desire to laugh, "you decided to respect my position because you were given reason to believe it might be stronger than it appeared." Away from Myste, he had resumed his more formal style of speech. "That was wise—as well as courageous. While honest admissions are being made, I will admit in my turn that I have often suspected your father of wisdom." His eyes glinted with momentary mischief. "His courage, however, came as a pleasant surprise."

"Unfortunately," he went on promptly, speaking now to the group around his standard, "we will be in battle again at any moment, and before that moment comes I must say that my position is also weaker than it appears."

Facing the champion, he asked, "How should I address you?"

The champion frowned. "You mean name or rank? I'm Darsint, First Battle-Officer, Unified Expeditionary Force cruiser *Scourge*."

"Darsint," King Joyse pronounced. "Your offer of aid is very welcome. I need it badly. I doubt, however, that I will ever be able to help you."

Darsint's frown deepened.

Instinctively, Elega caught her breath. What was her father doing now? Yet a glance at Myste reassured her: Myste appeared grave, but undistressed. Geraden was nodding slowly, as if to confirm what King Joyse said. Terisa seemed to be watching the foot of the valley distractedly, expecting harm.

"I am sure," King Joyse explained, "my daughter has told you that you were brought here by translation—by mirror. But the glass responsible for your presence was broken." Perhaps tactfully, he didn't mention that Darsint himself had broken it. "In addition, the only mirror we had which resembled that glass has also been shattered, by the enemies we now confront. As a result, I have no immediate aid to offer.

"I doubt that Master Gilbur can be persuaded to reveal how your mirror was made. Geraden is therefore our only hope." King Joyse didn't look at Geraden. "And I do not doubt that he will be able to reshape his mirror exactly, if we are victorious—if he is given time and peace."

Geraden continued nodding.

"But that only raises another difficulty," went on the King, "which is time itself. Our mirrors show Images of place, not of person. And the Images can be adjusted only over relatively small distances. Once Geraden has reshaped his glass, we will have the power to return you, not to your people or your home, but only to the place where you were found.

"How many days have passed since you were forced among us? And how many more will pass before Geraden is given time and peace? Will your 'cruiser'—will this *Scourge*—remain where it was, waiting for you?"

"Pythas," Darsint muttered darkly. "God-rotting piece of real estate. Should have left it alone while we had the chance. UEF needs a staging-area in that sector—but nobody needs a staging-area that bad."

King Joyse pursued his point. "Is it not more likely that your *Scourge* will be gone? that we will consign you to death among your enemies if we return you after so many days?"

"Shit, yes." The champion appeared to be chewing his lip below the rim of his visor's opening. "Pythians had us on the run when I got snatched. Plasma beams like I've never seen." He indicated his damaged armor. "*Scourge*'ll be long gone."

"So I can promise you nothing," King Joyse concluded, "except that I will use you as hard as I can—and serve you as faithfully as I am able.

"Will you help us?"

Elega's chest hurt for air, but she kept holding each breath as long as she could, hoping that her father's candor wouldn't drive Darsint away.

The champion didn't take long to make up his mind. "Oh, well," he sighed like a disappointed nightingale. "Myste warned me. She's still the only friend I've got. And you're her father. She thinks you're worth saving.

"Too bad I can't do it." The twisting of his face resembled a grin; he may have been indulging in a piece of UEF humor. Elega wasn't sure: his features were as hard to read as stone. "Weaker than I look. Like you. Handguns don't have the range you need—or the capacity. There's a limit to the number of people I can strangle personally. Can't stop what you've got coming." Inside his helmet, he nodded toward High King Festten's army. "And my rifle's about discharged—"

The blaring of the sackbut interrupted him.

At once, six catapults started winding back their arms.

Simultaneously, the wardrums began to beat their rhythm into the valley.

With a sharp look in that direction, Elega saw the Cadwal front advancing, preparing itself to pour through the breaks in the ridge. Too soon: the King and his champion weren't ready. And she hadn't had a chance to learn how Myste and Darsint and the Termigan came to be here—how they came to be together.

"But I'm not helpless." By degrees, it became more obvious that Darsint's expression was intended as a smile. "Might have enough charge left to take care of those toys for you." He gestured up at the siege engines. "Might even put a little God-rotting fear into your God-rotting enemies."

He stopped as if he were waiting for someone to catch the joke and laugh.

After a moment, King Joyse did laugh—a short, hard chuckle, not of humor, but of recognition. "'A little God-rotting fear.' I like the sound of that. Someday you must explain 'God-rotting' to me.

I suspect it is a phrase Castellan Lebbick would have enjoyed, if he had known it.

"Please do 'take care of' the catapults." King Joyse considered the Cadwal position, the readiness of the engines. "As soon as possible."

Still grinning that twisted, beaky grin, Darsint pulled his rifle off his back.

Involuntarily, a number of the guards and soldiers retreated a step.

Elega wished that Prince Kragen had dismounted, that he stood beside her. Like the Termigan, however, he stayed on his horse so that he could ride into battle at an instant's notice.

The champion checked a blinking red light on his strange weapon, thumbed a button. "Range isn't a problem." When he spoke softly, his voice sounded more than ever like birdsong. "Not against wood. But I'd have to get closer—if I weren't such a good shot."

Elega distinctly saw him wink at Myste.

For some reason, his wink reminded her that he was responsible for the burn-scar on Myste's cheek, the mark which seemed to transform Myste's expression from dreamy romance to decisiveness.

The wardrums picked up their pace.

Abruptly, Darsint raised the rifle to his shoulder, sighted along it.

During the space between one heartbeat and the next, his weapon let out a straight burst of fire.

Elega and Terisa and Geraden and everyone anywhere near the pennon turned in time to see one of the catapults catch the burst and fly to pieces. Chunks of timber and strands of rope sailed soundlessly off the rampart, shedding flames as they fell.

Elega thought she heard the hammering of the wardrums falter. Maybe she had imagined it.

"One," Darsint announced flatly.

He aimed again, fired again.

Its legs broken, his target leaned forward, started to topple; then its arm snapped under the stress.

"Two."

With some difficulty, Elega restrained an impulse to cheer. Everyone else was silent, clenched in awe and suspense.

Frowning, Darsint rechecked his rifle; he fired again. A blazing line sped as straight as a die toward the next catapult.

Apparently, the team of Cadwals at the engine panicked. They tried to throw before their catapult was ready. A load of scattershot sprayed harmlessly down the wall as fire reduced the catapult to wreckage.

"Three."

This time, there was no question about it: the wardrums faltered. A moment later, they stumbled into confusion as their drummers lost the beat. Instead of reorganizing themselves, resuming their insistent drive, they stopped altogether.

Several of the guards cleared their throats and began to cheer hoarsely. A ragged shout of approval, raucous with urgency and relief, spread out across the valley.

Well done, Darsint! Elega crowed to herself. By the stars, we will teach High King Festten what it means to oppose us!

The champion fired again; another engine collapsed.

"Four."

Frowning harder, Darsint peered at his rifle, pushed buttons, thudded the stock with the heel of his hand.

Through the mounting cheers, Prince Kragen called, "Darsint, is it wise to empty your weapon now? This battle has hardly begun. You will need your strength."

The champion gave another twisted grin. "It's never wise to take low ground and let enemies throw rocks at your head."

He lifted his rifle; from its muzzle came another shot of flame. "Five."

Over the tumult came the sackbut's blare, sounding retreat. The Cadwal front began to withdraw. As if they were already victorious, the King's guard and Prince Kragen's soldiers cheered more ferociously.

Nevertheless everyone around the pennon had seen how Darsint's fifth shot sputtered and fizzled. When he shrugged, aimed at the last catapult, and tried to fire, his weapon produced nothing except a spray of sparks, quickly gone.

He shrugged again, tried again: nothing. Automatically, he reslung the rifle across his back. To no one in particular, he said, "Anybody got a portable cyclotron I can adapt to charge this thing?"

Smiling, Myste moved close to him and put a hand on his armor as if to congratulate or console him.

By degrees, the cheering died as everyone realized that the last catapult wasn't going to fall.

If King Joyse felt any disappointment, however, he didn't show it. "That was well done, Darsint," he asserted, "well done indeed.

Let the High King beware. His fortunes have begun to turn. Now
he and his allies will know that you are here, and that you are with
us."

"They will also know," put in the Prince, "that his weapon has
no more force."

"But they cannot know how many weapons he has," Joyse retorted confidently, "or what his capabilities are. They will wait now.
They must. High King Festten and Master Eremis will consult together. When they strike again, they will attempt something extravagant—a sign of growing desperation."

Her father was amazing, really, Elega thought. Trapped in this
valley, hugely outnumbered, with Darsint's resources effectively exhausted, and the Congery's as well, he somehow made everyone who
heard him feel that he couldn't be beaten.

"In the meantime, my lord Prince," he continued, "we have a
good opportunity to strengthen our defenses. We must make the
best use we can of every obstacle to the High King's advance."

Prince Kragen nodded once, grimly ready. "As you say, my lord
King." His manner was severe: only the particular brightness of his
gaze betrayed his pleasure in the things he and Elega had planned
and hoped for together, in the validation of the risks he had persuaded the Alend Monarch to accept. "I will undertake the matter."

Gripping his reins, he turned his horse.

"I'll come with you," said the Termigan before anyone else
could speak. His flat eyes and dour expression gave no hint that he
had ever considered the Prince an enemy. "I didn't ride all this way
to sit around watching other people work."

"My lord Termigan." King Joyse's tone made both the lord and
Prince Kragen stop. "You have not yet told us how you happen to
be here, or why. And I have not had a chance to thank you. For
bringing two hundred men to my side, I am grateful. For bringing
Darsint and my daughter here safely, I am forever in your debt."

The Termigan jerked at his horse's head. "Sternwall is lost," he
snapped. For the first time, Elega noticed the froth on the beast's
mouth, the exhaustion in the beast's eyes. "I had no intention of
coming. Geraden told you that. I held on as long as I could. But
when I lost Sternwall I didn't have anywhere else to go.

"You're the only hope my Care has left—you, and your Imagers"—he looked like he wanted to spit—"and your alliance with
Alend." Forcibly, he seemed to recollect that he was talking to his

King. "My father practically built that city with his bare hands. I'm sorry I don't have better manners."

His mount stumbled as he wrenched it around. Nevertheless by simple willpower he pulled the beast into a trot as he rode away toward the foot of the valley.

King Joyse and Prince Kragen met each other's eyes. "Use him carefully," murmured the King. "I have lost two good lords already and have no wish to lose another."

The Prince replied with a bleak smile. "In Alend, old soldiers still talk about what a terrible thing it was to do battle against the lord of the Care of Termigan. I will use him carefully."

Bowing to the King, waving to Elega, Prince Kragen followed the Termigan.

Elega wanted him back. The knowledge that he was in no immediate danger didn't comfort her. At the same time, however, she felt a small shiver of eagerness because she knew that now she would get to hear Myste's story.

While the forces of Cadwal waited, and Prince Kragen did what he could to shore up the King's defenses, Elega and Myste withdrew to the Tor's tent, looking for a quiet place to talk. Terisa and Geraden were with them—and King Joyse as well, which surprised Elega because she expected him to be busy with matters of battle, and pleased her because it demonstrated that he trusted the Alend Contender, son of an old foe.

Darsint accompanied them also. In a way that made the mere idea of refusing him seem unimaginable, he insisted on staying with Myste.

Outside, the remaining catapult threw at intervals: a stubborn assailant, and quite useless. For the most part, the King's men were able to stay out of the engine's range. Eventually, it became clear that the catapult's only real purpose was to remind the guards and soldiers that High King Festten intended to destroy them.

But Elega wasn't thinking about destruction at the moment. She was marvelling at her sister, who had somehow become a force to be reckoned with in the struggle between kingdoms. Like Torrent, she had found a way to make a difference.

Elega was keenly proud of her.

"Did you really threaten your sister?" King Joyse asked as soon as everyone was settled. "Did you really threaten to unleash Darsint against the whole Alend army?"

The light of lanterns dimmed Myste's beauty. Inside the tent, she seemed less sure of herself, more easily embarrassed. A bit shamefacedly, she answered, "I fear so. I made an effort to be careful—to say less than I meant, rather than more. But I am certain Elega understood me."

Happily, Elega nodded. "I was glad of it, however—when I recovered from the shock. I needed as many arguments as possible to set before the Alend Monarch."

No doubt about it: Myste was definitely blushing. "Still I am relieved you did not put me to the test. My threats became hollow almost at once. As soon as we parted—as soon as you helped me from the Alend camp—Darsint and I left. We were not there to take any action against you."

"No?" Elega was surprised. "I would have sworn you were watching everything I did for days afterward."

"Where did you go?" Geraden put in. Like Terisa, he appeared to have some special reason to be pleased by Myste's presence. Perhaps it was because he loved families. Not for the first time, Elega noticed that he had changed enormously. The sense of *ability* in him was unmistakable. In retrospect, she was ashamed that she had ever treated him with scorn.

Myste glanced a bit awkwardly at her father. "Elega told me what I needed to know," she said slowly. "When I heard the High King was marching, not to Orison, but into the Care of Tor, I felt that my way became clear. Darsint and I went to help the Perdon, if we could."

The Perdon, who fought a suicidal battle against the forces of Cadwal because his King had abandoned him.

"'I have always believed that problems should be solved by those who see them,'" Terisa said, quoting softly. Her eyes shone as if she, too, were proud of Myste.

King Joyse didn't react to the implications of what Myste and Terisa said, however. He only smiled at them, and at Elega, basking in their company. "That was well done, Myste," he murmured. "Go on."

His attitude relieved Myste. "There is little to tell, really," she said more easily. "We traveled as best we could, but the High King's army was between us and the Perdon. We were saving Darsint's fire, since we knew it would soon be depleted, so instead of attacking High King Festten from the rear we attempted to pass around him to the fore. By the time we succeeded, the Perdon had already been trapped and killed.

"That was a hard time for us. Seeing my distress"—her eyes were wide with fondness—"Darsint wanted to assail the Cadwals, to hurt them as much as he could alone." Darsint nodded. "But I felt certain that his force must not be wasted, and I required him to withhold. Together, we waited and watched, gathering as much knowledge of the High King's movements as we could without betraying our presence.

"When your army came, we were once again on the wrong side, unable to reach you directly. This time, however, our position was fortuitous. Circling the High King's forces, first to the south, then to the west, we encountered the Termigan and his men.

"Without him, we would not have been able to join you, except by a ruinous expenditure of Darsint's fire."

Geraden interrupted again. "Did he explain himself? When Terisa and I asked him to come, he refused." He looked to Terisa for confirmation. "He was pretty convincing about it."

Myste shook her head. "He told us only what he has already suggested to you. He held to Sternwall as long as he could, but at last the pits of fire in the ground left him nothing of his father's Seat. With what fighting men he could spare from the care of his people, he set out across-country to Esmerel, intending"—she faltered momentarily, then resumed in a quiet, sad tone—"intending, I think, to both use and end his hate in one swift blow against Master Eremis.

"I cannot truly vouch for the state of his mind," she added. "I can only say that he was not easily persuaded to join us, to join his purpose to ours."

"I've seen that look before," Darsint muttered. "Had his death all planned—until he met us. Now, who knows?" The champion may have shrugged inside his armor.

"It was not Darsint's presence that persuaded him," Myste continued. "He is savage against all Imagery. And I do not think he was moved by the knowledge that you were here." She faced her father frankly. "He is another lord who believes he was abandoned by his King. But for some reason your alliance with Alend changed him. He finds—Father, I must say this. I fear he finds his old enemies easier to trust."

A shadow passed across the King's face. "Who can blame him?"

Awkwardly, Myste finished her story. "Once he was persuaded, however, he did not hold back. Since then, we have spent our time searching for a way past the Cadwals which would spare Darsint's fire. Without the Termigan's aid, we could not have reached you as we did."

As she spoke, King Joyse's expression cleared. "That is well," he said when she was done. "If we are defeated, my lord Termigan will be able to do whatever he wishes with his hate. And if we are victorious, he will know that we could not have won without him. That may do much to heal him.

"In the meantime, daughter, you have brought us new hope. Did you know that your meeting with Darsint was augured?"

Elega looked at King Joyse sharply. *Augured?*

Both Terisa and Geraden were grinning.

"Havelock cast an augury," Joyse explained, "in which you appeared, on your knees before Darsint as if you were begging him not to kill you."

Darsint shifted his weight uncomfortably. "She did kneel. I was hurt—out of my head. Couldn't get my eyes in focus. Everything was changed, enemies everywhere. Someone came, I fired. Nearly God-rotting killed her.

"Then I heard her voice. A woman. On her knees. Felt like shooting myself when I saw what I did to her."

Distinctly, as if he wanted no mistake on this point, he said, "She saved my life." There was a threat in his tone. He had no intention of letting Myste be harmed again.

For a moment, the King's blue eyes blurred. "When you disappeared from Orison," he continued to Myste, "I knew in my heart where you had gone—and I was afraid. That is why," he explained to Terisa, "I was so harsh with you, when I asked you to account for her absence. I could not resolve my fear of the truth.

"In fact," he went on, addressing Myste again, "when I first realized that the champion in Master Gilbur's glass was the same as the figure in Havelock's augury, I almost decided to shatter that glass. To spare you. So that Darsint would not be translated. Havelock had great difficulty dissuading me. Allowing that translation to take place—trusting the risks I had chosen—" His smile was sad and relieved and strong all at the same time. "That did not come easily. If I had let the Fayle urge me to stop the Congery, my determination might have faltered."

Geraden cleared his throat. "Adept Havelock tried to tell us about that augury—tried to tell Terisa. I'm still not sure why. All he managed to do at the time was scare us. But maybe he was trying to make us understand you better. As well as he could, in his condition—"

Dryly, King Joyse replied, "Perhaps. Don't underestimate him. At his worst, he's still the best hop-board player I know."

Without preamble, Terisa said, "There's got to be something we can do."

At once, the King shifted his attention to her. "My lady?"

"They're all here." She didn't seem to be speaking to him, or to anyone. Her eyes studied the air; her attention was inward. "All the pieces are in place. Myste and the champion. Elega and Prince Kragen. The Masters. Lebbick's army. He and the Perdon and the Tor all did what they were supposed to do before they were lost— sacrificed so the rest of us would come to this position. Even Torrent did her part. Everyone is doing what you want them to do, what you gave them the chance to do.

"Except Geraden and me."

Again, King Joyse asked softly, "My lady?"

No one else spoke. Geraden studied Terisa intently; Myste watched her with shining eyes.

"We've done what we can," Terisa said. "We helped bring about this position. But now we're useless. We might as well be pushed off the board."

Now she met King Joyse's gaze. "What do you want from us?"

He smiled at her as if she were wonderful. "My lady, I can beat the High King. I want you to defeat Master Eremis."

Before she could react—before Geraden or Elega or anyone else could say anything—Castellan Norge strode through the tent-flaps, unannounced and hurrying.

"My lord King," he said with as much urgency as his phlegmatic manner could convey, "you'll want to see this. Something's going to happen."

So quickly that he may have been trying to escape the questions Terisa and Geraden wanted to ask, King Joyse left his chair and followed the Castellan out of the tent.

Elega hesitated momentarily; she thought she ought to say something to Terisa and Geraden—or even to Myste and Darsint. But her heart was with her father, with the battle and Prince Kragen; she couldn't remain behind.

Outside, she hardly noticed that the rest of the people in the tent joined her only a moment later.

The valley was full of midmorning sunshine. Only midmorning, after all that had happened— Above the ramparts, the sky was immeasurably blue, as clean and complete as springtime. The air was turning subtly but unquestionably warmer, and under the sunlight the night's thick snowfall had gone slushy. Where the army had trampled the snow, a few small stretches of dark, wet dirt were beginning to appear. The stream down the center of the valley ran more loudly, taking in water from the snow-melt.

Like King Joyse and his companions around the pennon, every Mordant and Alend from the valley foot to Esmerel watched what could be seen of High King Festten's army.

The Cadwal forces appeared to be withdrawing.

No, not withdrawing: dividing. The High King parted his men into a new formation, half on either side with a space of clear ground between them as wide as the valley itself.

"Does he think he can lure us out there?" Norge inquired. "Does he think we're crazy enough to let him hit us from both sides?"

"No," King Joyse snapped, unintentionally brusque. "He is making room."

"Eremis is going to translate something," Terisa breathed to Geraden. "If I go down there, if I get close enough— If I can figure out the Image, the way I did at the crossroads, I might be able to break his mirror."

She wasn't talking to the King, but he heard her anyway. "You will not, my lady," he said at once. "If you fail, you will be the first victim. That risk is too great, even for me."

Geraden put his arm around her. He may have been trying to reassure her. Or maybe he was making sure she didn't sneak away.

Anticipation and dread knotted the atmosphere. King Joyse had said, *They will attempt something extravagant*— Everyone who had ever heard stories of the old wars knew that Imagers were capable of atrocities which could freeze blood in the heart.

Nevertheless when the next attack came no one was ready for it.

Because she was expecting something, concentrating hard, Terisa felt just a suggestion of the visceral cold of translation. Eremis' mirror was focused too far away to touch her strongly. She tightened her grip on Geraden.

In the clear space between the sides of the Cadwal army, a monster appeared.

She had seen it before. Every member of the Congery was familiar with it.

Huge eyes, insatiable and raging. Teeth dripping poison in a maw big enough to swallow houses. A vast, sluglike body. Slime-streaked sides.

Once, during the old wars, that beast had destroyed an entire village, eaten it hut by hut. The worm was too big to be killed, too big even to be hurt. Given time, it could have consumed anything. But King Joyse had captured the mirror from which the monster came, and Adept Havelock had translated the beast back to its cave in the Image.

Now Master Eremis had the mirror, and the beast was furious.

The creature gave a roar of hideous outrage, howling so fiercely that the walls of the valley rang. Then it slithered forward and began devouring the rubble that blocked High King Festten's approach, attacking the mounds as if piled rock offended it.

In spite of training and experience, determination and courage, the King's army broke into panic.

The monster's teeth among the rubble were as loud as detonations, inescapably destructive. Already the archers hidden in the mounds had to leap and run, risk snapping their legs or backs to get away. And when the rock was gone, the creature would enter the valley—

It would consume the entire army itself. Or it would drive guards and soldiers to the walls, where High King Festten's men could crush them at leisure. Or it would force them out of the valley, where the Cadwal army could fall on them from both sides. *Something extravagant*— This was extravagant, all right. But it wasn't desperate. It was a masterstroke, completely unanswerable; defeat as stark and terrible as the creature's teeth.

Helpless to save themselves, the Alend and Mordant ranks came apart like water and began spilling in all directions. Their cries were everywhere; hoarse and frantic; doomed.

The sight set King Joyse afire. "Death's hatchetman, Eremis!" he roared in a voice that seemed to match the monster's, "this is foul!"

But he didn't waste time on indignation. Wheeling to Norge, he barked like a trumpet, "Find Kragen! Rally the men! Retreat! That beast is no danger yet! We must stop this panic!

"Bring my horse!"

Galvanized by the King's shout, Norge raced for his own mount while two dumbstruck guards hauled Joyse's suddenly frightened charger forward.

In a moment, both men were gone, spurring their horses into the face of an army transformed to tumult and chaos. King Joyse didn't rage at his enemies; he didn't shout at his men. He simply rode hard, rode *conspicuously,* straight for the foot of the valley, with his sword bright in his hands, so that as many soldiers and guards as possible would see him and think he wasn't beaten.

"There's got to be *something* we can do," Geraden repeated, fretting at his helplessness like a boy.

Terisa chewed her lip. "I said that already." She hardly heard him, however. She was listening to the sound of the monster's teeth in the rubble—a savage, crushing noise which seemed somehow louder than the army's panic—and trying to think about several different things at the same time.

Choose your risks more carefully.

I want you to defeat Master Eremis.

Problems should be solved by those who see them.

I've got the strongest feeling—

And something else; something that refused to come clear. There was too much noise, too many people were shouting around her, too many people were going to die—

Something so stupidly obvious that she was going to kick herself as soon as she figured it out.

Master Barsonage was at Geraden's side. His eyes had a wild and aimless stare; he looked like a man who had wandered here after having his brains baked out in the desert. "Now I understand," he said, not—apparently—because anyone was listening to him, but because he had to say something, needed to hear a reasonable voice. "When we rescued you from the ruin of our meeting hall, Eremis used that glass to help clear away the stone. I thought his choice was odd, but now I understand. He was making his beast mad, teaching it to hate stone."

Something—

"Why did none of us realize that he must be the maker of that glass? Or an Adept?"

In spite of herself, she stopped to absorb what the Master said. He was right: Eremis must be an Adept. Or he had been working against King Joyse longer than anyone realized; had conceived his ambitions at a younger age. Unexpected abilities—

"But how did he get possession of the mirror?" asked the mediator. "I thought it was among those broken when he shattered Geraden's glass. He must have captured it then. That must have been one of the reasons for his attack on the laborium.

"Why did none of us think to see whether all the mirrors we lost were among those broken?"

It was unexpected: that's why. What Eremis did was unexpected. His abilities were unexpected. No one could expect the unexpected. By definition.

Then she had it, had it so suddenly that she seemed to reach her conclusion without taking any of the steps which led to it.

Yes.

Oh, *yes.*

"Geraden." She grabbed his arm, pulled him around to face her. "We've got to get back to Orison."

Geraden stared at her in shock; his jaw dropped. For one moment that felt sickening, like a fall from a bad height, she thought he was going to protest, Do you want to run away? Then that danger passed, and as quick as it was gone another took its place; she could see it in his face: What are you *talking* about?

Oh, Geraden, don't ask, we haven't got *time!*

But he was Geraden, the man she loved; instinctively, he had always put her needs ahead of his confusion. Instead of making protests or demanding explanations, he said, "We don't have a mirror."

"Master Barsonage does." With the ballroom of Orison in the Image.

"Flat glass. You can use it. I'll go mad."

That was right. Oh, shit. "Are you sure there aren't any others? Didn't the Congery bring *any* other normal mirrors?"

Hurry. Please. The creature was going to come through the rubble at any moment. And both King Joyse and Prince Kragen were down at the foot of the valley, vulnerable to those teeth—

As if the fact that he didn't know what was going on only made him more resolute, Geraden wheeled toward the mediator.

"Master Barsonage. Do you have another mirror? Did the Congery bring any other mirrors?"

Barsonage blinked some of the wildness out of his eyes. "Why?"

"Do you have one?"

"Why do you want it?"

Terisa pushed herself beside Geraden, tried to make the mediator notice her. "We've got to get back to Orison."

She was putting too much pressure on him; her demand seemed to increase his air of being lost. In a hoarse, dry tone, he asked, "Will you abandon King Joyse to his doom?"

Geraden clenched his fists, breathed, "*No,*" as if he were defending her.

Unfortunately, that just put more pressure on Master Barsonage. Terisa shook herself, forced down her fear, tried to give the mediator a better answer.

"I need to use Havelock's mirrors."

She had other reasons as well, but she couldn't take the time to think about them, much less explain them.

At least now she had the Master's attention. The effort to think clarified his expression, made his expression at once sharper and more human.

"What will you do?"

Hurrying past illogic, impossibility, uselessness, she replied, "Find Master Eremis' stronghold. Stop him."

Now Geraden stared at her the same way Master Barsonage did. At the same moment, they both asked, "How?"

"Unexpected abilities—" she began, fumbling for words, "unexpected actions— He can't expect the unexpected. You said so yourself."

Strictly literal, Master Barsonage returned, "I said nothing of the kind."

No. Listen. Let me think. "I mean me." Why couldn't she think? The monster devouring the rubble might have been eating her mind away. "I've done something unexpected. Twice."

Abruptly, with the beast already halfway through the piled stone, and the valley in panic, and Geraden and Master Barsonage staring at her as if she were demented, her sense of urgency and horror became too great for confusion. She knew how to think; she knew how to survive. She knew how to fight.

As if she were calm, she said, "When I got away from Master Gilbur, that wasn't really unexpected. By then we knew I had some kind of ability. But when I changed the Image in the flat glass in the laborium—the first day after I came to Orison—that was unexpected. And when I changed another Image to escape from Master Eremis, changed it across all these miles—that was unexpected. We've never even tried to explain it."

"Talent—" suggested Master Barsonage thinly.

She shook her head. "I don't mean that. I'm talking about something else." She faced Geraden squarely. "When you tried to translate me home, I ended up near the Closed Fist. That was your doing. You're the one who works with curved glass. But it was the Closed Fist in spring. It was augury. You changed the Image across time as well as distance.

"But when *I* changed the flat mirror," in shock, by reflex rather than conscious choice, "my Image showed the Closed Fist the way it really was at the time. In winter. How did I do that? How did I know what it looked like in winter?"

Geraden watched her as if she had staggered him and he was struggling to keep his balance. "I never thought of that."

"And when I escaped from Eremis—" Now she addressed Master Barsonage as well. "I used the same mirror that got me away from Gilbur. That makes sense. I was familiar with the Image. But the Image itself had changed in the meantime. The only time I actually saw it, when I used it to get away from Gilbur, it was full of wind. But when I used it to get away from Eremis, there was no wind. The Image was different. How could I change the Image in that mirror when I didn't even know what that Image looked like—when the Image I remembered was gone?"

Master Barsonage gaped. He would have looked foolish if the situation weren't so desperate.

"You mean," Geraden murmured softly, eagerly, on the verge of a revelation, "that's part of your talent. You don't need exact knowledge to change Images exactly. Something in you compensates for the things you don't know."

Right. Now she was focused entirely on the mediator, urging him to believe her, urging him to act. "I'm familiar with at least one of Havelock's mirrors. And I can't concentrate here, with that thing coming to get us." And she had at least one other reason. "I need to get back to Orison. So I can make an Image—an approximate Image—that might take us to Master Eremis' stronghold. It was dark, I couldn't see. But I remember a lot of details anyway. Maybe they'll be enough."

For a moment, Master Barsonage went on staring at her as if her ideas were inconceivable, imponderable. He had the soul of a fence-sitter: he didn't like hazardous decisions. Just when she was about to start yelling at him, however, he lifted his head and smiled, and all the wildness fell away from him.

"Why did you not say that from the first?"

Turning, he headed toward one of the Congery's wagons, shouting for other Masters to join him as he ran.

Terisa was about to follow when Geraden snatched her exuberantly into his arms, whirled her in a circle with her feet off the ground and her breath gasping. "I knew it!" he shouted to the blue sky and the chaos and the slug-beast. "I knew we weren't supposed to be here!"

Even though she couldn't resist kissing him, she was thinking, Put me down you idiot we've got to *go.*

He put her down. Together, they raced to the wagon.

The Masters were unpacking a mirror which showed a limitless sea glittering under hot sunlight.

"I brought it on a whim, really," Master Barsonage explained as the other Imagers set the glass as securely as possible in the wet snow. "It served us so well when we rescued you from the champion's destruction of our meeting hall, I thought perhaps it could serve us again. When you demanded a mirror, I was reluctant to risk it. I was trying to imagine how it might be used to drown that monster."

"I won't break it," Geraden promised. He was already beside the mirror, already stroking his fingertips along its beautiful woodwork. Despite the running and cries of the men, the desperate commands of the officers, the loud ruin of the monster's teeth, he seemed to have no difficulty concentrating. To Terisa's eyes, he shone with confidence and strength which made everything possible.

Nothing happened to the Image of the sea. Waves went on rolling their long, slow unrest from edge to edge of the frame; the heavens remained an immaculate blue unmatched by any color in the world except the sky's hue above the valley.

"Ready?" he asked Terisa over his shoulder. Without looking away from the glass, he extended his hand to her.

Where were Havelock's rooms, Havelock's mirrors? What had happened to Geraden's talent?

No, she told herself, he can do it this way, everything's all right. He had the ability to use mirrors for translations which had nothing to do with their Images. That was how he had come to her in the first place, how he had showed her the Closed Fist, how he had rescued himself from Orison. All she had to do was trust him.

Choose your risks—

She took his hand, started moving at once toward the glass so that she wouldn't falter.

But she was holding her breath as the Image opened to embrace her like the sea.

Of course she didn't fall into the sea: Geraden had too much control over his talent; he was in no danger of going that far wrong. Instead, she faded as if she had winked out of existence.

Holding his hand with all her strength, pulling him after her, she evaporated through the transition of mirrors, the instant, eternal plummet and soar between places of being; the vast redemptive and ruinous dark which her parents had taught her to know and fear and love by locking her in the closet.

When she came out of the translation, she lost her balance and collapsed in a heap, drawing Geraden helplessly after her—breaking his brief hold on the mirror's frame, his only attachment to the world of the valley.

For some strange reason, she landed on a thick carpet.

A synthetic carpet, running from wall to wall on both sides of her.

Adept Havelock didn't have a carpet like this in his rooms. No one had a carpet like this anywhere in Orison.

Across the deep, woven pile, she saw that she was surrounded by people: women in gowns; men in tuxedos. Some of them had yelled recently, dropped glasses full of ice and alcohol onto the carpet. They were all still now, however, motionless, staring frozen at Geraden and her with shock on their polished faces.

Until she recognized the angle of the hall leading to the bedrooms, and the shape of the entryway to the dining room and kitchen, she didn't realize that she was back in her old apartment.

Back in her old world.

FIFTY:
CAREFUL
RISKS

 eraden was sprawled halfway across her; his weight held
her down. Instinctively, she arched her back, tried to
shift him so that she could get her legs under her. He
didn't move. Staring at the strange carpet, the chrome-
and-wicker furniture, the astonished men and women in their inexplicable clothes, he murmured, "Glass and splinters. What have I
done?"

She thought the answer was obvious.

He had brought her back to her old condominium. And during
her absence time had passed; *months* had passed. Never one to cling
to a useless investment, her father must have sold her apartment as
soon as he felt sure she wasn't coming back. And the new owners
had redecorated it, of course—

All her mirrors were gone—every conceivable link to Mordant,
every way back—

On the other hand, what imaginable reason could Geraden have
for bringing her back *here?* for bringing her back here *now?* This
wasn't just an accident: it was an absolute disaster.

There was no way back.

"Get up," she urged as if his weight were suffocating her. "Oh,
God. Oh, shit. Get up."

"Call the police," a frightened woman pleaded.

"Call security," suggested someone else.

"Who *are* they?"

Geraden got up.

As he rose to his feet, the people in the gowns and tuxedos flinched; some of them retreated farther. A shoe kicked a glass, sent it rolling across the tile on the kitchen floor. Terisa could hear ice being crunched underfoot, as if that noise were louder than the voices.

"Call *security*, I said."

"How did they get *in* here?"

"I don't know. They just appeared, that's all."

"What have we been *drinking?*"

Her heart beat so hard that she had trouble finding her balance, trouble making her legs lift her upright.

"What have I done?" Geraden repeated softly; he was appalled to the bone.

"Miss Morgan?"

No, she was wrong again, she had jumped once again to the wrong conclusions. The ice wasn't louder than the voices: she had no difficulty at all hearing Reverend Thatcher.

He was there, squirming his way out of the press of people, a small, old man in a shabby suit. His pulse beat in the veins under his pale skin. He came a few steps toward her, then stopped; his eyes watered with surprise and relief and embarrassment.

"Miss Morgan?"

Her father was right behind Reverend Thatcher. His expression made him look like a startled barracuda.

Terisa gaped at him while her pulse faltered and her heart quailed.

Geraden, please. Oh, please. Get us out of here.

"Miss Morgan." Reverend Thatcher seemed to face her through a veil of tears. "We thought you were dead. Kidnapped—lost— I went to your father."

She had always considered her father mercilessly handsome in a tuxedo. His appearance was a weapon he knew how to use. And it made his anger more brutal; it implied that no one had the right to ruffle him.

He came out of the rich crowd as if he were stalking her.

She wanted to run. Dash into the bedroom. Hide under the bed.

It wasn't her bedroom anymore.

Oh, Geraden.

"He was going to sell your apartment anyway," Reverend Thatcher explained, driven by a need to justify himself. "I persuaded him to sell it for charity. For the mission. He's going to auction it tonight. To raise money for the mission."

Without warning, she nearly lost her fear.

Reverend Thatcher had persuaded her father? He had gone to her father and *persuaded* him, confronted him? Lonely and pitiable as he was, the small, old man must have risen to something approaching heroism, in order to confront her father like that—in order to best him.

This time, she didn't need the call of horns to help her see the change in Reverend Thatcher, the valor underlying his superficial futility. She and Geraden had blundered into his night of triumph.

"You *know* these people?"

"Who *are* they?"

"I don't care. Get them out of here."

Or else her father had relented in some way? He cared about her enough to be made vulnerable by losing her?

That idea changed everything. She believed in his unlove. It was fundamental to her. Could she have been wrong about him? Was there another part of him, a part she didn't understand, a part he didn't see himself when he looked in the mirror?

If he cared about her, how could she ever leave him?

No. He thrust Reverend Thatcher aside with such force that the old man stumbled. Chewing his anger, he demanded, "Terisa Morgan, how *dare* you embarrass me like this?"

"Terisa," Geraden asked as if he were panting, "do these people *know* you? Where are we?"

"You disappear without telling anyone," her father spat. "You abandon your job, your apartment, you abandon *me,* you don't have the simple decency to ask permission, you don't tell anyone where you're going, and then you show up like this, in front of my friends, when I'm trying to get a good price out of them for this place. Dressed like *that?* How *dare* you?"

Geraden, *please.*

Her father looked like he was going to hit her. "I'm *ashamed* of you."

That was too much. Nothing was changed. She had found depths in herself which no glass could reflect; but her father was

only what he appeared to be. Reverend Thatcher positively soared
in her estimation. Instead of cowering or crying or pleading, she faced
her father squarely.

But she didn't speak to him. Just for an instant, she wanted to
hurt him somehow, say or do something which would repay him for
his years of mistreatment. Almost immediately, however, she realized that there was no need. Simply not being afraid of him was
enough.

"Geraden," she said deliberately, "this is my old apartment.
Where you found me the first time." She didn't care how badly her
voice shook, or how near she came to tears. "This is my father. That's
Reverend Thatcher. I've told you about them.

"If there's any way you can get us out of here, you better do
it now."

"I don't care," a strident voice repeated. "*I'm* calling security."

"No!" both her father and Reverend Thatcher protested at the
same time.

Nevertheless she heard the sound of the phone snatched off
the hook, the sound of dialing—

"*Stop!*"

When Geraden stepped in front of her, he seemed taller than
she remembered. Or perhaps her father had become shorter. Geraden's voice rang with authority, and everything about him was
strong; his heart never quailed; even his mistakes hinted at glory.

"Do not call. Do not move. Do nothing. We will be gone in a
moment."

Everyone froze. The man holding the phone dropped it. Even
her father lost the power of movement. Like his guests, he stared at
Geraden and her with his mouth hanging open.

Casually, as if she weren't frantic inside, and had completely
forgotten panic, Terisa remarked to Geraden, "I thought you said
you can't shift mirrors across distances."

He didn't look at her. He didn't look at anyone: he closed his
eyes, trusting his authority—or sheer surprise—to protect him while
he concentrated. He had a king's face, and every line of it promised
strength.

Quietly, he muttered, "Well, I've got to *try*, don't I?"

Her father closed his mouth; he swallowed hard. Snarling deep
in his throat, he said, "I'm going to punish you for this—"

As if he were immensely far away, Reverend Thatcher retorted,

"Mr. Morgan, that's absurd. She's come back. We all thought she was dead, and now she's *come back*. We should be delighted."

Before anyone could respond, Geraden abruptly flung his arms wide. For no good reason except his own urgency, he cried, *"Havelock, we trust you!"*

Then he vanished.

Someone let out a vague shriek. Several of her father's guests gasped or flinched. Others appeared to be on the verge of fainting.

Suddenly, Terisa wanted to sing. Oh, he was wonderful, Geraden was wonderful, and nobody was going to be able to stop her, never again, she was never going to be afraid of her father again.

While she still had the chance, she turned to Reverend Thatcher.

"You can have your auction. Make him give you every penny he gets. I want you to have the money. It's a good cause, the best. And I might not come back. If I do, I certainly won't live here."

After that, without transition, she dropped into the quick, immeasurable plunge of translation.

Once again, Geraden had done the right thing.

As usual, she lost her balance; but he caught her as she stumbled out of the mirror, so that she didn't fall.

The change of light made her blink: electric illumination was gone, replaced by a few oil lamps. As her vision came into focus, she found that she was in the shrine or mausoleum which Adept Havelock had made out of the room where he stored his mirrors.

Where she needed to be.

What did he celebrate here? she wondered obliquely. What did he mourn?

But she had no time to spare for the Adept. Geraden held her hard, as if he had no intention of ever letting her go again.

"Glass and splinters, Terisa!" he breathed, pressing his face against her hair, "I'm sorry, I don't know what went wrong, thank the stars Havelock was watching his mirrors, I didn't mean to take us *there*—"

Already the Image of her apartment in the mirror he and the Adept had used was fading.

She kissed him to make him stop. "Don't apologize. You rescued us—that's what counts." That, and Reverend Thatcher's ability to extract money from her father. And the fact that she was no longer afraid. Part of her still felt like singing. "It was worth it.

"We've got to hurry. King Joyse doesn't have much time."

He met her gaze. For a moment, she could see the characteristic struggle between chagrin and eagerness going on inside him; self-distrust and hope at each other's throats. Almost at once, however, he smiled, and his eyes cleared, as if the acceptance he met in her turned the tide of the conflict.

"Right," he said like a man who couldn't think of any reason to be alarmed by the prospect of entering Master Eremis' stronghold. "Let's get started."

Together, they turned toward Havelock.

The Adept wasn't alone. He had Artagel with him.

Artagel was dressed for battle, and he was grinning.

Havelock had apparently been cleaning the room again. In one hand, he brandished a rather limp featherduster; he wore an apron several sizes too large for him to protect his still-spotless surcoat. Twisting his features as if he wanted to howl, he poked his duster at Terisa and Geraden, and said, "I *told* you to trust me.

"Don't you realize yet that I'm the one who planned all this? I planned it *all*. Joyse is the only man alive who could have *done* it, but I *planned* it. No matter how crazy I get, I'm the best fornicating hop-board player in Orison, *bar none*.

"*Remember* that, for a change."

Terisa couldn't resist: she asked, "You mean you knew we were coming?"

For once, the Adept was tolerant of questions. "Of course not. But I considered the possibility. What do you think planning *is?*"

"It's good to see the two of you again," Artagel interrupted happily. "I gather things have finally gotten desperate enough for some dramatic Imagery. A few of the Cadwals we've been taking prisoner in the ballroom look actively horrified.

"What're you trying to do?"

"Go to Eremis' stronghold, if we can get there," answered Geraden. "He isn't in Esmerel. Nyle isn't there. That was a trap. But Terisa thinks she can make an Image of the place Eremis took her. If she can, maybe we can find it and get in."

"Good." Facing his brother boldly, Artagel said, "This time, you aren't going to get rid of me so easily. Whatever you have in mind, you're going to need a bodyguard. And I am sick to the teeth"—he flashed his grin—"of being in command of this useless pile of rocks."

Geraden started to protest, but Terisa stopped him. This was another of her reasons for returning to Orison. Two days ago—was it only two days ago?—he had said, *When the fighting really starts, we'd better be sure we've got somebody with us who handles a sword better than I do.* One of his "strongest feelings." Instead of trying to explain, however, she said, "Let him do what he wants. We don't have time to argue with him."

As if to demonstrate her point, she left Geraden's side and went to the mirror she wanted, the flat glass reflecting a sanddune in Cadwal.

"Besides," Artagel whispered to Geraden behind her, "Havelock says you need me. He got me down here. I didn't have any idea you were coming back."

"What makes you think you're ready for Gart?" demanded Geraden hotly. "He's already beaten you twice. And you're still hurt."

Artagel chuckled. "What makes you think the two of you are ready for Eremis and Gilbur and Vagel? We've all got to do what we can. And," he added more soberly, "you may not have time for Nyle. Maybe I'll be able to help him."

Geraden apparently found that argument difficult to refute. As if to relieve a personal anxiety, he changed the subject. "How's the siege?"

"No trouble," Artagel replied. "Margonal is a model enemy. Yesterday he sent me a dozen sides of beef. Sovereign's courtesy. I sent him a cask of the King's best wine. We're becoming friends. As long as Orison doesn't panic, I'm not needed here."

Terisa set herself in front of the glass she had chosen and tried to relax.

Now that she had assumed this responsibility, it promised to be more difficult than she had allowed herself to imagine. She needed to conceive an Image of a place she had never seen, a place she knew only in small pieces, by feel. And during the relatively short time she was there, she hadn't exactly been concentrating on exact, concrete details. It had been dark—dark— Master Eremis had chained her to the wall; he had talked to her, threatened her, touched her. The arch-Imager Vagel had visited her. She had found and spoken to Nyle. And all the time her attention, her talent, had been directed elsewhere, groping for an answer to her fear—reaching out to the room in which she stood now, rather than teaching itself to recognize her prison.

She could make the mirror's desert Image melt into darkness: that was easy. But there were many different kinds of darkness in the world, in many different places. How could she be sure that the Image she conceived wasn't buried away inside the heart of some mountain, or lost in the depths of the sea?

Light: she remembered a faint, ambient illumination, a glow from an imperfectly sealed window above the bed. That was a start. How large was the bed? What was it made of? She had no idea. But the chain— Roughly ten feet of it, long enough to permit the exercises Eremis intended; stapled to the wall at the head of the bed. What else did she know?

Vaguely, the location of the doorway.

The distance between her fetter and Nyle's.

And she could remember exactly what those two iron staples felt like. Nyle's short chain. His wrist in its manacle. The rough, warm fabric of his sleeve—

Wait a minute. Wait a minute.

Images focused on places, not on people. But Nyle had been chained to the wall; she assumed he was still chained to the wall. Didn't that make him part of the place, an essential component of the Image she needed?

If she could remember what he looked like—

That, too, was easy: he looked like Geraden; slightly shorter; Geraden aged or embittered by disappointment and pessimism. *Geraden reduced to despair by Eremis and Gilbur,* no, don't think about that now, don't be distracted, take a deep breath, concentrate. She even remembered what Nyle was wearing.

A brown worsted cloak which covered him from neck to ankles, to keep the blood and the knife Eremis had given him hidden.

If she put together an Image of Nyle chained in that position, in those clothes, that close to the bed and her chain and the window, about that far from the door— Would it be enough?

She wanted to ask Geraden, but she knew he didn't know the answer. No one had ever measured her talent; no one knew what she could do. And there was only one way to learn. She had to test herself and see what happened.

She had to do the same thing to herself that King Joyse had done to her.

She wondered where he got his courage.

But she had no time for doubt. Geraden and the Adept and Artagel were watching her silently; they may all have stopped breathing. And back in the Care of Tor, in the valley of Esmerel, more lives and hopes were lost with every moment she delayed.

One deliberate piece at a time, she began to construct the Image.

Fortunately, before she made a mistake, she felt a sting of recollection.

Clothes—clothes— There was something wrong with Nyle's clothes.

Of course. Nyle wasn't wearing the clothes she remembered. After the physician Underwell had been butchered, disfigured, he had been dressed in Nyle's clothes. Otherwise no one would have jumped to the conclusion that the dead man was actually Geraden's brother.

Her pulse beat in her throat so hard that she had trouble speaking.

"What did Underwell have on? When he went to treat Nyle?"

The three men behind her shifted their feet; she heard their boots distinctly on the stone floor. "My lady?" Artagel responded uncomfortably, as if he thought she might be losing her wits.

"Don't ask," she breathed. "Just tell me. I've got to concentrate."

"If I told Joyse once, I told him a dozen times," remarked the Adept, "don't trust women." He sounded especially happy. "They've got their hearts in their finery and their brains in their loins."

"You've seen it," Geraden put in at once. "It's kind of a uniform. All the physicians wear it. So they're easy to spot when they're needed. A gray doublet. Cotton breeches." His voice trailed off; he may not have had much confidence in his ability to describe clothing.

He had said enough, however. A gray doublet with long sleeves and rough-spun fabric; not the worsted cloak she remembered.

As if by an act of will, she added that detail to the Image in her mind.

All she needed, she kept reminding herself, all she needed was a close approximation. Her unexpected abilities would take care of the rest.

Gradually, the mirror's reflection dissolved from hot sunlight to an almost impenetrable blackness.

How dare *you embarrass me like this?*
I'm ashamed of you.
I'm going to punish you—
Ha! she snorted reflexively. Try it.

She had a cramp between her shoulder blades. Every muscle in her body was knotted around itself. There were too many different kinds of dark in the world, too many different kinds of pain.

Studying the lightless Image, she said, "I need a lamp."

"What for?" inquired Artagel.

She wanted to repeat, Don't ask. I've got to concentrate. This time, however, it was important to be understood. Geraden had to be ready.

"I can use flat glass. You can't. I'm going to translate myself— there." Into a blackness she couldn't read, even though she peered at it until her temples throbbed. "With a lamp. If I don't lose control over this mirror, you'll be able to see where I am. Geraden can make another Image. A normal Image."

As she spoke, Geraden brought her a lamp. She risked a glance at him, risked losing her concentration— He was intent and keen, tight with determination; she couldn't imagine him losing heart. Nevertheless a shadow of fear darkened his gaze.

"Are you sure?" he whispered.

She shook her head. "Being sure is a weakness. Let Eremis have it."

Let her father have it.

Surprised by the steadiness of her hands, she accepted the lamp. Its flame seemed to come between her and the glass, changing the adjustment of her vision so that now she couldn't see anything.

An almost impenetrable blackness—

Oh, well.

Before she had time to think of any more reasons why she might fail, she opened the Image and stepped into it—

—into the disorienting, endless, momentary absence between existence and existence.

When she hit the floor, she nearly dropped the lamp.

The cramp in her back hampered her, kept her from moving her arms freely. As a result, she had to struggle for balance, and her jerky movements almost threw the lamp out of her hands.

She caught herself, caught the lamp, drew a gasping breath.

There was a door in front of her, a wooden door banded and

barred like the entrance to a cell. Her lamp was the only light in the room; her small flame sent shadows dancing across the raftered ceiling, down the stone walls. Like every other part of the world, the room was chilly.

Immediately, she turned to look around, at the place where the bed and the window and the iron staples were supposed to be—at the place where Nyle was supposed to be—

The sight of him suspended there in his manacles filled her with such triumph that she nearly shouted.

Geraden, hurry, I did it, *I did it!*

She didn't realize that she was losing her grip on the mirror in Orison until the details of Nyle's appearance struck her.

His face was chalky, not physically battered, but nonetheless haggard and abused. His eyes stared at her, dark pits from which the intelligence had been burned out. In spite of her sudden arrival, he slumped against his chains, unable to lift his weight off the manacles. Old blood crusted his wrists. A small caked pool marked the stone between his feet. Master Gilbur had strange tastes. Nyle looked like a man who had been used until the only part of him left alive was his sense of horror.

And that was the fate Master Eremis had intended for her. He had planned to reduce her to that condition, in order to hurt both her and Geraden as much as possible.

"Oh, Nyle!"

No, *concentrate,* don't think about it! In swift fright, she flung her attention back to Adept Havelock's mirror room, back to the glass which had translated her here. *Keep the Image.* There was light in Nyle's prison now, she held the lamp up, Geraden could see the scene, he could copy it in a curved mirror—if he was fast, if he did it before Nyle's blank, dead stare made her start to weep and rage—

If he didn't end up someplace else entirely—

Without warning, Artagel came through at a run.

Unable to anticipate the floor underfoot after the plunge of translation, he stumbled as if he were hurling himself at the door. His reflexes saved him from a collision, however. Recovering his balance almost instantly, he spun toward Terisa and Nyle. He had lost his grin in shock and surprise.

When he saw Nyle, he froze momentarily. The eagerness in him, the readiness for battle, seemed to shatter. Then he sprang past her and began trying to tear Nyle's fetters out of the wall with his bare hands.

Geraden was already there.

She didn't see him arrive, didn't see how he emerged from his translation; she only saw him throw himself at the cot as if he had gone mad. Coughing curses, he picked up the cot and crashed it against the wall, hammered and belabored it against the stone until the frame and legs broke into pieces the size of clubs.

With one of the legs, he went at Artagel and Nyle as if he meant to beat them both senseless.

Shouldering Artagel aside, he jammed the end of the leg into the nearest staple and levered it savagely out of the wall.

The iron staple sang like a sword as it skittered across the floor.

Nyle collapsed into Artagel's grasp.

Panting, "Bastards bastards bastards," Geraden attacked the second staple. It let out a thin, metallic scream as it pulled loose.

He and Artagel hunched over Nyle. Clenched sounds came between their teeth, as if both of them were weeping.

Terisa thought for a moment that Nyle was unconscious, too badly abused to understand what was happening. But then, in a voice made hoarse and ragged by howls, he croaked, "Geraden? Artagel? Is it really you?"

Fiercely, Geraden whispered, "We're here. We're here. Terisa brought us. As soon as you can stand, I'll translate you back to Orison."

Too late, Terisa heard the door open, saw light from the corridor outside wash against her and the Domne's sons.

She whirled frantically away as a voice like silk said, "If you can do that, it will be miraculous. I am going to cut your heart out before you can make the attempt. In my experience, dead men make poor Imagers."

Stark against the unexpected light, the man seemed to have no face, no features. The longsword he held looked black and fatal, a blade of darkness.

Terisa recognized him anyway.

Gart.

Crouched over Nyle, Geraden and Artagel were insignificant, pitiable, in the shadow of Gart's silhouetted strength.

Despite that, however, Artagel drawled without moving, "Don't tell me Eremis knew we were coming. I won't believe it."

"No," conceded Gart, as smooth as his blade. "Yet even co-incidence conspires to help victors. I was sent to bring Nyle to the Image-room. Master Eremis considered that you might do something desperate—although seeing you I doubt that he grasps how truly desperate you have become—so he wished to have your brother made ready to use against you.

"He may not be delighted to hear that I have slain you. He wishes that pleasure for himself. But I will answer for your deaths to the High King."

"I'm sure you will." Slowly, keeping his hands away from his sword, Artagel rose to his feet, left Nyle in Geraden's arms. Light from the doorway burned along the tears on Artagel's cheeks, lit sparks in his eyes. His fighting grin was gone; he seemed to have no heart left for it. "You're forgetting just one thing."

"And what is that?" the Monomach inquired maliciously.

Artagel shrugged. "We aren't dead yet."

As hard as she could, Terisa flung her lamp at Gart's head.

His quickness was appalling. As if he had known what she would do, he batted the lamp away from his face with the flat of his blade.

Nevertheless the lamp struck his shoulder. Flaming oil splashed down his chest, bright on his black leather armor.

In that instant, Artagel attacked.

So swiftly that his leap and the sweeping pull with which he drew his sword looked like one movement, wildly, almost in a frenzy, crying out his rage and hurt, he hacked at the burning man.

His assault was too sudden, too furious; Gart had trouble countering it. The High King's Monomach beat at the fire with one hand, trying to put it out before it took hold of his armor; with the other, he parried Artagel's blow awkwardly, barely succeeded at blocking it away from his head.

His whole weight behind the blow, Artagel swung again.

And again, as fast as he could.

Gart seemed to erase the flame, as if his touch were enough to extinguish it. Nevertheless he couldn't meet Artagel's attack one-handed. He was driven backward, into the doorway. And the door was too narrow for his strokes. His sword took chips out of the doorpost; the impact slowed him, so that he almost failed to lift Artagel's cut over his shoulder.

That counter left him off balance.

At once, Artagel drove forward with one foot and booted Gart in the chest.

Gart slammed against the far wall of the corridor and recoiled to the side, reeling to get his legs braced under him.

Artagel went through the doorway after him, steel on steel, steel on stone, out of sight to the left.

Terisa was already at Geraden's side. "Come on," she gasped, "come *on*." With both hands, she heaved at him, trying to raise him to his feet.

Clutching Nyle, Geraden surged upright.

They staggered together; Geraden struggled to hold Nyle; Nyle fought to help himself. Still gripping the cot leg he had used as a lever, Geraden hauled his brother toward the door.

In the corridor, Artagel fought for his life.

Gart had recovered; he was beginning to return the attack. And the wildness of Artagel's first assault was useless for defense. As a result, the nature of their combat changed. He was forced to meet Gart's skill with his own, instead of with frenzy.

He was still hampered by the tightness in his side.

And Gart had already beaten him twice.

The corridor clanged with blows, swirled with sparks. Artagel barely prevented the Monomach from returning to the doorway.

"*Come on,*" Terisa urged.

Geraden cast one white, urgent look at Artagel's back, then dragged Nyle in the opposite direction.

Terisa followed, pushing Geraden and Nyle to move faster.

Through the clamor of steel, they reached a corner.

As soon as they rounded it, the noise diminished.

They passed more doors: storerooms, cells, guards' quarters. Terisa thought they must be near the chamber where Master Eremis had his glassworks. Unless it was in the opposite direction. What was the "Image-room"? *Where* was it?

At the fourth door, Geraden stopped. He wrenched it open: a storeroom, apparently; bedding and pillows. More roughly than he intended, he thrust Nyle inside.

"Hide!" he hissed. "Let us do the fighting! All you have to do is stay hidden, so they can't threaten you."

Nyle gave his brother a look of dumb, helpless anguish. Then he stumbled into the dark, and Geraden jerked the door shut, catching it just in time to make it close softly.

Pale and extreme, he faced Terisa. "I hope to the stars," he panted, "we know what we're doing."

She grabbed at his hand and drew him into a run again, on down the corridor.

Know what we're doing.

I want you to defeat Master Eremis.

Artagel wouldn't last much longer: she knew that. Yet she and Geraden were still alive because of him. And Eremis didn't know they were coming. Maybe King Joyse and Prince Kragen had already been crushed. But she had promised in her heart that she would kill Master Eremis. The men who had treated Nyle like *that* were going to die.

The cot leg in Geraden's fist looked too short, too weightless, to do any good. Nevertheless he held it like a man who intended to find a use for it.

She needed a weapon of her own; she didn't have anything to fight with except her empty hands.

She had no idea how big the stronghold was, how to find her enemies. She and Geraden kept running anyway, beyond the range of Artagel's valiant struggle, around corners, along passageways. Geraden no longer seemed to be breathing hard: he had settled into a state of exertion where nothing could stop him. She saw suggestions of the Domne in him, hints of Tholden, as if he had all his family's strength. Her own lungs were being torn open, but she didn't care. Details like that had lost their importance; she had left them behind with her father.

Then the corridor opened into a place of more light; a room with many windows, full of sunshine.

A large, round room, as large as the Congery's former meeting hall in Orison; high, with its domed ceiling encircled by clerestories so that the bright morning shone in from all sides; reached by several entrances around the walls, as if this chamber were the center of the stronghold, the hub around which all Master Eremis' activities turned; and full of mirrors.

The Image-room.

Tall mirrors of many kinds stood in a wide circle around the center of the chamber, meticulously spaced ten or so feet apart, and facing inward, so that they could all be watched—so that they were all ready to be used—by the men in their midst.

Master Eremis.

Master Gilbur.

The arch-Imager Vagel.

Terisa thought that she and Geraden were running loudly, panting like engines. Apparently, however, their approach was relatively quiet. None of the men noticed them. Eremis and Gilbur and Vagel were all studying a flat glass which stood with them in the middle of the circle.

That mirror showed the great slug-beast as it entered the valley of Esmerel.

The mounds of rock which had blocked the creature's advance were gone, devoured; now the monster squirmed along its slime into the valley foot.

Almost directly under the beast's jaws rode King Joyse, holding his sword up like a banner. From this perspective, he seemed already in reach of the vast, venomous fangs. He was shouting commands or appeals which didn't convey anything through the glass. Small with distance, he looked at once extravagant and pathetic, like a weather vane dancing in the onset of a hurricane.

"Do your best, Joyse," growled Master Gilbur. "Withdraw your men. Rally them if you can. Then it will be Festten's power that actually destroys you, rather than ours."

Terisa and Geraden had slowed, almost stopped. He raised a finger to his mouth, urging silence; she nodded. They crept forward behind the Imagers, into the ring of mirrors.

The first mirror they saw from the front showed the side of a rocky mountain. The slope had a dark scar across it, as if a landslide had recently taken place. This was the source of the avalanches Eremis had used against Vale House and the Congery's chasm.

Grinning like Artagel, Geraden issued his challenge to his enemies by swinging his cot leg at the glass.

The mirror shattered like a cry; glass sprayed singing to the stone.

At the sound, the three Imagers spun.

Only Master Eremis showed any surprise. He may have had a secret liking for surprises: they tested him, gave him new chances to exercise his abilities. His expression when he saw Terisa and Geraden bore an unmistakable resemblance to joy.

"Astonishing," he murmured. "I did not believe that such talent existed in all the world."

Unlike Eremis, Master Gilbur had only one reaction to the unexpected. Clenched like his back, his features brandished their old scowl, their black and unalterable fury. One powerful fist dove into his robe, brought out a dagger as long as Terisa's forearm; the dagger which had killed Master Quillon. Deep in his contorted chest, he snarled curses like a hunting lion.

The arch-Imager's mouth hung open, but he didn't look surprised. He looked hungry, avid for some bloody sustenance he had been too long denied, insatiably destructive. His chin was wet with drool, and his eyes smoldered like the eyes of a lover lost in cruelty.

Before any of the Imagers had time to move, Terisa pushed the nearest mirror onto its back. As it fell, she saw a bitter landscape running with lava. Then the scene broke into splinters and ruin.

"If you do that again, my lady," Master Eremis said amiably, "I swear I will rip Geraden's balls off and make you eat them."

"Try it," retorted Geraden. He sprang to the next glass, clubbed it to shards.

Roaring, Master Gilbur charged at him.

Geraden dodged behind another mirror, pulled it over. Unfortunately, that left him open to Gilbur's attack. The dagger stabbed for his heart.

He saved himself by staggering to the side, slipping on chips of glass, crashing to the floor in a splash of slivers. Master Gilbur sprang after him, hammered the dagger at him. He rolled away, scrambled his legs under him, scuttled toward the wall—just out of reach. He had lost his club; he was weaponless against Gilbur's tremendous strength, the Imager's long blade.

"Stand still and die, dogshit!" Master Gilbur panted.

He drove Geraden backward.

Terisa faced Eremis and the arch-Imager alone.

She knew how to fight them: without thinking about it, without planning anything, she *knew*. She could never break enough of their mirrors to save King Joyse. They would kill her long before she did that much damage. And she would accomplish nothing if she shifted the Image which showed the King's peril. Nevertheless she had glass to oppose Eremis and Vagel with, mirrors at her disposal which they couldn't see. All she had to do was stay alive.

And concentrate—

I want you to trust me.

—concentrate on the flat glass in Havelock's rooms, the mirror with the Image of the sand dune. If she put this scene, this room, into that glass, the Adept could see it. He would see it, if he hadn't fallen completely victim to his insanity. And then he could translate both Eremis and Vagel to Orison.

Trust me.

Eremis would lose his mind. And Vagel would be in Orison, with no way back here. He might use one of Havelock's mirrors to avoid capture, but he would cease to be a threat.

All she had to do was *concentrate.*

She stood still. Instinctively, she raised her hands as if to show Master Eremis she was no longer a threat to his mirrors.

The way he looked at her made her blood labor like sludge in her veins.

To keep himself from being pinned to the wall, Geraden had to retreat toward one of the exits. Apparently hoping to draw Master Gilbur after him, he turned suddenly and fled, running hard down the corridor.

Cunning despite his rage, Master Gilbur stopped. There was no harm Geraden could do anywhere except in this room.

Clutching his dagger, Gilbur returned to the ring.

To the Image in Terisa's mind.

She held it steady, hoping now that Havelock would wait until Master Gilbur came within reach, within range of Eremis' destruction. She had no pity of any kind left in her.

At that moment, *a touch of cold as thin as a feather and as sharp as steel slid straight through the center of her abdomen.*

"Hee-hee!" a thin voice cackled. "Wait for me, Vagel! I'm coming."

Adept Havelock burst out of the air at a run.

"I'm *coming!*"

Oh, *no!*

He was a madman full of glee. His feet seemed to find the stone without any possibility of misstep, as if losing his mind made him immune to all the other hazards of translation. His apron flapped about his ankles as he ran.

As swift as joy, he sped for the arch-Imager.

In both fists he clutched his featherduster as if it made him mighty: a sword or scepter no one could oppose.

That surprised Vagel; it took him too suddenly for any reaction except panic. Once, in the past, Havelock had cost him everything but his life: now the mad Adept wanted his life as well.

Havelock was oblivious to everyone else. He didn't see Terisa. He didn't seem to notice that Master Eremis had stretched out a casual foot to trip him; he was only after the arch-Imager. Vagel, however, had flinched away; he headed for one of the exits with all the speed his old legs could produce.

Veering to follow, the Adept unconsciously avoided Eremis' foot.

"I'm *coming!*"

One after the other, they disappeared down the corridor, taking Terisa's only hope with them, her only way to fight.

"Ballocks and bull-puke!" rasped Master Gilbur. "Does every Imager left in the world now do these impossible translations?"

"I think not," Eremis replied, grinning ferally. "I think that was our lady Terisa's doing. I doubt, however, that she intended to bring the Adept here. *Her* thought was that he would translate us away— to Orison and madness." Rage and joy mounted in him as he spoke. "We are fortunate that Havelock is himself already mad, inaccessible to such cleverness."

Spitting obscenities, Gilbur started toward Terisa.

"No!" Master Eremis snapped at once. "The lady Terisa is mine. I will attend to her."

Gilbur stopped, facing Eremis.

"The destruction of King Joyse," Master Eremis continued, nonchalant and brutal, "I leave to you." He gestured around the mirrors. "Enjoy it as much as you wish. For me, there is more plea- sure"—he showed his teeth—"in *undoing* an Imager with her un- precedented capacities than in slaughtering a mere King.

"When Gart returns with Nyle, use them as you think best.

"My lady." Raising one long arm, he pointed at a passageway behind her. "Go there."

Because she had nothing left, Terisa turned and did as she was told.

Out in the valley, the destruction of King Joyse was proceeding as planned.

He had no weapon to combat the monster his enemies had unleashed. It finished eating its way through the rubble of the av- alanche, then came on into the valley, hungry for other prey. The last time someone—Eremis?—had translated this beast, it had been considerably less ravenous. And noticeably less irate. Master Eremis must have found the means to make it very angry.

How old would he have been at the time of that previous translation? Fifteen? *Ten?*

Was it possible for a boy so young to be that good an Imager? Or that full of malice?

King Joyse didn't know. And the answers didn't matter. What mattered was the army, his men and Prince Kragen's. They were going to die quickly and horribly if he couldn't wrestle them back under control, quench their panic. And they were going to die anyway, unless someone found a defense against this creature.

One thing at a time. Death later was preferable to death now. During the interval between now and later, anything might happen. Someone might think of a way to hurt the beast. Or it might accidentally get hit by a throw from the catapult, might change direction. Or it might die of old age and indigestion.

The army had to be saved *now*.

So he drove his charger as close to the monster as he dared; so close that his mount snorted foam and quivered; so close that he could feel the beast's breath sweep over him, could smell its intense, rank stink. And there he raised his voice like a trumpet against the hoarse screaming and the panic, the white-eyed and unreasoning dread.

"Retreat! *Retreat,* I say!" Retreat wasn't rout. "Find your captains! Rally to your captains! This beast can't outrun you!" It cannot silence *me,* and I am nearer to it than you are.

Behind him, the creature lifted its maw and howled. Somehow, he sent his call through the roar, demanding and clarion.

"You must retreat in order!"

The scene in front of him still looked like chaos. The shouting went on, full of fear. But he had an experienced eye: he could see the state of the army changing. Some of the captains held their ground and yelled for their men; more and more men began struggling through the press toward their captains. The army was like an augury in reverse, an Image resolving toward coherence out of a swirl of prescient bits.

Then riders came toward the King, goading their horses hard.

Prince Kragen. Castellan Norge.

Almost under the teeth of the creature, they met, reined their mounts. Norge's horse was frantic: it wheeled in fright, snorting as if it were deranged. A moment later, however, he fought it under control.

King Joyse held his sword high, in salute and defiance.

The sight of the three leaders there as if they were impervious to Imagery and horror seemed to have a palpable impact. Suddenly, the surge of men was transformed: no longer a rout interrupted by islands of order, it became an army vigorously quelling its own chaos.

"Well done, my lord King!" panted the Alend Contender. "I thought we had lost them."

"What now?" put in the Castellan. "How can we fight that thing?"

"We must not lose them again!" King Joyse returned. "Keep them to the center of the valley. Keep them moving steadily. We are bottled in this valley, but if we are pushed far enough we will attempt to win through the neck."

Howling again, the monster heaved itself forward.

In a group, King Joyse, Prince Kragen, and the Castellan spurred thirty yards up the valley, then stopped once more.

"Retreating won't save us!" cried Norge. "We can't get out the defile! Festten wouldn't do this if he didn't have an ambush ready. As soon as you try, we're lost." As if as an afterthought, he added, "My lord King."

The King restrained a sarcastic retort. "Then we must not let ourselves be pushed so far," he said with more mildness than he felt. The flash in his blue eyes may have been urgency—or it may have been a wild love of risk. "Get archers up the walls, as many as you can. If that beast has eyes, perhaps we can put them out."

Castellan Norge didn't waste time saluting. He dug his spurs into his mount and sped away at a dead gallop.

"A thin hope, my lord King," Prince Kragen commented tensely.

"I am aware of that," King Joyse allowed himself to snap, "my lord Prince." Then, however, he moderated his tone. "Suggestions are welcome."

Prince Kragen scowled over his shoulder at the beast. "If the Congery cannot save us, we cannot be saved."

King Joyse nodded grimly. "Then may the stars send Master Barsonage inspiration, or everything I have loved must perish."

His eyes continued flashing.

After a moment, Prince Kragen caught the King's mood and smiled himself.

Watching their father and the Alend Contender from the distance of the pennon, the ladies Elega and Myste stood like reflections of each other, holding their breath together when the monster roared or moved, exhaling in shared appreciation of what King Joyse and the Prince accomplished.

As the army fought down its panic, Elega murmured, "I did not believe that we would ever see him like this again."

"I hoped for it," replied Myste softly. "I could not bear to give it up. That is the difference between us. I cannot live without old hopes. You are willing to let them go in order to conceive new ones."

At the moment, Elega had no idea whether she considered this an accurate observation or not.

"Wouldn't catch me doing that," Darsint commented sourly. He stood a step or two behind Myste, apparently watching for threats in all directions. "Haven't got the guts. Fighting I can do. But stand like that so the men won't panic? Make myself a target?" He seemed to be talking primarily to himself; nevertheless Myste turned to hear him. "Maybe that's what went wrong on Pythas," he added. "Couldn't rally my men."

"It was a different situation," said Myste, "in a different place. You did everything any man could have done there."

Darsint looked at Myste strangely. He took no discernible comfort in her words. Elega had the impression that Myste had unwittingly aggravated whatever troubled him.

"That's what you people do, isn't it," he muttered like a distressed songbird. "*He* does it. Both of you. You do 'everything.'"

"We would if we could," answered Elega, more for her own benefit than to argue with him. "Unfortunately, we're women."

Down the valley, the monster surged forward; she thought both the King and Prince Kragen would be taken by those appalling fangs. But they rode out of reach in time, keeping themselves like a bulwark between the beast and their army, a defense which had nothing to do with physical force.

"And even if we could fight like men," Elega continued, "even if we were allowed, we couldn't do anything against that creature. If it is to be stopped, the Masters must do it."

Master Barsonage had already informed her, however, that he

had no hope left. A short way below her on the hillside, he had set up the mirror which had translated Terisa and Geraden away, the glass full of ocean. Eventually, he would try to hinder the beast with a rush of water. But he didn't expect much success. And none of the other mirrors remaining to the Congery could do anything against a creature that size.

As for Terisa and Geraden—

Where they were concerned, Elega would have been glad to hope; but she didn't know what to hope *for*. Her lack of confidence in Geraden was lifelong, hard to change. And Terisa also was no fighter.

Darsint made an uncomfortable noise in his throat, as if she had offended him somehow. Or frightened him.

"It is not your burden," Myste whispered to him gently. "You have already done more than we could have asked—more than most of us would have believed possible. And your rifle is exhausted. Doubtless that is the reason Master Eremis decided to risk his monster."

This observation didn't comfort the champion much, either.

Elega was watching her father and Prince Kragen so hard, focusing on them so exclusively, that she almost didn't see what was about to happen to them.

A shout of warning jerked her attention back a step, widened her angle of vision. With a cry she didn't hear herself utter, she saw riders come up both sides of the monster into the valley, dozens of them, hundreds; riders with red fur and alien faces, with four arms and two scimitars, their blades raised for blood; mounted creatures like the ones which had once attacked Terisa and Geraden, riding now to sweep around in front of the slug-beast against King Joyse and the Prince.

"Father!" Myste wailed into the turmoil.

But she only had one man to lose, only her father. Elega was going to lose Prince Kragen as well, and then the High King's victory would be assured regardless of whether or not the army relapsed to panic. Norge had men moving back down the valley, back toward the Prince and King Joyse, but they were too slow, too late. For a moment, Elega's vision went dark around the edges. She had the distinct impression that she was going to faint.

Then Darsint's metalled hand caught her by the shoulder,

turned her. She couldn't see his face; she was trying to pull away, trying to watch the foot of the valley. Yet he held her.

"Protect her." His voice sounded like a warble. "You can do it better than any of this lot. Understand? I love her. Can't let her be hurt."

Harder than he may have intended, he pushed Elega at Myste.

The sisters collided, hugged each other to keep themselves from falling.

Darsint set off at a run.

He headed for the stream and used it as a path: it was relatively clear; few of the men were milling in the cold water. Uneven ground and unsteady rocks made his armored feet slip and his strides lurch, so that he looked like a damaged machine hurrying toward a breakdown. Nevertheless the power still in his suit was enough to give him speed; he ran as fast a horse.

Not fast enough to save King Joyse and Prince Kragen, of course. At that pace, however, he might reach the foot of the valley in time to help avenge them.

Unfortunately, the Cadwals at the last catapult saw what he was doing. They threw scattershot at him as soon as he came within range.

Stones caught the sunlight, the bright metal; soundless amid the shouts and clamor, they hit hard. In spite of his armor, he went down on his face in the chuckling brook.

King Joyse and Prince Kragen wheeled when they heard the shout which had warned Elega. Kragen spat a curse at the sight of the red-furred creatures. Their hate was vivid, even through the monster's loud advance. And they were so many— He and King Joyse would never be able to get away. And the men Castellan Norge had already sent to rescue them had too far to come.

But the King smiled, and his eyes grew brighter. "As I said," he remarked in a voice only Prince Kragen could hear, "the High King grows desperate. He dares not fail. And men who dare not fail cannot succeed."

Prince Kragen considered this a foolish piece of philosophy— and gratuitous as well—but he had no time for it. He had no time to regret that he was about to die, or that he had failed his father, or that he would never hold Elega in his arms again. His hands snatched out his sword as he kicked his charger into a gallop, heading not toward the impossible safety of the army, too distant to do him any good, but rather straight at the nearest creatures, the front of the attack.

For the space of two or three heartbeats, he had a chance to be surprised and a bit relieved by the fact that King Joyse was right beside him, longsword ready, eyes bright for battle. Then the Alend Contender and the King of Mordant crashed alone into a vicious wall of scimitars and fought, trying to take as many of their enemies as possible with them when they died.

Once again, Elega was concentrating too exclusively on her father and Prince Kragen to see Darsint struggle back to his feet. She was holding Myste tightly: she only knew that something new had happened by the way Myste's body reacted.

Lumbering like a wreck, Darsint continued down the stream.

He couldn't run now. Myste had helped heal the wounds on his body, but nothing in this world could have helped him repair the holes which the Pythians had burned in his armor, and those holes made him vulnerable. He was hurt again now, listing to the side, stumbling occasionally; the power inside his suit may have been damaged.

He kept going anyway.

Prince Kragen and King Joyse kept going as well.

In fact, they kept going so well that the Prince felt a rush of joy at the way their swords rose and fell, the way their blows struck; the surge of their horses through the attack. The red-furred creatures had eyes in the wrong places, with whiskers sprouting all around them; they had too many arms, too many scimitars. And their hate was palpable in the fray, a consuming lust. Nevertheless they were flesh-and-blood: they could be killed. And they weren't especially skillful with their blades; they relied more on fury than on expertise.

The Prince and King Joyse cut into the heart of the attack and kept going, kept fighting shoulder to shoulder, as if between them they had discovered something indomitable.

It was amazing, really, how many cuts they ducked or parried or slipped aside; how far into the furred bodies they delivered their swords; how their crazy charge made the mounts of the creatures falter and shy. And it was amazing, too, how well the King fought. Prince Kragen himself was much younger—presumably much stronger. Yet King Joyse matched the Alend Contender blow for blow, swung and thrust his longsword as if the weight of steel transformed him, restored him to his prime. Now his beard was splashed with blood; cuts laced his mail; grue stained his arms. And yet he kept all harm away from his companion on that side.

For a few precious moments, they succeeded against unbeatable odds.

And while they succeeded, Prince Kragen found that King Joyse made sense to him at last. If everything else was lost, still no one would ever be able to change the fact that the King of Mordant and the Alend Contender had died side by side instead of at each other's throats.

Their success had to end. Two men simply couldn't survive against so much mounted and murderous savagery. And yet they did survive. The momentum of the battle changed suddenly, and Prince Kragen felt another singing rush of joy at the realization that he and King Joyse were no longer alone.

The Termigan had appeared in the midst of the fray.

He had all his men with him.

The look on his face was as keen as a cleaver; he had the hands of a butcher. The way he slaughtered his enemies justified every story the Prince had ever heard of him. And his men were beyond panic. They had seen Sternwall eaten alive by Imagery, and nothing could frighten them. During the first attack of the slug-beast, they had waited with their grim lord down near the foot of the valley, readied themselves to strike. They may have intended to strike at the monster itself. The red-furred creatures were a more possible enemy, however, and the last force of Termigan had hurled itself into the fighting without hesitation.

The lord and his men kept Prince Kragen and King Joyse alive until Norge's reinforcements arrived.

There were nearly a thousand of the creatures. Castellan Norge had sent less than half that many men to the rescue. The thought that King Joyse and Prince Kragen were already lost had filled the valley with alarm again, paralyzing a large portion of the army. And the men who sprang to Norge's call had to contend with horses that were wild with fear, terrified by the slug-beast and the alien creatures. In one sense, the Castellan was lucky to send as much help as he did to his King. In another, he was unlucky that he couldn't muster enough strength to turn the battle.

Nevertheless he achieved a goal which had never crossed his mind: he thinned out the combat directly in front of the monster; thinned it sufficiently to let Darsint through.

In the middle of the fray, Darsint shambled, hardly able to force one foot ahead of the next. He must have been in better condition than he looked, however. Every creature which attacked him, he shot with one of his handguns, aiming and firing almost negligently, as if he could do this kind of fighting in his sleep. When he missed, scimitars rang off his armor without hindering him; he appeared unconscious that he was struck. He wasn't interested in mere blades and horses.

His target was the slug-beast.

Guns ready, he paused before the monster's gaping maw. But he wasn't hesitating: he may have been afraid to hesitate. Instead, he was making some kind of adjustment inside his suit.

Before anyone except Myste realized what he meant to do, his suit produced a burst of power that enabled him to leap past the dire fangs straight down the beast's throat.

FIFTY-ONE: THE
THINGS MEN DO
WITH MIRRORS

F acing Gart's sword in the stone-walled corridor, Artagel felt that he was looking down the throat of death.

The High King's Monomach had recovered from the fire of the lamp, and from the first extremity of Artagel's attack; now he had his balance again, his command of steel and weight. Moment by moment, he seemed to grow stronger.

The lanterns which lit the passage made his eyes yellow; they gleamed like a beast's. His hatchet-nose faced his opponent, keen for blood. The scars on his cheeks, the initiation-marks of his craft, were pale streaks against the bronze hue of his skin. Though he was assailed by the best swordsman in Mordant, he wasn't even sweating. His blade moved like a live thing: as protective as a lover, it caught and countered every blow for him, as if to spare him the effort of defending himself.

His teeth showed, white and malign, between his lips; loathing stretched all the mercy out of his features. Yet Artagel felt sure that Gart's abhorrence had nothing personal to do with him. It involved no resentment of Artagel's reputation, no envy of his position, no particular desire to see him dead. In Gart, the lust for killing was a professional characteristic untainted by individual emotions.

Artagel had heard rumors about the training undergone by Apts of the High King's Monomach, the privations and hurts and dangers imposed on small boys to make them sure of what they were doing, sure of themselves; to harden their loathing. That was what gave Gart strength: his detachment; the impersonality of his passion. His heart held nothing which might confuse him.

Artagel, on the other hand, *was* sweating.

His hands were slick with moisture; under his mail, his jerkin clung to his skin. His sword had gone dead in his grasp, and his chest heaved with the exertion of swinging the blade. The tightness in his side had become a band of hot iron, fired to agony, and that pain seemed to sap the resilience from his legs, the quick tension from his wrists, the life from his weapon.

A flurry of blows, as loud as forgework, bright with sparks. A measuring pause. Another flurry.

There was no question about it: Gart was going to kill him.

Artagel didn't face this prospect with quite the same approval Lebbick had felt.

He couldn't afford to be beaten, absolutely could not afford to fail. If he went down, Gart would go after Terisa and Geraden. He would go after Nyle. They would all die, and King Joyse himself wouldn't stand a chance—

But when he thought about Nyle, remembered what had been done to his brother, his heart filled up with darkness, and he flung himself at Gart wildly, inexpertly. Only the sheer fury of his attack saved him from immediate death. Fury was all that kept him going; nothing but fury gave strength to his limbs, air to his lungs, life to his steel.

A quick, slicing pain brought him back to himself—a cut along the bunched muscle of his left shoulder. He recoiled from suicide as blood welled out of the wound. A minor injury: he knew that instinctively. Nevertheless it *hurt*— It hurt enough to restore his reason.

Not this way. He was never going to beat Gart this way. The truth was obvious in the effortless action of Gart's blade, the feral smirk on his face; it was unmistakable in the glint of his yellow eyes.

In fact, Artagel was barely able to keep Gart's swordpoint out of his chest as he retreated down the corridor, gasping for breath, battling to recover his balance. The Monomach's blade wove gleams and flashes of lantern-light as if his steel were somehow miraculous, like a mirror.

All right. Artagel couldn't beat Gart this way. Actually, he couldn't beat Gart at all. But he had to prolong the struggle as much

as possible, had to buy time. Time was vital. So he needed some
other way to fight. He had to start thinking like Geraden or Terisa,
*but not about Nyle, no, don't think about Nyle, don't give in to the dark-
ness.* He had to do something unexpected.

Something to ruffle Gart's detachment.

Down in the depths of Artagel's belly, a knot loosened, and he
began to grin.

Geraden wasn't grinning.

When Master Gilbur didn't follow him, he wasn't surprised. Just
disappointed. He had no idea in the world what he would have done
if the Master had chased him. Gilbur knew the stronghold, after all,
and Geraden could never hope to beat him in a test of violence. But
at least the hunchbacked Imager would have been away from the
mirrors, unable for the moment to do King Joyse any more damage.

That hope had failed, of course. Instead of drawing Master Gilbur away, Geraden had in effect abandoned Terisa, left her to contend with Master Gilbur and Master Eremis and the arch-Imager
alone.

Wonderful. The perfect climax to a perfect life. Now all he had
to do was blunder into a squad of guards somewhere and get himself
uselessly killed, and the story of his life would be complete.

Now it's your turn, the Domne had said. *Make us proud of you.
Make what we're doing worthwhile.*

Geraden had succeeded brilliantly.

He couldn't resist thinking like that. He had suffered too many
accidents; the logic of mishap seemed irrefutable. Nevertheless he
was too stubborn to accept defeat. He loved Terisa too much, and
his brothers, and the King—

In the name of sanity, remember to call me "Da."

As soon as he was sure Master Gilbur had given up the chase,
he turned down a side passage and began to double back toward the
Image-room.

Unacquainted with the stronghold, he spent several maddening
moments hunting his way. Where were the guards? Surely Master
Eremis had guards, servants of the High King if not of Eremis himself? Why hadn't he encountered them already? At last, however, he
reached another of the entrances to the Image-room.

From the entryway, he saw that Master Gilbur was the only one
there.

Just for a moment, while his heart lurched in his chest and a cry struggled in his throat, he thought, Terisa *Terisa!* Master Eremis and Vagel had taken her to rape and torture her, just like Nyle, *just like Nyle.* He had to go after her, he had to find her, help her, he absolutely and utterly could not bear to let them destroy her.

At the same time, unfortunately, he noticed what Master Gilbur was doing.

The Imager had his back to Geraden. That was fortuitous. Plainly, he didn't know or care what Geraden might do. He was carrying a glass out of the center of the ring of mirrors.

The flat mirror which showed Esmerel's valley.

He was carrying it toward a mirror which stood in the direct, clean light from one of the windows. Sunshine illuminated the Image vividly.

The scene which the glass reflected swarmed with cockroaches.

Geraden remembered those creatures. They had nearly killed him, and Terisa, and Artagel. Nevertheless the horror of that memory gave way at once to a new dismay when Master Gilbur set the flat glass down before the other mirror and stepped back to consider his intentions.

In the flat mirror, Geraden saw King Joyse and Prince Kragen directly under the rearing jaws of the slug-beast.

They were engaged in a desperate struggle against huge numbers of red-furred creatures with too many arms holding too many scimitars.

The King and Prince Kragen weren't alone: the Termigan was with them, and his men. They were covered with blood, battling furiously. Yet they couldn't expect to survive against so many alien warriors. And if the red-furred creatures didn't get them, the slug-beast would.

And Master Gilbur planned to translate a new threat into the fray. He was considering the focus of his mirrors so that he could move his flat glass in among the swarming cockroaches and translate them straight onto King Joyse's head.

Lord of the Demesne. Sovereign of Mordant. And Geraden's father's friend.

Remember to call me "Da."

Terisa needed him. He let her go. Once, hard, with both fists, he punched himself in the forehead.

Then he moved.

Swallowing panic and love and regret, he left the entryway and crept toward the ring of mirrors.

If Terisa could have seen him then, she would have recognized the iron in his face, the look of despair—and of brutal determination.

He was quiet; but he went quickly. To the mirrors he and Terisa had broken, to the cotleg he had dropped. Snatching up the club from a pool of splinters, he threw it with all his strength at the flat glass.

Unluckily, his boots crunched a warning among the shards and slivers; and Master Gilbur heard it. With astonishing swiftness, the Imager spun around, flung up his arm—

—deflected the cotleg.

It skimmed past the top of the mirror's frame and skittered away across the stone, out of reach.

"Balls of a dog!" Gilbur spat. Already, he had his dagger in his fist; his face was a clench of darkness. "Do you never give up?"

Geraden heard the cotleg knock against the wall as if that sound were the last thud of his heart. Another failure: his last chance gone wrong. Now he wouldn't be able to help King Joyse *or* Terisa, and they would both be lost. And if he didn't escape now, his own death was inevitable. No matter what happened, he would never be able to outfight Master Gilbur.

Nevertheless the augury drew him. This was his fate, his doom. Instead of fleeing, he stepped forward, into the ring of mirrors, until he was *surrounded entirely by mirrors, all of them reflecting scenes of violence and destruction against him.*

There he stopped.

"Why should I give up?" he asked as if he were just making conversation. "Why should I want to make it easy for you?"

Master Gilbur snarled an obscenity. Cocking his dagger, he prepared to charge.

At once, Geraden barked, "I wouldn't do that if I were you."

In surprise, the Master paused.

"I don't have anywhere else to go," Geraden explained. "I don't have anything else to hope for. Oh, I suppose I could run away. I could try to hide somewhere. You don't seem to have any guards. I might be able to stay alive for a while. But I'll never escape. I'll never find Terisa.

"If you chase me, I'll just break as many mirrors as I can before

I die. You've already lost four. How many more are you willing to risk? Do you think there's a chance I might be able to get them all?"

Obviously, Gilbur's first impulse was to attack: that was plain in the way his teeth showed through his beard, the way his knuckles whitened on his dagger. Almost immediately, however, he appeared to grasp the other side of the situation. Someone was bound to come soon, and then Geraden was lost. In the meantime, why risk damage to years of powerful work?

Instead of charging, he lowered his blade.

"You are wrong, puppy," he rasped. "We have guards. They will be here in a moment."

"Oh, I don't think so." Geraden fought to keep any hint of relief out of his voice. Time: that was all he wanted. A respite for King Joyse. A chance for something to happen. "I'm sure you have them, plenty of them. But I'll bet they're all outside, protecting this place just in case someone tries a sneak attack. Watching the defile. You and Eremis and Vagel are so stupidly sure of yourselves, you never expected to be attacked from inside."

Then, because he wanted to see how far he could goad the Imager, he asked, "Where's Gart?"

Master Gilbur's eyebrows knotted involuntarily. "Do not look behind you, pigshit boy. He may be there already. He has gone to fetch your dear brother Nyle—who, I may say, has given me considerable pleasure during his visit here."

The flat mirror's Image showed the great monster writhing in a paroxysm of rage and hunger.

"I don't think so," Geraden repeated. *Nyle.* He wanted to laugh so that he wouldn't do anything foolish, wouldn't go mad and try to attack the Imager; but he could barely keep himself from snarling. "Terisa and I already rescued Nyle. We did that first. If Gart isn't here, the men we brought with us must have got him." If Gart isn't here, Artagel must still be alive, still be fighting. "Or else High King Festten has plans he hasn't told you about. You must have noticed that his reputation for treachery is older than you are."

Unfortunately, Master Gilbur *was* able to laugh. "Pure vapor," he rasped with a guttural chuckle. "Mist and moonshine." He took a couple of nonthreatening steps, not toward Geraden, but to the side, away from the flat glass and the cockroaches. "You have not rescued Nyle—you do not know where he *is*. The room where I have enjoyed him is kept dark. You have never seen it. Therefore you could not find it, or translate him away.

"Gart will join us soon."

"Believe that if you can," retorted Geraden. *He* believed it; and the thought made all his muscles feel as weak as water. Yet he kept his gaze and his voice steady. "Just tell me one thing. Those red-furred creatures." They continued pouring around King Joyse and the Prince, hacking savagely. The Termigan's men and Norge's appeared vastly outnumbered. And the slug-beast— "You didn't just translate them this morning, did you? How did you get them mounted? How did you get them to serve you?"

The slug-beast had reared up as if it strove to stand on its tail.

"No, we did not," conceded Master Gilbur maliciously. "In that, at least, you are right. Those things—they call themselves *callat*. Eremis has worked with them at some length. They have become what you might consider his 'personal guard.' A complex and difficult negotiation was required before he agreed to commit his callat to Festten's support."

Too late, Geraden realized what the Imager was doing.

In the flat mirror, the rearing monster came down like a tower, crashed straight and limp to the ground. Its maw seemed to miss King Joyse and Prince Kragen; some of the callat were caught by its weight and crushed. But through the glass the reverberation of impact had no sound. And the beast made no effort to surge forward, devour more prey. It lay still with a strange curl of smoke rising between its teeth.

Master Gilbur reached one of the other mirrors in the ring.

He grasped its frame with his free hand, began snarling nonsense.

Out of the glass, like shot from a catapult, came hurtling a gnarled, black shape, no larger than a small dog, with claws like hooks at the ends of its four limbs and terrible jaws which filled half its body.

Master Eremis did like surprises. In a sense, he even liked unpleasant surprises. They raised the stakes, increased the challenge: they made him show what he could do. But there was nothing unpleasant about Terisa's unexpected arrival—or Geraden's either, for that matter. Master Gilbur could handle Geraden. And Terisa was beaten. He had seen her defeat in her eyes, had seen the light of intelligence

and determination start to fade. She was his at last, *his,* and every
spark of resistance left to her would only increase the fun of possessing her.

As he directed her toward his private quarters, watching from
behind the way her hips moved inside her uncomplimentary gar-
ments, remembering the sweet shape and curve of her breasts, and
the particular silken sensation between her legs, he thought that she
would be more satisfying than any woman he had ever destroyed.

Saddith's death had been satisfying, of course: deft, inescapable,
and almost infinitely clever. Nevertheless it had lacked the personal
touch. He hadn't destroyed her himself; he had only arranged events
so that she would suffer and die. On the unfortunately frequent
occasions when he had found it necessary to make love to her, the
exigencies of his plans had required him to treat her gently, almost
kindly, so that she would believe he might help further her social
ambitions. He was man enough, however, to meet even her boring
tastes in fornication. And with Terisa there would be no limits—
Nothing would inhibit the extravagant flavors of pain and debase-
ment he meant to elicit from her.

He felt so primed and poised that he could hardly refrain from
dancing as he followed her toward his rooms.

Obedient to his will, she entered his quarters and stopped in
the center of the one, big chamber where he had his bed, his instruments of enjoyment, and his copy of the flat mirror which showed
how matters progressed in the valley of Esmerel.

There King Joyse and Prince Kragen were about to go down
under a tide of callat. Or they would be driven within reach of the
monster rearing impressively over them.

Good. In fact, perfect. Eremis would like watching his enemies
die while Terisa wept and wailed.

"Remove your clothes," he told her, enjoying the harshness of
his tone. "You have evaded me too long, and the recompense I
demand has grown correspondingly large." If he took off his own
clothes, she would see just how large it was. "Nakedness is the very
least of the gifts your fine body will give me today."

Sunlight came from a series of windows along one wall, where
he occasionally let men stand to observe his exercises. Today, of
course, everyone was busy with battle or guard duty; but he was glad
to have his victory to himself. Outside was only a rugged hillside, a
freedom Terisa would never reach. The whole stronghold was aus-

tere, and he hadn't had time to procure rugs. But the sun warmed the chill of the stone floors, shedding brightness over his victim and the mirror.

She didn't obey. And she didn't pay any attention to the windows; as far as he could tell, she didn't notice them at all. Instead, she turned to the glass, as if it had more power over her than anything else did.

For the first time since they had left the Image-room, he saw her face.

Perhaps she wasn't beaten after all. Something in her conveyed a definite sense of evaporation, as if she were on the borderline of disappearing. Her expression was slack; her eyes, vaguely focused. And yet he also seemed to see something else, something secretive and wonderfully enticing. It may have been a covert hope: the hope, perhaps, that she could shift the Image in the mirror (but of course that wouldn't do anything to help either her or King Joyse); or the hope that Eremis would foolishly give her the chance to translate him away (but to do that she would have to physically thrust him toward the glass, and he was stronger than she was, much stronger); or the hope that she could use the mirror to escape herself (but he had no intention of giving her the opportunity).

Or maybe she was nourishing a hidden and hopeless desire to do him harm.

Whatever she concealed, it was exactly the spice he coveted. For a moment, he let her disobey him simply because he couldn't decide whether to kiss her gently or tear her clothes apart.

Studying the mirror, she asked in a thin, disinterested tone, "Where did you get those creatures? The ones that attacked Geraden and me. How did you get them to serve you?"

Master Eremis was happy to answer her. "The callat. They were a fortuitous discovery—as all things are fortuitous for men who can master life. They were first discovered among Vagel's Imagers in Cadwal, but no use was made of them. Apparently, every faction in Carmag feared that they might prove to be a decisive force—for someone else. However, after I had redeemed Vagel from his tenuous exile among the Alend Lieges, he remembered the formula and shaped a new mirror.

"The callat are indeed a powerful force, as you can see"—Eremis enjoyed a glance at the glass himself, although most of his mind was fixed on Terisa—"but not as powerful as the Cadwals feared. Their numbers are not great enough to make an army.

"They are renegades in their own world. Actually, they are in danger of extermination by what I can only describe as a race of groundhogs. Very large groundhogs. And the callat are too bloody-minded to make peace. They can only fight or die.

"Witnessing their danger, I translated one or two of them and began bargaining. In exchange for escape from their enemies"—Eremis shrugged aside the fact that he had never intended to let the callat live, had meant from the start to use them in a way which would destroy them—"they agreed to serve me."

Slowly, Terisa nodded. He wondered if she understood: she seemed to be thinking about something else.

"They come from a completely different world," she said. "They have a history of their own, motives of their own. Do you still claim they didn't exist until Vagel shaped the mirror?"

Her question drew a chortle from the Master. He made no effort to conceal that he was inexpressibly pleased with himself. "My lady, did you ever truly credit that piece of sophism?"

She regarded him gravely, as if she wanted to hear what he would say—and didn't care what it was.

Still chuckling, he continued, "No man of any intelligence—of whom there are only a few, I admit—has ever thought that the Images we see in mirrors do not exist. That position, with all the arguments supporting it, was forced on us by King Joyse, by his demand that the Congery should define a 'right' use of Imagery. Because he took it as proven that *if* Images were real in themselves *then* they must be treated with respect, forbearance—in effect, must be left alone—he allowed those who disagreed with him no ground on which to stand except that those Images have no independent existence.

"But of course his central tenet is so foolish that it is also unanswerable. He might as well claim that we must not breathe because we should not interfere with the air, or that we must not eat because we should not interfere with plants and cattle. The truth is that we have the *right* to interfere with Images because we have the *power* to interfere. It is *necessary* to interfere. Otherwise the power has no use, and it dies, and Imagery is lost.

"That is the law of life. Like every other thing which breathes and desires and chooses, we must *do what we can*."

Eremis licked his lips. "Terisa, I have sampled your breasts, and they are delectable. You must have an exceptionally vacuous mind, if you ever believed that you do not exist. I told you you were unreal only to make it as difficult as possible for you to discover your talent."

As he spoke, he studied her, looking for her secret reaction, the truth she wished to conceal. Her eyes were too dark, too lost: they didn't betray anything. As far as they were concerned, she was already gone.

But her pretty, cleft chin tightened as if she were clenching her teeth.

Delighted by this evidence of anger, he reached out and bunched his fists in her unflattering leather shirt. He regretted, really, that she hadn't had a chance to wash her hair; but everything else about her was perfect. He was going to tear the shirt away. Then, before he began to hurt her, he would do things to her breasts which would make her ache for him in spite of her secrets. He would surprise her with the pain, as she had surprised him.

For some reason, however, she had turned her face away. She wasn't even afraid enough of him to watch what he was doing. Instead, she gazed darkly at the mirror.

Unintentionally, he glanced there in time to see the slug-beast come down from its full height, collapse like soundless thunder in the valley and lie still. Involuntarily, he held his breath, waiting to see the monster move again, waiting to see it pounce forward and devour King Joyse and the arrogant Alend Contender. But the beast remained as limp as a carcass. Odd smoke curled briefly out of its maw and drifted away along the breeze.

"Excrement of a pig!" Eremis breathed. Forgetting Terisa, he turned to the mirror, gripped the frame with both hands, studied the Image intently. "That is impossible. You doddering old fool, that is *impossible*."

"Interesting," Terisa remarked as if she had never been less interested in her life. "Maybe 'all things' aren't as 'fortuitous' as you think."

Eremis thought he saw the Image of the valley begin to waver around the edges, thought he saw the rampart walls and the last catapult start to melt—

That also was impossible. He wasn't sure of what he was seeing.

He didn't delay to be sure. Swinging at once, he backhanded her across the side of the head so hard that she fell like a broken doll. She lay on one side in the warm sunshine, huddling around herself, with her hair spread out on the stone, and one hand cupped weakly over the place where she had been hit; she may have been weeping.

"If you try that again," he spat, "if you touch that glass with one more hint of your talent, I swear I will call Gilbur here and let him rape you with that dagger of his."

Perhaps she wasn't weeping: she didn't make a sound. After a moment, however, she nodded her head—one small, frail jerk, like a twitch of defeat.

Despite his monster's unexpected demise, Master Eremis recovered his grin.

Artagel, too, was grinning, but for an entirely different reason.

Despite the blood which streamed from his cut shoulder, he beat back the hot, steel lightning and force of Gart's next attack. That defense cost him an exertion which seemed to shred his wounded side. Twice he only saved himself because the corridor was too narrow for perfect swordwork, and he was able to block Gart's blade away against the stone. But at last he managed to disengage.

Before the High King's Monomach could come at him again, he retreated several quick strides, then relaxed his stance and dropped the point of his sword.

Gart paused to scrutinize him curiously.

Trying not to breathe in whooping gasps that would betray his weakness, Artagel asked, "Why do you do it?"

Gart cocked an eyebrow; he advanced a step.

Artagel put up a hand to ward off the Monomach. "You're going to kill me anyway. You know that. You can afford to send me to my grave with my ignorance satisfied. Why do you do it?"

Swayed, perhaps, by the admission of defeat, Gart paused again. "Why do I do what?"

With an effort which felt desperately heroic, Artagel tried to laugh. He failed, of course. Nevertheless he did contrive to sound cheerful as he said, "Serve."

The tip of Gart's blade watched Artagel warily as the Monomach waited.

"You're the best," Artagel panted, "the best. You lead and train a cadre of Apts who all want to be as good as you, and some of them may even have almost that much talent. You could be a power in the world. I'll wager you could unseat Festten anytime you want. You could be the one who decides, instead of the one who serves. Why do you do it?"

Gart considered the question for a moment. "That is who I am," he pronounced finally.

"But why?" demanded Artagel, fighting for a chance to regain his breath, his strength. "What does Festten give you that you can't get anywhere else? What does being the High King's Monomach get you that isn't already yours by right? You could *choose* who you're going to kill. If I were you, I'd be embarrassed by the amount of time you've spent recently trying to kill a woman. Whose decision was that? Why did you have to demean yourself like that?"

A snarl pulled tighter across Gart's teeth.

"I tell you, you could be a *power*. Don't you have any self-respect?"

The Monomach came at him like a gale in the constricted passage, suddenly, without warning; and the only thing that saved him was that he wasn't surprised. He got his longsword up, parried hard, tried to riposte. Gart slipped the blow aside and swung again. Artagel felt steel ruffle his hair as he ducked; Gart's blade rang off the wall; Artagel hacked at the Monomach's legs fast enough to make him jump.

Somehow not stumbling, not clutching at his torn side, Artagel disengaged again, retreated down the corridor.

"That," said Gart as if he had never been out of breath in his life, "is who I am."

"But the point is, you *serve*," protested Artagel. "You're nothing more than a servant, a *weapon*."

"Listen to me," Gart articulated dangerously. "I will not say it again. *That is who* I am."

"With *your* abilities?" Artagel's voice nearly rose to a cry. "I don't believe it. You're content to be a *servant?* You're content to be *used* like a thing with no mind, no pride? Aren't you a man? Don't you dream? Haven't you got ambitions?"

It was probably madness to goad the Monomach like this; but Artagel didn't care. For the first time since their contest began, he was having fun.

"No wonder you're so hard to kill. Inside, where it counts, you're already dead."

In response, Gart whirled his blade with such speed that the steel blurred into streaks of lantern-light. "Oh, I have dreams, you fool," he rasped. "I have dreams.

"I dream of *blood*."

So fiercely that nothing could stop him, he hurled himself at Artagel.

Now Gart was the mad one, the frenzied attacker, swinging as if he were out of control; Artagel was the one who couldn't do anything except parry and block—and try to keep his balance.

Unfortunately, the Monomach's fury only made their struggle more uneven. *He* wasn't wounded; *he* hadn't been weakened by a long convalescence. And at his worst he never forgot his skill.

As if by translation, cuts appeared on Artagel's mail, his leggings. A lick along his forehead sent blood dripping into his eyes. Reeling, almost falling, he slammed into the corner where the corridor turned, hit so hard that the last air was knocked out of his lungs.

He barely saved himself, *barely,* by diving out of the corner, rolling to his feet and running, his lungs on fire, his eyes full of sweat and blood, no life in his limbs, running until he gained enough ground to turn and plant his feet and stand there wobbling and face Gart for the last time.

The fun part of the fight was over.

Moved by instincts he didn't know he had, Geraden went down as if he had been clubbed.

The first vicious black shape missed him; its own momentum carried it beyond him, momentarily out of reach. And the second—

But Master Gilbur was bringing a whole stream of the beasts into the Image-room, translating them at Geraden as fast as they could leap. The Master's teeth gnashed the air, and his face burned, as if he were on his way to ecstasy.

A whole world of creatures like that. Of course. Ravening as if they had already eaten their way through all their natural prey. Terisa had shattered a mirror to end an attack like this; but that mirror wasn't this one. No, she had broken the flat glass which showed the intersection outside Orison. The original mirror, the source of the creatures, remained intact.

Obviously.

Flipping to the side, scrambling his legs under him, stumbling as if he would never regain his balance, Geraden struggled out of the direct spring of the creatures.

Three, five, nine of them, he lost count. Sliding in his boots as if the sunlit stone were ice, he rounded the edge of a mirror, wheeled behind it.

He was too frantic to think. And he had no chance against Master Gilbur anyway. All he knew was that he had to hurt the King's enemies as much as he could before he died. Gilbur clearly believed the gnarled shapes would get him before he did much harm. No doubt the Master was right. But every bit of damage might help. Any mirror Geraden could break might be the crucial one, the one that made sense of the Congery's augury—the one that gave King Joyse a chance against his doom.

The slug-beast had been killed. Surely anything was possible—

From behind, without knowing or caring what its Image was, Geraden took hold of the mirror and wrenched it onto its back.

And caught it before it hit the floor.

Inspiration: unexpected insight. As if the mere touch of the mirror's frame had shocked him, everything inside his head seemed to take fire and become new.

Not damage. If damage was all he tried to do, Gilbur had no reason to fear him. He would be dead in moments.

Imagery, on the other hand—

The first black shapes were already scrabbling over the stone to fling themselves on him. And more came furiously, avid for flesh. Master Gilbur turned his mirror in order to translate the creatures straight at Geraden.

Burning with inspiration, Geraden heaved the mirror upright again and opened it just as the nearest creature hit the glass.

Gone. As if the shape had never existed. Translated somewhere, he had no idea where, he still hadn't had a chance to so much as glance at the scene in the mirror.

Another and another, in rapid succession: gone. The gnarled creatures seemed to have no minds—or at least no sense of danger. Their hunger overwhelmed all other instincts; maybe they were starving to death in their own world. They hurled themselves into the glass as if it were Geraden's flesh.

The fire blazing up inside him felt like joy and triumph.

Four five six—

Master Gilbur bellowed something savage and sprang to a different mirror.

The last few shapes came at Geraden madly, their jaws stretched open, and Master Gilbur brought wolves rushing into the Image-room, wolves with spines along their curved backs and malign purpose in their eyes, wolves that were too big for Geraden's shield and would be forced by their sheer size to attack him over or around the mirror; and at that moment Geraden made the mistake of realizing what he was doing.

He was doing something worse than the translation of alien evils into his own world: he was translating them somewhere else, into a place completely unready for them, completely innocent. Whatever lived and moved in the Image he held was now being assaulted by vicious and entirely unexpected creatures for no good reason except to save his life.

No, this was wrong, it was *wrong,* he had no right to do it. These creatures, and the wolves, and anything else Gilbur might produce were only malignant because they had been translated, only because they were out of place. In their own worlds, they didn't deserve to be slaughtered. And no one else deserved to be slaughtered simply because Geraden was desperate.

Shoving the mirror away, he dove to the side.

The last black shapes struck the glass hard and slammed it onto its back. As they bounded up from the splinters to continue their attack, they left behind a shattered Image of their fellow creatures dying horribly in the acid of bitten ghouls.

A hunting snarl throbbed through the air; jaws slavered. Geraden scrambled across the ring of mirrors, trying to stay ahead of the gnarled shapes and the wolves.

Strange things were happening in the Image of Esmerel's valley. The slug-beast was definitely dead, no mistake about that. And its death altered the terms of the conflict. High King Festten committed all his forces to a killing charge. In two thrusts, seven or eight thousand men on each side of the supine monster, he sent his army to catch King Joyse while there was no escape, while the confused and lesser strength of Alend and Mordant was trapped between the defile at one end of the valley and the tremendous corpse blocking the other.

King Joyse should already have been crushed under the weight of the callat. He was still up and fighting, however. Prince Kragen was with him, and the Termigan, and Castellan Norge; but they weren't enough to keep him alive. No, he endured because the monster's death had galvanized his army: that impossible rescue from certain destruction had transformed panic into hope and fury. As fast as their horses or their legs could move them, his men came to support their King; the first several hundred of them had already charged in among the callat.

The Cadwals hadn't yet had time to catch up with the red-furred creatures. The callat had to face the recovered force of King Joyse's army alone.

Geraden dashed past the flat glass with black shapes on his heels. Master Gilbur seemed to be having trouble finding wolves. He had translated three, no, four into the Image-room; but now he was studying the Image, scanning its focus rapidly in search of more predators. The use he and Eremis had made of the wolves previously must have depleted their population.

Four would be enough, of course. The gnarled shapes would be enough. Geraden couldn't keep ahead of them, couldn't fight—

Not this way.

The first wolf appeared to rear straight up in front of him, springing for his head. Urgently, he wrenched himself aside. His boots skidded out from under him; he thumped down on his back, sliding beneath the attack.

The wolf landed among the black creatures.

They didn't care what they ate; they only wanted food. Swiftly, they all pounced on the wolf.

At once, their struggle became a whirl, a snarling dervish, a mad ball of claws and fangs. The wolf was big, powerful; the shapes sank their hooks and teeth in and clung.

With the air knocked out of his lungs, Geraden lay still.

As if they recognized a mortal enemy, the other wolves sped to help their fellow.

Master Gilbur spat curses, then crowed obscenely as he located more wolves.

Geraden couldn't breathe. He could hardly move his limbs. Nevertheless he had to act now, had to grab this brief chance. He might never get another one.

Talent was a remarkable thing: he was learning more about it all the time. He was an Adept of some kind; he could use other people's mirrors. And he had rescued himself and Terisa out of her

former apartment, out of a world which had no Imagery. All he had
to do was concentrate, take Master Gilbur by surprise.

In a way, it helped that he couldn't breathe. It almost helped
that the struggle between the wolves and the gnarled creatures was
only ten feet away, and that the wolves were winning, crunching the
bones of the smaller beasts. The extremity of his plight left no room
for doubt or hesitation.

He turned his head toward the mirror and studied the Image,
fixed it in his mind: a forest full of harsh shadows, slashed by light
there and *there;* boughs angling upward; underbrush of a kind he had
never seen before. During the spaces between his heartbeats, he
memorized the scene.

Master Gilbur hunched beside the mirror, clutching the frame
with one fist, crooning to the glass. A feral ecstasy lit his features,
as bright as fire, as consuming as lava.

When the first of the new wolves started through the mirror,
Geraden closed his eyes and shifted the Image in his mind.

And the Image in the mirror shifted.

He didn't know what he shifted it to, and he didn't care. Instinctively, he must have selected some place or vista to fill the mirror: he couldn't imagine a blank glass. But that detail was unimportant. What mattered was that he could reach out with his talent, that
by surprise if not by strength he could break Master Gilbur's hold
on the glass.

It worked. The Image melted while the wolf was still caught in
the prolonged instant of translation.

The wolf was cut in half.

The mirror shattered.

Gilbur wheeled to confront Geraden. For a moment, the brutal
Imager actually gaped. Then rage knotted his face, and he let out a
roar which seemed to strike the air dumb, leaving the battle of the
wolves without a sound.

He turned to the next mirror in the ring.

From its dark depths, he brought out a burst of lightning so
hot that it scorched the stone floor; a blast of thunder so loud that
it thudded in Geraden's tight lungs; a wind so hard that it seemed
to hammer him down even though he hadn't tried to rise, hadn't
tried to move.

The Imager was translating a storm into the chamber.

Using it to buffet and confuse and overwhelm Geraden until
Master Gilbur could get to him and drive a dagger into his heart.

Now that he had Terisa down on the floor and hurt, Master Eremis
thought he would begin to take advantage of her. He found, however, that he had trouble pulling his attention away from the mirror.

He liked surprises: they were tests, opportunities. Yet the death
of the slug-beast nagged at him. That was an unforeseen development. Of course, the creature could have collapsed for any number
of reasons which had nothing to do with the battle. Nevertheless its
demise suggested that he had underestimated his enemy's
capabilities.

And King Joyse's forces were rallying now. That was perfectly
predictable—but still frustrating to watch. Festten had made the right
decision: to launch a full-scale assault while the armies of Mordant
and Alend were still in disarray. Unfortunately, his men were too
far away to save the callat. And King Joyse and Prince Kragen were
doing entirely too good a job of pulling their forces into order to
meet the Cadwal charge.

Soon the battle would degenerate into a simple contest of steel
and determination.

King Joyse would lose, of course. Festten had him heavily outnumbered. And Gilbur had an impressive array of mirrors at hand.
Yet Master Eremis wasn't pleased. On the scale of armies, Gilbur's
remaining resources were relatively minor. And if the Cadwal victory
weren't ultimately achieved by Imagery, the High King would become more difficult to rule in future. He would trust his own strength
more, Eremis' less. He might begin to think he could dispense with
Master Eremis altogether. And Gart was somewhere in the
stronghold—

The Master was prepared for all these eventualities. Nevertheless he didn't find them especially attractive.

Carefully, Terisa got to her feet, so that she, too, could look at
the mirror. She had the smudge of a growing bruise on her cheekbone, but it only made her lovelier. When she had been hurt enough,
she would be intolerably beautiful.

Master Eremis considered hitting her again. But that was too
crude, really. He expected better of himself: more imagination,
greater subtlety. And he wanted to see what his enemies were going
to do.

He wanted to see what Gilbur was going to do.

It would be something violent, something effective. Considering Gilbur's susceptibility to rage of all kinds, however, it might also be something premature. Master Eremis didn't want to see Joyse die too soon, too easily.

At the moment, there was no danger of that. The callat were beaten: Joyse was able to disengage, with Kragen, Norge, and the unanticipated Termigan. They rode a short way up the valley, conferred with each other briefly, then began shouting orders which conveyed nothing through the glass. And their army seemed to come into order around them almost magically.

None too soon, Kragen spurred away to command the defense to the right of the monster's corpse. Norge went to the left, with the Termigan beside him. Well, Joyse was an old man. No doubt he needed rest. He didn't appear to be resting, however. Instead, he rode everywhere, organizing his men.

For some reason, he divided them into three forces: one to support Kragen; one for Norge and the Termigan; one for himself.

"I don't understand," said Terisa thinly, in that impersonal, disinterested tone.

Master Eremis felt that he was beginning to comprehend her. That tone didn't indicate defeat. It was a sign of withdrawal: not of retreat, but of hiding, of covert intentions. Perhaps she thought that if she could go far enough away in her mind, he wouldn't be able to hurt her. Or perhaps she hid so that she could take him by surprise.

A small thrill of anticipation ran through his veins, and he shifted his weight slightly onto the balls of his feet.

"Have you ever understood anything?" he countered with amiable sarcasm.

His scorn didn't seem to touch her. She may have been too distant to hear it accurately. In the same tone, she said, "You have all these flat mirrors, but you don't use them very well."

Another surprise: one with exciting possibilities. What was she thinking?

"Do we not?" he asked casually.

"You have a glass that shows Vale House." Despite her dullness, her voice was strangely distinct. "You could have taken Queen Madin yourself. You could have brought her here as a hostage. She would have been more use to you than Nyle."

Oh, that. Master Eremis was mildly disappointed; he had hoped for something a bit more interesting. "A predictable idea," he commented acidly, "and not precisely brilliant. If I had done that, I would have given up the wedge I wished to drive between Joyse and Margonal. I would have given up the obstacles I wished to place in your path.

"I must confess I am still somewhat surprised that Margonal let you into Orison. That was not a reasonable decision, in view of the news you carried." He paused to let Terisa volunteer an explanation, but she didn't speak. No matter. He would get all the answers he wanted from her eventually. "I am sure," he resumed, "I came very close to achieving exactly what I desired with the Queen.

"If, on the other hand, I had done as you—and Festten—advise, I might have gained nothing. The Queen would have been in my hands—and the translation would have made her mad. Damaging hostages is a blade with two edges. Her madness might have hurt Joyse enough to weaken him. Or it might have incensed him enough to disregard her. Then the effort of attacking her would have been wasted."

There remained the question of what had happened to the Queen. And the question of how Joyse had contrived to rejoin his army, after his disappearance from Orison. But those answers could wait as well. Thinking about his own tactics brought new joy to the Master's loins. The satisfaction he wanted from Terisa was long overdue.

"But you have this mirror now," she said as if she couldn't see her peril in his eyes. "Why don't you just translate King Joyse and Prince Kragen? Make them mad? Then you can't lose. Without them, the army will collapse. And you can lock them up the way you did Nyle. You can laugh at them until they die."

Oh, how she pleased him! She made him laugh. "I will do that, I assure you," he promised. "At the right moment, I will do it, and it will give me more pleasure than you can conceive."

In the mirror, along the sides of the monster, the forces of Cadwal and Mordant and Alend met for their last battle.

"At first, of course," Eremis explained, "I had to be cautious. You taught me to respect your talents. If I had given you the chance, you might have broken my mirror. But that danger ended when you came here. When you gave yourself into my power."

Initially, the fight was even. The walls of the valley and the bulk of the slug-beast narrowed the ground, restricted the number of

Cadwals able to advance together. And Joyse's men fought as if they were inspired. Even Kragen and that dour loon the Termigan seemed inspired. For a time, at least, Festten lost a lot of men and gained nothing.

"Now I wait only to let these armies do each other as much harm as possible. Joyse cannot win, but before he dies he may give Festten a victory as costly as any defeat. That will humble even the High King's arrogance. It will make him too weak to think he can command or refuse me."

Then, inevitably, the defenders on the left began to crumble. Norge went down; he disappeared under a rush of Cadwal hooves. In spite of his native grimness, the Termigan was forced backward. Their men tried to retreat in some semblance of order, but the Cadwals surged after them, overtook them, hacked them apart. Festten's strength started flooding into the valley.

"So I will let the battle progress a while. I will wish Joyse all the success he can manage. And then"—Eremis was so delighted that he wanted applause—"at the crucial moment I will translate him away to the madness and ruin he deserves."

He wasn't particularly surprised to see Festten himself lead the second wave of the assault. The High King had an old and overwhelming desire to see Joyse die; he would have been ecstatic to kill his nemesis himself. Eremis considered, however, that Festten was taking a useless risk. The Master had no intention of allowing the High King the gratification he craved.

There was something odd in the way Terisa regarded Master Eremis, something that resembled hunger. Softly, she asked, "Have you hated him all your life? Even when you were just a kid? the first time you translated that monster? Did you hate him even then?"

"Hate him?" Eremis laughed again. "Terisa, you mistake me. You always mistake me." The pressure inside him was rising, rising. "I do not hate him. I hate no one. I only despise weakness and folly. As a youth, when I shaped the mirror which showed what you call 'that monster,' I translated it merely as an experiment. To learn what I could do. Later I was forced to abandon my glass in order to avoid being captured with it, and that vexed me. I promised then I would retaliate.

"But I do not waste my time"—he was growing deliciously ready for her—"I *assure* you that I do not waste my time on hate."

She continued to gaze at him with her curious blend of absence and hunger. She had her back to the windows and the sunlight; perhaps that was what made her eyes look so dark, her beauty seem so fatal.

Huskily, bringing the words up from far down her throat, she said, "Let me show you what I can do."

With one hand, she reached out and gently touched her fingertips to the unmistakable bulge in the front of his cloak.

He felt like crowing.

Frantically, Artagel fought to prolong his life, keep himself on his feet for one more moment, just one, then another if he could do it. He was the best swordsman in Mordant, wasn't he? Surely he could keep himself alive one more moment at a time?

Maybe not. The pain in his side had become a fire that filled his lungs, so that he seemed to snatch each raw breath through a conflagration. His sword kept turning in his hands; blood and sweat ruined his grip. His legs had lost their spring; he had no more strength to do anything except shuffle his boots over the stone. Sometimes his heavy lurching from side to side dashed water and blood off his brows, cleared his vision; most of the time, however, he had trouble seeing.

How had the corridor become so narrow? He couldn't seem to get a full swing, no matter what he did.

Gart, on the other hand, didn't appear to be experiencing any difficulty. His brief, wild fury had faded. In fact, the pace of his attacks was slower now, more deliberate; more malicious. He was toying with his opponent. Yellow glee shone in his eyes, and he grinned as if he were crowing inside.

What a way to die. No, worse than that: what a way to be beaten. Artagel was a fighter; he had lived most of his life in the vicinity of death. For him, it was at once so familiar and so unimaginable that he couldn't be afraid of it. But to be beaten like this, utterly, miserably—

Oh, Geraden, forgive me.

If only, he thought dumbly, if only he hadn't been hurt the last time. If only he hadn't spent so much time in bed.

Terisa, forgive me.

But it was stupid to wish for things like that. Foolish regret: a waste of time and energy and life. Gart had beaten him the last time, too. And the time before that.

I will regret nothing.

He retreated down the passage, past more doors than he could count; stumbling, barely on his feet. By bare will, he kept his sword up for Gart to play with.

If anybody thinks he can do better than this, let him try.

That was enough. As unsteady as a drunk, he stopped; he locked both hands around his wet swordhilt.

I will regret nothing.

Almost retching for air, he jerked forward and did his absolute best to split Gart's head open.

Negligently, Gart blocked the blow.

Artagel's eyes were full of blood: he couldn't see what happened. But he knew from the sound, the familiar echoing clang after his swing, and from the sudden shift of balance, that he had broken his sword.

One jagged half remained in his fists; the other rang away across the floor, singing metallically of failure.

"Now," Gart breathed like silk. "Now, you fool."

Involuntarily, Artagel went down on one knee, as if he couldn't stay on his feet without an intact weapon.

The High King's Monomach raised his sword. Between streaks of Artagel's blood, the steel gleamed.

For some reason, a door behind Gart opened.

Nyle came into the passage.

He looked like Artagel felt: abused to the bone; exhausted beyond bearing. But he held the chains of his manacles clenched in his fists, and he swung the heavy rings on the ends of the chains at Gart's head.

The instincts which had made Gart the High King's Monomach saved him. Warned by some visceral intuition, some impalpable tremor in the air, he wrenched himself aside and started turning.

The rings missed his head, came down on his left shoulder.

They hit him hard enough to strike that arm away from his sword. But he did most of his fighting one-handed anyway, despite his weapon's weight. While his left arm fell numb—maybe broken— his right was already in motion, bringing his blade around to sever Nyle's neck.

Nyle!

In that moment, a piece of time as quick and eternal as a translation, Artagel brought up the last strength from the bottom of his heart and lunged forward.

With his whole body, he drove his broken sword through the armhole of Gart's armor.

Then he and Nyle collapsed on Gart's corpse as if they had become kindred spirits at last.

He had the peculiar conviction that he needed to prevent Gart from rising up after death and shedding more blood. A long time seemed to pass before he recovered enough sanity to wonder whether Nyle was still alive.

The crash and burn of Master Gilbur's storm seemed to blot out Geraden's senses, smother his will. He couldn't remember the last time he had taken a breath. On the other hand, air wasn't especially important to him at the moment. Lightning struck the stone so close-by that it nearly scorched him; he could feel the shock like a tingle in the floor. Darkness swept the sunlight away: thunder tried to crush him.

Well, the storm daunted the wolves, held them at bay. That was some consolation. And if it continued to mount in this enclosed space, it would begin to topple the mirrors.

Master Gilbur didn't appear to care any longer what might happen to his mirrors. He was roaring like the blast, and his hunched back strained to lift his head as high as possible, gnash his jaws at the ceiling.

With a massive concussion, all the windows blew out. At once, the pressure around Geraden eased, and he started breathing again.

Too bad: the loss of the windows might save the mirrors. Unless the roof came down.

Gilbur had to be stopped. Geraden had the distinct impression that the Imager was going mad, transported by power. A storm like this, constricted like this, could conceivably level the whole building.

Geraden had done it once. Could he do it again?

Forget the thunder that deafened him, stunned his mind. Forget the lightning, the near-miss of fire hot enough to incinerate his bones. Forget wind and wolves and violence.

Think about glass.

Despite the storm, Gilbur's only real weapon was the mirror itself, a piece of normal glass. It had a particular hue blended of sand and tinct; a particular shape created by molds and rollers and heat. His talent had made it what it was. His talent opened it like a blown-out window between worlds. But Geraden also had talent. He could feel the mirror, see its Image in his mind as if by the simple intensity of his perception, his imagination, he made it real.

He didn't know how to halt the translation. But he could shift the Image.

No. Gilbur was resisting him. Forewarned by what had happened to the mirror of the wolves, the Imager clung to this glass grimly, forced the translation.

Don't give up. Don't get confused. No matter how it felt, this wasn't a contest between lightning and flesh, thunder and hearing, wind and muscle. Those things were irrelevant. The struggle was one of will and talent. Gilbur may have been mad, exalted by hate, but he had no experience with this kind of battle; none of the Masters had ever been trained to fight for control of their translations in this way.

And Geraden had gone wrong so often in his life that it had become intolerable. He loved too many people, and they had been too badly hurt.

In one moment briefer than a heartbeat, the Image shifted.

Severed in midpassage, the storm blasted the glass to powder.

Geraden couldn't hear anything: the abrupt silence seemed louder than thunder. He saw Master Gilbur cursing him, spitting apoplectic fury at him, but the oaths made no noise. The sprinkling fall of glass-dust was mute. The wolves bared their fangs, and their chests heaved, but their snarling was voiceless.

While Geraden struggled to his feet, Gilbur moved to another mirror.

For one stunned instant, Geraden gaped at the Image and didn't understand. What power did Gilbur see there? The glass showed an empty landscape, nothing more: a barren stretch of ground riddled with cracks, tossed with boulders, but devoid of anything that breathed or moved or could attack.

Then, as Master Gilbur got his hands on the frame and began to snarl his concentration-chant as if it were fundamentally obscene, Geraden saw the ground in the Image jumping.

The boulders rocked and heaved, lifted from the dirt; the edges of the landscape vibrated.

Earthquake.

Gilbur's mirror showed a place in a state of ongoing cataclysm, of almost perpetual orogenic crisis—the kind of crisis that built and broke mountains, shouldered oceans aside, shattered continents.

He was translating an earthquake.

"No!" Geraden cried through the mounting tectonic rumble. "You will not do this!"

"Stop me!" bellowed back the Imager, impervious to authority, or reason, or self-destruction. "*Stop me,* you puny bastard!"

The stronghold would go down in moments: it hadn't been built to withstand an earthquake. That would end the translation. As soon as the ceiling fell, Gilbur would be crushed; his mirror would be crushed.

But in the meantime everyone else inside would die. Terisa and Eremis. Artagel and Gart. Nyle. Geraden himself. And the tremor might trigger the collapse of the surrounding hills. The devastation might spread for miles before it faded.

Yes! Geraden had no idea whether or not he shouted aloud. I will *stop* you! He ignored the accelerating tremble under his boots, the deepening, rocky groan in the air; he accepted Gilbur's challenge. *You will not do this!*

With all the force he possessed, he took control of the glass, arrested the translation.

This time, Master Gilbur was ready for him; braced and powerful; completely insane. The virulence of the Imager's will to open the mirror shocked through Geraden, burned him like fire, nauseated him like poison. The mirror itself was merely held, locked between opposing talents; but everything Gilbur brought to the battle seemed to strike straight into Geraden.

Rages he had never felt, needs he had never understood, lusts he had never imagined; loathsome things, destructive things; fears so inarticulate and consuming that they deformed the Master's essential being.

Long years ago, before King Joyse brought him to the Congery, Gilbur had been an Imager living alone in the Armigite hills, interested only in his own researches. But he had been attacked; and in the struggle the roof of his cave had fallen on him, pinning him under a block of stone. He had lain there for hours or days until Eremis had rescued him.

During that time, he had suffered like the damned.

Excruciating pain in the long, lonely dark; a horror of death elevated to agony by every terrible fear he could imagine; screams no one would ever hear, even though they went on for the rest of his life.

He had come through that experience mangled in spirit as well as in body. It had made him who he was: hungry and violent; eager for power; devoted to Eremis. Many times since joining the Congery, he would have gone amok, if he hadn't been restrained by Eremis' presence—or crippled by the suspicion that it was Eremis who had attacked him in the first place. Now he hurled all his twisted needs and desires into his translation; hurled them all at Geraden.

They should have been enough to make Geraden quail. But they weren't. In an odd, unforeseen way, he was prepared for them.

He, too, had once been buried alive, under the rubble of Darsint's escape from Orison. He had tasted pain and horror, hopeless suffocation. And now, as then, other people's needs were more important to him than his own.

If Gilbur's translation succeeded, Terisa and Artagel and Nyle would die. Everyone in and around the stronghold would probably die. Without the help Geraden and Terisa could give, King Joyse might die, taking Mordant and eventually Alend with him.

So Geraden ignored the harsh anguish Gilbur sent at him. He closed his mind to his visceral fear of trembling stone. He shut the wolves out of his awareness.

Will-to-will, he met Master Gilbur's madness and held the mirror, sealing the glass in the onset of translation, keeping the earthquake back.

That was Gilbur's chance. If he had let go of the mirror then and used his dagger, he could have killed Geraden almost without effort.

But he didn't let go. Maybe he couldn't. Or maybe somewhere down at the bottom of his heart he wanted to be stopped. Whatever the reason, he clung to the glass frame, clung to his translation, and tried to make his hate stronger than Geraden's determination.

In the end, it wasn't his hate that failed him: it was his body. Without warning, while he strained and raged, a pain as heavy as a spear drove through the center of his chest.

He blanched; his hands slipped from the mirror; involuntarily, he clutched at his heart. Slowly, his jaw dropped, and his eyes began to gape. Reaching for air he could no longer find, he stumbled to his knees as if the ground had been cut out from under him.

His whole face twisted as if he wanted to curse Geraden before he died. But he had lost his chance. He was already dead as he toppled to the stone.

The wolves would have killed Geraden then. He was too shaken to defend himself, too deeply shocked. Artagel and Nyle arrived in time to save him, however. Artagel was exhausted, of course, hardly able to lift his arms; but he had Gart's sword, and it seemed to give him strength. And Nyle swung his chains crazily, which made one or two of the wolves hesitate, giving Artagel the opportunity to dispatch them.

The three brothers hugged each other long and hard before they went to look for Terisa.

"No." Master Eremis caught her by the wrist and pulled her hand away from him. "Not yet. I am not ready to trust you." But he was ready to do everything else to her. "I have not forgotten that you once kicked me."

She continued to gaze at him as if he hadn't spoken. The combination of hunger and absence in her eyes didn't change.

Again, he wondered what she had hidden away in the secret places of her heart. Was that where she kept her fear? Or did she still have surprises left in her?

He was ready for everything about her, ready to take away everything she had. Before he was done, she would confess her secrets, all of them, she would give him everything about herself, hoping that it would save her. But nothing would save her. He was going to take all she had and leave her empty.

Now, however, she wasn't looking at him any longer. Her attention had returned to the mirror.

Kragen still held his ground, blocked the right side of the valley with more success than Eremis had expected from him; but the defense to the left continued crumbling. The forces of Alend and Mordant seemed to dissolve under the Cadwal charge. Hurrying to take advantage of this opportunity, the Cadwals gathered speed.

High King Festten followed them, bringing all his reinforcements to that side. In moments, Festten himself rode past the dead length of the slug-beast, entering the valley at a hard canter.

As soon as the High King was in reach, Joyse struck. With the third portion of his army, he came down the valley like a hammer and smashed into the front of the charge.

At the same time, Kragen abandoned his position. Leaving behind only enough men to keep his side of the valley closed for a short time, he brought the rest of his strength against the Cadwal incursion.

And the Termigan did the same from the other side.

He was retreating, his men were scrambling for their lives, they

were already beaten—and suddenly they turned and became a co-
herent force again and attacked. Backed by the rampart wall, they
drove into the Cadwals near the narrowest point of access to the
valley—

—hit so hard, so unexpectedly, that they cut Festten off.

With four or five thousand of his men still outside the valley,
out of reach, the High King found himself facing his old enemy in
battle.

Here for a short time at any rate the conditions of combat were
almost even: the numbers of the armies were nearly equal. Nevertheless there was nothing equal about the way the men fought.

The Cadwals had been taken by surprise, outmaneuvered; their
greatest weapon, the slug-beast, was dead; they couldn't retreat.
Their consternation was obvious through the mirror, as vivid as a
shout. And the forces of Mordant and Alend struck as if they knew
that while King Joyse led them they could never be defeated.

They didn't know that Joyse was as good as dead, that Eremis
could translate him to madness at any time. They only knew that he
was leading them again, and fighting mightily, that no one had ever
seen him lose. His spirit seemed to sweep them with him, carry them
all to power.

Almost immediately, what should have been an even fight began
to look like a victory for the King.

Terisa cleared her throat. Softly, but precisely, so that each word
was unmistakable, she asked, "Do you hear horns?"

Horns?

Eremis studied her narrowly. He didn't care about the battle,
not anymore; the fire in him needed a different outlet. No matter
what happened in the valley, Joyse's doom was *here:* this mirror would
ruin him. And if Festten was beaten first, so much the better. Eremis
was done with that alliance. It had served its purpose.

But she wasn't looking at him.

He wanted her to look at him. He wanted to see fear in her
eyes.

With his hands on her shoulders, he turned her.

Still she wasn't afraid. The hunger she had revealed earlier was
gone. Blankness filled her gaze.

No, Terisa, he promised, there is no escape that way. There is
no part of you so secret that I cannot find it and hurt it.

To get her attention, he unclasped his cloak and let it drop, then undid his trousers so that she could see the size of his passion against her.

Still her eyes showed no fear. She looked past him or through him as if she had gone blind.

Fiercely, he caught hold of her, closed his arms around her, sealed his mouth on hers. He meant to kiss her until she resisted— or melted—

But she was already limp. All her muscles had gone dead. Her lips felt cold, as if the blood in her heart had become ice.

He gripped her brutally, so furious at her for defying him this way that he wanted to break her back, punish her at once, absolutely. He was strong enough: he could do it. Crushing his forearms across her spine, he tried to find the place where she could still feel pain.

An unexpected movement caught the corner of his eye.

She turned her head toward it as if she knew what it meant.

Before he had time to think, he looked at the mirror.

The movement was there; but it wasn't the movement of armies, it wasn't in the Image. The Image itself was moving, modulating—

While he watched, the scene which the glass reflected became a large room with a bed and instruments of enjoyment; stone floors; sunshine.

At the center of the scene, facing Eremis, stood a tall, naked man with a nose that was too big, cheekbones that sloped too much toward his ears, a thatch of black hair too far back on his skull. Despite their usual intelligence and humor, the man's eyes were wide, almost gaping.

His arms held an unattractively dressed woman. Her body sagged against him as if the last of her strength had faded away.

Her eyes, on the other hand—

They were no longer blank. She had gone so far down inside herself that she had reached a place of unexpected power. Darkness seemed to spill from her gaze like a void overflowing, a black emptiness reaching out to gather him in.

He was seeing himself, and her; that was his own Image echoed in the flat mirror. It had a luminous quality, a precise perfection, which startled him like a revelation, as if it were all he needed to know.

Let me show you what I can do.

The last thing he felt before his mind vanished into eternal translation was a sense of complete astonishment.

FIFTY-TWO:
NO MORE
FIGHTING

erisa seemed to hang limp there in Master Eremis' frozen embrace for a long time.

At one point, she thought she remembered a peculiar tremor under her feet, a trembling in the stone.
It was gone before she noticed it, however, and her recollection of
it was uncertain.

Nevertheless the effort of trying to think helped bring her back.

Now she remembered something else, something she couldn't
be mistaken about: the sound of horns.

She had heard them plainly, winding through her heart: the
music of hunting, the bold summons of music; the call to risk and
beauty. Even though mirrors couldn't transmit sound, the horns had
come to her while she watched King Joyse ride into battle; she had
heard the horns as she had seen him fight. They had lifted her up—

The memory of them lifted her now, restored her to herself.

It was time to move.

She didn't know what had happened to Artagel and Geraden,
but she wasn't afraid; not yet. Gart would have stopped Geraden if
he could. And Master Gilbur would have attacked King Joyse by
Imagery if he could. Since Gilbur had done nothing—except make
the floor tremble?—Geraden and Artagel must still be alive. She
wanted to see them, however, all three of the brothers. She wanted

to feel Geraden's arms around her and look at Artagel's face and find out how Nyle was.

She took one last look at her Image, making sure of herself. Then she released her hold on the mirror, so that it could resume its natural reflection.

After that, she began to squirm out of Eremis' grasp.

He was as hard as stone, still erect and rigid; every part of him was tight with unsatisfied ambition and striving. As a result, she found it difficult to get away from him. Nevertheless, because he couldn't react to her movements, he couldn't keep her.

After a moment, she was free.

He went on standing as though she were his forever—as if he had only turned his head momentarily from her best kiss to glance at the mirror before consummating their embrace.

Vaguely, she wondered if he might be in pain, if he had enough of himself left to feel outrage or loss. She doubted it.

Then Geraden and Artagel and Nyle entered the room.

Despite their obvious exhaustion, they had all come to fight for her. Artagel held his sword poised; Nyle swung his chains; Geraden's face was full of threats. They all came forward to fling themselves at Master Eremis. But when they saw that he wasn't moving, that he couldn't move, and she was unharmed, Geraden gave a shout of joy, Artagel blinked in happy astonishment, and Nyle dropped his chains.

Oh, Geraden. Oh, love. Mute with relief and constricted weeping, she hugged him and hugged him while Artagel thumped her back boisterously and Nyle shed quiet tears of his own.

None of them asked any questions. They were all happy to wait a while to find out what had happened.

On the other hand, after a moment they all found themselves looking at the mirror.

Its focus had to be adjusted before they could see King Joyse. He had ridden so far down the valley, was so heavily engaged among the Cadwals, that he was momentarily out of view. When they located him, however, they saw almost at once that he might win this battle.

His forces and the High King's still seemed roughly equal in numbers. But the Termigan and his men continued to block the left side of the valley; the soldiers Prince Kragen had left in place sealed the right side. As a result, High King Festten wasn't receiving any reinforcements.

He needed reinforcements. The Cadwals simply weren't fighting as well or as hard as their opponents. King Joyse and the Prince attacked them from two sides, and the Termigan cut at their rear, and the rampart wall and the slug-beast's corpse hemmed them in: they had no room to maneuver, no avenue of escape. And the men of Alend and Mordant fought as if they couldn't be beaten.

At the sight, Artagel's face shone, and Geraden cheered, "Look at him! Didn't I tell you he was worth serving?" He had apparently forgotten that Nyle might have a different reaction. "Didn't I?"

Terisa still needed to weep. At the same time, a fierce exultation rose in her. She had to struggle to make her throat work. "Something I want to do."

Unable to explain, she waved Geraden and Artagel and Nyle back from the mirror. She moved it so that Master Eremis no longer blocked her way. Nearly in tears, nearly crowing, she adjusted the focus of the Image up to the rampart, to the last catapult.

The engine was ready to throw—and both King Joyse and Prince Kragen appeared to be within range.

Striking her only blow of the battle, Terisa translated a strut out of the catapult's frame. The timber was under such pressure that it came through the glass like a shot and slammed against the far wall.

Without the strut, the engine wrenched itself apart.

This time, both Geraden and Artagel cheered. Some of the men in the valley looked like they might be cheering.

That helped; but she still couldn't unknot her grief and joy. If she remained where she was, with Master Eremis like that in front of her, she might begin sobbing wildly.

"Let's go," she said.

Artagel nodded at once and turned to support Nyle. But Geraden looked at the erect Imager, and at the cloak on the floor, as if he were embarrassed by pity.

"Shouldn't we cover him?"

Terisa shook her head. "Leave him alone. He's probably happy that way."

In surprise and relief, Geraden gave a shout of laughter.

Artagel laughed, too, a loud, long hoot of mirth. Even Nyle managed a wan smile.

Suddenly, the knot inside Terisa loosened, and she started laughing as well.

Happy that way. Ready and capable and full of himself until he died. Giggling and chuckling, she and the Domne's sons laughed all the way back to the Image-room.

In the center of the damaged ring of mirrors, they found Adept Havelock. He sat on the bare stone as if he had appeared there by translation. His eyes were strangely focused, and his face wore lines of sorrow; he looked like a man who had lost an old friend.

His arms held the arch-Imager.

Vagel had what looked like a tree limb driven through his belly. He was covered with blood, obviously dead.

Havelock was singing to him softly.

"I understand," the mad, old Imager crooned as if he were comforting a child. "I understand everything. Everything."

Terisa felt a renewed desire to weep, but it didn't last long.

The flat glass showed King Joyse surging through the press of Cadwals toward High King Festten. He wasn't using his sword anymore: he didn't seem to need it. His charge alone was enough to make the Cadwals give ground. They were being routed.

The destruction of the last catapult had struck them like an announcement from the stronghold that Master Eremis and Master Gilbur and the arch-Imager Vagel were defeated. And the forces of Mordant and Alend gave the Cadwals no space or time in which to rally. The High King appeared to be screaming furiously, but he couldn't make the wall of men around him hold.

"He's going to do it," Artagel breathed happily. "He's going to beat Festten."

"With Prince Kragen," Terisa said for Nyle's benefit, pointing out the alliance between Mordant and Alend. "They're doing it together."

Nyle stared as if he couldn't trust his eyes.

For a moment, Terisa thought that someone should talk to him. There was a great deal he didn't know, a number of things he needed to hear. But she still didn't have the heart for explanations; not yet.

"Can we go there?" she asked Geraden. "To the valley?"

The only man she could think of who might have the power to do Nyle some real good was King Joyse.

"We don't know where it is from here," Geraden replied thoughtfully. "And there have *got* to be guards around here somewhere. We're bound to run into them, if we try to go on foot." His smile came to him easily. "Of course, we've got plenty of mirrors."

Nyle looked apprehensive. In a tone of mock-boredom, Artagel said, "Don't worry. There's really nothing to this translation business, once you get used to it."

Terisa found herself laughing again. Geraden laughed as well, and Artagel chuckled.

She feared that she wouldn't be able to stop laughing if they didn't go soon. The things she had endured and suffered in the past few days required some kind of outlet. But Geraden sobered when he looked at Adept Havelock. After a moment of uncertainty, he went to stand near the Adept.

"Vagel is dead," he said carefully. "You finally beat him. We're going to join King Joyse. Will you come with us?"

Havelock didn't raise his head. Briefly, however, he stopped crooning. In a surprisingly lucid voice, he said, "You go ahead. I'll stay here for a while. If things go badly at the last minute, I can use these mirrors to take care of Festten. That should guarantee Joyse's victory."

Almost at once, he added, "Not that he needs me to guarantee anything for him."

Softly, he began singing again.

Geraden shrugged. With a bemused expression on his face, he returned to Terisa, Artagel, and Nyle.

He was becoming more familiar with his talent, more practiced. He needed only a few seconds to take one of the curved mirrors and shift it until its Image showed the hillside in the valley where King Joyse had set his pennon—the hillside where Myste and Elega, Master Barsonage and the Congery stood to watch the battle. When he was ready, he bowed sententiously to Terisa and his brothers, and gestured for one of them to go first.

Activity was a kind of outlet. Promptly, Terisa moved to face the glass.

Before she stepped into it, however, she met Geraden's intent, glad gaze and said, "If you go wrong this time, you are really and truly going to owe me an apology."

While he was still laughing, she accepted the translation.

As usual, she lost her footing when the quick, infinite passage was over. Ingloriously, she stumbled and fell to her knees in the slush of melting snow.

Myste and Elega cried out when she appeared; but Master Barsonage reached her first. Choking on solicitude, astonishment, and hope until he was completely unable to speak, he helped her to her feet.

She had time to see the fierce triumph on Elega's features, the vindication and the dark loss in Myste's eyes. Then Nyle and Artagel appeared beside her and had to be helped out of the muck.

At once, Artagel whipped out Gart's sword and held it high. "The blade of the High King's Monomach!" he shouted.

The guards around the pennon started cheering.

To the accompaniment of hoarse cries, fervent applause, Geraden arrived.

He fell flat on his face as if the slush were a pig wallow. This time, however, the lady Elega helped him regain his feet; she beamed at him. At last, she had learned how to ignore his minor mishaps.

For some reason, the chagrin in his smile seemed wonderful to Terisa. It seemed to suggest that he had come through his experiences with a whole heart.

Then other cheers echoed up from the valley foot. King Joyse had reached the High King; he had knocked Festten's sword aside, pulled the Cadwal tyrant off his mount.

Frantically, the High King's men began to surrender as fast as they could.

They had good cause: outside the valley, their reinforcements were scattering. Maybe the destruction of the last catapult had taken the resolve out of them. Or maybe Havelock had performed some other translation to frighten them. Whatever the explanation, thousands of men stopped trying to batter their way into the valley and headed instead for the maze of the hills.

Without reinforcements, the Cadwal position became hopeless. High King Festten's men gave up to save their lives.

King Joyse had won what should have been an impossible victory.

Cheering spread up the valley, resounded from the ramparts into the clean sky. Abruptly, Master Barsonage let out an uncharacteristic yell, and the Imagers began congratulating each other delightedly. Elega's eyes spilled happy tears; Artagel flourished Gart's sword; Geraden hugged Terisa until she thought her ribs might crack. For a moment, the only unhappy people on the hillside were Myste, who had lost Darsint, and Nyle, who had helped bring King Joyse to the brink of defeat.

Almost at once, however, an unexpected silence followed the

shouting up from the foot of the valley. Terisa and Geraden craned their necks without letting go of each other; for a moment, their view was blocked by the press of men. Fortuitously, a gap appeared just in time to let them see the slug-beast open its maw as if it had come back to life.

Struggling mightily, the champion forced open the monster's evil teeth and staggered between them.

Immediately, he wrenched off his helmet and flung it aside. For a while, he stood gasping as if he had come close to suffocation. Then he pressed several studs down the sides of his armor, and all the metal folded away and fell to the ground, leaving him dressed in what may have been his underwear.

"God-rotting suit," he panted harshly. "Ox-supply gave out. Like everything else."

"Do you mean," Artagel asked in amazement, "he actually let that thing *eat* him?"

Several of the guards nodded.

The cheering started again, louder this time.

Myste's face seemed to flare with joy. She left the hillside at a run, racing to rejoin Darsint.

Gradually, the tumult gave way to a new kind of order. The surrendering Cadwals were organized and guarded, marched aside. High King Festten was put on another horse with his hands tied behind him. He had lost his golden helmet; without it, he appeared much smaller. Between King Joyse and Prince Kragen, with the Termigan beside them, he was brought up the valley to the hillside and the King's pennon.

Terisa had never seen King Joyse seem more like a man who deserved horns. He wasn't alone in his triumph, however. Prince Kragen had come through his personal doubts and risks to a look of achievement nearly as sharp-edged as the King's. And the Termigan positively glowered with satisfaction. In fact, the battle and its outcome had done him so much good that he couldn't contain himself. As soon as he and his companions reached the hillside, he ignored protocol and common sense by surging ahead of King Joyse and Prince Kragen.

He brought his charger directly to Terisa and Geraden, did a curvet that nearly knocked them down; then he settled his mount. "You gave me good advice," he said loudly, so that everyone could hear the lord of Termigan approach as close as he was able to an apology. "I should have listened sooner."

Geraden laughed again. "You listened soon enough, my lord Termigan."

The lord's flinty features almost grinned as he withdrew to let King Joyse and Prince Kragen speak.

The Prince didn't seem particularly interested in speaking. He had already jumped off his horse to embrace Elega; he was too busy hugging her to think about anything else for a while.

From horseback, regally, King Joyse faced Terisa and Geraden, Artagel and Nyle.

"You have a story," he said, "which I am eager to hear. For the moment, however, tell me only the result. What have you accomplished?"

"My lord King," replied Artagel at once, "the High King's Monomach is dead."

"And Master Gilbur is dead," Geraden said.

A moment later, he added, "Adept Havelock has killed the arch-Imager Vagel."

Terisa cleared her throat. She wanted to say, What about Nyle? Can't you see what happened to him? He needs help.

But the King's blue gaze held her; the memory of horns held her. As well as she could, she said, "Master Eremis looked at his own Image in a flat mirror. I don't think he's going to bother you anymore."

King Joyse's smile was as bright and cleansing as the warm sunlight and the ineffable sky.

When he looked at Nyle, however, his smile went away.

He dismounted; he strode toward Nyle sternly, like a sovereign with a traitor to punish.

Then he stopped.

Instead of speaking harshly, he murmured, "Nyle, forgive me."

Nyle's face twisted helplessly. "Forgive—? My lord King, I betrayed you."

"Yes!" King Joyse retorted at once. "You betrayed me—as my daughter Elega betrayed me—as the Congery betrayed me. And because I was betrayed this victory became possible. Everything you did against me, you did out of love and honor. And for that reason everything you did played its part in the saving of my realm. You betrayed me to do Mordant good, Nyle. *I* failed you. I failed to see

your importance, your *worth,* when my esteem would have been to
your benefit.

"I could not have protected you from hurt. But I could have
helped you place a higher value on yourself."

Nyle tried to answer; there may have been a number of things
he wanted to say. But he couldn't control his weeping.

Both Artagel and Geraden put their arms around him.

King Joyse turned away to address everyone within earshot.

"Nyle has suffered," he announced in tone both grim and elated,
sorry and glad. "Do you hear me? He is not a traitor. He has suffered
as the Perdon suffered, and as the Tor suffered, and Castellan Lebbick, because his love is strong and he did not understand."

As he spoke, his voice carried farther and farther, until it
reached the walls and the armies, the men of Mordant and Alend
and Cadwal throughout the valley.

"A great many good men have suffered and died, among them
Master Quillon, who served my purposes when I could risk them
with no one else, and Castellan Norge, who served Orison and Mordant and all of you with his life. And with their pain they have pur-
chased a victory which we could not have gained otherwise.

"Remember that they were hurt for us! Remember that we have
freedom and victory and *life* because of them!

"And because all of you fought like heroes!

"Now the world is ours, and we must heal it. From this day, let
us make our world a place of peace."

When he finished, the cheering went on for a long time.

After the wounded had been cared for as well as the circumstances
allowed, and the men of the three armies had been fed by supplies
translated from Orison, King Joyse ordered all of High King Festten's
captains, in addition to his own and Prince Kragen's, to join him
while he heard the tales Terisa and Geraden, Artagel and Nyle had
to tell. He asked the Prince and Elega, Myste and Darsint to describe
what they had done. He told his own story again, so that his actions
would be as widely understood as possible. Then he returned the
Cadwal captains to their men.

He sent several hundred of his guards to find and subdue Master
Eremis' stronghold. And he sent other riders to go among the hills,
announcing to any hidden or belligerent Cadwals the same amnesty
he offered the men who had surrendered: return to their homes or

not, join him or not, as they chose, without fear of being hunted down or coerced. King Joyse feared no one and intended to shed no more blood.

Then the Congery began producing hogsheads of ale and casks of wine, and everyone who remained in the valley of Esmerel was invited to the King's celebration.

That night in the Care of Tor there was no more fighting.

EPILOGUE: CROWNING THE PIECES

S ome time later, as spring turned toward summer, Terisa and Geraden rode out of Orison to the stand of trees among the hills where they had first been attacked by callat—where the horsemen of her dream had first appeared to her in the wrong guise, just as they had later come to her in the wrong place, doing the wrong things.

The late cold and snow which had hampered the march to Esmerel had done considerable damage to fruit trees and flowers and early vegetables across the Demesne and the Care of Tor; but there were no signs of chill-blight here. The trees were rich green and elegant, shading the long grass beneath them with easy sweetness; and through the grass wildflowers peeped like delicate and unexpected possibilities. A low breeze ruffled the foliage enough to make the trees murmur, keep the air cool; not enough to disturb the tranquility of the place.

Terisa had brought Geraden there because she wanted to hear horns again. She had a decision to make, and she thought that the keen music which had once lifted her out of herself in a dream, opening her heart to him and King Joyse and Mordant, would help her.

That dream had been a strange kind of augury, at once accurate and misleading: false on both occasions when it had been fulfilled, and somehow true in conflation, as if each occasion had contributed a piece of the truth.

Nevertheless she would have liked to have another dream to go by, an Image reflected in a mirror made of the pure sand of dreams. She needed a sense of direction, of purpose; a hint to guide her.

She had to decide whether to stay where she was. Or to return to her former life.

Geraden was being studiously, almost grimly noncommittal. She would have liked to hear him ask her to stay: that, too, might have helped. But he was determined to respect her wishes, bring no pressure to bear on her decision. Oh, he wanted her to stay; she knew that. But he also wanted her to be happy. He had always been that way, caught up in what she needed or wanted, instinctively willing to let her lead him. And the stronger he became, the more confidence he gained, the less he demanded for himself.

Her happiness wasn't something he could achieve by asking her to subordinate her desires to his own.

Unfortunately, his determination to let her reach her own decision only seemed to make the decision itself more difficult.

She wanted to hear horns.

The woods held a gentle music of their own, but it wasn't the call which thrilled her spirit, the potent blend of melody and hunting. The wildflowers bobbed their heads in the light breeze, nodding to her as if they understood, but revealing nothing. She thought of her former life as a struggle between Reverend Thatcher and her father—a battle to help the ruined and destitute of the world against rapacity and unconcern, against men who inflicted misery for their own benefit simply because they were able to do so. And the more strength Reverend Thatcher showed, the more she wanted to help him.

There were things she could do in her old world.

Mordant, on the other hand, was at peace. And likely to remain so for a long time.

She loved it anyway. She didn't want to give it up.

Geraden, help me.

Even though she knew he didn't want to answer, she asked, "What should I do?"

He had reached a point where he apparently found it impossible to meet her gaze. Looking away through the trees as if he were searching for the place where the callat had first shown themselves— a place hard to recognize in a scene full of leaves and grass and wildflowers—he murmured, "I get the impression Darsint is content to stay."

"He might as well be," she replied with more asperity than she intended. "He doesn't have a way back. You can return him to the Image where you found him—to Pythas—but you can't return him to his people. And his suit doesn't have any power. He couldn't defend himself.

"I don't have that problem. You could send *me* back."

Glumly, Geraden nodded.

Without warning, loneliness welled up inside her, and her eyes brimmed with tears. Oh, Geraden, love, can't you help me? Softly, so that he wouldn't hear how she felt, she asked, "What are my choices?"

He shrugged. "I can translate you home. Your father must have sold the apartment by now. You'll have to start your life over again." Almost at once, however, he added, "But it might not be so bad. I could visit you sometimes. You could visit me. We know how to do that."

His voice faded into the rustle of leaves.

"Or?" she insisted.

"Or you can stay here." For a moment longer, he held his face away, refused to look at her. But then, like a man who couldn't stop himself, he turned toward her. "You can stay here and marry me."

Through her tears, his eyes looked abashed and brave, accessible to joy or pain; troubled, sweet, and precious. And when he gazed at her like that, she heard the unmistakable sound of horns.

So they were married in high summer, in the great ballroom of Orison, the hollow hall which had seen no use for years until the Masters had turned it into a staging-area for supplies during the march to Esmerel.

As if regretting the neglect of those joyless years, King Joyse made the ballroom festive for the occasion: the walls were decked with banners and streamers; fragrant rushes were strewn upon the floor; fires in fine braziers gave the air a sheen of gold, while flames in the huge hearths took the old chill out of the stones; musicians arrayed themselves along the balconies, practicing flourishes and dances until every corner of the place seemed to sing and tremble.

All this was organized by the lady Torrent. She was still shy— the dangers and privations she had endured to help rescue her mother hadn't changed that—but she had discovered in herself a reflection of her mother's firm will, as well as the organizational skill to make people and objects come together at the right time. Like her sister Myste, she had rapidly become Terisa's friend, and they had spent many happy hours planning the wedding, to Geraden's alternating chagrin, amusement and delight.

Nonetheless she was still baffled by her new status: she hardly knew what to do with the fact that King Joyse had proclaimed her his heir and successor. Her talents, he declared, were the ones Mordant would need most when he was gone. Publically, she demurred, claiming that she only wished he would live forever. Privately, however, she found that she had a number of ideas about how Orison and Mordant should be ruled.

But even more impressive than the color and music and celebration which Torrent produced was the list of personages who came to the wedding.

Naturally, King Joyse and Queen Madin presided. From time to time, they held hands; and the Queen seemed to dote on Terisa and Geraden as if one of her own children were getting married. According to rumor, however, their reunion had been a stormy one for a long time after her return to Orison. She was said to have been furious at his treatment of her, his refusal to share his secrets with her, to involve her in his plans; and all his protestations and explanations had just made her angrier. This was only rumor, of course. It was true, however, that he had sometimes emerged from their private rooms looking like a man who would have preferred almost any warfare to this peace.

Nevertheless by the time of the wedding they had resolved or accepted their differences, and had begun to enjoy each other's company again. Perhaps he had aided their reconciliation by naming Torrent to succeed him. From their raised seats at one end of the ballroom, they smiled approval at the assembly, and at each other, and were satisfied.

First among the guests—not in nominal rank, but in actual status—were Prince Kragen, the High Regent of Cadwal, and his Consort, the lady Elega. As a couple, they were the basis on which King

Joyse and the Alend Monarch had built their new alliance, their new peace. In an effort to insure that no new tyrant came to power in Cadwal, and that the three kingdoms would be held together by bonds of authority and family as well as of common interest, the Monarch's son and the King's daughter had been set on Festten's former Seat in Carmag.

This arrangement had been Joyse's idea, but Margonal had accepted it readily enough. He was learning to understand the way his old enemy thought. And he had ideas of his own—

Blind, weary, content—and unwilling to face the rigors of a second journey to Orison—the Alend Monarch had sent his new Contender to stand in his place at the wedding: a man who now could claim precedence over everyone in Orison except King Joyse and Queen Madin, because of his position as Margonal's representative and potential successor.

The new Alend Contender was Nyle.

Arriving for the ceremony, he still appeared perplexed and a bit daunted by his circumstances. But when Kragen had been installed as High Regent in Carmag, Margonal had needed another Contender; and the Alend Monarch had sensed in Nyle a man with a newborn but almost ferocious instinct for caution. Caution, the Monarch had declared, was the fundamental requirement for anyone who meant to rule over Scarab and the Alend Lieges. Kragen had shown himself altogether too prone to risks, and Margonal wished to replace him with someone who lacked that flaw.

Nyle had refused the honor—or the responsibility—at first. He didn't deserve it, he wasn't worthy. Eventually, however, King Joyse had confronted him with a royal command, and he had felt himself forced to acquiesce.

The reports which King Joyse had since received from the Alend Monarch indicated that Nyle was proving to be exactly the Contender Margonal wanted, despite his self-distrust.

Behind the Alend Contender, and behind the High Regent and his Consort, stood Castellan Darsint and his new bride, the lady Myste.

King Joyse and Queen Madin would have gladly combined the marriage of Darsint and Myste with that of Terisa and Geraden; but Darsint had flatly declined a public ceremony. On the other hand, he hadn't hesitated to accept the place of Castellan.

Chains of command, the procurement of supplies, the movement and housing of men and animals, discipline and defense: these were things the Congery's champion understood in his bones. And his role in the battle of Esmerel gave him an enormous personal credibility which carried him past the uncertain days while he was learning his new job. In addition, he had Myste's advice and support; and despite (or perhaps because of) her "romantic notions" she had a sense of practical ethics which tempered and guided his authoritarian instincts.

After the Castellan and his lady, the lords of the Cares were arranged in an order of precedence which depended solely on the parts they—or their predecessors—had played in the King's war. First were the Tor, the Perdon, and the Termigan; next, the Fayle and the Domne; last, the Armigite.

The new Tor was one of the old lord's younger sons—in fact, the only one of his sons who wanted the position. But the old Perdon had died without children; and his widow had positively refused to look at the prospect of being the first female lord in Mordant's history as anything except a cruel burden. "You have lost me my husband and my friends, my lord King," she had protested harshly. "Will you now deprive me of quiet as well?" So King Joyse, with a glint in his eyes which occasionally suggested humor, and occasionally malice, had named Artagel as the Perdon.

Artagel's protests had been considerably louder than those of the old lord's widow; but King Joyse had only smiled and insisted, glinting. And at last, in exasperation, he had snapped, "Be reasonable, Artagel. You can't be the best swordsman in Mordant for the rest of your life. The years won't let you. And those scars are never going to be as resilient as whole flesh and muscle. It's about time you had something else to do."

So Artagel had relented with an ill grace which had gradually faded as he realized that his new position in Scarping made it possible for him to have a home—and maybe even a family?—of his own at last.

As for the Termigan, everyone had expected him to refuse to attend the wedding, not out of any animosity, but simply because he was too busy rebuilding Sternwall. Nevertheless he had not only come, but he had come politely. Furthermore, he had brought with him an entire wainload of Rostrum wine as a marriage present: a gift which some people considered fit for a King; altogether too fine for mere Geraden and Terisa.

The Domne and the Fayle came next, old friends pleased in each other's company. But of Geraden's family no one else had made the trip to Orison: Tholden was consumed with the task of laying out and constructing a new Houseldon; Wester didn't enjoy travel; Minick couldn't leave his shy wife; Stead couldn't spare the time from his other pursuits. No one had accompanied the Domne except Quiss. Forthright and irrefusable as always, she had claimed that he couldn't hope to make the journey without someone to take care of him. Upon arriving in Orison, however, she had made it clear that her real reason for coming was to see Terisa and Geraden again, and to hear about everything they had done, and to give them the benefit of her advice.

The Domne himself didn't seem to feel compelled to give anyone advice. On the other hand, he was so happy and proud that he made Geraden's face shine and gave Terisa the glad impression that the whole family was present in the old lord's person.

Last of the lords came the Armigite, remarkably subdued in his manner and dress, miserable in his isolation. After the battle of Esmerel, everyone who spoke to King Joyse—in fact, everyone in Orison—had an opinion concerning how the Armigite should be treated. Among them, the Alend Monarch had counseled leniency: after all, the Armigite's imprecise loyalties had allowed the Alend army to reach Orison intact, with obvious (if unforeseen) benefits for both Alend and Mordant. In contrast, Darsint had recommended beheading: treachery deserved death. At last, however, King Joyse had settled on the worst punishment of all: he had decided to do nothing; to treat the Armigite as if his worse offenses were so trivial that they weren't worth noticing.

The Armigite spent most of his time before and after the festivities trying to get someone to talk to him; but no one was willing to be bothered.

Below and beside King Joyse sat Adept Havelock, in a place of honor—and of discretion, as well, a place from which he could withdraw easily if necessary. Since the battle of Esmerel, he seemed to have settled comfortably into his role as the madman of Orison. No longer obsessed by the need for lucidity, he had become able to relax and enjoy himself in odd ways. As a result, his madness appeared to grow more benign, driving him to fewer extremes, permitting him more satisfaction.

He never spoke of his struggle with the arch-Imager, never told how he had beaten Vagel. And he never explained why he had chosen to risk everything in personal combat with Vagel, instead of simply translating his old enemy and Eremis and Gilbur to Orison, as Terisa had intended. If anyone asked him a question, however, any question at all, he often replied with a complete, clear, and quite inappropriate description of everything he and King Joyse had done to meet Mordant's need.

So the celebration went forward, full of music and orations, dancing and wine, vows and homage. On the Congery's behalf, Master Barsonage rejected any unseemly ostentation for the Masters. For himself, however, he claimed the right to stand as Terisa's father during the ceremony. Happy and fustian in a remarkably red robe, he accompanied Terisa through the formalities, and made speeches on her behalf, and generally behaved as if he were as proud as the Domne.

Thus the arch-Imager Terisa of Morgan and Adept Geraden of Domne were married like the princess and the hero in a fable: grandly (some said gloriously) surrounded by family and friends and honor and respect, in a world which they had helped bring to safety. She had lost her father's wealth in order to gain her own power, and the enchantment which had held her was gone. And he had inherited something better than Cares or kingdoms, which was himself: his courage and his willing heart had come into their true birthright.

In the ceremony of marriage, they made a number of vows, all of which added up to the same thing: they promised to help each other hear horns.

About the Author

Born in 1947 in Cleveland, Ohio, *Stephen R. Donaldson* made his publishing debut with the first Covenant Trilogy in 1977. Shortly thereafter, he was named Best New Writer of the Year and given the prestigious John W. Campbell Award. He graduated from the College of Wooster (Ohio) in 1968, served two years as a conscientious objector doing hospital work in Akron, then attended Kent State University, where he received his M.A. in English in 1971. Donaldson now lives in New Mexico.

MINERALS

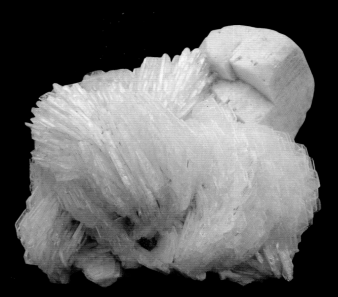

MINERALS

An Illustrated Exploration of the Dynamic World of Minerals and Their Properties

George W. Robinson, Ph.D.
Earth Sciences Division
Canadian Museum of Nature

Photography by
Jeffrey A. Scovil

Mineral specimens from
the collection of the
Canadian Museum of Nature

■

A Peter N. Nevraumont Book

SIMON & SCHUSTER

New York   London   Toronto   Sydney   Tokyo   Singapore

SIMON & SCHUSTER
Rockefeller Center
1230 Avenue of the Americas
New York, New York 10020

Canadian
Museum
of Nature

Musée
canadien
de la nature

Text copyright © 1994 by Canadian Musem of
Nature/Musée canadien de la nature
Photographs copyright © 1994 Jeffrey A. Scovil

10 9 8 7 6 5 4 3 2 1

Printed in Hong Kong by Everbest Printing Company
through Four Colour Imports.

Library of Congress Cataloging in Publication Data

Robinson, George W. (George Willard), 1946-
    Minerals / by George W. Robinson :
photography by Jeffrey A. Scovil.
        p.   cm.
    ISBN 0-671-88002-0
    1. Minerals.   I. Scovil, Jeffrey A.   II. Title.
QE372.2R63   1994
549—dc20   94-6344
                                             CIP

This book was created and produced by
Nevraumont Publishing Company
New York, New York

President: Ann J. Perrini

Book and jacket design: José Conde, Kanazawa City, Japan
Figure illustrations: Jane Axamethy

Contents

The Earth

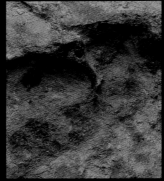

PART I

and Its Minerals

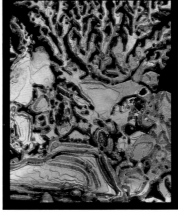

chapter one

Thinking like a Geologist

EVEN in childhood I was fascinated by the natural beauty of minerals and intrigued by their seemingly endless diversity of colors and shapes. Finding and studying these treasures of nature became a lifelong obsession. Later I learned that minerals, along with the familiar landscape of mountains, valleys, plains, and oceans that we all too often take for granted, are the natural consequence of billions of years of interaction between dynamic global forces and the materials that make up the planet. What are these forces and materials, and how do they interact? These are the questions that have enticed and will continue to motivate me and other earth scientists for generations to come.
❲ The devastating blasts of Krakatoa or Mount Saint Helens, cataclysmic earthquakes in Italy or California, seasonal avalanches in British Columbia or the Alps, or periodic floods by the Mississippi or Yellow Rivers are continual reminders of the powerful geological forces at work around us. While we mourn our losses, we also perplexedly fail to learn from them and continue to build our homes and cities on major faults and floodplains in defiance of nature. The geological record provides overwhelming evidence that these processes have been and will continue to be operative for millions of years.
❲ The record also shows that numerous dynamic relationships exist between these forces and the materials that make up the Earth. Study has taught me that the same geological forces that cause earthquakes in San Francisco, volcanos in Iceland, or black smokers along the Juan de Fuca ridge beneath the Pacific Ocean, also provide the heat, pressure, and other requirements for making minerals. How do I know what these requirements and materials are? How can I tell that one particular rock or mineral must have formed in an

ancient sea and another in an ancient lava flow? By observation and experimentation. Many geological processes can be observed directly. We can watch mountain streams tumble pebbles as they flow downhill to the plains. We can watch a thin crust of salt form along the edge of a mud puddle and cracks develop as the mud dries up. We can watch a volcano erupt. If I encounter a field full of rounded pebbles at the base of a mountain, I don't suspect that the site is an ancient volcano or mud puddle! Common sense and the law of **uniformitarianism** tell me otherwise.

Simply stated, the law of uniformitarianism says that *the present is the key to the past*. Because streams carry pebbles downhill today, they probably did so yesterday, last week, last year, and even a million years ago. Thus, even if there is no flowing water within a hundred kilometers of the pile of pebbles I came upon, logically I can assume that water once flowed here. Although now it may seem merely to state the obvious, when first proposed by James Hutton in 1785 and systematized by Sir Charles Lyell in the 1830s, the law of uniformitarianism not only revolutionized geology but established it as a hypothesis-testing science, based on observation and reasoning. Seeing is believing. Witnessing lava cool before our eyes to form solid rock provides the direct evidence we need to infer a similar origin for ancient lava flows or cinder cones we may encounter elsewhere.

Some things, such as atoms, gamma rays, or the center of the Earth, we can't see, so we must rely on indirect means to visualize their properties. A bat can't see an insect flying past him in the night sky, yet it is able to locate the insect and track its position with sound waves. Similarly, I can't see atoms, yet by diffracting X rays from a tiny crystal of a particular mineral, I am able to learn how its atoms are arranged internally. I can't see, smell, hear, feel, or taste gamma rays, so when I go to the field in search of radioactive minerals, I bring a Geiger counter that can detect them. The fact that many of the Earth's properties and processes, including some of those that characterize and make minerals, cannot be detected or observed directly by human senses does not preclude their existence.

Even though I can't watch most minerals forming, I can predict how and where they might originate. This is not magic. If I know that a certain kind of cake requires baking at 175°C for 45 minutes, then I also know what kind of oven I'll need to make it, and that a refrigerator won't be required. Likewise, if I know the physical and chemical conditions that a mineral needs to form, then I need only look for possible places in the Earth that provide those conditions. If a temperature of 1,500°C is required to synthesize a particular mineral in the laboratory, then looking for that mineral in rocks that form at lower temperatures would make little sense. Sound, straightforward reasoning such as this, taken a step at a time and tested in the field, is the modus operandi of the geologist.

During the last half of the twentieth century, geophysical data from the study of earthquakes and gravity measurements combined with detailed geological mapping of the Earth's surface and ocean floors has provided

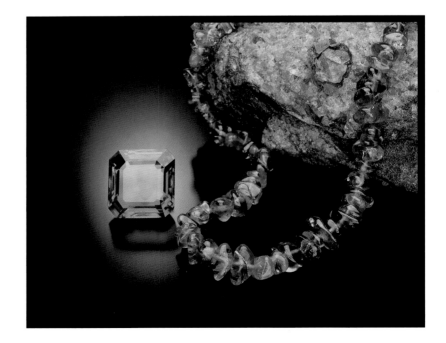

PLATE 1

Nickel-Iron meteorite.
Canyon Diablo, Arizona. 12 x 13 cm.
(Geological Survey of Canada
specimen)

By studying meteorites such as this one,
geologists are able to learn about the
composition of the Earth and its history.

PLATE 2

Olivine, variety peridot.
Mogok, Burma (faceted gem,
44.73 ct); San Carlos Indian
Reservation, Arizona (necklace and
specimen, 7 x 8 cm).

Olivine is a common mineral in the
Earth's mantle and in some meteorites.

geologists with a whole new concept of the Earth's structure. We now know that the Earth is layered, as an egg is. It has a relatively thin, light, outer **crust** or "shell," which is underlain by a denser **mantle** (the white of the egg), with an even denser "yolk," or **core.** The solid crust on which we live averages 30 to 50 kilometers thick beneath the continents, but only 6 to 8 kilometers thick beneath the oceans. The mantle, which is also solid, is approximately 2,900 kilometers thick, but the core, with a radius of 3,400 kilometers, has a liquid outer portion. Naturally we know more about the crust than we do about any of the other layers, since we can directly sample and analyze the crust. Some direct sampling of mantle rocks also has been possible because pieces of them are sometimes transported to the Earth's surface by volcanic eruptions, but most of what we know about the mantle and core we have learned indirectly from geophysical measurements and the study of meteorites [PLATE 1].

You are probably now asking yourself, What can we possibly learn about the inside of the Earth by studying meteorites from outer space? To answer that question, I will pose another: How did the Earth form in the first place? Of course, no one knows for sure, but the theory upheld by most geologists today suggests that all the planets in our solar system formed by the coalescence and accretion of matter by gravitational attraction. The first particles to combine were probably very small, but as more accumulated, the increase in gravitational attraction due to increased mass attracted larger pieces of matter, such as meteorites and small would-be planets forming at the same time. In fact, the moon probably formed when one such "planet" collided with the Earth, breaking off a section that eventually became the moon.

Ancient meteor-impact craters on the surfaces of both the moon and the Earth are well documented, and meteorites are continually being found all over the Earth. Is it mere coincidence that two of the main minerals found in mantle rocks, olivine [PLATE 2] and pyroxene, are also those found in stony meteorites, or that the observed velocity of seismic waves traveling through the Earth's outer core matches that expected for a molten nickel-iron meteorite containing some silicon? Is it also mere coincidence that the age of the Earth based on the radioactive decay of lead isotopes is the same as that for nickel-iron meteorites: 4.5 billion years?

Much has been learned about the Earth by studying **isotopes.** Isotopes are atoms of the same element with different numbers of neutrons in their nuclei and thus different atomic masses. Some isotopes are unstable and tend to "decay" into more stable forms. To do so they emit energy in the form of radiation at a constant rate. If this rate is known, as it is for many isotopes, then by comparing the amounts of initial isotope and decay products present, we can calculate how much time has passed since the decay began. This process is the basis for the radiometric dating of rocks. In addition, as radioactive isotopes of potassium, uranium, and thorium in the Earth's interior decay into more-stable products, the energy they emit is converted into heat. Inside the Earth, temperature increases with depth, possibly reaching 5,000°C in the core. This increase in temperature with depth is known as the **geothermal**

gradient and averages about 30°C per kilometer in the Earth's crust.

Isotopes are useful geological indicators in other ways as well. Because they have different masses, different isotopes of the same element may partition differently in certain reactions or occur in different ratios in rocks from different parts of the Earth. Increasing knowledge of how various isotopes are distributed throughout the Earth and how they selectively partition from one another during certain chemical reactions is helping geologists interpret many phenomena.

Because heat always flows from hotter areas to cooler ones, within the Earth heat flows from its hot interior to its cooler surface. Much of this heat transfer is accomplished by **convection.** What is convection and how does it work? Here's a simple experiment to try. Prepare an ordinary cup of hot coffee with cream, milk, or whitener and wait a minute or two for motion caused by the stirring to stop. Now, taking care not to cause any motion in the cup, slowly lower a thin, clear ice cube into the coffee. Peer through the ice cube as if it were a glass-bottomed boat and watch what happens. In a few seconds you should see a swirling motion develop beneath the ice cube, which will start to move about, seemingly under its own power. You are observing convection at work. As heat is transferred from the coffee to the ice, it causes the ice to melt. Because the ice water is denser, it sinks toward the bottom of the cup and is replaced by rising, less-dense, hot coffee, which melts more ice, continuing the process. The relative motion set up in the cup by the rising and sinking liquid creates **convection currents** that cause the turbulent flow you see beneath the ice cube. As the convective motion increases, the resulting current is usually strong enough to move the ice cube across the surface of the cup.

A similar situation exists within the Earth. Heat flowing from the core through the mantle to the crust causes convection cells to develop. The crust responds by breaking apart and, like our ice cube, moving about. Of course, the crust moves much more slowly than our ice cube—only a few centimeters a year. This simple concept is the driving force behind what is probably the most important geological theory proposed in modern time: **plate tectonics**●

chapter two

Continents Adrift

T

HE **plate tectonic** theory proposes that the Earth's crust consists of large **plates** that "float" about its surface because of convective motion through the mantle beneath them. If this sounds a bit far-fetched, don't worry; I was not a believer at first either. After all, for convection to work there must be a flow of materials, and I told you earlier that both the Earth's crust and the mantle beneath it are *solid*. How can a solid flow? The answer lies in *time*, that unique, all-important parameter that separates geology from the other sciences. As humans, we have difficulty believing what we can't see happening. When we toss a stick into a river, we can watch it flow downstream because fluid flow in a river is easily observable within our human time frame and points of reference. A stick thrown onto a glacier, however, even if we stare at it for a month, does not seem to move. But the question remains, did the stick really not move, or did it move so little or so slowly that we couldn't see it happening? ⊄ Glaciologists have provided an unequivocal answer. Suspecting that solid ice does indeed flow, glaciologists have proven the point by driving a straight row of posts across the surface of a glacier and marking reference points on land in line with the row at each of its ends. After several months, when the line of posts is surveyed, it is no longer straight, but is bowed outward near its midpoint. With more time, the bow becomes pronounced and visually obvious. The solid ice is flowing, but too slowly for human perception. Given enough time and a slow, steady application of force (in this case, gravity), the solid ice "bends" rather than breaks. Sealing wax, which is also solid, will shatter if given a quick blow by a hammer but will bend, or flow, with a slow, steady application of force, especially if warmed. The same is true of most solid metals. Might not a solid (especially one at 1,200 to 2,500°C), such as the Earth's mantle, also be capable of maintaining a similar slow rate of convective flow?

If you are still a little uncertain about the plausibility of plate tectonics, there is a good deal more tangible evidence supporting the theory. For the plates to "float" they would have to be less dense than the rock beneath them. This is exactly the case. Although the composition of crustal rocks varies widely, in general we find that the continents are **granitic** in composition, while the ocean basins are **basaltic.** Granites contain more lightweight elements, like sodium, aluminum, silicon, and potassium, than do basalts, which contain more of the denser elements calcium, iron, and magnesium. Therefore, the average density of granite is less than that of basalt. Peridotite, which is one of the most common rocks in the upper mantle, has a density greater than that of either granite or basalt. Thus, considering only differences in density, the observed positioning of the continents on top of the oceanic crust, which is on top of an even denser mantle, makes sense.

From deep-sea submersibles scientists have been able to watch submarine volcanic eruptions produce oceanic crustal basalts along midoceanic ridges. Studies of these rocks show that bands of basalts with identical magnetic properties and ages are symmetrically distributed at equal distances on either side of the ridge, with progressively older basalts as one travels farther from the ridge. This compelling evidence for a spreading seafloor is corroborated by calculations indicating that North America and Europe are moving apart at a rate of about one centimeter per year. A quick look at a world map shows that the shapes of opposing continental margins do appear to fit together. Fitting continents back together reveals much more evidence suggesting that they were once joined. Rocks of similar age and structure on opposite sides of the oceans match up, as do rocks containing similar fossil assemblages, glacial features, and magnetic alignment of iron-bearing minerals.

All the evidence points to the conclusion that the continents were formerly joined together and have drifted to their present positions like ships on a sea of moving basaltic plates. But what happens to the continents and plates as they move about? As FIGURE A shows, there are three possibilities: (1) they spread apart, (2) they slide past one another, or (3) one sinks beneath the other. The first scenario produces midoceanic ridges and volcanos, such as those in Iceland. The second produces long fractures along which there is movement, such as the San Andreas **fault** that parallels the California coastline. The frequent earthquakes experienced in California result from the sudden release of energy and fracturing of rock as the plates slide by one another. The third case is exemplified off the east coast of Japan, where a deep-sea trench marks a zone of **subduction.** There a westward-moving oceanic plate **subsides,** or sinks beneath the Asian continent, carrying along with it a good deal of sediment piled on the ocean floor. The deeper the sediment and oceanic crust sink beneath the continent, the hotter they get, until they finally melt. Surrounded by much-denser rock, the less-dense,

Plate Boundaries.

When two plates meet, they spread apart (e.g., East Pacific Rise), slide past one another (e.g., San Andreas Fault), or pass beneath one another (e.g., west coast of South America).

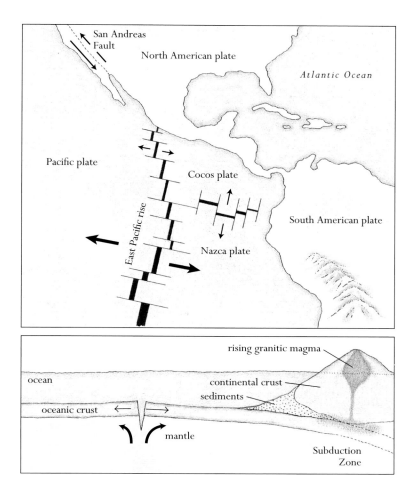

until they finally melt. Surrounded by much-denser rock, the less-dense, molten rock, known as **magma,** follows zones of weakness back toward the surface, where it eventually may erupt as one of Japan's many volcanos.

Because the Earth's crustal plates ferry the continents about its surface, continental collisions also occur. When two continents collide, huge mountain ranges are formed, as crustal rocks are either folded like an accordion or scraped off one continent and piled atop those of the other. The Himalayas formed by such a collision between India and Asia, the Alps by the collision of Africa with Europe.

Why did I say that the plate tectonic theory was probably the greatest geological discovery in modern time? Because it accounts for and ties together so many different geological phenomena. It explains the cause and global distribution of volcanos and earthquakes, the shape of the continents, why we find fossils of ancient marine organisms high and dry on mountaintops, and even why we find certain plants and animals on one continent but not another. It also provides a rational explanation for the evolution and distribution of many minerals, but to understand why, we must first understand what a

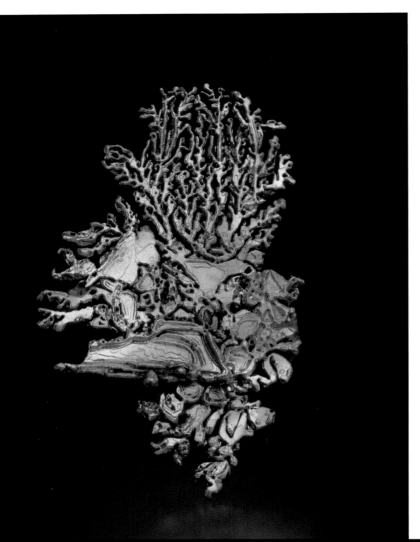

PLATE 3

Gold.
Grass Valley, California. 2 x 3.5 cm.

*Gold is one of the few minerals that occurs
as a native element. Most minerals are
compounds, composed of two or more
elements.*

PLATE 4

Calcite.
Herja, Transylvania, Romania.
5 x 7 cm.

*Calcite is stable over a broad range of
temperature and pressure. These spherical
aggregates of calcite crystals are only one
of its many forms.*

chapter three

Minerals

MOST **minerals** are *naturally occurring inorganic solids with defined chemical compositions and crystal structures.* I usually think of them as nature's inorganic chemicals and the Earth as nature's laboratory. A few minerals, such as gold, sulfur, or diamond [PLATES 3, 12, 63, and 135], exist as individual **native elements,** but most are **compounds,** composed of two or more elements chemically bonded together. Like all chemicals, minerals have specific ranges of stability with respect to heat, pressure, acidity, oxidation, and numerous other parameters. If one or more parameters change, some minerals may no longer be stable and will change to form different minerals that are stable in the existing conditions. In that regard minerals are like people. They like to be "comfortable" in their surroundings. No one working in a foundry wants to wear a heavy overcoat, even on a cold winter day, until, of course, it comes time to go outside and walk home. We respond to changes in our environment, and so do minerals. ❰ The plate tectonic model described in Chapter 2 provides many combinations of parameters and the means to change them. For example, at midoceanic ridges there is high heat flow but low pressure; submarine trenches provide little heat but enormous pressure; the collision of continents places dissimilar rocks in contact with one another and provides great lateral pressure; a subducting plate exposes huge areas of rock and sediment to increasing heat and pressure while a rising body of magma created when they melt provides a localized source of heat but not much pressure; and so on. *The wide range of physical and chemical parameters provided by natural geological environments and the availability of specific chemical elements ultimately dictate which minerals will be produced.* ❰ It doesn't matter to a growing crystal of calcite [PLATES 4, 40, 49 and 107] where it forms, as long as its surroundings provide its essential

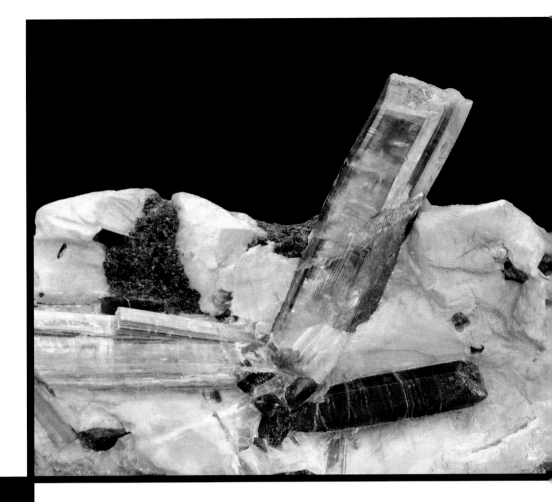

PLATE 5

Kyanite (blue) **and Staurolite** (brown) **in Mica Schist.**
Monte Campione, Ticino, Switzerland. 6 x 8 cm.

Because they form exclusively under conditions of high heat and pressure, kyanite and staurolite are used by geologists to interpret the history of metamorphic rocks.

PLATE 6

Mesolite on Apophyllite.
Poona, Maharashtra, India.
4 x 6.5 cm.

Sprays of delicate crystals like this mesolite can form only by unimpeded growth into open spaces, such as gas bubble cavities in basaltic lava flows.

ingredients and a stable environment for its growth. Calcite may form equally well in an igneous rock, such as a carbonatite at several hundred degrees Celsius, in a vein in a metamorphic rock like slate at only 200°C, or in a cavity in limestone, a sedimentary rock, at only 20°C. (Igneous, metamorphic, and sedimentary rocks are discussed in Chapter 4.) Calcite has a broad range of stability with respect to heat and pressure. The physicochemical conditions in each of these extremely different geological environments overlap the stability field for calcite, so calcite may occur in any of them. Therefore, by itself, the discovery of a calcite crystal in a rock tells us very little about the geological history of the rock.

Some minerals, however, have more-restricted limits of stability and therefore occupy only a few geological niches. The conditions of high heat and pressure required to form diamonds, for instance, exist only in the Earth's mantle. Stishovite, a rare form of silica (SiO_2), forms only under extremely high pressures, such as realized in rocks that have sustained a meteor impact. Andalusite, sillimanite, and kyanite [PLATES 5 and 112], all of which have the chemical formula Al_2SiO_5, are stable only at specific ranges of pressure and temperature and thus are extremely useful to geologists in deciphering the geological record of rocks that contain them.

Minerals are all around us; the Earth's rocks are composed of them. If minerals are so common, though, why do well-formed crystals seem so rare? Why is it, in spite of hiking over miles of rocks, you have probably never encountered spectacular crystals like those pictured in this book? To understand why this is so, we must look carefully at the underlying mechanism that forms all minerals: **crystallization.** Simply stated, crystallization is the organization of atoms from random into ordered, symmetric arrangements. It is the crystal structure that determines all the properties of a mineral: its shape, color, hardness, and even how it breaks. No two mineral species have the same kind of atoms arranged in the same way.

Most of the magnificent crystals housed in museums and illustrated in this book crystallized in a fluid medium in open spaces. Nonrestrictive surroundings are essential for the growth of large, perfect crystals [PLATE 6]. Time and the availability of essential chemical constituents are also crucial. All other factors equal, large crystals require more time to grow than small ones, but if supplied with the proper ingredients for too long a time, continued growth results in the crystals heading each other off to form a mass of interlocking crystals without well-developed forms. Given all these requirements, it is apparent why large, perfect crystals are scarce in nature: in most geological settings their essential constituents are seldom supplied in the right amount, at the right rate, and at a suitable temperature and pressure with sufficient time or space for them to develop ●

PLATE 7

Azurite (blue) **and Malachite**
(green).
Bisbee, Arizona. 6 x 8 cm.

Azurite and malachite form as a result
of the oxidation of earlier-formed copper-
bearing minerals such as chalcopyrite
[see PLATE *8].*

PLATE 8

Chalcopyrite and Calcite.
Groundhog mine, Vanadium, New
Mexico. 4 x 5 cm.

These crystals formed in open space by
precipitation from an aqueous solution.

chapter four

The Rock Cycle

ALTHOUGH in general we can say that the genesis of minerals is controlled by crystallization, this statement does not explain the distribution of minerals within the Earth. Such an explanation can be obtained only by considering crystallization in context with geological processes. Only then does it become clear why certain minerals occur where they do. A dynamic balance exists between constructive and destructive forces within the Earth. Vulcanism and continental collisions build up mountains; weathering and erosion tear them down. In the process rocks, and the minerals that comprise them, are recycled. Even a hard, durable rock like granite is not immune to these forces. ❰ The very moment granite is exposed to the Earth's surface, physical and chemical weathering begin to take their toll. Repeated heating and cooling by the sun causes the outermost surface of the rock to expand and contract, physically weakening it until it splits off (of course, the granite could always fall victim to a quarrying operation, which would greatly accelerate the process). As rain falls on the granite, it chemically breaks down its **feldspars,** the most abundant mineral group in the Earth's crust, into clays, releasing grains of quartz and other minerals. These smaller particles are carried from the mountains to the plains by wind, water, or ice, and eventually by rivers to the sea, where they accumulate as layers of sediment. With continued accumulation, sediments compact under pressure to form **sedimentary** rocks, which are eventually carried back toward the continent by the moving plates. ❰ When these rocks reach the continent, some may be carried downward with the plate as it plunges beneath the continent. As they continue their downward journey, increased heat and pressure recrystallizes both the sediments and the

The Rock Cycle.

Rocks are continually recycled by geological processes. Magma crystallizes to make igneous rocks, which are broken down and carried as sediments to the sea by weathering and erosion. The sediments compact to form sedimentary rocks, which recrystallize under heat and pressure, forming metamorphic rocks. Continued heating causes melting, which forms a magma, completing the cycle. Water may be driven from the rocks at various points along the way, producing aqueous solutions.

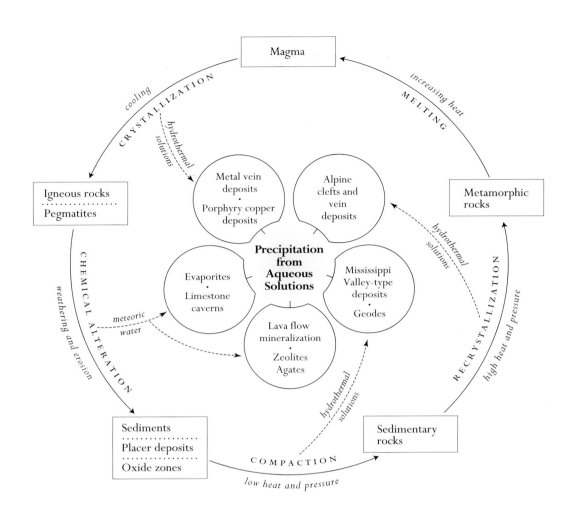

oceanic crust into **metamorphic** rocks. As the rocks descend even deeper, the rising temperature causes them to melt, forming a **magma.** The magma, which is under pressure and is less dense than the surrounding rock, rises upward to form an igneous rock—maybe a granite—as it cools and completes the cycle [FIGURE B].

Of course, there are many shortcuts and side roads that can be taken along the way. For example, igneous rocks may be recrystallized into metamorphic rocks or remelted to form magma without ever having been eroded. Igneous rocks are not the only ones subject to erosion. Sedimentary and metamorphic rocks are equally susceptible and may be recycled directly back to the sea as sediments. Life, too, enters the geological picture. Consider for a moment where each of the calcium atoms in your bones or teeth may have been in the geological past. Perhaps they were once dissolved in an ancient sea, where they were removed by a mollusk and incorporated into its shell as aragonite ($CaCO_3$). When the mollusk died, its shell would have fallen to the sea floor, where it could have been buried for millions of years in the sediment. The aragonite would probably recrystallize into calcite (also $CaCO_3$), while the imprint of the shell remained as a fossil record of former life. As more sediment accumulated, the increased heat and pressure due to burial would have formed limestone. Millions of years later, the processes of uplift and erosion could expose the limestone to the Earth's surface. There it could be discovered and quarried by humans, who might blast it apart and haul it off in a truck to a kiln, where it would be roasted to make lime (CaO) for use as a soil conditioner. Vegetables grown in the conditioned soil could take up some of the calcium, which your body might assimilate when you ate them.

Although these hypothetical calcium atoms in the aragonite, calcite, limestone, and lime represent only a miniscule fraction of the materials that make up the Earth, they illustrate an important point: They may be constituents of very different things depending on the time at which they are observed within an ongoing, natural process of recycling. Eventually, given enough time, the rock cycle is usually completed.

Completing the rock cycle requires that some minerals be created and others destroyed. As FIGURE B shows, the cycle involves four major processes: (1) **crystallization from molten rock,** (2) **precipitation from aqueous solutions,** (3) **chemical alteration of preexisting minerals,** and (4) **recrystallization by heat and pressure.** In the first of these, atoms of different elements are naturally sorted and recombined to form specific minerals as molten rocks cool to form igneous rocks. The minerals that form depend on the composition of the magma and what happens to it as it cools. Minerals such as diamond [see PLATE 12] form deep within the Earth at high temperatures and pressures and therefore are early to crystallize from a magma. Other minerals, such as beryl or topaz [see PLATES 20 and 23], form much later, at lower temperatures and pressures.

The second process centers on the role of water in dissolving, transporting, and recombining various chemical elements to make minerals as different as gold, halite (rock salt), or opals [see PLATES 3, 37, and 41], depending on the source of the water and the kinds of rocks through which it flows. The third process involves specific chemical processes, such as oxidation or changes in acidity, that result in the creation of new minerals like azurite from old ones like chalcopyrite, formed previously by other processes [PLATES 7 and 8]. The fourth process embodies the roles of heat and pressure in restructuring the atoms of previously formed minerals into new arrangements to make various minerals in metamorphic rocks [see PLATE 5]. Some minerals, such as emeralds [see PLATES 20, 120, and 133], may form by more than one process or require combinations of several processes to form. Finally, living organisms also play a role in the creation of some minerals, such as sulfur [see PLATE 135].

The remainder of this book has been organized around the mineral-forming processes that I just described. It is imperative to remember, however, that this scheme of classification is simply one of convenience; it is not inviolable. No definite boundaries have been established between these processes. As with many natural phenomena, often explanations of the genesis of minerals offer more shades of gray than black or white. Many questions have no clear-cut answers. For example, at exactly what point does the heat and pressure

PLATE 9

Goethite.

Bennington, Vermont. 15 x 18 cm.

The formation of these stalactites of goethite required at least two mineral-forming processes: chemical alteration and precipitation from an aqueous solution.

required to compress sediments into sedimentary rocks become enough to call them metamorphic rocks instead? At what point does recrystallization by heat and pressure in a semisolid, plastic state leave off and partial melting to form a magma begin? These points are all arbitrary, and my judgment may differ from that of other geologists. Where the line is drawn is not important. What is important is understanding how each process works and its relationships to the others.

Often more than one process is involved in the formation of a particular mineral. For example, consider the formation of the simple iron-oxide mineral goethite [PLATE 9], which forms the familiar brown rust stains commonly seen on rocks of all types. The first requirement is a source of iron, such as the iron sulfide pyrite [see PLATES 65, 78, and 109]. When pyrite comes in contact with groundwater containing dissolved oxygen, it oxidizes into iron sulfate, which further oxidizes in solution and precipitates goethite (i.e., goethite separates from the solution, since it is insoluble). Operative are at least two processes: chemical alteration and precipitation from aqueous solution. Which process is more important to form goethite? The question is irrelevant because both are essential.

As human beings we tend to see all things relative to our own brief lifetimes. Slow change appears to us as no change and therefore goes unnoticed. Most rocks and minerals change at an imperceptibly slow rate, but they do change! Thus, the specimens illustrated in this book are a snapshot in time, subject to transformation by geological processes. Although they may currently reside in human hands, they did not always, nor will they likely forever remain. To explain the genesis of minerals, a geologist must work like a detective, interpreting clues left behind by the processes that formed them. He or she must look for a motive, opportunity, and means to solve the mystery. In the case of minerals, the motive is their inherent tendency toward chemical and physical equilibrium with their surroundings. Opportunity is provided by the diverse geological environments created by plate tectonics and other geological processes; the means are the four main mineral-forming processes: crystallization (see Part II), precipitation from aqueous solutions (Part III), chemical alteration (Part IV), and recrystallization (Part V) ●

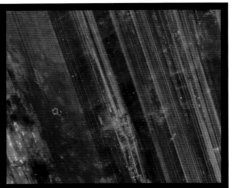

Minerals

from Molten Rock

chapter five

Crystallization

FE W things are more spectacular or memorable than a volcano in full eruption. It is also probably the most obvious example of rocks in the making, and the most common answer to the question, how do rocks form? My first encounter with lava was at the site not of an active volcano, but rather an extinct one in northern Arizona. Although the site contained no molten rock, rising steam, sulfurous fumes, intense heat, or raining cinders, I could feel the presence of all these things, for their evidence was all around me. ❦ To my left lay a great, black field of jagged, toffee-surfaced blocks of lava. Here and there large sheets of the black rock had been bulldozed into ridges by the river of molten rock that once flowed beneath them. In the distance to my right was a conical hill of reddish-brown cinders, burning bright in the afternoon sun. Cinders littered the landscape. It was as though all the clinkers I had ever seen on all the railroad lines in my life had been gathered up and scattered across this unfamiliar landscape. It could be nothing else; this was a volcano! Fascinated with the landscape and geological features that until then I had seen only in books and films, I spent an hour taking photographs and walking around, just observing and getting acquainted with this marvelous but alien landscape. One thing I didn't do, though, was look for crystals, for I knew I was not apt to find them here. ❦ A lava field seldom contains large, well-formed crystals of any mineral, since the few minutes to hours that it takes for the molten lava to solidify is usually not enough time for large crystals to form. **Magma** is molten rock; **lava** is magma that comes to the Earth's surface. In general, the faster magma cools, the smaller are the individual crystals that are formed. Often very fine-grained rocks result. Although the rapid cooling of volcanic rocks is not conducive to producing large, well-formed crystals, occasionally we do find such crystals in them. Some of the world's best and largest crystals of leucite occur in lava from the Roccamonfina volcano in the Campania region of Italy, which last erupted in A.D. 276, and large, gem-quality crystals of labradorite are mined from the lavas of extinct volcanos near Plush, Oregon. How do these crystals get so big, if they have so little time to crystallize?

The answer is simple: they do not crystallize at the Earth's surface, even though the rock enclosing them does. Think for a moment of a volcano as simply a safety valve, much like the one on a steam pressure cooker. When the valve on the pressure cooker fails, the drastically lower pressure outside the pot causes not only steam and super-heated water but also bits of partially cooked food from the bottom of the pot to eject. Leucite and labradorite have relatively high melting points, and the crystals had probably already grown to their present size and shape within a subsurface chamber of magma before the volcano erupted. The sudden release of pressure brought about by eruption of the volcano caused the already formed crystals to be carried to the surface along with the lava, just as the solid food is ejected from the bottom of the pressure cooker. Close examination of such crystals typically reveals that their **matrix,** the rock that encloses them, is indeed much finer grained, since it crystallized much more rapidly. Much has been learned about crystallization in magmas by studying such crystals, since their compositions reflect the prevailing chemical conditions at the time of their formation.

In addition to the length of time a magma takes to cool, an equally important and obvious factor that determines what kind of minerals can form is the composition of the starting material. If a particular element is not present in a magma, no mineral containing that element can form when the magma eventually cools. Although some ancient, primordial magmas may well exist in the Earth's mantle or outer core, most magmas probably form by the melting of preexisting rocks. Such melting usually takes place either in the Earth's mantle, where there is sufficient heat, or in the crust above the mantle, where because of their compositions, the rocks have lower overall melting temperatures. For example, as basaltic oceanic crust and sediments are dragged down a subduction zone by tectonic motion, they are heated until they melt. Because the sediments are largely derived from the weathering of granitic rocks from the continental crust, they contain more silicon and aluminum than does the basalt. Thus when they melt, the sediments provide additional silicon and aluminum to the magma, producing magmas more granitic in composition than would the melting of oceanic crust alone. Japan's Mount Fuji probably formed in such a manner. It is composed of andesite, a volcanic rock intermediate in composition between basalt and granite.

The crystallization of magma involves transitions from the liquid to solid state. Relatively unordered atoms or groups of atoms in the liquid must become ordered into solid, crystalline structures as they lose heat energy. But which atoms or elements fit together as the magma cools, and what minerals

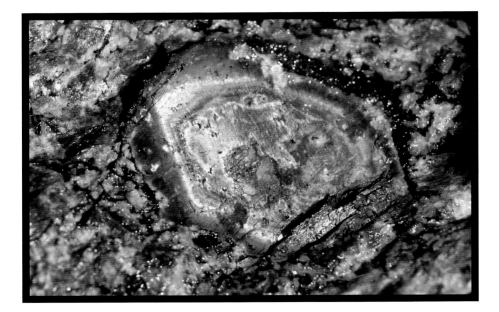

Labradorite (a plagioclase feldspar).
Nain, Labrador. 6 x 9 cm.
(Photograph by Michael Hamilton,
Geological Survey of Canada)

*Differentiation of magma caused
compositional zoning between calcium and
sodium in this crystal of labradorite.
Because visible light behaves differently as
it passes through the different zones, it
produces this spectrum of colors.*

do they form? One of the first scientists to investigate these questions was
Canadian geologist Norman Bowen, who as early as 1922 drew some fundamental conclusions about how minerals crystallize in a cooling magma, many
of which still hold. Like many other geologists, Bowen had observed that certain minerals (e.g., olivine, pyroxene, and plagioclase) often form distinct
layers of crystals in igneous rocks, but could not explain how and why this was
so. Bowen suspected that the removal of these minerals from the magma by
crystallization caused the chemical makeup of the remaining magma to
change, thus limiting the number of subsequent crystals that could form, but
he had no hard evidence, no proof. Since he obviously could not visit a magma
chamber many kilometers beneath the Earth's surface to see firsthand how
minerals crystallize, Bowen decided to do the next best thing: synthesize a
magma chamber in his laboratory, where he could control the composition of
the magma as well as its temperature and pressure.

Bowen combined the appropriate amounts of the various chemical constituents of a rock, placed them in a sealed container made from a nonreactive
material (such as platinum) that could withstand high temperatures, and melted the ingredients to make a "magma." By controlling the temperature, he
could quickly stop the melting, instantly "freezing" the magma into solid
"rock." He could then separate and analyze the resulting minerals, along with
their glasslike matrix, whose composition represented that of the residual, or
remaining "magma." By repeating the experiment at successively lower temperatures, Bowen was able to recreate the paths of crystallization for many
minerals.

Beginning with a "magma" of basaltic composition, Bowen noted that minerals with high melting points (such as pyroxene, olivine, spinel and ilmenite)
were the first to crystallize. He also observed that as calcium and magnesium
were removed from the magma by the crystallization of plagioclase feldspars

and olivine, the remaining liquid became progressively enriched in sodium, potassium, and iron. This observation was possible because such compositional trends are recorded in zoned crystals of these minerals, which grow outward from their centers, resembling rings of a tree [PLATE 10]. The cores of the plagioclase crystals contained more calcium than did their rims, which were enriched with sodium. Similarly, olivine and pyroxene crystals showed an outward decrease in magnesium relative to iron content. At lower temperatures minerals such as amphiboles, micas, potassium feldspar, and quartz crystallized.

In addition to quantitatively describing crystallization in a magma for the first time, the qualitative geological implications from Bowen's experiments were staggering. He had shown that many different igneous rocks could evolve from the same initial magma! For the first time geologists understood why basalts like the famous Palisades north of New York City showed accumulations of dense olivine crystals in their lower halves and lighter, calcium-rich plagioclase crystals in their upper portions, or why certain volcanos in Iceland first erupt basaltic lavas, followed by increasingly silicic lavas.

To really appreciate and understand what is going on as minerals crystallize from a magma, we need to look more closely at the atomic level. Because the two most abundant elements in the Earth's crust are silicon and oxygen, the most common kind of magma is a **silicate** magma, which solidifies to form silicate minerals. As the magma cools, silicon and oxygen atoms join together in the shape of a tetrahedron, with one oxygen atom (O) at each of its four corners and a single silicon atom (Si) in its center. Such SiO_4 **tetrahedra** are the building blocks of silicate minerals. In the liquid magma diverse metal atoms, such as potassium, iron, or magnesium, with various sizes and charges are surrounded by networks of SiO_4 tetrahedra, between which they must fit to form crystals. Not all of them make it.

Atoms with unusual sizes and charges do not fit easily into the structures of the minerals that are crystallizing. As various minerals form, rejected atoms are left behind in the residual part of the liquid magma, where they increase in relative concentration. Atoms of any minor chemical elements in the magma will either be incorporated or excluded from a mineral's structure based on how similar they are to the mineral's major constituent atoms [FIGURE C]. It's analogous to tricking a parking meter or vending machine into accepting a metal washer of similar proportions to a coin. The closer the two atoms are in size and charge, the greater the likelihood that one can substitute for the other. For example, the trace element nickel is incorporated early into olivine (magnesium iron silicate) because nickel "feels" like magnesium or iron to a growing olivine crystal. Similarly, elements such as barium and lithium are rejected by early-forming minerals but are incorporated into later-forming potassium-dominant feldspars or micas whose structures are better suited to accommodate them.

By the end of the crystallization sequence, the residual liquid no longer resembles the original magma at all. It is greatly enriched with water, fluorine,

ACCEPTED ATOMS

Silicon (Si^{4+})

Magnesium (Mg^{2+})

Iron (Fe^{2+})

Oxygen (O^{2-})

REJECTED ATOMS

Potassium (K^+)

Beryllium (Be^{2+})

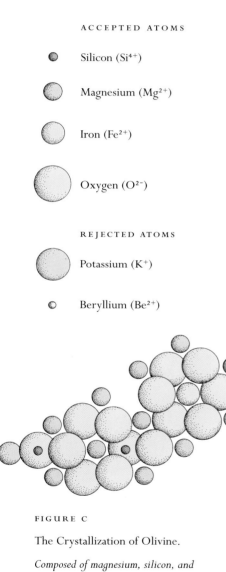

FIGURE C

The Crystallization of Olivine.

Composed of magnesium, silicon, and oxygen atoms, olivine is one of the first minerals to crystallize as a silicate magma cools. Often olivine also contains iron, since iron atoms are similar in size and charge to magnesium atoms. Other elements, such as potassium or beryllium, do not easily fit into the structure of olivine, and therefore remain in the magma to form different minerals later at lower temperatures.

Magmatic Processes.

Many things can happen to a magma when it intrudes a rock. Pieces of the intruded rock may break off and be assimilated by the magma. Volatile components may diffuse into or out of the magma. Other chemical components, soluble at higher temperatures, may even segregate and form a separate magma. All these processes change the composition of the magma and influence which minerals form.

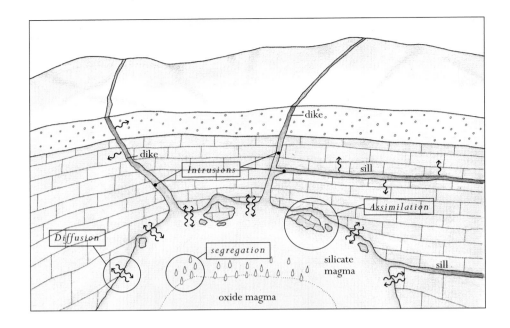

and other volatile components, along with other "incompatible" elements that were present in the original melt. Elements such as boron, beryllium, niobium, tantalum, zirconium, tin, tungsten, thorium, or uranium, whose atoms are of unusual size or charge, become concentrated. The residual melt is made up of these "rejects." A colleague describes the crystallization of minerals as "the law of constant rejection" (although I'm sure his students probably think he's referring to dating). The further crystallization of this leftover, water-rich magma full of the "rejects" may result in deposits of many strategically important metals, and when conditions are favorable, produces many of the large, perfect crystals of exotic mineral species pictured in this book.

The progressive change in the composition of a magma due to the removal of various constituents is known as **differentiation.** Hundreds of geologists since Bowen have continued to study differentiation by recreating magma chambers in their laboratories using sophisticated high-temperature and pressure-confining cells called bombs. Occasionally, one lives up to its name! Although many principles of differentiation have been eloquently refined since the days of Bowen, many questions remain unanswered. Reproducing in the laboratory the conditions thought to exist in a natural magma chamber is certainly very difficult, but maintaining them for geological time is impossible. Some "slow" reactions we will never be able to observe. Furthermore, in natural systems there are far too many variables to anticipate or to control in a simulated environment; too many things can go wrong. We seldom observe predicted differentiation going to completion because usually something happens to interrupt it. What might those interruptions be? Let's go back to the kitchen and see.

When I make a pot of vegetable-beef soup, I can deviate a great deal from the basic recipe in my cookbook and still end up with a vegetable-beef soup. I may even wish to convert my soup to stew by adding some flour or cornstarch, and I may have to adjust the heat, since each time I add new ingredients, I am really creating a new soup, with a new composition and new properties. Like

PLATE 11

Magnetite in Carbonatite.
Oka, Quebec. 4.5 x 6 cm.

This unusual texture is probably due to the segregation of two liquids that could not dissolve completely in one another during the cooling of a carbonate-rich magma.

Bowen, who controlled the composition and temperature of his laboratory "magmas," I can control the ingredients and temperature of my soup, but in the natural world, no one can be in control. When magma intrudes rock, pieces of the rock may break off and mix with it, adding new ingredients to the "soup." Known as **assimilation** [FIGURE D], this process can have profound physical and chemical effects on the magma. Not only are new chemical components added to the magma from the rocks assimilated, but other elements are removed from the magma because various minerals are forced to crystallize as heat is lost to the colder, assimilated rocks.

Diffusion of materials between a magma and the rock that surrounds it also may occur, changing the compositions of both. To understand this process, pretend you came into my house as I was cooking my soup. Chances are you could smell the onions, spices, and other volatile ingredients in the air and could deduce what my supper was going to be. Were it not for diffusion, the uniform spreading out of molecules from areas of higher concentration (the pot) to areas of lower concentration (the air in the house), this would not be possible. Diffusion may occur in either direction. When a rock is intruded by a magma, elements such as lithium or beryllium, which exist in higher concentrations in the magma than in the rocks surrounding it, may diffuse into the rock.

Even without assimilation or diffusion, as a magma differentiates, changes in its composition and temperature may result from the **segregation** of two or more immiscible fluids [see FIGURE D]. Like a bottle of well-shaken salad dressing—which eventually separates into oil, vinegar, and spices—oxide-, sulfide-, or carbonate-dominant magmas may segregate, or "unmix," from an originally silicate-dominant magma [PLATE 11]. Each of the segregated magmas may differentiate further and produce completely different minerals. Because of differences in density, heavy minerals such as chromite, ilmenite, platinum and various metal-sulfide species may settle out and concentrate to form deposits of mineable size ●

chapter six

Gems from the Deep

NOW that we have explored generally how minerals crystallize from molten rock, it's time to turn our attention to some specific minerals that formed that way, one of the most popular of which is diamond [PLATE 12]. (So far, only Superman has succeeded in making it from coal!) Traditionally, primary diamond occurrences have been limited to the relatively uncommon, though widely distributed, igneous rock, kimberlite (named for Kimberley, South Africa, where diamonds have been mined for over a century). More recently, diamonds have been discovered in another kind of igneous rock, lamproite, and they are currently being mined from at least one such deposit at Argyle, in Western Australia. Both kimberlite and lamproite are thought to have formed 150 to 200 kilometers beneath the Earth's surface, in the upper mantle, where the extremely high temperature and pressure required to produce diamonds exist. For years it was assumed that diamonds must somehow form in kimberlitic or lamproitic magmas. Recent studies, however, have produced overwhelming evidence to the contrary, proving that the diamonds did not form in either of these rock types! ◖ Although we cannot directly determine the age of diamonds themselves with present technology, we can date other minerals (e.g., garnet) that crystallize from the magma at the same time and are trapped as inclusions in the diamonds. Relatively new microchemical techniques capable of detecting minute quantities of certain radioactive isotopes that are sometimes present in garnets have shown that garnet inclusions in diamonds from Kimberley, South Africa (and by analogy, the diamonds themselves), are as much as 3.2 billion years older than the kimberlite in which they occur. No way could these diamonds have crystallized from the same magma as the

PLATE 12

Diamond crystal in Kimberlite.
Mir Pipe, Yakut, Russia. 6 x 8 mm.

Although embedded in kimberlite, this diamond crystal did not originally form in this rock.

kimberlite! An intrusion of kimberlite (or lamproite) simply provides a convenient shuttle service to transport the diamonds, which it incorporates as inclusions along the way, to the Earth's surface. Diamonds probably form in the mantle, as huge slabs of basaltic oceanic crust are carried down zones of subduction at continental margins in accordance with the model of plate tectonics. As the basalt slabs are forced beneath the continental crust, they are subjected to a tremendous change in temperature and pressure, which transforms them into a rock known as eclogite. The wide variation in carbon isotopes of diamonds from eclogites suggests that the carbon that constitutes them may be derived from carbonate-rich sediments and / or organic material dragged downward along with the oceanic crust. Maybe Superman is onto something after all!

Placer deposits are another well-known source of diamonds, although the diamonds clearly do not form in them. Placer mining employs water to separate gems or precious metals from gravels; perhaps the most familiar example is gold panning. Placer deposits result from weathering and erosion. (The diamond deposits around Diamantina, Minas Gerais, Brazil, near the Orange River in South Africa, and in the famous Golconda mines in Maharashtra, India, are all of this type.) At the Earth's surface, peridotites and kimberlites are broken down into soils by weathering. In the process, diamonds and other resistant minerals, such as pyrope garnet and chrominum-rich minerals, that may accompany them are freed. Because these minerals are relatively hard and similar in density to diamonds, they are transported with diamonds by erosion, and are useful as prospecting indicators. The diamonds that have been recovered from placer deposits are some of the world's finest, which according to Darwin's theory of natural selection we might predict, since only the fittest survive the harsh processes of weathering and erosion.

Many other gem minerals form by crystallization from magma. Like diamond, most have high melting points and relatively simple chemical compositions. A few of the more common gems that form this way are some rubies and sapphires, spinel, zircon, pyrope garnet, olivine (peridot), and chrome diopside [PLATE 13]. Also like diamonds, many of these minerals occur as distinct inclusions in volcanic rocks, and many have subsequently been concentrated or relocated in placer deposits by weathering and erosion ●

chapter seven

Carbonatites: Unusual Rocks with

Unusual Minerals

CARBONATITES, a group of unusual igneous rocks, often host rare minerals. No one knows exactly how carbonatites form, but most geologists believe they are derived from the mantle. As their name implies, carbonatites are composed chiefly of carbonate minerals, most commonly calcite. This composition sets carbonatites apart from all other igneous rocks, which are composed predominantly of silicate minerals. Another distinguishing feature of carbonatites is that they normally contain relatively high concentrations of strontium, niobium, thorium, and rare earth elements. These elements may combine to form such exotic species as pyrochlore [PLATE 14] and other minerals of interest to both scientists and collectors because of their unusual compositions and rarity. Many are also of economic importance. Niobium is used in manufacturing alloys with great strength and resistance to high temperatures, and both niobium and the rare earth elements are becoming increasingly important in the superconductor industry. Other more-common elements, such as iron, titanium, and phosphorus, have also been mined from carbonatites in the form of magnetite, rutile, and apatite. ❖ Minerals that form in carbonatite magmas share similar crystallization trends with those that form in other magmas. Species with high melting points, such as magnetite and rutile, form before those with lower ones, such as amphiboles or micas. Because carbonatite magmas also may differentiate, certain minerals crystallizing from them may show compositional changes with time, just as pyroxene and olivine do in basalts [see Chapter 5]. Although the actors may have changed, the story line has not. ❖ One of the most mineralogically interesting carbonatite occurrences I have ever visited was exposed by the Francon quarry on Montreal

PLATE 14

Pyrochlore crystals in Calcite.
Veshnovorgorsk, Chelyabinsk Oblast,
Russia. 5 x 6 cm.

*Pyrochlore forms in carbonatite magmas
rich in niobium, an element important to
our space-age technology.*

PLATE 15

Weloganite.
Francon quarry, Montreal, Quebec.
4.5-cm crystal.

*Named for W. E. Logan, founder of
Canada's Geological Survey and National
Museum, weloganite is known to exist in
only a few deposits formed by
differentiation of alkalic magmas.*

Island, Quebec. Unlike most carbonatites, those in the Francon quarry occur as **sills.** A sill is a flat, sheetlike intrusion of igneous rock that is parallel to the layers of the intruded rock. The Palisades sill north of New York City is a famous example. Because the carbonatites in the Francon quarry formed sills, when the magma intruded the enclosing rock (in this case a limestone), the magma was quickly chilled and solidified at its upper and lower contacts, effectively sealing it off from its surroundings. In the process, however, volatile components such as water, fluorine and carbon dioxide were sealed in with the magma, enabling differentiation to evolve an unusual, late-stage fluid, enriched in volatiles and rare elements, by the "law of constant rejection." Differentiation in most carbonatites never reaches such a late stage. Lighter than the surrounding magma, "bubbles" of this fluid segregated and rose toward the top of the sill, where they accumulated to form a layer of "pockets," or cavities. The pockets range in size from a few centimeters to nearly half a meter across, and almost all are lined with exotic, well-crystallized minerals, ten of which have been identified as species new to science. At present the quarry is being reclaimed as a landfill site, but the proliferation of specimens it provided in its twenty years of production will be admired and studied for generations.

Probably the most famous mineral found at the Francon quarry is the rare species weloganite [PLATE 15]. Not until we examine weloganite's composition, however, does it become apparent why it formed in this unusual carbonatite. Chemically, weloganite is a hydrated (i.e., it contains water) strontium-sodium-zirconium carbonate. In general, minerals containing water are stable only at relatively low temperatures (around 200°C or less), which are achieved only during the last stages of magmatic differentiation. Weloganite also contains strontium and zirconium, two elements whose atoms are of unusual size and charge and therefore do not fit easily into most crystal structures. Thus, these elements are relegated to forming what minerals they can — in this case, weloganite — at the latest possible time in the crystallization sequence ●

PLATE 16

Euclase.
Minas Novas, Minas Gerais, Brazil.
3 x 4 cm.

Because beryllium atoms are so small, they are rejected by early-formed minerals in granitic magmas and are left to form exotic minerals, such as this euclase, near the end of the differentiation process.

PLATE 17

Columbite and Albite.
Governador Valadares, Minas Gerais, Brazil. 1.5 x 2 cm crystal.

Like so many minerals found in granitic pegmatites, columbite contains an element of unusual size and charge: niobium. Columbite is found in only certain granitic pegmatites, but albite is common in most.

chapter eight

Granitic Pegmatites

PEGMATITES are very coarse-grained, intrusive igneous rocks that are more or less equivalent in gross composition to their parent rocks—somewhat like a tossed salad as compared to vegetable juice. For example, granite is an igneous rock composed largely of feldspar, quartz, and mica; so is **granitic pegmatite.** The main difference between these two rocks is the size of the individual crystals of feldspar, quartz, and mica that comprise them. In granite, the size of the grains (crystals) of these minerals averages 1 to 5 millimeters, but in granitic pegmatites, grains 1 to 5 centimeters in diameter are common, if not small. Granitic pegmatites, which are derived from a magma with the composition of granite, are by far the most common kind of pegmatite—so common that unless specified otherwise, the word "pegmatite" alone has come to imply "granitic pegmatite." Don't forget, though, that almost any kind of magma can produce a pegmatite. ❦ Many pegmatites form tabular, intrusive structures known as **dikes** [see FIGURE D]. Dikes and sills form in the same way: by intrusion of magma. The difference is in their structural relationship to the rock that they intrude. Dikes cut across the layers of rock they intrude; sills lie parallel to them. Not all pegmatites form dikes. Germany's famous Hagendorf South pegmatite, for example, is turnip-shaped. Some pegmatites form small, localized segregations within the host rock, which often contain a central open void, or crystal pocket. Known as **miarolitic cavities,** these pockets probably form by the separation and accumulation of volatile components in the magma during the last stages of crystallization. In general, miarolitic cavities occur in pegmatites that form at relatively shallow depths in the Earth's crust because the higher pressure associated with greater

PLATE 18

Red Beryl.
Wah Wah Mountains, Utah.
I X I.2 cm.

In spite of numerous occurrences of topaz rhyolites worldwide, crystals of red beryl have been found in only one or two such deposits in Utah, suggesting that the conditions for their formation are not easily duplicated.

PLATE 19

Spessartine in Rhyolite.
Ely, Nevada. I-cm crystals.

Spessartine is one of the most common species of garnet in both topaz rhyolites and granitic pegmatites, since both these rocks originate from magmas with similar compositions.

depths is not conducive to the segregation and accumulation of volatiles. This pressure inhibits the formation of miarolitic cavities in the same way that standing on bread dough would prevent it from rising.

Pockets similar to miarolitic cavities occur in pegmatite dikes when the water content of the magmatic fluid is too high to remain "dissolved" in the magma. The excess water separates out along with some of the rare elements, forming pockets—the source of many gem crystals and fine mineral specimens. Ironically, the very water that is necessary to create these pockets can also cause their destruction. At higher temperatures water exists as steam, and if its vapor pressure increases until it exceeds the confining pressure imposed by the surroundings, an explosion occurs, just as it would in a steam boiler tank. The resulting physical and thermal shock causes earlier-formed crystals in the pocket to shatter. That's why in most gem pockets the gem crystals are found detached from the walls or as shards of broken and healed crystals. If the gem pocket did not rupture, however, it would likely stew in its own juices and engulf its contents, since many of the earlier-formed gem crystals would not be stable under such chemical conditions and would dissolve. Like predator and prey, that which destroys also ensures survival.

In spite of voluminous research on pegmatites, geologists still are not sure why they come about and why their individual mineral grains develop such large crystals. In rare cases these crystals may attain lengths up to 15 meters, as demonstrated by spodumene crystals at the Etta pegmatite in the Black Hills of South Dakota, or the 10-meter-long crystal of beryl found in 1950 at the Bumpus quarry, near Bethel, Maine. Extremely slow cooling rates, optimum conditions for diffusion, and the presence of water and various fluxing agents (chemical components that promote crystal growth) have all been proposed as mechanisms to promote crystal growth. Probably all these factors play roles of varying importance depending on the situation.

Because they form late in the crystallization of a magma, pegmatites frequently contain minor concentrations of unusual minerals. By the time a granitic magma differentiates to the pegmatite stage, the residual melt is typically enriched with water, fluorine, and other volatile components, as well as uncommon elements such as boron, lithium, beryllium, niobium, tantalum, and others, provided they were present in the original magma. It is these elements that are responsible for such exotic minerals as euclase or columbite [PLATES 16 and 17], in addition to a number of gem minerals. Occasionally a magma that might form a granitic pegmatite beneath the Earth's surface finds its way above ground and erupts as the volcanic rock, rhyolite. One variety, topaz rhyolites, are very rich in fluorine, and in addition to topaz may host unusual minerals such as bixbyite, red beryl, and spessartine garnet [PLATES 18 and 19]. The occurrence of these minerals in structurally "late" features such as cavities and open spaces along fractures suggests that the fluorine, manganese, beryllium, and other elements required for their growth accumulated in a late-stage fluid that probably existed as a vapor when the

PLATE 20

Beryl.
Minas Gerais, Brazil (golden, 4 cm; aquamarine, 7 cm); Jos, Nigeria (emerald, 5 cm).

The colors in these three gem varieties of beryl are regulated by very minor amounts of impurity elements: iron in the case of aquamarine and golden beryl; chromium or vanadium in the case of emerald.

PLATE 22

Chrysoberyl.
Espírito Santo, Brazil. Gem, 10.77 ct; crystal, 2.5 x 4 cm.

This unusual star-shaped crystal is the result of twinning, a process in which two or more single crystals grow together in a symmetrical relationship.

PLATE 21 *(opposite)*

Elbaite.
Tourmaline Queen mine, Pala, California. 10-cm crystals.

The dramatic change in color in these crystals of elbaite, a lithium-rich tourmaline, is probably due to a change in the manganese and iron concentrations in the fluid in which it grew.

PLATE 23

Topaz.
Kleine Spitzkoppe, Namibia (crystal,
4 x 4 cm); Mason County, Texas
(gem, 48.35 ct).

*Topaz is one of many gem minerals mined
from granitic pegmatites throughout the
world.*

PLATE 24

Almandine.
Hedgehog Hill, Peru, Maine.
6 x 9 cm.

*Perhaps the most common species of garnet
in granitic rocks, almandine crystals such
as this one have been found in many of
New England's pegmatites.*

minerals crystallized from it because of the rapid decrease in pressure encountered at the Earth's surface.

Not all rhyolites or granitic pegmatites contain exotic minerals. Like granites, which consist largely of quartz, feldspars, and mica, some granitic pegmatites are mineralogically simple. The type of pegmatite that forms depends largely on two factors: the chemical makeup of the original magma and the depth at which it forms. In general, pegmatites that are derived from granites already enriched in boron, lithium, and rare elements and that form at medium to shallow depths in the Earth's crust show the most complex and diverse assemblages of minerals.

As a genetic group, no other type of deposit is known to host a more varied array of important gem minerals than do the granitic pegmatites. They are the primary source of aquamarine, tourmaline, chrysoberyl, and topaz, as well as significant producers of almandine and spessartine garnets, some emeralds, and a long list of less familiar gems [PLATES 20 to 24]. The range of colors, clarity, superior hardness, and relatively high refractive indices of these minerals make them ideal gemstones. Some are varieties of the same mineral species. For example, aquamarine, emerald, heliodore, and morganite are each a differently colored variety of the species beryl [see PLATE 20]. Similarly, kunzite and hiddenite are the lavender and green varieties of the species spodumene.

Individual gems or crystals of some of these minerals may show two or more zones of different colors. In the tourmaline species elbaite [see PLATE 21], one color variant occurs with sufficient regularity to have earned the name "watermelon" tourmaline because of its pink interior and green rim. The ability of certain elements to induce color in minerals has earned them the name **chromophores.** The color in all these gem minerals is caused by extremely *minor* amounts of contaminant chromophores such as iron, manganese, chromium, vanadium, or copper, but it is their *major* element constituents that define the species. The dramatic color zonation exhibited by multicolored and watermelon tourmaline reflects changes in the availability of chromophores to the growing crystal. Color zonation may be due to crystal structural preferences for specific chromophores or may indicate an abrupt change in fluid composition, as might occur during pocket rupture.

Granitic pegmatites have become so well known for their exotic and gem minerals that we too often forget that they also produce some of the world's finest examples of their primary constituents: feldspars, quartz, and micas. Were it not for the industrial demands for these more common minerals, most pegmatite deposits would never have been worked! Most granitic pegmatites host two different kinds of feldspars: the potassium-rich species, orthoclase or microcline [PLATE 25], and the sodium-rich species, albite [PLATE 26].

Every known color variety of quartz has been found in granitic pegmatites. One of the most common is smoky quartz [PLATE 27]. Granites in general, and their pegmatites in particular, contain above-average concentrations of the

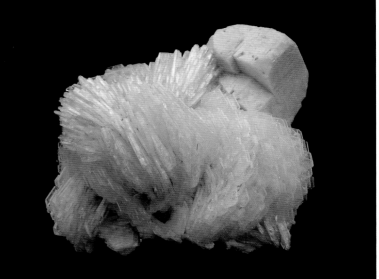

PLATE 25

Microcline, variety amazonite.
Pikes Peak, Colorado. 7 x 12 cm.

*The Pikes Peak area of Colorado is famous
for its crystals of amazonite, which form in
open voids in granite, known as miarolitic
cavities.*

PLATE 26

Albite (white) **and Microcline**
(beige).
Minas Gerais, Brazil. 15 x 18 cm.

*Together these two feldspars constitute
much of the volume of all granitic
pegmatites.*

PLATE 27 *(opposite)*

Smoky Quartz and Albite.
Middle Moat Mountain, North
Conway, New Hampshire. 4 x 4 cm.

*These crystals of smoky quartz and albite
were collected from a miarolitic cavity in
granite by the author, circa 1966.*

PLATE 28

Rose Quartz.

Minas Gerais, Brazil. 8 x 14 cm.

Unlike other varieties of quartz, rose quartz crystals such as these are found exclusively in granitic pegmatites.

PLATE 29

Muscovite.

Conselheiro Penã, Minas Gerais, Brazil. 7 x 13 cm.

Because of the abundance of potassium, aluminum, and silicon in granitic magmas, muscovite is one of the most common micas produced when the magma cools to form a granitic pegmatite.

PLATE 30 *(opposite)*

Molybdenite.

Malartic, Quebec. 1.5 x 2 cm.

Sulfide minerals such as this crystal of molybdenite are usually found in hydrothermal vein deposits rather than in pegmatites.

PLATE 3 1

Triphylite.
Smith mine, Newport, New
Hampshire. 2.5-cm crystal.

*Well-formed crystals of triphylite such as
this one are rarely preserved in granitic
pegmatites because they are chemically
attacked by late-stage, residual fluids near
the end of a pegmatite's crystallization
sequence.*

PLATE 3 2

Monazite.
Joaquim Felicio, Minas Gerais, Brazil.
2.5 x 3 cm.

*Monazite, a phosphate of cerium, often
contains uranium, thorium and other rare
elements typical of granitic pegmatites.*

radioactive elements uranium and thorium, as well as some radioactive potassium in their feldspars and micas. With time, the radiation emitted from these elements causes quartz that contains trace amounts of aluminum substituting for some of its silicon atoms to appear a dark, smoky color. Rose quartz [PLATE 28] is also common and sometimes extremely abundant in granitic pegmatites. After much investigation the prevailing theory is that its pink color is due to the presence of titanium or manganese substituting for silicon. Less commonly, citrine quartz and amethyst are found in some pegmatites.

Only three species of mica are common in granitic pegmatites: muscovite [PLATE 29], biotite, and to a lesser extent lepidolite, which is restricted to lithium-bearing pegmatites, and often accompanied by the lithium-rich tourmaline, elbaite. Biotite and muscovite are more widespread. Unlike muscovite, biotite seldom forms pocket-type crystals because in most pegmatites biotite crystallizes before the pocket-forming stage begins.

Many other minerals are found in individual granitic pegmatites. Some are common, others exceedingly rare. Occasionally unexpected minerals appear in granitic pegmatites. For example, excellent crystals of molybdenite occur in a pegmatite near Malartic, Quebec [PLATE 30], and well-formed silicic edenite crystals occur in the McLear pegmatite near DeKalb Junction, New York. The chemical constituents required to form such minerals can usually be traced to the source rocks of the magma or to assimilated rocks. Some pegmatites host significant quantities of phosphate minerals. The most common is fluorapatite, although some pegmatites contain large pods of lithium-, manganese-, or iron-rich phosphates such as amblygonite, lithiophilite, or triphylite [PLATE 31]. Less-common phosphates, such as xenotime or monazite [PLATE 32], may be locally abundant in pegmatites, as are simple oxide minerals such as rutile or cassiterite (tin oxide). Some pegmatites in Western Australia have even been commercially worked for tin ●

chapter nine

Agpaitic Pegmatites

NAMED for Agpat, a locality in southern Greenland, **agpaites** are feldspar-rich igneous rocks with unusually high concentrations of alkali metals, especially sodium, and low concentrations of aluminum and silica. Agpaites are often found near carbonatites. In addition to feldspars, the common rock-forming minerals in agpaites reflect their unusual chemistry and often include sodium-rich species such as nepheline and sodalite. Differentiation of agpaitic magma generally parallels that of other magmas, with pyroxenes crystallizing before amphiboles, which crystallize before micas. Because of the high alkali metal content of the magma, however, the specific minerals formed are different. The main pyroxene mineral is the sodium-rich species aegirine [PLATE 33], and the sodium-rich amphibole tends to be arfvedsonite. ❰ By the time an agpaitic magma differentiates to a pegmatite stage, it has usually become enriched with zirconium, as well as titanium, niobium, thorium, strontium, barium, beryllium, and rare earth elements because these elements do not fit easily into the structures of the early-formed minerals. Because of their unusual chemistry, agpaitic pegmatites host a long list of uncommon to exceedingly rare minerals, some of which (e.g., eudialyte) may be potentially useful as a source of zirconium. Other rare species in these rocks constitute a veritable treasure trove for scientists and collectors. Intrusive complexes of agpaitic rocks are known around the world, but the most famous are those in Russia's Kola Peninsula, in southern Greenland, in Norway, and at Mont Saint-Hilaire in Quebec. ❰ Conditions of formation for several species common in agpaitic pegmatites must be similar, for their mutual presence and relative orders of formation in the crystallization sequence appear similar even in widely

separated occurrences. For example, when collecting at the famous locality of Narssârssuk in southern Greenland, I was struck by similarities between many of the minerals I found there and those I had seen at Mont Saint-Hilaire, Quebec, which I had visited only a few weeks earlier. At both localities well-formed crystals of similar minerals occur in miarolitic cavities in a gray, nepheline-bearing rock. Frequently the rock coarsens and displays a pegmatitic texture around the cavities. Since crystallization in these cavities must proceed from the outside in, the earliest minerals form at the outer margins of the pockets and the last to crystallize fill the pocket interiors. The major constituents of the pegmatite band surrounding the pocket at both localities are typically potassium feldspar and aegirine, showing that these were the first minerals to crystallize.

Well-formed crystals of eudialyte are also among the early-formed minerals, and the main plagioclase feldspar at each locality is the sodium-dominant species albite, most of which crystallized after the potassium feldspar. I was surprised to find transparent, pale pink albite forming overgrowths on the potassium feldspar at Narssârssuk, since I had previously seen that association on only a few specimens from Mont Saint-Hilaire. These minerals were succeeded by a series of uncommon minerals, such as elpidite [PLATE 36], that are rich in zirconium and other elements whose atoms are of unusual sizes or charges. Among the last minerals to form in these pockets were natrolite, quartz, and various carbonate minerals, such as synchysite [PLATE 35] and calcite. Although my observation of these trends in crystallization at both Narssârssuk and Mont Saint-Hilaire is

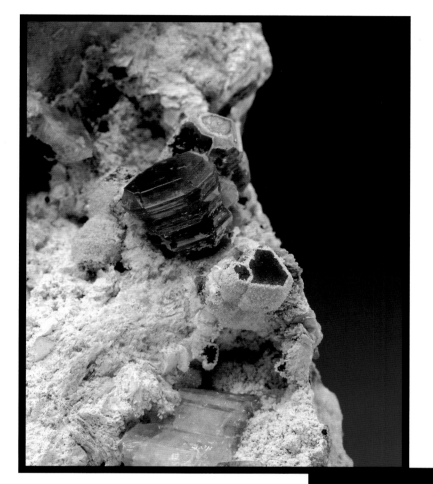

PLATE 35

Synchysite and Albite.
Narssârssuk, Greenland.
2.5 x 4.5 cm.

*Minerals like synchysite that contain
rare earth elements, carbonate, fluorine, or
other volatiles are among the last to
crystallize from a magmatic fluid. Albite
usually forms earlier.*

PLATE 36

Elpidite.
Mont Saint-Hilaire, Quebec.
10 x 14 cm.

*To date, the quarries at Mont Saint-
Hilaire have produced the world's finest
specimens of this rare sodium-zirconium-
silicate mineral.*

PLATE 34

Serandite (orange) **and Analcime**
(white).
Mont Saint-Hilaire, Quebec.
8 x 22 cm.

*Of all the rare minerals found at Mont
Saint-Hilaire, serandite is perhaps the
most renowned. Globally, analcime is a
much more common mineral, though few
localities have produced crystals as large
and sharp as those from Mont Saint-
Hilaire.*

purely empirical, their similarity leads me to speculate that such a crystallization sequence may be characteristic of agpaitic pegmatites.

Of all known occurrences of agpaitic pegmatites, no single one has produced as many mineral species (nearly 300 at the time of this writing, 28 of which are new to science) or as many large, well-crystallized specimens as Mont Saint-Hilaire, Quebec, has. No other locality has produced equally splendid rosettes of catapleiite crystals (up to 20 cm) or similarly fabulous crystals of orange serandite [PLATE 34]. Mont Saint-Hilaire is one of the world's most important mineral localities, but why? What unique set of circumstances brought about its mineralogical importance?

Commercial quarrying operations there have removed a large volume of rock, providing collecting opportunities for hundreds of people, and many keenly interested private collectors have brought their finds to the attention of professionals who could identify them properly. Nature has had significant input, too. Three episodes of magmatic intrusion are evident at Mont Saint-Hilaire. Partial assimilation of rock inclusions from earlier intrusions by later intrusions, as well as assimilation of overlying sedimentary rocks diversified the compositions of the magmas. Of key significance, however, is that before it was emplaced, the last intrusion of magma encountered and mixed with a brine, which explains both the enrichment of sodium, manganese, chlorine, and bromine in these rocks and the high volatile content, which was required to produce the explosively fractured rocks that characterize them. Of great importance, too, is that this final magma evolved to a pegmatite stage.

The formation of pegmatites was no doubt facilitated by the addition of volatiles from at least three sources: the original magma, the brine, and the overlying sediments. Finally, the pegmatite stage was able to express itself in more than one way at Mont Saint-Hilaire: as dikes, miarolitic cavities, and infillings in fractured rocks, depending on the quantity of fluids involved, the concentration of volatiles, and the confining pressure and mobility of fluids within the enclosing rock. All these factors combined to produce many small, unique pegmatites, each of which differentiated by the "law of constant rejection" to form the myriad exotic, rare minerals for which Mont Saint-Hilaire is famous ●

chapter ten

Summary of Crystallization
in Magmas

W E have examined one important process by which minerals are formed: the crystallization of magma, or molten rock. Most magmas are created when heat from the Earth's interior melts rocks in the upper mantle or crust. As a magma cools, crystallization organizes randomly arranged atoms or groups of atoms in the liquid magma into orderly, symmetric arrangements to form crystals of individual minerals. Those with the highest melting points are the first to form, followed by minerals with successively lower melting points. As different minerals crystallize, they remove specific chemical elements from the melt, changing its composition. The elements removed are those whose atoms are of a size and charge suited to fit the available spaces in the structures of the forming crystals. The continual compositional change in the magma through the selective removal of specific elements by crystallization is known as differentiation. ❰ Atoms of unusual size or charge do not fit into the forming crystals and thus accumulate in the liquid fraction of the melt along with water and other volatile components. The resulting late-stage magmas often produce the most interesting and diverse minerals. The specific minerals that form depend largely on two factors: the initial composition of the magma, and its cooling history. Contamination by assimilation or diffusion, as well as segregation of immiscible components, can alter a magma's chemistry, and too-rapid cooling can halt differentiation. Generally, rocks that host more-interesting and diverse minerals have cooled more slowly, taking more time to differentiate and growing larger crystals. Some of the largest crystals known are found in granitic pegmatites, where their growth probably was promoted by slow cooling, the fluxing action of boron or other elements, and favorable conditions for diffusion due to the presence of volatiles ●

PART III

Minerals
and
Water

chapter eleven

Dissolution and Precipitation

W ATER is perhaps the most important substance on the Earth. It is a unique compound that makes soil out of mountains, drives chemical reactions, and supports life as we know it. Without water, not only would no life exist on the Earth, but probably there would not be as many well-crystallized minerals. As we learned in Part I, minerals are nature's inorganic chemicals, and like chemicals stored in jars in a laboratory, most minerals require water to dissolve them and enable them to react with one another. For example, salt, the mineral halite [PLATE 37], is a compound composed of two elements, sodium and chlorine. In a crystal of halite, the atoms of these two elements exist as **ions.** Ions are atoms that have gained or lost one or more of their electrons and, as a result, have an electric charge. An ion with a positive charge (i.e., an atom that has lost electrons) is known as a **cation.** A negatively charged ion (i.e., an atom that has gained electrons) is called an **anion.** In halite sodium cations are bonded to chloride anions. ❦ Because of their unique shape, water molecules (H_2O) have opposite charges on the ends. Thus, the reason I can dissolve a spoonful of salt in a glass of water is that the water molecules pull the sodium and chloride ions apart. The sodium cations are attracted to the negatively charged oxygen ends of the water molecules, and the chloride anions to the positively charged hydrogen ends. This process of separating the sodium and chloride ions, thereby placing them into solution, is called **dissociation.** Because the solvent is water, the resulting solution may be described as **aqueous.** ❦ The degree to which a substance will dissolve in water — its **solubility** — depends on how strongly its constituent atoms are bonded together. If their own attractive force is greater than that of the

water molecules, dissociation does not take place and the substance does not dissolve. Temperature can also be a factor. From experience I know that I can dissolve more salt in warm water than in cold water, but no matter how hot the water, eventually no more salt will dissolve. When that point is reached, the solution is **saturated.** What happens if the water cools or evaporates? In evaporation, the agent that caused dissociation of the sodium and chloride ions and kept them apart, the water itself, leaves the solution. In the absence of water the ions are free to bond together again to form salt crystals, which **precipitate** from the solution.

Regardless of the compound involved, the underlying principle remains the same: at any given temperature there exists a critical level of concentration beyond which no more of that compound's constituent ions can be held in the amount of water available. If this concentration is exceeded, precipitation must occur. Whether the solution is in a glass on my kitchen counter, in a mud puddle in my driveway, or in a fault zone half a kilometer beneath the Earth's surface is irrelevant.

Probably the easiest way to make something precipitate from an aqueous solution is simply to remove the water. This is precisely what happens when **evaporite** minerals form in saline marshes, salt lakes, or seasonal lakes, called **playas.** Such lakes can be found by the hundreds in basins and prairies in semi-arid climates where the rate of evaporation is very high. Their sizes range from a few meters to several kilometers across, and the number of minerals that form in them from a few to several dozen. Utah's Great Salt Lake is a familiar example. Dissolved salts, derived from the chemical weathering of rocks, are carried by rivers and streams to the lakes, which have no outlets. There the salts accumulate until their concentrations exceed their limits of solubility and crystals of various minerals, such as halite, sylvite, gypsum, or borax, begin to precipitate. The least-soluble minerals are the first to precipitate, the most-soluble the last. Bodies of seawater that have been cut off from the ocean may also undergo evaporation, resulting in **marine evaporite** deposits.

In addition to halite, gypsum is one of the most common and economically important evaporite minerals [PLATE 38]. The sparkling pure white sand that forms the dunes at White Sands National Monument, New Mexico, is composed of tiny gypsum crystals that probably formed in Lake Lucero, a playa located a few kilometers to the west, and were carried by wind to their present resting place. Large flowerlike aggregates of gypsum crystals, appropriately called desert roses, also occur there and in other deserts, such as near the border between Tunisia and Algeria in the Sahara, or in parts of the Chihuahuan Desert in northern Mexico. Their interesting shapes make these specimens desirable as decorative curios for tourists, but to a geologist they have a very different significance: because they form by precipitation from an aqueous solution, their existence proves that the area was not as arid in the geological past. Borates, too, are commonly associated with evaporite deposits and include minerals such as borax and colemanite [PLATE 39], which are mined from large deposits in the Death Valley and Mojave Desert regions of southern California.

PLATE 38

Gypsum.
Swan Hill, Victoria, Australia.
9 x 15 cm.

The parallel, horizontal bands of crystals in this specimen probably represent several periods of crystallization due to changing water levels in a shallow, seasonal lake known as a playa. As the water evaporated, concentrations of dissolved calcium and sulfate ions increased until crystals of gypsum precipitated.

PLATE 39

Colemanite.
Boron, California. 3.5 x 7 cm.

The source of the boron required to make colemanite and other borates in many seasonal lakes (playas) is probably linked to volcanic activity and supplied by nearby hot springs that once flowed into the basins.

PLATE 40

Calcite.
Carter County, Montana. 8 x 10 cm.

The iciclelike form of these calcite stalactites is graphic evidence of formation by precipitation from dripping water.

PLATE 41 *(opposite)*

Opal.
Barcoo River area, Queensland, Australia. 4 x 5 cm.

The play of color in opal results from the diffraction of light by an orderly arrangement of similarly sized spheres of silica.

There are numerous other places where minerals form by dissolution and precipitation. The eerie, cool, dark silence of Carlsbad Caverns, a fairyland of magnificent cave formations, seems about as far removed from the clear, warm, sunlit pools of water at Yellowstone National Park's Mammoth Hot Springs as one can imagine. Yet the same geological process is occurring at each place: the dissolution and precipitation of calcium carbonate. Among the more alluring of geological wonders, limestone caverns are also the product of dissolution by and precipitation from aqueous solutions. As rainwater falls through the air, it dissolves minute amounts of carbon dioxide, producing a weak solution of carbonic acid. Less commonly, acidic water derived from other sources, such as a magma, also may be present. Following fractures and openings in the rock, the acidic water slowly dissolves calcium carbonate (calcite) from limestone, thereby widening its path as it goes. With sufficient time, large openings develop into an intricate system of underground caverns.

In open areas above the water table, contact with air causes some of the water to evaporate. When this happens, the dissolved carbon dioxide is lost from the solution, and calcium carbonate precipitates because it is not soluble in the purer water. When the calcium-charged water drips from an isolated point on the ceiling of the cave, the beautiful iciclelike formations we know as **stalactites** are born [PLATE 40]. Like annual rings of a tree, the concentric bands nearly always visible in cross sections of stalactites attest to their mechanism of growth [see PLATE 139]. At Mammoth Hot Springs the groundwater that forms the pools flows through a large area of limestone before emerging as springs at the Earth's surface. As it trickles over the precipice facing the valley below, the water evaporates, losing its dissolved CO_2 and causing calcium carbonate to precipitate in the form of an elegant terrace resembling a petrified, white waterfall.

Like calcite, quartz (or silica, SiO_2) is nearly insoluble in pure water at normal surface temperatures but becomes more soluble in warmer and more-alkaline solutions. Silica makes up much of the porous, white mineral matter that accumulates around geysers and hot springs and is the major constituent of most petrified wood, but perhaps the most intriguing and valuable form of silica is opal [PLATE 41]. Chemically, opal is $SiO_2 \cdot nH_2O$, where n denotes a variable amount of water that can range up to about 20 percent by weight. The most important deposits of precious opal, such as those in Australia, form when silica is dissolved from SiO_2-rich sediments by groundwater as a result of chemical weathering. The groundwater trickles downward until it reaches an impermeable layer, where it accumulates in cracks and cavities. In dry seasons the supply of water is cut off, and the silica separates as submicroscopic spheres that accrue in a gel-like suspension. As long as the rate of evaporation is fairly constant, all the silica spheres reach about the same size. As they pile up into layers, the spheres form an orderly array, as would equal-sized glass marbles if dropped into a bathtub of water. A small amount of water is usually trapped in the spaces between the spheres, but as evaporation continues, the whole mass eventually solidifies to form opal.

PLATE 42

Barite.
Frizington, Cumbria, England.
7 x 16 cm.

Barite, together with calcite, aragonite, and other minerals, is often found in the iron deposits in western Cumbria, England, since all these minerals form by the same process as the iron deposits: precipitation from aqueous solutions.

PLATE 43

Manganese Oxide dendrites on Limestone.
Solnhofen, Bavaria, Germany.
12 x 14 cm.

Like a miniature river delta, groundwater containing dissolved manganese randomly spread along a flat, planar surface in this limestone, leaving behind a trail of manganese oxide when it dried up.

PLATE 44

Rhodochrosite.
Hotazel, Cape Province, South
Africa. 2 x 2.5 cm.

The introduction of carbon dioxide to
water containing dissolved manganese
was probably responsible for the formation
of these crystals of rhodochrosite on
manganese-oxide ore.

PLATE 45

Wavellite.

Avant, Arkansas. 4 x 6 cm.

Wavellite is a phosphate mineral that can form when water containing dissolved phosphorus encounters aluminum-bearing minerals in a rock.

PLATE 46

Variscite.

Fairfield, Utah. 12 x 15 cm.

The yellowish parts of this specimen of variscite are made of crandallite, wardite, and other phosphate minerals that formed as solutions penetrated cracks in the variscite, liberating some of its phosphorus and replacing it in the process.

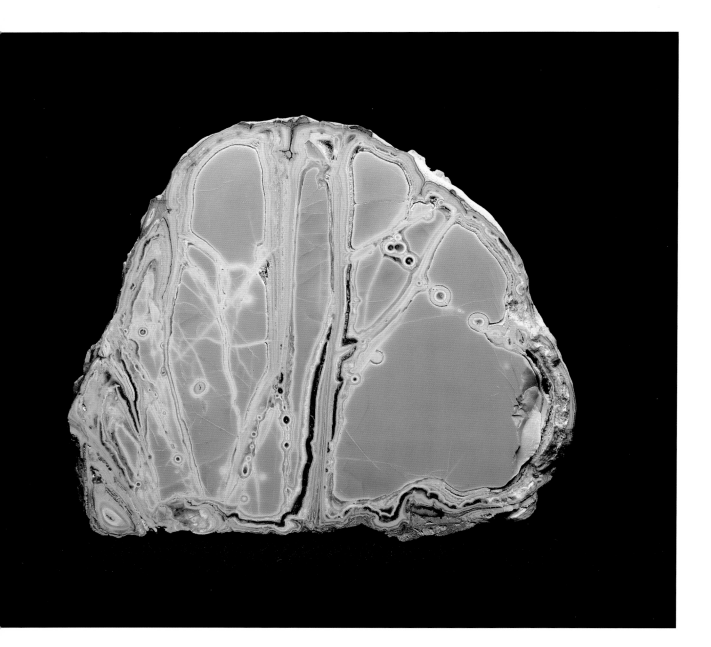

In the mineral world examples of dissolution and precipitation of the same compound are relatively uncommon, since most natural aqueous solutions contain other dissolved elements that interfere and cause the formation of additional minerals. One of the most common of these elements is iron, which may combine with other elements to form minerals such as hematite (Fe_2O_3), goethite [α-$FeO(OH)$], siderite ($FeCO_3$), or pyrite or marcasite (both FeS_2) when it precipitates. Which mineral forms depends largely on how acidic or basic the solution is and on the availability of dissolved oxygen, sulfur, and carbon dioxide, which determines whether oxides, sulfides, or carbonates can form. Stalactitic and **botryoidal** (resembling a bunch of grapes) growths of goethite [see PLATE 9] and hematite commonly fill voids in sedimentary iron deposits and are indicative of precipitation from solution.

Other minerals, such as calcite, aragonite, and barite [plate 42], often occur with the iron minerals in these deposits, as do a variety of manganese oxide minerals (e.g., pyrolusite and manganite), which normally precipitate after the iron minerals because they are more soluble and remain in solution longer. Occasionally the beautiful red manganese carbonate mineral rhodochrosite is encountered [PLATE 44]. Other manganese oxide minerals, such as romanechite or hollandite, commonly precipitate on fracture surfaces in rocks to form fernlike growths known as **dendrites** [PLATE 43]. Groundwater circulating through phosphorus-rich rocks may dissolve some of the phosphate from them and deposit it elsewhere in the form of various phosphate minerals, depending on what other kinds of rocks or minerals the groundwater encounters. Reaction with clays or aluminum-containing rocks brings about the precipitation of aluminum-bearing phosphates, such as wavellite or variscite [PLATES 45 and 46]. Reaction with iron-rich rocks forms iron phosphates, such as rockbridgeite, strengite, or vivianite [PLATES 47 and 67]. The presence or absence of any of these minerals at a given locality depends on whether their constituent ions were present in sufficient quantity to exceed their limits of solubility ●

chapter twelve

Hydrothermal Solutions

IN nature's laboratory, aqueous solutions may vary from a few drops to an ocean in volume, from near freezing to several hundred degrees in temperature, and may be at the Earth's surface or several kilometers beneath it. Similarly, the compositions of these solutions may range from nearly pure water, to water saturated with many dissolved materials. Geologists broadly categorize these solutions as either **hydrothermal** or **meteoric,** based on their temperature and mode of occurrence. Generally, meteoric water is derived from the atmosphere, such as rainwater, and makes up most of the water we see on the Earth's surface or a short distance beneath it, such as the groundwater in a well or sinkhole. Meteoric water is the type responsible for the minerals we have discussed up to now. Hydrothermal water, as its name implies, is much hotter. Its evolution is more complex than that of meteoric water [FIGURE E], and it is usually hidden well beneath the surface of the Earth. ⁌ Sometimes meteoric and hydrothermal water are difficult to distinguish because one may mix with or contribute to the other. Certainly the water in some hydrothermal solutions originally was meteoric. Hot springs and geysers are familiar examples. These geological wonders typically occur in areas of recent volcanism, where a source of magma lies relatively close to the Earth's surface. As groundwater seeps downward through channels and cracks in the rock in these areas, it comes closer to the magma and is warmed by it. Even without a near-surface body of magma, as we descend into the Earth's crust beyond the first 1 to 2 kilometers the temperature increases. Therefore, any meteoric water that sinks into the crust or is buried along with sediments accumulating in a geological basin, inevitably will be warmed. The temperature it must reach to be considered hydrothermal water is a matter of opinion.

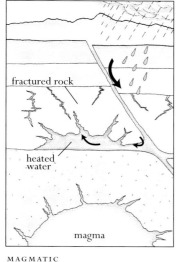

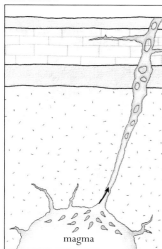

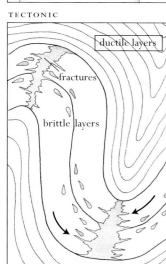

FIGURE E

Sources of Hydrothermal Solutions.

There is no single, universal source for hydrothermal solutions. Some are simply hot meteoric water. Others may evolve from magma or be driven from the rocks by heat and pressure during burial or tectonic events.

Hydrothermal solutions also may be generated by magmatic or tectonic processes [see FIGURE E], and the vein-type deposits they produce historically have supplied a significant percentage of the world's gold, silver, copper, and other metals. The idea that mineral deposits might form by deposition from hot, watery solutions is not new. As early as 1546 the "father of mineralogy," Georgius Agricola, proposed that veins of ore minerals form by rainwater circulating deep into the Earth's crust and depositing dissolved minerals in open channels. A century later the French philosopher René Descartes postulated that these mineralizing solutions originate from molten rock deep in the interior of the Earth. Who was correct? They both were. In Part II we saw how differentiation concentrates certain metals and volatile components, such as water, in the leftover, residual magmatic fluids. These hot, aqueous fluids are one type of hydrothermal solution, and the metal vein-type deposits they form are found in and around large bodies of granitic rocks throughout the world. We also find similar metal-bearing hydrothermal vein deposits in folded mountain belts and other zones of high tectonic activity, such as along plate boundaries, where there are no apparent magmatic or meteoric sources available. In these cases the tectonic activity itself provides the heat and pressure required to "squeeze" out and force the water through the rocks.

Mineralization by precipitation from aqueous solutions, whether hydro-thermal or meteoric, follows a common pattern. Water travels through open spaces or permeable sections of the Earth's crust, such as along faults or through porous rocks, dissolving soluble minerals as it goes. If the water is hot, it dissolves even more minerals. As we will see in Part IV, the solution may chemically alter the rocks through which it passes and itself be changed in composition by these reactions. Whenever one of the components dissolved in the solution exceeds its solubility limit, it precipitates. Any number of factors, such as evaporation of the water, falling temperature or pressure, reaction with the wall rock, or mixing with other solutions, can cause the solubility limits of one or more dissolved components to be exceeded.

This process is the general way that minerals crystallize from aqueous solutions. Remember, though, that the specific chemical reactions involved in mineral dissolution, transport, and deposition are governed by complex physical and chemical mechanisms, many of which are still poorly understood. Not the least of these is the process of crystal growth itself. Because they typically grow unimpeded in open spaces, crystals precipitated from aqueous solutions are frequently very well formed and are among the most spectacular examples of the mineral world●

chapter thirteen

Warming the Rain

AT the Earth's surface weathering and erosion are constantly at work, wearing down mountains into soil. Running water, probably the single most important agent of erosion, carries the soil from the mountains to the plains or sea, where it accumulates as sediment. It is not surprising, then, that sediments commonly contain up to 20 percent water trapped in pore spaces. On the continents sediments tend to collect in broad, low areas known as **basins.** The basins themselves often contain marine sediments, indicating their former existence as seafloors that were uplifted by tectonic movements as the continents evolved. As sediments accumulate in basins, they are compacted under their own weight and warmed by the Earth's heat as they are buried deeply under more sediments or occasional lava flows. Such burial may result in temperatures as high as 250 to 300°C, causing organic materials and hydrated minerals like gypsum or clays to give up more water. Of course, additional water may always flow into the basin from above or from along its margins following porous layers. As the water is warmed by burial, its ability to dissolve the minerals it contacts increases. Evaporite minerals, such as halite and gypsum, are common in sediments and are a source of soluble chlorides and sulfates, which form a **brine** when they dissolve. The addition of these ions to the solution greatly increases its capacity to dissolve metals such as copper, lead, and zinc by forming complex ions that are more stable (i.e., less likely to precipitate) at lower temperatures. ◖ Driven by differences in pressure, temperature, and elevation, solutions may travel great distances through basins, following porous sediments or the open spaces of fractured rocks. Carbonate rocks, such as limestones or dolostones (limestones in which calcite is replaced by

PLATE 49

**Galena on Dolomite and
Sphalerite.**
Joplin, Missouri. 2-cm crystal.

*The repeated association of these minerals
in MVT deposits around the world suggests
that their origins are closely linked.*

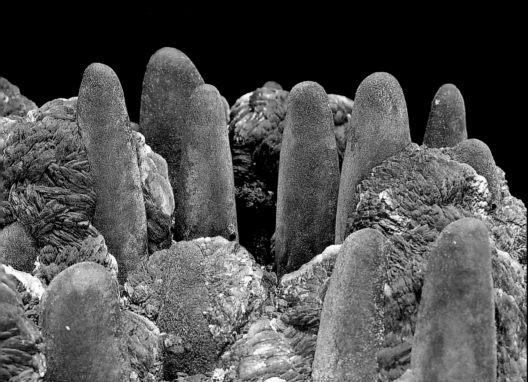

PLATE 50

Marcasite.
Shullsburg, Wisconsin. 15 x 20 cm.

*The presence of stalactites of marcasite and
other minerals in MVT deposits underscores
the importance of precipitation from
aqueous solutions in their formation, since
stalactites require dripping water to form.*

PLATE 51

Fluorite and Sphalerite.
Denton mine, Hardin County, Illinois.
12 x 19 cm.

*The occurrence of sphalerite and fluorite
together on a limestone matrix is an
association typical of specimens from MVT
deposits.*

dolomite), are especially susceptible to invasion by these solutions because they are highly soluble and are porous. As the solutions enter open spaces, they are cooled by a reduction in pressure. They also may react with the rocks or other solutions that they contact or be cooled by upward transport. Any one of these events can cause dissolved minerals to precipitate as their saturation limits are exceeded. Perhaps the most famous hydrothermal deposits formed in this manner are called **Mississippi Valley Type (MVT)** deposits, named for the region of the central United States where they have been studied in detail. Some of the world's finest examples of galena, sphalerite, calcite, marcasite, and fluorite have come from these deposits [PLATES 48 to 51].

Some of my most memorable mineral collecting was in the Mid Continent mine near Treece, Kansas, which exploited one of many MVT deposits in the tristate district of Missouri, Kansas, and Oklahoma. Stepping into the infamous "iron maiden," as the local mine operators had christened the oversize tin can being used as an elevator, I was lowered 100 meters below the Earth's surface into an entirely different world. As I walked through the underground maze of tunnels, the light from my lamp was reflected by numerous small fracture fillings of galena and sphalerite, the two main ore minerals at the mine, and here and there a natural black asphalt oozed from cracks in the dolostone. Eventually I came to an area where the rock was much more fractured; in fact, all that held it together were well-formed crystals of sphalerite and calcite. Farther along I encountered even larger openings, some extending nearly 15 meters, completely lined top and bottom with golden-yellow calcite crystals up to 30 centimeters long. Elsewhere I found galena crystals as much as 15 centimeters across and a 2-meter wide fracture zone entirely filled with slabs of rock covered with pink dolomite crystals. Perched upon the dolomite were small, brassy-yellow crystals of chalcopyrite and larger individual crystals of sphalerite, galena, and calcite. It was a mineral collector's dream!

A mineral collector's dream, however, can be a geochemist's nightmare! Explaining the origin of MVT deposits is difficult. Since the two predominant sulfide minerals in MVT deposits, galena (PbS) and sphalerite (ZnS), are nearly insoluble in water, how can they travel in solution to their site of deposition? If lead or zinc ions encounter sulfide ions, as they must to form galena or sphalerite, precipitation is nearly instantaneous. These properties of galena and sphalerite imply that crystals as large as those I found at the Mid Continent mine should never have formed, since rapid precipitation nearly always produces very small crystals. How then do such large crystals of galena and sphalerite form in an MVT deposit? This is the question that plagues the geochemist.

There is no single, simple answer. What is needed for these large crystals to form is a mechanism that slowly introduces sulfide ions to the solution at the site of metal precipitation. Analyses show that most subsurface brines contain very low amounts of sulfur, which is nearly always in the form of sulfate (SO_4^{2-}) rather than sulfide (S^{2-}) ions. From experimental studies we know that

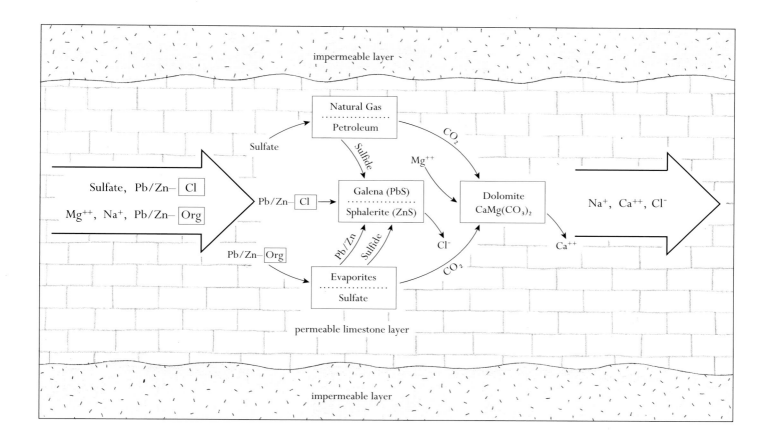

Figure F diagram labels:

impermeable layer

Natural Gas
Petroleum

CO₂

Sulfate

Mg⁺⁺

Sulfide

Sulfate, Pb/Zn— Cl

Mg⁺⁺, Na⁺, Pb/Zn— Org

Pb/Zn— Cl

Galena (PbS)
Sphalerite (ZnS)

Dolomite
CaMg(CO₃)₂

Na⁺, Ca⁺⁺, Cl⁻

Cl⁻

Ca⁺⁺

Pb/Zn— Org

Pb/Zn

Sulfide

CO₂

Evaporites
Sulfate

permeable limestone layer

impermeable layer

FIGURE F

Mineralization in MVT Deposits.

Because the lead and zinc sulfides galena and sphalerite are nearly insoluble in water, these metals probably travel in solution as complex ions with chlorides or organic molecules. Reactions between organic molecules and sulfate minerals may provide the sulfide necessary to form the galena and sphalerite, to liberate chlorides, and to cause dolomite to precipitate. Fluid inclusions in minerals from MVT deposits commonly contain chlorides, sulfates, and organic molecules, and dolomite is nearly always present in the rocks.

PLATE 52

Barite on Calcite.
Pennington County, South Dakota.
5-cm crystal.

The occurrence of this barite crystal in a type of geode called a septarium suggests that it was formed by precipitation from groundwater percolating through sediments.

both lead and zinc travel in brine solutions as chlorides and may do so with certain organic compounds as well. We also know that certain organic compounds can convert sulfate to sulfide and that when sulfate is removed from solutions containing dissolved calcium, magnesium, and carbonate ions, dolomite [CaMg(CO₃)₂] readily precipitates.

Interestingly, fluid inclusions in minerals from MVT deposits typically contain abundant chlorides as well as organic compounds. Was all the asphalt and pink dolomite I saw in the Mid Continent mine there just by chance, or does each play a definite role in the creation of an MVT deposit? Do lead and zinc travel as chlorides along with dissolved calcium, magnesium, carbonate, and sulfate ions until the solution encounters organic compounds that convert sulfate to sulfide, causing the precipitation of dolomite, sphalerite, and galena? Or is sulfide added to the solution by thermal decomposition of petroleum, bacterial reduction of sulfates, or another mechanism? All are possible, and all have been suggested as probable mechanisms for the development of MVT deposits [FIGURE F].

There are many other examples of hydrothermal mineralization by solutions derived from sediments. In the midwestern United States, such mineralization in beds of limestone has led to the formation of hollow, crystal-lined nodules called **geodes.** The area around Keokuk, Iowa, is particularly well known for the number of fine specimens it has produced. Resembling a cantaloupe on the outside, when broken open the geodes are found to be lined with inwardly projecting crystals of quartz, calcite, barite [PLATE 52], celestine, or other minerals. Similar hollow structures, called **septaria,**

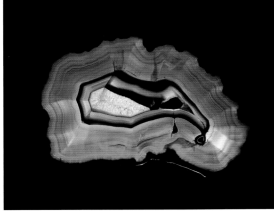

PLATE 53

Mordenite on Cristobalite in Basalt.

Poona, Maharashtra, India.
6 x 10 cm.

Once thought to have originated from basaltic magmas, mordenite and most other zeolite minerals found in basaltic lava flows are now believed to have crystallized from meteoric solutions.

PLATE 54

Stilbite.

Poona, Maharashtra, India. 5 x 7 cm.

Stilbite, here in the form of a bow tie, is one of the most common zeolite minerals in basaltic lava flows.

PLATE 55

Agate.

Rio Grande do Sul, Brazil.
14 x 23 cm.

The variously colored bands in this agate are due to impurities such as iron and manganese oxides.

PLATE 56

Amethyst.

Artigas, Uruguay. 6 x 10.5 cm.

The stalactitic form of this amethyst specimen suggests that it formed in a cavity by precipitation from an aqueous solution.

PLATE 57

Native Copper.
Keweenaw Peninsula, Michigan.
10 cm.

*Like zeolites and agates, the occurrence of
native copper crystals such as these in
basaltic lava flows for years led geologists
to believe they precipitated from magmatic
rather than meteoric solutions.*

often contain similar minerals. How and why geodes form is not completely
understood. They tend to form around fossils, which probably provide the
initial opening for mineral-bearing solutions to enter. As the organic remains
in the fossil decompose, microchemical environments with characteristics
different from those of the enclosing sediment may be established, causing
various minerals to precipitate.

Sometimes things are not as they seem. Because of the widespread occurrence of zeolites, agates, amethyst, and native copper in basaltic lava flows
[PLATES 6 and 53 to 57], formed by the crystallization of magma, one might
conclude that these minerals also form by magmatic rather than hydrothermal
processes, especially any involving meteoric water. But this is not the case.
As molten rock spreads across the Earth's surface during a volcanic eruption,
two obvious things happen: first, the lava warms the area beneath it, and second, in doing so the molten rock is cooled along its lower contact, like hot
fudge poured onto a cold table. If the lava encounters water (rain, snow, a
lake, or ocean), it will cool even faster and form a glass, since there is not
enough time for crystallization to occur. Rising bubbles of gas often become
"frozen" in place, forming layers of cavities as the lava cools, and continued
flow can fracture already solidified portions. If a larger body of water is
encountered, bulbous **pillow** structures (named for their shape) may develop.

Gas bubbles, pillows, and areas of fractured rock all provide open spaces
through which water can flow. As the lava cools, water preferentially reacts

Hydrothermal Mineralization
in Lava Flows.

*Minerals such as zeolites, amethyst, agate,
and native copper that are common in
basaltic lava flows form by precipitation
from aqueous solutions that permeate open
spaces such as fractures or gas bubble
cavities in the basaltic lava.*

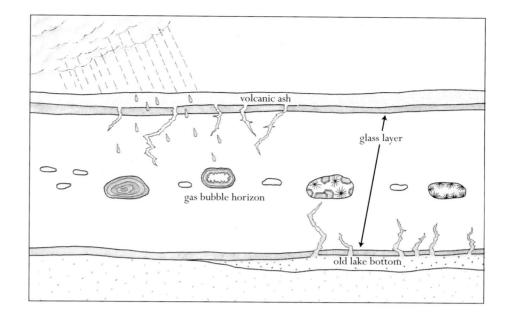

with the glass faster than with the rock (since the atoms in the glass are not
bonded together tightly in crystal structures) and leaches iron, magnesium,
aluminum, silicon, calcium, potassium, and sodium ions from it. Similar reactions occur when water filters through volcanic ash. After the entire body has
cooled sufficiently, various minerals begin to crystallize from the hydrothermal solution that has filled the open spaces [FIGURE G]. Often much of the
iron and magnesium is removed as a thin layer of blue-green clay precipitates.
If the solution is unusually high in dissolved silica, minerals such as amethyst,
jasper, bloodstone, or agate may fill the opening. When the temperature cools
to about 200°C, zeolite minerals will begin to crystallize as their levels of
saturation are exceeded.

Zeolites are a group of about fifty minerals, the more common of which
include analcime, chabazite, heulandite, natrolite, mesolite, mordenite, and
stilbite [see PLATES 6, 53, and 54]. Most zeolites are aluminosilicates of calcium, sodium, or potassium, as are the minerals prehnite, datolite, pectolite,
and apophyllite [PLATE 6], which frequently accompany them. Since water is
an integral part of their structure, zeolites are stable only at relatively low
temperatures. That's why they generally form at temperatures below 200°C.
Many zeolites can exchange cations (atoms that have lost electrons) with surrounding solutions because they have large "holes" in their crystal structures.
This feature has led to their commercial application as molecular sieves in
devices ranging from water softeners to medical dialysis units●

chapter fourteen

Beyond Pegmatites

IN Part II we learned that as a magma cools, minerals crystallize from the melt, changing the composition of the remaining liquid by removing specific elements from it, and that near the end of the differentiation period, fluids capable of generating pegmatites with exotic minerals may form. Sometimes, however, pegmatites are not formed, or if they are, the differentiation process may continue beyond the pegmatite stage. The last remaining liquids become enriched in water and volatile components such as fluorine, chlorine, and sulfur, along with metals such as tin, tungsten, gold, silver, uranium, and other elements that could not be incorporated into the structures of the earlier-formed minerals because of their unusual sizes or ionic charges. Such remaining liquids represent one more source of hydrothermal solutions and are the type most frequently cited as "classic" examples of hydrothermal solutions. ❏ These solutions emanate from the magma and travel away from it, following permeable rocks or openings along faults and fracture systems and forming hydrothermal vein deposits. Accompanying steam may develop sufficient pressure locally to blast its way through to an area of lower pressure, creating a **breccia pipe** (breccia is a rock composed of sharp, angular fragments cemented together). The resulting rapid decrease in pressure causes the solution to cool, which in turn may cause various minerals to precipitate. Breccias also may be created by grinding and fracturing of rocks due to movements along faults in the Earth's crust or by collapse when supporting rock is dissolved away. The open spaces between the blocks of broken rock in breccias provide an ideal environment for solutions to migrate and crystals to form. The chrysocolla specimen in PLATE 79 graphically illustrates this process.

PLATE 60

Tetrahedrite (black) **with Bornite**
(purplish), **Chalcopyrite** (golden),
and Quartz (white).
Herodsfoot mine, Liskeard,
Cornwall, England. 5 x 6 cm.

Except for quartz, all these minerals
are important ores of copper and are
commonly mined from vein deposits formed
by precipitation from hot, metal-bearing,
aqueous solutions.

PLATE 61

Nickel-Skutterudite.
Schneeberg, Saxony, Germany.
3 x 4 cm.

As hot, metal-bearing solutions that
emanate from magmas migrate farther
from their sources, silver and nickel cobalt
arsenide minerals such as this one may
precipitate.

PLATE 62

Rhodochrosite (pink) **and Fluorite** (green).
Silverton, Colorado. 3 x 4 cm.

Studying the distribution of certain isotopes of oxygen, hydrogen, and other elements reveals that meteoric as well as magmatic solutions may have played a role in the formation of these and other minerals in the mines of the San Juan Mountains, Colorado.

The most obvious proof that solutions forming a hydrothermal mineral deposit evolved from a magma is a direct association of the deposit with igneous rocks. Often such an association is clear, but if the solutions had to travel some distance from their parental magmas, the connection is less apparent. A clue to the heritage of such deposits may be gleaned from the minerals they contain. Because they evolve by differentiation, the minerals in such deposits are those last formed by that process, such as quartz, as well as minerals containing the elements that were the "leftovers" isolated by the "law of constant rejection." As the solutions move farther from their sources and begin to lose heat to their surroundings, minerals are formed as dissolved components reach their respective levels of saturation and precipitate. Solutions derived from granitic magmas frequently precipitate fluorine-bearing species such as fluorite, topaz, and fluorapatite [PLATE 58]; oxides of uranium, tungsten, and tin [PLATE 59]; sulfides of iron, copper, lead, zinc, silver, antimony, arsenic, and other metals [PLATES 60, 61, and 64]; and even some native metals, such as gold, silver, copper, arsenic, and bismuth [see PLATES 63 and 74].

Similar patterns of hydrothermal mineralization occur in widely separated locations. Mines in the counties of Devon and Cornwall in southwestern England have been exploited for tin since the Bronze Age. There the major ore of tin is cassiterite [see PLATE 59], which occurs in veins in granite, along with a wealth of other metallic minerals: major ores of tungsten, such as wolframite and scheelite; copper-bearing sulfide minerals, such as chalcopyrite, chalcocite, bournonite, bornite, and tetrahedrite [see PLATE 60]; the lead and zinc sulfides galena and sphalerite; and dozens of others.

PLATE 64

Stibnite.
Baia Sprie, Transylvania, Romania.
6 x 9 cm.

Antimony minerals such as stibnite usually precipitate from hydrothermal solutions at relatively low temperatures, which helps explain their occurrence in veins distant from their parental magmas.

PLATE 65

Pyrite and Quartz.
Butte, Montana. 2.5 x 4 cm.

The simple iron sulfide pyrite is perhaps the most common metallic mineral in hydrothermal vein deposits, proving that not all such deposits contain valuable metals.

PLATE 63

Gold.
Botes, Transylvania, Romania.
6 x 6 cm.

Many gold-bearing quartz veins such as those in Transylvania are believed to form from hot, aqueous solutions derived from magmas.

An equally important and historic mining center is in the Erzgebirge highlands near the border of Germany and the Czech Republic, where tin, copper, silver, and other economically important metals have been mined since 1168. These deposits also consist of veins in or emanating from granitic rocks. As in England, in the Erzgebirge highlands species such as cassiterite, wolframite, scheelite, apatite, and topaz occur in the earlier-formed tin- and tungsten-rich veins, whereas sphalerite, chalcopyrite, and galena, along with a number of silver-, nickel-, uranium-, cobalt-, and arsenic-bearing minerals [see PLATE 61] are found in later-formed veins, at greater distances from their source.

Similar mineralogical trends are visible in the tungsten mines of Panasqueira, Portugal, among other places. In each of these regions, the granites intruded tectonically active zones along folded mountain chains or plate boundaries. High-temperature minerals like wolframite and cassiterite precipitate from the solution before minerals such as the sulfides, whose elements remain in solution by forming complex ions that are stable at lower temperatures. Acting like a time-released drug, this process is what gives rise to the elemental zoning observed in these deposits.

Other genetically similar deposits are found in volcanic and tectonically active zones throughout the world. Some, such as those in the San Juan Mountains of Colorado or in Transylvania, Romania, have also been significant producers of gold, silver, and other minerals [PLATES 62 to 64]. One such group, known as **porphyry copper** deposits because they occur in or adjacent to quartz-monzonite porphyries or related granitelike rocks, can be found all along the Pacific Rim, from the Canadian Cordillera, through the Rockies, into Arizona and New Mexico, and extending south as far as Peru and Chile [PLATES 8, 62, and 65].

Because of their obvious close association with volcanos and igneous rocks, these deposits have traditionally been considered examples of hydro-thermal solutions derived from magmatic sources. Today, however, we know that this is not always completely true. The fluid inclusions contained in the minerals from some of these deposits and their oxygen and hydrogen isotope compositions point to the same conclusion: meteoric water has played an important role in their genesis. At some localities the data suggest that meteoric and magmatic hydrothermal waters mixed; at others the magma probably only provided the heat required to raise the temperature of meteoric water sufficiently to enable it to leach metals from the surrounding rock and redistribute them in cooler, fractured rocks it encountered as it migrated away from the heat source. The occurrence of a mineral in a vein of an igneous rock does not alone prove that it was formed by an igneous process●

chapter fifteen

The Effect of Tectonism

WHEN plates collide, tremendous compressional forces cause some to break and others to be folded like an accordion, depending on their composition and degree of brittleness. When the accompanying heat and pressure are great enough, existing minerals recrystallize, producing metamorphic rocks. Among other effects, this same heat and pressure can liberate water from the rocks, which flows into areas of lower pressure such as fractures or other open spaces. As it flows through the rocks, the heated water dissolves some of the minerals it encounters, forming a hydrothermal solution. The minerals that precipitate from such hydrothermal solutions depend on several factors: the initial composition of the fluid released, the composition of the rocks through which they flow, how long they are in contact with these rocks, the pressure and temperature, and the rate at which the pressure and temperature change at the site of crystallization.
¶ Because they are derived from the rocks in which they are found, the minerals in this type of hydrothermal deposit must have a chemical makeup consisting of combinations of the elements in those rocks. (No matter how hard you squeeze a tea bag, it will never give you coffee.) This point is well illustrated by two famous and very different localities, one in central Arkansas, the other just 35 kilometers from the Arctic Ocean, in Canada's Yukon Territory. At the Arkansas location, about 300 million years ago the collision of the African and North American plates caused the birth of the Ouachita Mountains, leading eventually to the creation of the entire Appalachian range. Today, we find hundreds of widespread veins of quartz crystals [PLATE 66] in the Ouachitas, especially in the area between Hot Springs and Mount Ida, Arkansas. Quartz crystals are abundant here because

the rock that was tilted and fractured by the ancient tectonic forces that formed the Ouachitas is relatively pure sandstone, composed almost entirely of one mineral: quartz. The hydrothermal water that was activated as a result of the tectonic activity had little else available to dissolve and precipitate.

Rocks of the Rapid Creek-Big Fish River area in the Yukon Territory host more complex examples of minerals formed from hydrothermal solutions activated by tectonic processes. These rocks consist mainly of iron-rich sandstones, mudstones, and shales that contain an unusually high amount of phosphorus. Deformation and fracturing of these rocks occurred during uplift of the northern Rocky Mountains about sixty million years ago. Hydrothermal solutions activated by the tectonism flowed through the rocks, leaching silica, iron, phosphorus, and other elements from them. When the solutions reached the open fractures, these elements were redeposited as quartz, siderite, and a large suite of unusual phosphate minerals, among them some of the world's finest lazulite and wardite crystals. Calcium-bearing phosphates like collinsite formed in fractures in the calcium-rich mudstone, iron-rich phosphates such as vivianite [PLATE 67] formed in veins in the iron-rich rocks, and complex assemblages formed in veins cutting across several types of rock.

The quartz veins in Arkansas and the phosphate minerals in the Yukon both formed at relatively low temperatures and pressures. When the prevailing temperature and pressure confining the hydrothermal solution are higher, other minerals form instead. If those parameters later change, the changes are reflected in the minerals that follow. Nowhere is this better illustrated than in the famous **alpine cleft** deposits found throughout the Alps in Switzerland, Austria, France, and Italy.

High in the Swiss Alps near the Grimsel and Furka passes, some of the world's finest crystals of quartz and pink fluorite have been collected from clefts in granitic rocks. One of the most famous finds was made over a century ago by a team of **strahlers** near the Tiefen Glacier. Strahlers are highly skilled mountain guides who specialize in finding and collecting minerals from alpine clefts, a Swiss tradition that has prevailed to the present. Suspicious about a quartz vein high above them in the cliff face, the Tiefen Glacier team made their way up the wall, where they excavated the vein for several days. Eventually they encountered a small, dark hole, which when opened up, proved to be one of the largest alpine clefts ever discovered. Measuring 6 x 4 x 2 meters, the cleft was full of soft, dark green chlorite embedded with huge, perfectly formed crystals of quartz weighing more than 100 kilograms and nearly a meter long. For the next eight days almost the entire population of the nearby village of Gutannen pitched in to assist in removing the crystals. Some of these wondrous specimens can be seen today in the Natural History Museum in Bern.

Although they seldom find crystals of such proportions, present-day strahlers continue to collect equally fine but smaller crystals of quartz, pink fluorite, hematite [PLATE 68], and other minerals from similar occurrences throughout the Alps. Clefts containing minerals with more varied compositions, such as anatase, brookite, titanite [PLATE 69], or epidote [PLATE 70], occur in

PLATE 69

Titanite (yellow) **and Orthoclase** (white).
Stubachtal, Salzburg, Austria.
3.5 x 5 cm.

The tiny, green flakes of chlorite adhering to the other minerals on this specimen are characteristic of alpine cleft deposits.

PLATE 70

Epidote.
Untersulzbachtal, Salzburg, Austria.
4 x 4.5 cm.

Overlooking the Grossvenediger Glacier high in the Austrian Alps, this famous alpine cleft deposit has produced what most experts agree are the world's finest crystals of epidote.

PLATE 68

Hematite.
Cavradi, Grisons, Switzerland.
3.5 x 5 cm.

Crystals of hematite such as this one, known as eisenrosen, or "iron roses," are classic examples of alpine cleft minerals. The tiny red crystals aligned on their faces are the mineral rutile.

PLATE 71

Benitoite (blue) **and Neptunite**
(black).
San Benito County, California.
4 x 5 cm.

*The proximity of compositionally different
rocks is probably what provided the
unlikely combination of elements (K, Na,
Li, Fe, Mn, Ba, Ti, Si and O) contained in
these rare minerals.*

PLATE 72

Jordanite (silver) **and Sphalerite**
(amber) **in Marble.**
Lengenbach quarry, Binn, Valais,
Switzerland. 3 x 4 cm.

*As tectonic forces gave birth to the Alps,
they also provided the means to generate
the hydrothermal solutions responsible for
these and many other minerals.*

rocks possessing a greater diversity of elements as source materials for the hydrothermal solutions. At the famous locality for epidote in the Untersulzbachtal in the Austrian Alps, tectonic activity that metamorphosed layers of sedimentary and volcanic rocks approximately thirty million years ago also produced clefts lined with epidote and other minerals. The presence of calcium, aluminum, iron, and silicon in the nearby rocks and the elevated temperature and pressure provided by the collision of the African and European plates enabled the epidote to form. The occurrence of bent as well as broken and healed epidote crystals suggests that the tectonic forces remained active during crystallization of the cleft minerals. Ironically, the same tectonic forces that provided the conditions necessary to form the clefts also halted their development, for their continued lifting up of the land enabled erosion to wear it away, thus decreasing both temperature and pressure by removal of the overlying rock.

Many other minerals form from hydrothermal solutions generated by tectonic forces, each following a similar pattern. The tectonic setting provides the heat and pressure to liberate the water, and the enclosing rock provides the chemical elements that form the solution. Therefore, the more variable and numerous the rocks, the more unusual and exotic the minerals that form. Sometimes the assemblages are unique. The rare barium titanium silicate mineral benitoite [PLATE 71] occurs with neptunite in natrolite-filled fractures in serpentine only near the headwater of the San Benito River in California. The Lengenbach quarry near Binn, Valais, Switzerland, is home to jordanite [PLATE 72] and some other very rare lead arsenic sulfide minerals, since those were the elements available from the surrounding rocks. Similarly, the beautiful magenta mineral kämmererite [PLATE 73] occurs in fractured chromite at Erzurum, Anatolia, Turkey, because the chromite and surrounding serpentinite provided chromium, magnesium, iron, aluminum, and silicon, its essential ingredients. Even some of the gold in the California mother lode district [see PLATE 3] probably formed when hydrothermal solutions activated by tectonic forces and/or local magmatic intrusions leached it from the surrounding rocks and redeposited it in fractures and openings in quartz veins ●

PLATE 73

Clinochlore, variety kämmererite.
Erzurum, Anatolia, Turkey.
3.5 x 4 cm.

Kämmererite (chromian clinochlore) is found in fractures in the rocks at this locality because the rocks contained its essential ingredients: chromium, magnesium, iron, aluminum, and silicon.

chapter sixteen

Summary of Water's Role

in Mineral Formation

BECAUSE of its unique structure, water causes many ionic compounds, including some minerals, to dissociate into their component ions, creating an aqueous solution. Increasing the temperature may enable more ions to be dissolved, but eventually saturation occurs, preventing further dissolution. When their limit of solubility is exceeded, minerals precipitate out of solution as individual cations and anions bond together to form crystals. The slower the precipitation, the greater the likelihood that large, well-formed crystals will develop. Decreasing temperature or confining pressure, evaporation, and mixing with other solutions are common natural processes that induce precipitation. ❧ As meteoric water flows over and through rocks, it dissolves some of their minerals, causing the rocks to weather and be eroded. The dissolved minerals are carried by rivers and streams to the sea or to an inland basin, where a playa lake may form. Tectonic uplift also may isolate part of an ocean, forming an inland sea. If the rate of evaporation exceeds that of rainfall, the lake or sea dries up and forms an evaporite deposit. The first minerals to precipitate are the least soluble; the most-soluble minerals precipitate last. Important deposits of salt, gypsum, and borax form in this manner. ❧ Erosion transports sediments to topographically low areas known as basins, where they accumulate. When burial is sufficiently deep, heat mobilizes the water within the sediments, creating a hydrothermal solution. Evaporites in the sediment may dissolve to form a brine that enables metals such as lead, zinc, or copper present in the sediments to form complex ions with either chlorides or organic molecules in the brine. Such metal-bearing solutions can be driven considerable distances by changes in temperature or pressure, dissolving even more metals until they cool or encounter anions that cause the metals to precipitate. Lead-zinc MVT deposits, as well as the native copper deposits in the Keweenaw Peninsula of Michigan, probably formed in this way.

Hydrothermal solutions also may evolve as an end product of magmatic differentiation, particularly in granitic magmas. These solutions are typically enriched in volatile components such as fluorine, sulfur, and water and carry metals whose ions are of unusual size or charge, which precluded their incorporation by earlier-formed minerals. Hydrothermal solutions may also be produced by tectonic forces as water is driven from their enclosing rocks into fractures created by the forces. Minerals that form in this type of deposit always contain the same elements that are present in the host rocks because the solutions from which they precipitate are derived from those rocks●

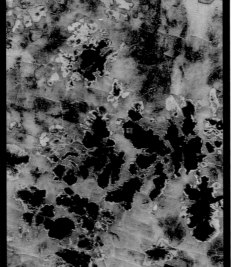

PART IV

Chemical Alteration

chapter seventeen

Equilibrium and Chemical Reactions

MOST of us are already familiar with the effects of chemical alteration. It's the reason we have to take our cars to body shops to repair the damage from rust, and why we periodically have to polish our tarnished silverware. Iron in the steel used to make cars reacts with oxygen in the air to form iron oxide, or rust; silver reacts with sulfur in foods, in water, or in the atmosphere to make silver sulfide, which appears as a dark tarnish. Why do these reactions occur? In the conditions to which they are exposed, neither the iron nor the silver is stable. They "want" to be in a more stable, "comfortable" state for the imposed conditions, a state where there is no tendency to change spontaneously. Chemists know this state as **equilibrium**. ◖ In nature, native iron is comparatively rare at the Earth's surface, but where it does occur it rusts, just as the iron in our automobiles does. Likewise, iron meteorites nearly always have a well-developed outer coating of iron oxide [see PLATE 1], and native silver, which is relatively common in nature, almost always has a dark, tarnished surface of silver sulfide (the mineral acanthite) if it has been exposed to groundwater or to the atmosphere [PLATES 74 and 140]. ◖ Minerals are merely some of nature's solid chemicals, and they react with various chemical elements and compounds in their environment, including each other. The laws governing these reactions are the same as those that govern all other chemical reactions. Water promotes chemical reactions between minerals by aiding in their dissolution and providing a medium in which their constituent ions are free to move about and react. Dissolving salt in water results in a solution containing sodium cations and chloride anions. What happens, though, if the water already has other cations or anions in it? What determines whether a given

PLATE 74

Native Silver and Calcite.
Silver Islet, Lake Superior, Ontario.
2 x 5 cm.

The tarnish on these natural wires of silver formed by reaction with sulfur, just as it does on the silverware in your kitchen drawer.

cation will react with a particular anion to form a new compound?

Chemicals or minerals react because the **products** of their reaction are more stable in the existing environment than are they, the **reactants.** Like a ball rolling down the stairs, a chemical reaction does not stop until the final "step" is reached. The final step in this case is the point at which one of the reactants has been completely consumed or there is a change in the existing conditions that effectively establishes a new environment. Sometimes a reaction that should take place fails to come about. For example, a ball can remain precariously balanced on the top step for a very long time. We know the ball inevitably will roll down the stairs because it is unstable in its present position, but exactly when this will happen is uncertain. All that is needed is a little boost to get things going. To chemists this boost is known as **activation energy.**

In the mineral world, crystals of sulfur [see PLATE 135] may be in contact with oxygen in the air for eons without changing because without activation energy sulfur reacts with oxygen so slowly that nothing seems to be happening. Heat accelerates the process, producing sulfur dioxide by the chemical reaction commonly known as burning. When a ball rolls to the bottom of the stairs, some of its stored **(potential)** energy is converted to mechanical **(kinetic)** energy. In giving up stored energy, the ball (or in our case, the sulfur and oxygen molecules) reaches a lower, more stable energy state for the existing conditions.

A ball will roll down the stairs just as well in your house as in mine. Sulfur burns equally well in a test tube in the laboratory or on the edge of a vent from an active volcano. The chemical alteration of minerals may take place in any geological setting or in any kind of rock—igneous, sedimentary, or metamorphic. The only requirements are a condition of disequilibrium and a source of activation energy. Heat is one of the all-time great activators of chemical reactions, but it is not the only form of energy. Light, too, can initiate chemical changes in certain sensitive minerals such as proustite or vivianite. Even mechanical energy can initiate some chemical reactions; that's why dropping a bottle of nitroglycerin is not recommended!

At equilibrium there is no tendency for spontaneous change. Reactants and products are in a state of balance. It's as if we had ten equally energetic volleyball players, five on either side of the net, each throwing a ball over the net. Players on the left represent reactants; those on the right represent products. Under these conditions the number of balls thrown from left to right by the "reactants" is exactly counterbalanced by those coming in the opposite direction from the "products." The "game" is in equilibrium. How can we make more balls travel to the right? One way is to call out another player or two from the reactants' bench. Or we could let those players rest and achieve the same effect by removing one or two members of the products team from the court. The same is true for chemical reactions in equilibrium.

A chemical reaction may be driven in one direction or the other by increasing or decreasing the concentrations of reactants or products. As we saw in Chapter 11, this is the principle that governs the formation of evaporite minerals. At saturation the precipitating crystals of solid halite are in a state of equilibrium with their dissolved component ions, Na^+ (sodium) and Cl^- (chloride). Adding water, a reactant, causes the reaction to shift toward its products (i.e., dissolved ions), so more halite dissolves. Introducing more dissolved ions, the products, causes the opposite reaction to occur: halite precipitates. The removal of a reactant (water) by evaporation can also reverse the reaction and cause halite to precipitate, as it does in a playa lake ●

PLATE 75

Tincalconite pseudomorph after Borax.
Boron, California. 6 x 9 cm.

This specimen of chalky-white tincalconite was formed by dehydration of transparent, lustrous borax crystals.

PLATE 76

Metatorbernite pseudomorph after Torbernite.
Musonoi mine, Kolwezi, Shaba, Zaire. 2 x4.5 cm.

Like the tincalconite in PLATE 75, these metatorbernite crystals formed by dehydration of torbernite and have retained the outward crystal form of that mineral.

chapter eighteen

Drying Out

MOST chemical reactions responsible for the creation of minerals involve water. Among the simplest are **hydration-dehydration** reactions. You are probably already familiar with one example from the mineral world, but you may not realize it. Calcium sulfate exists naturally in two common forms: gypsum ($CaSO_4 \cdot 2H_2O$), which contains two water molecules per formula unit, and anhydrite ($CaSO_4$), which has no water. Gypsum is quarried and roasted to drive off its water, then powdered and sold as plaster of Paris. What do we do with it? Add water to make gypsum again! Because the roasting drives off water, it is a **dehydration** reaction. The second reaction, adding water, is **hydration.** ❧ Calcium sulfate is not the only mineral with variable states of hydration. Common in mineral collections are large, well-formed groups of opaque, chalky-white crystals labeled as borax from Boron, California, or other localities. But such labels are wrong. Borax ($Na_2B_4O_7 \cdot 10H_2O$) contains ten molecules of water per formula unit, and its crystals are transparent and glassy. Although the specimens in question may have been borax when they were collected, with time they have dehydrated into the mineral tincalconite ($Na_2B_4O_7 \cdot 5H_2O$), which is more stable in the dry conditions of storage [PLATE 75]. Similarly, the heavily hydrated uranium minerals autunite and torbernite often dehydrate into meta-autunite and metatorbernite [PLATE 76]. ❧ Specimens such as these, that although different from the original mineral, have retained its crystal shape, are called **pseudomorphs** (*pseudo* = false, *morph* = shape). They are direct, tangible evidence of chemical alteration. Because they are composed of one mineral formed *after* the other, pseudomorphs are commonly described as minerals "after" the original mineral—for example, tincalconite after borax or metatorbernite after torbernite ●

chapter nineteen

Neutralization Reactions

L

IKE water, acids and bases may influence the solubility of some compounds, and hence their tendency to participate in a chemical reaction. In water hydrogen ions (H^+) are bonded to hydroxyl (OH^-) ions to make HOH, more commonly written as H_2O. In **acids** hydrogen ions are bonded to different anions, such as Cl^- (chloride) in hydrochloric acid (HCl), or SO_4^{2-} (sulfate) in sulfuric acid (H_2SO_4). **Bases** contain OH^- bonded to a cation other than H^+. A familiar example is household lye, which is sodium hydroxide (NaOH). Aqueous solutions of acids therefore contain higher concentrations of H^+ than do aqueous solutions of bases, which contain more OH^-. The concentration of H^+ or OH^- in the solution, which determines how strongly acidic or basic it is, is measured on the **pH scale.**
❦ The pH scale ranges from 0 to 14. The lower the pH value, the more acidic the solution (i.e., the greater the concentration of H^+); the higher the pH value, the more basic the solution (i.e., the greater the concentration of OH^-). At pH = 7, at ordinary room temperature, the concentrations of H^+ and OH^- are equal, and the solution is **neutral,** neither acidic nor basic. Pure water (HOH) is neutral because it has equal concentrations of H^+ and OH^-. ❦ Acids and bases react with many minerals, as well as with each other. The reaction of a base with an acid is called **neutralization.** In water lye dissociates into Na^+ and OH^-, and hydrochloric acid dissociates into H^+ and Cl^-. When a solution of lye is added to a hydrochloric acid solution to neutralize it, the H^+ and OH^- react to make H_2O, leaving the Na^+ and Cl^- dissolved in the resulting solution. ❦ Neutralization reactions occur in nature as well as in the laboratory. As rain droplets coalesce and fall through the atmosphere, for example, small amounts of oxygen, carbon dioxide, sulfur dioxide, and other gases may dissolve in them, producing weak

acids. By the time the rain reaches the Earth's surface it is ready to begin chemically altering some minerals. As the acidic rainwater seeps into the ground, it dissolves salts and organic acids, increasing its acidity. The resulting solution, called **groundwater,** can chemically weather minerals in the rocks that it contacts. As a result, feldspars are decomposed into clays, sulfide minerals into sulfates, and silicate minerals like olivine or pyroxene into serpentine.

We benefit from these reactions in many ways. Not only do they help make soil and provide the mineral nutrients essential for plant growth, but when conditions are favorable, they also produce deposits of bauxite or garnierite, important ores of aluminum and nickel. The large bauxite deposits of Arkansas and Suriname and garnierite deposits of New Caledonia probably formed in this manner. On the down side, as rain falls through polluted air, it dissolves more of some gases (such as sulfur dioxide) than we would like, resulting in **acid rain.** Fortunately, nature has a way of controlling that, too — at least sometimes.

The pH of a solution greatly affects the solubility of some minerals. In areas where the underlying rock, known as **bedrock,** is limestone, lakes appear to be less affected by acid rain than those where the bedrock consists of igneous rocks such as granite. Why? Limestone is made of calcite, which dissolves more readily in acid solutions than in neutral water because of the increased number of H^+ ions available to help dissociate it. The abundant H^+ ions in an acidic lake combine with the HCO_3^- supplied by the dissolved calcite to form H_2CO_3, which breaks down into H_2O and CO_2. In the process the pH level increases to a more desirable, neutral value. The leftover culprits of acidity in acid rain, SO_4^{2-} ions, combine with Ca^{2+} to make calcium sulfate, which is relatively harmless to the lake.

This natural process has taught us that dumping crushed limestone into lakes suffering from the effects of acid rain can help restore their pH to neutral. The same neutralization reaction occurs on the outsides of some buildings, where acid rain has reacted with the $CaCO_3$ in their concrete or mortar, producing a white, powdery, surface coating of calcium sulfate, or gypsum. You seldom have to travel far to find minerals!●

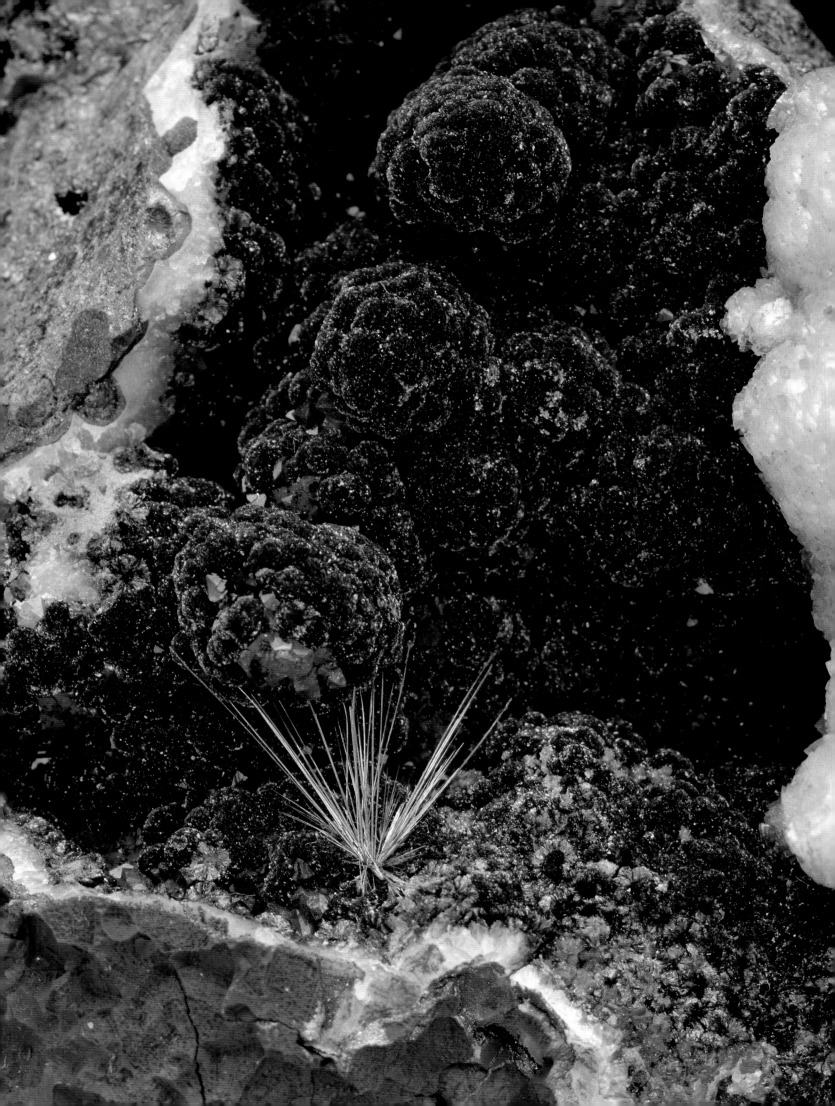

chapter twenty

Oxidation-Reduction Reactions

W HEN iron rusts or sulfur burns, the iron and sulfur combine with oxygen and are therefore said to be **oxidized.** The terminology seems logical, since they combine with oxygen. What really happens, however, is that the oxygen robs the iron and sulfur atoms of some of their electrons. In the broad, chemical sense, **oxidation** is the loss of electrons from an atom. In rusting, atoms of neutral, metallic iron (Fe^0) are oxidized to either ferrous (Fe^{2+}) or ferric (Fe^{3+}) cations by giving up either two or three of their electrons to oxygen atoms. Similarly, when sulfur burns, each neutral sulfur atom shares four of its electrons with two oxygen atoms to make the compound sulfur dioxide (SO_2). Because both iron and sulfur *lose* electrons, they are considered oxidized. But what about the oxygen? It experiences an opposite effect; it *gains* electrons. The gain of electrons is known as **reduction.** ❡ Whenever something is oxidized, something else must be reduced. This is what happens in **oxidation-reduction** reactions ("redox" reactions for short). In the rusting of iron, iron is oxidized and oxygen is reduced. When sulfur burns, sulfur is oxidized and oxygen is reduced. The total number of electrons lost by oxidation equals those gained by reduction, since formation of a stable compound requires that the total positive and negative charges of its constituent atoms are equal. It's like buying and selling: without seller and buyer agreeing on an equitable price, there can be no transaction. ❡ Other, more-complicated redox reactions can occur between iron minerals, as a colleague and I learned while studying the mineralogy of the Sterling iron mine near Antwerp, New York. This old, water-filled hematite mine was one of our favorite collecting spots. Although we never found any of the spectacular specimens of millerite

PLATE 77

Stilpnomelane (velvety green-brown) and **Millerite** (brassy needles).
Sterling mine, Antwerp, New York.
4 x 4 cm.

Millerite from the Sterling mine is world famous, but its associated minerals are more important in deciphering the origin of the deposit. The oxidation of some of the iron in the stilpnomelane was accompanied by the reduction of part of the iron in the hematite (red) to form the mineral magnetite (black).

[see PLATE 77] for which the locality is famous, we did collect other interesting minerals that provided clues about the role of redox reactions in their formation. Since these minerals were all iron-rich, the first question to address was the source of the iron that formed the hematite ore. The answer was in the surrounding rock.

The Sterling mine is situated in a body of granitic gneiss (a metamorphic rock with the composition of a granite) that contains local concentrations of the iron-sulfide minerals pyrite and pyrrhotite. Groundwater containing dissolved oxygen readily attacks these minerals, oxidizing them to soluble iron sulfates and liberating sulfuric acid in the process. Immediately adjacent to the pyrite-bearing gneiss is a large body of marble. If such an acidic solution were to encounter marble, the calcite in the marble would neutralize the solution, thereby increasing its pH. A higher pH (i.e., an increase in OH^- concentration) would cause precipitation of iron hydroxide, which is relatively unstable and, with time, dehydrates into hematite or goethite. At the Sterling mine stalactitic and botryoidal hematite appears to be one of the earliest-formed minerals, suggesting that such precipitation from solution did occur. Perfectly formed crystals of hematite coat some of the stalactites or line crystal pockets in the ore, suggesting that they formed after the initial precipitation.

However, there is something strange about these hematite crystals: they are magnetic, but hematite should not be attracted by a magnet. Why are these hematite crystals magnetic? Rather than hematite, these crystals are magnetite pseudomorphs after hematite. In hematite (Fe_2O_3) all the iron is ferric (Fe^{3+}), but in magnetite (Fe_3O_4) one of the iron atoms is ferrous (Fe^{2+}). The only way to change hematite into magnetite is by reduction, which implies that oxidation is occurring somewhere else, but where? The answer this time was among the "interesting" minerals we had collected: stilpnomelane [PLATE 77].

Stilpnomelane may contain both ferrous and ferric iron. The Sterling mine contains two kinds of stilpnomelane—one green, the other golden brown—but both must have formed after the hematite crystals, since stilpnomelane is always found coating the crystals. When we analyzed the two stilpnomelanes, we found that the green variety, which tended to be associated with the magnetite-poor ore, contained significantly less ferric iron than the golden-brown variety, which was associated with the magnetite-rich ore. Thus, the electrons made available from the oxidation of Fe^{2+} to Fe^{3+} in the stilpnomelane probably reduced some of the Fe^{3+} in the hematite to Fe^{2+}, resulting in the formation of magnetite.

With many minerals oxidation proceeds in a much less complicated, more direct manner. When groundwater containing dissolved oxygen percolates downward following fractures in a hydrothermal vein or rock containing native metals or metal-sulfide minerals, those previously formed, or **primary** minerals, often are oxidized. The minerals that form from them are referred to as **secondary,** and the portion of the vein affected by the oxidation is called an **oxide zone.** Oxide zones normally develop in the upper portion of a vein,

PLATE 78

Pyrite in Shale.
Goldfield, Western Australia.
8 x 10 cm.

The occurrence of pyrite in black, organic-rich shales is common, indicating the prevalence of oxygen-poor, reducing conditions.

The Development of an Oxide Zone.

As groundwater containing dissolved oxygen trickles through fractures in veins bearing metallic-sulfide minerals, many of the metallic minerals are oxidized. Oxide zones usually develop above the water table, where more air is available. In the more-reducing conditions below the water table metal-sulfide minerals may precipitate again, forming a minable zone of enriched ore. (After Mason and Berry, 1968, Elements of Mineralogy, page 141.)

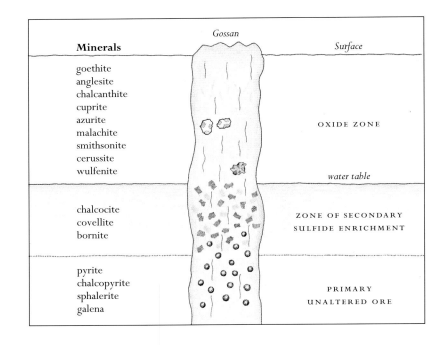

Minerals	
goethite anglesite chalcanthite cuprite azurite malachite smithsonite cerussite wulfenite	OXIDE ZONE
	water table
chalcocite covellite bornite	ZONE OF SECONDARY SULFIDE ENRICHMENT
pyrite chalcopyrite sphalerite galena	PRIMARY UNALTERED ORE

above the water table, where oxidizing conditions tend to prevail because air is usually present [FIGURE H]. Below the water table conditions are more reducing, since the available oxygen is limited to only the small quantity that remains dissolved in the water. Native metals and sulfide minerals are particularly susceptible to oxidation and commonly form oxides or sulfates, some of which may dissolve in the water, causing the metals to be leached away or to migrate below the water table, where under reducing conditions they may precipitate again as different minerals. Zones of **secondary enrichment** formed in this manner may concentrate metals into economically important ore deposits. The rocks in and around the vein from which the soluble minerals have been leached acquire a porous, often rusty appearance, forming a **gossan,** or "iron hat." A gossan often denotes the presence of an ore deposit beneath it. Such structures are often staked by prospectors in search of future mines.

Somewhat analogous are the sediments at the bottom of a lake or sea, where the chief source of oxygen is that dissolved in the water above the sediment. The accumulation and subsequent decay of organic matter depletes the water of available oxygen and forms black, carbon-rich sediments. Therefore, as one goes deeper into the sediment, conditions become increasingly reducing. That's why minerals such as pyrite, that favor reducing conditions, form deeper in the sediment than do minerals such as goethite, hematite, or siderite, that require a more oxidizing environment. The universal presence of pyrite nodules in black, carbonaceous shale [PLATE 78] illustrates the influence of reduction on iron mineralization in such geologic environments ●

chapter twenty-one

Lights, Camera, Action!

THE cast is ready and knows the script, but has the
stage been properly set? Just because all the right
ingredients are present does not mean they will react.
The physical and chemical parameters must not be at or
near equilibrium, and reaction must lead to a more stable
assemblage. What are some of the physical and chemical
factors that determine which minerals form? The compositions of the primary minerals determine the elements
available to be released as cations or anions by oxidation.
The concentration of dissolved oxygen and the presence or
absence of acids (i.e., the pH) may affect the degree of oxidation possible. Dissolved cations or anions already present in the
groundwater may cause the precipitation of some minerals if
their solubility limits are exceeded. The presence or absence of a
particular anion in the solution often determines whether an available cation is transported by the solution because some anions may
render the cation insoluble, thus removing it from the cast of players.
❿ Temperature also has an effect on the solubility and hence on the
concentrations of cations and anions, as well as on the rates of their
reactions. Usually an increase in temperature increases the rate of a
chemical reaction. The grain size of the reactant minerals also influences
the rate of reaction. Small grains collectively provide more surface area and
thus react more quickly than larger grains do. The availability of fractures
and the porosity of the rock determine where and how far solutions can
penetrate. Locally, the permeability and composition of a rock can be highly
variable and can cause the deposition of quite different minerals only
centimeters apart. ❿ Finally, there is our old geological friend, time. The
longer the reactants are exposed to each other, the longer they can react.

PLATE 79 *(above)*

Chrysocolla (blue) **and Tenorite**
(black) **in Breccia.**
Silver City, New Mexico. 7.5 x 9 cm.

*The fractures in this rock provided
convenient avenues for copper-bearing
solutions to enter and deposit these
minerals.*

PLATE 80 *(left)*

Cuprite (red) **on Native Copper.**
Ray, Arizona. 2.5 x 4.5 cm.

*Oxygen dissolved in groundwater is
probably responsible for the oxidation
of this copper into cuprite.*

Canada has thousands of metal-sulfide mineral deposits, but almost no oxide zones are associated with them, in spite of abundant fresh air and water. Why? The hard, dense Precambrian rock that hosts most of these deposits is relatively impermeable to oxygen-laden groundwater, the relatively low average temperatures impede oxidation reactions, and erosion by the glaciers from the last great ice age probably scoured away any shallow oxide zones that might have developed.

Many factors may be involved in even the simplest geochemical system. For example, if water containing dissolved oxygen comes in contact with native copper, the most likely minerals to form are copper oxides such as tenorite or cuprite [PLATES 79 to 81]. Whether the outcome is tenorite or cuprite depends largely on how much oxygen is dissolved in the water; cuprite requires less oxygen to form than does tenorite. Because groundwater also frequently contains dissolved carbon dioxide, two other minerals, the carbonates azurite and malachite [PLATES 7 and 82], commonly form. Together these two species probably account for most of the blue and green stains associated with copper-bearing mineral deposits. Which of the two forms usually depends on the concentrations of oxygen, carbon dioxide, and water. Although azurite has a broader range of stability than does malachite among these chemical parameters, it favors drier, less-oxidizing conditions, which are not always readily provided or maintained in oxide zones (because drier areas require more air than water and therefore generally have readily available oxygen). An increase in pH, on the other hand, as may occur when groundwater encounters limestone, can sometimes favor malachite stability. Malachite thus

PLATE 81

Cuprite (red) **and Chrysocolla** (blue).
Mashamba West, Shaba, Zaire.
2.5 x 4 cm.

*Similar geochemical trends occur in widely
separated oxide zones throughout the world.
The precipitation of the copper silicate
chrysocolla following copper oxides is demonstrated by both the tenorite in PLATE 79 and
this cuprite.*

PLATE 82

Azurite and Malachite.
Apex mine, St. George, Utah.
8 x 10 cm.

*Hollow molds of former gypsum crystals
coated by blue azurite, partially replaced by
green malachite, record a history of chemical
change.*

PLATE 83

Smithsonite.
Kelly mine, Magdalena, New Mexico.
4 x 7 cm.

*When groundwater with dissolved oxygen
filters through a near-surface ore deposit
containing sphalerite or other zinc-rich
sulfide minerals, it may oxidize some of them,
putting zinc into solution. If the solution also
contains dissolved carbon dioxide, or if it
encounters limestone, the zinc-carbonate
mineral smithsonite may form.*

PLATE 84 *(right)*

Hemimorphite.
Iglesias, Sardinia, Italy. 6 x 8 cm.

*Although pure hemimorphite and smithsonite
[see PLATE 83] are colorless or white, both
minerals occur in a wide range of colors
resulting from trace amounts of elements such
as cobalt or copper.*

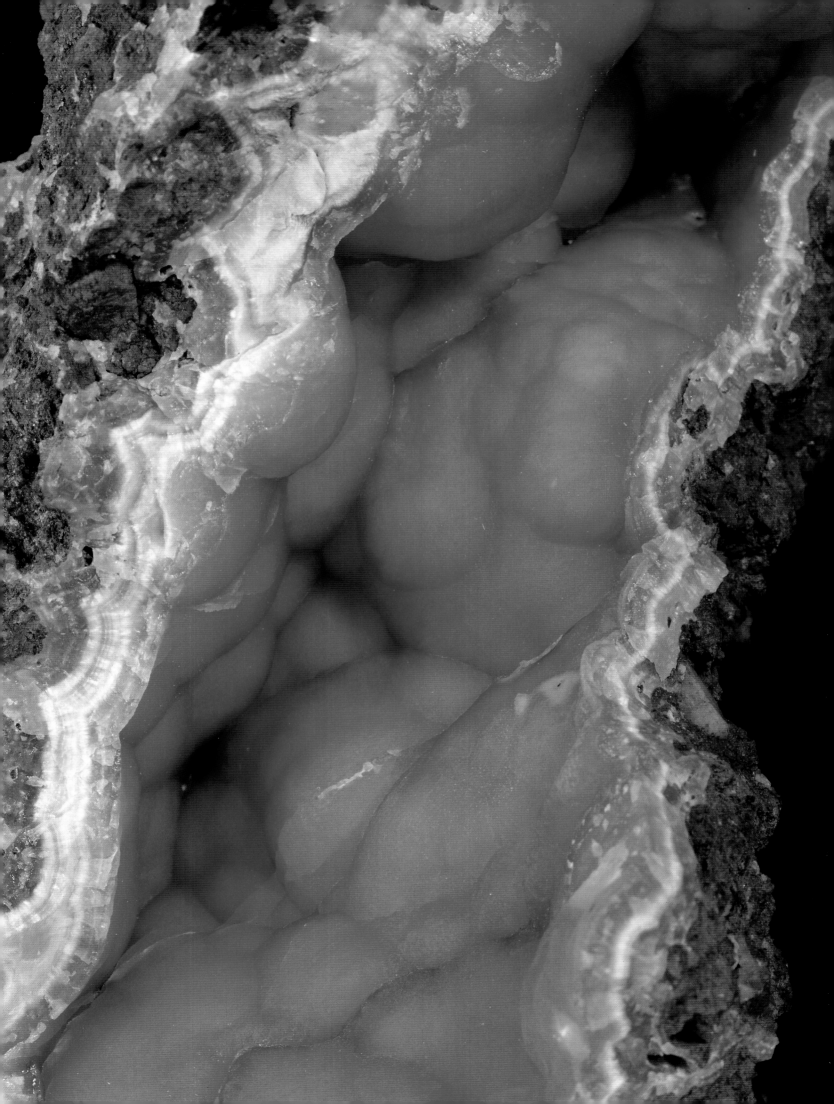

PLATE 87

Cerussite.
Tsumeb, Namibia. 4.5 x 7 cm.

Resembling delicate snowflakes, these twinned crystals of cerussite probably formed when lead, leached from galena, reacted with groundwater containing dissolved carbon dioxide.

is often more abundant than azurite and replaces it as pseudomorphs [see PLATE 82]. These examples show that the composition of the groundwater and of the rock it encounters can be just as important in determining what secondary minerals form in an oxide zone as the composition of the primary minerals themselves.

Now let's turn the camera to some other actors. So far, we have considered what minerals might form when a single element (e.g., copper) is exposed to a relatively "pure" groundwater containing only dissolved oxygen and carbon dioxide. Most hydrothermal vein deposits, however, contain several metal-bearing minerals, and groundwater nearly always contains a considerable variety of dissolved cations and anions. The ubiquitous presence of pyrite, chalcopyrite, galena, and sphalerite in hydrothermal vein deposits provides iron, copper, lead, and zinc ions to most oxide zones. More-complex sulfide minerals, such as tetrahedrite or tennantite, provide antimony and arsenic.

With a greater diversity of cations and anions available to react, a greater number of secondary minerals are able to form. Among the simpler and more common of these are the zinc carbonate and zinc silicate minerals smithsonite and hemimorphite [PLATES 83 and 84] and the lead sulfate and lead carbonate minerals anglesite and cerussite [PLATES 85 to 87]. Lead is rather immobile because it forms relatively few compounds that are soluble in water. Unless it can form complex ions with sulfur or chlorine, which keep it in solution, lead normally does not travel far. Instead it forms relatively simple secondary minerals close to its point of origin in oxide zones. Gold, too, is a very insoluble and inert element that must form complex ions in order to travel in solution. As a result, it forms no know secondary mineral species.

PLATE 88 (left)

Olivenite on Quartz.
Wheal Unity, Gwennap, Cornwall,
England. 4 x 5 cm.

Originally deposited by hot, aqueous
solutions, earlier-formed sulfide minerals
containing copper and arsenic were
oxidized at lower temperatures to make
this copper arsenate mineral.

PLATE 89 (right)

Aurichalcite.
79 mine, Hayden, Arizona.
5.5 x 6.5 cm.

The presence of limestone at this mine was
probably instrumental to the formation of
aurichalcite [(Zn,Cu)$_5$(CO$_3$)$_2$(OH)$_6$],
since it provided a source of carbonate
(CO$_3$) and the means to neutralize acidic
solutions in which aurichalcite would
dissolve.

Dozens of other secondary copper, lead and zinc minerals are found in oxide zones, each with limits of stability with respect to oxidation and pH. For example, secondary minerals of zinc—such as the arsenate hydroxides, adamite [$Zn_2(AsO_4)(OH)$] and legrandite [$Zn_2(AsO_4)(OH) \cdot H_2O$] [PLATE 90], and the carbonate hydroxides, aurichalcite [$(Zn,Cu)_5(CO_3)_2(OH)_6$] [PLATE 89] and rosasite [$(Cu,Zn)_2(CO_3)(OH)_2$]—favor basic conditions and require a highly oxidizing environment for their formation. All these minerals contain OH⁻ as an essential ingredient, and both their arsenic and their copper exist in states of high oxidation. It is not surprising that all four of these minerals occur both at the Ojeula mine, near Mapimi, Durango, Mexico, and at Tsumeb, Namibia, since at each locality primary zinc, copper and arsenic sulfide minerals (e.g., sphalerite, tennantite or arsenopyrite) were exposed to aerated groundwater which oxidized them, providing the cations and anions essential to form these minerals. Limestone ($CaCO_3$) at each locality probably provided the dissolved carbonate required for the aurichalcite and rosasite, and neutralized any acids, thereby increasing the pH of the solution, and so its (OH)⁻ concentration. The chemically similar species, olivenite [$Cu^{2+}_2(AsO_4)(OH)$] [PLATE 88], is well known from Tsumeb, and has also been reported from Mapimi.

Virtually all metallic minerals are subject to chemical alteration. Given the proper pH range and oxidizing environment, dissolved aluminum, silicate or phosphate ions in the groundwater may react with copper, for example, to form minerals such as chrysocolla, liroconite, or turquoise [PLATES 79, 91, and 92]. Lead may combine with less-common anions to form equally colorful

PLATE 90

Legrandite.
Ojuela mine, Mapimi, Durango,
Mexico. 4 x 6 cm.

*Oxidation of primary sulfide minerals such
as sphalerite and arsenopyrite provided the
essential ingredients to form this rare
secondary zinc arsenate mineral.*

PLATE 91

Liroconite.
Wheal Gorland, Gwennap, Cornwall, England. 2.5 x 3 cm.

The world's finest examples of this rare copper aluminum arsenate mineral are from Wheal Gorland.

PLATE 92

Turquoise.
Gabbs, Nevada. 5.5 x 6 cm.

Nodules of turquoise such as this one form when acidic, copper-bearing groundwater reacts with aluminum- and phosphorus-rich minerals in porous volcanic rocks.

PLATE 93

Crocoite.
Dundas, Tasmania, Australia.
8 x 8 cm.

*The occurrence of these crystals of crocoite
on a rusty gossan matrix is typical of many
minerals found in oxide zones.*

PLATE 94

Wulfenite.
Mammoth-St. Anthony mine,
Tiger, Arizona. 4 x 6 cm.

*This colorful lead molybdate mineral occurs
in the oxide zones of many of Arizona's old
copper, lead, and silver mines.*

PLATE 95

Pyromorphite.
Cornwall, England. 3.5 x 4.5 cm.

The presence of pyromorphite, a lead phosphate chloride, on a porous, spongy quartz matrix suggests that the small cavities now in the quartz were probably once occupied by lead-bearing sulfide minerals that were leached away by groundwater containing dissolved oxygen, chloride, and phosphate.

PLATE 96

Mimetite.
San Pedro Corralitos, Chihuahua, Mexico. 7 x 10 cm.

The outward structure of this mimetite suggests that it precipitated from an aqueous solution, but its composition indicates that chemical alteration played an equally important role in its formation.

PLATE 97

Vanadinite.
Mibladen, Morocco. 3 x 5 cm.

*Because pyromorphite and mimetite
[see PLATES 95 and 96] have atomic
structures and color ranges similar
to vanadinite, identifying these three
minerals without chemical analysis
can be extremely difficult.*

PLATE 98

Cuprosklodowskite.
Musonoi mine, Kolwezi, Shaba,
Zaire. 6 x 6 cm.

*Under the right conditions the oxidation
of earlier-formed copper- and uranium-
bearing minerals can result in the
formation of this rare copper uranyl
silicate mineral.*

minerals, such as wulfenite, crocoite, pyromorphite, mimetite, or vanadinite [PLATES 93 to 97]. Uranium, cobalt, nickel, and antimony, as well as many other metals, also form secondary mineral species [PLATES 98, 99, and 102]. Some of these minerals are locally abundant, but globally they are uncommon because relatively few locations simultaneously have all the elements and the restricted chemical parameters essential for their formation.

Although chemically complex, these minerals are the natural and predictable consequence of the oxidation of a hydrothermal vein deposit. Theoretical modeling through laboratory simulations of such complex systems is possible but complicated. It is extremely difficult to anticipate and account for all factors in even the simplest natural environments. Even the climate may control the presence or absence of some species, such as chalcanthite [PLATE 100], which is readily soluble in water and therefore preserved only at localities in arid regions, such as Chuquicamata, Chile, or the southwestern United States. All too frequently more variables are operative in natural geochemical systems than are suspected. Perhaps that's why the theoretically impossible frequently seems to occur in nature ●

chapter twenty-two

Which Comes First ?

Studying the order in which secondary minerals form in oxide zones provides important clues to the chemical parameters that prevailed during their formation. This order, or succession, of mineral species, known as the **paragenetic sequence,** is discerned by observing what minerals crystallize on the surfaces of or replace other minerals. Pseudomorphs are perfect examples. The minerals constituting the pseudomorph formed after the original species, whose shape is retained. Goethite after pyrite [PLATE 101], for example, is proof that the iron sulfide pyrite formed first and was subsequently oxidized and replaced by goethite, an iron oxide hydroxide. ◖ Deciphering the paragenetic sequence usually requires only a good microscope, a notebook, and the patience to make and record careful observations on as many specimens as possible from the occurrence. Since the idea is to look for repeated, characteristic patterns, large numbers of **representative** samples must be examined. Otherwise the true picture may be distorted. For a geologist to determine the paragenetic sequence of a locality based on only a few samples from one small area would be equivalent to a visitor from outer space who, after arriving on this planet in the middle of the Sahara Desert, reports that the Earth is a hot, dry, planet devoid of life. When done carefully, simple paragenetic observations can reveal much about the genesis of a mineral deposit. One of my favorite mineral localities — a small, abandoned antimony mine in Ham Sud Township, Wolfe County, Quebec — illustrates this point well. ◖ At this locality veins of quartz containing native antimony (Sb) bear cavities containing small crystals of stibnite (Sb_2S_3), some of which appear to be replaced by kermesite (Sb_2S_2O). Crystals of valentinite and

PLATE 101

Goethite pseudomorph after Pyrite.
Windover, Nevada. 3.5 x 7 cm.

The perfect preservation of the distinctive, striated crystal faces on these former pyrite crystals by goethite leaves little doubt concerning their identity.

PLATE 102

Valentinite (white), **Kermesite** (red), **Stibnite** (black), **and Native Antimony** (silver).
Ham Sud Township, Wolfe County, Quebec. 4 x 5 cm.

Deciphering which minerals form before or after others may provide clues to changing chemical conditions during their formation. In this specimen native antimony was first oxidized by sulfur-bearing solutions to make stibnite, an antimony sulfide. As oxidation proceeded, solutions progressively richer in oxygen formed kermesite, an antimony sulfur oxide, followed by valentinite, an antimony oxide.

senarmontite (both Sb_2O_3) grow on the kermesite [PLATE 102], and the whole assemblage is frequently coated by stibiconite [$Sb^{3+}Sb^{5+}_2O_6(OH)$]. Take a minute to examine the formulas for these minerals. Initially only the native element, antimony, was present. Early in the paragenetic sequence sulfur reacted with antimony to make stibnite, but the sulfur was gradually replaced by oxygen as the prominent anion in the system, and kermesite and other oxide minerals formed.

That conditions became progressively more oxidizing is demonstrated by the sequential increase in the number of electrons lost by antimony, from zero in native antimony to three in stibnite, kermesite, valentinite, and senarmontite, and finally to five in the stibiconite. The presence of OH^- in stibiconite further suggests an increase in pH and/or a drop in temperature (minerals formed at high temperatures seldom contain OH^-) occurred. These observations are in accord with the geological setting. The veins themselves are locally sheared and fractured, indicating movement during or after they formed. The fracturing created openings for oxygenated water to enter and form the observed sequence of secondary minerals as erosion of overlying rock exposed the veins ●

chapter twenty-three

Chemical Alteration in Igneous
and Metamorphic Rocks

CHEMICAL alteration is not confined to oxide zones and near-surface environments. In granitic pegmatites minerals like tourmaline, beryl, microcline, spodumene, or uraninite that form early in the crystallization sequence frequently may appear corroded or replaced by other minerals. Such minerals are no longer stable in the fluids present near the end of the crystallization of the pegmatite. Tourmaline may be replaced by micas or cookeite, beryl by bertrandite, spodumene by eucryptite, and uraninite by gummite, a bright orange mixture of secondary uranium oxides [PLATE 103]. The dissolution of these minerals replenishes the fluid with lithium, boron, beryllium, aluminum, uranium, and other elements to form even more exotic, rare minerals that are stable at lower temperatures. ⬤ Probably the most famous minerals to form in this manner are the secondary phosphate species that arise from the alteration of primary phosphate minerals like amblygonite or triphylite [see PLATE 31]. The secondary phosphates that form depend largely on what cations are available in the fluid, on the temperature, and on whether conditions are oxidizing or reducing. Other physical and chemical constraints may be important for individual species. The available cations are a function of what primary minerals were attacked by the solution. If the environment is not very oxidizing, triphylite may be altered into ferrous iron phosphates such as ludlamite or vivianite, but under oxidizing conditions ferric iron phosphates like heterosite, rockbridgeite, or strengite may form. None of these minerals requires the addition of elements other than those present in the original primary phosphates from which they are derived. In most pegmatites, however, many other cations are available, so

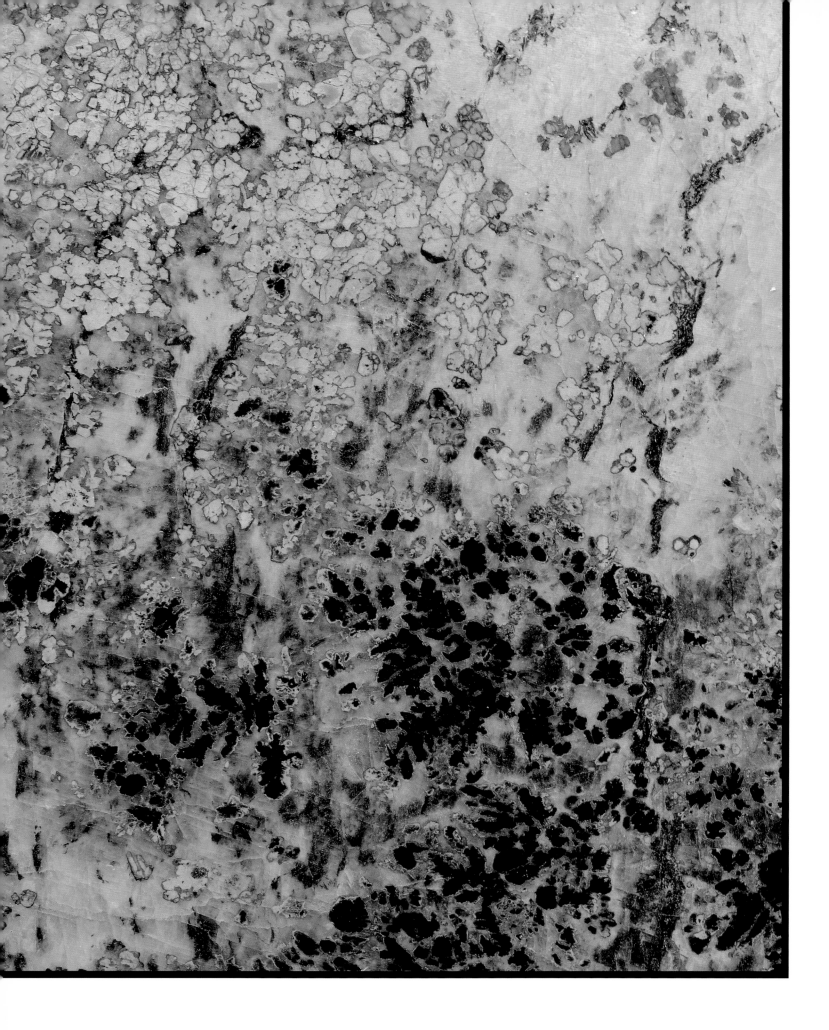

PLATE 104

Eosphorite on Rose Quartz.
Taquaral, Minas Gerais, Brazil.
3.5 x 5 cm.

Eosphorite is a common secondary phosphate mineral that forms by the chemical alteration of earlier-formed phosphate minerals, such as lithiophilite and triphylite [see PLATE 31], in some granitic pegmatites.

PLATE 105

Hydroxylherderite.
Virgem da Lapa, Minas Gerais, Brazil.
1.5-cm crystal.

The corroded white feldspar under this crystal of hydroxylherderite provides evidence of chemical attack and dissolution of earlier-formed minerals in this granitic pegmatite. Hydroxylherderite is a secondary phosphate mineral formed by the dissolution of earlier-formed calcium-, berylium- and phosphorus-bearing minerals.

PLATE 103 *(left)*

Gummite (orange) **and Uraninite** (black).
Ruggles mine, Grafton, New Hampshire. 6 x 7 cm.

Gummite forms by the chemical alteration of uraninite. All of the orange mineral in this polished slab of pegmatite was once black, as proven by the remnants of unaltered uraninite that form the cores of some of the grains of gummite.

PLATE 106

Water and carbon dioxide are probably responsible for the chemical alteration of part of this green, glassy diopside crystal first into tremolite (white), and later the tremolite into talc (gray).

many chemically more-complex minerals can form. For example, adding aluminum to triphylite that is in the process of being altered may result in the formation of childrenite or eosphorite [PLATE 104], whereas beryllium, from the dissolution of beryl, might form a secondary beryllium phosphate such as hydroxylherderite [PLATE 105].

Evidence of chemical alteration is visible in many metamorphic rocks, too. Certain minerals, which formed originally under conditions of much higher temperature and pressure, are subsequently exposed to more-aqueous conditions at lower temperatures and pressures, in which they are not as stable. As expected, they react to form species that are more stable in the new conditions. Because these reactions occur in response to a declining temperature and pressure, the process is sometimes referred to as **retrograde metamorphism.**

One of the best examples of retrograde metamorphism I have encountered is at a small outcrop of metamorphosed sedimentary rocks in a pasture near DeKalb, New York. This locality is famous for its transparent, green, gem-quality crystals of diopside [see PLATE 115], which formed under conditions of high temperature and pressure when calcium-, magnesium-, and silica-rich sediments were metamorphosed, over a billion years ago. The diopside occurs in small crystal pockets filled with a mixture of tremolite, calcite, talc, and quartz. Unfortunately, fresh, gem-quality crystals are uncommon here because most of the crystal pockets have been exposed to solutions that have altered much of the diopside into the mineral tremolite. Many crystals show further breakdown of the tremolite into talc [PLATE 106], quartz, and calcite, probably due to continued reaction with carbonated water. Other common examples of retrograde metamorphic reactions include the alteration of micas into chlorites or vermiculite, cordierite into chlorite or mica, and olivine into serpentine ●

chapter twenty-four

Replacement Deposits

REGARDLESS of their origins or how they are mobilized, solutions containing dissolved minerals nearly always bring about some sort of chemical reaction as they travel through permeable rocks. Frequently the reaction results in the replacement of one or more minerals by others. The specific reactions and how much rock gets replaced depend not only on physical and chemical parameters such as temperature, pressure, pH, and oxidation potential, but also on the compositions of the solution and of the rock being invaded, the permeability of the rock, and how long the solution and rock are in contact. The longer the ions can penetrate the rock by diffusion, the more extensive the replacement will be. Given sufficient time to equilibrate with their surroundings, such solutions can replace enormous volumes of rock, completely changing their composition and appearance. The wall-rock alteration that accompanies the emplacement of a hydrothermal mineral deposit may provide an important exploration guide, since a zone of alteration exposed on the surface may be easier to detect than an ore body buried beneath it.

❡ One of the classic examples of a rock formed by chemical replacement is dolomitic limestone, or dolostone. Dolomite [PLATE 107], the essential mineral constituent of dolostone, is calcium magnesium carbonate [$CaMg(CO_3)_2$]. Although several theories regarding the formation of dolomite have been proposed, none is universally accepted. All explanations agree, however, that it involves the replacement of some calcium in the calcite ($CaCO_3$) of the limestone by magnesium traveling in solution. Seawater is generally considered the primary source of this magnesium. Evidence of dolomite formation is often present in limestone (or dolostone) quarries in

PLATE 107

Calcite (golden) **on Dolomite** (pink).
Sainte-Clotilde-de-Châteauguay, Quebec. 20 x 20 cm.

The occurrence of large golden calcite crystals on pink dolomite in the Beekmantown dolostone of Quebec and in MVT deposits in the midwestern United States suggests that similar environments prevailed at each location.

PLATE 108

Quartz.
Middleville, Herkimer County, New York. 4 x 5 cm.

It's easy to see how these quartz crystals got the name "Herkimer diamonds"!

the form of a "pocket layer," a particular layer of sediment that contains crystal-lined cavities called pockets or **vugs.** Quarries in the Beekmantown, Lockport, and Little Falls dolostones that cover much of central New York and southeastern Ontario and Quebec frequently encounter such layers in their operations. In addition to dolomite, these pockets often contain crystals of quartz [PLATE 108] and minor amounts of the same kinds of minerals found in MVT deposits, since they form in a similar manner. Where magnesium replacement is more extensive, magnesite ($MgCO_3$) forms. Such magnesite deposits have been found in Brumado, Bahia, Brazil, and Eugui, Navarra, Spain.

Carbonate-rich rocks such as limestone, dolostone, or marble are frequently victims of other chemical replacement reactions, involving acidic, metal-bearing solutions. These solutions sometimes cause the formation of ore deposits of lead, zinc, or iron by gradually dissolving the carbonate minerals. The addition of the carbonates to the solution changes its pH and composition, causing the metals to precipitate in situ, thereby replacing the original rock or specific minerals in it. Some important examples of deposits formed in this way include the Magma mine at Superior, Arizona; various mines in the mining districts of Leadville, Colorado, and Santa Eulalia, Chihuahua, Mexico; and the Nanisivik mine on the western end of Baffin Island, Northwest Territories, Canada. The Nanisivik mine is famous for

PLATE 109

Pyrite.
Nanisivik, Northwest Territories.
3.5 x 5 cm.

*At the Nanisivik mine beds of dolostone
were replaced by sphalerite and pyrite,
some of which contains pockets filled with
crystals such as these. The unusual shape
of these crystals was inherited from earlier-
formed, twinned crystals of marcasite,
over which they grew.*

its unusual pyrite crystals [PLATE 109], which occur in ice-filled pockets.
The pockets are filled with ice because the mine itself is situated in permafrost
(permanently frozen ground) that extends to a depth of nearly 500 meters!

The unusual shape of these pyrite crystals is related to the way they
formed. At Nanisivik, metal-bearing, sulfide-rich solutions permeated a bed of
dolostone and replaced it with pyrite, sphalerite, and galena, creating the ore
that is mined there. Originally acidic, the solutions became more basic by reaction with the dolostone. Marcasite and pyrite (both FeS_2) have different crystal
structures. Because marcasite exists in more acidic conditions than those
favored by pyrite, at Nanisivik marcasite preceded pyrite as the stable form of
FeS_2. Flat, star-shaped, twinned crystals of marcasite are common at Nanisivik
and often form a substrate upon which the pyrite crystals grow. The orienta-
tion and shape of the pyrite crystals is therefore inherited from the marcasite
crystals, which act as a template. Most pyrite crystals, which usually do
not overgrow and replace marcasite, more closely resemble those from Butte,
Montana [see PLATE 65], than those from Nanisivik.

Hundreds of other examples of chemical alteration are known in the mineral world. Whether pyrite-replaced beds of limestone or tincalconite-replaced
borax crystals, pseudomorphs provide irrefutable evidence that a change has
taken place. As long as the physical and chemical parameters are favorable and
the products of the reaction are more stable for the given conditions than are

PLATE 111

Quartz replacing Riebeckite.
Girqualand West, Namibia. 5 x 8 cm.

The texture of the original fibrous riebeckite has been perfectly preserved by quartz to form this popular gem material, tigereye.

PLATE 110

Stibiconite pseudomorph after Stibnite.
Catorce, San Luis Potosi, Mexico. 13 x 22 cm.

Probably once shiny and metallic like the stibnite in PLATE 64, these crystals were chemically altered into white, powdery stibiconite by oxygenated groundwater.

the reactants, almost any type of mineral can replace any other. Pseudomorphs may or may not make immediate "chemical sense," however. For example, it seems logical that stibiconite replaces stibnite [PLATE 110], since both minerals are antimony compounds, but why should quartz (SiO_2) replace chemically unrelated minerals such as fluorite (CaF_2) or barite ($BaSO_4$), as it does at Ouray, Colorado, or riebeckite (a Na-Fe-Mg silicate) to form the popular gemstone tigereye [PLATE 111], as it does at Griqualand West, Cape Province, South Africa? The formation of such pseudomorphs often involves a series of reactions induced by compositional changes in the solutions responsible for their creation. The minerals that make up the pseudomorphs must be more stable under the changed conditions, but the number of intermediate reactions required to arrive at these pseudomorphs may never be known. Nor can we be sure that the pseudomorphs we see represent a final, stable equilibrium for the conditions, since our collecting may have intercepted them en route to final equilibrium •

chapter twenty-five

Summary of the Chemical
Alteration of Minerals

I N reviewing why minerals are subject to chemical alteration, remember that minerals are themselves nothing more than chemicals and that they are stable only under certain sets of conditions. When the conditions change, so do the minerals. The chemical factors that affect these conditions are varied. They include parameters such as pH, the oxidizing or reducing potential of the system, and the presence or absence of specific chemical constituents. Sometimes reactions require activation energy to progress. Another essential requirement is water, which is capable of dissociating ionic compounds into their constituent cations and anions, thus making them more reactive. Physical parameters—most importantly pressure and temperature, as we will see in Part V—also affect overall conditions. Natural geological environments provide a great range of temperatures, pressures, and chemical parameters, which result in a corresponding variety of possible reactions among minerals. ❰ Some reactions, such as hydration or dehydration of a species due to changes in temperature or relative humidity, or the simple oxidation of a metal into its oxide, are relatively simple; others are much more complicated. From the Earth's surface to the water table, conditions are generally oxidizing; below the water table they are more reducing. The oxidation of metallic minerals in hydrothermal veins often results in an oxide zone in the uppermost parts of the deposit. Sulfides are oxidized to sulfates, many of which are water-soluble and therefore can be carried in aqueous solutions through permeable rocks and can react with other elements to make more complex mineral species. When the oxidized metal ions encounter reducing conditions, as they might below the water table, they may precipitate as sulfides again, sometimes in concentrations of economic importance.

Chemical alteration also occurs in magmatic and metamorphic environments, where early-formed minerals are exposed to changing conditions in which they may no longer be stable. Different minerals react in different ways when exposed to changing chemical parameters. The availability of activation energy, the presence of water, the permeability of the rock, the size of the individual grains of minerals in the rock, variations in acidity, oxidizing or reducing nature of the environment, the presence or absence of specific cations or anions, and the amount of time available for reactions to occur all influence chemical reactions. Each mineral has limits of tolerance to these variables, and each will react when those limits are exceeded in an attempt to reach a lower-energy, more stable state of equilibrium with its surroundings. No mineral is immune to chemical alteration given the right physical and chemical conditions ●

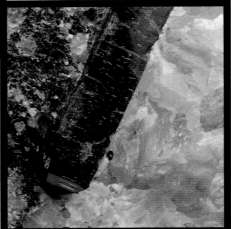

PART V

Recrystal-
lization

chapter twenty-six

Heat and Pressure

I T ' S three days after Thanksgiving, and we have a problem: how do we serve the leftover turkey this time? Should we heat it up again and serve it plain, or should we slice it and mix it with other ingredients to make turkey salad or a hot casserole? Whatever we decide, one fact remains the same: the turkey has already been cooked once and will require either reheating or the addition of new ingredients to make a new dish. Like our leftover turkey, previously formed minerals may be changed by reheating and/or combining them with other ingredients to make new minerals. Since the minerals already crystallized once before, they are said to **recrystallize** when heat and pressure involves them in the process a second time. ❰ Where does recrystallization take place? In all probability at this very moment minerals are recrystallizing about seven kilometers below our feet or anywhere else with sufficient heat and pressure to cause individual minerals to react chemically with one another or reorganize the atoms in their structures to make new minerals. Beyond the first one or two kilometers from the surface, the temperature in the Earth's crust increases with depth at an average rate of about $30°C$ per kilometer. We all know that rocks are heavy. The weight of several kilometers of rock is enormous and is the primary reason that pressure increases with depth. Depending on the density of the rock, a typical increase of pressure with depth in the Earth's crust ranges from 250 to 300 atmospheres per kilometer (1 atmosphere = 1,013 millibars, or 14.7 pounds per square inch at sea level). On the average, then, the minerals in the rocks seven kilometers below us are being subjected to temperatures and pressures of about $200°C$ and 2,000 atmospheres. Exposing minerals to this much heat and pressure is the equivalent of placing your hand on a hot coil on your kitchen stove and then parking 540 cars on top of it. It's enough heat and pressure to make you want to change the situation; it's also enough heat and pressure to initiate recrystallization in most rocks.

There are, of course, other sources of heat and pressure. When a magma intrudes a rock, for example, much heat is generated, and the pressure may increase locally because of the physical force applied by the magma. On a grand scale we know from plate tectonics that the continents are on the move. The pressure from weight and the stored thermal energy in the Earth's crustal plates is tremendous, and changes in pressure and temperature will be inevitable when these plates come in contact with one another. Furthermore, the changed conditions may persist for tens of millions of years. Because the plates themselves are recycled, so are the rocks in them. Today's marble may have been yesterday's limestone, today's garnet yesterday's beach. The recrystallization of minerals is an ongoing process.

In Parts I, II, and III, I emphasized that minerals are stable only within specific ranges of chemical and physical conditions but concentrated on the chemical conditions. In this section I will show how the two important physical parameters, heat and pressure, influence the recrystallization of minerals. Heat and pressure are two different things. **Heat** is a form of energy; **pressure** is the amount of force acting on a given unit of area. Like changes in chemical parameters, changes in temperature and/or pressure may cause an existing assemblage of minerals to become unstable and to recrystallize into one that is stable under the new conditions. Because heat and pressure are two different variables, they can affect the stability of an assemblage of minerals by acting independently or together ●

chapter twenty-seven

Metamorphism

WHEN subjected to heat and pressure, a rock may change both physically and chemically. The directed compression imposed by the collision of the Earth's plates causes crystals of platy minerals like mica or elongate crystals like amphiboles to align in parallel planes, changing the texture of the rock. (You can witness the effect by squeezing randomly stacked cards or pencils between two books.) If high enough, the pressure will crush and smear the mineral grains, increasing their total surface area and releasing trapped fluids. These fluids are critical for recrystallization. Because we usually focus our attention on the minerals, we too easily forget about the fluids. ❡ Without fluids there would be very little recrystallization because the reactions would proceed too slowly, even in terms of geological time. Increased surface area of mineral particles and the presence of fluids facilitate chemical reactions, which may be activated by heat. Some minerals respond to heat and pressure by reorganizing the atoms in their structures into a more stable arrangement; others react chemically with one another to make a new assemblage of minerals. The net result is that the whole character of the rock may be changed. Recrystallization by heat and pressure can induce both textural (physical) and mineralogical (chemical) changes in rocks. ❡ As in all other geological processes, time is also a critical factor. The longer a rock is exposed to heat and pressure, the more pronounced their effects will be. Like crystals growing in a magma or in an aqueous solution, crystals forming by recrystallization grow larger with time. The changes induced by recrystallization, however, must be accomplished in the solid state. The rock may behave like plastic, preserving swirls and folded layers created by imbalances in pressure, but it

PLATE 112

**Kyanite pseudomorphs after
Andalusite.**
Lisens Alp, Tyrol, Austria. 6 x 8 cm.

*An increase in pressure or a decrease in
temperature was needed to transform these
former andalusite crystals into kyanite.*

must not melt, for if it does, a magma forms and crystallization proceeds by
the igneous process differentiation. It is the solid-state transformation of one
rock into another in response to changes in the physical and chemical conditions around it that geologists call **metamorphism** (meaning "change in
form"). The process that brings about the change is recrystallization. Both
the geographic extent and relative intensity of metamorphism can vary widely.
The effects of metamorphism may be seen over very large areas (**regional**
metamorphism), or they may be confined to within a few meters or kilometers of an igneous intrusion that brings about only a local increase in heat and
pressure (**contact** metamorphism).

It's easy to see how melting sets limits for recrystallization at high temperatures, but what about at low temperatures? Drawing the line between
high and low temperatures is not easy. Both metamorphic and sedimentary
rocks form under heat and pressure. How then do we determine which
temperature-pressure ranges result in sedimentary rocks and which induce
metamorphism? The only objective criterion is the presence or absence of
specific minerals. We recognize the onset of metamorphism, for example,
by the appearance of one or more metamorphic **indicator** minerals.

The presence of indicator minerals and the changed textures in the rock
enable a geologist to recognize where recrystallization has taken place. Some
minerals, such as chlorite or quartz, may be stable in both sedimentary and
metamorphic rocks, so taken alone, their presence tells us little about the

temperature or pressure conditions under which the rock formed. Others, such as andalusite, kyanite [see PLATE 5], or sillimanite, are ideal indicators because their presence proves that a recrystallization reaction indicative of a specific range of pressure and temperature has occurred.

Andalusite, kyanite, and sillimanite have the same formula: Al_2SiO_5. The arrangement of the aluminum, silicon, and oxygen atoms within them, which is dependent upon pressure and temperature, is what makes them different. In general, andalusite forms under conditions of lower pressure than the others, kyanite forms at higher pressure, and sillimanite at higher temperature and higher pressure. These minerals demonstrate how temperature and pressure may act independently or together to recrystallize Al_2SiO_5. Andalusite may recrystallize into kyanite by a decrease in temperature or an increase in pressure, or into sillimanite by an increase in either or both of these variables. Similarly, kyanite may recrystallize into sillimanite by a decrease in pressure or an increase in temperature.

The famous andalusite crystals from Lisens Alp, Tyrol, Austria, are proof that such changes occur [PLATE 112]. Although for many years they were thought to be among the best examples of large, sharp andalusite crystals in the world, when X-rayed, many of these specimens exhibit patterns indicative of kyanite! Rather than pure andalusite, these crystals are kyanite pseudomorphs after andalusite, and could have formed only by an increase in pressure or a decrease in temperature after crystallization of the original andalusite.

Andalusite, kyanite, and sillimanite are good examples of indicator minerals because each forms within specific ranges of temperature and pressure. The mutual coexistence of two of these minerals in equilibrium greatly narrows the range, and the rare occurrence of all three in equilibrium defines a unique point at about 600°C and 6 kilobars of pressure. This type of theoretical information provides a powerful tool for solving geological problems, but it is not without its limitations. Experimental conditions only *approximate* natural ones, and the values obtained from them must be used with caution. The presence of trace elements and other chemical components in the natural environment, as well as unanticipated physical complications can change things dramatically!

Nevertheless, if we are mindful of such limitations and account for them, a sound, theoretical understanding of what *should* happen to certain minerals when exposed to specific temperatures and pressures provides us with a means to test geological hypotheses. At present the study of metamorphic rocks is one of the most important branches of the geological sciences because it is crucial to our understanding and assessment of the plate tectonic model of Earth dynamics. If we can predict how specific minerals should recrystallize as they accompany a plate on its way down to the mantle, we can look for the predicted results among the rocks in plates that have made the journey ●

chapter twenty-eight

Composition

INDEPENDENT of how much or how long heat and pressure are applied to a rock is one other important and by now obvious factor that determines what minerals will form: the chemical composition of the rock being recrystallized. (After all, we can't make a ham sandwich from leftover turkey!) The fewer the initial ingredients, the fewer the potential products of recrystallization. In the simplest case, of course, only one mineral is present. Pure sandstones or limestones, which are composed almost entirely of the minerals quartz or calcite, respectively, fall into this category. When sandstone and limestone recrystallize into their metamorphic equivalents, quartzite and marble, their textures may change and coarsen, but their constituent minerals remain the same. Recrystallization of chemically more-diverse rocks, such as shale or impure limestone, has a greater variety of potential outcomes. ❡ Shale is composed largely of clay minerals and quartz (SiO_2). Clay minerals have various compositions and contain aluminum, sodium, potassium, calcium, magnesium, iron, and other elements. The quartz and clay minerals in shale are stable over a broad range of pressure up to about 300°C, so until that temperature is reached, few new minerals form. The physical appearance of the shale may change as fluids are driven off and it becomes more compact and brittle, but as the temperature increases, chemical changes produce various metamorphic indicator minerals. One of the first is pyrophyllite, which forms by the reaction of quartz with the clay mineral kaolinite. At around 400°C pyrophyllite breaks down into Al_2SiO_5 (in the form of either andalusite or kyanite, depending on the pressure), quartz, and water. ❡ By this time the shale has probably become much harder and more compact and acquired a

Almandine in Mica Schist.
Wrangell, Alaska. 2.5-cm crystals.

When aluminum-rich sediments are subjected to moderately high temperature and pressure, crystals of almandine garnet may form as the sediments are transformed into metamorphic rocks.

Cordierite.
India. 13 x 14 cm.

Known as iolite or water sapphire, this attractive blue gem mineral forms when aluminum- and magnesium-rich rocks are subjected to high temperature and pressure.

shiny luster, the result of alignment of the platy clay minerals. It has become the metamorphic rock, slate. With increasing temperature and pressure, the slate will become even shinier, and its layers will probably deform as it recrystallizes into yet another rock, phyllite. Between 400 and 500°C chlorites and micas begin to appear, and the rock is transformed from phyllite into schist. Crystals of almandine garnet [PLATE 113] also may form at this time, especially with an increase in pressure. From 500 to 700°C additional minerals, such as staurolite, cordierite, or sillimanite [PLATES 5 and 114] may form, along with clots or distinct bands of feldspars and quartz, changing the rock from a schist into a gneiss.

In the late 1800s a Scottish geologist, George Barrow, found this precise sequence of minerals in northern Scotland, where shales have been metamorphosed by high heat and pressure. Starting where the effects of metamorphism were the least and progressing to where they were the most intense, Barrow found that the rocks changed from shale to slate, to phyllite, chlorite schist, mica schist, and finally gneiss. He also observed that the minerals in these rocks appeared in the following order: chlorite, biotite mica, almandine garnet, staurolite, kyanite, sillimanite. A very similar sequence exists between eastern Vermont and the White Mountains of New Hampshire, and many others have been documented elsewhere.

The composition of an impure limestone is quite different from that of shale and consists predominantly of calcite with variable amounts of dolomite, quartz, clays, and other minerals. Since these minerals provide calcium, magnesium, silicon, and aluminum as "ingredients," these same elements must constitute the new minerals formed by recrystallization. Exposing an impure limestone to increasing temperature and pressure usually results in the silicate minerals talc, tremolite, diopside, and forsterite. Because the carbonate content of limestone normally exceeds its silicate content, "excess" calcite left over from the reactions that form these minerals is common, which explains why they are often enclosed in coarsely recrystallized calcite [see PLATES 123 and 128].

Because the carbonates calcite and dolomite release carbon dioxide when they break down, the concentration of CO_2, as well as that of H_2O, becomes important in regulating the possible reactions. At very high temperatures, calcite and quartz may react to form the calcium silicate wollastonite and CO_2. However, since CO_2 is a product of the reaction, it must be removed for the reaction to proceed. (Remember the volleyball players from Chapter 17; the game could be won by adding players to the reactants team or removing them from the products team.) An environment of low pressure (likely provided by contact metamorphism), into which the CO_2 can escape, or the presence of water to dilute the CO_2 concentration accomplishes this task.

When limestones rich in silica and magnesium recrystallize, rocks such as tremolite-diopside schists (often with interbedded quartzite) may result. Such rocks are found at a number of localities in St. Lawrence County, New York, where well-formed crystals of diopside and tremolite [PLATES 106 and 115]

PLATE 115

Diopside.
DeKalb, New York. 4 x 4 cm.

These gem-quality crystals of diopside probably formed by the recrystallization of a sandy dolostone under conditions of high heat and pressure.

PLATE 116

Lazurite.
Sar e Sang, Nuristan, Afghanistan.
2-cm crystal.

Known to the gem trade as lapis lazuli, lazurite has been mined in northeastern Afghanistan since biblical times.

PLATE 117

Corundum, variety ruby.
Mysore, India. 3 x 4 cm.

These rubies probably formed by the recrystallization of aluminum-rich rocks at very high temperatures and pressures.

occur in small pockets or seams. The famous diopside locality dear DeKalb and uvite locality near Richville (Gouverneur township) are classic examples. By contrast, if little silica is available, the presence of aluminum may lead to the formation of the oxide minerals spinel or corundum, since it is the silicate minerals that normally incorporate the aluminum. The ruby deposits of Mogok, Burma, which have yielded fabulous gem-quality ruby corundum and spinel crystals for centuries, are probably the most famous example. The presence of evaporite minerals in carbonate-rich sediments may lead to the formation of another important gem, lapis lazuli, which is composed of the ultramarine blue mineral lazurite [PLATE 116].

Any rock—igneous, sedimentary, or metamorphic—can be recrystallized. The minerals that form depend on the composition of that rock, the amount of heat and pressure to which it is subjected, the availability of fluids to promote recrystallization, and the allowance of sufficient time for the process to occur. The diversity of minerals that can result is enormous. Rocks such as peridotite, that are rich in magnesium silicate minerals, may recrystallize to form deposits of talc, serpentine, or chrysotile asbestos. Given the right conditions, the recrystallization of aluminum-rich rocks yields rubies or sapphires [PLATE 117]. Seafloor sediments containing local concentrations of manganese may recrystallize into rhodonite [PLATE 118]. At Franklin, New Jersey, metamorphism of manganese- and zinc-rich sediments in contact with limestone has produced a unique zinc ore deposit consisting of coarsely crystallized franklinite, willemite, and zincite [PLATE 119], along with numerous more-exotic species. Hundreds of other examples of regional metamorphic minerals could be cited, from actinolite to zussmanite, but the basis of their formation is the same: each is more stable in the imposed conditions of temperature and pressure than were the initial minerals from which it formed●

chapter twenty-nine

Complex Recrystallization

SO FAR, I have talked only about minerals that form during the large-scale, regional recrystallization of rocks, driven by heat and pressure supplied by burial or tectonic forces. All the essential ingredients of recrystallization have been contained in the rocks themselves. Essentially, I have been only reheating the turkey. Now it's time to make a casserole by adding ingredients from outside sources. This is exactly what happens during **contact metamorphism** within a few meters of a small igneous intrusion or a few kilometers of a larger one [FIGURE 1]. ❧ The magma provides not only heat but also new ingredients to the rock that it intrudes by the injection and diffusion of fluids. While the heat induces recrystallization, the fluids bearing chemical components may react with one or more of the minerals in the rock, chemically replacing them. Both processes are commonly grouped together under the umbrella of contact metamorphism because both are confined to an area in contact with the intrusion. This contact zone of recrystallized and chemically replaced rock physically manifests itself as a band or **aureole** around the intrusion. Because any type of magma can intrude any type of rock, the possibilities for many different and exotic mineral species to form are great. Let's look at a few recipes for mineral casseroles. ❧ As we learned in Part II, the magmatic fluids that form granitic pegmatites become enriched in volatiles and light elements such as lithium, boron, and beryllium by the "law of constant rejection." When such a magmatic fluid intrudes a rock, these elements tend to diffuse into the rock because their small atomic size and mass usually permits their access to even the smallest permeable spaces. These elements form highly reactive ions that chemically alter the rock and form

PLATE 120

Beryl, variety emerald.
Malisheva mine, Yekaterinburg,
Sverdlovsk Oblast, Russia.
3-cm crystal.

Emeralds in mica-schist deposits have a
complex genesis, involving both magmatic
and metamorphic processes.

FIGURE I

Contact Metamorphism.

When a magma intrudes a rock, chemical components are often exchanged, and the local increase in heat and pressure recrystallizes the rock in contact with the magma. A common example is the intrusion of a dolomitic limestone by a silicate magma to form a rock known as skarn. Silicon and aluminum from the magma react with calcium and magnesium in the limestone to make minerals such as diopside and grossular in a halo, or aureole, around the magma.

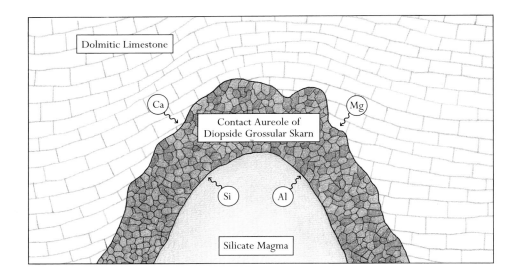

Dolmitic Limestone

Ca

Mg

Contact Aureole of Diopside Grossular Skarn

Si   Al

Silicate Magma

new minerals. Lithium-bearing amphiboles such as holmquistite, and the magnesium tourmaline, dravite, which are often found in rocks adjacent to intrusions of granitic pegmatites, are two examples. The lithium or boron required to make these minerals is supplied by the invading magmatic fluid; most of the other elements are provided by minerals already present in the rock.

When a beryllium-bearing fluid from a granitic magma invades a silica-poor rock such as amphibolite or serpentinite, a mica schist-type beryl deposit may result. The significance of such deposits is that the rocks that are intruded often contain minor concentrations of chromium or vanadium, two elements that may be incorporated by the beryl to produce emeralds [PLATE 120]. The legendary emerald mines of Cleopatra, near the Red Sea in Egypt, are of this type and are among the oldest mines known, having produced emeralds for Cleopatra, and possibly even King Tutankhamen, over 3,300 years ago. Similar deposits in Russia, Brazil, and other countries are the major producers today. In some of these deposits the rare variety of chrysoberyl, alexandrite, is also mined. Named for Russian emperor Alexander II, this unique gemstone appears green in daylight but red in artificial incandescent light ●

chapter thirty

Skarns: Trash or Treasure?

IN Part IV we learned that at low temperatures limestone is susceptible to chemical replacement by metal-bearing solutions. At higher temperatures, near intruding magma, limestone typically recrystallizes into coarse-grained marble, while iron, aluminum, silicon, sodium, potassium, and water supplied by the magma react with the limestone to make silicate minerals containing those elements. The resulting recrystallized rock, called **skarn** [see FIGURE 1], may host a wide variety of mineral species. The word skarn is derived from the Swedish for "waste" or "trash." It originally referred to the silicate-rich band of waste rock (i.e., the contact metamorphic aureole) surrounding more-valuable ore. ❑ One person's trash is another's treasure. Some skarns may contain economically recoverable ore minerals such as magnetite, cassiterite, scheelite, sphalerite, or chalcopyrite, or provide local concentrations of manganese, phosphorus, uranium, and other metals. Many skarns contain large, well-formed crystals enclosed in recrystallized calcite, or marble. The crystals of ilmenite from Arendal, Norway, or Bancroft, Ontario, on the other hand, may not occur in sufficient quantities to be valued for their titanium content, but they are valued by scientists and collectors as some of the largest well-formed crystals of ilmenite known. Likewise, the spinel crystals from Amity, New York, may be too dark and opaque for use as gemstones, but they are among the finest large crystals of spinel in the world. ❑ The minerals that form in a skarn depend on temperature and pressure, as well as on the compositions of both the magmatic fluid and the original limestone with which it reacts. The heat transferred to the limestone from the magma may increase the temperature in the contact zone to nearly that of

PLATE 121

Uvite.
Powers farm, Pierrepont, New York.
7 x 12 cm.

The origin of the skarnlike assemblage of minerals at this famous locality is not well understood because much of its geology is concealed by overlying sand that was deposited by glaciers approximately ten thousand years ago.

PLATE 122

Uvarovite.
Outokumpu, Finland. 2-cm crystals.

Most garnet is red, but when rocks containing small amounts of chromium are recrystallized under heat and pressure, the rare green garnet, uvarovite, may form.

PLATE 123

Diopside (green) and Phlogopite (brown) in Calcite.
Bird's Creek, Ontario. 5 x 9 cm.

These calcium- and magnesium-rich silicate minerals are typical of skarns that form in dolomitic limestones.

PLATE 124

Fluor Silicic Edenite.
Wilberforce, Ontario. 4 x 4 cm.

The fluorine in this complex species of amphibole is a reminder of the importance of volatile components such as fluorine and water in promoting recrystallization reactions.

the magma itself. Therefore, it is not unusual to find feldspars, garnets, pyroxenes, or olivines in a contact aureole, since these minerals also are stable in high-temperature magmatic environments. The concentrations of water, carbon dioxide, fluorine, and other volatile components have a great influence on the total pressure and regulation of possible reactions between the various minerals present. The fewer the chemical constituents available, the fewer and simpler the minerals that can form. The simplest of these are anhydrous minerals, such as magnetite or wollastonite, that contain only one or two metal cations. Vesuvianite and uvite tourmaline [PLATE 121] are examples of chemically more-complex species found in skarns.

Given the elements most often involved in the formation of a skarn, and recalling some of the minerals formed by magmatic processes, it is not too difficult to predict which minerals might be found in skarns. For example, garnets form at relatively high temperatures and include species rich in calcium, aluminum, and iron, elements common in skarns. The calcium-rich garnets grossular, andradite, and uvarovite [PLATE 122] thus all occur in skarns. Like garnets, the pyroxenes, amphiboles, and micas most often encountered in skarns are rich in calcium, iron, and magnesium. Examples include the pyroxenes hedenbergite and diopside [PLATE 123]; the amphiboles tremolite, actinolite, and edenite [PLATE 124]; and the micas biotite and phlogopite [see PLATE 123]. Composed of similar elements, the minerals epidote and vesuvianite also are common in some skarns.

Potassium and plagioclase feldspars both occur in skarns, as does scapolite, because the combination of an impure limestone and a magmatic fluid rich in silica provides all the ingredients necessary to make these minerals. The calcium-dominant scapolite, meionite [PLATE 125], is especially prevalent in skarns because of the universal abundance of calcium in limestones. Large, well-formed crystals of scapolite have been found in hundreds of localities. One very different and interesting occurrence, however, stands out from all the rest: Mars. Some geologists believe that scapolite is present on Mars because infrared spectra from certain areas of the planet's surface closely resemble those of scapolite. Assuming that scapolite does exist on Mars, the requirements for its formation on the Earth, particularly the fluid phase necessary to promote crystallization, suggest that at one time in the geological past Mars had a very different atmosphere and perhaps even lakes or oceans, the remains of which may now be stored in its polar ice caps.

Because they result from recrystallization, chemical alteration, and replacement occurring simultaneously, skarns are among the most complex deposits known. In some of the billion-year-old metamorphosed sediments of northern New York State and southeastern Ontario and Quebec are a number of classic mineral localities that contain typical skarn minerals. Specimens of uvite, titanite, zircon, uraninite, fluorapatite, and other species from these occurrences can be viewed in nearly every major natural history museum in the world [PLATES 121 and 123 to 128]. Marble is usually present at or nearby most of these localities, but in some cases the skarns form curious, calcite-cored veins that cut

PLATE 126

Zircon.
Silver Queen mine, near Perth,
Ontario. 4-cm crystal.

*In skarns, the occasional occurrence of
minerals such as zircon, that are typical of
magmatic deposits, is a reminder of their
complex origin.*

PLATE 127

Uraninite.
Cardiff mine, Wilberforce, Ontario.
2-cm crystal.

*Some of the largest well-formed crystals of
uraninite in North America come from
metamorphic calcite-fluorite veins in the
billion-year-old rocks of the Wilberforce
area in southeastern Ontario.*

PLATE 128

Fluorapatite in Calcite.
Yates mine, Otter Lake, Quebec.
2 x 6 cm crystal.

*Did the phosphorus required to form this
fluorapatite crystal come from nearby
sediments or from the igneous rocks with
which its calcite matrix was in contact?*

across or are included within the adjacent metamorphosed sediments rather than the marble. Although the veins often contain large, well-formed crystals, most of the minerals are the same species that occur in the adjacent rocks.

Various theories on the origin of these veins have been proposed, but none is universally accepted. The veins are similar to skarns in that they occur locally in metamorphic rocks, usually near marble, and they contain skarnlike mineral assemblages developed in contact zones between silicate-rich and coarsely recrystallized carbonate-rich rocks. Often, however, no source of igneous-derived fluids is apparent. One interpretation, of course, is that an igneous source does not exist. Perhaps the fluids are derived tectonically, and these deposits are but one more example of how more than one geological process can create conditions conducive to the formation of the same suite of minerals.

Sometimes the mountain may come to Mohammed. We have seen how skarn minerals form when a magma intrudes a carbonate rock such as limestone. On a smaller scale, however, a somewhat reverse process can happen. Because they are of sedimentary origin, limestones can't really "intrude" magmas, but pieces of limestone may be incorporated into a magma as inclusions. The net result is often very much the same: a similar geological environment of high temperature and relatively low pressure results in new minerals being formed as the limestone is recrystallized and chemically altered by fluids from the magma. The resulting minerals are those typical of skarn deposits. Two examples of such occurrences are the blocks of recrystallized limestone ejected by Mount Vesuvius, Italy, and the marble inclusions that occur in the nepheline syenite at Mont Saint-Hilaire, Quebec. Probably the most famous mineral formed in such a manner is the namesake of Mount Vesuvius, vesuvianite [see PLATE 130], which occurs along with other common skarn minerals at both localities ●

chapter thirty-one

Rodingites

LIKE skarns, rodingites have a complex origin. In Chapter 15 I explained how some hydrothermal solutions evolve from tectonic processes to produce alpine cleft and related vein-type deposits. The essential elements of the minerals in the clefts and veins were provided by the enclosing rock, the gross character and composition of which remained relatively unchanged. As these same solutions travel farther from their points of origin and encounter rocks of different compositions, however, they may chemically alter the enclosing rocks, producing new suites of minerals. **Rodingites** are one example of rocks formed in this way. ❡ Although their origin is not completely understood, it is generally agreed that rodingites represent chemically altered granitic dikes that are associated with metamorphosed oceanic crustal rocks scraped off a tectonic plate during continental collisions [FIGURE J]. Rodingites occur in folded mountain chains throughout the world. The elevated temperature and pressure provided by the converging plates liberate hydrothermal solutions that chemically alter the olivine and pyroxene in the magnesium-rich oceanic crustal rocks into serpentinite and convert some of the granitic dikes into rodingites. The more-famous and better-studied rodingites of North America are in the northern Appalachians, which extend from northern Vermont, through southeastern Quebec, to Newfoundland. Similar occurrences can be found in the Ural Mountains of Russia, Pakistan, and numerous localities in northern Italy and southern Tyrol, Austria. ❡ Some of the world's finest examples of grossular, diopside, vesuvianite, clinochlore, and other minerals have come from these deposits [PLATES 129 to 131]. Many of these minerals from widely separated localities such as

Asbestos, Quebec; Eden Mills, Vermont; and Asbest, Russia, are indistinguishable from each other, suggesting that similar geological conditions once existed at each of these places. Grossular from each of these localities ranges in color from pale pink to bright orange; some specimens are even emerald green. Green grossular owes its color to chromium, originally present in the magnesium-rich rocks as chromite and made available to the grossular by the fluids moving through and chemically altering the rocks. The cores of many of the green grossular crystals from Asbestos, Quebec, contain a tiny grain of chromite. Andradite garnet also occurs in some rodingites. The most famous locality is probably Val Malenco, Lombardy, Italy, where the green, gem variety known as demantoid has been found. Excellent crystals of epidote, clinozoisite, prehnite, pectolite, and many other minerals also have been found in rodingites.

Skarns and rodingites are not the only rocks formed by the action of chemically reactive fluids during metamorphism. The movement of hydrothermal solutions along contact zones between rocks of different com-

PLATE 131

Diopside (pale green) **with Clinochlore** (micaceous green) **and Grossular** (orange).
Mussa Alp, Piedmont, Italy.
3.5 x 4.5 cm.

The same tectonic forces that created the Alps also mobilized hydrothermal solutions to make these minerals and others in a belt of serpentinite that stretches across northern Italy into Austria.

PLATE 132

Charoite.
Chary River, northwest Aldan, Yakut, Russia. 8 x 10 cm.

Complex reactions between alkalic rocks and marble resulted in this attractive, unique gem mineral.

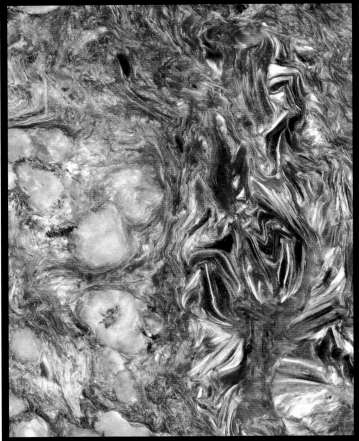

The Formation of Rodingites.

a. When plates collide, pieces of oceanic crust are sometimes thrust over continental crust. b. With time the oceanic crust may become incorporated into a mountain chain, as the plates continue to move. c. Granitic magma formed by melting sediments dragged down a subduction zone rises and intrudes the old slab of oceanic crust as dikes. d. Heat and pressure cause hydrothermal solutions to be driven from the rock. The solutions chemically alter the oceanic crustal rock (e.g., peridotite) into serpentinite and the granitic dikes into rodingites.

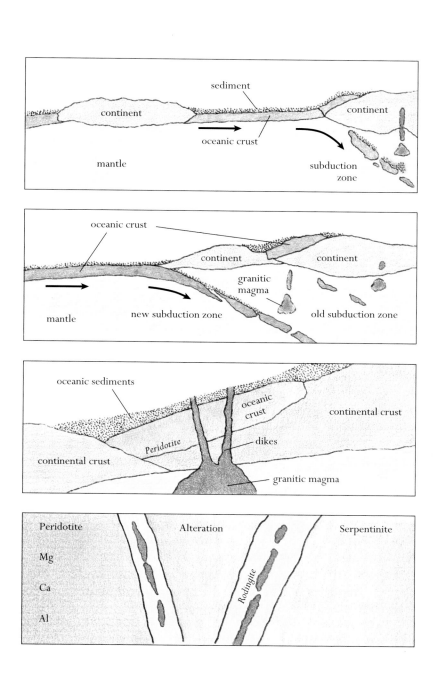

positions frequently results in the chemical alteration of one or both rocks. This type of alteration is especially evident in tectonically active areas such as folded mountain chains, where changes in temperature and pressure are experienced. The commercial deposits of talc in the Appalachians of Vermont and in southern Quebec probably formed in such a manner along contacts between serpentinite and various indigenous rocks, as did deposits of nephrite jade in similar geological settings. The huge almandine garnet crystals exposed at the Barton mine on Gore Mountain, near North Creek, New York, also are believed to be the result of chemical replacement along a contact zone, in this case between an olivine metagabbro and metasyenite. Charoite [PLATE 132] is found in chemically altered rocks at the contact of a nepheline aegirine syenite with limestone in the Chary River area, northwest Aldan, Yakut, Russia. Occurring as large masses of interlocking lavender crystals associated with several other rare minerals, charoite is used as both a gemstone and an ornamental rock. To date, the deposit remains unique●

chapter thirty-two

Summary of Recrystallization

MANY minerals are not stable when exposed to high temperature and pressure and respond by reorganizing their own atoms into new, more-stable structures or by reacting chemically to form new minerals that are more stable under the prevailing conditions. This natural process of recycling old minerals into new ones is known as recrystallization. Recrystallization is facilitated by the presence of (usually water-rich) fluids in the rock, although the process itself occurs in the solid state. The metamorphic rocks that result are changed both chemically and physically. The parallel alignment of platy and rodlike minerals in response to directed pressure usually imparts a layered structure to these rocks. ❏ The three most important factors that determine which minerals form during recrystallization are temperature, pressure, and the chemical components available from the minerals and fluids in the rock. After metamorphism, rocks often show progressive zones of changing mineral assemblages that correlate with gradients in temperature and pressure. The presence of indicator minerals denotes specific conditions of temperature and pressure. The greater the number of chemical components involved, the greater the variety of minerals that may form. ❏ In more-complex systems, additional chemical components may be introduced by the intrusion of a magma or its accompanying diffusion. Since the area affected is confined to that in contact with the intrusion, the resulting process is called contact metamorphism. Within the contact zone, or aureole, there is usually evidence of chemical replacement of one mineral by another. Contact metamorphism is characterized by high temperature but relatively low pressure. Skarns are one of the most familiar examples of contact metamorphism, and result when a magma intrudes a carbonate-rich rock, such as limestone or dolostone. The carbonate rock supplies calcium, magnesium, and carbon dioxide to the system, while the magma supplies silicon, aluminum, iron, sodium, potassium, and various volatile components. The resulting skarn is thus rich in silicates of those elements. The presence of other minor chemical constituents enables numerous more exotic minerals to form. The conditions of contact metamorphism may be mimicked by other geological processes, such as the incorporation of pieces of limestone by a magma and their subsequent recrystallization under conditions of high temperature and low pressure.

Various geological settings may provide the conditions necessary for recrystallization. Both temperature and pressure increase as one progresses into the Earth's crust from its surface. Thus, simple burial of sediments in deep basins may be enough to initiate recrystallization. As sediments and oceanic crustal rocks are carried along the Earth's tectonic plates, they are also subjected to changes in heat and pressure. These changes are especially evident at plate boundaries, where plates collide. Hydrothermal fluids may be released by such tectonic activity and chemically alter the rocks they contact, making new minerals. Magnesium-rich rocks such as peridotites are often transformed into serpentinite during the process, while associated igneous rocks such as granite may be converted into rodingites. Rocks of dissimilar compositions also may be placed in contact with each other by activity along faults. Fluids migrating along their contact under the elevated temperatures and pressures of metamorphism may promote recrystallization. Numerous geological environments are conducive to recrystallization, each providing a mechanism for change in its governing parameters: temperature, pressure, and available chemical components •

Summary

# of Mineral-forming Processes

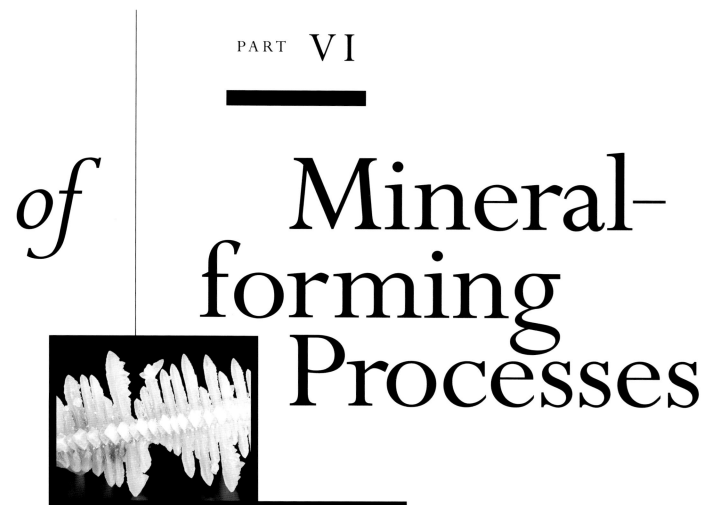

PLATE 133

Beryl, variety emerald.
Muzo, Colombia. 4-cm crystal.

Several mineral-forming processes were required to make this crystal of emerald.

PLATE 134

Cubanite.
Henderson mine, Chibougamau, Quebec. 3-cm crystal.

It is hard to believe that the iron, copper, and sulfur constituting these lustrous, rare crystals of cubanite were probably once a black cloud of sulfide "smoke" spewed from a hydrothermal vent kilometers beneath the ocean.

chapter thirty-three

Interaction of Mineral-forming

Processes

MINERALS are chemical compounds having specific ranges of stability with respect to physical and chemical factors such as heat, pressure, pH, and oxidation. These ranges are broad for some minerals, such as quartz and calcite, but narrow for others, such as diamond and gypsum. Often more than one geological environment provides conditions conducive to the formation of a particular mineral. That's why vivianite and other phosphate minerals may occur in such radically different geological settings as granitic pegmatites in Brazil or quartz veins in shale in northern Canada. More than one geological or mineral-forming process may be required to make some minerals. Nowhere is this better illustrated than in the famous emerald deposits of Colombia, or the volcanogenic massive sulfide deposits of the Canadian shield. ❡ The emerald mines of the Muzo and Chivor districts of Colombia have been actively worked since the mid-1500s, but only now are we beginning to understand how the deposits probably formed. A good part of the reason for our longstanding ignorance is that these deposits are totally unlike any other known occurrences of beryl, including other emeralds. Instead of occurring in granitic pegmatites or mica schists, emeralds in Colombia [PLATE 133] occur in veins of calcite and albite in black, organic-rich shales and limestones — sedimentary rocks normally indicative of relatively low temperatures and pressures. Even a few rare specimens of emerald replacing fossil snails have been found! Because all other occurrences of beryl are related to magmatic fluids, for years a similar origin was surmised for the solutions that deposited the Colombian emeralds. However, recent research offers a very different and plausible explanation. ❡ By studying the compositions and distribution of specific isotopes in fluid inclusions in these emeralds, we now know that the hydrothermal solution from which the emeralds crystallized does not have a magmatic origin at all. Instead it is more akin to a localized, higher-temperature version of a Mississippi Valley Type deposit. In MVT deposits metals are leached from sediments in geological basins by brines, which carry them in solution to their site of deposition. There chemical reactions (perhaps involving organic molecules) cause the metal-bearing minerals to precipitate.

In Colombia, tectonic forces deformed and fractured the organic-rich shale and limestone that hosts the emerald deposits, creating openings and releasing brines trapped in the sediments. The beryllium and other essential elements needed to form the emeralds were probably present in the sediments themselves and entered the brine complexed with organic molecules. As the somewhat acidic brine cooled in the fractures, it reacted with the limestone, which neutralized the brine and caused various minerals, including emeralds, to precipitate. The fortuitously present sulfur (probably in the form of hydrogen sulfide, H_2S) scavenged the available iron and precipitated it as pyrite, thereby preventing iron from being incorporated by the crystallizing emeralds. If that had happened, the color of the resulting beryl would probably have been a much more ordinary blue-green.

Volcanogenic massive sulfide deposits have an even more complex history. To see how some of these deposits form, we must journey to the bottom of the ocean where two of the Earth's plates are actively spreading apart, such as along the Mid-Atlantic or Juan de Fuca Ridges. Scientists traveling in deep-sea submersible vessels have visited both locations, collecting samples and recording their findings on videotape. In addition to witnessing underwater volcanic eruptions and discovering some new, interesting life forms, these scientists discovered and filmed a geological wonder that has revolutionized how geologists interpret the origins of many ore deposits: **black smokers.** Like smokestacks on a factory roof, these strange pipelike structures billow out clouds of what appears to be dense, black smoke, which, when analyzed, is found to be a very fine precipitate of sulfide minerals.

As seawater seeps down through cracks in the basaltic oceanic crust on the ocean floor, it is warmed by the magma below [FIGURE K]. The resulting hot, salty solution dissolves some of the metal-bearing minerals in the basalt. As if in a giant percolator, the solution is heated and forced back up through the cracks in the rock, dissolving more minerals, until ultimately it encounters the ice-cold seawater. Unable to remain in solution because of the abrupt change in temperature, the metals precipitate out as metal-sulfide minerals such as pyrite, chalcopyrite, galena, and sphalerite. The larger the chimneys grow, the more unstable they become, and eventually they topple over in a mound, but the finely dispersed sulfide "smoke" may spread out over a considerable area and settle as finely banded layers on the seafloor.

The finely dispersed sulfide minerals produced by black smokers are gradually buried by other marine sediments and carried away from their birthplace as the plates slowly drift apart. Eventually the sulfide-rich sediments reach a continent, where they are either carried downward along with the subsiding plate or are scraped off onto the continent. In the first case they descend toward the mantle and are heated until they melt, forming a sulfide-rich magma. Under pressure the

Volcanogenic Massive Sulfide
Deposits.

*a. Near mid-oceanic ridges where two
plates spread apart, magma heats
seawater, which infiltrates fractures in the
oceanic crust and dissolves metals from the
rock. The heated water is forced upward
under pressure and erupts from the seafloor
as what is known as a black smoker. The
"smoke" is really a fine precipitate of
sulfide minerals that settles to the bottom
as sediment. b. The sulfide-rich sediment is
carried by the moving plate to a continent,
where it may be scraped off and recrystallized into a massive sulfide deposit in a
forming folded mountain chain.*
*c. Alternatively, the sediment may be
carried down a subduction zone and
melted to form a sulfide-rich magma,
which rises and forms a massive sulfide
deposit by crystallization and segregation.*

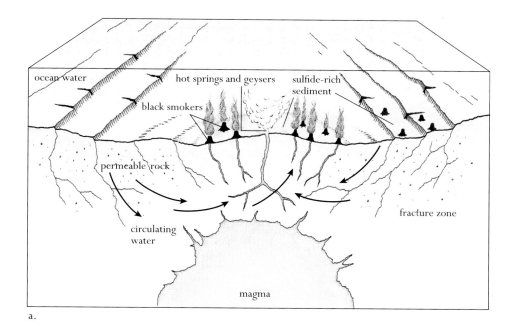

a.

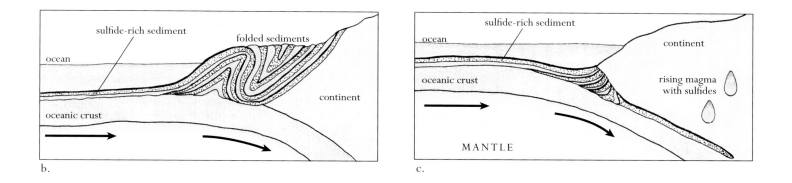

b.

c.

magma rises along faults and fractures into the crust above it, where it eventually may form an ore deposit. In the second scenario, the sulfides are subjected to
substantial heat and pressure from the tremendous force exerted by the converging plates and are recrystallized. Continued tectonic activity causes the sulfides to be folded and fractured as they are uplifted and incorporated into a
forming mountain chain.

The fracturing also opens channels for tectonically activated hydrothermal
solutions to enter and precipitate a second generation of sulfides, locally enrich-
ing the grade of the ore. The cubanite crystals in plate 134 probably formed in
such a manner. As uplift continues, erosion wears down the rocks covering the
deposit, exposing it to the surface and providing some lucky prospector with an
opportunity to become a millionaire. Some of the world's richest mines are
thought to have formed in this way. The repeated association of such massive
sulfide deposits with volcanic rocks and marine sediments along both modern
and ancient continental margins is more than just coincidence; it's a consequence of the recycling of the Earth's minerals by plate tectonics ●

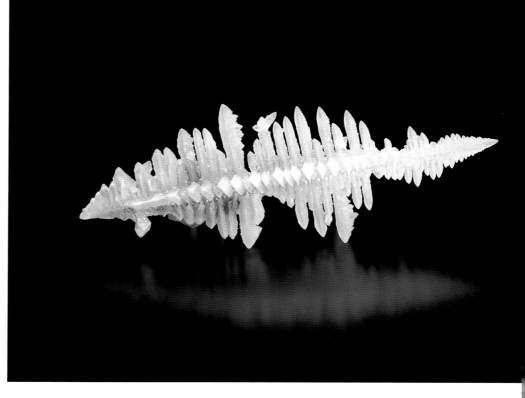

Sulfur.

Perticara, Sicily, Italy. 3-cm crystals.

Once thought to be of volcanic origin, we now know that these crystals of sulfur formed by a biological process, as bacteria chemically converted the sulfate in minerals like anhydrite into elemental sulfur.

Sal Ammoniac.

Ravat, Tadshikistan. 1.5 x 5 cm.

This type of skeletal crystal commonly results from rapid growth, which is characteristic of sublimation, the transition of a substance directly from a vapor to the solid state. In this case the vapor came from burning beds of coal.

chapter thirty-four

Biogenic Minerals

IN addition to the tectonic forces that recycle rocks and make minerals, we must reckon with another "force," the rather incredible "geological force" of life itself. In Part IV I gave examples of how oxidation-reduction reactions govern the genesis of certain minerals. Another very interesting, though less obvious, variant of such reactions — that provided by certain microorganisms — also leads to the formation of minerals. Plants and animals have respiratory systems that oxidize food aerobically (i.e., using oxygen) to produce energy. Anaerobic bacteria, however, do not have this capability. They derive their energy by the process of **chemosynthesis.** ❦ Anaerobic bacteria can take advantage of elements with multiple oxidation states, such as iron and sulfur, by effecting a change in the oxidation state. The energy released in the process sustains the life of the bacteria. For example, some bacteria can oxidize native sulfur or sulfide-bearing minerals into sulfates. The reverse process is accomplished by other bacteria, which reduce sulfates to sulfides. The white staining frequently seen on old limestone or concrete buildings is a result of the first of these reactions. Sulfate produced by bacteria oxidizing sulfides in the limestone reacts with calcium in the limestone or concrete to make gypsum (calcium sulfate), which forms the powdery white coating. The products of sulfur-reducing bacteria commonly occur as pyrite or other sulfide minerals in dark, organic-rich shales [see PLATE 78]. Because the genesis of such minerals is biologically driven, they are said to have a **biogenic** origin. ❦ Another, and economically more important, example of a biogenic mineral is native sulfur itself [PLATE 135]. Once thought to be of volcanic origin, most of the world's major sulfur deposits, such as those in Poland, in Sicily, or

along the Gulf coast of the southeastern United States, are now known to have been created by sulfate reduction by microorganisms. The biogenic origin of native sulfur was determined using isotope analysis. The most abundant isotope of sulfur is ^{32}S, but ^{34}S is also relatively common. Bacteria preferentially act on the lighter ^{32}S isotope, which causes a relative increase in the concentration of the heavier isotope, ^{34}S, in the "unused" sulfate. By measuring the concentrations of these two isotopes in the sulfur and sulfate, we can establish whether or not the reaction has been driven by bacteria.

In the Sicilian sulfur deposits, it is believed that beds of gypsum and anhydrite (both calcium sulfates) provided the sulfate that was reduced to sulfide (probably in the form of H_2S) while organic material was oxidized, liberating carbon dioxide. The carbon dioxide dissolved in water, forming carbonic acid (H_2CO_3), which reacted with the calcium ions derived from the gypsum and anhydrite to form aragonite or calcite (both $CaCO_3$). The frequent presence of hydrocarbons in close association with all these minerals lends credence to the theory that they are biogenic.

The crystals of sulfur, sal ammoniac [PLATE 136], and other minerals from Ravat, Tadshikistan, have different biological roots. These minerals form from vapors given off by burning beds of coal below the Earth's surface. Following fractures to the surface, the vapors cool rapidly, and the minerals form by **sublimation** (i.e., crystallization from a vapor directly to a solid). Certain calcium phosphate minerals (e.g., hydroxlapatite, monetite or brushite) are thought to derive their phosphorus from accumulations of bird droppings (called guano) from the large colonies of birds that inhabit some coral islands. The droppings are a source of soluble phosphorus that reacts with the calcium carbonate in the underlying coral to produce these minerals.

Similar reactions are known to occur in limestone caves that contain large accumulations of bat excrement (also called guano). Iron and aluminum phosphates such as strengite, phosphosiderite, and variscite have been found in guano deposits where iron- or aluminum-rich minerals are present beneath the droppings. Near Kerch, on the Crimean peninsula of Ukraine, well-formed crystals of vivianite and anapaite occur in casts of fossil shells [PLATE 137]. Vivianite occurs with other phosphate species in fossil shells at Mullica Hill, New Jersey, and the large crystals of vivianite found in clay in Richmond, Virginia, in the 1960s were reported to have been associated with fossilized whale bones.

Microorganisms are not the only life forms responsible for biogenic minerals. Interference in geological systems by fungi, plants, and animals — including humans — also causes minerals to form. The ancient mines of Laurium, Greece, located on the Aegean Sea approximately 40 kilometers southeast of Athens, have been worked for lead, silver, and zinc since 600 B.C. Slag produced from smelting the ore was dumped into the sea, where unrecovered lead reacted with seawater to form laurionite, penfieldite, and other rare minerals in cavities created by gas bubbles in the slag. All sorts of secondary sulfate minerals form on the walls of mines, where mining operations

PLATE 137

Anapaite.
Kerch Peninsula, Crimea, Ukraine.
4 x 5 cm.

Did the dissolution of the fossil shells lead to the formation of this specimen of anapaite by providing the necessary calcium or by locally changing the pH to a range more favorable for anapaite to form?

PLATE 138

Cuprite on Copper.
Britannia mine, Britannia Beach,
British Columbia. 9 x 17 cm.

*Are these minerals? The copper
precipitated from water flowing over an
iron pipe unintentionally left behind in
the process of mining. The cuprite formed
naturally by reacting with oxygen from the
air, just as it probably did to form the
crystals in PLATE 80.*

have exposed primary sulfide minerals to moisture and air. Without human intervention, none of these minerals would have formed where they did.

As we drive down the highway in our cars and trucks, exhaust contaminated with lead from gasoline additives settles onto the roadside, where it reacts with phosphates in the soil to make plumbogummite. And how many kinds of minerals do you suppose might eventually form in our landfills and garbage dumps? Will any of them become an ore body? Even within our own bodies mineral processes are at work. Hydroxylapatite forms an essential part of our bones and teeth, and the less fortunate among us may be manufacturing struvite or weddellite in the form of urinary stones.

The formation of minerals by biogenic processes presents mineralogists with a philosophical problem: when is a mineral not a mineral? There are probably as many definitions of minerals as there are textbooks about them, but all the definitions have some common criteria: minerals must occur naturally, be a solid phase, and have a definite chemical composition and crystal structure. Some definitions also include caveats that minerals must be inorganic or be formed by inorganic processes. Hence purists may question the validity of biogenic or post-mining products [PLATE 138] as mineral species. Even most purists, however, have a hard time accepting that imposing such a rigid definition excludes such classic examples as the sulfur crystals from Sicily, the calcite forming the chalk in the white cliffs of Dover, England, and perhaps all marine dolomite from minerals.

Where human activities result in the formation of minerals, we must consider intent. If the intent of the activity is to produce the species (e.g., a furnace-grown diamond or ruby), then most mineralogists would probably consider it a synthetic compound, not a mineral. By this definition, the biogenic aragonite constituting a natural pearl would be considered a mineral, but the same compound in a cultured pearl would not because, without deliberate human intervention, the oyster would not have produced the pearl ●

chapter thirty-five

What Have We Learned?

YOU now know that some minerals form by a single process, others by several. You have also seen that considerable overlap and interaction may exist between these processes and the forces (including life!) that drive them. My decision to include or exclude any given mineral from the discussion of the main geological processes has been arbitrary and, of course, is limited by how much scientists know about its genesis. Often I can attribute the genesis of a mineral to a particular mineral-forming process with confidence based on its physical structure, associated species, or analogy to similar specimens of known origins. These conclusions usually are correct, but they may be wrong, especially if extended too far. ❡ For example I am confident that the famous rhodochrosite stalactites from Catamarca Province, Argentina [PLATE 139], form in open voids by precipitation from aqueous solutions because all other stalactites form in that way and because rhodochrosite is common in deposits of hydrothermal origin. I am not comfortable, though, speculating on whether the source of the aqueous solution that formed these specimens is meteoric, magmatic, or tectonic because I have never visited this locality, performed any fluid-inclusion or isotope studies on the rhodochrosite, or read an account of such studies. Similarly, I believe that the famous large stibnite crystals from the Ichinokawa mine on the island of Shikoku, Japan, as well as the classic examples of wire silver from Kongsberg, Norway [PLATE 140], also formed by precipitation from aqueous solutions, but I can only guess about the source of the antimony or silver required to make these minerals, or about the derivation of the solutions. ❡ The twentieth century has seen incredible advances in science and technology, ranging from humankind's first powered

PLATE 139

Rhodochrosite.

Catamarca, Argentina. 6 x 8.5 cm.

Its formation by precipitation from aqueous solution may be inferred from the structure of this rhodochrosite stalactite, but the sources for the solution or the manganese and carbonate it must have contained cannot.

PLATE 140

Wire Silver.

Kongsberg, Norway. 8 x 10 cm.

Although this silver specimen is from one of the world's most famous mineral localities and silver mining districts, many of the specifics concerning its origin remain a mystery.

flight to its first footsteps on the moon. By understanding how minerals form in nature, we are now able to synthesize many of them and can even improve some of their desired properties by doing so. We have made great strides in understanding how nature operates, but as each new discovery answers a question, it nearly always raises numerous others. We have gained considerable knowledge of how matter behaves in relatively simple, closed systems, and from the laws of thermodynamics we can successfully predict which minerals should be stable at a given set of parameters for that system. Unfortunately, nature seldom provides such simple, closed systems. A quick look at the silicon-oxygen system proves the point.

Silica (SiO_2) may appear as one of several different minerals, depending on temperature and pressure. At atmospheric pressure, low quartz, high quartz, tridymite, and cristobalite crystallize at progressively higher temperatures. At significantly higher pressures, coesite or stishovite may form. (The existence of the latter two species was predicted before their actual discovery in nature.) At the Earth's surface, low quartz is the stable form of SiO_2. Tridymite should exist only at temperatures from 870 to 1470°C, yet tridymite still persists in volcanic rocks formed in that temperature range at the Earth's surface tens of thousands of years ago, because it lacks the activation energy required to recrystallize into low quartz.

Opal, another silica-rich mineral, forms under near-atmospheric conditions of low pressure and temperature and should therefore form as low quartz. X-ray studies of opal indicate, however, that the much-higher-temperature mineral cristobalite, is the species usually present. How can this be? The answer is that although they are SiO_2, the opals formed in a complex system containing more than just silicon and oxygen. The system includes water, aluminum, and alkali metals, which, when incorporated in only minor amounts into the structure of the crystallizing SiO_2, favor a cristobalite-like structure.

The world of mineralogy is full of surprises and unanswered questions. Knowing positively how a given mineral has formed and why is the exception rather than the rule. Because minerals and the elements they contain have become essential to our everyday lives, research will undoubtedly continue to reveal new information about their properties, potential uses, and formation in nature. Knowledge of how minerals form is fundamental to locating future ore deposits and to synthesizing substitutes for crucial minerals whose natural occurrences are being depleted. *Homo sapiens* is in a unique position: no other organism has such an ability to understand and control its environment. Understanding the Earth's basic geological processes and their relationship with the biosphere and with human activity is essential to our own survival●

Recommended Reading

American Geological Institute. 1962. *Dictionary of Geological Terms.* Garden City, NY: Dolphin Books, Doubleday. A concise, handy reference for all audiences.

Bancroft, Peter. 1973. *The World's Finest Minerals and Crystals.* New York: Viking Press. Intended primarily for mineral collectors, this is an easily read text.

Bancroft, Peter. 1984. *Gem and Crystal Treasures.* Fallbrook, CA: Western Enterprises. A unique blend of travel, history, and descriptive mineralogy focusing on most of the world's most important mineral localities; for both general and informed audiences.

Brownlow, Arthur H. 1979. *Geochemistry.* Englewood Cliffs, NJ: Prentice-Hall, 1979. A modern, broad-based approach to geochemistry for an advanced audience.

Carmichael, Ian S. E., Francis J. Turner, and John Verhoogen. 1974. *Igneous Petrology.* New York: McGraw-Hill. A thorough discussion of magmatic processes and the genesis of igneous rocks; advanced level.

Cattermole, Peter, and Patrick Moore. 1985. *The Story of the Earth.* Cambridge: Cambridge University Press. A modern physical geology text written for a general or informed audience.

Cocks, L. R. M., and P. H. Greenwood, eds. 1981. *Chance, Change and Challenge: The Evolving Earth.* Cambridge: Cambridge University Press. A compendium of papers on the evolution of the Earth and its geological systems; for an informed audience.

Degens, Egon T. 1989. *Perspectives on Biogeochemistry.* New York: Springer-Verlag. A comprehensive review of the interaction between the living and nonliving world; advanced level.

Desautels, Paul E. 1968. *The Mineral Kingdom.* New York: Madison Square Press, Grosset and Dunlap. A nontechnical approach to the fascinating world of minerals; written for a general audience.

Ehrlich, Henry Lutz. 1981. *Geomicrobiology.* New York: Marcel Dekker. A technical discussion of some of the more important biogenic minerals; advanced level.

Fleischer, Michael, and Joseph A. Mandarino. 1991. *Glossary of Mineral Species 1991.* Tucson: The Mineralogical Record. A handy, alphabetical listing giving the chemical formula and a published reference for all known mineral species.

Frye, Keith, ed. 1981. *The Encyclopedia of Mineralogy.* Stroudsburg, PA: Hutchinson Ross. A comprehensive, advanced reference manual.

Guilbert, John M., and Charles F. Park, Jr. 1986. *The Geology of Ore Deposits.* New York: W. H. Freeman. A comprehensive review explaining the genesis of nearly every kind of ore deposit; intended for an informed to advanced audience.

Jackson, Kern C. 1970. *Textbook of Lithology.* New York: McGraw-Hill. A thorough treatment of the fundamentals of physical geology for a general but informed audience.

Kearey, Philip, ed. 1993. *The Encyclopedia of the Solid Earth Sciences.* Oxford: Blackwell Scientific Publications. A modern, comprehensive reference manual for all audiences.

Keller, Peter C. 1990. *Gemstones and Their Origins.* New York: Van Nostrand Reinhold. An informative, well-illustrated text explaining the genesis of some of the world's most important gem deposits; for both general and informed audiences.

Lapedes, Daniel N., ed. 1978. *McGraw-Hill Encyclopedia of the Geological Sciences.* New York: McGraw-Hill. A comprehensive reference manual for all audiences.

Mason, Brian. 1958. *Principles of Geochemistry.* New York: John Wiley and Sons. One of the classic texts describing the chemistry of the Earth and its geological processes; for an advanced audience.

Mason, Brian, and L. G. Berry. 1968. *Elements of Mineralogy.* San Francisco: W. H. Freeman. A traditional but popular mineralogy textbook; for an informed audience.

Mottana, Annibale, Rodolfo Crespi, and Giuseppe Liborio. 1978. *Guide to Rocks and Minerals.* New York: Simon and Schuster. A handy pictorial guide for a general or informed audience.

Nickel, Ernest H., and Monte C. Nichols. 1991. *Mineral Reference Manual.* New York: Van Nostrand Reinhold. A handy, alphabetical listing giving chemical and physical data with reference citations for all known mineral species.

Pough, Frederick H. 1960. *A Field Guide to Rocks and Minerals.* Boston: Houghton Mifflin. One of the most popular texts among amateur mineralogists; for general and informed audiences.

Redfern, Ron. 1983. *The Making of a Continent.* New York: Times Books, New York Times Book Company. A well-illustrated text explaining the principles of plate tectonics; for general to informed audiences.

Roberts, Willard Lincoln, Thomas J. Campbell, and George Robert Rapp, Jr. 1990. *Encyclopedia of Minerals.* 2d ed. New York: Van Nostrand Reinhold. A comprehensive reference manual for all audiences.

Sinkankas, John. 1964. *Mineralogy for Amateurs.* New York: Van Nostrand Reinhold. A comprehensive, easily read, popular text for general and informed audiences.

Sofianides, Anna S., and George E. Harlow. 1990. *Gems and Crystals from the American Museum of Natural History.* New York: Simon and Schuster. A well-illustrated, easily read text focusing on the occurrence, properties, history, and lore of common and uncommon gemstones; for general or informed audiences.

Strahler, Arthur N. 1981. *Physical Geology.* New York: Harper and Row. A thorough treatment of the fundamentals of physical geology for a general but informed audience.

Tindall, James R., and Roger Thornhill. 1975. *The Collector's Guide to Rocks and Minerals.* New York: Van Nostrand Reinhold. An easily read text intended for a general audience.

Turner, Francis J. 1968. *Metamorphic Petrology: Mineralogical and Field Aspects.* New York: McGraw-Hill. A thorough, advanced discussion of metamorphism and metamorphic rocks.

Verhoogen, John, Francis J. Turner, Lionel E. Weiss, and Clyde Wahrhaftig. 1970. *The Earth: An Introduction to Physical Geology.* New York: Holt, Rinehart and Winston. A comprehensive, advanced physical geology text.

Wilk, Harry, and Olaf Medenbach. 1986. *The Magic of Minerals.* New York: Springer-Verlag. Superb photographs highlight this introduction to the world of minerals; for general and informed audiences.

Winkler, Helmut G. F. 1979. *Petrogenesis of Metamorphic Rocks.* 5th ed. New York: Springer-Verlag. A thorough, advanced discussion of metamorphism and metamorphic rocks.

Appendix: Some Additional Minerals and How They Form

There are currently about 3,800 known mineral species. In selecting those discussed in the preceding chapters, I have tried to strike a balance between minerals and localities that are familiar, and those that best illustrate a particular geological process. As a result, some important minerals had to be omitted, along with many additional examples of ways that given species might form. The following table lists some of these minerals, their localities, and modes of genesis. Although some, such as carletonite or cumengite, are globally rare species, they have been included because they are often seen in collections. I have used general mineral names to imply a series of species, especially when the species have common modes of origin (e.g., "allanite" implies allanite-(Ce) and allanite-(Y); "axinite" implies ferro-, magnesio-, or manganaxinite). Similarly, polymorphs with similar modes of origin, such as atacamite and paratacamite, have been listed simply as "atacamite." The process/type code used in the table is given below, and the numbered references follow the table. Where possible, I have tried to provide nontechnical references that describe the occurrence of the species and its associated minerals. References giving more complete and scientific descriptions for each species may be found in the *Encyclopedia of Minerals, Mineral Reference Manual,* and *Glossary of Mineral Species,* which are cited in the Recommended Reading list. A visit to nearly any university or museum library will provide many more.

....

Processes and Types

M	· crystallization from magma		C	· chemical alteration
ag	· agpaitic pegmatite		bi	· biogenic
cb	· carbonatite		ox	· oxidation-reduction
df	· differentiation		re	· chemical replacement
gr	· granitic pegmatite		hp	· hydrothermal alteration in
vx	· volcanic extrusive			pegmatite

P	· precipitation from aqueous solution		R	· recrystallization
al	· alpine cleft		rd	· rodingite
ev	· evaporite		rm	· regional metamorphism
mvt	· Mississippi Valley type		sk	· skarn
mt	· meteoric		cm	· contact metamorphism
hy	· hydrothermal (mg · magmatic,		vs	· recrystallized volcanogenic
	me · meteoric, tc · tectonic,			massive sulfide deposit
	bs · basalt flow mineralization)			

....

Species	Locality	Process/type	References
Acanthite	Cobalt, Ontario	P/hy	14,78,148
	Freiberg, Saxony, Germany	P/hy-mg	5,6,121,180,202
	Guanajuato, Mexico	P/hy	6,151,202
Andorite	Oruro, Bolivia	P/hy-mg	5,32,202
Ajoite	Ajo, Arizona	C/ox	194
	Messina District, South Africa	C/ox	21
Allanite	Madawaska, Ontario	M/gr	171
	Fahlun, Sweden	M/gr	42,212
	Olden Twp., Frontenac County, Ontario	R/cm	171
	Otter Lake, Quebec	R/cm	115
	Trimouns, France	P/al	173
	Eifel District, Germany	M/vx	83
Alstonite	Alston, Cumbria, England	P/mvt + C?	149
	Hardin County, Illinois	P/mvt + C?	122,177

Species	Locality	Process/type	References
Anhydrite	Naica, Chihuahua, Mexico	P/hy	151
	Simplon Tunnel, Switzerland	P/al	5,149,203
	Stassfurt, Saxony, Germany	P/ev	19,149
Annabergite	Laurium, Greece	C/ox	105
Anthophyllite-gedrite	Fiskenaesset, Greenland	R/rm	159
	Nuuk, Greenland	R/rm	2
Antlerite	Chiquicamata, Chile	C/ox	33,149
Artinite	Staten Island, New York	P/hy-tc?	91,167
	San Benito County, California	P/hy-tc	31
Astrophyllite	St. Peters Dome, Colorado	M/ag	140,152
	Mont Saint-Hilaire, Quebec	M/ag	85,125
	Narssârssuk, Greenland	M/ag	159
Atacamite	Wallaroo, South Australia	C-ox	162
	Atacama, Chile	C-ox	33
Augelite	North Groton, New Hampshire	C/hp	135,184
	Rapid Creek, Yukon Territory	P/hy-tc	176
	Oruro, Bolivia	P/hy-mg	32
	Mono County, California	P/hy	223
Augite	Salzburg, Austria	P/al	6,183
	Ariccia, Roma, Italy	M/df	42
	Franklin, New Jersey	R/sk	58,59,146
	Eifel District, Germany	M/vx	83
Austinite	Gold Hill, Utah	C/ox	106
	Mapimi, Durango, Mexico	C/ox	151
Autunite	Spokane, Washington	C/ox	166
	Autun, Saône-et-Loire, France	C/ox	149
Axinite	Bourg d'Oisans, Isère, France	P/al	49
	New Melones Lake, California	P/al	160
	Polar Urals, Russia	P/hy-tc	185
	Luning, Nevada	R/sk?	49
	Bungo Province, Kyushu, Japan	R/cm	181
	Vitória da Conquista, Bahia, Brazil	P/hy-tc	25
Babingtonite	Westfield, Massachusetts	P/hy-bs	147
	Bombay, Maharashtra, India	P/hy-bs	40
	Paterson, New Jersey	P/hy-bs	156,157
Beryllonite	Stoneham, Maine	C/hp?	135,155
	Paprok, Nuristan, Afghanistan	C/hp?	175
Betafite	Betafo area, Madagascar	M/gr	148
	Bancroft, Ontario	R/sk (M/cb?)	102,171
Bismuthinite	Jefferson County, Colorado	M/gr	148
	Cornwall, England	P/hy-mg	52,148
	Kingsgate, New South Wales Australia	P/hy-mg	53
Blödite	Soda Lake, California	P/ev	154
Boleite	Boleo, Baja California, Mexico	C/ox	6,151
Boracite	Lüneburg, Hannover, Germany	P/ev	19,149
Boulangerite	Noche Buena, Zacatecas, Mexico	P/hy	151
	Trepca, Serbia	P/hy	120
	Madoc, Ontario	P/hy-me?	16,130
Brazilianite	Minas Gerais, Brazil	C/hp	5,6,135
	North Groton, New Hampshire	C/hp	41,135,184
	Rapid Creek, Yukon Territory	P/hy-tc	176
Brewsterite	Strontian, Scotland	P/hy	196
	Yellow Lake, British Columbia	P/hy-bs	196
	Harrisville, New York	P/hy-tc	172

Species	Locality	Process/type	References
Brochantite	Bisbee, Arizona	C/ox	68
	Bingham, New Mexico	C/ox	192
Brucite	Brewster, New York	P/hy-tc	88,91
	Texas, Pennsylvania	P/hy-tc	63,148
	Asbest, Russia	R/rd	174
	Asbestos, Quebec	R/rd	77
Buergerite	San Luis Potosi, Mexico	M/vx	47,151
Cacoxenite	Hagendorf, Bavaria, Germany	C/hp	135
	Indian Mountain, Alabama	P/mt	12,67
	Coon Creek, Arkansas	P/mt	103
Calaverite	Cripple Creek, Colorado	P/hy-mg	6,187,217
	Calaveras County, California	P/hy	154,217
Caledonite	Tiger, Arizona	C/ox	6,17
	San Bernardino County, California	C/ox	39
	Leadhills, Lanarkshire, Scotland	C/ox	64
Cancrinite	Bancroft area, Ontario	C/re	84
	Mont Saint-Hilaire, Quebec	M/ag	85,125
	Eifel District, Germany	M/vx	83
	Point of Rocks, New Mexico	M/vx	43
Carletonite	Mont Saint-Hilaire, Quebec	R/cm	85,125
Carnotite	Colorado Plateau area, Utah, Colorado, New Mexico, Arizona	C/ox	78,149
Cavansite	Owyhee Dam, Malheur County, Oregon	P/hy-bs	208
	Poona, Maharashtra, India	P/hy-bs	111
Chondrodite	Amity, New York	R/rm	99
	Brewster, New York	R/sk	88,91
Chlorargyrite	Broken Hill, New South Wales, Australia	C/ox	127,224
Cinnabar	Almaden, Ciudad Real, Spain	P/hy	37
	Hunan & Kweichow Prov., China	P/hy	5,6,168,181
	Coast Range, California	P/hy	154
	Idria, Slovenia	P/hy-mg	7
Clinoclase	Tintic District, Utah	C/ox	126,149
	Liskeard, Cornwall, England	C/ox	52
	Majuba Hill, Nevada	C/ox	92,93
Cobaltite	Cobalt, Ontario	P/hy	14,78
	Tunaberg & Håkansboda, Sweden	R/sk	1,6
Conichalcite	Mapimi, Durango, Mexico	C/ox	151
	Gold Hill, Utah	C/ox	106
Covellite	Butte, Montana	P/hy-mg	6,148
	Summitville, Colorado	P/hy-mg	109
	Alghero, Sardinia, Italy	P/hy	148
Creedite	Santa Eulalia, Chihuahua, Mexico	P/hy	6,151
Cryolite	Ivigtut, Greenland	M/gr	6,159
	Mont Saint-Hilaire, Quebec	M/ag	85,125
	Francon quarry, Montreal, Quebec	M/cb	29
Cumengite	Boleo, Baja California, Mexico	C/ox	6,151
Cyanotrichite	Grand Canyon, Arizona	C/ox	117
	Moldawa, Banat, Romania	C/ox	149
Danburite	San Luis Potosi, Mexico	P/hy	151
	Russell, New York	R/sk	91
	Anjanabonoina, Madagascar	M/gr	221
Dawsonite	Francon quarry, Montreal, Quebec	M/cb	29
	Mte. Amiata, Tuscany, Italy	P/hy	149
	Mont Saint-Hilaire, Quebec	M/ag	85,125
Descloizite	Grootfontein, Namibia	C/ox	215
	Santa Eulalia, Chihuahua, Mexico	C/ox	151
Diaspore	Chester, Massachusetts	P/hy-tc	123
	Mugla Province, Turkey	P/hy-tc	136
Dresserite	Francon quarry, Montreal, Quebec	M/cb	29
Dumortierite	Alpine, California	R/rm	154
Dyscrasite	St. Andreasberg, Harz, Germany	P/hy-mg	6,121,148
	Príbram, Czech Republic	P/hy-mg	6,107
Edingtonite	Bathurst, New Brunswick	P/hy-tc	76
	Dumbartonshire, Scotland	P/hy-bs	196
	Ice River, British Columbia	M/ag	74
Enargite	Butte, Montana	P/hy-mg	6,148
	San Juan County, Colorado	P/hy-mg?	109,141
	Quiruvilca, La Libertad, Peru	P/hy-mg	118
Enstatite (Hypersthene)	Jackson County, No. Carolina	M/df	222
	North Creek, New York	R/rm	66,91
	Eifel District, Germany	M/vx	83
	Summit Rock, Oregon	M/vx	82
Epistilbite	Berufjord, Iceland	P/hy-bs	196
	Bombay, Maharashtra, India	P/hy-bs	40,196
Euxenite	Quadeville, Ontario	M/gr	102,171
	Madawaska, Ontario	M/gr	171
	Ampangabe, Madagascar	M/gr	148
	Iveland, Aust-Agder, Norway	M/gr	148,212
Fergusonite	Madawaska, Ontario	M/gr	102,171
	Iveland, Aust-Agder, Norway	M/gr	212
	Baringer Hill, Llano County, Texas	M/gr	186
Forsterite	Zabargad Island, Egypt	P/hy-me + C	6,100,214
	Notre-Dame-du-Laus, Quebec	R/cm	198
Francevillite	Mounana, Gabon	C/ox	28
Gadolinite	Falun, Sweden	M/gr	42,212
	Hiterö, Vest-Agder, Norway	M/gr	42,212
	Brunet & Llano Counties, Texas	M/gr	38,186
	Graubünden, Switzerland	P/al	70
Gahnite	Rowe, Massachusetts	R/rm	42
	Topsham, Maine	M/gr	57
	Franklin, New Jersey	R/sk	58,59,146
Glauberite	Camp Verde, Arizona	P/ev	195
	Searles Lake, California	P/ev	153,154
Glaucophane	Coast Range, California	R/rm	154
Gmelinite	Two Islands, Nova Scotia	P/hy-bs	196
	Flinders, Victoria, Australia	P/hy-bs	18,196
	Paterson, New Jersey	P/hy-bs	156,157,196
Gormanite - souzalite	Rapid Creek, Yukon Territory	P/hy-tc	176
Goyazite	Minas Gerais, Brazil	C/hp	135
	North Groton, New Hampshire	C/hp	135,184
	Rapid Creek, Yukon Territory	P/hy-tc	176
	Binnental, Valais, Switzerland	P/hy-tc	6,69,188
Graftonite	Grafton, New Hampshire	M/gr	41,135
	Black Hills, South Dakota	M/gr	135,170
Graphite	Ticonderoga, New York	R/cm	91,114
	Sri Lanka	R/rm	148
	Crestmore, California	R/sk	89

Species	Locality	Process/type	References
Greenockite	Bishopton, Renfrew, Scotland	P/hy	148
	Granby, Missouri	P/mvt	148
	Paterson, New Jersey	P/hy-bs	156,157
	Llallagua, Potosi, Bolivia	P/hy-mg	6,8
Gyrolite	Poona, Maharashtra, India	P/hy-bs	40
Halotrichite	Mojave, California	C/ox	154
Hambergite	San Diego County, California	M/gr	54,112
	Anjanabonoina, Madagascar	M/gr	219
	Gilgit, Pakistan	M/gr	98
Hanksite	Searles Lake, California	P/ev	153,154
Harmotome	Strontian, Scotland	P/hy	196
	Andreasberg, Harz, Germany	P/hy	196
	Vaasa, Finland	P/hy	196
Hauerite	Raddusa, Sicily, Italy	P/mt + C/bi?	5,148
Hauyne	Eifel District, Germany	M/df	83
	Mte. Somma, Vesuvius, Italy	M/df	42
Hessite	Botes, Transylvania, Romania	P/hy-mg	6,148
Hornblende	Aussig, Bohemia, Czech Republic	M/df	42
	Lake Harbour, Northwest Territories	R/sk	75
	Cornopass, Switzerland	R/rm	203
	Eifel District, Germany	M/vx	83
	Summit Rock, Oregon	M/vx	82
Howlite	Windsor & Iona, Nova Scotia	P/ev	97
	Boron, California	P/ev	3,4,6,139,163
Huebnerite	Pasto Bueno, Peru	P/hy-mg	6
	San Juan County, Colorado	P/hy-mg?	109,141
	Alpine County, California	P/hy	161
Hureaulite	Minas Gerais, Brazil	C/hp	50,135
	Black Hills, South Dakota	C/hp	135,170
	Mangualde, Beira, Portugal	C/hp	135
Hutchinsonite	Quiruvilca, La Libertad, Peru	P/hy-mg	118,210
	Binnental, Valais, Switzerland	P/hy-tc	6,69,188
Hyalophane	Busovaca, Bosnia	P/al	225
	Binnental, Valais, Switzerland	P/hy-tc	6,69,188
Hydromagnesite	Staten Island, New York	P/hy-tc?	91,167
	Soghan mine, Kerman, Iran	P/hy-tc?	9
Hydrozincite	Mapimi, Durango, Mexico	C/ox	151
	Goodsprings, Nevada	C/ox	149
Ilvaite	South Mountain, Idaho	R/sk	165,204
	Seriphos, Greece	R/sk	61,204
	Elba, Italy	R/sk	204
Inesite	Trinity County, California	P/hy	51,154
	Kuruman District, Cape Province, South Africa	P/hy	79,200,220
Iron	Disko Island, Greenland	M + C/ox	148,159
Jadeite	Tawmaw, Burma	R/rm & C	100
	San Benito County, California	R/rm & C	100
Jamesonite	Noche Buena & Nieves, Zacatecas, Mexico	P/hy	151
	Wolfsberg, Harz, Germany	P/hy	148
Jeremejevite	Swakapmund, Namibia	M/gr	209
	Mt. Soktuj, Siberia, Russia	M/gr	181
Kernite	Kern County, California	P/ev	3,4,6,139,163
Kinoite	Christmas, Arizona	C/ox	221

Species	Locality	Process/type	References
Kornerupine	Harts Range, Northern Territory, Australia	R/rm	128
	Fiskenaesset, Greenland	R/rm	158,159
	Betroka, Tulear, Madagascar	R/rm	42
Kröhnkite	Chuquicamata, Chile	C/ox	33
Kulanite	Rapid Creek, Yukon Territory	P/hy-tc	176
Laumontite	Bombay, Maharashtra, India	P/hy-bs	40,196
	Paterson, New Jersey	P/hy-bs	156,157,196
	Minas Basin, Nova Scotia	P/hy-bs	196
	Bishop, California	P/hy	144,154
Lawsonite	Tiburon Peninsula, California	R/rm	154
Lazulite	North Groton, New Hampshire	C/hp	135,184
	Minas Gerais, Brazil	C/hp	135
	Rapid Creek, Yukon Territory	P/hy-tc	176
	Werfen, Salzburg, Austria	P/hy-tc	142,149
	White Mountains, California	P/hy	223
	Graves Mountain, Georgia	R/rm	35
Lead	Långban, Sweden	P/hy	134,148
Leadhillite	Granby, Missouri	C/ox	149
	Tsumeb, Namibia	C/ox	215
	Leadhills, Scotland	C/ox	64
Levyne	Spray, Oregon	P/hy-bs	196
	Faeroe Islands	P/hy-bs	15,196
Libethenite	Cornwall, England	C/ox	52
	Mindola, Kitwe, Zambia	C/ox	108
	Libethen, Slovakia	C/ox	149
Liddicoatite	Antsirabe, Madagascar	M/gr	6,219
Linarite	Red Gill, Cumbria, England	C/ox	36
	Graham County, Arizona	C/ox	96
	Bingham, New Mexico	C/ox	192
Ludlamite	Rapid Creek, Yukon Teritory	P/hy-tc	176
	Cobalt, Idaho	P/hy	165
	North Groton, New Hampshire	C/hp	135,184
	Municipio de Aquiles Serdán, Chihuahua, Mexico	P/hy	6,151
Magnetite	Balmat, New York	P/hy	30
	Chester, Vermont	R/rm	71
	French Creek, Pennsylvania	R/sk	63
	Bancroft, Ontario	R/cm	171
	Eifel District, Germany	M/vx	83
	Mineville, New York	M/df	91
	St. Gotthard Pass, Switzerland	P/al	5,203
Margarite	Chester, Massachusetts	P/hy-tc	123
Mercury	Almaden, Ciudad Real, Spain	P/hy	37
	Sonoma & Sanata Clara Counties, California	P/hy	154
	Idria, Slovenia	P/hy-mg	7
Microlite	Amelia Courthouse, Virginia	M/gr	133
	Minas Gerais, Brazil	M/gr	27
Milarite	Val Guif, Grisons, Switzerland	P/al	203
	Jaguaraçu, Minas Gerais, Brazil	M/gr	216
	Gunanajuato, Mexico	P/hy	6,151
Millerite	Halls Gap, Kentucky	P/hy-me	129
	Malartic, Quebec	R/vs + M/df?	189
	Siegerland, Germany	P/hy	19,148
	Orford Township, Sherbrooke County, Quebec	R/cm	193
	Gap mine, Lancaster County, Pennsylvania	M/df + P/hy	63,148

Species	Locality	Process/type	References
Molybdenite	Climax, Colorado	P/hy-mg	211
	Kingsgate, New South Wales, Australia	P/hy-mg	53
	Aldfield, Quebec	R/sk	199
	Renfrew area, Ontario	R/sk	199
Mottramite	Tsumeb, Namibia	C/ox	215
Narsarsukite	Narssârssuk, Greenland	M/ag	159
	Mont Saint-Hilaire, Quebec	M/ag & R/cm	85,125
Nickeline	Cobalt, Ontario	P/hy	14,78,148
	Port Radium, Northwest Territories	P/hy	197
	Freiberg and Schneeberg, Saxony, Germany	P/hy-mg	121,182
Okenite	Poona, Maharashtra, India	P/hy-bs	40
Orpiment	Hunan Province, China	P/hy	168
	Humboldt County, Nevada	P/hy	191
	Quiruvilca, La Libertad, Peru	P/hy	118
Osumilite	Sardinia, Italy	M/vx	81
	Eifel District, Germany	M/vx	81,83
	Lane County, Oregon	M/vx	81
Pachnolite	Ivigtut, Greenland	C/hp	6,159
Palygorskite	Metalline Falls, Washington	P/hy	22,164
Paravauxite	Llallagua, Bolivia	P/hy	6,8
Pargasite	Pargas, Finland	R/cm	212
Parisite	Muzo, Columbia	P/hy	6,206
	Quincy, Massachusetts	M/gr	149
	Mineral County, Montana	P/hy-mg?	113
Pentlandite	Sudbury, Ontario	M/df	48
	Malartic, Quebec	R/vs	189
Perovskite	Zlatoust, Ural Mtns., Russia	R/cm	5,181
	Magnet Cove, Arkansas	R/cm	148
	Gardiner Complex, Greenland	M/cb	94
	Jacupiranga, São Paulo, Brazil	M/cb	131
	Val Malenco, Lombardy, Italy	R/rd	13,70
	Eifel District, Germany	M/vx	83
Petalite	Minas Gerais, Brazil	M/gr	26
	Oxford County, Maine	M/gr	57,155
	Elba, Italy	M/gr	6,145
Petzite	Nagyag, Romania	P/hy-mg	6,148
	Goldhill, Colorado	P/hy	148,217
Phenakite	Minas Gerais, Brazil	M/gr	23
	Anjanabonoina, Madagascar	M/gr	219
	Chatham, New Hampshire	M/gr	179
	Mount Antero, Colorado	M/gr	86
	Takowaja, Urals, Russia	R/cm	181
	St. Gotthard area, Switzerland	P/al	203
Phillipsite	Melbourne, Victoria, Australia	P/hy-bs	196
	Monument, Oregon	P/hy-bs	196
Phosgenite	Monteponi, Sardinia, Italy	C/ox	5,149
	Cromford, Derbyshire, England	C/ox	20
	Laurium, Greece	C/ox (bi)	105
	Tsumeb, Namibia	C/ox	215
	Tiger, Arizona	C/ox	17
Phospho-phyllite	Potosi, Bolivia	P/hy	5,6
	Hagendorf, Bavaria, Germany	C/hp	135
Phospho-siderite	Black Hills, South Dakota	C/hp	135,170
	Pleystein, Bavaria, Germany	C/hp	149
(Metastrengite)	Indian Mountain, Alabama	P/hy-me	12,67
Pollucite	Bernic Lake, Manitoba	M/gr	196
	Oxford County, Maine	M/gr	155,196
	·Nuristan, Afghanistan	M/gr	10,196
	Island of Elba, Italy	M/gr	6,145,196
Polybasite	Arizpe, Sonora, Mexico	P/hy	151,202
	Freiberg, Saxony, Germany	P/hy-mg	6,121,182
	Guanajuato, Mexico	P/hy	6,151,202
Powellite	Keewenaw Peninsula, Michigan	P/hy-bs	213
	Nasik, Maharashtra, India	P/hy-bs	110
	Tungsten, Nevada	R/cm	149
	Randsburg, California	C/ox	154
Proustite	Chañarcillo, Atacama, Chile	P/hy-mg	6,34,202
	Freiberg, Saxony, Germany	P/hy-mg	6,121,182
	Pribram & Joachimstal, Bohemia, Czech Republic	P/hy-mg	6,190
	Cobalt, Ontario	P/hy	14,78,148
Pseudo-malachite	Shaba Province, Zaire	C/ox	62
	Libethen, Slovakia	C/ox	149
Pumpellyite	Keewenaw Peninsula, Michigan	P/hy-bs	213
Purpurite	North Groton, New Hampshire	C/hp	41,135,184
Pyrargyrite	Freiberg, Saxony, Germany	P/hy-mg	6,121,182,202
	Andreasberg, Harz, Germany	P/hy-mg	6,121,202
	Fresnillo, Zacatecas, Mexico	P/hy	151,202
	Huancavelica, Peru	P/hy-mg	202,218
	Guanajuato, Mexico	P/hy	5,6,151,202
Pyrrhotite	Santa Eulalia, Chihuahua, Mexico	P/hy	151
	Riondel, British Columbia	P/hy-me?	73
	Nova Lima, Minas Gerais, Brazil	P/hy-mg	124
	Kapnic, Romania	P/hy-mg	6,148
	Trepca, Serbia	P/hy	120
	Sudbury, Ontario	M/df	48
	Malartic, Quebec	R/vs	189
Realgar	Hunan, China	P/hy	168
	Humboldt County, Nevada	P/hy	191
	King County, Washington	P/hy	5,45,164
	Kapnik, Romania	P/hy-mg	6,148
	Binnental, Valais, Switzerland	P/hy-tc	6,69,188
Rhodizite	Antandrokomby, Madagascar	P/gr	205
Roselite	Bou Azzer, Morocco	C/ox	6,150
Samarskite	Iveland, Satersdalen, Norway	M/gr	148,212
	Mitchell County, No. Carolina	M/gr	222
Sapphirine	Fiskenaesset, Greenland	R/rm	158,159
	Betroka, Madagascar	R/rm	42
Scholzite	Hagendorf, Bavaria, Germany	C/hp	135
	Reaphook Hill, South Australia	P/hy-me? + C/ox	95
Schorl	Bovey Tracey, Devon, England	P/hy-mg	52
	Oxford County, Maine	M/gr	56,155
	North Groton, New Hampshire	M/gr	41
	Chester, Vermont	R/rm	71
	Riverside County, California	M/gr	65
Scolecite	Nasik, Maharashtra, India	P/hy-bs	40,196
	Minas Basin, Nova Scotia	P/hy-bs	196
	Rio Grande do Sul, Brazil	P/hy-bs	196
	Cowlitz County, Washington	P/hy-bs	196
Scorodite	Tsumeb, Namibia	C/ox	215
	Concepción del Oro, Zacatecas, Mexico	C/ox	6,151
	Djebel Debar, Constantine, Algeria	C/ox	149
Serendibite	Johnsburg, New York	R/cm	178
Shattuckite	Bisbee, Arizona	C/ox	68

Species	Locality	Process/type	References
Shortite	Green River, Wyoming	P/ev	132
	Mont SaintHilaire, Quebec	R/cm	85,175
Siderite	Nova Lima, Minas Gerais, Brazil	P/hy-mg	124
	Mont Saint-Hilaire, Quebec	M/ag	85,125
	Durham, England	P/mvt	104
	Tavistock, Devon, England	P/hy + C/re	5,52
	Pikes Peak, Colorado	M/gr	55,140
	Allevard, Isère, France	P/al	6
	Rapid Creek, Yukon Territory	P/hy-tc	176
Siegenite	Viburnum Trend, Missouri	P/mvt	116
	Siegen, Westphalia, Germany	P/hy	19,148
Sodalite	Bancroft, Ontario	C/re	84
	Mont Saint-Hilaire, Quebec	M/ag	85,125
Sperrylite	Noril'sk, Siberia, Russia	M/df	46,137
	Sudbury, Ontario	M/df	48
	Transvaal, South Africa	M/df	5
Sphaero-cobaltite (Cobaltocalcite)	Shaba Province, Zaire	P/hy	119
	Concepción del Oro, Zacatecas, Mexico	P/hy	6,151
Stannite	Potosi & Oruro, Bolivia	P/hy	6,8,32
Stephanite	Arizpe, Sonora, Mexico	P/hy	151,202
	Freiberg, Saxony, Germany	P/hy-mg	121,182,202
	Pribram, Bohemia, Czech Republic	P/hy-mg	6,190
Strontianite	Hardin County, Illinois	P/mvt	6,122
	Francon quarry, Montreal, Quebec	M/cb	29
	Strontian, Scotland	P/hy	149
	Winfield, Pennsylvania	P/hy/me	44
	Jamesville, New York	C/bi	44
Sturmanite	Kuruman District, Cape Province, South Africa	P/hy	200
Sugilite	Kuruman District, Cape Province, South Africa	P/hy?	200
Sussexite	Franklin, New Jersey	R/sk	58,59,146
Sylvanite	Cripple Creek, Colorado	P/hy-mg	6,187,217
	Nagyag, Transylvania, Romania	P/hy-mg	6,148
Tantalite	Alto Ligonha, Mozambique	M/gr	6
	Taos County, New Mexico	M/gr	87
	San Diego County, California	M/gr	54
	Gilgit, Pakistan	M/gr	98
Tarbuttite	Broken Hill, Zambia	C/ox	143
	Reaphook Hill, South Australia	C/ox & P/hy	95
Tellurium	Vulcan, Colorado	P/hy	148,169
	Kalgoorlie, Western Australia	P/hy	148
	Moctezuma, Sonora, Mexico	P/hy	60
Tennantite	Tsumeb, Namibia	P/hy	215
	Binnental, Valais, Switzerland	P/hy-tc	6,69,188
	Concepción del Oro, Zacatecas, Mexico (incorrectly ascribed to Naica, Chihuahua)	P/hy	207
Tephroite	Franklin, New Jersey	R/rm	58,59,146
Thenardite	Camp Verde, Arizona	P/ev	195
	Searles Lake, California	P/ev	153,154
Thomsenolite	Ivigtut, Greenland	C/hp	6,159
Thomsonite	Goble, Oregon	P/hy-bs	196
	Renfrewshire, Scotland	P/hy-bs	196
	Asbestos, Quebec	R/rd	77
Thorianite	Fort Dauphin area, Madagascar	R/sk?	5,148
	Otter Lake, Quebec	R/cm	115
	Bancroft area, Ontario	R/cm, M/gr	102

Species	Locality	Process/type	References
Thorite	Bancroft, Ontario	R/cm	102,171
	Eifel District, Germany	M/vx	83
Torbernite	Shaba Province, Zaire	C/ox	6,62
	Mitchell County, North Carolina	C/hp	222
	Gunnislake, Cornwall, England	C/ox	52
Tridymite	Summit Rock, Oregon	M/vx	82
	Thomas Range, Utah	M/vx	82
	Eifel District, Germany	M/vx	83
Trona	Green River, Wyoming	P/ev	132
Tugtupite	Kvanefjeld, Greenland	M/ag + C/hp?	90,159
	Mont Saint-Hilaire, Quebec	M/ag + C/hp?	85
Tyuyamunite	Colorado Plateau area, Utah, Colorado, New Mexico, Arizona	C/ox	78,149
Ulexite	Boron, California	P/ev	3,4,6,139,163
Uraninite	Port Radium, Northwest Territories	P/hy	197
	Joachimstal, Bohemia, Czech Republic	P/hy-mg	6,78
Uranophane	Bancroft, Ontario	C/ox	102,171
	Grants, New Mexico	C/ox	78
	Kolwezi, Shaba, Zaire	C/ox	62
Vauxite	Llallagua, Potosi, Bolivia	P/hy	6,8,218
Veszelyite	Phillipsburg, Montana	C/ox	201
Villiaumite	Isle of Los, Guinea	M/ag	149
	Kvanefjeld, Greenland	M/ag	159
	Mont Saint-Hilaire, Quebec	M/ag	85,125
	Point of Rocks, New Mexico	M/vx	43
Vivianite	Potosi and Oruro, Bolivia	P/hy	6,8,32
	Cobalt, Idaho	P/hy	149,165
	Trepca, Serbia	P/hy	120
Wardite	Taquaral, Minas Gerais, Brazil	C/hp	6,24,135
	Rapid Creek, Yukon Territory	P/hy-tc	176
Wavellite	Llallagua, Potosi, Bolivia	P/hy	8
Whiteite	Rapid Creek, Yukon Territory	P/hy-tc	176
	Custer, South Dakota	C/hp	72
Willemite	Santa Eulalia, Chihuahua, Mexico	C/ox	151
	Tsumeb, Namibia	C/ox	215
	Mont Saint-Hilaire, Quebec	M/ag	85,125
Witherite	Hardin County, Illinois	P/mvt	6,122
	Alston, Cumbria, England	P/mvt?	5,6
	Hexam, Northumberland, England	P/mvt?	44
	Seneca County, New York	C/bi	44
Wurtzite	Llallagua, Potosi, Bolivia	P/hy-mg	6,8
	Butte, Montana	P/hy-mg	6,148
	Thomaston, Connecticut	P/hy-tc?	80
Zinnwaldite	Zinnwald, Bohemia, Czech Republic	P/hy-mg	6
	Pikes Peak, Colorado	M/gr	140
Zoisite	Merelani, Arusha, Tanzania	P/hy-tc+C/r e	5,6,11,101
	Ducktown, Tennessee		78
	Telemark, Norway	R/vs	212
	Alchuri, Baltistan, Pakistan	R/rm P/hy-tc?	138

Appendix References

1: Adolfsson, Stig G. 1973. "Håkansboda Copper and Cobalt Deposit, Sweden." *Mineralogical Record* 4 (1): 38-39.

2: Appel, Peter, W. Uitterdijk, and Aage Jensen. 1987. "Notes and New Techniques: A New Gem Material from Greenland: Iridescent Orthoamphibole." *Gems & Gemology* Spring: 36-42.

3: Aristarain, L. F., and C. S. Hurlbut, Jr. 1972. "Boron Minerals and Deposits, Part I." *Mineralogical Record* 3 (4): 165-172.

4: Aristarain, L. F., and C. S. Hurlbut, Jr. 1972. "Boron Minerals and Deposits, Part II." *Mineralogical Record* 3 (5): 213-220.

5: Bancroft, Peter. 1973. *The World's Finest Minerals and Crystals.* New York: Viking Press.

6: Bancroft, Peter. 1984. *Gem and Crystal Treasures.* Fallbrook, CA: Western Enterprises.

7: Bancroft, Peter, Joze Car, Mirjan Zorz, and Gregor Kobler. 1991. "Famous Mineral Localities: The Idria Mines, Slovenia, Yugoslavia." *Mineralogical Record* 22 (3): 201-208.

8: Bandy, Mark Chance. 1976. *Mineralogy of Llallagua, Bolivia.* Tucson Gem and Mineral Society Special Paper 1. Tucson.

9: Bariand, P., F. Cesbron, and H. Vachey. 1973. "Hydromagnesite from Soghan, Iran." *Mineralogical Record* 4 (1): 18-21.

10: Bariand, Pierre, and J. F. Poullen. 1978. "Famous Mineral Localities: The Pegmatites of Laghman, Nuristan, Afghanistan." *Mineralogical Record* 9 (5): 301-308.

11: Barot, N. R., and Edward W. Boehm. 1992. "Gem-Quality Green Zoisite." *Gems and Gemology* 28 (1): 4-15.

12: Barwood, Henry. 1974. "Iron Phosphate Mineral Locality at Indian Mountain, Alabama." *Mineralogical Record* 5 (5): 241-244.

13: Bedogné, Francesco, and Renato Pagano. 1972. "Mineral Collecting in Val Malenco." *Mineralogical Record* 3 (3): 120-123.

14: Berry, L. G., ed. 1971. "The Silver-Arsenide Deposits of the Cobalt-Gowganda Region, Ontario. *Canadian Mineralogist* 11 (1): 1-429.

15: Betz, Volker. 1981. "Famous Mineral Localities: Zeolites from Iceland and the Faeroes." *Mineralogical Record* 12 (1): 5-26.

16: Bideaux, Richard A. 1970. "Mineral Rings & Cylinders." *Mineralogical Record* 1 (3): 105-112.

17: Bideaux, Richard A. 1980. "Famous Mineral Localities: Tiger Arizona." *Mineralogical Record* 11 (3): 155-181.

18: Birch, W. D. 1988. "Zeolites from Phillip Island and Flinders, Victoria." *Mineralogical Record* 19 (6): 451-460.

19: Bode, Rainer, and Artur Wittern. 1989. *Mineralien und Fundstellen Bundesrepublik Deutschland.* Haltern: Doris Bode Verlag.

20: Burr, Peter S. 1992. "Notes on the History of Phosgenite and Matlockite from Matlock, England." *Mineralogical Record* 23 (5): 377-386.

21: Cairncross, Bruce. 1991. "The Messina Mining District, South Africa." *Mineralogical Record* 22 (3): 187-199.

22: Cannon, Bart. 1975. *Minerals of Washington.* Mercer Island, WA: Cordilleran Publishing.

23: Cassedanne, J. P. 1985. "Recent Discoveries of Phenakite in Brazil." *Mineralogical Record* 16 (2): 107-109.

24: Cassedanne, Jacques P., and Jeannine O. Cassedanne. 1973. "Minerals from the Lavra da Ilha Pegmatite, Brazil." *Mineralogical Record* 4 (5): 207-213.

25: Cassedanne, Jacques P., and Jeannine O. Cassedanne. 1977. "Axinite, Hydromagnesite, Amethyst and Other Minerals from near Vitória da Conquista (Brazil)." *Mineralogical Record* 8 (5): 382-387.

26: Cassedanne, J., and J. Cassedanne. 1981. "The Urubu Pegmatite and Vicinity." *Mineralogical Record* 12 (2): 73-77.

27: Cassedanne, J. P., and Jack Lowell. 1982. "Famous Mineral Localities: The Virgem da Lapa Pegmatites." *Mineralogical Record* 13 (1): 19-28.

28: Cesbron, F., and P. Bariand. 1975. "The Uranium-Vanadium Deposit of Mounana, Gabon." *Mineralogical Record* 6 (5): 237-249.

29: Chamberlain, Steven C. 1991. "Die Mineralien des Francon-Quarry, Montreal Island, Quebec, Canada." *Mineralien-Welt* June: 59-69.

30: Chamberlain, S. C., and G. W. Robinson. 1993. "Unusual Occurrence of Magnetite Crystals from the Balmat District, St. Lawrence County, New York." *Rocks and Minerals* 68 (3): 122-123 (abstract).

31: Cisneros, S. L., R. E. Witkowski, and D. L. Oswald. 1977. "Artinite from San Benito County, California." *Mineralogical Record* 8 (6): 457-460.

32: Cook, Robert B. 1975. "The Mineralogy of the Department of Oruro, Bolivia." *Mineralogical Record* 6 (3): 125-137.

33: Cook, Robert B. 1978. "Famous Mineral Localities: Chuquicamata, Chile." *Mineralogical Record* 9 (5): 321-333.

34: Cook, Robert B. 1979. "Famous Mineral Localities: Chañarcillo, Chile." *Mineralogical Record* 10 (4): 197-204.

35: Cook, Robert B. 1985. "Famous Mineral Localities: The Mineralogy of Graves Mountain Lincoln County, Georgia." *Mineralogical Record* 16 (6): 443-458.

36: Cooper, M. P., and C. J. Stanley. 1990. *Minerals of the English Lake District.* London: Natural History Museum.

37: Crawford, Jack W. 1988. "Famous Mineral Localities: The Almaden Mines, Ciudad Real, Spain." *Mineralogical Record* 19 (5): 297-302.

38: Crook, Wilson W., III. 1977. "The Clear Creek Pegmatite: A Rare Earth Pegmatite in Brunet County, Texas." *Mineralogical Record* 8 (2): 88-90.

39: Crowley, Jack A. 1977. "Minerals of the Blue Bell Mine, San Bernardino County, California." *Mineralogical Record* 8 (6): 494-496.

40: Currier, Rock H. 1976. "The Production of Zeolite Mineral Specimens from the Deccan Basalt in India." *Mineralogical Record* 7 (5): 248-264.

41: Dallaire, Donald A., and Robert W. Whitmore. 1990. "Mines and Minerals of North Groton, New Hampshire." *Rocks and Minerals* 65 (4): 350-360.

42: Dana, Edward Salisbury, and William E. Ford. 1957. *A Textbook of Mineralogy.* 4th ed. New York: John Wiley & Sons.

43: DeMark, R. S. 1984. "Minerals of Point of Rocks, New Mexico." *Mineralogical Record* 15 (3): 149-156.

44: Dietrich, R. V., and Steven C. Chamberlain. 1989. "Are Cultured Pearls Mineral?" *Rocks and Minerals* 64 (5): 386-392.

45: Dillhoff, Richard M., and Thomas A. Dillhoff. 1991. "Realgar from the Royal Reward Mine, King County, Washington." *Rocks and Minerals* 66 (4): 310-314.

46: Distler, V. V. 1992. "Platinum Mineralization of the Noril'sk Deposits." *Canadian Mineralogist* 30 (2): 480 (abstract).

47: Donnay, Gabrielle, C. O. Ingamells, and Brian Mason. 1966. "Buergerite, a New Species of Tourmaline." *American Mineralogist* 51 (1): 198-199.

48: Dressler, B. O., V. K. Supta, and T. L. Muir. 1991. "The Sudbury Structure." In *Geology of Ontario,* Edited by P.C. Thurston, H.R. Williams, R.H. Sutcliffe and G.M. Scott, Ontario Geological Survey Special Vol. 4, 593-625. Ministry of Northern Development and Mines, Toronto.

49: Dunn, Pete J., Peter B. Leavens, and Cynthia Barnes. 1980. "Magnesioaxinite from Luning, Nevada, and Some Nomenclature Designations for the Axinite Group." *Mineralogical Record* 11 (1): 13-15.

50: Dunn, Pete J., Peter B. Leavens, B. Darko Sturman, Richard V. Gaines, and Carlos do Prado Barbosa. 1979. "Hureaulite and Barbosalite from Lavra do Criminoso, Minas Gerais, Brazil." *Mineralogical Record* 10 (3): 147-151.

51: Dunning, G. E., and J. F. Cooper, Jr. 1987. "Inesite from the Hale Creek Mine, Trinity County, California." *Mineralogical Record* 18 (5): 341-347.

52: Embrey, P. G., and R. F. Symes. 1987. *Minerals of Cornwall and Devon.* London: British Museum (Natural History).

53: England, Brian M. 1985. "Famous Mineral Localities: The Kingsgate Mines, New South Wales, Australia." *Mineralogical Record* 16 (4): 265-289.

54: Foord, Eugene E. 1977. "The Himalaya Dike System: Mesa Grande District, San Diego County, California." *Mineralogical Record* 8 (6): 461-474.

55: Foord, Eugene E., and Robert F. Martin. 1979. "Amazonite from the Pikes Peak Batholith." *Mineralogical Record* 10 (6): 375-376.

56: Francis, Carl A. 1985. "Maine Tourmaline." *Mineralogical Record* 16 (5): 365-388.

57: Francis, Carl A. 1987. "Minerals of the Topsham, Maine, Pegmatite District." *Rocks and Minerals* 62 (6): 407-415.

58: Frondel, Clifford. 1972. *The Minerals of Franklin and Sterling Hill: A Check List.* New York: Wiley-Interscience.

59: Frondel, Clifford, and John L. Baum. 1974. "Structure and Mineralogy of the Franklin Zinc-Iron-Manganese Deposit, New Jersey." *Economic Geology* 69 (2): 157-180.

60: Gaines, Richard V. 1970. "The Moctezuma Tellurium Deposit." *Mineralogical Record* 1 (2): 40-43.

61: Gauthier, Gilbert, and Nicolaos Albandakis. 1991. "Minerals of the Seriphos Skarn, Greece." *Mineralogical Record* 22 (4): 303-308.

62: Gauthier, Gilbert, Armand François, M. Deliens, and P. Piret. 1989. "Famous Mineral Localities: The Uranium Deposits of the Shaba Region, Zaire." *Mineralogical Record* 20 (4): 265-288.

63: Geyer, Alan R., Robert C. Smith, II, and John H. Barnes. 1976. *Mineral Collecting in Pennsylvania.* 4th ed. Pennsylvania Geological Survey General Geology Report 33. Commonwealth of Pennsylvania Department of Environmental Resources Topographic and Geologic Survey, Harrisburg.

64: Gillanders, R. J. 1981. "Famous Mineral Localities: The Leadhills-Wanlockhead District, Scotland." *Mineralogical Record* 12 (4): 235-250.

65: Gochenour, Kenneth. 1988. "Black Tourmaline from Little Cahuilla Mountain, Riverside County, California." *Rocks and Minerals* 63 (6): 440-444.

66: Goldblum, Deborah R., and Mary Louise Hill. 1992. "Enhanced Fluid Flow Resulting from Competency Contrast within a Shear Zone: The Garnet Ore Zone at Gore Mountain, NY." *Journal of Geology* 100: 776-782.

67: Gordon, Jennings B., Jr., and Curtis L. Hollabaugh. 1989. "Phosphate Microminerals of the Indian Mountain Area." *Mineralogical Record* 20 (5): 355-362.

68: Graeme, Richard W. 1981. "Famous Mineral Localities: Bisbee, Arizona." *Mineralogical Record* 12 (5): 258-319.

69: Graeser, Stefan. 1977. "Famous Mineral Localities: Lengenbach, Switzerland." *Mineralogical Record* 8 (4): 275-281.

70: Gramaccioli, Carlo M. 1979. "Minerals of the Alpine Rodingites of Italy." *Mineralogical Record* 10 (2): 85-89.

71: Grant, Raymond W. 1968. *Mineral Collecting in Vermont.* Vermont Geological Survey Special Publication No. 2. Vermont Geological Survey, Montpellier.

72: Grice, Joel D., Pete J. Dunn, and Robert A. Ramik. 1989. "Whiteite-(CaMnMg), a New Mineral from the Tip Top Pegmatite, Custer, South Dakota." *Canadian Mineralogist* 27: 699-702.

73: Grice, J. D., and R. A. Gault. 1977. "The Bluebell Mine, Riondel, British Columbia, Canada." *Mineralogical Record* 8 (1): 33-36.

74: Grice, J. D., and R. A. Gault. 1981. "Edingtonite and Natrolite from Ice River, British Columbia." *Mineralogical Record* 12 (4): 221-226.

75: Grice, J. D., and R. A. Gault. 1983. "Lapis Lazuli from Lake Harbour, Baffin Island, Canada." *Rocks and Minerals* 58 (1): 12-19.

76: Grice, J. D., Robert A. Gault, and H. Gary Ansell. 1984. "Edingtonite: The First Two Canadian Occurrences." *Canadian Mineralogist* 22 (2): 253-258.

77: Grice, J. D., and R. Williams. 1979. "The Jeffrey Mine, Asbestos, Quebec." *Mineralogical Record* 10 (2): 69-80.

78: Guilbert, John M., and Charles F. Park, Jr. 1986. *The Geology of Ore Deposits.* New York: W. H. Freeman.

79: Gutzmer, Jens, and Bruce Cairncross. 1993. "Recent Discoveries from the Wessels Mine, South Africa." *Mineralogical Record* 24 (5): 365-368.

80: Henderson, William A., Jr. 1979. "Microminerals." *Mineralogical Record* 10 (4): 239-241.

81: Henderson, William A., Jr. 1981. "Microminerals." *Mineralogical Record* 12 (6): 381-385.

82: Henderson, William A., Jr. 1985. "Microminerals of the Western Volcanics." *Mineralogical Record* 16 (2): 137-135.

83: Hentschel, Gerhard. 1983. *Die Mineralien der Eifelvulkane.* Munich: Christian Weise Verlag.

84: Hewitt, D. F. 1961. *Nepheline Syenite Deposits of Southern Ontario.* Toronto: Ontario Department of Mines.

85: Horvath, Laszlo, and Robert A. Gault. 1990. "The Mineralogy of Mont Saint-Hilaire Quebec." *Mineralogical Record* 21 (4): 284-359.

86: Jacobson, Mark I. 1979. "Famous Mineral Localities: Mount Antero." *Mineralogical Record* 10 (6): 339-346.

87: Jahns, Richard H., and Rodney C. Ewing. 1977. "The Harding Mine, Taos County, New Mexico." *Mineralogical Record* 8 (2): 115-126.

88: Januzzi, Ronald E. 1966. *A Field Mineralogy of the Tilly Foster Iron Mine at Tilly Foster, Brewster, New York.* Brewster, NY: The Mineralogical Press.

89: Jaszczak, John A. 1991. "Graphite from Crestmore, California." *Mineralogical Record* 22 (6): 427-432.

90: Jensen, Aage, and Ole V. Petersen. 1982. "Tugtupite: A Gemstone from Greenland." *Gems & Gemology* 28: 90-94.

91: Jensen, David E. 1978. *Minerals of New York State.* Rochester, NY: Ward Press.

92: Jensen, Martin. 1985. "The Majuba Hill Mine: Pershing County." *Mineralogical Record* 16 (1): 57-72.

93: Jensen, Martin. 1993. "Update on the Mineralogy of the Majuba Hill Mine, Pershing County, Nevada." *Mineralogical Record* 24 (3): 171-180.

94: Johnsen, Ole, Ole Petersen, and Olaf Medenbach. 1985. "The Gardiner Complex, a New Locality in Greenland." *Mineralogical Record* 16 (6): 485-494.

95: Johnston, Christopher W., and Roderick J. Hill. 1978. "Zinc Phosphates at Reaphook Hill, South Australia." *Mineralogical Record* 9 (1): 20-25.

96: Jones, Robert W. 1980. "The Grand Reef Mine, Graham County, Arizona." *Mineralogical Record* 11 (4): 219-225.

97: Joyce, D. K., R. I. Gait, and B. D. Sturman. 1994. "The Morphology, Physical Properties and Occurrence of Howlite from Iona, Nova Scotia." *Rocks and Minerals* 69 (2): 119 (abstract).

98: Kazmi, Ali H., Joseph J. Peters, and Herbert P. Obodda. 1985. "Gem Pegmatites of the Shingus-Dusso Area: Gilgit, Pakistan." *Mineralogical Record* 16 (5): 393-412.

99: Kearns, Lance E. 1978. "The Amity Area, Orange County, New York." *Mineralogical Record* 9 (2): 85-90.

100: Keller, Peter C. 1990. *Gemstones and Their Origins.* New York: Van Nostrand Reinhold.

101: Keller, Peter C. 1992. *Gemstones of East Africa.* Phoenix: Geoscience Press.

102: Kennedy, Irwin. 1979. "Some Interesting Radioactive Minerals from the Bancroft Area, Ontario." *Mineralogical Record* 10 (3): 153-158.

103: Kidwell, Albert L. 1989. "Phosphate Minerals of Arkansas." *Rocks and Minerals* 64 (5): 189-195.

104: King, Robert J. 1982. "The Boltsburn Mine, Weardale, County Durham, England." *Mineralogical Record* 13 (1): 5-18.

105: Kohlberger, William. 1976. "Minerals of the Laurium Mines: Attica, Greece." *Mineralogical Record* 7 (3): 114-125.

106: Kokinos, Michael, and William S. Wise. 1993. "Famous Mineral Localities: The Gold Hill Mine, Tooele County, Utah." *Mineralogical Record* 24 (1): 11-22.

107: Kolesar, Peter. 1990. "Dyskrasit-Kristalle aus dem Bergbau-Revier Pribram in der Tschechoslowakei." *Lapis* 15 (9): 19-26.

108: Korowski, Stanley P., and Cor W. Notebaart. 1978. "Libethenite from the Rokana Mine, Zambia." *Mineralogical Record* 9 (6): 341-346.

109: Kosnar, Richard A., and Harold W. Miller. 1976. "Crystallized Minerals of the Colorado Mineral Belt." *Mineralogical Record* 7 (6): 278-307.

110: Kothavala, Rustam Z. 1982. "The Discovery of Powellite at Nasik, India." *Mineralogical Record* 13 (5): 303-309.

111: Kothavala, Rustam Z. 1991. "The Wagholi Cavansite Locality near Poona, India." *Mineralogical Record* 22 (6): 415-420.

112: Larson, Bill. 1977. "The Best of San Diego County." *Mineralogical Record* 8 (6): 507-518.

113: Lasmanis, R. 1977. "The Snowbird Mine, Montana's Parisite Locality." *Mineralogical Record* 8 (2): 83-86.

114: Lauf, Robert J. 1983. "Graphite from the Lead Hill Mine, Ticonderoga, New York." *Mineralogical Record* 14 (1): 25-30.

115: Leavitt, D. 1981. "Minerals of the Yates Uranium Mine, Pontiac County, Quebec." *Mineralogical Record* 12 (6): 359-363.

116: Le Font, Mark. 1984. "Siegenite from the Buick Mine, Bixby, Missouri." *Mineralogical Record* 15 (1): 3739.

117: Leicht, Wayne C. 1971. "Minerals of the Grandview Mine." *Mineralogical Record* 2 (5): 214-221.

118: Lewis, Richard W., Jr. 1956. "The Geology and Ore Deposits of the Quiruvilca District, Peru." *Economic Geology* 51: 41-63.

119: Lhoest, Joseph J., Gilbert Gauthier, and Vandall T. King. 1991. "Famous Mineral Localities: The Mashamba West Mine, Shaba, Zaire." *Mineralogical Record* 22 (1): 13-20.

120: Lieber, Werner. 1973. "Trepca and Its Minerals." *Mineralogical Record* 4 (2): 56-61.

121: Lieber, Werner, and Hermann Leyerzapf. 1986. "German Silver: An Historical Perspective on Silver Mining in Germany." *Mineralogical Record* 17 (1): 3-18.

122: Lillie, Ross C. 1988. "Minerals of the Harris Creek Fluorspar District, Hardin County, Illinois." *Rocks and Minerals* 63 (3): 210-226.

123: Lincks, G. Fred. 1978. "The Chester Emery Mines." *Mineralogical Record* 9 (4): 235-242.

124: Lucio, A., and Richard V. Gaines. 1973. "The Minerals of the Morro Velho Gold Mine, Brazil." *Mineralogical Record* 4 (5): 224-229.

125: Mandarino, J. A., and V. Anderson. 1989. *Monteregian Treasures: The Minerals of Mont Saint-Hilaire, Quebec.* Cambridge: Cambridge University Press.

126: Marty, Joe, Martin C. Jensen, and Andrew D. Roberts. 1993. "Minerals of the Centennial Eureka Mine, Tintic District, Eureka, Utah." *Rocks and Minerals* 68 (6): 406-416.

127: Mason, Brian. 1976. "Famous Mineral Localities: Broken Hill, Australia." *Mineralogical Record* 7 (1): 25-33.

128: McColl, Don, and Gladys Warren. 1984. "Kornerupine and Sapphirine Crystals from the Harts Range, Central Australia." *Mineralogical Record* 15 (2): 99-101.

129: Medici, John C. 1981. "The Halls Gap Millerite Locality." *Rocks and Minerals* 56 (3): 104-108.

130: Melanson, Frank, and George Robinson. 1982. "The Fluorite Mines of Madoc, Ontario." *Mineralogical Record* 13 (2): 87-92.

131: Menezes, Luiz Alberto Dias, and Joaniel Munhoz Martins. 1984. "The Jacupiranga Mine, São Paulo, Brazil." *Mineralogical Record* 15 (5): 261-270.

132: Milton, Charles. 1977. "Mineralogy of the Green River Formation." *Mineralogical Record* 8 (5): 368-379.

133: Mitchell, Richard S. 1977. "Some Noteworthy Minerals from Virginia." *Rocks and Minerals* 52 (5): 221-229.

134: Moore, Paul B. 1970. "Mineralogy & Chemistry of Långban-Type Deposits in Bergslagen, Sweden." *Mineralogical Record* 1 (4): 154-172.

135: Moore, Paul Brian. 1973. "Pegmatite Phosphates: Descriptive Mineralogy and Crystal Chemistry." *Mineralogical Record* 4 (3): 103-130.

136: Moore, Thomas P. 1987. "Notes from Germany." *Mineralogical Record* 18 (2): 159-163.

137: Moore, Thomas. 1992. "What's New in Minerals: Tucson Show." *Mineralogical Record* 23 (3): 273-281.

138: Moore, Thomas. 1993. "What's New in Minerals: Tucson Show." *Mineralogical Record* 24 (3): 219-230, 237.

139: Muessig, Siegfried. 1959. "Primary Borates in Playa Deposits: Minerals of High Hydration." *Economic Geology* 54: 495-501.

140: Muntyan, Barbara L., and John R. Muntyan. 1985. "Minerals of the Pikes Peak Granite." *Mineralogical Record* 16 (3): 217-230.

141: Murphy, Jack A. 1979. "The San Juan Mountains of Colorado." *Mineralogical Record* 10 (6): 349-361.

142: Niedermayr, Gerhard. 1986. "Mineral Localities in Austria." *Mineralogical Record* 17 (2): 105-110.

143: Notebaart, C. W., and S. P. Korowski. 1980. "Famous Mineral Localities: The Broken Hill Mine, Zambia." *Mineralogical Record* 11 (6): 339-348.

144: Novak, G. A., and S. G. Oswald. 1971. "Laumontite from the Pine Creek Mine, Bishop, California." *Mineralogical Record* 2 (5): 222.

145: Orlandi, Paolo, and Pier Bruno Scortecci. 1985. "Minerals of the Elba Pegmatites." *Mineralogical Record* 16 (5): 353-363.

146: Palache, Charles. 1935. *The Minerals of Franklin and Sterling Hill, Sussex County, New Jersey.* United States Geological Survey Professional Paper 180. United States Department of the Interior, Washington.

147: Palache, Charles. 1936. "Babingtonite and Epidote from Westfield, Massachusetts." *American Mineralogist* 21: 652-655.

148: Palache, Charles, Harry Berman, and Clifford Frondel. 1944. *The System of Mineralogy of James Dwight Dana and Edward Salisbury Dana, Yale University 1837-1892.* 7th ed. Vol. 1. New York: John Wiley and Sons.

149: Palache, Charles, Harry Berman, and Clifford Frondel. 1951. *The System of Mineralogy of James Dwight Dana and Edward Salisbury Dana, Yale University 1837-1892.* 7th ed. Vol. 2. New York: John Wiley and Sons.

150: Pallix, Gerard. 1978. "Famous Mineral Localities: Bou-Azzer, Morocco." *Mineralogical Record* 9 (2): 69-73.

151: Panczner, William D. 1987. *Minerals of Mexico.* New York: Van Nostrand Reinhold.

152: Pearl, Richard M. 1974. "Minerals of the Pikes Peak Granite." *Mineralogical Record* 5 (4): 183-189.

153: Pemberton, Earl H. 1975. "The Crystal Habits and Forms of the Minerals of Searles Lake, San Bernardino County, California." *Mineralogical Record* 6 (2): 74-83.

154: Pemberton, Earl H. 1983. *Minerals of California*. New York: Van Nostrand Reinhold.

155: Perham, Jane C. 1987. *Maine's Treasure Chest: Gems and Minerals of Oxford County*. West Paris, ME: Quicksilver Publications.

156: Peters, Joseph J. 1984. "Triassic Traprock Minerals of New Jersey." *Rocks and Minerals* 59 (4): 157-183.

157: Peters, Thomas A., Joseph J. Peters, and Julius Weber. 1978. "Famous Mineral Localities: Paterson, New Jersey." *Mineralogical Record* 9 (3): 157-179.

158: Petersen, Ole V., Ole Johnsen, and Aage Jensen. 1980. "Giant Crystals of Kornerupine." *Mineralogical Record* 11 (2): 93-96.

159: Petersen, Ole V., and Karsten Secher. 1993. "The Minerals of Greenland." *Mineralogical Record* 24 (2): 4-67.

160: Pohl, Demetrius, Renald Guillemette, and James Shigley. 1982. "Ferroaxinite from New Melones Lake, Calaveras County, California, a Remarkable New Locality." *Mineralogical Record* 13 (5): 293-302.

161: Prenn, Neil, and Peggy Merrick. 1991. "The Monitor-Mogul Mining District, Alpine County, California." *Mineralogical Record* 22 (1): 29-40.

162: Pring, Allan. 1988. "Minerals of the Moonta and Wallaroo Mining Districts, South Australia." *Mineralogical Record* 19 (6): 407-416.

163: Puffer, J. H. 1975. "The Kramer Borate Mineral Assemblage, Boron, California." *Mineralogical Record* 6 (2): 84-91.

164: Ream, Lanny R. 1985. *Gems and Minerals of Washington*. Renton, WA: Jackson Mountain Press.

165: Ream, Lanny R. 1989. *Idaho Minerals*. Coeur d'Alene, ID: L. R. Ream Publishing.

166: Ream, Lanny R. 1991. "Two Autunite Localities in Northeastern Washington, The Daybreak and Triple H & J Mines." *Rocks and Minerals* 66 (4): 294-297.

167: Reasenberg, Julian. 1968. "New Artinite Find on Staten Island, New York." *Rocks and Minerals* 43 (9): 643-647.

168: Ren, Kai-Wen. 1980. *Minerals in China*. Shanghai, China: Shanghai Scientific and Technical Publishers.

169: Rickard. T. A.; annotated by Arthur E. Smith and Richard A. Kosnar. 1983. "Across the San Juan Mountains." *Mineralogical Record* 14 (4): 243-249.

170: Roberts, Willard Lincoln, and George Rapp, Jr. 1965. *Mineralogy of the Black Hills*. South Dakota School of Mines and Technology, Bulletin No. 18. Rapid City, SD.

171: Robinson, George, and Steven C. Chamberlain. 1982. "An Introduction to the Mineralogy of Ontario's Grenville Province." *Mineralogical Record* 13 (2): 71-86.

172: Robinson, George W., and Joel D. Grice. 1993. "The Barium Analog of Brewsterite from Harrisville, New York." *Canadian Mineralogist* 31 (3): 687-690.

173: Robinson, George W., and Vandall T. King. 1990. "What's New in Minerals?" *Mineralogical Record* 21 (5): 481-492, 501.

174: Robinson, George W., and Vandall T. King. 1993. "What's New in Minerals?" *Mineralogical Record* 24 (5): 381394.

175: Robinson, George W., Vandall T. King, Eric Asselborn, Forrest Cureton, Rudy Tschernich, and Robert Sielecki. 1992. "What's New in Minerals?" *Mineralogical Record* 23 (5): 423-437.

176: Robinson, George W., Jerry Van Velthuizen, H. Gary Ansell, and B. Darko Sturman. 1992. "Mineralogy of the Rapid Creek and Big Fish River Area, Yukon Territory." *Mineralogical Record* 23 (4): 4-47.

177: Rossman, George R., and Richard L. Squires. 1974. "The Occurrence of Alstonite at Cave in Rock, Illinois." *Mineralogical Record* 5 (6): 266-269.

178: Rowley, Elmer B. 1987. "Serendibite, Sinhalite, Sapphirine, and Grandidierite from the Adirondack Mountains, at Johnsburg, New York." *Rocks and Minerals* 62 (4): 243-246.

179: Samuelson, Peter B., Kenneth H. Hollmann, and Carlton L. Holt. 1990. "Minerals of the Conway and Mount Osceola Granites of New Hampshire." *Rocks and Minerals* 65 (4): 286-296.

180: Sansoni, Gerhard. 1993. "Über Akanthit, insbesondere aus dem Freiberger Revier." *Mineralien-Welt* 4 (2): 36-40.

181: Scalisi, Philip, and David Cook. 1983. *Classic Mineral Localities of the World: Asia and Australia*. New York: Van Nostrand Reinhold.

182: Schröder, Boris, and Ulrich Lipp. 1990. "Der Uranerzbergbau der SDAG-Wismut im Roum Schneeberg-Aue-Schlema und seine Mineralien (II)." *Mineralien-Welt* Heft 3 (November-December): 20-44.

183: Seemann, Robert. 1986. "Famous Mineral Localities: Knappenwand, Untersulzbachtal, Austria." *Mineralogical Record* 17 (3): 167-181.

184: Segeler, Curt G., Anthony R. Kampf, William Ulrich, and Robert W. Whitmore. 1981. "Phosphate Minerals of the Palermo No.1 Pegmatite." *Rocks and Minerals* 56 (5): 197-214.

185: Skobel', L. S., I. I. Nekhanenko, and N. P. Popova. 1993. "Axinitfunde in der Lagerstätte Puiva, Polarural." *Mineralien-Welt* 4 (5): 33-37.

186: Smith, Arthur E. 1991. "Texas Mineral Locality Index." *Rocks and Minerals* 66 (3): 196-224.

187: Smith, Arthur E., Jr., Ed Raines, and Leland Feitz. 1985. "Great Pockets: The Cresson Vug, Cripple Creek." *Mineralogical Record* 16 (3): 231-238.

188: Stalder, H. A., P. Embrey, S. Graeser, and W. Nowacki. 1978. *Die Mineralien des Binntales*. Bern: Naturhistorisches Museum der Stadt Bern.

189: Staveley, R. C. 1976. "Minerals of Marbridge Mines Limited." *Mineralogical Record* 7 (4): 174-178.

190: Stobbe, J. 1981. "Famous Mineral Localities: Príbram, Czechoslovakia." *Mineralogical Record* 12 (3): 157-165.

191: Stolburg, Craig S., and Gail E. Dunning. 1985. "The Getchell Mine, Humboldt County, Nevada." *Mineralogical Record* 16 (1): 15-23.

192: Taggard, Joseph E., Abraham Rosenzweig, and Eugene E. Foord. 1989. "Famous Mineral Localities: The Hansonburg District, Bingham, New Mexico." *Mineralogical Record* 20 (1): 31-46.

193: Tarassoff, P. 1993. "History and Mineralogy of the Orford Nickel Mine, Orford Township, Quebec." In *Proceedings of the 20th Annual Mineralogical Symposium*, 27 (abstract). Rochester, NY: Rochester Academy of Science.

194: Thomas, William J., and Ronal B. Gibbs. 1983. "Famous Mineral Localities: The New Cornelia Mine, Ajo, Arizona." *Mineralogical Record* 14 (5): 283-298.

195: Thompson, Robert J. 1983. "Camp Verde Evaporites." *Mineralogical Record* 14 (2): 85-96.

196: Tschernich, Rudy W. 1992. *Zeolites of the World*. Phoenix: Geoscience Press.

197: Tyson, Rod. 1989. "The Port Radium District, Northwest Territories, Canada." *Mineralogical Record* 20 (3): 201-208.

198: Van Velthuizen, Jerry. 1993. "The Parker Mine, Notre Dame du Laus, Quebec." *Mineralogical Record* 24 (5): 369-373.

199: Vokes, F. M. 1963. *Molybdenum Deposits of Canada*. Geological Survey of Canada Economic Geology Report No. 20. Geological Survey of Canada, Ottawa.

200: Von Bezing, K. L., Roger D. Dixon, Demetrius Pohl, and Greg Cavallo. 1991. "The Kalahari Manganese Field: An Update." *Mineralogical Record* 22 (4): 279-297.

201: Waisman, Dave. 1992. "Minerals of the Black Pine Mine, Granite County, Montana." *Mineralogical Record* 23 (6): 477-483.

202: Wallace, Terry C., Mark Barton, and Wendell E. Wilson. 1994. "Silver and Silver-bearing Minerals." *Rocks and Minerals* 69 (1): 16-38.

203: Weibel, M. 1966. *A Guide to the Minerals of Switzerland*. New York: Interscience, Wiley.

204: Weiner, K. L., and Rupert Hochleitner. 1987. "Steckbrief: Ilvait." *Lapis* 12 (4): 7-9.

205: Weiner, K. L., and Rupert Hochleitner. 1990. "Steckbrief: Rhodizit." *Lapis* 15 (2): 7-9.

206: White, John S. 1971. "What's New in Minerals." *Mineralogical Record* 2 (5): 231.

207: White, John S. 1972. "Tennantite-Tetrahedrite from Naica, Chihuahua, Mexico." *Mineralogical Record* 3 (3): 115-119.

208: White, John S. 1974. "Mineral Notes: New Minerals." *Mineralogical Record* 5 (2): 74.

209: White, John S. 1975. "What's New in Minerals?" *Mineralogical Record* 6 (1): 38-40.

210: White, John S., and J. A. Nelen. 1985. "Hutchinsonite from Quiruvilca, Peru." *Mineralogical Record* 16 (6): 459-460.

211: White, W. H., A. A. Bookstrom, R. J. Kamilli, M. W. Ganster, R. P. Smith, D. E. Ranta, and R. C. Steininger. 1981. "Character and Origin of Climax-Type Molybdenum Deposits." *Economic Geology* 75th Anniversary Vol.: 270-316.

212: Wilke, Hans-Jürgen. 1976. *Mineral-Fundstellen*. Vol. 4, Skandinavien. Munich: Christian Weise Verlag.

213: Wilson, Marc L., and Stanley J. Dyl, II. 1992. "The Michigan Copper Country." *Mineralogical Record* 23 (2): 4-72.

214: Wilson, W. E. 1976. "Famous Mineral Localities: Saint John's Island, Egypt." *Mineralogical Record* 7 (6): 310-314.

215: Wilson, Wendell E., ed. 1977. "Tsumeb! The World's Greatest Mineral Locality." *Mineralogical Record* 8 (3): 1-128.

216: Wilson, W. E. 1981. "What's New in Minerals?" *Mineralogical Record* 12 (3): 177-186.

217: Wilson, W. E. 1982. "The Gold-containing Minerals: A Review." *Mineralogical Record* 13 (6): 389-400.

218: Wilson, W. E. 1982. "What's New in Minerals?" *Mineralogical Record* 13 (1): 39-42.

219: Wilson, Wendell E. 1989. "The Anjanabonoina Pegmatite, Madagascar." *Mineralogical Record* 20 (3): 191-200.

220: Wilson, W. E., and Pete J. Dunn. 1978. "Famous Mineral Localities: The Kalahari Manganese Field." *Mineralogical Record* 9 (3): 137-153.

221: Wilson, W. E., and J. S. White. 1976. "What's New in Minerals?" *Mineralogical Record* 7 (2): 55-59.

222: Wilson, W. F., and B. J. McKenzie. 1978. *Mineral Collecting Sites in North Carolina*. Information Circular 24. Raleigh, NC: North Carolina Geological Survey.

223: Wise, William S. 1977. "Mineralogy of the Champion Mine, White Mountains, California." *Mineralogical Record* 8 (6): 478-486.

224: Worner, H. K., and R. W. Mitchell, eds. 1982. *Minerals of Broken Hill*. Melbourne: Australia Mining & Smelting.

225: Zebec, Vladimir, and Marin Soufek. 1986. "Hyalophan von Busovaca, Jugoslawien." *Lapis* 11 (1): 28-31.

Index

Acknowledgments

In the year it has taken me to write this book, I have received much encouragement, advice, and assistance from many individuals, to whom I am extremely grateful. First and foremost, I owe a great deal of thanks to my wife, Susan, for the original illustrations on which the figure illustrations were based, and for her encouragement, critical reading, and infinite patience while I spent many an evening and weekend at the word processor. Second, I would like to thank Jeffrey Scovil, with whom it was a pleasure to work and whose exceptional photographic talent has added much to the book. I am also indebted to Michael Hamilton of the Geological Survey of Canada, who provided the photograph of labradorite [PLATE 10]. The suggestions of Steven Chamberlain, T. Scott Ercit, Joel Grice, William Henderson, Richard Herd, Louis Moyd, Peter N. Nevraumont, Terri Ottaway, Jeffrey Scovil, Art Soregaroli, Richard Taylor, and Brad Van Diver greatly improved the manuscript. Patricia M. Leasure and Linda Cunningham at Simon and Schuster were early and enthusiastic supporters of the book. I would also like to thank José Conde for his exquisite book design, and Stephanie Hiebert for her expert copyediting. Finally, I would like to thank Dawn Arnold and Cathy Ripley for their technical support throughout the project, and my assistant, Michel Picard, for the extra work he assumed in my absence.